Julia
Involved

Julia Involved

THREE JULIA PROBYN NOVELS

The Lighthearted Quest

The Portuguese Escape

The Numbered Account

by Ann Bridge

McGraw-Hill Book Company, Inc.

NEW YORK   TORONTO   LONDON

JULIA INVOLVED
A Trilogy
© Ann Bridge 1962
All rights reserved

Library of Congress Catalog Card Number: 62–17639
First Edition of Julia Involved
07745

Contents

THE LIGHTHEARTED QUEST   1

THE PORTUGUESE ESCAPE   229

THE NUMBERED ACCOUNT   481

The
Lighthearted
Quest

"I simply can't think how to get hold of him," said Mrs. Monro dolefully, leaning forward in her chair to poke unskilfully at the fire of rather damp logs, which hummed and sizzled faintly in the wrong sort of grate for wood.

"Have you advertised?" asked Mrs. Hathaway. As she spoke she picked up the tongs, arranged the logs better, and pushed some bits of bark from the log-basket in between them; then kneeling down she began to ply the bellows.

"Yes," said Mrs. Monro, with a sort of weak pride. "In the *Times*, and the *Telegraph*, and the *Continental Daily Mail*—Edina said I ought to try that."

"Quite right. And how long ago was that?" asked Mrs. Hathaway, continuing to blow the fire, in which the bark now began to burn rather more hopefully.

"Three weeks the Continental one, and five the others, and there's still not a word. But now that his Uncle's dead, Colin simply *must* come home —I can't run this great place alone."

This was at least the eleventh time in the course of a single conversation that Mrs. Monro had said that her son Colin must return to run the property in Argyll, which would be, and indeed effectively now was, his. Since her husband's death her brother-in-law, Colonel Monro, had taken charge of it for his young nephew, but when he took pneumonia and died the crisis had arisen; and Mrs. Monro, as usual when a crisis arose, had sent for Mrs. Hathaway.

"When did Colin write last?" Mrs. Hathaway asked.

"Oh, *ages* ago; at least nine months. He is so naughty and unkind; it's really *wrong*," said Colin's mother.

Mrs. Hathaway in her heart agreed, but she kept to the main issue.

"Where did he write from, then?"

"Let me think—was it Tangier, or Casablanca, or Cadiz?—or that place with the funny name? Wait—I'll look," said Mrs. Monro, getting up and walking across the worn and faded carpet, with its hideous pattern of bunches of roses tied with ribbon on a black ground, to her cluttered Victorian escritoire, where papers bulged untidily from all the pigeon-holes and lay piled in heaps, obstructing the drawers. She poked and pulled and peered ineffectually, while Mrs. Hathaway looked on with the mixture of pity and irritation which her friend always aroused in her.

"No, I can't find it. How tiresome," said Mrs. Monro, stuffing papers back into quite different orifices from those whence she had removed them. She opened a drawer, muttering "This is only bills. Oh no, here it is," she exclaimed in triumph, and returned to her chair. "Look, it *is* from the place with the funny name—Cuter, I should call it, but Edina says it's pronounced Theeoota." She handed the letter over.

Mrs. Hathaway read it with attention. It was short, and uninformative to a degree which to her suggested some form of deliberate concealment. The boat was all right, though they had had a spot of engine trouble; business had been fairly good; one of his partners had gone home—none of them was mentioned by name, Mrs. Hathaway noticed—but he and the others were well; the weather was splendid, and he was her loving son, Colin.

"Tell me again what exactly the 'business' is," Mrs. Hathaway said, folding up this unsatisfactory missive and handing it back.

"Selling oranges, or bananas," said Mrs. Monro. "They go in and buy them in one place, and then sail off and sell them in another. I remember he said about eighteen months ago that they had done very well in Marseilles; that was what made Edina think of the *Continental Daily Mail*, because it's published in Paris."

Mrs. Hathaway passed over this characteristic *non sequitur*.

"I shouldn't have thought there was much profit to be made out of selling oranges round all those Mediterranean ports," she said. "They grow them in Africa as well as in Spain, and even in that extreme south-west corner of France, I believe. And if he was going to pick up bananas he'd have to go right out to the Canaries. How big is the boat?—big enough for that?"

Of course Mrs. Monro had no idea how big the boat was. Edina might know, she said; but Edina was out seeing about draining those fields on McNeils' farm, that poor John had been so keen on—"It was standing over those wretched drainers, in the East wind, that made him ill and killed him," said Mrs. Monro, beginning to dab at her eyes.

"Does Colin ever ask you for money now?" Mrs. Hathaway asked, ignoring her friend's all-too-easy emotion.

"No," said Mrs. Monro, perking up and putting away her handkerchief. "That's the extraordinary thing. He did ask for three hundred pounds to help to buy the boat, right at the beginning—but since then he's never asked for a penny. So you see there *must* be money in selling oranges, Mary, whatever you say." Mrs. Monro quite often caught the drift of more that was said than her friends ever expected her to, Mrs. Hathaway knew. She considered this last item in silence. For Colin not to ask for money for at least three years was, as his mother said, extraordinary;

but nevertheless this business of orange—or banana—selling sounded strangely unconvincing.

"May I see the letter again?" she said, and having looked at it—"Does he never give any sort of address?" she asked. "This just says 'Ceuta'."

"No—that's all he ever says and I write '*Poste Restante*, Cadiz,' or whatever it is."

"And he never says where he's going next, so that you could catch him with a telegram?"

"No. He really is very naughty and unkind," said Mrs. Monro, beginning to sniff and fumbling for her handkerchief again. "He used to at first, now I come to think of it; but he hasn't now, for a long while."

A gong boomed through the house, announcing lunch; the two ladies went downstairs, past windows on which rain beat violently, borne on a westerly gale. The fire in the dining-room was worse than that in the sitting-room upstairs, and the deaf and immensely aged butler who crept round on flat feet, handing rather surprisingly good food, somehow added to the general sense of depression—obviously, Mrs. Hathaway thought, it would be useless to try to make him get up a good fire.

"What is this cook you have?" she asked, as a flaked pastry *vol-au-vent* full of some meat, heavily flavoured with garlic, succeeded a delicious omelette.

"Oh, isn't she awful? She's a Spaniard, and one can't say a word to her," said Mrs. Monro. "She *will* put all these flavourings in, and I can't stop her, because she can't understand."

"I think her food is frightfully good," said Mrs. Hathaway. "May I have some more of this?" She got up, the aged butler having retired.

"Oh yes do, if you can bear it. Forbes hates her food—he makes her grill him a chop every day."

"Forbes always was a silly old ass," said Mrs. Hathaway, tucking into her second helping of garlic. "You're frightfully lucky, Ellen, to get food like this. But why on earth does she stay up here?—your cook? I should have thought a Spaniard would have frozen to death."

"Oh, she likes having the Macdonalds' chapel just next door; she goes to Mass there every single morning. Ronan Macdonald talks a little Spanish too, and she likes that—but he won't translate for *me*," said Mrs. Monro resentfully.

There was a sound of dogs scuffling and being rebuked in the hall outside; after a pause the door opened and Edina Monro came in, a tall girl with very dark straight hair cut close to her head, grey eyes, and a dead-white skin—she wore cream-coloured corduroy slacks and a blue seaman's jersey.

"Is there some lunch for me? I had to come in, it's too wet for the men to go on," she began—"Oh, Mrs. Hathaway, it's nice to see you. Did you have an awful trip?"

"It was a bit rough coming round Ardlamont Point, but I don't mind that," said Mrs. Hathaway, getting up, with the manners of her generation, to shake hands with the girl. "How are you, Edina? You look well."

Miss Monro in fact did look well; there was nothing unhealthy about her intensely white skin, to which not even hours out of doors in a howling gale gave the faintest tinge of colour.

"Thank you; yes I am very well," said Edina, as she spoke going over and pressing the bell after a brief inspection of the food on the side-table. "Plenty I see," she muttered, "thank God for Olimpia." "Yes, this revolting climate is in fact incredibly healthy," she said to their guest, pulling up a chair and sitting down beside her. "Forbes, get me a very *hot* plate, and then come and lay me a place," she said, as the butler appeared at the door, a resentful expression on his old face. "And tell Olimpia that we shall want coffee."

"Dear, we don't need coffee after lunch," said Mrs. Monro.

"Oh yes we do—I see you hadn't ordered it, even for your poor friend after her long journey! Really, Mother, you are barbarous."

"I'm sure Forbes doesn't like the way you speak to him," said Mrs. Monro, changing her ground.

"No, why should he? But he does what I tell him, which is more than he does for you," her daughter replied tranquilly—"Spoilt, lazy old bastard." Mrs. Hathaway could not restrain a tiny laugh; she liked Edina very much.

"Well he is, you know," the girl said, encouraged by the laugh. "But at least one doesn't have to carry in trays, or wash up, thank God."

A *crème brûlée*, faultlessly made, followed the *vol-au-vent*; Mrs. Hathaway, accustomed to the mutton-and-milk-pudding rigours which normally prevailed at Glentoran, mentally echoed Edina's thanks to her Creator for the Spanish cook. Over the coffee, which the girl made Forbes bring up to the sitting-room, the subject of finding Colin again arose.

"Mother, you'd better go and rest; it's past your time," said Edina, after Mrs. Monro had recapitulated at some length most of what she had said to her guest before lunch—"I made you late, I know, but off you go. You'll be wretched this evening if you don't have it." And with a sort of kindly firmness she hustled her parent off, finding her book and spectacles for her.

"There—now we can talk," the girl said with satisfaction, returning to the fire, on which she placed two or three more logs. "It is good of you to come up," she said. "Poor Mother is in a frightful state."

"That's very understandable," said Mrs. Hathaway. "But Edina, tell me one thing—how much good would Colin be at running this place, even if you could get him back?"

"Oh, you know, I think he might manage all right. He didn't do too badly at Cambridge, or at Cirencester. He's capable enough; it's just that he likes changing—he doesn't seem to care about sticking to one thing."

"He would have to stick to this," said Mrs. Hathaway. "The land is one thing that can't be left to itself."

"Well he might, now. There wasn't much point in his sticking up here while Uncle John was running it perfectly, and loving doing it."

Mrs. Hathaway meditated.

"You wouldn't take it on yourself, Edina?" she presently asked. "Robertson was singing your praises all the way from the pier: 'Miss Edina gets a grup on things,' he said," she added smiling.

"Oh yes, I get a 'grup' all right," said Edina cheerfully, "but it's not really the sort of thing I care to do, nor what I was educated for, at vast expense. And I'm not sure that we can afford it, really."

"How do you mean?"

"Well, there's not much more than a living for two to be got off this place, and in London I'm making fifteen hundred a year. I give Mother *her* dress-allowance these days," said Edina, with a grin.

"Good Heavens! Fifteen hundred a year!" Mrs. Hathaway was startled. She knew that Edina had taken a good degree in Modern Greats at Oxford, and that she was working at some job in London, but she had never imagined that her young friend was making a living on that scale. "What do you do?" she asked, with interest.

"Oh, I'm in advertising—the new high-powered sort. In its rather phoney way it's really very interesting, and now that we're beginning to get into T.V. it's going to be more interesting still, and better paid."

"*Better* paid? Gracious."

"Oh yes. I'm due for a rise to two thousand pounds in June, unless my coming off up here bitches it," said Edina. "They gave me three months leave, when I said I had to have it, without a murmur, so I dare say it will be all right. But I want to get back as soon as I can, rise or no rise; there are some rather tricky things coming up soon that I specialise in, and I don't want anyone else to handle them and probably rot them up—and nor do my bosses," she added.

Mrs. Hathaway observed, with slight surprise, that there was nothing objectionable about Edina's complete self-confidence; it was entirely objective.

"Yes," she said after a pause. "I see that you really oughtn't to be held up here. But have you any ideas as to how to get hold of Colin?"

"No—that's what's so tiresome. Maddening boy! Have you, Mrs. H.?"

"Well, I've been thinking about it, since your Mother told me what she knows—which is little enough," said Mrs. Hathaway. "And I have got the impression that there is something rather funny about the whole thing."

"Funny or phoney?"

"Well both, really. Anyhow writing is no good, since his last address is nine months old; and advertising is no good, because either he doesn't see the papers, or if he does he doesn't choose to answer. I think someone will have to go and find him."

This time it was Edina who was startled. She opened her grey eyes very wide.

"That's a thought! But I don't quite see how anyone would set about it. You mean go and enquire at all these film-scenario ports?"

"Yes. And the boat must be registered—what's her name, by the way?"

"Oh, that damnable child has never even told us that!" Edina exploded. "He really is too tedious."

"Well, all the more reason for on-the-spot enquiries," said Mrs. Hathaway. "Three or four young Englishmen, cruising about and selling oranges or bananas or whatever they do sell—I don't really much believe in the orange part, myself—ought to be tolerably identifiable."

"You know, I believe you really have got something there," said Edina. "But who's to do it? Would you go?"

"Oh no, I should be useless at badgering consulates and accosting harbour-masters, or whatever one does to find missing yachts—it would have to be someone young and enterprising."

"Anyone in mind?" Edina enquired, eyeing Mrs. Hathaway rather suspiciously.

"Yes. Julia, I thought," that lady replied.

"Julia? Do you think she'd be any good? Well yes, I suppose she might —she's not really half as stupid as she looks," said Edina. "But would she go? She has oodles of money of course—but one's only allowed a hundred pounds, and I should think all this foraging around in Tangier and places would cost a lot."

"That's why I think Julia would be so suitable. She's a journalist, and they can get extra foreign allowances for trips."

"She's a pretty half-baked journalist; only this free-lancing for weeklies, and the *Yorkshire Post* now and then," Edina objected.

"Oh, my dear child, I'm sure that doesn't matter a bit. I know a woman who writes for most terrible magazines, things you've never even heard the names of, and she is always rushing off to Cannes and St. Moritz and so on to write up the film-stars and their clothes and all that—she gets colossal foreign currency allowances, I know."

"I see. Yes, well then Julia is quite a thought. She could get away all right, I expect. I don't suppose her papers would mind," said Edina, rather cattily.

Mrs. Hathaway laughed.

"All right—let's ring her up tonight," Edina went on. "The sooner we find him the better, for me as well as for Mother. Only I still wonder if Julia is up to it."

"Oh, don't underestimate Julia. You don't really know her much, do you?"

"Well no. One has one's own friends, somehow. Do you know her well?"

"Yes—her mother was a friend of mine," said Mrs. Hathaway, rather slowly. It flicked into Edina's mind, belatedly, that she had heard that after Mrs. Probyn's death and Major Probyn's re-marriage, Mrs. Hathaway had befriended Julia, their only child. Colin and Edina were not very closely related to her. Julia's mother had been their father's first cousin, and had often brought her to Glentoran when they were all children; but after Mrs. Probyn's death all that had ceased—the Monros had never greatly cared for Major Probyn, and liked his second wife even less. Julia had been left a considerable fortune by her grandmother, so that she was able to lead a quite independent life, not shackled to her father and stepmother; she worked as a journalist because it amused her, not because she was in any need of earning her living, and she had been abroad a good deal, as Edina, feeling rather exculpatory, now pointed out to Mrs. Hathaway—one didn't see so much of people if one never knew whether they were there or not, she explained.

"Yes, of course," said Mrs. Hathaway pleasantly. "I don't blame you for not knowing Julia, Edina—I'm only pin-pointing the fact that you don't! *C'est une constatation,* as the French say."

Edina laughed, relieved. How sensible and *nice* Mrs. Hathaway was.

"I wonder if she would go," she went on. "Shall we put it all up to her on the telephone, or try to get her to come up? It's rather a long business to explain."

"We'll see how she reacts," said Mrs. Hathaway. "It would be better if she came, I think, if she can get away at once. Another reason why she would be a good person to go," she pursued, "is that she's a very fair linguist; her French is excellent, and she speaks quite tolerable Spanish too."

"Oh well then, do let's get her to come up," said Edina, "to brace up Olimpia. She cooks quite differently after Ronan's been talking to her, though I believe he only knows about twenty-eight words."

"He must have been talking to her this morning," said Mrs. Hathaway. "That *lovely* lunch."

Julia, when telephoned to, made no difficulties at all about coming up. Mrs. Hathaway, who by common consent did the talking, merely said that they were all in trouble about Colin, who couldn't be got hold of just now; they thought Julia might be able to help, perhaps, and was there any chance of her coming up to talk it over? "To be much good," said Mrs. Hathaway, with her customary clarity, "it ought to be *soon*."

"Oh yes, I'll come at once. If I take a sleeper tomorrow night—no, that means two days. I'll fly to Renfrew tomorrow, the first flight I can get, and wire for a car to bring me on; that will save a day. Unless I ring up, if I *can't* get a seat, I'll see you about tea-time tomorrow. It will be lovely to be at Glentoran again. How's Aunt Ellen?"

"As easy as that," said Mrs. Hathaway, having retailed these plans to the other two.

"Well, it must be nice to be able to splash money about like that," said Edina.

"Yes—and sensible, too. Julia is rather good about knowing what to spend on," said Mrs. Hathaway. She turned to Edina with a small smile. "Bottle up your prejudice till she comes—you are far too sensible yourself to let my approval of Julia put you against her," she said—and Edina, who had been doing exactly that, did cause her vague hostility to subside.

"I still don't see how Julia is to find him, Mary," said Mrs. Monro.

"One finds very little without looking for it, Ellen," replied Mrs. Hathaway. "Do you mind if I go to bed? I feel rather like it, after the journey."

Julia Probyn arrived next day, not at tea-time, but as they were sitting down to lunch—a scrunch of carwheels on the gravel outside the dining-room windows announced the advent of a huge Chrysler, driven by a smart chauffeur.

"I'll go, Forbes," said Edina to the old butler, who was bumbling round with dishes with his usual maddening slowness; "lay another place"—and she went out. A moment later she returned, ushering in her young relation.

"Dear Aunt Ellen, I do apologise for being so early," said Julia, kissing

her aunt affectionately. "I rang up the air-line last night and got a cancel-
lation for the first flight, such luck—so I told them to tell Renfrew to have
a car ready, and here I am." She turned to kiss Mrs. Hathaway with even
more warmth. "How blessed to see you. And Aunt Ellen, can my driver-
man have some lunch?"

"Of course," said Edina, answering for her parent. "Just come and mutter
some of your Spanish to our cook, and she'll be your slave."

"Really, Edina—" Mrs. Monro began in protest; but her daughter ruthlessly led the guest out across the hall and through the red baize door to the
back regions. Julia, smothering mirth, spoke solemnly in elegant Castilian
to Olimpia, whose haughty features relaxed at the familiar accents in
which she was asked to provide food for the chauffeur—bowing, smiling,
she expressed her desire to do everything she could.

"*Le agradezco mucho su amabildad,*" said Julia, eyeing her sternly, and
returned to the dining-room, telling her driver on the way to wait in the
hall till Forbes should summon him to his meal. "Don't smoke," she added
casually, earning Edina's silent approbation.

Julia was tall, and built on full if graceful lines; her large smooth oval
face usually held very little expression; this mattered less because of her
perfect, faintly tawny complexion, as lightly flushed with colour as a
nearly-ripe apricot, the exquisite level line of her mouth, and above all her
immense grey-blue eyes, which somehow seemed to promise all sorts of delightful expressions, though entirely without her volition. (Her friends
called them doves' eyes, her enemies likened them to the eyes of cows.)
Her hair was a sort of tawny blonde, a most peculiar shade; she wore it
drawn back plainly from her shapely forehead, to hang, a deplorable
length, half-way down her shoulders, where it ended in flowing curls, like
liquid treacle. To complete this exotic appearance she was beautifully
dressed, and had long perfect legs. During lunch Edina studied her, fascinated. She usually spoke very slowly, without actually drawling, and her
deep voice was as devoid of expression as her face. Except that her fair-
ness had this curious tawny leonine quality she was, Edina thought, the
arch-type of the dumb blonde.

The other exception to the type was the fact that she was nothing like
as dumb as she looked; this emerged during the discussion of her mission,
which took place after lunch, when Mrs. Monro had again been despatched to rest by her daughter. Mrs. Hathaway and Edina had no need
to stress the urgency of Colin's return, since Mrs. Monro had dealt with
that aspect with wearisome thoroughness during lunch, and indeed until
she retired; they concentrated on telling the little they knew—about the
boat or yacht, the friends, the orange or banana-selling, and the ports at

which he was known to have touched during the past three years. Julia listened, largely in silence—at last she said:

"In fact you really haven't a clue as to where he may be now?"

"No, not the faintest."

"Detection!" said Julia, delighted, a gleam of interest at last showing in her face. "Pure detection! What a frolic! Yes, of course I'll go; I'd love to escape this hellish winter. And Colin used to be such a darling—I'd adore to find him. I expect I shall."

"How shall you begin?" enquired Mrs. Hathaway.

"Could we look at a map?" said Julia. "I'm rather vague about where all these places are, and how to get to them."

Edina brought an atlas, in which Julia underlined various ports with a rose-tipped finger—"Casablanca, Tangier with Gib. almost opposite," she murmured; "Ceuta, yes, and Malaga up round the corner—and then Oran and Algiers and all those places. *I* see."

"We never heard of his going to Oran or Algiers," said Edina; "it was more Malaga and Gib. and Cadiz, and Tangier and Casablanca—down that end."

Julia lit a cigarette, slowly as she did everything, and blew out smoke. "I shall begin with Africa, I think," she pronounced.

"Why?"

"Well, Morocco and Algiers are news just now, with all these assassinations and bomb-throwings and skirmishes and things, and I shall have to get the papers lined up in order to get an extra currency allocation." Edina nodded approvingly—they had not yet raised this point with Julia; obviously there had been no need to.

"*Ebb and Flow* and *The Onlooker* can't run to special correspondents out there, but they would be sure to love articles and call them 'from our correspondent in Morocco' without paying a farthing extra," she pursued, a slow smile making her beautiful mouth even more beguiling. "So they would give me the right chits to push across the counter to those elderly virgins in the Bank of England."

Edina laughed.

"I can do Spain later," Julia pursued, "if I draw a blank on the coasts of High Barbary."

"How shall you go?—fly?" Mrs. Hathaway enquired. She was delighted, secretly, that Julia was showing up so well.

"Oh no, I think not. Some boat—if I'm going to look for a boat I'd rather start on a boat, to get the feel of the thing, if you follow me. I'll ring up some of the lines later—if you'll let me?" she said to Edina, who registered suddenly how agreeable these pretty manners were; she knew that Julia would pay for her calls, but the question was graceful. "Of course," she said.

Julia got up and went over again to the atlas, and gazed at it.

"The Lynches are in Casablanca," she said. "They might know something. He's in some bank, and banks know a lot."

"I shouldn't have thought Colin used a bank much, except to wheedle the manager into letting him overdraw," said Edina.

"Where's his account now? Still in Cambridge, or up here, or where?" Julia asked. "Is it still open?"

"Goodness, we never thought of that. I've no idea. It used to be in Duntroon, with a pay-in and pay-out account in some bank at Cambridge, like I had at Oxford."

"Well, let's ring up Duntroon now, and see if it's still there."

This was done, by Edina. Mr. MacIntyre, the agent, protesting that it was against the regulations, nevertheless vouchsafed the information— "just for you privately, Miss Monro, since I know ye all so well"—that Mr. Colin had closed his account some nine months ago; the balance had been transferred to the Banque Régie Turque in Casablanca.

"There you are!" said Julia triumphantly. "Where a man's bank-account is, there shall his body be also, at least occasionally. We're getting warmer."

"Can there really be a branch of the Banque Régie Turque in Casablanca?" Mrs. Hathaway asked. "It seems most extraordinary. I thought that was purely a Turkish thing."

"Well, Mr. MacIntyre would never pay sixpence into a non-existent Bank," said Edina—"There must be. Look!" she exclaimed suddenly—"Nine months ago. But that's just when he stopped writing!"

"Who, Colin?" Julia asked.

"Yes—at least we've never heard since then. He didn't write all that often before, but there's never been such a long gap as this."

"Well, this may be where Paddy Lynch will come in," said Julia—"one banker will sometimes talk to another banker. I'd certainly better look in at Casablanca. But Edina, why don't you write to him there, care of the Banque Régie Turque? It seems the firmest address you've had."

"Well we could," said Edina dubiously—"but he never answers. If you're going out I should hardly have thought it worth while."

"Oh very well. In that case, Edina, I think I'll start getting onto the shipping lines: some of them must have offices in Glasgow."

"It's frightfully expensive before the cheap time begins," said Edina.

"Ah, and they're shut when it does. No, on we go; I'll try to remember to put the charges to expense account," said Julia, with another of those slow pleasing grins. "I'll have them all A. D. & C."

The shipping lines were not very fruitful. Most of the big liners no longer call at Gibraltar when outward bound for Australia or the Far East, and the few that do were booked out till mid-March with sun-seeking Britons. Julia established this fact in a way that amused Edina and Mrs. Hathaway. The bookings were mostly made in London, the shipping clerks told her; they couldn't really say in Glasgow—with languid firmness Julia told them to ring up London, and call her back "collect". "Oh, reverse the charge, if you don't know what 'collect' means," she intoned slowly. "This is urgent—I'm the Press. Do please get on with it." They got on with it, and reported these negative results. Julia, scribbling pounds, shillings and pence on the telephone pad, said—"Well, that's useless."

"Why not try a cargo-boat?" said Mrs. Hathaway. "I believe they go to all sorts of small places, and if you want to get the 'feel', as you say, of a banana-boat, or whatever Colin's is, that should be just the thing."

"A good idea," Julia agreed.

"Do you get sea-sick?" Edina put in. "Cargo-boats can be pretty small— I had some chums who went to Greece on one, and it was tiny."

"No—never sea-sick. Yes, a cargo-boat is undoubtedly the thing, but I expect I could fix that more easily in London. In fact, Edina, I think I'd better flash off again tomorrow and get onto it; poor Aunt Ellen, she's in a dismal frenzy herself, and I'm sure driving you frantic—quite apart from your firm howling for you. Do you mind if I ring up Renfrew for a passage? Oh, what a pity—it is so nice up here. I do love Glentoran."

CHAPTER II

"WELL THIS IS the London Docks, lady," said the taxi-man to Julia a week later, pulling up at a huge gateway beyond which black-looking buildings loomed through a grey downpour of rain. "Know which shed you want?"

"Number Nine," said Julia, consulting a paper which the shipping company had given her.

"Ought to be a policeman," said the taxi-driver.

"Hoot," said Julia.

When the driver hooted a policeman appeared from a sort of sentry-box by the gates, and asked what Julia wanted.

"The *Vidago*."

"May I see your ticket, please?" He inspected it, and looked curiously at Julia through the cab window; then directed the driver.

"Go along as far as you can, straight, and then turn right. You'll see her lying." The taxi passed through the big gates, and proceeded slowly over cobbles gleaming in the rain; the buildings formed a sort of canyon, its floor nearly as wet as a river-bed; short broad spaces led off it on one side, piled with crates and wine-barrels; more wine-barrels cluttered the canyon-floor itself—Julia had never seen so many wine-barrels in her life. At length they reached a transverse road; the taxi turned right, and in a few seconds came to the water, where nearly a hundred yards away a ship lay moored alongside the berth.

"That'll be her," said the driver.

Julia stared at the boat with the curiosity which everyone feels about a ship they are to travel on. She was prepared for it to be small, for she knew the *Vidago* to be only thirteen hundred tons, but she was startled by its extreme dirtiness. All the paintwork that should have been white was smeared with black grime, or stained and mottled with rust; it looked very unappetising.

The driver got out, turning up his collar, and began to unstrap her suitcases.

"Oh leave those," said Julia. "I don't want them put down in this mess." The quayside was quite as filthy as the ship, and wetter. "I'll go and find a steward or someone—wait, please." And she walked off towards the boat along the strip of cement between the water and the open-fronted shed from which goods were embarked, a big resonant place as dirty as everything else, full of crates of goods and, she noted, tractors—innumerable tractors. Her progress was presently blocked by a crane, from whose control cabin, forty feet above her head, a monkey-faced man in blue jeans peered out at her curiously; to circumvent this obstacle she took to the shed, where four or five men were languidly mounting crates on out-size luggage-barrows; re-emerging onto the quay she found herself at the *Vidago*'s gangway. This was almost surrealist, she thought; it consisted of a sort of ladder of black slimy wooden steps, with dirty ropes for hand-rails, mounting to the deck of the *Vidago* at an angle of some thirty-five degrees. Julia surveyed it with distaste, and instead of attempting the disagreeable ascent, stood still and shouted.

A porthole close above her was pushed open, and a huge red face poked through it. "Who d'ye want?" it enquired.

"Someone to bring my luggage aboard," said Julia.

"Och, I don't know that there's anyone here—they're mostly ashore," said the red face.

"But we're sailing at four. I'm the passenger," said Julia.

"We're only sailing tomorrow, no the nicht," the face pronounced; it then withdrew, closing the porthole.

"Oh, *God!*" said Julia, crossly and loudly. She stood for a moment, undecided what to do next. To spend the next twenty-four hours in these surroundings was a dismal prospect; on the other hand her taxi was going to cost a fortune, with all that luggage—it seemed absurd to pay it twice over. (Mrs. Hathaway was quite right about Julia's sensible views as to what it was worth spending money on.) She determined to get most of her stuff on board at once, somehow, and walked back towards the taxi; passing as before through the cargo-shed she looked round for a barrow, found one, and wheeled it out along the quay—as she passed below the crane she was once more hailed from above, this time by the monkey-faced man in the cabin atop of it.

"Want help with your baggage, Miss?"

"Yes please," Julia called up; on reaching the taxi she and the driver began to pile her suit-cases onto the barrow. They had just finished this task and she was paying off the cab when two individuals came up simultaneously—one the crane-driver, the other a tall man with a curly brown beard, in a very shabby nautical uniform and a peaked cap.

"Can I help?" the newcomer asked.

"Oh, I think this kind person is going to take my stuff aboard the *Vidago* for me—there seems to be no one else to do it," said Julia coldly. She was feeling extremely cross.

"I'm the mate of the *Vidago*," said the bearded man. "I'll send the boy along—this chap can't go aboard. But we're not sailing till tomorrow, you know."

"I know nothing of the sort," said Julia, more coldly still. "Your passenger-manager or whatever he calls himself told me yesterday at six o'clock to be here at three sharp, to sail at four, and I have no contrary instructions."

"Ah yes, but there's been a hold-up," said the bearded man. "Very sorry." He spoke with a very cultivated accent, which contrasted sharply with his shabby appearance.

"I'm sorry too, but I can't help that," said Julia—"I and my luggage are coming aboard *now*, according to schedule. Carry on—take it to the gangway," she said to the crane-driver.

A grin appeared in the depths of the mate's beard.

"Oh very well," he said.

"If your 'boy' can drag this up your ladder and put it in my cabin, he had better," said Julia, walking off after the crane-driver and the barrow; the mate, his grin expanding in his beard, followed.

Her cabin when she reached it, after negotiating the precipitous gangway and following the mate along decks as black and filthy as the rest of the ship, proved a rather agreeable surprise. It was quite a sizeable little room, containing besides a substantial bunk with drawers below it a hanging-cupboard, a desk-cum-chest of drawers, a fitted basin, and a big padded sofa built against the bulk-head.

"Fine," said Julia, looking round her. "But my luggage won't all go in here. Stop," she said firmly to the boy, who was beginning to pile her cases onto the sofa—"only bring in what I tell you. Yes, the typewriter, and those two small ones; that's all for here." She turned to the officer, who loomed, still grinning slightly, in the passageway outside, and asked—"Where does the rest go? You would hardly have a baggage-room, with only one passenger?"

"No, afraid not."

"Well, will you have it put somewhere—*dry*," said Julia calmly.

"Is the pilot's cabin unlocked?" the first officer asked the boy.

"Yessir."

"All right—put it in there."

The pilot's cabin was next door to Julia's, similarly furnished and equally large; she supervised the stowing of the rest of her luggage in it, remarking, "Very handy," to the mate.

"You all right now?" he asked, still looking amused.

"No. I must have the keys to lock both these cabins. You can't leave cabins unlocked in port," said Julia. "And then I want to telephone, as there's this delay. Is the ship connected up by telephone?"

"No—not a liner, you know," said the mate. "But you could ring up from the agents' office on the quay."

"Where is that?"

"I'll show you,"—and the keys having been produced by the boy, he led her down the gang-ladder again and along the shed to a small door with a roughly-painted label outside which read "Forres Line. No Admittance".

"Thanks," said Julia briefly; the bearded man, still grinning slightly, raised his hand to his cap and walked off.

The office was a grubby little hole in which a red-haired individual sat at a desk, telephoning; another, wearing a felt hat and a stained raincoat, stood by the window, which was smothered in cobwebs, holding up long yellowish sheets of paper to catch the last light of the winter's afternoon, and occasionally calling out figures to the one at the telephone, who repeated them down it; a third was tinkering with a very small electric fire, on which he succeeded in balancing a kettle just as Julia walked in. They all looked up, and the man at the telephone, saying "Hold on," asked if she wanted anything?

"To telephone, when the line is free; to the head office," Julia replied.

The man with the kettle, who was very old, removed a pile of ledgers and a couple of beer-bottles from a chair, of which he dusted the seat with his sleeve before offering it to her; she sat down and waited. Presently the lists came to an end, and the man at the desk asked her who she wanted at head office.

"The passenger manager."

The passenger manager was 'not available'.

"Find out when he will be, please, and tell him to ring back. Miss Probyn to speak to him." "Can I wait here?" she asked.

"Oh, surely. Have one of mine," said the man at the window, as she pulled out her cigarette case. He looked at her subdued elegance curiously. "You're not for the *Vidago?*"

"Yes."

Julia enjoyed her wait in the Forres Line's quay-side office, in spite of her irritation over the delay in sailing. The old man brewed very strong tea on the electric fire, laid on its side, and they gave her a cup, thick with the glutinous oversweetened condensed milk beloved of the merchant navy—she found time to wonder how the manufacturers contrived to introduce its peculiar and revolting flavour into this product, with which she was to become painfully familiar in the next few days. In spite of her toughness and temper Julia could be quite a good mixer when she chose, and it always interested her to know how operations were carried on in jobs and trades unfamiliar to her; she soon beguiled the three men in that grubby little room sufficiently to learn not only the reason for the *Vidago's* delayed sailing, but a good deal about dock-side labour as well.

"The rain, you see," said the red-haired man at the desk. "It came on heavy about eleven, and you can't load in rain."

"Oh, why not?"

"Soaks the holds; rots or rusts the cargo, and anyhow this dock's shift's short-handed today."

"Oh, why is that?" asked Julia, sipping the old man's brew, which reminded her of a mixture of senna and stewed prunes.

"The fight in Belfast," said the man at the desk.

"Really? How come?" enquired Julia.

What she learned fascinated her. One of the dockers named Murphy had for a brother a prize-fighter, who was appearing that night in a big fight in Belfast; so Murphy and his closest pals had chartered a private plane to fly to Northern Ireland to see the show, and large numbers of their comrades had gone off by special train to Liverpool, to cross by boat for the same purpose. This, more than the rain, had held up the loading of the *Vidago*. Julia hugged herself. The poor underpaid dockers, always striking for a living wage! Whoever heard of the so-called idle rich hiring private planes and trains nowadays? These views however she kept to herself.

At length the telephone rang; the passenger manager, at last 'available', was on the line.

"Oh Mr. Scales," said Julia taking up the instrument—"Miss Probyn here—yes, down at the docks. Why didn't you let me know that the boat isn't sailing till tomorrow?"

Mr. Scales was evasive. Really, he was extremely sorry, but he hadn't known in time to let her know.

"But the rain came on, and the men stopped work, at eleven—that meant there wasn't a hope of getting her out on tonight's tide," said Julia inexorably; she had picked up a lot of information over her tea. "I only left home at two. Surely there would have been time?—in three hours?"

Mr. Scales could almost be heard to wriggle down the telephone. He hadn't heard quite at eleven o'clock; he really was very sorry it had occurred.

"Well, I call it a very poor show," said Julia. "Don't you instruct your dockside staff to keep you informed when this sort of thing happens, so that you can warn your passengers?"

"That'll mean a raspberry for me," muttered the red-haired man, grinning cheerfully, however.

Mr. Scales meanwhile was asking what Miss Probyn meant to do? Could he do anything to help her?

"I expect so. Have you a car?"

Yes, Mr. Scales had a car.

"Then you could come and fetch me, couldn't you, and take me back to the West End?"

"You're not thinking of sleeping on board, then?"

"Yes, certainly I am—my flat is shut, and I don't see any point in paying for a room at a hotel because of this muddle," said Julia firmly. "But I can spend the evening with friends. No, no hurry—so long as I start about six. Right—thank you." She rang off.

"It won't really mean trouble for you, will it?" she asked the red-haired man. "What time *did* you tell the office?"

" 'Bout twelve—and they know damn well up there that if the stevedores go off before twelve they never come back till after the dinner-hour, not if the sun was blazing."

"Scales is new," said the man in the rain-coat. "He doesn't know the works yet."

"Have you any idea what time we shall get off tomorrow?" Julia asked him.

"Not much before ten p.m., I'd say." He turned to consult a dog's-eared tide-table which hung on the wall by the window, near which he had remained standing all the time. "No, about ten she should be moving down into the Pool. But they'll want you on board by nine."

"Oh, *what* a bore!" said Julia. "I did want to go down the river by daylight. Oh well—and now can I have another call, please?"

She tried to ring up Mrs. Hathaway, but that lady was out and would be out all the evening. Julia cast about in her mind who to try next: she had said goodbye to everybody, her flat was shut and her maid gone off to relations in the country; she felt as if her life in London had already, for the time being, come to an end. At last she bethought her of someone to whom she hadn't said goodbye, nor even announced her departure, out of a cowardly desire to avoid what she privately phrased 'bother', when she was in a rush of packing and arrangements. For after a hurried routing round among cargo-lines she had come on the *Vidago,* sailing for Tangier in under a week and carrying one passenger; she had seized on this chance, but the ensuing days had been a frenzied scurry of what she called 'lining-up' the papers for which she wrote, securing her currency allocation, getting the appropriate visas on her passport and all the rest. The person to whom her thoughts now turned was a young man in the Treasury, who in a rather indeterminate way was an admirer—that is to say she had refused him once, he had sulked for some months, and latterly had begun to hang round her again. He was very nice; it was even possible that some day she might decide to marry him—meanwhile she had rather a bad conscience about having kept him in the dark regarding her trip, and he would, if free, certainly be delighted to take her out to dinner and a movie. So she asked for another call. (She made no offer to pay—this was all the Forres Line's fault, anyhow.)

"Is that the Treasury? Mr. Consett, please . . . Geoffrey? Oh good . . . Dinner tonight? Yes, I'd love to; in fact I was going to suggest it. What time, and where? . . . Oh, could you make it a bit earlier? Sevenish for drinks? . . . No, not at the flat—it's shut . . . Because I'm going away . . . Well, to Morocco, actually—I'll tell you all about it at supper . . . No, don't bother to pick me up . . . Because I'm at the London Docks!" (Here Julia tried unsuccessfully to stifle a giggle.) "No, I'm being brought in to S.W.1. —someone's doing penance! . . . Oh, Geoffrey, don't be sour—I can't explain it all now, and I won't try! Where shall we dine? . . . The Oviedo?

Right—but I shan't dress . . . Well then come to my club at seven, for drinks. Goodbye." She rang off.

Both Julia's telephone conversations had brought grins of pleasure to the faces of the other three occupants of the little office—a young lady, going on that little tub the *Vidago,* first ticking-off the Head Office and then giving back-chat to someone in the Treasury! When she got up and shook hands with them all, with thanks for their tea and their hospitality, each one wrung her hand warmly. "It's been a pleasure. Come in any time," said the old man.

"Oh, I daresay you'll see more of me tomorrow," said Julia airily. "Goodbye, and thank you again."

She went back to her cabin, unpacked and put on a dark frock, with an eye to the gang-ladder, and did her face; on her way up she had yelled for 'the boy', and told him to send Mr. Scales to her cabin when he should arrive. But before that she had another encounter. Emerging to scout about for her escort she almost ran into a small elderly man with grey hair, a smooth grey face, and several gold bands on his sleeves.

"Is it Miss Probyn?" he asked.

"Yes."

"Ah, good evening. I'm sorry we're not starting on time," said this person. "I hope it's not putting you about too much."

"Well, I thought the office might have told me about it," said Julia, who believed in rubbing it in to companies or corporations.

"Won't you come and have a drink?" said the grey-haired man, opening a teak door in the corridor a few yards from her own.

"I'd love to, if someone will tell Mr. Scales where to find me," said Julia, passing through the door. The large, comfortably furnished room in which she found herself told her that she was in the captain's cabin; it had several of the built-in sofas, a big desk, some arm-chairs, and a cupboard in the wall with a shelf below holding a wooden rack of glasses.

"Scales will find you here all right," said the captain slowly, moving over to the cupboard—he spoke even more deliberately than Julia herself. "What will you drink?—gin or whisky?"

"Whisky, please."

"Do you like soda?" he asked, holding up a tumbler to the light and squinting at it; as he spoke he opened the lower part of the cupboard, pulled out a spotless cloth, and began to polish the glass.

"Yes please."

The captain pushed a bell, meanwhile unlocking the upper cupboard and taking out a bottle of Black-and-White; when the boy tapped on the door he said, "Tell Andrews to bring some soda."

"He's ashore, Sir."

"Is Mr. Harris on board?"

"Yessir—I think so, Sir."

"Then tell him I want some soda, please."

"Yessir."

There was something about the slow formality of Captain Blyth's manner of speaking to his ship's company which was to impress Julia throughout the trip; it began to impress her that first evening when Mr. Harris, who was the chief steward, appeared and said apologetically that Andrews must have gone off with the keys, and he could only find one bottle of soda, which he had borrowed off Mr. Reeder. All Captain Blyth said was—"Thank you. Get some."

"In port, things slow down a bit. The men all like to get ashore, and of course drinks aren't served till we get outside territorial waters," he said, bringing the whisky and soda over to where Julia sat on one of the sofas, and setting them on a table fixed to the bulkhead at her side. "Now, tell me how you like this."

The time passed pleasantly—Julia's lingering vexation gradually melted away under the captain's slow, cheerful chat. He had a flat, quiet manner and spoke in a gentle, flat voice. He himself liked gin, he said, proceeding to drink it; the agents in the ports mostly liked whisky, and you wouldn't believe how much they would drink; moreover they liked to sit up all night, whereas he, himself, hated staying up late, unless he had to be on the bridge, which was a different thing. He expressed a courteous hope that Julia would be comfortable, and mentioned various people in Tangier who always came out on his ship—"come time after time, the Watsons do. He's a nice man, Mr. Watson—and she's nice, too."

Mr. Scales proved to be a very young man, to Julia's surprise; when she was arranging her passage he had contrived on the telephone to sound almost paternal. When the boy announced him Captain Blyth said, "Oh, I must give you your pass," in his soft voice, and sat down at his desk and unlocked a drawer—everything in his cabin seemed always to be being unlocked and locked again.

"Pass? whatever for?" asked Julia curiously.

"Can't get into the docks at night without. There. Hope you enjoy yourself." He came out with her along the deck to the gangway. "Sorry everything's in a bit of a mess—clean up when we get to sea," he said. "Don't slip, now—that's awkward, that gangway is."

It took Mr. Scales and his small car, caught up in the evening jam of westbound traffic from the City, rather a long time to transport Julia to the discreet club, mostly peopled by women twice her age, for which Mrs.

Hathaway had put her up; Mr. Consett was waiting for her, the porter said. Unhurried, Julia went in and found him sitting in the big chintzy drawing-room, reading *Antiquity*.

"I'm sorry I'm late—the traffic in the City was awful, and my penitent didn't drive very well," she said.

"I've not been here long. Who is your penitent, and why?" asked Mr. Consett, locking *Antiquity* away in a black brief-case with the royal cypher on it.

"A *very* incompetent young man—will you have whisky or a Martini?" —"A Martini and a tomato-juice, please," said Julia to the severe elderly waitress, "and we're not dining here."

"Goodness, Julia, what an aunt-heap this place is!" Mr. Consett said in a lowered tone as the waitress moved away, glancing round at the other occupants of the room.

"Well yes. But the drinks are reasonably good."

"'A very incompetent young man' you were saying," Mr. Consett prompted her.

"Yes, in the shipping office." She related Mr. Scales's crime. Mr. Consett gazed at her indignantly.

"In fact, you were going to slide off without so much as letting me know! What a *Schweinhund* you are, Julia."

"What is a *Schweinhund*?" asked Julia, sipping her tomato-juice—her languages did not extend to German.

"A mixture of a cur and a swine," said Mr. Consett measuredly. "No, really, Julia—you are *monstrous*."

"I was in such a rush," she said, turning the dove's rather than the cow's eyes onto him. "I hadn't a moment to see anyone, Geoffrey; truly I hadn't. Fixing my newspapers, and the visas, and getting extra Travellers' Cheques, and finding a boat to go on—you can't think what an absolute *scrum* it's been."

"Why Morocco, anyhow?" the young man asked. He was very tall; pallid, with thick fair hair, a square intellectual face, and pale blue eyes, he usually looked as severely detached from this world as a youthful St. John the Evangelist in an early Flemish predella.

Julia explained the nature of her quest; Geoffrey Consett immediately became extremely un-detached.

"What is this Colin? A boy-friend? Otherwise, why do you go hooshing off to find him in this completely wildcat way? I never heard such rubbish."

"Oh Geoffrey, don't be a clot! People aren't usually boy-friends in at all a *heavy* way if they go off for three years at a time, and never write. But in fact I've hardly seen anything of Colin since he was at Eton."

"Eton? What surname?"

"Monro, you silly. He's Aunt Ellen's son. And I'm only going because Uncle John has gone and died, and Aunt Ellen is in such a fuss, and poor wretched Edina—who makes twice *your* salary, I may say—has got to stay and run Glentoran till someone can find Colin and make him come back and look after his own infernal estate. Not but what it's a most darling place," said Julia.

"Colin Monro—yes, I remember him; he was in Merryweather's," said Geoffrey, temporarily disregarding all but the Etonian aspect of Julia's remarks. "A pig-headed creature."

"Oh, was he? Well, he's a poor correspondent."

Mr. Consett, during the second round of drinks and over dinner at the Oviedo, continued to cross-examine Julia about Colin and her trip. At one point he asked how the orange-selling venture had been financed. Julia had no idea, but unguardedly let out the fact that nine months earlier the balance of Colin's account at Duntroon had been transferred to the Banque Régie Turque at Casablanca. Mr. Consett pounced on this piece of information like a peregrine on a pigeon.

"Transferred it to Casablanca? How big was the balance?"

"I haven't the smallest clue," said Julia. "Why?"

"Because it's illegal, for a sum of any size. My dear Julia, surely *you* know about currency restrictions?"

"Well yes, for travelling. I never thought of that," said Julia candidly. "But old Mr. McIntyre at the Bank of Scotland in Duntroon would never do anything illegal, from what Edina says."

"I must look into this," said Mr. Consett, with more animation than he had yet shown—"the Bank of England will know. Nine months ago, you say?"

"Oh Geoffrey, *please* don't go making trouble! Edina and Aunt Ellen have quite enough bothers on their plate as it is, without you stirring up the Bank of England with your beastly bureaucratic spoon."

"My dear Julia, do be your age! What all these papers employ you for I can't think," said Geoffrey. He often tried, rather helplessly, to impose his superior knowledge on his love by way of subduing her—a futile process always, and particularly unsuccessful in Julia's case. "If what has been done is within the regulations it can't make trouble," he pursued; "and I agree that the Bank of Scotland are about the last people in the world to slip up. But if the sum was of any size there would have to be special permission for the transfer, and to obtain that reasons would have to be given. I think I might be able to find out what those reasons were. It certainly wouldn't be given for hawking oranges!"

"I wish you wouldn't use words like 'obtain'," said Julia petulantly.

"Oh darling, what a clown you are! Don't you see that I may be able to help you in this lunatic search-party of yours?" the young man said, reaching for her hand across the table.

Many hands, and often, are held in the Oviedo—Julia was not in the least embarrassed, and suffered poor Mr. Consett to clasp, and even to kiss her long fingers with their glistening pale-pink tips. Satisfied for the moment —and the waiter arriving with a fresh dish—the young man returned to the subject of her journey, in a more tranquil spirit.

"Where are you sailing to, on your cargo cockleshell?" he asked.

"Tangier—it seems to be the only place boats stop at, going that way. And it's quite a good jumping-off place for all the rest, I gather."

"An excellent one; and a most darling place in itself—like Glentoran," he said, smiling his rather unexpectedly warm smile. "They're doing some very interesting bits of excavation there, too."

"What sort? Neolithic?" Julia knew very little about archaeology, but her prolonged acquaintance with Geoffrey Consett had resulted in her having to hear a good deal about it, and she had picked up some of the words.

"No, no—Roman, and some possible Phoenician too; old La Besse has been working on a fascinating site which is undoubtedly Roman on the top storey, so to speak, but shows signs of Phoenician stuff below that. The amusing thing is that it seems to have been a factory."

"A factory? Goodness, what on earth of?"

"Wine, oil, and they think salt fish—there are pits that suggest fish-pickling more than anything else." He suddenly became enthusiastic. "You ought to see all that, Julia—I envy you going off there now. Look out for old La Besse."

"Who's he?"

"It's not a he, it's a she. An immensely old Belgian lady with a beard! And she sticks at it—she's out on that site day after day, with her rag-time team of Berber labourers, for six or seven hours at a time."

"When were you there?" Julia asked—"I never heard about all this."

"Oh, last winter," said Mr. Consett, trying unsuccessfully not to look too conscious. Last winter had been during the period when he was sulking after being refused by Julia. "She's tremendous fun," he went on rather hastily—"and all that stretch of coast is simply stuffed with Phoenician graves, too."

"What are they like?" Julia enquired, less out of any particular interest in Phoenician graves than from a good-natured desire to co-operate in covering up the embarrassment about last winter.

"Dug out of the rock, I believe, I never saw much of them—I hadn't time. They're mostly rifled; the Berbers go at them like mad."

"What on earth for?"

"Oh, the jewellery. Exquisite golden things turn up sometimes."

"How enchanting!" said Julia; her eyes shone, kindled by the thought of jewellery in any form. "I'd love to see those."

"I'll give you a letter of introduction to Mme La Besse," said the young man—"I'll air-mail it to Tangier. Where shall you be staying, by the way?"

"The Villa Espagnola—moderate, but Cook's say the food and beds are all right."

Mr. Consett jotted the address down.

"There are other things you must do in Tangier if you are going to be there, Colin or no Colin," he said, rather sententiously. "For one, you must go up to the Kasbah, the old Moorish city, on a Friday to see the Mendoub go to the Mosque for his devotions. He has a lovely cavalry guard, all over tassels."

"Who's the Mendoub?"

"The Sultan's representative in the International Zone—a sort of Viceroy, on the smallest possible scale. The Kasbah's lovely, anyhow; the Terence Monteiths have a house there which is quite delicious—look out for them too."

"The Monteiths have a place next door to Glentoran," said Julia—"but I don't suppose I shall meet them."

"Oh you will—everyone usually meets everyone in Tangier. And don't on any account miss old Lady Tracy—she's lived there for a hundred years, and knows everything; in fact she's quite likely to be able to throw some light on Colin."

"Not an old lady of a hundred, surely," said Julia sceptically.

"You don't know Lady Tracy," said Geoffrey Consett with finality.

CHAPTER III

THE *Vidago* got off more or less on time the following night. Julia stayed down at the docks till the ship sailed; it occurred to her that there might be the makings of an article for *Ebb and Flow* in dockside life, so she put on a dirty old featherweight silk macintosh, such as can only be bought in Italy, visited her new friends in the office, and chatted with the crane-driver and the stevedores in the shed; she learned all the details of the fight, anxiously listened to over the wireless by everyone she met, though Murphy's army of backers had not returned—"oh, they won't show up now till Monday," said the red-haired man in the office. She had various drinks; the first was with the crane-driver, who had taken a fancy to her, at lunch-time; with delightful hesitation he asked if she ever fancied a glass of port?—and when she said she did, led her out to a small cheerful pub, where the fight was also being discussed eagerly. Her lunch she ate on board in the small saloon, along with Captain Blyth and the officer with the beard, who proved to be the Mr. Reeder whose soda the chief steward had 'borrowed' for her the night before; this meal, as it was to do throughout the voyage, took place at twelve-thirty—Julia was late, and when apologising to the Captain explained that she had been having drinks with the crane-driver. She noticed that the mate eyed her rather curiously on hearing this.

"At 'The Prospect of Whitby' I suppose," said the Captain.

"Oh no—is that near here?"

"Not far off. You ought to see it, if you don't know it."

It rather surprised Julia that the Captain of the *Vidago* should be so accessible before sailing; liners' captains, in her experience, kept themselves *incommunicado* except when on the high seas. But she had still a lot to learn about the ways of cargo-boats: both the hours of meals on board, and the general uncertainty which governs their movements. She was late again for supper, a form of high tea, not having realised that it would be at five-thirty; to repay much hospitality in the little office she had gone over at about five p.m., taking with her a bottle of Bourbon, a farewell offering from an American officer who had fallen under her spell—Julia hated the whisky, but thought it might go down well in the office, which it did; therefore she was late. But it was over a Scotch with the Captain at nine that she had her real shock. He mentioned casually that they would be putting in at 'Casa'. (He pronounced it 'Cahssa'.)

"Where's that?"

"Casablanca."

"Goodness, are we going to Casablanca?"

Julia had booked to Tangier, understanding that that was the *Vidago's* first port of call; she listened with impatience to Captain Blyth's slowly-pronounced explanation of some failure to deliver part of the cargo for 'Tangiers', as he called it, and how instead they had loaded up with tractors and saloon cars for 'Cahssa'. If they were putting in at Casablanca she might be able to see Paddy Lynch, and cause him to make enquiries about Colin through the Banque Régie Turque; but then, if Geoffrey's probings at the Bank of England yielded any fruitful results, she ought to know what they were before accosting Paddy.

"How long shall we have at Casablanca?" she asked, practically cutting into the Captain's softly-spoken sentences.

"About twelve hours—maybe twenty-four. You never know to an hour or so."

Julia got up, moving a good deal faster than she normally moved.

"Where can I get to a telephone?" she asked. "Do excuse me, but if we're going to Casablanca I ought to get hold of someone at once. The office will be shut of course—damn!"

There was a telephone kiosk by the other dock gates, nearer the ship, the Captain told her. Julia remembered those gates, that was the exit which she and the crane-driver had used on their way to the pub.

"Well, if you will forgive me, I'll fly and telephone," she said.

"You'll be back by nine-thirty, won't you?" the Captain said. "I oughtn't to let you off the ship now, it's ten past nine."

"Oh yes, I'll be back in loads of time. How sweet of you. That perishing Mr. Scales might have told me about going to Casa of course—what a blot the man is," said Julia, hurriedly downing her whisky; she heard the Captain's slow chuckle as she hastened out.

She was out of luck. When she had pattered through the rain to the red kiosk, a desolate little monument to who knows what ardent or despairing last-moment conversations, and put in her three pennies, there was 'No Reply' from Geoffrey's flat. Julia said "Damn" again, pressed Button B., and tried the Garrick—the Club porter, after a prolonged interval, informed her that Mr. Consett was not in the Club. She stood for a moment or two in the cold stuffy little wood-and-glass box, smelling of stale tobacco-smoke, casting about in her mind as to where else she could try, but no brilliant idea occurred to her. Julia had a strongly-held theory, upon which she often acted with success, that in any crisis there is always something clever to do if one can only calm down and think what it is—she therefore calmed down and thought hard, in that telephone box by the London Dock gates; but nothing occurred to her except a strong desire to go and ask kind fatherly Captain Blyth what on earth she could do to get a message ashore at that time of night? Julia did not then know that the *Vidago*'s captain was commonly known as 'Cheery Blyth', or to his ship's company simply as 'Cheery'; but in her moment of need she felt the want of his cheerful kindness, and after splashing back over the wet cobbles and scrambling and slipping up the greasy gang-way, she boldly tapped on his door.

"Gracious, you *are* wet," he said, as she entered on his "Come in." "Get your call all right?"

"No. In fact I'm in rather a jam. I suppose there's no earthly means of getting a letter ashore, now?"

"Take off that wet mac thing—I'll dry it in my bathroom," said the Captain; he took it from her and disappeared through an inner door. Returning—"You'd better have some whisky," he said levelly; "don't want to start off with a cold."

"But *can* I get a letter ashore?" Julia asked, as he poured her out a stiff glass.

"O' course—the pilot will take it when we drop him, down the river; easiest thing in the world," said Cheery Blyth, cheerfully.

"Oh, splendid. What time will that be?"

"Some time after midnight. Now you'd better put in your own soda, and get it right."

Blessing the kindly little man, warmed and comforted, Julia sat contentedly in his cabin till a fair rather sleek-haired young man entered to announce that the *Vidago* was about to get under way. Captain Blyth ignored this information till he had effected a rather formal introduction —"Miss Probyn, this is our second officer, Mr. Freeman; Freeman, this is our passenger, Miss Probyn." After which he went leisurely into his inner cabin and emerged in an oilskin and a cap heavy with gold braid, Julia's mackintosh over his arm.

"Oh, thank you. But whom do I give my letter to?" Julia asked.

"Put it on my desk—I'll leave my door open, and see that it goes."

By now Julia felt sure that it would. She went to her cabin and scribbled a note to Geoffrey, telling him that they would be calling at Casablanca, and that he should therefore hurry up his enquiries at the Bank of England, and airmail the results to her. Then the idea struck her—where should he write *to*? Poste Restante? A considerable experience of the difficulty attending the extraction of letters from Postes Restantes in France and the Iberian Peninsula had made Julia cautious; she decided that Geoffrey's letter had better be sent care of Paddy Lynch—she must just risk the Lynches being away. She would have written to Paddy too, but she hadn't enough stamps left for airmail, and the Captain and apparently everyone else were either on the bridge or for'ard ringing bells and shouting, as the *Vidago* nosed and edged her way through incredibly narrow locks and channels, gently bumping, sometimes, against the stone sides, on her way to the open river. Tying a scarf round her head Julia went on deck and watched this process for a while. Deck hands ran to and fro, slinging hempen fenders over the side when a bump seemed imminent; arc-lights fizzed above dark water, dirty with refuse of all kinds; figures in oil-skins moved about on the wet cement which in this strange world represented land, shouting directions—once one of them bellowed for 'the keys', and some keys tied to a piece of wood were flung down to him. That small circumstance intrigued Julia very much; but it was wet and cold, and on the whole rather monotonous—she went back to her snug little cabin, turned in, and slept.

Julia thoroughly enjoyed her voyage on the *Vidago*. Crossing the Bay of Biscay in January is not normally regarded as a pleasure-trip, but the weather was not excessively bad, and the little vessel rode well, lightly surmounting huge seas that would have dealt shuddering blows to a big liner. Indeed in every way, Julia felt, a small cargo-boat had immense advantages over the leviathans on which she had hitherto done her ocean travel. Personal relations, if slight, were genuine as far as they went; one met the officers at all meals anyhow, and chatted as human beings do over their food—what was wholly and mercifully absent was the forced and bogus heartiness found on large passenger-boats, with their ghastly organised deck-games and evening gaieties. She spent much of her time in her cabin—since except the gloomy little dining-saloon there was nowhere else to sit—or in the pilot's cabin next door, which she used as a study-cum-luggage room, tapping away at an article on 'Dock-side Diversions' for *Ebb and Flow*. Now and again, for air, she went on deck; she asked Captain Blyth if he minded slacks on board—such already was her feeling for the little Skipper—when he said "No, very sensible," she wore them, with a duffle-coat and fleece-lined rubber zip-boots to the knee superimposed for her outings. Julia had swithered about taking those boots on a journey into sunshine, it seemed so silly; but she had decided to 'for the Bay'—in fact they were to stand her in good stead on many journeys in Morocco.

The first time that Mr. Reeder, the mate, encountered her on deck thus equipped, he looked her up and down and said—"Jolly good boots. Where did you get the duffle-coat?"

"Buntings, in High Street, Kensington," said Julia—"they go in for war surplus."

She asked him about the shipping that dotted the horizon in all directions—the eastern approaches to the Bay seemed almost as full of traffic as Piccadilly—and had pointed out to her tankers, long, low, and ugly; tramps of various sorts, apparently all familiar to Mr. Reeder: "That's a John Doe Line," he would say of some spot on the sky-line; "they're small coal-boats." Near the French coast, off Ushant, lively little fishing craft bobbed about on the grey-blue waters, causing Julia to opine that it must be frightfully difficult to avoid them at night, especially in fog.

"Not any more—radar's made all that easy," he said.

"Oh, have *you* got radar?"

"Naturally," he said, rather huffily.

"I wish I could see it," said Julia.

"You must ask the Old Man about that," said Mr. Reeder, repressively. "I've no objection to passengers on the bridge, in fact I like the company, but it can't be done unless he says so."

Of course Julia asked Captain Blyth at the very next meal, which was one of those rather indigestible spam-and-salad, cake-and-scone collations at the distasteful hour of five-thirty p.m., if she could go up on the bridge some time to watch the radar functioning.

"Yes. Better come up tomorrow night, when we shall be off Finisterre— then you'll see the land on it as well as the ships."

They slogged down across the Bay, that evening and that night; next morning Julia awoke to see a rather thin watery sunlight seeping in at her cabin window. She scrambled hastily out of her bunk—a drawer, half-pulled out below it, she had learned to use as a ladder—and ran across to the window to look out. Yes, sun it was, albeit rather faint as yet; in London one had forgotten that such a thing as sunshine existed. And the sea was blue too—faintly blue; anyhow not that cold steely grey. She felt extraordinarily exhilarated as she climbed back into bed just as Andrews, the steward, tapped on the door with her morning tea; he came in wearing his usual rig-out of shirt-sleeves, no collar, a puce pull-over, and a dark stubbly chin. "It looks a nice morning, Miss," he said—Andrews was evidently slightly exhilarated too.

So was everyone else. A sort of joy pervaded the ship at the sight of the sun; it took the very practical form of doing some washing. A positive efflorescence of washing broke out on both decks, and at the mid-day meal there were prolonged arguments between Mr. Struthers, the lanky Chief Engineer, Mr. Freeman, the fair-haired second officer, and Reeder as to the best way of washing woollens—*Lux* or *Tide*, and how hot the water should be. The Captain contributed a story of a very nice young fella who had been given a cardigan knitted by his mother, which he had boiled in soda—everyone laughed politely. Julia decided to do some washing herself: by plaintively asking Mr. Reeder where and how she could hang her things, as she had no clothes-pegs, she caused him to run a line for her across the boat deck under the bridge—"When your stuff's ready I'll hang it for you without pegs," he said briefly.

"Ready in half-an-hour," said Julia equally briefly; and half-an-hour later she watched with amusement the big bearded mate attaching her nylon effects to the line. He did this by a most ingenious method: inserting the point of the marlin-spike on his clasp-knife into the cord, he unlayed it enough to slip one corner of a garment through, and did the same to a second corner; the cord, springing back into place, held the sweater or petticoat as in a vice, far more strongly than any clothes-peg.

"That's grand," said Julia admiringly, watching a selection of her wardrobe flapping and fluttering, completely secure, in the brisk breeze. "How clever. Thank you so very much."

"Ah," said Mr. Freeman, pausing on his way up to the bridge to take his four-hour trick to observe these proceedings, "but that will leave nicks on the shoulders of jerseys. Now my wife, she always reeves an old stocking through the sleeves of her jerseys, and pins that to the line at the middle and ends—so the jersey itself doesn't get nicked, see?"

"That sounds very clever," said Julia politely—"but I haven't any old stockings with me, and I'm sure this will be perfect." Reeder however, for whose benefit the last remark was intended, had stalked indignantly away.

"*Oh* what fun," Julia thought, retiring to the pilot's cabin to type out more items concerning "Dockside Diversions" before Andrews went round the boat ringing a hand-bell to announce lunch—again she compared these direct simplicities with the atmosphere on large liners, to the latter's disfavour.

That night she had her usual whisky with the Captain about nine-thirty. Andrews always brought cocoa and biscuits to all cabins at eight-fifteen; Julia had amended this, in her case, to having her thermos filled with her own *Nescafé*, which blanketed the insupportable flavour of the condensed milk better than cocoa—and being in a thermos, she could take it when she liked, which was when she was finally installed in her bunk. (She was much struck by the lack of such amenities, apparently willingly endured by the merchant navy.) At ten-thirty that evening—"Well, let's go up," said Captain Blyth, "if you really want to see the radar carrying on." And up they went.

A radar screen is more like a small television set than anything else. In the darkened chart-room behind the bridge proper—where a seaman stood at the wheel, and Mr. Reeder, his beard muffled in a scarf, strode up and down looking both business-like and sulky—there was no light except that from a shaded lamp, falling on the chart spread out on the big table against the bulk-head. The Captain went first to this, and studied the pencil line drawn on it to indicate the ship's course; he went out in front, glanced at the bearings on the illuminated compass in front of the helmsman, and then spoke to Reeder. "Have we picked up Torinan yet?"

Reeder moved rapidly over and stuck his wrist watch into the faint light of the binnacle.

"Three minutes ago, Sir."

"H'm." He went across to the port side of the bridge, remarking—"Like to come and see?" to Julia over his shoulder.

Julia went with him. Several steady lights, small and yellow, pricked the darkness, but after a few seconds a much more powerful one, infinitely far away, winked, flashed, paused—and then winked and flashed again.

"That's Torinan. One always gets it a bit before Finisterre."

"How do you know which light it is?" Julia asked.

"By the number of flashes, and the intervals between. I'll show you"— and leading her back into the chart-room he reached down from a shelf a grey paper-backed volume, rather thumbed and dog's-eared from much use, entitled, Julia saw—"Admiralty List of Lights, Vol. IV." He licked a tobacco-stained finger and turned the pages. "There's Torinan."

Julia bent over the chart-table and read, muttering the words aloud:— "Toriñana. 1740. Octagonal tower on white square building, 29 ft. high. I.W. Character and period G.P. Occ. (3) Miles seen in clear weather, 20. Light 5.5 seconds, eclipse 1 second, light 1 second, eclipse 1 second, light 5.5 seconds, eclipse 1 second."

"There you are, you see," said Captain Blyth. "Check the flashes with a second-hand, and you know at once. Now we'll see if Spain is showing yet."

With him Julia peered at the dark glassy screen, on which small luminous objects showed here and there; he explained to her the meaning of the concentric rings of green light surrounding the central point which was the ship, and how each ring stood, at the present adjustment, for ten miles.

"Then that ship," said Julia, indicating a white object like a small maggot, "will be about five—no, four miles away."

"That's right. Four or three-and-a-half. Of course if you get really close you can magnify it." He twiddled a knob, the green rings seemed to shift, the maggot was ever so slightly enlarged—"Now that's set at five miles," said Captain Blyth.

"Yes—oh, obviously now it's three-and-a-half—no, three."

"Well, we're both moving, you see."

Julia was entranced by this magical gadget. "Can you make the range larger too, so one can see further away?" she asked.

"Yes. We'll pick up Spain." He twiddled the knob again, and suddenly the whole screen went dark.

"Silly thing," said Captain Blyth mildly. "We'll have to get Sparks." He pressed a bell on the chart-table, and lit a cigarette, quite unperturbed. To the man who presently appeared, looking rather sleepy and dishevelled, he said—"Fetch Sparks."

A moment or so later the wireless officer, also looking sleepy and dishevelled, appeared. "Sparks, this damn thing's conked out," said the Captain
equably. "Fix it."

Julia was familiar with Sparks, the wireless officer, a curly-headed boy
from the Midlands; she sometimes went and sat with him in his cabin, next
door to the pilot's and full of curious instruments, to listen to whichever
English news service he could best pick up at the moment, through the
singing tappings in Morse which never seemed to stop for an instant.
Sparks, whose real name was Watson, was a happy youth, utterly devoted
to his job; he would sit by the hour, head-phones clipped round his curly
brown skull, listening-in to the inter-ship messages which fill the ocean air
with etheric chit-chat. Now however his cheerful face wore a rather sulky
expression as he fiddled with the radar, removing and replacing valves—it
was getting on for eleven-thirty, and Sparks had been fast asleep. However when he had finished he said, "All right now, Sir, I think," very
respectfully.

"Thanks," said Captain Blyth. Once again he twiddled a knob; the
illumined maggots seemed to increase, and right up at the edge of the
screen appeared some faint curved lines of light, more like the petals of a
chrysanthemum, Julia thought, than anything else. The Captain pointed at
them with his thumb.

"That's Spain—Finisterre. It'll show up better when we get nearer."

"Can I stay and see?"

"'Course, if you like. But I think I'll go to bed." He went out again to
the bridge, looked at the binnacle, peered over the port side at the flashes
from Toriñana Lighthouse; returned to the chart-room, laid the protractors
on the chart, ruled a line and made an X in pencil, below which he wrote
the time—23.23. Then he called, "I'm going below, Reeder," and vanished
down the companion-ladder.

A moment or so later Reeder ceased his pacing of the bridge and came
into the chart-room, where Julia was still peering, fascinated, at the radar
screen.

"Oh—you're still here."

"Yes, the Captain said I could stay—I want to see the land come clearer
on this. Oh, could you explain one thing?"

"I expect so—what is it?"

"All this fuzz of little white dots round the ship herself, just like the
Milky Way."

Reeder laughed shortly.

"That's what we call the clutter—it's the ship's own disturbance in the
water."

"Oh—oh how funny."

"Why funny?"

"Because all the other things it shows, like ships and land, are solid—this is only bubbles in the water, like you see over the side. And talking of that, did you notice that there's phosphorescence in the water tonight?—not a lot, just an odd spark, but it's there all right."

"Yes. The beginning of southern waters. Lovely," said Mr. Reeder. He glanced rather keenly at her. "You're fairly observant."

"Not really, a bit—madly vague, in fact. Thanks"—as he gave her a cigarette, and lit one for himself. "Do you like southern waters?" she asked then—Mr. Reeder seemed in a more unbending mood than his usual abrupt aloofness, tonight.

"Yes, adore them—sub-southern, that is; I loathe the tropics. That's why I stick to this run—Spanish ports, Moroccan ports!"

When he spoke of sticking to the *Vidago*'s run Julia recalled how Captain Blyth had said of him, over one of their nightly drinks, that Reeder was 'one of the most efficient officers in the merchant navy. He could have had his master's ticket any time these last eight years, but he won't go up for it. Can't understand the fella'. With this in mind—

"Why do you like the Spanish and Moroccan ports so much?" she asked.

"The sun—and the girls! Anything with black hair drives me wild!" said Reeder frankly. "Can't abide blondes—funny, isn't it?"

Julia laughed. But suddenly an idea struck her. "Do you get to know much about other ships in all these ports?—yachts and things like that?"

"Don't know what you mean by 'things'—one hears about some of the yachts, of course. Why? Do you want a yacht?"

"No, but I'm looking for one."

"What's her name?"

"The lunatic part is that I don't even know that," said Julia, more slowly than usual.

"Then I don't see how you are going to find her, unless you know the owner's name. What sort of yacht is she?—steam or sail?"

"Some sail and some engine, I think—I've no idea how big, either. It's all quite mad, but I absolutely must find her. I do know one of the owners' names, but not whether it's registered under that."

"*She's* registered," Reeder corrected. He seemed to hesitate for a moment, and then said—"Why have you got to find her? None of my business, of course."

Julia now plumped for telling this abrupt, rather cranky, man the reason for her quest—after all she needed any help she could get, and the Captain's unsolicited testimonial caused her to regard Reeder as a trustworthy person. In her near-drawling tones she related the whole story: Uncle John's death, and the consequent crisis at Glentoran; Aunt Ellen's distress, Edina's frustration at being stuck in Argyll, and her anxiety to get back to her rich job—finally, Colin's alleged orange-selling, and his failure to write for the last nine months. Reeder listened in silence; at the end he spoke.

"Of course they aren't selling oranges at all—you realise that?"

"No, I don't. I don't realise anything. What would they be doing, if not that?"

"Smuggling, of course."

"*Smuggling!*" said Julia in astonishment, raising her delicate eyebrows. "Smuggling *what*, for goodness sake?"

"Almost certainly currency out of Tangier; watches and cameras, probably, out of Gibraltar. Watches and cameras are duty-free there; they cost about a third of what they do elsewhere. Or American cigarettes."

While Julia stood silent in front of the radar machine, digesting this quite new idea, a seaman in shirt-sleeves came into the chart-room, bearing a dirty high-sided wooden tray with a pot of tea, some chipped cups, and a jug of the horrible condensed milk—Reeder poured out a cup, which he told the seaman to take out to the helmsman; then he offered Julia one.

"Oh no thanks, I think tea is quite too revolting, with this unutterable milk—how you all bear it I can't imagine! But do have a go yourself; I have my thermos of *Nescafé* down below."

Reeder laughed, and poured himself a cup of the dreadful brew. Drinking it, rather to Julia's surprise he reverted to the subject of Edina. "She must be quite a considerable girl, to be earning such a huge screw. How old did you say she is?"

"I didn't say. But in fact she's twenty-five."

"Formidable," said Reeder. "And now she's running the farm?"

"Well they have three farms in hand, actually; she's running those, and the saw-mill and lime-mill—and of course she has to supervise the other eight farms, see to gates and fences and so on; and then the hill sheep, naturally. They simply can't afford a factor, with taxation what it is. Who can?"

"Sheep, eh? What sort? Black-faced on the hill, I suppose?"

"Yes, and some cross lambs on the low ground."

"Do you winter those away?"

"No, it's not worth it. Why, do you know about farming in the Highlands?"

"Not there, but I was brought up on a place in Northumberland." Julia was momentarily struck by his use of the word 'place' rather than 'farm'. "Good heavens!" Mr. Reeder pursued—"What a job for a girl! I should say being a mate is a picnic to it."

"I couldn't agree more. I think life on this ship is one long picnic—if you leave out the food," said Julia.

Reeder laughed again, heartily this time.

"Well, I wish you all luck in your search," he said. "Anyhow you'll be making it in some of the most delightful places in the world. Tangier, is it, that you're making your base? Know it?"

"No—I've never set foot in North Africa. Rather a thrill, really. But any hints and tips will be gratefully received," said Julia, with a hint of her beguiling grin. She felt sure that if Mr. Reeder vouchsafed any information or suggestions about Tangier they would be on quite different lines to Geoffrey's. She was not wrong. He stared rather hard at her, for a moment or two, in the faint reflected glow from the light over the chart-table; then—

"Well, I will give you one," he said at last. "I don't suppose it would normally be given to young ladies, but then I know nothing about young ladies!"

"Well, what is it?" Julia asked with a sort of tranquil impatience. "Don't bother over-much about young ladyhood, because I'm congenitally hard-boiled."

"That was rather my impression, in spite of your appearance," Reeder said, grinning a little through his beard. "Well go sometime when you're in Tangier to Purcell's Bar—it's a good place, one of the nicest there is."

"Good drinks?"

"Yes, first class; no wood-alcohol to put your eyes out. And Purcell is a most delightful type—*sabe todo*."

"Oh he does, does he? Might he know Colin?"

Mr. Reeder displayed panic, unexpectedly.

"Oh, for God's sake don't go walking into Purcell's Bar and asking about smugglers!" he said hastily. "That would put the lid on. No—but when you've salted him, just drifting in and having a gin-and-something for a bit, you might throw a fly over him about your smuggling cousin. He might know or he might not; my bet is that he *would* know, but whether he tells you or not is anybody's guess."

"My guess is that he might—people do tell one things," said Julia. "But I'll go very slowly, I promise you. Thanks."

At that point Mr. Freeman came stumping up the ladder and walked into the chart-room—he checked at the sight of Julia.

"Oh, hullo," he said—"I didn't expect to find you here."

"Studying radar," said Julia. She turned again to the screen. Up in the top left-hand corner the chrysanthemum-petals were now quite clear and strong, and spread much further down towards the ship. "Oh look, Mr. Reeder—Spain's showing up beautifully now."

Reeder however did not look; instead he went out onto the bridge, glanced at the binnacle, at his wrist-watch, and then came back and did things on the chart with the protractors, as Captain Blyth had done making a pencil X and writing '23.59 hours' below it.

"There you are," he said to Freeman. "Over to you now. Wish you joy of your trick"—and he strode out; his heavy steps could be heard clattering down the ladder.

"I think I shall say Goodnight too," said Julia and betook herself to her cabin. In bed, sipping her coffee and smoking a last cigarette, she meditated on what Reeder had told her. It was quite a new idea that Colin might be smuggling—and would probably make him harder to trace, she thought; he might even be using a false name. But then—if so, why in the world should the Bank of England allow him to transfer his account to Casablanca? Smuggling currency was about the last thing that the Bank would either smile upon or promote. All very queer—and still thinking how queer it was, and what fun to be trying to unravel so odd a mystery, she fell asleep.

Casablanca, where the *Vidago* eventually tied up at about nine one morning, gives a rather false first impression of North Africa. What one sees—what Julia saw—as the ship moves along the coast to slip in behind the long long mole which protects the harbour is first the hideous factory zone to the north of the city, and then a conglomeration of high, featureless, cream-coloured modern blocks, near-sky-scrapers, which constitute the town itself. This is very disillusioning. It might be a lesser New York; lesser, and less ugly than the fantastic Manhattan skyline, but not in the least anyone's idea of Africa, or any part of the Old World. From the deck Julia observed it all—as they approached the dock-side she noticed that the local workers, at least, looked very different to Mr. Murphy's friends at the London Docks: not only had they very dark skins, some indeed being obvious negroes, but many of them wore long-skirted garments, and on their heads small brightly-coloured skullcaps, knitted or crocheted in patterns resembling Fair-Isle, and very dirty.

"Good gracious me, what an extraordinary place," she muttered to herself. "Not at all what I expected."

THE ARAB DOCKERS, in their curious garb, were considerably quicker off the mark than their *confrères* in London. The hatch-covers had been got off while the *Vidago* was idling along inside the mole, awaiting the signal to berth, and in no time at all crane-drivers in fancy dress were slinging tractors, endless tractors, out of one end of the ship and small saloon cars, mostly painted a pale green, out of the other; the moment these last touched solid ground swarms of Moors ran them off the rope nets which held the wheels, manhandled them across the wide quay-side, and parked them in neat rows between the warehouse sheds. It was a pleasant lively sight, in the bright southern sunlight, and Julia stood watching it with satisfaction—this might make a nice tail-piece to "Dockside Diversions", she thought, if *Ebb and Flow* had the guts to print anything which in the least reflected on English labour.

Almost the moment they tied up a very obvious Englishman in a trilby hat had come aboard, and disappeared into the Captain's cabin; he presently reemerged, accompanied by Captain Blyth, who brought him up to Julia and made one of his little formal introductions:

"Miss Probyn, this is our agent, Mr. Bond; Mr. Bond, this is our passenger, Miss Probyn. Mr. Bond has a letter for you, Miss Probyn"—and the agent, after shaking hands, gave Julia a letter addressed in Geoffrey Consett's familiar hand, simply to 'Miss Julia Probyn, M.S. *Vidago*, Casablanca.' To her surprise it bore no stamp or post mark.

"Oh, thank you. How did this come, Mr. Bond?"

"It was sent down by hand to the office—from one of the Banks, I believe."

Julia bore it away to her cabin and read it. Like Casablanca, the letter was not at all what she expected. In the first place it was typewritten. Mr. Consett began by explaining that to make sure of its reaching her he had sent it with a covering one to Mr. Lynch at the Banque Anglo-Marocaine, telling him that she was on the *Vidago*—"then he can contact the agents and get it to you at once." "Sensible creature," Julia commented approvingly. But for the rest of the letter she had no approval at all—she read it, frowning, with mounting vexation.

"I made enquiries in the quarter I spoke of," Mr. Consett wrote, "but I think you had better leave that line of enquiry alone. As you know, banks are not allowed to divulge any particulars about their clients' accounts to third parties—it is like the seal of the confessional; and though the Bank of

England is practically a Government department since it was nationalised,
that rule holds for it too. I regret now very much that I made the suggestion
at all—it was foolish of me. My only excuse is that at the time I was thinking of something else." The letter ended very formally—

"Yours ever
Geoffrey Consett."

"Dictated," said Julia angrily. "All official rubbish!" She picked up the
envelope from the sofa beside her, intending to crumple it up and throw
it into the wastepaper-basket which she had forced Andrews to extract
for her from the Chief Steward—she felt a need to crumple and throw
something—when she noticed that there was another sheet in the envelope;
this was written in Geoffrey's hand.

"Oh darling, you know what I was thinking of that last evening—*you!*
I do wish you hadn't gone away; London really *is* a desert without your
beautiful blank foolish face in it. And anyhow, even if you do find your
second or third cousin, or whatever he is, I doubt if he will come home
quite as soon as you or his family would wish—Edina may have to sacrifice
her magnificent salary, so much larger than mine, for a bit longer! But
whatever you do don't start your Irish bank-clerk chum snooping round—
I do implore you to leave the whole thing alone, from the banking angle."

"One for me, one for the file!" said Julia contemptuously. Poor Geoffrey—
he was so frightful when he went all official. "Divulge!" she muttered
disgustedly, looking at the type-written letter again. Then she re-read the
P.S. Taken together, the two letters made her smell a rat. If Geoffrey didn't,
like Reeder's friend in the bar at Tangier, *sabe todo,* he knew a good deal
more than he was willing to say, even to her. Now quite intelligent young
women like Julia often develop a peculiar and really irrational remorselessness towards young men who are their self-professed slaves, but with
whom they are not yet in love; she was unreasonably vexed with Mr. Consett for his official caution and propriety. She sat in her snug little cabin,
that she had become so fond of, smoking and thinking. Geoffrey was of
course a complete clot to imagine that she wouldn't try to make Paddy
Lynch find out all he could; *he* wasn't the Bank of England, and nor was
she—her job was to find Colin. But the whole business about the B. of E.
was most peculiar. Whatever Colin's present occupation was it probably
wasn't smuggling—Reeder must have been wrong about that—since it had
official sanction; indeed someone at the Bank must know a good deal about
it if they could put Geoffrey in a position to hint to her, in the privacy of
his P.S., that Colin probably wouldn't come home at once. What could it
be?

Anyhow, she decided, glancing at her watch, she had better take some steps about contacting Paddy, even if she did in the end decide to use a certain discretion in tackling him; and also find out from the Captain how long they would have in "Casa".

At that point there was a tap on her door, and Andrews, as he frequently did, entered without waiting for any "Come in".

"Car's come for you, Miss," he said.

"What car?"

"Couldn't say, I'm sure. I was just told to tell you that the car's waiting for you on the dock-side."

"Thank you, Andrews. Say I'll be there in five minutes."

She stepped out on deck for a moment, to make up her mind about the temperature. It was not yet ten, and there was a light breeze off the sea, but it was already getting gently warm; by mid-day, in a city, it would probably be hot. She exchanged her woolly for a blouse, her brown shoes for green sandals, matching her broad-brimmed felt hat—that most useful of travelling companions, which had crossed the Bay rolled up into a green cone among her stockings; throwing her pale tweed overcoat across her arm, she went on deck in search of Captain Blyth.

She found him still in conversation with the agent, leaning on the rail watching the cars and tractors being unloaded.

"Oh Captain dear, someone's sent a car for me. That probably means hospitality—so how long have we got here?"

"Well, we shan't be sailing till tomorrow, anyhow."

"Oh, grand—a night ashore! What fun."

"That's what the crew always think at Cahssa," said the Captain. "And they come aboard again at three in the morning as green as grass, and plucked clean as chickens!—and all they say is that they had *fun*." He spoke in his usual gentle accents of this aspect of human folly in his crew.

Mr. Harris, the Chief Steward, whom Julia had hardly seen since her first evening on board, when he pinched the bottle of Mr. Reeder's soda for her, now came bustling up rather pompously, holding out a note to the Captain.

"This has come for Miss Probyn, Sir," he said.

"Well give it to her, then," said Captain Blyth flatly—Harris, looking foolishly formal, handed the envelope to Julia.

"Oh, will you excuse me?"

The note was from Mr. Lynch. He would be busy at the bank till one, but was sending his car and chauffeur to show her the sights of Casablanca during the morning, and to bring her to his house for lunch. "Ali speaks tolerable French. The Librairie Farrère is the best place for picture post-cards. It will be uncommonly nice to see you again."

Julia said to the Captain—

"I'm going ashore for lunch. I'll be back before tomorrow morning, anyhow."

"O.K. Don't get shot up!" replied Captain Blyth tranquilly.

"Which is Mr. Lynch's car?" Julia asked Harris. There were two cars near the foot of the gangway, a small black Ford and a beige one considerably larger than the sea-green saloons which were continually being swung up out of the bowels of the ship.

"Oh, the black one's mine," said the agent, hearing her question. So Julia ran down the gangway and got into the beige car, the chauffeur politely holding the door open for her.

Ali was a neat little Arab with a flattened hook nose, a small Chaplin moustache, and dark brown eyes full of a rather sceptical intelligence, indeed his whole expression conveyed a not unfriendly scepticism; he wore a trim chauffeur's jacket over baggy dark-blue trousers, and a red fez. Julia told him to go to the Librairie Farrère. This was a huge bookshop in the business quarter among the tall blocks of buildings which made the streets look like canyons of golden sandstone. Here she turned over masses of picture-postcards, mostly displaying palm-trees, camels, and views of Marrakesh, none of which seemed very appropriate for despatch from this African version of New York; however she bought a few, and then realised that she had no Moroccan currency—whatever that might be. It proved to be a special African type of franc, and the grey-haired woman who served her had no hesitation in changing a £1. note—however she only got 800-odd francs for it.

"Not a thousand?" asked Julia, in her excellent French.

"Ah no, Mademoiselle—not in the Maroc. A thousand is the *French* rate."

Back in the car, Julia learned with astonished amusement in what Ali's idea of the sights of Casablanca consisted. He drove her briefly through the Mella, the Jewish quarter, which was too tumble-down and dirty even to be picturesque, with low one-storey houses and many street markets; but thereafter they proceeded to visit the hospitals of the city, which stood more on the outskirts, in large airy tree-shaded avenues. He took her to nine in all, ending up with the Animal Dispensary! "Hospital for Arab Men," Ali would say complacently, pulling up before high iron gates and indicating a series of modern buildings in spacious grounds full of flowering shrubs and trees; or "Hospital for Arab Children". There were hospitals for Europeans too, of course, but the little chauffeur made the longest pause of all outside "Hospital for Arab Women". He pointed out to Julia the Moorish trained nurses, unveiled and in European dress, but not in uniform, passing in and out through the gates, their up-to-date tartan-covered bags of medical appliances strapped to the carriers of their bicycles, explaining how they went into Arab homes, giving piqûres, applying dressings, administering medicines and treatment. "Do much good," said Ali, with such conviction that Julia was considerably impressed; she sat in the car for some time watching these lively hatless girls, their modern dress and hair-do contrasting so strangely with their dark-skinned un-European faces, chatting at the big gates to numerous Moorish women, presumably their patients—the latter veiled to the eyes and smothered in voluminous white draperies which, as Edith Wharton said long ago, caused them to resemble nothing so much as animated bundles of washing.

After the Animal Dispensary, however, she struck. Among the post-cards she had bought was one of Marshal Lyautey unveiling a memorial plaque to Charles de Foucauld, and she wanted to see it; she had what she herself would have called 'rather a thing' for that strange being, the cavalry officer turned White Father, whose missionary efforts had been so wholly unavailing, his political effect on the pacification of North Africa so great. She showed Ali the picture and bade him take her there. The Foucauld monument stands in a particularly busy avenue; Ali approached it from the wrong side and pulled up level with it, but across the road.

"Wait," said Julia; she hopped out, threaded her way through the traffic and stood quietly for a few moments in front of the memorial, behind its small hedge of bushes. It seemed to bring her monkish hero—so unlike all the pseudo-romantic business of the novelists who write up the Foreign Legion—strangely near. Julia was seldom impulsive, except when moved by temper, but now she did an odd thing: she knelt down on the dusty gravel and said a prayer for the repose of the soul of the saintly eccentric. Ali eyed her curiously when she returned to the car.

Casablanca in recent years has become a zoned city, carefully controlled by the Municipal Council. Factories may only be erected on the northern side—and only factories; impossible to get a permit to build a house there. Out to the south on gently rising ground lies the residential zone, spreading all the time—hotels, some blocks of flats, but mostly villas, of all shapes and sizes, in pretty gardens full of flowering shrubs; in that climate every-thing grows so fast that this modern quarter has not in the least the un-finished aspect of a new garden suburb in England—shrubs rise from the ground practically with the speed of the Hindu magician's mangrove-tree, while creepers with exotic blossoms smother the walls almost before the plaster is dry. Here no shops may be built; an impassioned petition from the residents was necessary even to get a permit for a petrol-station to be opened for local use.

Out to this pleasant district Ali proceeded to drive Julia, along avenues of older, larger, more sedate houses; she gazed about her with a lively interest, veiled by her customary vacant expression. Paddy Lynch's house was a medium-sized villa in the new quarter, covered in flowering roses, climbing geraniums, and some creeper with dark-green leaves and flowers precisely the colour of tangerine-peel; Paddy himself, lanky, black-haired, with lake-grey eyes set in an Irish smudge of dark eyelashes was standing waiting for her at the top of a flight of concrete steps—as the car pulled up he ran down to greet her.

"Julia! How splendid! No need to ask how you are—you're radiant!"

"Dear Paddy," said Julia, giving him a cool kiss. "This is so nice."

"Nita's away, such a shame; she'd have loved to see you."

"Why?"

"Oh, a baby—and though a Frenchman produces such splendid pasteurised milk for us all, she thought she'd rather have it in England, and see if she can nurse it herself. But come in."

"Good idea, nursing," said Julia, as her host led her into a large sun-filled room; at the further end, through an archway, was another room with a table set for lunch.

Over drinks—"What on earth are you doing in Morocco?" Mr. Lynch asked.

"Sunshine—and articles for my medium papers."

"Why aren't you staying here? I gather you're going on to Tangier. You ought really to stop and do Marrakesh and Rabat and all that; you could stay with me and I'd drive you over for a week-end."

"I'd love to do that later on; I'm all booked at Tangier now, hotel and everything. Tell me, Paddy, how are things here now?" Julia asked, with a mental eye on her articles.

"Oh, very quiet—there hasn't been an assassination for at least ten days."

Julia laughed.

"Well, that's quiet for Casa," said Mr. Lynch, laughing too. "By the way, what time do you sail?"

"Only tomorrow morning."

"Why not come and stay here tonight, then?"

"Oh no Paddy dear, thank you so much—unpack and re-pack, so exhausting. But I'll lounge in your nice garden this afternoon, if I may, and have supper with you if I'm asked."

"Of course you're asked. Only it will be a bit late because I have to go to a cocktail-party this evening. I know—why don't you come too?"

Julia made a small face.

"I feel rather like Sir Anthony Eden about cocktail-parties. Will it be diplomatic or amusing?"

"Well, the Binghams are nice people—he's in the Banque Régie Turque."

Julia managed to repress a start—when she spoke it was with a real drawl.

"Oh very well—anything to oblige. But I shall have to go back to the boat and change," she said, with a glance at her coat and skirt.

"Need you? You look perfect." She nodded vigorously. "Very well; Ali can take you down about six, and bring you back to pick me up. What did Ali show you, by the way? *Splendeurs et misères de Casablanca?* That's the classic round."

"No; he showed me nothing but hospitals," said Julia, and related her morning. Mr. Lynch laughed, but this curious form of sight-seeing aroused his interest.

"That's a rather significant tribute to the French," he said. "Hospitals and after-care are one of their real achievements in Morocco. It's like drawing teeth, of course, to make the Arabs go to a hospital or a clinic the first time; but once they've been nothing will keep them away. Ali's wife nearly died with her last baby but two, and I simply bunged her into the *Hôpital pour Femmes Arabes* by main force—now he won't hear of her having a child at home. It's a most frightful pity, this muck-up about the Sultan, because the French are doing such a superb job here. Ah, here's Mahomet and the lunch."

Another Arab, in the baggy blue cotton breeches to which Julia was beginning to get accustomed, topped by an impeccable white jacket and a fez, stood bowing in the archway leading to the dining-room; as they sat down Julia observed that though in all other respects so neat, the servant's jaw and chin were covered with several days' stubbly black growth. After he had left the room, Mr. Lynch, forking in mouthfuls of a delicious risotto, pursued his theme.

"Did you notice Mahomet's beard?"

"Well yes."

"That's all part of the trouble. He used to keep shaved, clean as a whistle; especially on Fridays, when he went to the Mosque. Today's Friday—and just look at him."

"I did," said Julia candidly. "But what has Mahomet's not shaving got to do with the new Sultan?"

"Everything!" said Paddy Lynch explosively. "At the Mosque they pray for the Sultan as their Imam, sort of High Priest, ye-know—but the French have ousted the one they recognise and believe in, and put in someone else. 'Tis as though you were to ask Cat'lics to pray for the intentions of a new Pope, put in by the Russians, with the true Holy Father exiled some other place!" In his excitement Mr. Lynch relapsed surprisingly into his native idiom.

"Then why did the French do it?"

"Oh, the ould fella was just hopeless!—wouldn't sign any decrees, even those for reforms that the people themselves wanted; he was holding everything up. The French could hardly help themselves—'twas a regular *impasse*. But the cure is worse than the disease—now a lot of the Moors have stopped wanting even reforms, if they come from the French. Nationalism and traditionalism, fighting now on the same side, and the next minute fighting one another! But you can't touch a Moslem's faith—and that's what the Administration has done, God help them." He sighed, gustily.

Mr. Lynch's words about the Moslem's faith reminded Julia of the curious look Ali had given her after she had prayed at the Foucauld memorial, and she told her host about the small episode.

"Did you do that? Oh good. No, Ali won't have thought it in the least odd; on the contrary, it will have impressed him a lot. They think Christians fearfully irreligious—and to see one praying at the shrine of a Christian marabout will have bucked him up no end."

After lunch a telephone call came for Mr. Lynch, who hurried away; Julia sat on the verandah among stone troughs full of pink geraniums, revelling in the hot sun, or browsed among her host's books—she also gave some thought to what use she could best make of a cocktail party in the house of someone belonging to the Banque Régie Turque. It was stupid of her not to have found out how high up Mr. Bingham was, but she had been so interested in Ali and Mahomet, and the whole Moroccan set-up, that she hadn't. Oh well, time enough on the way. She was now glad that when Paddy asked her what she was doing in Morocco she had not told him, flat out, that she was looking for Colin Monro—it had been on the tip of her tongue to say so. But she might do better with a total stranger, over lots of drinks, especially if he was a foreigner. Mr. Bingham was obviously English or Irish—then why in the Banque Régie Turque? —but he would inevitably invite all his colleagues to his party.

He had done so, as Julia ascertained after a hurried dash down to the *Vidago*, where in the pilot's cabin she routed out a rather spectacular black and gold cocktail-dress, very décolleté, and black French sandals with straps threaded with gold. She looked out a hat, but decided against it— she knew that her hair, in certain circles, was one of her strong suits, however much Edina might rail against its length, and she might want her

strongest suit to-night. When they called at the villa to pick up Mr. Lynch
she knew that she had done right: his glance as he looked at her was one of
those involuntary tributes that are far more telling than any words. However, he used words too.

"Goodness, Julia, you will smash them! Have you any idea how beautiful you can make yourself when you try?"

She blew him a kiss.

"A pretty fair idea, dear Paddy—thanking you!"

"So I should suppose. A strengthener before the effort?"

"Oh dear no—I want to keep my head, in a strange town."

On the way down—"What exactly *is* Mr. Bingham in the Banque Régie
Turque? Do tell me," Julia said.

"Oh, very senior. I think you'll like him, and his wife is a charmer."

"Why is he in a Turkish Bank?"

"Oh, that's a long story. Buxtons were invited, practically, to come here,
and refused—I can't imagine why. It was very mistaken. So the Banque
Régie Turque stepped in, and a very good thing they have made of it;
they very wisely took on Bingham to handle the English side of things."

"I see. And who are his colleagues? Turks?"

"Oh, French and all sorts. There's a very amusing Armenian—you must
meet him."

"What's his name?"

"Panoukian."

As they spun down a long boulevard Julia said, very casually—

"Have you run into my cousin Colin Monro out here?"

"Monro? No, I don't think so. What does he do?"

"Nothing very much, so far as I know. He sails a bit about all these
ports, I think—oranges, or something."

"Oh, one of these amateur smugglers," said Mr. Lynch, rather contemptuously. Julia was struck by his jumping instantly to the same conclusion
as Reeder. "They're such a bore, always getting into prison or some row,
and wanting to be bailed out. They're a perfect pest to the Consulate."

Julia held her tongue, and decided to concentrate on Mr. Panoukian for
the moment. Obviously Paddy knew nothing—anyway, Colin's account
wasn't in his bank.

The Binghams' was a very large house on one of those earlier and
staider avenues between the city proper and the flowery new garden suburb
—as they walked up the flagged entrance-way a muffled roar of voices
greeted them. Julia paused in the warm darkness, and sniffed—"Paddy,
what is this heavenly smell?"

"Lemon-blossom," replied Mr. Lynch; he stepped onto a flower-bed to pluck a spray from a tree. "There, you can tuck that in behind your sun-burst," he said—"Is it diamonds or Woolworth's?"

In the house the party was huge, and already in full blast; Julia stud-ied the company with interest. The women's clothes were very smart, but their hats, oddly, not nearly so good, and their hair and faces either over-done, or not really done at all. Registering such things was a sort of Pavlov reflex with her, but when Paddy introduced their host she concentrated on him. Mr. Bingham was an enormous man, at least six foot three, with iron-grey hair and a huge pale moon of a face, in which a pair of lively grey eyes shone—he flourished a tumbler of whisky-and-soda, rather to Julia's surprise.

"Honoured, Miss Probyn. A great pleasure. What will you drink?"

"Oh, I'd like to follow your example," said Julia, in her slowest tones. "I'll come with you," she said as he moved off towards the buffet.

"Now that's a sensible girl! Would you ever get it, if you didn't come with me? And aren't you wise to choose whisky. Scotch or J.J., by the way?"

"Oh J.J. please," said Julia. She had already decided that her host was an Irish Bingham, and probably in a fairly receptive state, early as it was in the evening; it would be a sound move to opt for Irish whisky, which in fact she loathed. While he was fetching her drink she made a second rapid decision as to her preliminary approach, and when he returned with her glass acted on it at once.

"Mr. Bingham, where is the money here? Who makes it, and from what?" He stared at her.

"Good God! Whatever makes *you* ask a thing like that?"

"Oh, didn't Paddy tell you I'm a journalist? And where the money is is rather a primary question about a place, don't you think? I shan't quote you, naturally, but that's the first thing I need to know."

"Of course you're quite right," Mr. Bingham said; as he spoke he moved through an archway, holding up a looped curtain for Julia to pass, and took up a position by a bookcase in the next room. "Well, phosphates apart—you know Morocco produces twenty per cent of the world's output of phosphates—the big *quick* money is mostly made in this town," he began.

"From?"

"Real estate: land values in this place keep soaring like in Shanghai in old days, or in some American boom town; and petrol-stations, and the smart shops, and a bit of night-life."

"Is any made outside Casa?"

"Oh yes; Agadir is developing very fast too—and the citrous fruit in-dustry is becoming quite a big thing. And besides dried peas, they're starting canned peas too, and tinned fish; the French are very go-ahead about all that, and it gives a lot of employment, and brings money into the country."

"Anything else?" Julia asked.

"Well, no one really knows yet what's going to happen about the oil industry."

"Oil! You mean petroleum? Do they get *that* here?"

"Oh yes—there's that big cracker-plant at Petit-Jean. But I fancy," Mr. Bingham said, leaning towards Julia confidentially, "that the petrol yield may not come up to expectation. Faults in the limestone bedding, they say—don't really understand all that myself. But I gather Morocco is never likely to become a second Kuwait."

"That's all most useful," said Julia. "I can't thank you enough, Mr. Bingham."

"Don't you want to write any of it down?" her host asked, looking at Julia with a sort of two-edged interest.

"Oh dear no. It stays here," said Julia, tapping her big white forehead. Mr. Bingham laughed. "That's the lot, is it? No small handy side-lines?"

"Well there is one little side-line—no two."

"Oh, what are they? Readers like side-lines," said Julia professionally.

"Well it's a funny thing, but there's getting to be quite a trade in Moorish stuff—you know, antiques, leather goods and brass and so on. All that used only to be on sale in Fez or Marrakesh, but quite recently the merchants up there have started sending their sons or nephews down to the coast, to Port Lyautey and Rabat and this place, and even to Mogador and Agadir to open up shops—and you'd be surprised what they're making out of it. A lot of the sons could buy father out now, after only two or three years."

"Fascinating," said Julia. "I must look up these sons! And what's the second side-line?"

Mr. Bingham again looked confidential, and leaned further towards Julia along the top of the book-case.

"Well, they're doing quite a bit—curious thing—in some of these rare metals."

"What, uranium?"

Mr. Bingham looked slightly embarrassed. "Well not pitchblende"—he hemmed a little. "Don't get that here, but they find a lot a queer things, some of the ones with numbers and fancy names—elements, don't you call them?"

"Oh, like titanium and molybdenum?"

"What a girl you are! Yes, they do mine molybdenum, and antimony and cobalt as well. Cobalt of course is enormously valuable; it's worth about a guinea a pound. The French concessionnaires are mining that in a biggish way. Wait—I'll bring you the other half."

In Mr. Bingham's absence Julia *résumé*-d what she had heard and stowed it away neatly in her mind. There wasn't much in phosphates and chick-peas, even canned ones, for an article, and Casablanca night-life had been done to death, but there could be a story in the curio-sellers' rich sons, and possibly in these metals. A guinea per pound was a nice sort of price to write up. When Mr. Bingham returned with their glasses— "Do go on about the cobalt and molybdenum," she said.

"Cheers!" said her host, drinking to her. "I like intelligent girls! I hear they're finding newer stuff than cobalt too," he added.

"Who are? The French?"

"The French have the regular concessions, of course, but—well, don't quote me," he said again, "but it was the Germans who began on these new things."

"What, before the War?"

"No no, just a year or two ago—the East Germans, they say. But other people have started in now as well, on the Q.T., I gather, and without bothering about concessions too much—though everyone connected with it seems to keep their mouths fairly tightly shut."

"Could I use that at all? I mean, if no one will talk, how do I get a story?" Julia asked.

"Ah, that's up to you," said her host, rather belatedly looking discreet. "I've said too much already, I daresay. But I've given you the tip—a nod's as good as a wink, as we say in the Twenty-Six-Counties! And I should think you could make a mule talk, if you gave your mind to it!"

"Oh, how sweet you are! And you have helped me so much. But I'm sure I ought not to monopolise you any longer," said Julia—"You've been so liberal. Push me off onto someone else now."

"Who'd you like to meet? The Prefect and the City Fathers?"

"Well really I'd rather talk to your partners. Haven't you any Turks about? I think it's so frightfully odd and amusing, finding the Banque Régie Turque here," Julia said, with Mr. Panoukian well in mind.

"Oh, there are good reasons for that. But if you insist on Banque Régie Turque bankers—Hey!" Mr. Bingham called, above the roar of voices. "Panoukian! Come over here."

A short slender man with a greenish-white face, dressed in a tightly-waisted suit, with a carnation in the buttonhole, and sharply-pointed shoes, obeyed this summons.

"Panoukian, let me introduce you to Miss Probyn, a friend of Paddy Lynch's. She's a journalist, and she wants to know about Morocco, but

she only wants to learn it from bankers!" said Mr. Bingham expansively—
he then moved away.

Julia deployed her rather varied arts on Mr. Panoukian, who was clearly
highly intelligent; his queer topaz-coloured eyes looked at her with the
expressionless steady glare of one of the great cats, a lion or a panther;
but he shot out information and sympathetic wit in faultless English,
and on a higher level than Mr. Bingham's. They got on very well—so
well that at last Julia decided to plunge. Leaning a little towards him
on that same confidential bookcase, she said—

"Mr. Panoukian, I believe you could help me. Would you?"

"My dear lady, if I can, the thing is done," he said, with an exceedingly sweet smile.

"Oh thank you. Indeed I *do* hope you can, for we are in such trouble,"
said Julia, turning the eyes of a distressed dove onto the Armenian. "Look
—I feel as if I can trust you; may I be perfectly frank?"

"It is almost always wiser to be perfectly frank, especially if one wants
help," said Mr. Panoukian. "In theory the English understand this, and
nous autres do not—in fact I often find the reverse to be the case."

Julia laughed a little, but promptly returned to her role of distressed
damsel.

"I'm looking for someone—a distant cousin, whom I haven't seen for
years. He hasn't written home now for months and months, and his poor
mother is distracted; she needs him, too, because the man who used to
look after their very large property has just died, and there is no one to
see to things. So I have come out to try to find him."

"The journalism is a blind, then?"

"Oh no—it finances me. *You* must know all about our currency restrictions in England."

"Yes. How fortunate for the unhappy mother that you are a journalist!"
Mr. Panoukian said—was it with a hint of mockery? On that assumption—

"Oh, please don't be unkind!" said Julia.

"I am not. Who could be unkind to you? But please tell me one thing—
with this perfect frankness which we agree is so useful: why do you imagine that *I* can help you to trace your missing cousin?"

"Because he has an account with you; here, in Casablanca."

Was it her imagination or did a sort of veil, an almost imperceptible
blankness come over those yellow eyes when she said that?

"Indeed! And may I know his name?"

"Of course—how could you help me, otherwise? His name is Colin
Monro," said Julia.

This time there was no doubt about it. Mr. Panoukian's topaz eyes

seemed visibly to lose all expression before her own; it was as if a blind
shutter of refusal were drawn down over that whole curious visage. She
did not have to wait for his words to know that she had failed, that this
was a dead end; she hardly listened when he said, slowly—

"Monro? I must look that up. Where are you staying?"

Mr. Panoukian was not a mule, he was one of the greater cats—and
she could not make him talk. But *why* not? she asked herself, as they
drove back to a late supper. To her surprise Mr. Lynch drove her himself;
the chauffeur had disappeared.

"Where's Ali?" she asked.

"I sent him home—I always do if I'm going to be at all late."

"But why?"

"So he won't get stoned," said Paddy casually. "He lives in the new
Medina, the modern Moorish quarter, and everyone knows he works for
a foreigner; if he comes back late the thugs stone him."

"Paddy, it's not *true!* In a modern town, today?"

"Oh yes, it's happened three or four times. If I have to keep him late
for some official do I send him home in a taxi."

Over coffee after supper, in the rather chilly drawing-room—the electric
power had failed for some reason, as it constantly did, Julia learned—she
confided to her good friend Paddy the real reason for her coming
to Morocco, and asked if he would do anything he could to trace Colin.
(Whatever Geoffrey might say, she had got to find him.)

"His account's with the Banque Régie Turque, is it? Is that what you
were making eyes at Panoukian about?"

"Yes," said Julia, unruffled. "I made all the eyes I've got, but it was
no use."

"No, I shouldn't expect it to be. You'd have done better with old Bingham—you really have enslaved him! What did Tony say?"

"Tony?"

"Tony Panoukian."

"Said he'd look up the account. But I saw—I mean I'm practically certain
—that he *did* know about Colin, and wasn't going to tell—his whole face
sort of shut up, went dead-pan, at the name."

"Have you any idea what young Monro really is up to?"

"No, not a clue. *You* said smuggling, and so did the mate on my boat—
but I can't believe it's really that, because" . . . here Julia paused, wondering how much to say. Recalling Mr. Panoukian's dictum about perfect
frankness, she decided to plunge.

"Because what?" Mr. Lynch asked, while she hesitated.

"Well, I told a chum in the Treasury about Colin's account having been transferred here, and he volunteered to find out the reason for permission being given from the Bank of England."

"A rather *young* man, I deduce," said Paddy Lynch.

"Yes. Well, I got a most totally clottish officialese letter from him this morning, the one he sent via you—*typed*, would you believe it?—telling me to leave it all alone from the banking angle. From which I deduce," said Julia, fitting another of Mr. Lynch's cigarettes into a small delicate silver-and-ebony holder, "that not only does the B. of E. know all about his job, and bless it, but that it is something peculiarly hush. Otherwise why the panic? Geoffrey's letter was panic-stricken."

"In the typed officialese?"

"Oh no—the panic was in an M.S. P.S.," said Julia, grinning a little, while a faint and becoming blush stole over her apricot-tinted cheeks.

"H'm. I think I see."

"And your horrible Panoukian person shutting up like a *clam* at the very sound of Colin's name confirms that, wouldn't you say? If it was all open and in the clear he'd have said, 'Oh yes, of course—I'll send you his address tomorrow,' don't you think?"

"Um. Yes. I daresay you're onto something. Have you got the letter from your Treasury pal on you?"

"No, I left it on board, locked up. He said I was on no account to start you snooping," added Julia, with a giggle.

"That won't worry me," said Mr. Lynch. "I'm an Irish citizen; I've no commitments to the Old Lady of Threadneedle Street, certainly none to over-ride those to the *young* lady, Julia my dear! I'll snoop for all I'm worth. Give me your Tangier address, by the way—and the telephone number."

"I'll have to post you that; I don't know it."

"Then remember to airmail it. Surface mail from Tangier takes an eternity."

"All surface mail takes an eternity since airmail began—I think they put the letters on ox-wagons," said Julia—and Mr. Lynch laughed.

He drove her down to the docks himself. Having been fetched and carried by Ali, Julia had not troubled to register exactly where her ship lay, and they had to cruise about under the arc-lights for some time till she spotted the small neat shape of the *Vidago*.

"Golly, what a comic little tub!" said Mr. Lynch. "I must say I think you're pretty devoted, Julia, to have crossed the Bay in winter on that! Who is the devotion to, the missing man? Is he worth it?"

"I've no idea. We were both pretty immature when I saw him last. No," said Julia reflectively—"I think the devotion is to a place rather than to any person. I've been happier at Glentoran than anywhere else on earth, I simply adore it—and it can't carry on without Colin to run it. So I'm going to find him."

CHAPTER V

TANGIER FROM THE SEA presents a far more agreeable aspect than Casablanca. A line of ochre-coloured cliffs stretches away towards Cape Spartel on the right, in the centre the mass of white, indubitably Moorish houses of the Kasbah, climbs steeply up a hill; to the left the modern town slopes, also agreeably white and clean, down to the bay and harbour, and beyond to the east rises the Djebel Musa, Hercules' African pillar—so much more pillar-like than its European opposite number, Gibraltar, which from Tangier is barely discernible in the distance, vaguely resembling a lion crouching very low indeed.

Julia stood on deck with Mr. Reeder, admiring this pleasant scene spread out in the sparkling sunshine, while he pointed out the various features of it to her. "I envy you a bit, staying here," he said. "Charming place. How long *shall* you be here?"

"I've no notion. It depends on how soon I find my cousin."

"Ah. Yes. Well, I wish you luck in your quest. Don't forget Purcell, he may be able to help you—but go slowly."

"I will."

"I do hope you succeed, if only for your other cousin's sake—Edina, did you say? Pretty name; curious, too."

"It's a family name."

"She must be a tremendous girl, to be able to run a place like that, and yet earn such a huge screw on her own as well," said Mr. Reeder thoughtfully. "Worth knowing. What is she like?"

"Her hair is jet black," said Julia with malice.

"Oh God! She's not tall, by any chance?"

"Very tall—and as slim as a willow."

"Help!" said Mr. Reeder. "I should be sunk if I met her."

"I expect so—she sinks a lot of people," said Julia.

After fond farewells to Captain Blyth and the rest of the ship's officers Julia went ashore. Andrews, typically, loaded up "the boy" with so many of her possessions at once that her typewriter nearly fell off the gangway into the water; she shouted a cold, slow reproof at him from the quay, which caused him to bring the rest of her luggage down himself. (She saw Captain Blyth's tranquil grin at this episode as he stood at the rail below the bridge.) More tractors and more saloon cars were being slung ashore, also a piece of deck-cargo which had amused Julia throughout the voyage: several wooden cases of lighter-fuel, which might not be stowed below, and had remained lashed on the main deck. Evidently the cigarette-lighters of Tangier could now be filled.

The Villa Espagnola to which a taxi bore her was really a small hotel, situated at the top of the town at the far end of the big Boulevard, the main shopping street, where this peters out into a residential quarter of large houses in gardens, where most of the Legations are situated; as she unpacked, the great fronds of palm-trees on a level with her window tossed their heads like restless horses in the sea-breeze close outside, and the scent of roses came up from the garden below—by craning her neck a little she could just see the white mass of the Kasbah, a pile of gleaming rectangular blocks, each block a house, poised precariously on the steep slope of its hill. All pretty good as a change from London in January, Julia thought—in her calm fashion she exulted a little.

But she was never one to waste time and as Purcell's Bar was obviously going to be a slow process, she made a call there her first job. The Spanish proprietor looked a little startled when she asked the way to it, but gave her directions—down through the Medina and the Socco Chico, the Small Market, and then a street on the right, close above the harbour.

Julia had the sensible habit of always buying a plan of any new town the moment she arrived in it; her hotel however had none, so she set off without. Everyone in Tangier speaks Spanish, so she had no difficulty in asking her way to the Socco Chico, revelling as she went at the sight of teams of donkeys laden with unrecognisable merchandise blocking the road for Chrysler cars, or more of those women smothered in white draperies, and men in dark-brown woollen jellabs, straight from neck to ankle, and topped with wide straw hats looped up and trimmed with cords and tassels of wool. Heavenly fun, she thought; delicious entertainment of the eye—no wonder Colin and Reeder liked this part of the world.

But when she tried to go through the Medina to the Socco Chico the heavenly fun became a little too much of a good thing. The old Moorish city of Tangier is a network of steep cobbled alleys, so narrow that the passage of a single donkey sends the thronging pedestrians scrambling into the open-fronted shops for safety; even without a donkey's passing it was hard to push one's way through the swarms of people—Moors and Jews, men and women—and the smells were unwonted and strong; moreover there were so many twists and turnings that she soon felt in danger

of being hopelessly lost. She beat a retreat uphill, and managed to find
her way back into the big open market lying immediately above, the Gran
Socco; here she took a taxi, which circumnavigated the impossibly steep
angle and narrowness of the Moorish shopping quarter, and drew up in
a quiet, narrow, modern street, where a small and discreet notice said
"Purcell's Bar".

She found this to be quite a small place, a narrow room with a bar
along one side leading through into a larger one, both with small glass-
topped tables and modern leather-covered chairs—it was all as quiet as
the street and as discreet as the notice, rather to her surprise; she had
expected something more exotic or more rough-and-tumble. It was early
in the evening; she took a seat in the narrow room opposite the bar, ordered
a drink, and then sat demurely sipping it while she took stock of her surroundings. The man who served her wore an ordinary dark suit, but his
face was far from ordinary: negro blood was obvious in the wide mouth
and broad mask, but his hair was brown and straight, his skin merely
of a European sallowness, his eyes grey. When he brought Julia her drink
he spoke perfect English, but having done so he busied himself quietly
among his bottles, not making conversation after the manner of his kind.
This struck her; and indeed there was about the whole man a quiet dignity,
combined with a look of strong intelligence, which was impressive. Could
this, she wondered, be Purcell himself? If merely a barman he was an
unusual one.

Her question was answered by the entrance of a little Moor in fez, baggy
blue trousers, and scarlet jacket, who carried a basket full of bottles and
spoke in Arabic to the grey-eyed man; he was promptly set to washing
and polishing glasses, and from the demeanour of them both it was obvious that the half-negro was the boss. Julia studied him with fresh interest.
He certainly had the look of a person who might know everything, and
would keep his mouth shut on what he knew, she thought, recalling
Reeder's words. A few minutes later she received fresh confirmation of
his identity. The muslin-veiled door onto the street opened again to admit
a small rather seedy man, who somehow had the word 'spiv' written large
all over him; he leaned over the bar and greeted the man behind it with
the words, "Look here, Purthell, old man"—then he caught sight of Julia
and lowered his voice, so that the rest of his communication was lost
to her. Julia was pleased—this was the sort of type she had expected to
find in Purcell's Bar. But he was not made very welcome—Purcell listened
coldly and shook his head more than once. The newcomer had a very
slight cast in one eye; presently he cocked the other at Julia, clearly asking
who she was?—Purcell shook his head again, repressively, and said some-

thing which drove the small cross-eyed representative of the underworld out of the bar. (Julia felt an instantaneous conviction that this miserable little creature belonged to Tangier's underworld, whatever that might amount to, and that Purcell, like King David's wife, despised him in his heart.)

She was sufficiently interested by what she had already seen to sit on, in hopes of more—she asked for another drink, and when Purcell brought it observed that it had been a beautiful day—he agreed, with almost royal politeness, and expressed a hope that she was enjoying Tangier. Julia said that she was. But just then the door opened again and five or six men came in: of various ages, they were all speaking English and wore English-tailored suits; two or three had the quality for which we use the blunt word 'pansy' written as large on them as 'spiv' had been written on the seedy little man. They were manifestly *habitués*—they perched on stools along the bar and asked for "the usual, please, Purcell". One in particular struck Julia rather pleasantly—he was very tall, with flaming red hair and no look of a pansy at all about him; he wore a dark blue blazer above white flannel trousers, and removed a pair of sunglasses after he had settled on his stool. She listened for some time to the conversation of this bunch—all residents, she gathered, since they were discussing their gardens: the bashing of their tulips by a recent storm, and why daffodils would grow so superbly in Tetuan, only fifty miles away, and yet "absolutely *not*, my dear" in Tangier. She hoped for a mention of the Monteiths, for from the glances discreetly cast at her she realised that to form an acquaintance would be easy—but none came. Oh well, these people might come in useful some time—you never knew. She was satisfied with her evening when she left, with a word of thanks to Purcell.

Next day she embarked at once on what the police call "routine enquiries". She went first to the British Consulate-General, a medium-sized but stately yellow-washed house standing among palm-trees in a commanding position, with open spaces all round it. Most of the other seven Powers who operate the International Zone at Tangier call their missions Legations; the English, with a typical arrogant modesty, describe theirs as a Consulate-General, though the Consul-General enjoys the local rank of Minister. This distinction is rather chic and slightly annoys the more flamboyant colleagues of the British representative; they would hate to be mere Consuls-General themselves, but realise that in Tangier it is really grander *not* to be a Minister—in self-defence they ostentatiously address him as "Your Excellency" or "M. le Ministre".

A very tall Moor, splendid in a dark-blue robe down to his feet, met her at the gate-house which commands the entrance, and led her through

a flowery garden to offices behind the house proper, where she had an
interview with a very young and most courteous vice-consul.

"Colin Monro? No, I'm pretty certain that he hasn't made his number
here, but I'll check in a moment, if you like. What was he doing?"

Julia, still under the influence of Mr. Panoukian's remarks about the
value of frankness, said—

"Well I think they were probably smuggling, though they called it
selling oranges."

"Oh, did they? Out here they usually pretend to be fishermen, if they
bother with a disguise at all. If you will wait one moment, I'll check." He
vanished through a door.

"No," the vice-consul said, when he returned—"He didn't get imprisoned
and ask us to bail him out. I'm so sorry I can't help. How long are you
staying?"

"Till I find him," said Julia.

"Ah. Yes. Have you put your name in the book? Oh, but you should
do that"—and he led her out through a spacious hall where a couple of
Moors clad in tunics, fezzes and baggy breeches of brilliant scarlet were
polishing the marble floor. "Here," the young man said—and Julia inscribed her name and "Villa Espagnola" in a large album.

Having drawn a blank at the Consulate-General, she tackled the harbourmaster, who was supposed to be found in an office down near the
quay. This was a far less courtly proceeding and took much longer; however at last, using a great deal of Spanish and many blandishments Julia
achieved access to an official of sorts. Here, though she felt more hamstrung
than ever by her ignorance of the name of Colin's boat, she got a bit
further. Yes, the harbourmaster's chief clerk told her, there was an English
yacht, with several Señores on board, hanging about Tangier; he too consulted files, after which he informed Julia that the boat was called "The
Frivolity". No, she was not in the harbour now; he thought they had gone
to Gibraltar. The Ingleses bathed in the sea a great deal, he volunteered,
diving off the boat itself; imagine such a thing! This encouraged Julia,
for Colin was a strong and impassioned swimmer. Had the Señor seen
them, she asked. Oh yes, many times. Were any tall and dark? Indeed
yes—one extremely tall, and very dark. And did the Señor know their
names?

But here the clerk was less helpful: Julia could not be sure whether
he was being evasive or really did not know. One, he said, with some
confidence, was certainly a lord—but that was as far as he would go.
He indicated politely that the office was now about to close for the lunch-
eon-hour—this, Julia guessed from past experience in Spain, would cer-

tainly last till four p.m. at least, so with grateful thanks she took her leave and withdrew to Purcell's Bar, most conveniently close by, for a drink and meditation.

As before she was the only patron, except for the red-haired man who had impressed her favourably the evening before, who sat in the furthest corner of the inner room, drinking beer and reading a book. In this agreeable solitude Julia decided to seek some information from Purcell, and when he brought her drink she asked him how one got to Gibraltar?

"By the Ferry—it goes every day."

"Can one go in the morning and come back the same night?"

No, that one could not do; the ferry went about midday, and only returned the next morning.

"How lunatic," said Julia. "Why? Why not come back the same night? It can't take very long to steam across there."

Purcell's strange face with the negro bones and the intelligent European eyes took on a most peculiar expression—combined, it seemed to Julia, in equal parts of vivid comprehension, some secret amusement, and reprobation.

"It just is so," was all he said, however.

"Oh well—how tiresome. And could you tell me where one can stay in Gibraltar?—a cheap hotel?"

Purcell's peculiar expression was if anything accentuated as he said— "There is really only one possible hotel in Gibraltar—the Rock; and it is not cheap."

"How much a night, do you know? This is very kind of you," said Julia, "but one has to be careful these days, on a travel allowance."

"Wagons-Lits Cooks could tell you exactly, but I believe about fifty shillings a night."

"Fifty shillings a *night!* Merciful God!" Julia exploded—"How appalling." Purcell gave a tiny laugh. "The proprietor of the Rock Hotel is a first cousin of the ferry-owner, I presume," she said—at which Purcell laughed out loud, causing the red-haired man in the inner room to look up in surprise. Laughter was rare with Purcell, Julia surmised.

However, these huge prices—the ferry cost about a pound each way too, she gathered—decided her against going to Gibraltar on what might prove to be a wild-goose chase: after all she had no certainty that the tall dark young man on the *Frivolity* was really Colin, though she knew that he numbered more than one youthful peer among his intimates. Instead she went in the afternoon to Cook's, checked on the exorbitant prices, and then forced a very ill-mannered and recalcitrant clerk to ring up the harbourmaster at Gibraltar to find out if the *Frivolity* was there.

At Gibraltar, on the other end of the line, all was ease. Julia spoke herself with someone who talked English, and learned that the yacht she wanted had sailed that very morning for Malaga—however she was expected back in about ten days' time, and was then thought to be proceeding to Tangier.

Fair enough, Julia said to herself, as she walked out of the Wagons-Lits office and strolled up a sunny street towards the Place de France; best wait till they come back, staying inexpensively at the Espagnola, and meanwhile work up Geoffrey's local contacts, using his letters of introduction to Lady Tracy and Mme La Besse. And see the local sights, and continue to put salt on Purcell's tail by repeated visits to his very nice bar, till it became possible to consult him. In Tangier, in hot sunshine in January, this seemed a very agreeable programme; and after taking a black coffee at a small table on the pavement outside the Café de France, on the Place, she went back to her small hotel in high good humour and typed out "Dockside Diversions"; she was just in time to airmail it from the English Post Office in a street below the Consulate-General, where the stamps sold are ordinary English ones with the word TANGIER printed in heavy black across the face. It was then, as always, crowded with a mob of all nationalities, who wished to profit by the cheap postal rates—sixpence for an airmail letter to the British Isles, for example.

This feature, and the whole business of England having its own post-office in the absurd international setup that Tangier is, delighted Julia. In common with most of her generation, the post-war, neo-New Young, she had a thoroughly considered respect and admiration for her country; Julia's contemporaries would never be found passing resolutions not to fight for King and Country. And even in the short time that she had been in Tangier, in conversation with the inmates of her little Spanish hotel Julia had learned something which amused and pleased her even more than the existence of the English Post office—namely the astonishing impression created by the visit of the Royal children to Gibraltar. The Spanish press had been uttering all sorts of menaces about what would happen if the Queen herself dared to set foot on what, in defiance of treaties, they deemed to be the soil of Spain; her Majesty however not only stepped ashore herself, but for good measure sent those royal midgets, Prince Charles and Princess Anne, up the Rock to see the monkeys. The foreign element in Tangier could not get over this example of *le phlegme britannique;* they found it quite over-powering.

"These little children!—to take such a risk!"

This had never struck Julia while at home—monkeys are monkeys, and all children love them. But the effect on foreign opinion of this expedition she found very gratifying.

Next morning she set out to call on Lady Tracy, taking Geoffrey's letter of introduction—to which, in the rather old-fashioned elegance of manners which he affected, he had clipped his visiting-card, with "To introduce Miss Julia Probyn" written across the top. The address was some unpronounceable Arabic street-name; Julie caused the *patron* of her little pub to read it out to her taxi-driver, who could not, it seemed, read himself; on hearing it he said, in Spanish, that the Señorita must prepare herself to walk. Julia had prepared herself for almost anything, but the approach to Lady Tracy's house succeeded in startling her. The Kasbah at Tangier rises right up to the very lip of that line of cliffs of ochreous earth which overhangs the approach to the Straits; but beyond it, westwards, other houses have been planted on this vertiginous ridge, between the yellow cliff-fall to the sea and the steep approach from the landward side—and in such a house Lady Tracy lived. After grinding up a yellowish muddy street between small whitewashed houses which turned blank walls to the roadway, the taxi paused practically in mid-air, reversed several times, and came to rest facing back towards Tangier proper—the taxi-man then indicated to Julia that she must now proceed on foot down a concreted path, punctuated here and there by flights of steps, and that the pink *casa* at the end was the house which she sought. Julia picked her way down this slope, which was inundated now and again by douches of dirty water thrown from the houses overhanging it, whose washing flapped in the breeze off the ocean; an iron gate in a small garden gave access to Lady Tracy's front door.

This was opened by a Moor who bowed, took the letter which she held out, and ushered her into a hall or room built in the Moorish style, with narrow arches on slender pillars supporting a high ceiling, and rugs spread about on a floor brightly patterned in small tiles—through curtained archways she caught glimpses of other rooms. From the windows, also arched and with tiny pillars, the view was superb—out across the blue sea of the Straits to that ultra-couchant lion Gibraltar on one side; to the cliffy outline of Cape Trafalgar on the other. Turning back to the room Julia, seeking an impression of its owner, noted that the furniture was partly Moorish, with a few good English pieces; everywhere a clutter of photographs, some of famous people, stood about on small tables along with curios and brass trays; water-colours, some good, more less good, shared the wall-space with the typically Moslem decoration of pieces of brilliant embroidery and some very fine old rugs. There were several modern French books lying about, and a good deal of dust was present; the whole room, Julia thought, spoke of a vigorous personality—too vigorous to fuss about coherence in its surroundings, let alone dust.

The Moorish manservant had borne off Mr. Consett's letter to his mistress; after rather a long pause he reappeared, holding back the curtains of one of the arched openings to admit a very old lady indeed, dressed with as much inconsequence as the furnishings of her room in a welter of cardigans, scarves and shawls—she held Geoffrey's letter in one hand, the other she extended to Julia.

"My dear Miss Probyn, how very kind of you to come and visit me! And how good of my young friend Geoffrey to send you."

Julia lost her heart to Lady Tracy at once. By the time she left, nearly two hours later, she was completely subjugated. Here for once, for a wonder, was a purely golden character: full of intelligence in spite of her great age, and yet almost bursting with benignity; at no point, in spite of her free and lively comments on all manner of events and people, did she display the smallest contempt for those stupider than herself— who must, Julia reckoned, comprise at least ninety-five per cent of her acquaintance. Simplicity, and a sort of divine modesty characterised all her utterances, shrewd as they were. And Lady Tracy's character, Julia soon came to feel, explained the heterogeneous appearance of her room, and especially the bad water-colours; these had clearly been kept out of an affection strong enough to over-ride the chilly fads of mere taste. One in particular, close above the chair in which the old lady evidently always sat—judging from the litter of sewing, newspapers, half-cut books and knitting on the table beside it—constantly caught Julia's eye; faded and spotted with damp, it was nevertheless executed with the utmost spirit, and represented an exotic-looking boat under full sail, off a coast of savage mountains dotted whitely here and there with temples, villas, and mosques. At last she asked who had painted it?

"That? Oh Jane Digby; Lady Ellenborough, you know. Positively *heading*, you see my dear child, for the wilder shores of love. Don't they look wild?"

Julia, entranced by this, rapidly decided that no time need be wasted in "salting" Lady Tracy; she would cultivate her for all she was worth, for her own pleasure in such a rare being, but in the meantime she sought her advice immediately.

"Lady Tracy, Geoffrey sent me to you not only *pour me procurer un plaisir*—which he has done," she added smiling—"but because he thought you might conceivably be able to help me. May I pour out to you?"

"Oh yes, dear child, pour away—I am an absolute reservoir of out-pourings, though I can't imagine why."

"I can," said Julia; "I can already. Well, this is it"—and she unfolded her mission. At the end—"How *does* one set about finding a person on a yacht in Tangier?" she asked.

"Oh, in various ways. What are they doing? Smuggling? So many try to do that. Are you sure they are really smuggling?"

"No," said Julia, "I'm not sure of anything—it's all utterly vague. Smuggling is just a general suspicion which several people, like you, have thrown out. But I went up to the Consulate-General yesterday, and they certainly haven't been imprisoned; at least they didn't seem to know my cousin's name there."

"Well, that's something. You don't think your cousin and his friends are just young *rentiers* living out here on yachts to avoid paying English income-tax? There is so much of that in *le grand bidet*," said Lady Tracy, calmly.

"*Le grand bidet!* What on earth is that?" Julia asked, still more entranced by this phrase.

"Oh yes, that's what they call this end of the Mediterranean; its shape on the map, if you come to think of it, is rather like a biddy."

Julia laughed.

"What a pleasing name! Well anyhow, I don't think Colin can be tax-dodging; he's anything but a *rentier,* in fact I shouldn't think his income has ever been large enough to pay tax on at all. Don't people get up to two hundred and fifty pounds free?"

"I daresay, my dear—we don't have to bother much about that out here, thank goodness. Colin!" said Lady Tracy abruptly. "Colin what?"

"Colin Monro. His father was a cousin of my mother's, and I call *his* mother Aunt Ellen, and think of her as an aunt. They have a most heavenly place in Argyll—I really do love it," said Julia, in an unwonted burst of confidence. "And he's needed there now because the old uncle who used to cope—another cousin of my mother's—has gone and died."

"Ah yes—we all die in time," said Lady Tracy tranquilly. "My turn is really overdue." She turned to the table beside her chair and rang a small brass handbell which stood on it, saying—"I think we might have a glass of sherry to assist us in studying this problem."

A young and very beautiful Moorish girl, swathed in veils, answered the bell; she slid in through one of the archways, stepped noiselessly across the floor and stood behind Lady Tracy's chair; there she bent over her mistress, stroking her shoulder with the gesture of a loving child, and bending down asked her in Arabic what she wanted? Julia could not understand the words, but the sense of them was clear—even more clear was the complete devotion of the handmaiden to her mistress; there was a sort of Biblical beauty about the whole thing, small and unimportant as it was, such as

Julia had never seen in the modern world. She was still under the spell of this when the sherry was brought, poured out, and handed to her by that beautiful creature, who looked as she imagined Ruth or Jephtha's daughter to look, or some other gentle Old Testament heroine.

"Colin Monro," Lady Tracy mused, sipping her sherry. "No, I don't remember the name. I will think, and perhaps ask. I don't always ask, one sometimes hears more without."

"You don't know the owners of the *Frivolity?*" Julia asked. "I got a faint idea that he might be on her, but it's only a guess. She's in and out of here, I know."

"Oh, I believe they are all much older, and mostly very rich; hardly your cousin's galère, I should have thought. But I have never met them, and I can't recall their names. One is a peer, I think. My dear child, what a task this is for you!"

"Yes it is—and I really have got to succeed. But any sort of detection is rather fun, don't you think?"

"Oh yes—the greatest possible fun. It will be so kind if you will let me detect with you, as far as I can from this chair."

"Oh *please* do," said Julia, with fervour. "Dredge up the sediment from your reservoir—I'm sure you will come on some dead cat that will furnish a clue."

Lady Tracy laughed; really a high, old, but infectious chuckle. Then she became practical all of a sudden.

"How are you going to live? This may take some time, and a hundred pounds goes nowhere in this place."

Julia mentioned her invaluable papers.

"Oh, that is splendid. How clever you must be! I take *Ebb and Flow* —it's somewhere on that chair, I think." Julia found it for her, on the seat of a splendid Chippendale armchair, of which one broken leg was propped up by a beautiful little Moroccan coffer of crimson velvet, studded with silver nails. "Ah yes—thank you. A good paper. But can they *remit* to you here?" the old lady asked astutely.

No, it was only the extra allowance, Julia admitted.

"Well, that is better than nothing, of course; much better. But I was thinking—let us get Feridah to give us some more sherry," Lady Tracy said, tinkling the brass handbell; once again the beautiful girl glided in, stroked her aged mistress, and re-filled their glasses. Julia felt as if she were in some quite fresh version of the Arabian Nights, sitting in this Anglo-Moorish house—was it old or a modern imitation, she wondered?—perched above the ocean's rim somewhere between the Pillars of Hercules and the Garden of the Hesperides, with this marvellous old lady.

"Do you have only Moroccan servants?" she was moved to ask.

"Yes. They suit me better. 'Abdeslem who let you in is my steward, and butler, and general factotum, a wonderful person; and then little Feridah is what in old days in England used to be called one's body-servant—which she is: she dresses me and all that. And I have a notable cook called Fatima—you must come and taste her food sometime. And there are all sorts of hangers-on who pretend to weed the garden and feed the chickens, and of course chiefly take a percentage of my peas and eggs." She gave her chuckle. "It is all much more peaceful and happy though than what most of one's friends go through. But let us get back to you, my dear child."

"Oh well if we must," said Julia. "I think your household is much more amusing than me."

Lady Tracy patted Julia's hand.

"We must be practical," she said. "I was thinking that if you took some job here, you would be making money to live on, in the first place. Would you take a job?"

"Oh Lord yes, if I could get one. What had you in mind?"

"Can you type?" Lady Tracy asked.

"Yes rather—I have my typewriter with me."

"Shorthand?"

"No," said Julia with distaste—"not shorthand."

"Ah well—I daresay that wouldn't matter. You could memorise the gist of letters, and take notes and so on—and if you are a writer, I feel sure you could make up very good letters yourself."

"Do *you* want a secretary?" Julia asked, hopefully.

"Oh no, dear child; I have only a very small correspondence—nearly all my friends are dead. But tell me—what languages do you speak and write?"

"Really well, French and Spanish—Italian only moderate."

"Excellent. Let me hear you speak a little French and Spanish."

Julia, rather embarrassed, nevertheless pulled herself together and first asked her hostess in Spanish about the age of her house, and then in French what brought her originally to Tangier? Lady Tracy laughed, clapped her hands, and without answering either question said in English—

"That will do, perfectly. How unusual in an English girl to speak such good Spanish—and it is so essential here. Now listen, my dear Miss Probyn. I can see that you are tolerant of old people, and for the post I have in mind that is important. I have an old friend, very able but very crotchety and very vague; she works extremely hard and has a large correspondence, mostly in French, and she is badly in need of a secretary. I may as well tell you at once that none of them stay with her very long," said Lady Tracy, with a fine little smile; "but you have no thought of staying for ever, and a person of your upbringing is more likely to be patient and gentle than those little girls who do do shorthand, but seem to have so few other interests."

"Perhaps—yes, probably," said Julia. "What does your difficult friend work *at*, Lady Tracy?"

"Well my dear, I believe it is archaeology," said Lady Tracy, looking rather amused.

"Goodness, can it be Madame La Besse?"

"Yes. Do you know her, then?"

"No, but Geoffrey told me about her; in fact he gave me a letter to her, too."

"Ah yes—I remember that he was very much interested in all that; he spent a lot of time with poor Clémentine out at her excavations. Well, so much the better; she was very fond of him, so you will have a golden entrée—though no entrée, golden or not, generally lasts very long with her, poor thing," said Lady Tracy philosophically. "Well, I will write to her too, and recommend you. Are you interested in archaeology?"

"No, not a bit," said Julia frankly—"but that won't prevent me from typing her letters to learned societies in perfectly good French, unless it's *too* technical; and even then I can make her spell out words like mesolithic."

Lady Tracy laughed again.

"My dear child, I see that you will be *perfect* for this. Now I will write her a note, and you shall take it to her with her beloved M. Consett's letter tomorrow. I am sure she will engage you, and I shall tell her that she must pay you a *large* fee. Then you can live more or less free; and what is more important, you will have a cover, as I think they call it, for your presence here."

"Do I need cover?" Julia asked, rather startled both by the idea and the word itself, in the mouth of Lady Tracy of all people. "Can't I just be here, like any other tourist?"

"I think cover is *always* a good thing," said the surprising old lady. "But it is especially useful when one is making enquiries. You have been making them already—at the Legation, from the harbour-master—for a missing young man in a mystery yacht, whose name you don't even know. Don't you suppose that all the relevant circles in this tiny place will already be discussing this fascinating fact?"

"No, it would never have occurred to me," said Julia.

"Oh well, you may be sure they are. And a beautiful young lady is conducting the search!—*immensely* sensational," said Lady Tracy, what practically amounted to a grin appearing on her wise old face; this made Julia laugh.

"What are the 'relevant circles' as you call them?" the girl asked.

"Oh, Interpol, if they are smuggling—and the Zone Police and all sorts of other interests," said Lady Tracy airily. Then 'Abdeslem came in, bowing, with some enquiry; Lady Tracy told him to wait while she wrote a note to Mme La Besse, and Julia took it and went away, considerably cheered.

It will be noticed that she had not been *quite* frank with her new acquaintance; she had said nothing about the curious business of the Bank of England. It seemed to the girl more prudent not to do this, to begin with at any rate, especially as Lady Tracy was a friend of Geoffrey's; she remembered Paddy Lynch's comment on Geoffrey's youth in that connection. So she left that part out. She rejoined her taxi, poised at the crumbling edge of the cliff, and went skimming back to her hotel, wondering what Interpol was, and what "interests" could possibly feel concern in her affairs. She could have no idea what that particular piece of loyalty to Mr. Consett was going to cost.

CHAPTER VI

Julia did not take Lady Tracy's and Geoffrey Consett's letters to Mme La Besse next day, as she had intended. In the morning, writing an account of her trip to Mrs. Hathaway, a glance at the date showed her that it was Friday, and she decided to take Goeffrey's advice and go up to see the Mendoub pay his weekly visit to the mosque. On the advice of the *patron* of the villa she did not attempt to find her way up through the Kasbah; the mosque stands at the very top of the old citadel, and it is a toilsome ascent to it on foot up steep cobbled alleys and flights of steps—moreover, said the Señor Huerta, she would certainly lose her way. So she took a taxi, which after climbing through the high-lying modern quarter to the south passed through the citadel wall and twiddled its way by narrow streets to decant her at the upper end of an irregularly-shaped *place*, sloping slightly downhill; near the lower end of this was the mosque. But, said the taxi-man, who had conducted a brisk conversation with Julia in Spanish the whole way, let the Señorita first go to the *mirador* close by, and look out over the ocean—the Mendoub was always late, and she was early.

Julia took his advice and went out onto a small terrace, whose parapet wall overhung the cliff itself; below her the sea, blue as heaven under the hot sun, murmured gently about the yellow cliff-foot. The coast of Spain was a deeper blue, as willow-gentian is deeper than forget-me-nots—but what interested Julia more than the soft shapes of Gibraltar and Trafalgar was that she succeeded in descrying, away to her left and also perched on the cliff's edge, a pink-washed house which was certainly Lady Tracy's—her house was a mirador in itself.

Turning back into the *place*, she looked about her. The square slanted downhill in two directions, so that the buildings on her left lay below those on her right; they mostly presented blank whitewashed walls pierced by a single door, over each of which, incongruously, a blue-and-white enamel plaque carried a number. At the lower end a heterogeneous crowd was already gathered; Julia strolled down towards it over the hot stones, looking for a point of vantage from which to watch the proceedings, and if possible somewhere to sit. Both these requirements, she observed, were met by a short flight of steps leading up to a building with iron-barred windows; climbing the steps she perched on the parapet at the top. Almost immediately, however, an official in a green uniform followed by an Arab carrying a kitchen chair came over, planted the chair on the top step, and bowing politely urged Julia in French to sit on it. The official seemed too grand to tip, so Julia gave a coin to the Arab; then she lit a cigarette and settled down to see the fun.

There was plenty to look at. Immediately in front of her on the lower side of the *place*, which at this end extended still further down the slope in a sort of rectangular bulge, the Mendoub's guard was already drawn up, a line of Moorish horsemen on beautiful little barbs; the men had various weapons stuck and slung about their wild dress, and carried long staves with fanions a-top; the little horses were as betasselled as Geoffrey had led her to expect—tassels depended from saddles, from bridles, and wherever a tassel could be hung, all in bright colours in which red predominated. The guard was smaller than she had expected; only fifteen in all, but it was by no means the only part of the show. There were also two rows of elderly men dressed in robes of spotless cream, with hoods or cowls thrown back to reveal maroon skullcaps bound round with narrow snowy turbans; they stood on either side of the paved road which bisected the cobbles of the *place* from top to bottom, talking among themselves—beyond them a gaggle of populace and children, all strangely garbed, shouted and ran about, constantly harried and called to order by several policemen, and the official in green who had brought her the chair.

All this was amusing enough at first, but presently it began to pall. Half an hour passed, three-quarters of an hour, and still no Mendoub. Several Americans, shepherded by two rather officious Arab guides, arrived, and also took up their stance on the steps, crowding these uncomfortably; they had cameras which they held to their eyes as they photographed the Mendoub's guard, but they were restrained by the official in green from photographing the old men in white bournouses. They grumbled about that, and about the unpunctuality of the planes which were carrying them about Morocco and Spain; it was very hot; Julia began to get bored. And then something very peculiar happened.

Out onto the flat roof of one of the Moorish houses which bounded the bulge at the lower end of the square came two men, carrying canvas chairs which they proceeded to set up in the small shade cast by two bay-trees growing in tubs. They then disappeared, to reappear after a moment, each carrying a large cocktail-glass. The houses below the bulge were so much lower than the northern side of the *place* that their roofs were practically on a level with Julia, and she could see clearly all that took place; for a moment or two she watched the two men idly, envying them the deckchairs in which they presently sat down, the shade of the bay-trees, and above all their cocktails. Then suddenly she sat up very straight, as both rose and came and stood by the low parapet, looking down onto the crowd below. One was the red-haired man whom she had twice seen in Purcell's Bar, wearing as usual his white flannel trousers and dark blue blazer. But the other? The other was much younger, very tall and very dark; and Julia, incredulously, thought that she recognised Colin Monro. She stared and stared, through the glittering blinding sunshine; the range was about seventy yards, and moreover Colin had been four years younger when she last saw him, and this was a grown man. But the loose easy walk, the slouch—so like Edina's slouch—were exactly as she remembered the charming youth at Glentoran; and what she could discern of the face at that distance was Colin's face.

She sprang up from her kitchen chair, and started to go down the steps, disturbing the Americans, who protested loudly—not without reason. For at that very moment a vast cream-coloured motor-car nearly as long as a bus appeared at the upper end of the *place*, and moved slowly down it; the Arab guard sprang to attention, the two rows of old men hurriedly pulled the hoods of their white robes over their heads and stood in reverent attitudes; the police chivvied the crowding children away and awed them into silence, and then stood at the salute as the Mendoub, the local representative of the Sultan, who is Allah's representative on earth as far as Morocco is concerned, drove up to pay his devotions to Allah on high. Helpless, fuming, hemmed in by the eager transatlantic tourists, and in spite of herself awed by the moment, Julia stood, one eye on the two men on the roof, while she watched the proceedings. There was little enough to see— several elderly men in long robes emerged from the car, were surrounded and masked by the police, and shuffled off up a cobbled alley to the mosque. By the time they disappeared the two men on the roof opposite had also vanished, taking their chairs with them.

The moment that it was possible to do so Julia ran down the steps and tried to push her way through the crowd of women and children in order to find the entrance to the house on whose roof she thought she had seen Colin; but it was some moments before she could reach her objective, and when she did she was completely frustrated. Only one house had a door giving onto the lower, bulging corner of the square, and that was away to one side; she knocked at it, and after a long pause a veiled Arab woman with cross-eyes opened to her. The inner court revealed by the open door was dirty and filthy to a degree which really precluded that house being lived in by the red-haired man, with his immaculate trousers; nor could Julia exchange a word with the woman, who looked equally blank at the sound of English, Spanish, or French. Julia gave it up. Some distance away an archway led through into a cobbled alley, which was in fact the entrance from the Kasbah; Julia tried this. Here there was a plethora of doors—closed doors in blank walls; not only on both sides of the main alley, but in a sort of court leading off it—she counted at least eight. But in the confused rabbit-warren which an old Moorish city usually is it was impossible to determine which of the eight was the door of the house she wanted. She tried one, haphazard—it opened on another filthy little court-yard, on another Arab woman, though this time not cross-eyed; but she too understood nothing but Arabic. Poor Julia began to feel desperate. It was frightful to think of Colin perhaps being within a few yards of her, and not to be able to reach him. She went out again into the *place*, noted the position of the house with the bay-trees as well as she could, and returned to the alley. One house in the court leading off it seemed to correspond best to that position—moreover the door was of clean-grained wood, not covered with peeling paint, and the knocker was tidily blacked; Julia used this to knock loudly.

The door was opened almost immediately; through it, past the smartly-dressed Moor in a braided jacket who stood in the opening she caught a glimpse of a neat courtyard with white-washed walls and geraniums growing in big earthenware jars. This was much more the style, Julia thought, and it was quite hopefully that she addressed the elegant man-servant.

It is always a question in Morocco, and in Tangier especially, whether servants will respond best to Spanish or to French—on this occasion Julia opted for French.

"Monsieur is at home?" she asked.

"I will enquire, Mademoiselle," the Moor replied politely; he spoke excellent French. "Might I have Mademoiselle's card?"

Now visiting cards are one of the many things that have practically disappeared from England since the Second World War, when they could only be bought, with permits, by diplomats and officials—Julia, brought up without such things, had none. She said so, but gave her name; the servant bowed elegantly as he repeated it carefully—evidently a well-trained man, she thought. And then a still stranger thing happened. It struck her that she might as well ask for Colin at once and she said, quietly—"*En effet*, the person whom I desire to see is Monsieur Monro. I believe he is staying here."

When she said that, this well-trained Moorish man-servant, with no diminution of the elegance of his manners, and without uttering a single word, very quietly shut the door in her face.

For a moment or two Julia stood in that shadowed but nevertheless hot little court, utterly taken aback. One very seldom has a door shut in one's face by a servant unless one is a beggar, or in some other obvious way unsuitable for polite society—which Julia knew she was not. She had a moment of fury, an impulse to hammer savagely with that black-painted knocker on the tidy well-grained door. But she pulled herself together, and did neither. Slowly she turned away—and then turned back to see if there was one of those blue-and-white plaques with numbers over the door. There was not. And there was no street-name at the entrance to the little court; when she turned the corner and stood where she could see up the alley into the *place*, there was none there either. But at the angle where the court and the alley met she nearly bumped into a small lurking figure, European, with a hang-dog look—she recognised the seedy little man who had come into Purcell's Bar the first time she went there, by the cast in his eye. He glanced at her curiously before he scuttled off, silently, on rubber-soled feet, and was lost to sight among the gradually dissolving crowd in the square.

This tiny encounter rather upset Julia, coming on top of what had gone before. Had he *seen* that door shut in her face? The thought was disagreeable; somehow the whole thing was eminently disagreeable. She walked out into the square, suddenly extremely aware of heat, hunger, and fatigue—and how on earth was she to get back to the Espagnola? She really *couldn't* walk it. However this problem solved itself, rapidly. The Americans with whom she had shared those steps had gone, but one of

their Arab guides, whom she recognised, promptly accosted her; he con-
jured up a taxi out of space and escorted her to the Place Pasteur, all the
address she would vouchsafe. There, in English, he demanded an exorbitant tip—Julia said *"Par exemple!"* and gave him a very modest one; whereat
he smirked, bowed, and took himself off.

The Espagnola being under Spanish management really preferred its
patrons to lunch about half-past two, so Julia did not have to worry about
being late; this was as well, for she felt a little unnerved. Seeing Colin, if
it was Colin, was startling enough—and she felt pretty sure that it must
have been him, or why had the mere mention of his name caused that door
to be shut? She was troubled. The whole thing was so extraordinary, and
seeing the seedy little man from the underworld there, at that precise moment, was somehow the last, most disconcerting touch. *How* was she to
get hold of Colin?

Julia, finishing her tortilla and refusing cheese—after all she was not as
hungry as she thought, she found—fell back on her usual principle of
there being always some sensible thing to do: in this case, she decided
after reflection, the sensible thing was to take a nap. She did so, and
awoke refreshed and mentally restored; she had tea sent to her room, made
a leisurely toilet, and set off in good time for Purcell's Bar; if she went
early enough she would be sure to find him alone and—well, one never
knew.

Purcell was alone when she went in, sure enough; he greeted her with
a minute degree of extra friendliness, a sort of delicate accent on the
gradual progress in their acquaintanceship which really charmed Julia—it
occurred to her that she knew no one, in any walk of life, who would
have done this better, if indeed as well. Purcell observed that it was a hot
day, and while he shook her cocktail for her, neat and small behind his
bar, asked if she would like a piece of ice in it? Julia said she would, and
when he brought her drink with the clear cube swimming in the liquid
he also brought the bottle of Gordon's, and slipped in an extra dash, observing that in his view a washy cocktail was a horrible thing. These
agreeable attentions cheered Julia up considerably, and restored her nerve;
nevertheless, she resisted the gin-born impulse to ask Purcell some questions, and instead did a sort of mental summing-up. If she had really seen
Colin up in the Kasbah today he couldn't be on the *Frivolity*, so *that* was
out; and if it wasn't him that she had seen, why the closed door at the
sound of his name? Damn!—why hadn't she longer sight?

Purcell broke in on these reflections with a friendly query from behind
the bar—had she, he asked, been up today to see the Mendoub? This
struck Julia as being a sort of pointer for further action. Yes, she had gone,

she said; very interesting and very picturesque. Then she drawled out a question—"Who is that tall man with red hair whom I've seen in here once or twice? You know—he always wears white flannel trousers and a blue blazer."

Purcell hesitated for a moment before replying—did his fascinating Anglo-negro face bear for a moment something of the same withdrawn expression that she had seen on Mr. Panoukian's face down in Casablanca? She couldn't be sure, but there certainly was a perceptible hesitation before he replied.

"I know the person you mean," the bar proprietor said, "but I don't know his name."

"Oh, you must!" Julia protested. "He came in with all that bunch of pansies!" she added unguardedly—"They're locals."

Purcell gave a little laugh.

"Still I do not know his name. I do not know the names of everyone who comes here—not yours, for example! In any case this particular gentleman left Tangier early this afternoon; he came in to get supplies of whisky and gin before going off to the interior."

"Was there another man with him?"

Purcell eyed her a little curiously, she thought, when she asked that, but all he said was—

"No, he came alone, except for his chauffeur; they brought the car and took the cases away in it."

Julia reflected again for a moment.

"He has a house here, hasn't he?" she then asked.

"Ah, that I could not say. He may be staying at the Minzah—many people stay there. I only see him at intervals."

Julia was about to press her questions when that veiled door opened and let in several people, among them those she had seen on her first visit; she paid and went home.

Next day she took her letters of introduction round to Mme La Besse; she telephoned in advance, and was asked to come early, as the lady had to go out for the day. That suited Julia; this quest was evidently going to be a long job, and the sooner she started earning the better. Mme La Besse lived in a rather indeterminate little house standing in a small muddled garden, down a cul-de-sac high up in the modern quarter to the west of the town; from the main road at the entry to the cul-de-sac there was a splendid view, out over half Tangier lying far below, white among the green trees, with the misty blue of the mountains of the Rif in the distance; but from the house itself, low and muffled in its rather ugly small trees, nothing of this was to be seen. Mme La Besse was a short stout

woman with thick untidy grey hair, and dressed in ugly shapeless clothes;
her beard, of which Geoffrey had spoken, was very much in evidence, stiff
greyish bristles all over her chin. But she had a pair of very bright lively
pale-blue eyes and a thoroughly cheerful expression; this was accentuated
after she had read Geoffrey's letter.

"Ah, this dear Consett!—he is so charming. I like him enormously. He
says you are his friend—his fiancée, perhaps?"

"Decidedly *no*—but I too like him," said Julia. "He is very fond of you,
and greatly wished me to know you," she added courteously.

"*Le cher garçon!* and such an ardent archaeologist. And you?"

"I am afraid not—I am completely ignorant of all that."

"Ah well, never mind. Did he speak to you of my beard?" the old lady
asked unexpectedly.

"Actually he did," Julia said, embarrassed but candid. Mme La Besse
laughed, delightedly; she seemed to think her beard the best joke in the
world. When she laughed her whole stout flabby body shook like jelly,
and her rather ugly face became creased with mirth—Julia decided that
her new employer was rather likeable.

For employer and employed they at once became. Mme La Besse asked
if she could drive a car? The car proved to be a Chrysler, a make which
Julia had in fact only driven on her dash to Glentoran a couple of weeks
earlier; she had beguiled the long run from Renfrew to Argyll by driving
much of the way herself—this entitled her, she felt, to undertaking to drive
the La Besse machine, and she hardily agreed to do so. She for her part
bargained for a four-day week, in order to have time to write her articles—
she had already started one on Casablanca, and how money was made in
Morocco. Mme La Besse did not appear to be much impressed by journalism; indeed she gave the impression of not being easily impressed at all—
"*Tiens! Les petites feuilles*" was her only comment. But she agreed to engage Julia to work four days a week, for a very fairly handsome sum in
francs, which as Lady Tracy had foreseen would enable the girl to live
practically free at her Spanish pension; and she also made no fuss about
Julia's stipulation for an occasional week off if she wanted it.

The job was a curious affair. It comprised paying the bills (some of
them months old), dealing with the Spanish servants, doing the shopping
for the household, and buying the flowers—Mme La Besse had a passion
for flowers, and liked to have her untidy little house full of them all the
time. This was a thing Julia enjoyed; it involved constant trips down to the
Gran Socco, the big open-air market, where vegetables, fruit and cheeses
were to be bought, and where majestic Berber women, in those huge betasselled straw hats, sold flowers of every kind—roses, carnations, freesias,

heaths and myrtles; most charming of all one of them, in particular, delighted in concocting bright formal Victorian posies, with garden flowers and wild flowers all mixed together—Julia loved these, and always had one in her room in the hotel, but Mme La Besse preferred grander displays. No accounts were kept that Julia could see; she was given money to go shopping, and brought back the change, but her employer waved aside her neat sheets of reckonings. Nor was there a great deal of correspondence, though now and again she had to type out a few pages of reports on "l'excavation." It became clear to Julia that what Mme La Besse wanted was less a secretary than a mother's help, to deal with the practical affairs of life, leaving her free for more congenial occupations. Geoffrey was right, though—she was great fun.

Before the first week was out Julia to her great satisfaction was called on to drive the old lady down to "l'excavation"; she had not yet been outside the city at all, and was delighted at the chance of seeing something of the countryside. The site lay in the International Zone—in which the city of Tangier is embedded like the stone in a peach—on the coast, down beyond the air-port; Julia sent the Chrysler humming along a superb road, first through suburbs, then across open country through fields either ploughed, or blue with wild Spanish iris standing two feet high, and past streams along whose banks paper-white narcissus bloomed in huge milky clumps. When they turned out towards the ocean the splendid road degenerated, till it ended as no more than a yellow sandy track; cultivation ceased, and a fragrant heathy countryside, full of wild scillas, took its place. Set among the heaths and cistuses Julia presently saw an oblong of low stone walls, of a curious tone between deep cream and pale sand, sloping gently down towards the real sand of the shore, along which the green Atlantic breakers rose and poised, to tumble and fall in a thundering confusion of foam; the noise they made was splendid on that wild sweet-smelling shore, in the strong hot sunshine.

They parked the car near a small roughly-built shed, surrounded by a little courtyard full of the spouts and bases of amphorae, tiles, and archaeological bits and pieces of all sorts; in the shed itself, Mme La Besse explained, the more valuable objects were housed, padlocked. However they did not then enter it; the old enthusiast could not wait to show the newcomer the site itself. In fact it was charming, and laid out with the utmost ingenuity. At the upper end were three large underground cisterns, still holding water—two had vaulted cemented roofs, as the Romans built them, but the third was roofed with over-sailing courses of dry stone, unmortared; this, Mme La Besse stated, was the Phoenician style for such things. Julia asked how the water reached the cisterns, and was shown some sec-

tions of stone-cut drainpipes through which it had been led, from springs
a considerable distance away, up on the higher ground inland. In the next
enclosure below the cisterns—each activity, in this ancient factory, had had
a compartment to itself, on most modern lines—were shallow mortared
tanks for treading the grapes to make wine; Julia had once been up the
Douro to see the port vintage, and noticed with amusement that these
Roman or Phoenician structures were exactly like the *lagares* in which,
today, bare-legged Portuguese men in flowered cotton pants tread the
grapes to make port, the only difference being that in Portugal in the
twentieth century the raw wine is led off through pipes, whereas here a
small open channel, beautifully cemented, had led it away to an adjoining
tank several feet deep. "That must hold at least eight thousand gallons,"
Julia said, comparing it in her mind to farm tanks installed by the Monros
up at Glentoran.

"*Nine* thousand," said Mme La Besse proudly—"Consett said at least
nine thousand."

Two Berber labourers in straw hats were busily engaged in shovelling
sand out of the bottom of this receptacle and throwing it up over the side;
Mme La Besse shouted greetings to them in Arabic, and they shouted
back, happy and friendly. The sand kept on blowing in, Mme La Besse
explained; that must have been bad for the Phoenician wine, make it salty,
Julia observed, which made the old lady laugh and shake.

Next they inspected what Mme La Besse declared to be the *huilerie,*
the oil-mill, where olives were crushed before their oil was pressed out;
Julia was rather unconvinced by this, since there was little to be seen but
a large block of stone surrounded by a shallow circular trench or gutter,
mortared as usual. However the fishpits, which they visited next, were extremely convincing. A range of deep tanks, each some ten feet long by six
feet broad, and seven or eight deep, ran round three sides of another enclosure, all lined with beautifully fine close mortar; for fish, whether
swimming alive, pickling in brine, or steeping in oil they looked just the
thing, indeed it was hard to think of a purpose unconnected with fish to
which such structures could be put. Julia—perfectly ignorant of Roman, let
alone Phoenician remains—regarded everything she was shown with a
fresh and slightly sceptical eye; she listened, also a little sceptically, to the
old archaeologist's eager attributions. The little temple in the middle of
the whole lay-out, with its small elegant pillars, she was prepared to accept,
and could even pay a happy tribute to a civilisation which insisted on the
equivalent of a chapel built into the heart of its factories. But she felt less
sure about three long enclosures lying towards the lower, seaward end of
the rectangle of buildings, which Mme La Besse declared to have been

ware-houses for the finished products before they were shipped away—one for wine, one for oil, and one for the pickled fish.

"But how do you *know* that that is what they were for?" Julia asked in her usual slow tones, gazing at her employer from behind her immense dark sun-glasses.

"For what else should they be? And if you had seen the number of shards of broken amphorae that we cleared out of them, you would have thought the same! Oil and wine were certainly transported in amphorae; how they sent the fish we don't know—possibly in rush baskets lined with the leaves of palmettes."

"What are palmettes?" Julia asked.

"Oh, this plant from which the Moors make the *crin végétal* with which they stuff their mattresses—this countryside is full of it, you will see them when we have lunch," said Mme La Besse, rather irritably. She hustled Julia down to look at the baths at the lower end; these too were perfectly convincing, Julia had seen the like in England, when dragged by Geoffrey to observe Roman remains. Hot baths, cold baths, stone steps leading down into both; the tile-vaulted chambers of the hypocaust, where fires were kindled below the sudarium, the sweating-room, immediately above; neat herring-bone tiling floored most of these rooms, and here and there a fragment of gay frescoes, orange and white, still clung to the walls.

Julia surveyed all this with approval; if the place had really been a factory, these dispositions for the workers' comfort were admirable. "Fine; pit-head baths," she said—and then had to translate and explain to Mme La Besse about the English arrangements for coal-miners to wash before they went home from their work. But in spite of her lingering scepticism she was charmed by the idea of such a factory, functioning more than two thousand years ago. Standing there, fingering the curious pock-markings in the beautiful rough golden stone of the wall, for a little while she let her imagination run—an unusual thing with her, picturing those long-ago labourers toiling in the fish-pits or carrying laden amphorae down to the triremes or quinqueremes anchored at the mouth of the small river which ran out just below the site into a bay sheltered by a projecting headland, sweating under the strong sun, as she was sweating merely from walking about. Here, where fragrant scents from the heathy uplands filled the warm air, and the surf thundered on the sands below, there was no suggestion of dark Satanic mills; if one had to be a factory-hand, better to have been a Phoenician one, she thought. And vast earthenware jars full of flowery aromatic wine like that which she drank nightly—free of charge, since it was *vinho de mesa*—at the Espagnola was an amusing counterpart to the tractors and saloon cars which she had watched being decanted

from the *Vidago* onto this very coast—amusing, and somehow nicer, as
honest wine is nicer than any piece of machinery.

These meditations were only possible because the foreman who directed
the labourers had come up to ask some directions of Mme La Besse, but
they were soon interrupted; he went away, and the eager old lady led the
way down to where most of the actual digging was taking place, in front
of the sea-ward wall of the site. Here five or six more Berbers, in headgear
which varied from ragged turbans to torn straw hats, were clearing away
soil to lay bare curious stone slabs, some of them grooved, and several
small stone boxes or tanks sunk in the ground, with one sloping side, which
reminded Julia of nothing so much as the fitted wash-tubs in the laundry
at Glentoran; the men greeted Mme La Besse with gleeful pleasure, and
she chatted to them, with a word for each—clearly she was a general
favourite. The excavated soil, to Julia's astonishment, was wheeled away in
barrows to be riddled at some hundred yards' distance before being tipped
onto the fore-shore—no hope therefore, as even her ignorance recognised,
of being able to know with any exactitude where any particular object,
revealed in the wire sieve, had come from. Had Geoffrey seen this extraordinary proceeding, she wondered?—however she said nothing.

Mme La Besse was worried about those small stone tanks or boxes, and
asked Julia if she had any idea what they could have been used for? Julia
mentioned the laundry wash-tubs—"If you dug along behind them you
might find a spout or something that led the water into them," she said;
she had already been shown parts of the underground system of stone
channels through which water had been brought by gravity from the
cisterns at its upper end down to every part of the site, and had admired
its ingenuity. Mme La Besse was delighted with the laundry idea; she
whipped a mason's trowel out of her belt and began to dig herself, and
called up a Berber to help. Julia looked on, wishing that she had a trowel
or spade with which to dig too, while Mme La Besse, on her knees, continued to speculate aloud as to whether this could have been a laundry or
wash-house.

"I know!" Julia exclaimed suddenly.

"What do you know?" asked the old lady, squatting back on her heels
and wiping her perspiring face with an earthy hand.

"Won't this have been the place where they gutted the fish? Right down
here near the shore, you see, and keep the pickling chamber clean. London
fishmongers always clean fish in sort of sinks, with running water—you
can see them in the backs of the shops."

Mme La Besse was even more delighted with this second suggestion;
she stood up to pat Julia on the shoulder, and said that she was *une fille*

très intelligente, then shouted to the foreman to come over and discuss this new idea. Presently she abandoned the foreman, and led Julia off again—"You must see *all,*" she said, "and then we will have lunch."

There was not much more to see. Out on the open space, as yet undug, between the lowest wall and the sea lay several large blocks of that pock-marked limestone, placed there till either their use or their original positions could be established; one or two had large phalluses carved in relief on the sides, definitely proving, Mme La Besse thought, that they were Phoenician in origin. Julia, her hair spectacular in the sun, and in her huge dark glasses looking like a peculiarly vacant film-star said in her slow tones—

"Couldn't they be Mithraic, and Roman?"

The old woman cocked her head sharply at the young one.

"I thought you were so ignorant!" she said.

"Oh well, everyone knows about Mithras now, since that place in the City was being dug up," said Julia blithely.

"*Tiens!* Yes, well, it is possible that these are Mithraic—but I think not."

They lunched near the shed, sitting on the last fringe of the heathy slope where it fell away to the shore, and Mme La Besse showed Julia some low bushy dumps of palm-leaves which she said were the palmettes from which *crin végétal* was made. Julia was hungry, though the lunch was not very good; she made a mental note that if she was going to come to the site often she would organise the picnic food herself. However there was a bottle of the good red Moroccan wine which helped down the rather dry sandwiches and the lump of hard Moroccan cheese.

"What impression does the site make on you?" Mme La Besse asked.

"Fascinating! And so much has been done; I suppose to begin with—well, what was there to see?"

"Nothing!—except for a few fallen pillars among the cistuses."

"Extraordinary," said Julia. "What fun you must have had."

The old lady was pleased with these rather moderate tributes, and developed her theories while she masticated the withered sandwiches. The archaeological sites in England to which Geoffrey Consett had sometimes borne Julia in his little car had all been completely excavated, determined, and written up—she had not realised the part that speculation and intelligent interpretation has to play in archaeology. Now she did, and in her casual way she sympathised with her employer's problems; she was really rather moved when the old lady said—

"You like it out here? You will come often? I see that you have intuition, good ideas; you could be a great help to me in the excavation. This notion of cleaning the fish outside the walls—it is formidable!"

Julia asked nothing better than to spend as much time as possible out in this delicious place, thunderously musical with surf along the shore, sweet with wild scents—she said as much, and Mme La Besse patted her hand.

But while they lunched something else held her attention. When Mme La Besse had left the site to eat the Berber labourers also knocked off work; they went out onto the dry white sand of the upper shore and there knelt down with their faces towards Gibraltar—which also happened to be towards Mecca, more or less—and recited their mid-day prayers, bowing their foreheads to the ground, before they started to eat. Julia remembered what Paddy Lynch had said about a Moslem's faith, and how irreligious they considered Christians—well, there you were. If she were a Catholic she might have said the Angelus, and so might Mme La Besse. *Was* she a Catholic? Julia felt too lazy to ask—she drank another glass of wine and then, poking her head into the shade of a palmette plant, while her body relaxed in the sun, she fell into a doze.

CHAPTER VII

JULIA WAITED rather impatiently during the next few days for the promised letter from Paddy Lynch, which was to report the results of his "snooping" about Colin; she was busy with her work, she wrote away at her Casablanca article, but she had quite sufficient time to wonder why he didn't write, and to ponder uncomfortably over the episode up in the Kasbah. When at last Paddy's letter did come it was profoundly unsatisfactory.

"No go," he wrote. "I'm frightfully sorry—I did all I could. Johnny Bingham knows nothing, I'm sure of that—so it wouldn't have been any good your using those eyes of yours on him! Tony Panoukian certainly *does* know something, I can see, but he is keeping utterly mum about it. I was very much surprised, really. Your cousin must be on some tremendously hush job, because Tony will usually tell me anything I want to know. They've got his account all right—I got that, quick like the fox, from a clerk before I tackled the high-ups."

Julia thought Mr. Lynch's letter over carefully, sitting in her room at the Espagnola. She was thoroughly intrigued by this whole series of dead ends —a dead end at the Bank of England, two dead ends in Casablanca, that closed door (than which no end could be deader) in the Kasbah. What *could* be going on? She had said up at Glentoran, she remembered a little ruefully, that detection would be a frolic—but it wasn't really much of a frolic to be thwarted at every turn, and find out *nothing*, delicious as it was to be in Tangier in the sun among flowers, and much as she was enjoying her days out at *"l'excavation"*, searching for thresholds and floor-levels, digging herself with the trowel she had bought at Kent's Emporium, and writing up reports for the old lady.

Time was marching on, and she was getting nowhere. She remembered that Lady Tracy had also expressed a fondness for detection—from her chair; and that afternoon she chartered a taxi by the hour (Spanish-speakers can do this in Tangier) and went up to the house on the cliff.

Lady Tracy was out on the roof—which was flat and festooned with lines of washing—sitting in a deckchair and screaming jests over the low parapet at the Moorish occupants of some rather hovel-like little houses down on the slopes below. The cliffs here were, so to speak, in two tiers: first an upper cliff, then a talus of scree overgrown with grass, now full of grazing goats and those small houses dotted about; then a second vertical fall to the blue water, crashing ceaselessly against the yellow line of rocks.

"They are so *nice*," Lady Tracy said, when Julia had greeted her and been kissed, waving a gnarled old hand over the parapet. "From here I can watch every detail of their lives: the washing, the cooking—do you see that little stove out in the garden?—milking the goats, and the hunt for eggs. I *must* remember to tell Nilüfer that her brown hen has a nest in that big clump of thistle—do you see it, under the rock? The fact is, I know almost more about them than they know themselves, from this eyrie."

This was another pleasing facet of Lady Tracy's character, and Julia liked to think of her sitting on her roof-top, watching Moorish domestic life and enjoying long range conversations with her friends a hundred feet below. However she was glad when presently the old lady asked—"Well, and how is your search going?"

"It isn't going at all. I wanted to ask you if your detection had produced any results, because mine hasn't."

"Oh, I am sorry. And I am afraid I have been rather useless too. I have a nephew who goes about a lot, and often seems to know things, but unfortunately he is away just now—such a bore."

"Yes," said Julia, flatly. "It is, rather. You see I haven't the faintest idea what to do next. When do you expect your nephew to get back?"

"Dear child, I have no idea. One never knows, with him. He's a botanist, and goes flitting off after some flower or other like a butterfly! He knows just where to look for the rarities—which I don't suppose real butterflies care about," said Lady Tracy, looking vague. "I expect they just want honey, don't you?"

"I suppose so," said Julia, rather dully. She suddenly felt depressed; she had hoped a good deal from Lady Tracy's help, and now none seemed to be forthcoming.

The old lady saw her depression. She leaned over and patted Julia's hand. "My dear child, I am *sorry* not to have helped you. I will try to bestir myself somehow, even before Hugh comes back—and in the meantime, do remember what St. Paul said about possessing one's soul in patience. *Was* it St. Paul?"

"I can't remember."

"Tell me," said Lady Tracy, with a sudden switch of subject—"How are you getting on with Mme La Besse?"

"Oh, the dig is heaven," said Julia more cheerfully, "and she's great fun." Lady Tracy said that the Belgian was delighted with Julia and her help. "She says that you have intuitions!" she said with a gleam of amusement.

"Oh yes, I'm bursting with intuitions," Julia replied gaily. "And she's nothing like as tatty as you led me to expect—not so far at least."

"Ah, wait!" said Lady Tracy.

Julia decided to follow one of her intuitions that very evening. Since Lady Tracy had learned nothing—again Julia had failed to put the old lady in possession of *all* the facts, but she overlooked that point—the time had clearly come to ask Purcell flat out about Colin. It was too early for the bar to be open when she got back to the Espagnola, so she filled in the time by writing a much overdue letter to Edina; that is to say, knowing her Aunt Ellen she wrote two letters: a short boring one saying that she hadn't found Colin yet but hoped to soon, and how lovely Tangier was, and she had taken a job as secretary to support herself—and another for Edina's private eye.

"Colin is evidently up to something quite extraordinary," she wrote, "though so far I can't find out what, and nor can Paddy"—and she gave a lively version of her encounter with Mr. Panoukian. "I think he was probably *smuggling,* to begin with," the letter went on; "the mate on the boat, a most odd bearded type called Reeder, suggested it at once—and everyone I've seen since puts that up as a hypothesis, Consulate-General and all. *No one* sells oranges seriously, Mrs. H. was quite right about the smell of *that* rat; and out here they don't even call it orange-selling, they usually dress up as fishermen—that nonsense was just for home consumption." Then she pursued the theme of Mr. Reeder.

"He's really quite an enigma. Madly efficient, the Captain told me; he could be at the top of his profession by now—but he sticks on in this subordinate job because he loves this run—so he says. And I couldn't place him at all. He looks *terrible,* in a ghastly old uniform and with that beard, and he is crusty and curt to a degree; but he talks like a complete gent—really rather an ultra-gent, if you follow me—and he knows all about sheep, and wintering away and first-cross lambs. It seems he was brought up in Northumberland, where they have to do much what one does in Argyll about sheep." And she added as a P.S., in an access of leisurely mischief—

"He says anything with black hair drives him wild."

As she walked down to post this missive in the English Post office on her way to Purcell's Bar, through the calm bright evening air, and the golden light which conferred a certain beauty on even the dullest villas, Julia's depression suddenly left her. She was beginning to feel at home in Tangier, as if she "belonged"; and she liked the place more than ever—she was no longer afraid of losing her way in the old city, and after buying one of these delicious posies from her enormous flower-woman in the Gran Socco, who greeted her with cries of pleasure, she cut down through the swarming alleys to the Socco Chico, with its thronged cafés and strolling crowd of idlers, and made her way to the quiet little street where Purcell's notice so discreetly beckoned.

She was still too early—the muslin-veiled door was locked. Julia tapped on the glass with the stem of her bouquet; in a moment it opened, and the little Moor peered out. When he saw who it was he drew the door wide to let her in, with a bow and a greeting in what he conceived to be French—Julia felt still more at home. "Monsieur Purcell?" she asked, seeing no sign of him, as she sat down at her usual table; the Moor scurried away, and in a moment Purcell himself was there behind the bar, small, neat, calm and courteous, with a smile of welcome.

"Sorry if I'm too early, Mr. Purcell, but I wanted to talk to you," the young woman said. "Yes, a Martini, please."

"That will be a pleasure," said Purcell, pouring things into a mixer. "What pretty flowers!"

"Aren't they? There's a heavenly old Berber woman in the Gran Socco who always makes them—a giantess!"

"I know her," said Purcell, bringing Julia's drink round the end of the bar and setting it down on the table. "She is a witch with flowers."

"Yes, she is. Look, Mr. Purcell, sit for two minutes, till people come—I hate shrieking through space!"

Purcell sat.

"You won't drink yourself? You never do, I think?"

"No, I never do. I will have a cup of coffee, though." He called in a low voice, and ordered coffee from the little Moor.

"Mr. Purcell," said Julia, "did you ever know a young man called Colin

Monro, who was in and out of here for two or three years on a yacht with
some other young Englishmen?"

"Yes, naturally I knew him. He was often here; they hung about for
some time, as you say."

"What were they doing?"

"Oh, smuggling, of course. I am sure you know that already"—with a
fine glance.

"Well, I guessed it."

"Yes, that was it. But after a time I imagine they made the place too hot
to hold them; probably the Zone police got busy, or Interpol—they combine,
you know—anyhow those young men seem to have cleared out altogether.
I haven't seen anything of them for the last year—well, say ten or eleven
months."

The last four words clicked in Julia's head like a bolt into its slot. Ten
or eleven months—ten fitting in exactly with the transfer of Colin's account
from Duntroon to Casablanca. But another thing struck her about Purcell's
words. There was a lot of information, but all made somehow indefinite: "I
imagine", "probably", "they seem". In her turn she studied Purcell curiously, with a long slow look, in silence.

"May I ask, if it is not indiscreet, why you are interested in Mr. Monro?"
the man asked.

"Of course. He's my cousin, and we've had no news of him now for ages.
I hoped you might know something. Do you know the name of the yacht,
for instance?"

"No, I have no idea. Those sort of people do not talk much about themselves."

His face still puzzled her. *Sabe todo*, Reeder had said—and might be
reluctant to say what he knew. She determined to fire all her batteries, now
at last.

"Look, Mr. Purcell dear," she said with the eyes of a mourning dove—
"You've simply *got* to help me about this! I'm desperate. I must find him."

"Why are you desperate? Why must you find him?"

"I must find him because he's wanted at home, badly. Listen—please
listen." She poured out the story of Glentoran; Purcell did listen, in silence.
"Anyhow his mother is frantic—he's her only son," Julia ended. "Surely you
see?"

"Why do you not consult your friend Lady Tracy," Purcell asked.

At this instance of Purcell's all-knowingness Julia laughed; she couldn't
help it. She had a very pretty laugh, deep and gurgling, and slow, like her
speech, as if she were chewing and tasting her amusement—it made Purcell
smile.

"Why is that funny?" he asked, with genuine curiosity.

"Oh, a private joke. Anyhow, I did ask Lady Tracy, and she promised to help, and she hasn't been able to. Her nephew, who it seems *sabe todo*," —Julia grinned again, privately, at the phrase—"and might have been able to find out, has gone jaunting off after wild flowers, so he's no use."

Purcell's face, so mobile and expressive, once more seemed to Julia to register some impression which she could not fathom at the mention of the nephew and the wild flowers, but he said nothing.

"So there's no one to help me but you—don't for goodness sake suggest that I try Mme La Besse! I know there's no reason why you should help me; but I am really in trouble, and I ask you to."

He looked at her for some moments in silence when she said that; there was an expression, almost of compassion, on his queer face.

"It is *really* urgent, serious, that you get in touch with him?" he asked at last.

"Yes."

Still he studied her, as if trying to come to a decision.

"*Yes*," Julia said again, nodding her head.

He smiled.

"You are very persuasive. And I assume that you have some good reason for thinking that I can help you; I am curious about this, but I shall not ask what it is. I will do what I can, if you for your part will promise not to say *to anyone* that it is I who have told you what I now tell you."

"I promise that," said Julia quietly, though she was tremendously excited. Was she really going to learn something at last?

"Good. Well, if I were you I should go up to Fez—you have not been to Fez yet, have you?" Julia shook her head. "While you are there, simply *en touriste*, go to the shop of a very well-known dealer in curios called Bathyadis: any of the guides will take you to him. He may be able to tell you something—but speak to him alone, out of earshot of other people. If he cannot, or will not, tell you himself, he may at least put you in touch with a compatriot of yours, a Mr. St John."

Julia was all ears—this was quite unexpected. But another of those clicks took place in her head, and after thanking Purcell she said, quite light-heartedly and casually—

"Is Bathyadis one of the ones whose sons have started shops in Casablanca and Agadir and places?"

The effect on Purcell of this innocent question was electric—he started in his seat, for a moment he looked almost angry—or was it almost frightened?

"How do you know that?" he asked sharply.

"What, that they've started curio-shops down on the coast—the sons of the dealers in Fez and Marrakesh, I mean? Oh, someone was telling me about it in Casa, when I was asking who made money, how, out here."

"Who was this person, may I know?" He spoke with a curious urgency.

"A rather dumb bank-manager, to be exact," said Julia. "At a cocktail-party. Why? Is it important? I just thought it was fun that the sons and nephews had got so rich in two or three years that they could buy Papa out, now," she said, tranquillisingly.

Purcell appeared to be tranquillised; his expression relaxed.

"No, it is not important," he said. "And it is, as you say, an amusing development." He paused for a moment. "But it is a very recent one, which few people, even those living out here, know about—so naturally I was surprised that you, so newly arrived, had heard of it."

"Yes, of course," said Julia smoothly; but to herself—"Covering-up," she said.

"You have many contacts in Casa?" Purcell asked, now with all his usual blandness.

"Oh no—just one friend, in a bank. His wife and I were at school together," said Julia. "My boat put in there for twenty-four hours, so I looked them up. Horrible place, Casa, don't you think? I like this so much better."

"Ah, who would not?" said Purcell. "Tangier is unique."

At that moment the door opened to admit the young men whom Julia had now come to call "the bunch". At the first shadow on the muslin veiling, even before the tiny click of the latch, quick and silent as a cat Purcell was on his feet; before the door opened he was the other side of the table; and when the bunch entered, giggling and calling to one another, he was bending across assiduously and saying, for all to hear—"You are *sure* you will not have another, Mademoiselle?"

"Quite sure, thank you," said Julia, rising and taking a note from her purse. In fact the pansies could not have arrived more opportunely: she had got a line out of Purcell, and to continue to sit exchanging elegant cover-talk with him about the uniqueness of Tangier and the horribleness of Casablanca was the last thing she wanted. She had plenty to think about, and wanted time for that.

But thought, though amusing and exciting—*why* the fuss about the curio-dealing sons in the Atlantic ports?—it seemed quite inexplicable—did not take her very far. What was obvious was that she must go to Fez as soon as possible, and follow up this clue, faint and mysterious as it was. Next day she told Mme La Besse as she drove her out to the site, spinning along the blue-grey tarmac between the blue fields of irises, that she wanted to take a week's leave at once. The old lady was rather cross.

"What, already? But you have only just begun! Does my work bore you so soon?"

"No, *aucunement*—I adore the work," said Julia, heartily and truly. "But I must go now. I told you I might have to, dear Madame, as you will remember."

Mme La Besse grunted. "And where 'must' you go, now?"

"To Fez."

"Fez? *Tiens.* If you go to Fez you might do something useful to me," said the old Belgian, suddenly mollified and with a return to her usual childish eagerness.

"I should have the utmost pleasure in doing this, if it is within my power," said Julia, turning on some of her more elegant and formal French —she had already learned that this had a subduing effect on Mme La Besse when she became irritable. "Pray tell me, dear Madame, what it is that you desire of me."

Tame as a lamb, ardent as a little girl, Mme La Besse told her.

"I wish that you would go to Volubilis, the ruined Roman city near Fez. I am told that there is there a very good example of a Roman oil-mill, and I should like you to examine this with the greatest care, and write down a description on the spot, so that I may compare it with our little *huilerie* here. Perhaps," said Mme La Besse, peering hopefully sideways at Julia, "you could make a sketch?"

No, Julia could not sketch, and she had no camera; but she promised to take a tape-measure and bring back accurate measurements of the *huilerie.*

"And please observe closely, how it resembles or differs from ours here. Volubilis is said to have been built on the site of a Berber city, the name is derived from a Berber name. The Phoenicians were there also. I have a theory, though as yet I cannot prove it, that it was the Phoenicians who began the cultivation of the olive and oil-production in l'Afrique du Nord, long before the Romans; all information is therefore valuable."

Julia promised to do her best. Then she put a practical question.

"How far is Volubilis from Fez?"

"Oh, a nothing—sixty or seventy kilometres, perhaps."

"Is there a bus?"

"*Chère enfant,* how should I know? But in any case you could not travel in an autobus in le Maroc! You must take a car."

"Um," said Julia, wondering what this would be likely to cost. The trip to Fez would be pretty expensive, anyhow. But just then they arrived at the site, and the moment the Chrysler had been turned and parked near the shed, the old lady, glowing with enthusiasm over this new project, led Julia up to look at that so unconvincing oil-mill again. They stared together at the round block of yellow stone, the circular cemented channel, and at some other squarish blocks about whose use the old lady confessed herself at a loss—Julia for her part had no intuitions on this occasion. They stood speculating for some moments; a chilly wind had sprung up suddenly, and dark clouds were looming over the bronze-coloured mass of the headland which protected the bay on the south-west—Julia shivered.

"I think I'll go and fetch my coat," she said.

"Let us just go up to the wine-press enclosure, and see if Achmet and Abdul have got all the sand out of the big wine-tank," said Mme La Besse. "This wind will blow it in again, and I want to see the bottom."

The wine enclosure was the next above the one where they stood; they went into it and looked down into the deep tank. Abdul and Achmet had cleared out all the sand and were wheeling the last of it away in barrows; the bottom seemed to be covered with dark mud. Mme La Besse drew Julia's attention to some discoloration on the cemented sides, observing that to her it had a purplish look, like the stains of wine—Julia felt that to see this required the eye of faith, but did not say so. The two Berbers had carried away the short ladder they used for getting in and out of the pit; Mme La Besse lamented this, she wanted to climb down and examine the stained cement with the magnifying glass which, like her trowel, she invariably carried stuck in her belt. Julia volunteered to go for the ladder if she could be told the Berber word for it; Mme La Besse could not remember this for the moment, and while they stood undecided, on a sharp gust of wind down came the rain. Julia had only a cardigan—damn, if only she had fetched her coat.

"Here, under the wall—we shall get some shelter there," exclaimed the old lady, as she spoke unbuttoning her rather aged burberry; she drew it off and threw part over Julia's shoulders as they crouched together immediately above the tank under the low wall, which did afford a certain amount of shelter from the wind-driven rain. Julia thought she had never seen such a heavy downpour; the silver rods rebounded from the earth like hail, causing a white mist a foot high to rise above the surface of the ground; the rain hissed among the stones, and drummed—a different note— on the floor of the tank at their feet. Watching all this idly, and still rather cross at having been prevented from fetching her coat in time, the girl presently saw a sight which filled her with something like awe. The rain was so heavy that small runnels of water were soon streaming away downhill on all sides, and in a matter of minutes there was water all over the floor of the ancient wine-vat; the rain, hammering into this, brought it up in foam—and the foam was *red!*

"Look!" Julia almost gasped. "Mme La Besse, look at the tank!"

"Ah! You *see,*" the Belgian said, in slow triumph. That was all. The old woman was awestruck too, as well she might be; in silence, together, they watched a twentieth-century rainstorm stirring up lees of wine nearly two thousand years old.

Julia lost no time about setting off for Fez, though the more she thought about it, the more dubious the adventure seemed. Would Bathyadis tell her anything?—even how to find Mr. St John? On him, at least, she determined to try to secure a second string to her bow; she went up to the pink house on the cliff to consult Lady Tracy.

"Mr. St John? Oh yes, of course I know him," said the old lady. "He comes down here sometimes, though not as often as one could wish. Such an interesting man—he has lived in Fez for ages, fifteen years at least, and quite *among* the Moors; he has a house in the Medina. My dear child, if you could get him to take you about a little, he is the most perfect cicerone; he knows everything and everybody. Shall I give you a letter to him?"

"Oh yes, *do.* Do you think he would take me about to please you?"

"My dear child, once you have met I am confident that he will take you about to please *you*—or indeed to please himself," said Lady Tracy, bending her beautiful old eyes on the girl with a sweet aged archness. "I will write at once—" she rang her little brass bell as she spoke. "Feridah shall find my pad for me." Julia could see the pad on the table, poking out from under some knitting and *Life,* but refrained from mentioning the fact; she could never see enough of the lovely Feridah, who slid in, smiled through her veils at the visitor, stroked her mistress, and produced what was required. "When do you go?" Lady Tracy asked pausing in her careful deliberate writing.

"Tomorrow."

"By car?"

"Oh heavens no—by train."

"My dear, it is an *awful* journey! And do you realise that there is *no* restaurant car? Be sure to take a good picnic-basket and a bottle of wine, so that you don't starve."

Julia had not realised that the Moroccan State Railways seldom provide food for the traveller even on long journeys, and gratefully ordered herself an ample picnic meal on her return to the Espagnola. Señor Huerta had booked a room for her in a small hotel at Fez in the Medina, the old city, when she explained that she could not possibly afford the prices at the Palais Jamais, ravishing as she knew this to be; it was French-run, he said, and she would be all right there.

The storm which had so dramatically afforded proof of the authenticity

of the wine-vat out at the site continued to blow and deluge Morocco, and
when Julia went down to the station in good time for the three-thirty train
to Fez it was only to learn that it had not even arrived—there were floods,
the Espagnola porter told her; roads were washed away, and the train was
delayed. Julia sat rather gloomily on her suitcases in that curious place,
Tangier railway-station, watching the milling crowd of Moors, French
colons, tourists, and hawkers of cigarettes and sweets who filled it, and
used the time to inform herself about the journey from the hotel porter.
What about customs, for instance? Oh, there were plenty of *them*, the man
said grinning: customs out of the city of Tangier—the officers would come
presently, to those benches where people were placing their baggage, as the
Señorita saw for herself; customs again into the Spanish Zone; more customs on entering the French Protectorate of Morocco. It is a fact that the
town of Tangier and its surroundings have a certain resemblance to one
of those nests of wooden boxes beloved of the Chinese: the great French
Protectorate, stretching from the Sahara on the East to the Atlantic on
the West, and reaching southwards almost into Equatorial Africa, is the
vast outer box; the much smaller Spanish Zone is the next; then the
minute International Zone with the absurd little city at its heart. Absurd
only because this tiny entity is politically unique, an internationally-ad-
ministered territory of a bare two hundred and twenty-five square miles,
containing a population of only a hundred and seventy thousand souls;
yet this doll's-house unit has its capital, its diplomatic corps, a judiciary of
no less than eight judges, in fact most of the paraphernalia of statehood—
it is really much as if Bournemouth had become a state, full as the place
is of the delicate and the elderly.

About five the train from Fez came in; half an hour later it moved out
again. The Espagnola porter was surprisingly efficient, and while most of
the passengers were still screaming harassedly round the customs benches
Julia found herself relaxing in a first-class carriage, her suitcases in the
racks. Here she was presently joined by an exasperated and sweating individual who slung some rather military-looking baggage up on to the
opposite rack, cursed his Arab porter in American French, overtipped him,
and sank back into his seat to light a Chesterfield—with typical courtesy
he held out his pack to Julia before he did so.

"Oh thank you, but I'm smoking," said Julia. "May I later?"

Her travelling-companion, whose age she judged to be about thirty, next
began to ask about customs; thanks to the Espagnola porter Julia was able
to enlighten him. And was there a restaurant-car? No there wasn't, she told
him.

"Gosh! This is a hell country! How will I eat? With this hold-up I won't get to Port Lyautey till around two a.m.," said the American aghast.

Julia made no comment on this; instead she asked him what he was going to Port Lyautey for?

He was stationed there, it seemed, at the American Naval Air Base. Julia had not yet realised the highly important political fact of the huge American air bases in Morocco, but she pricked up her journalist's ears at once (with the *Onlooker* and *Ebb and Flow* well in mind) and set about cultivating the airman. Port Lyautey was sandy, she learned, and pretty up-state; there really wasn't much to it beside the Base; nor was there all that much to the Base—it was dull, apart from the jets. They had a library, but he had read mostly all the books; he amused himself by writing letters. Julia drew him out on the jets, about which he was enthusiastic—wonderful machines! They had given a number to the French for their base at Meknes and sent instructors up to teach the Frogs how to fly them—he had been doing that before he went on leave to take a look at France; he hoped to get sent up again. Meknes was a hick town, though it had a pretty gate —"Kinda arch, y'know; funny, but really pretty"—but when he went there he often drove over to Fez. "Fez is a swell town, so unique. Know it?"

Julia said she was going to Fez.

The airman at once said that he'd try to fix it to get sent up to Meknes right away—anyway he had four or five days' leave in hand; he'd gotten fed up with France and came back, so he might come up any time. Where was she staying?

Julia told him the name of her small hotel.

"That's in the old town, isn't it? A small French place? Oh, I'd not stay there if I was you. Little French hotels are awful. Ever stay in one? That's what drove me away, the French hotels. Their notions of *plumbing!*"

Julia laughed and said that she had lived in France, and didn't mind any of it, not even the plumbing. She continued to cultivate her Yankee acquaintance, with her usual regrettable eye to the main chance: if he came up to Fez with his car it might solve the problem of getting out to Volubilis and checking on the Roman *huilerie* for Mme La Besse. He was quite nice really, she decided; rather lonely, rather bored—bored, living in Morocco! Julia constantly kept one eye out of the window, observing the countryside, the houses, the flocks of white tick-birds in the sodden fields, the storks wading majestically across the flooded land, a group of animals she couldn't identify scampering beside a reed-bordered stream—could they be deer? Were there deer in Morocco? She asked her new acquaintance, who had already informed her that his name was Steve Keller, and that he had "done" two years there.

He didn't know—he knew strangely little about this place where he had lived so long. He had obviously never had any real curiosity whatever about the country or its inhabitants: the Moors were a crafty crowd, he said, but just the same what business had the god-damned French there, sitting on top of them and making money out of them? Julia, startled by this attitude, mentioned the hospitals in Casablanca as one instance of something the French had done *for* Morocco—it was, so far, the only thing she knew of that tremendous work. Oh well, maybe, Mr. Keller replied; he hadn't seen the hospitals, he didn't know. But he was against imperialism and colonialism, any place.

"Why?" Julia asked. "The French have done at least one good thing, which you've never managed to learn about in all this time—don't tell me the Arabs would organise hospitals on their own; they never have anywhere. What harm have they done to the Moors?"

He couldn't answer her. It was just this vague emotional feeling, supported by incuriosity and ignorance, with no more solid basis than an inherited mass-memory of one instance of a Colonial dispensation gone wrong, gone sour; but issuing in a mass-attitude which presented a blank wall to facts. Julia was startled and rather horrified—she had met several Americans, but all of a much more sophisticated type than the airman: either too well educated to be at the mercy of these primitive concepts, or too wise to give them expression. She relapsed into silence, a thing which always came easy to her.

Dusk began to fall, ending the resource of looking out of the window; the unheated train grew very cold—Julia was glad she had put on the fleecy zip boots admired by Mr. Reeder. She was hungry, and made up her mind to have supper; clearly she must offer some to her companion and as she lifted down her basket and began to unpack it on the little table under the window she said—

"Won't you have something to eat? I have lots. That is, if you don't mind sharing it with an impenitent imperialist, who is a convinced believer in the colonial system for backward races."

He laughed very nicely.

"You have me there! I am hungry." He fairly beamed as he watched her spread out a long loaf, a packet of butter, slices of raw smoked ham, tomatoes, and a jar of black olives, with a bottle of Moroccan red wine standing up in the midst.

They supped in amity, now talking again; Julia had a little thick travelling glass, Steve Keller fished an aluminum cup out of his baggage, from which they drank. The raw ham troubled his timid ignorance about strange foods. "Nonsense, it's delicious; what absurd ideas you have," said Julia firmly.

"It's *raw*," objected the American.

"Yes, and so are oysters—it's raw and it's *good*. No, you'll get no more bread till you've eaten a slice," the girl said, tucking the loaf back into her basket—and in fact when Mr. Keller had tried the raw ham he admitted that it *was* good.

Just as they were finishing supper the ticket collector came along—after snipping their tickets he informed them both that they must change at Petit-Jean. This was one thing on which the Espagnola porter had failed to enlighten Julia; she thought the train went through to Fez. They would reach Petit-Jean about 9.30 to change trains—oh, abundantly of time; yes, and plenty of porters. And when would they reach Fez? Julia asked. Ah, it was impossible to be precise—at one in the morning, or perhaps at two.

Julia groaned—this was going to be ghastly. Her little hotel was to have sent to meet her train at the normal time, but would they wait till one or even two a.m.? However, she put all that aside till the time came, with her usual calm.

When they reached Petit-Jean, they found that the collector was wrong both about the abundance of time for the change and the supply of porters. Of the latter there were none. Julia and Steve Keller tumbled out in the darkness on to a platform empty of everything but other distracted passengers tumbling out too, while a French voice screamed *"Départ pour Fez en deux minutes!"* The airman gathered up her suit-cases, gallantly abandoning his own luggage, and led her, running and stumbling, round to another stationary train, which proved to be the one for Fez; hastening after him, cumbered with her typewriter and food basket, on the further platform she bumped into a small man who swore at her in some guttural language as he recoiled from the painful impact of the basket. "The same to you, with knobs on!" Julia muttered—in the light falling from the high train windows she saw that he had a cast in one eye, and thought she recognised the seedy little man from Purcell's Bar. But there was no time to make sure—Steve was already throwing her cases up the four feet which always separate the doors of French trains, Heaven knows why, from ground level, and hollering to her to hurry. Discomfited, furious, panting, Julia climbed in after them just as the train drew out.

"Oh thank you *so* much!" she shouted at him through the window—and "See you in Fez Thursday," the American shouted back.

Fez is a strange city. Withdrawn, remote, secretive, it is so compressed, both within itself and by its gloomy encircling hills that it is one of the most difficult towns in the world to *see*—its most famous monuments, like the Karaouine Mosque, can never be entered by Christians (or any other infidel), and there are no open spaces from which to gaze even on the exterior of these wonderful buildings. The most the visitor can do is to climb to the top of one or other of the Madrasahs, or sacred colleges, and thence look out over the roofs of the greater wonders, and perambulate the narrow steep streets, catching a glimpse, here of a fountain, there of the carved doorway of a shrine. It is very revealing of the character of the place that the only views it permits of itself as a whole should be of its walls, seen from the slopes of the hills outside—Fez allows no view within those walls.

And yet it is full of magic: the magic of things half-seen in a dream, the magic of the barely visible or the partly remembered, which are the very stuff of dreams. Fez is full of rivers—seven, I believe—but they all run underground; the narrow alleys are full of the mysterious sound of invisible rushing water, but even the rivers may not be looked upon. These subterranean streams serve the useful purpose of sewers and also of rubbish dumps; here and there, under dank and clammy vaulted archways, one comes upon a mortared chute where the sound of the hidden water is extra loud—two women with baskets, or a mule-drawn cart, are to be seen emptying part of what Fez has done with and wishes to be rid of down the chute into the roaring hurrying stream, below and out of sight. Earth has not anything to show, not more fair, but more peculiar.

And the people are as strange and as secretive as the place. Hawklike Arab types predominate, striding along in silence on slippered feet, their stern splendid faces closed, inward-looking; the women's great sombre eyes look out from above swathing white veils with none of the languor or gay curiosity of the eyes which look out above veils in Tangier or Marrakesh; even the Berber women, unveiled and with deep blue designs tattooed on brow and chin seem, in Fez, to lack the bold chattering gaiety which they display elsewhere—sitting inviting the passer-by to inspect their wares in Tetuan, for example. And since the secretive, the mysterious, are apt to be also slightly sinister, or at least intimidating, Fez at first often creates a faintly alarming impression.

So at least it seemed to Julia Probyn—especially when the Oran express, into which she had to make another unexpected change at Meknes, decanted her at the station at half-past one in the morning. The railway of course has been kept well away from the mediaeval city, brooding within its walls; it only touches the new town. There were few passengers besides herself, and these got into cars and drove away; a solitary taxi was parked under the arc-lights on the space outside the station. This Julia hailed. It was free—it had not been sent by her hotel; an aged Arab with a beard, leaning in his jellabs by the station entrance heard her question, and vouchsafed in curious French that the hotel had sent a car earlier, but that it had gone away. So Julia drove off in the taxi, cold, weary, and in spite of her usual calm a little nervous—what, for instance, would the taxi cost at this unearthly hour? It cost five hundred francs; but after driving along what seemed miles of wall, and through innumerable gateways and archways, looming high and shadowy above her, it did at last deposit her at her hotel, where a lot of hammering and bell-ringing at length produced a sleepy servant who led her to a small but decent room—fifteen minutes after she entered it Julia was in bed and asleep.

Next morning, over the familiar French breakfast of rolls and butter, with chicory in the coffee, she wrote a note to Mr. St John enclosing Lady Tracy's letter, and saying that if it was not "a bore" she would so much like to see him—this the hotel undertook to send by hand at once. Señor Huerta at the Espagnola, and Lady Tracy too, had impressed on the girl that no European woman of *any* age could with propriety walk alone in the streets of Fez; anxious to lose no time—though the prices of her small hotel proved, mercifully, to be fairly moderate—Julia asked the management to lay on a French-speaking guide for eleven o'clock. When she went downstairs this individual was already waiting—a tall Arab in flowing robes, whose excessively handsome face was only slightly disfigured by a rather noticeable wart on one side of his high hawklike nose. He spoke fair French; but in spite of his handsomeness, or perhaps because of it—there are women who instinctively distrust handsome men—Julia disliked Abdul from the moment she set eyes on him, and she was really rather relieved when, in the middle of their colloquy as to where she should go and what she should see, the hotel porter announced that a Monsieur Anglais desired to speak with Mademoiselle, and she found herself face to face with Mr. St John.

Mr. St John, Julia decided at once, could not possibly be as old as he looked, or he simply couldn't have walked about at all. He looked incredibly old. He was very short, not much over five feet, with bushy snow-white hair and a face so brown, leathery, and wrinkled that he strongly resembled a lizard—but a very *nice* lizard; his expression was charming, benevolent and intelligent, in spite of his disconcertingly saurian face, with the little hooked poking nose, so like the nose of a questing tortoise. He spoke with extreme deliberateness and a curiously beautiful enunciation; his words came out like small carved beads of sound from his tight withered lips. Julia was fascinated by him, and by his brief way of dealing with Abdul, the guide.

"Another time," he said in French, waving a small claw-like hand in dismissal. "Today it is *I* who escort Mademoiselle." (The 'moi' in this speech was even more elaborately carved than the other verbal beads.) Abdul, clearly intimidated, gave a deeply respectful Moslem salutation and took himself off.

"Now that we are rid of this *shameless* exploiter and profiteer, what do you want to see?" Mr. St John asked.

"Well, Fez," said Julia. "But don't let me be a bore."

"That were impossible. And if Fez could bore me—which it never has yet—I should console myself by looking at you," the old man said, with a prehistoric twinkle from under his extraordinary dinosaurs' eyelids. "But do you, in the first place, wish to shop?"

"No, not really. You see I haven't much money for shopping—this hellish travel allowance!" said Julia. "But some time, when we've done the main sights, I should like to go to Bathyadis. I hear he has lovely things, and that one can look at them without buying too much."

"Ah, this delightful Bathyadis! A great friend of mine. Who told you of him?" Mr. St John asked, with a keen glance.

"Lady Tracy," Julia lied glibly. She had rather been caught on one foot by Mr. St John's turning up so promptly, and with her customary deliberation she decided not to rush matters, but to hold her fire and see what happened—she had intended to do a preliminary visit to Bathyadis alone and try out the ground before embarking on the Englishman at all. As it was, she would be passive today. Something might eventuate.

Quite a lot eventuated, as it turned out. Mr. St John, with a stout walking-stick, led Julia on a skilful round of Fez, which he accompanied by a learned and lively commentary: through *souks* full of leather, of copper, of pottery, of silks, of spices—each commodity in its separate street; past fountains with exquisite carved plaster above them, past the doors, equally ornate, of famous and forbidden mosques; under those vaulted echoing tunnels where the rushing noise of underground water filled the air, and women tipped rubbish into the subterranean streams. He told her of the seven rivers, and their names.

"Yes, but where do all these Alphs come out?" Julia asked, "if they do come out? They must look pretty ghastly when they emerge, with all this garbage in them; they'd really do better to stick to caverns measureless to man, don't you think?"

Mr. St John laughed, a dry articulated laugh such as a tortoise might give, if tortoises laughed.

"Dear young lady, how practical and factual you are! Do you know, I have never observed them after they emerge—which they certainly do, ultimately."

"Oh well, I expect you're wise," said Julia carelessly. She was beginning to get tired, young and strong as she was, after yesterday's journey and her short night; moreover Fez is built on two slopes of considerable steepness, so that when perambulating the old city half one's time seems to be spent in climbing Mount Everest, or descending something equally abrupt. She was much relieved when at last Mr. St John, turning into a courtyard with a fountain, and shops opening all round it, said—

"Here is Bathyadis'."

The shop was really two, and was not in the least like a European shop. It consisted of a couple of rooms, with most of both their fronts open to their full width on the court, causing Julia to wonder how the place could be shut up at night. One half was given over solely to carpets, the other was full of curios of every sort—silverware, antique jewellery in cases, lamps, brass trays, exquisite embroideries, woven saddle-bags and jellabs, and fine old leather-work; the whole place glowed and gleamed with colour like Aladdin's cave.

Bathyadis, in spite of his Greek-sounding name, was to all appearance a complete Moor, dressed in a long woollen robe with a fez on top— Goodness, that's why they're called fezzes, Julia thought to herself, now at last in the city that gives its meaning to the word; he had a splendid presence, a flowing grey beard, and courtly manners. He greeted Mr. St John by name in passable French and with evident pleasure, and invited them to sit down and have mint tea; Mr. St John looked enquiringly at Julia.

"Oh yes, do let's—I'm longing to take the weight off my feet," the girl said in English. Mr. St John nodded to Bathyadis and introduced him to Julia, who figured in the introduction, she recalled afterwards, as "a friend of mine."

They sat on a sort of bench covered with rich carpets. A youth in Arab garments brought the mint tea in glasses; it was sweet, scalding hot, and very minty—Julia thought it rather nasty, but sipped peacefully while Bathyadis and her escort talked. They spoke in French, and she listened idly, glad to be sitting down; Bathyadis was asking if Monsieur St John wanted to look at the tray again? No, not today, the old gentleman said— nevertheless the dealer had the tray brought out, a lovely antique one in wrought brass, of exquisite workmanship; Mr. St John continued to say No.

Meanwhile Julia's eye, roving round the cave-like gloom of the shop, was caught by a little coffer or trunk covered in plum-coloured velvet studded in a graceful pattern with silver-headed nails, for all the world like the one which propped up the broken Chippendale chair in Lady Tracy's house in Tangier; she thought it quite enchanting, and presently she drew Mr. St John's attention to it. "Would that be fearfully expensive?" she asked. "I'd love to have it, if I have to starve for a week!"

"The little trousseau-trunk, do you mean? Oh no, they are not in the least costly—two pounds, or two pounds ten at the most. They have become a drug in the market." He spoke to Bathyadis, and the little object was brought over by the youth who had fetched the tea, and opened for Julia's inspection; inside it was lined with some flowered material, there was a tiny lock and a delicate silver key.

"It's sweet," said Julia. "I will reflect upon it," she told Bathyadis in French, waving the pretty thing away.

"How wise you already are," said Mr. St John approvingly. "One should always tell an Arab that one will reflect upon a purchase; the longer one reflects, the less a given object costs."

"Why do you call them trousseau-trunks? And why are they a drug in the market?" Julia asked.

"For a sad reason, in answer to your second question. For centuries, here, the trousseau of a Moorish bride has always been carried in the wedding procession—on someone's head, usually—enclosed in one of these velvet coffers, varying in size of course according to the wealth and social status of the family; most of these little pieces of luggage are between two and three hundred years old, handed down with love and respect from mother to daughter from generation to generation. But recently," said Mr. St John, emitting a whistling sigh which again reminded Julia of a tortoise of her childhood, "it has become dated, out-moded, arriéré, to use these beautiful things for this purpose; it is considered much more chic, more up-to-date, to send down to Casablanca or to the New Town here, for some very dreadful modern suit-case in compressed fibre—if possible with an imitation of the skin of the lizard or the crocodile stamped on its surface—in which to carry the bride's trousseau to her new home."

"God, how revolting!" said Julia fervently.

"You are right. The Deity may with propriety be invoked to condemn this practice. However, it obtains; and that is why these lovely objects of art—for they are that—can now be bought at bargain prices."

"Well, I'll buy one next time I come. If I wait, shall I perhaps get it for thirty-five shillings?" Julia asked.

"Oh, you are admirable! I daresay you may. I will speak to him about it," Mr. St John said—and did so.

"Mademoiselle, my friend, desires a coffer, which you will sell her at the proper price—not at all the *prix de touristes*, you understand." The immediate result was to cause Bathyadis to have half the contents of the crowded shop pulled aside in order to display to Julia another trunk of the same sort, only in a more crimson shade of velvet, and five times bigger. "*Non, non,*" Julia said, laughing and shaking her head—the old Englishman for some reason grinned broadly at this point.

However Mr. St John, still speaking French, now asked a question of Bathyadis which caused Julia to sit up and listen. How was his son doing in Casablanca?

Oh, marvellously—he was making a fortune. Such a place for money, Casablanca! "But he is here, just for a week—you would like to meet him?"

Mr. St John said he would, and the Arab youth, who had been quietly putting back the displaced objects in front of the vast velvet trunk, was sent to fetch young Mr. Bathyadis. Julia hugged herself in silence—as easy as all that.

The young man when he arrived proved to be much less picturesque than his father, since he wore neat European clothes; but his manners were equally good. He greeted Mr. St John with the utmost warmth, thanking him with all his heart—rather to Julia's surprise this—for having made that wonderful suggestion. "Only a year and a half I am there, and already such gains! It is formidable!" More mint tea was brought to celebrate the occasion; the young man was presented to Julia, who said she would be going to Casablanca later, and would so much like to visit his shop and take her friends there—young Bathyadis whipped out a card and handed it to her; she stowed it away in her purse with great satisfaction. A second article on the Moroccan financial side-lines was practically in the bag, if she could only get onto that business of the rare minerals, somehow or other.

As they left, bowed out by old Bathyadis and his rich son, Julia had a small, unpleasant shock. Leaning against the wall in the open court-yard, in conversation with the Arab youth who had fetched the tea, was—this time quite unmistakably—the seedy little man with the cast in his eye whom Julia thought she had recognised when she bumped into him at Petit-Jean the night before. She walked quickly over, determined to tackle him; but with his beetle-like run he nipped out through the archway leading from the court to the street, and was gone.

"What is it?" Mr. St John asked, as she fell back, baffled, beside him.

"That revolting little man! I really believe he's following me," said Julia indignantly.

"Dear young lady, it should no longer surprise you that men follow you, surely?" said Mr. St John, with calm and slightly mocking benevolence.

"Oh, well—" said Julia; she was by nature all in favour of calm, and gave that up for the moment.

Mr. St John said that they would now visit the museum. The museum is at the top of Fez, or Everest, Bathyadis' shop is at the bottom; they toiled upwards. Julia began to feel extraordinarily tired—so tired that the sight of lush growths of plants on the tops of yellow plastered walls, and the trees that occasionally overhung them, could no longer charm her; she could think only of her back, which ached, of her feet, and the appalling cobble-stones in which her feet trod. But even in this near-coma of exhaustion, one thing drew and held her attention. Now and again, in fact quite often in their exhausting progress uphill they encountered some wonderful old man, swathed from head to foot in impeccable robes of creamy wool, a woollen hood covering his ice-white hair, and revealing his ice-white beard—they were the *cleanest* human beings that Julia had ever beheld, and moreover she observed that the crowds in the thronging alleys made way for them with reverent respect.

"What *is* that old man?" she was at last moved to ask Mr. St John, as they passed yet another of these ultra-clean white-clad figures.

"He is a leading member of one of the religious brotherhoods, which are such a feature of Muslim life here," Mr. St John replied.

"Religious life? For charity and so on, like the Spanish *hermandads?*"

"Originally, yes; and for that reason they are held in great veneration and wield a prodigious influence. But latterly, with the growth of nationalism and the disturbed state of public feeling, a good many of these brotherhoods, or the leaders of them, have begun to bend their organisations to political ends, alas!"—he ended with another of those whistling sighs. Julia was so much interested that she almost forgot her fatigue—this would be splendid for *Ebb and Flow.*

"I suppose they are rather anti the new Sultan, then?" she asked. "I mean, he's like a schismatic Pope, isn't he?"

"You are astonishingly well-informed"—he bent his bright lizards' eyes curiously onto Julia's lovely blank face. "Yes—well—well yes and no. The late Pope, as you so amusingly regard him, presented great difficulties to the Administration; but the installation of the schismatic one has presented even greater. And in spite of their strong religious leanings not all the Moulays—for I should explain that these leaders and many others besides, being descendants of the Prophet, are entitled to be called Moulay

This-or-That—are 'anti': amusing trans-atlantic word, but how briefly expressive! Where was I?" Mr. St John asked, suddenly lost in his own parentheses.

"You'd got to where not all the Moulays were anti-something, but you didn't say what—you got held up on the word anti," said Julia, amused.

"Ah—yes—thank you. Well, by no means all of them are 'anti', or against the French Administration, since it has brought such undoubted benefits to Morocco:—peace, stability, order, wealth; progress in agriculture, and in the development of natural resources such as oil and minerals—all things unknown here for two thousand years; moreover things which the Arabs and Berbers, delightful and splendid though they may be as individuals, are congenitally incapable of creating for themselves. And these men, wiser and more forward-looking than most of their compatriots, have tried to use their influence, both religious and political, to achieve co-operation with the French régime. Since the régime has installed a schismatic Sultan, or Pope, they have supported him too."

"That sounds very sensible to me; fine, in fact," quoth Julia.

"It *is* fine, it *is* sensible," said Mr. St John. "But what is the lamentable result? Do you read the papers, here? If so you will have seen that the Moulay X was murdered in Casablanca last week."

"No, I hadn't seen it. Good gracious, that must be since I was there! And everyone thought it was getting so quiet."

" 'Everyone' was wrong. This Moulay X was an excellent man, learned, wise and sufficiently statesman-like to realise that the best thing for Morocco, whatever mistakes the French may have made, was a long continuance of the Protectorate; and he threw all his weight into that end of the scale. But that sufficed for him to be branded as a quisling, and all he got for his pains was a bullet."

"Fired by whom?"

"A nationalist—or more probably a common assassin hired by the extreme nationalists—who are neither learned, nor wise, *nor* statesman-like," said Mr. St John, an astonishing bitterness suddenly infusing his clipped delicate accents. "So-called patriots!" he said angrily, tapping sharply with his stick against the corner of a house. "Oh," he said, with a sudden change of tone—"We have passed it. I am sorry."

"Passed what?"

"Marshal Lyautey's house. Would you like to see it?" He looked backwards as he spoke.

"Not if it means going down that hill again," said Julia firmly. "Another day, perhaps." They appeared to have reached the top of Mount Everest

at last, and had turned into a fairly level street whose surface was, thank
goodness, sand and not cobbles.

"Very well—we will go on to the museum—it is quite close by."

"Look, Mr. St John, couldn't we—I—go to the Museum some other
time? I'd far sooner go on hearing about the French and the Nationalists
than look at the finest museum in the world, if there is any place, besides
Bathyadis' shop, in the whole of Fez where one can *sit*," said Julia.

He was full of compunction.

"Of course—you are tired, and I am thoughtless! There is a charming
garden attached to the museum; we can sit there." And there in a few
minutes they did sit, on the curb of a fountain in the sun, among beds
full of bright flowers, with exotic trees growing darkly overhead against the
blue African sky.

"That's *lovely*," said Julia, stretching her feet out in front of her luxuriously. "Heaven fountain; heaven garden. Now please, would you tell me
what mistakes, exactly, the French have made? You said just now that
Moulay What-Not wanted to play in with the French, in spite of their mistakes. I thought from what I saw in Casa that they had done a lot for this
country—but of course I don't know anything yet."

"What did you see in Casablanca?" Mr. St John asked—his stress on the
full word was a minute rebuke, Julia felt.

"Oh, all those hospitals—" she described her morning with Ali.

"Yes, the French have done that: created wonderful social services in
the larger towns. And they are struggling to educate the Moors to a point
where they are fit for self-government, and to create a competent indigenous
bureaucracy; have you seen the great college that they have built at Rabat,
devoted entirely to courses in political administration?"

No, Julia had not yet been to Rabat.

"Well, you will see it. But—" the old gentleman paused, and emitted
another of those hissing sighs. "Their mistakes—how difficult they are to
analyse! Intellectual mistakes, spiritual mistakes, emotional mistakes—all
intangible, but how appallingly potent and dangerous intangibles can be!
That is what the modern world so fatally tends to forget, obsessed as it is
by material and economic progress. Spiritual values?—idealistic rubbish!
But they are the ultimate ones, even in things political." He darted a
diamond-bright lizard's eye onto Julia, seated beside him on the fountain's
rim, her face turned up lovingly to the sun with closed eyelids, her thick
tawny lashes resting on her apricot-coloured cheeks. "This really interests
you?" he enquired a little sharply.

"Yes. That's why I asked," said Julia, without opening her eyes. Mr. St
John chuckled—cool himself, the coolness of this young woman pleased

him. He pulled a small notebook out of his pocket, ruffled the pages, and said—

"Then I will read you a prophecy about the French mistakes in North Africa—made by one of the two men who loved it most, and understood it best. If you care, that is, to listen."

"I'm listening," said Julia, still without opening her eyes; and Mr. St John proceeded to read.

" 'If France fulfils her duty, if she behaves towards her peoples as mother and not exploiter, doing to others what she would wish done to her, she will have an admirable Empire. If she does not, the mass of the population will necessarily remain alien and aloof, without attachment to us, different from us in everything; it will be influenced only by the local aristocracy. This aristocracy, composed of the middle class, the small chiefs, and the marabouts will study in our schools, but without acquiring there any affection for us; from their schooling, owing to the ease of communications, will arise the idea of a patriotic union between all the lettered, educated, or distinguished people of the Barbary countries, from Fez to Tunis, all with a single aspiration—that of throwing us out.' "

The words rang, somehow, vaguely familiar in Julia's ears, but she could not place them at once.

"Goodness, that's accurate enough as a prophecy," she said. "It's exactly what *is* happening. Who wrote it?"

"It was written in the year 1911, please remark," said Mr. St John.

"Yes, but who by? Oh, I believe I know—was it de Foucauld?"

"You surprise me more and more! Yes, it was. Do you study him?"

"Well, I read that Fremantle book—so good, I thought—and the French life—not so good, wouldn't you say? But it was a long time ago, and I had rather forgotten. Good Heavens!" said Julia reflectively—"he *was* a prophet. But then he would be."

"Please note what he says about the 'ease of communications' at that time," said Mr. St John. "In 1911 there was no airmail, spinning a deplorably rapid web of postal deliveries all over North Africa—still less was there the even more lamentable diffusion of ideas by the wireless. Today every small town in Morocco can, and does, listen to false, vain, and utterly subversive broadcasts in Arabic from Cairo radio."

"Do they do much harm?"

"Infinite! It is largely, mainly, Egypt's fault that the situation here has got so completely out of hand. Egypt!" said Mr. St John, putting a serpent's hiss of contempt into the word. "Weak, effete; futile in armed conflict— look at her ignominious performance in the war with Israel!—and yet this vaulting ambition. *She* will lead the Arab world. The whole Egyptian army is not worth one corps of Moroccan tribesmen! But because she has the technical capacity to disseminate these ideas, she is a disruptive force throughout North Africa."

"Yes, I always gathered that the Gyppos were pretty wet," said Julia, still reflectively. "Some older friends of mine were there during the war, and they took a dim view of them, I must admit. But you still haven't told me what the French mistakes were," she persisted. "Did de Foucauld prophesy them too?"

"He indicated what would have to be done to avoid them—and it has not been done. This," said Mr. St John, turning to his little notebook again, "was written in 1915,"—and once more he read.

"'We French have in Africa two essential duties to perform. The first is the administration and civilisation of North-west Africa—Algeria, Morocco, Tunis, the Sahara are united for the first time in history, and form a single block. Our second duty is evangelisation—and we do, we might as well say, absolutely nothing about it. The White Fathers are fifty-six in all North Africa! . . . Moreover I do not know anyone, colonising farmer, officer, or missionary, who knows the indigenous population sufficiently well.' There you have it—the 'not knowing the people sufficiently well' has all along been one of the major French mistakes," said Mr. St John sadly.

"Could the Moslems have been evangelised? I thought it was next to impossible. Even Fr. de Foucauld never baptised a convert, did he?"

"No—and perhaps evangelisation, in his terms, was impossible. But they could have been loved and understood as he loved and understood them. His influence was incalculable—the influence of the Christian spirit; that, in spite of all the great good that the French have done, has been lacking, and that alone might have prevented what he foresaw so terribly clearly. Hear him again—how wise he was!

"'My thought is, that if the Moslems of our colonial Empire do not gently, little by little, become converted, a nationalist movement analogous to that in Turkey will arise; an intellectual élite will be formed in the big cities, taught à la française without having either French hearts or minds, an élite which will have lost its own Islamic faith, but which will keep the label in order to influence the masses. . . . Nationalist sentiments will be exalted by this élite, which when it finds an opportunity (such as would be provided by difficulties threatening France from without or from within) will use Islam as a lever to rouse the ignorant multitudes, and will try to create an independent African Moslem Empire.'"

"Goodness, what price Isaiah now? That *is* today, to a hair!" said Julia.

"Yes, it is. I give the French two more years here, at the outside."

"No!" Julia was shocked. Little as she yet knew of Morocco at first hand, the idea of the French leaving, or being driven out, and so soon, put coldly like that, appalled her. "Do you really think that, after all they've done?"

"I do indeed." Mr. St John sighed again, loudly, elegiacally. "Alas, alas!"

That was on a Tuesday. Julia would rather have waited longer before going to see Bathyadis again, but Steve Keller had said that he was coming up on Thursday, and if he arrived in time she thought they had better go to Volubilis and check on the *huilerie* for Mme La Besse at once; then she would have another day in which to tackle Mr. St John about Colin—always supposing that she got no satisfaction, or not as much as she needed, from Bathyadis. After which, unless one or the other could put her in the way of finding her cousin at once she would return to Tangier. Of course if either of them told her where to reach him she would throw everything aside and go; but Julia was getting rather dubious about all these clues and contacts which seemed to lead nowhere, and modest as it was, her little French hotel in Fez was a good deal more expensive than the Espagnola—moreover in Fez she wasn't earning.

The following morning, accordingly, she laid on Abdul, the handsome voluble Arab guide whom Mr. St John had so unceremoniously waved aside the day before, and told him to take her to Bathyadis. Abdul like all Arab guides had ideas of his own, and began by leading her to all sorts of irrelevant sights; Julia in her most *cassant* tones told him that M. Saint Jonne had already taken her through the street of the silks and the street of the spices, and would he please take her directly to the *magasin* of M. Bathyadis. All the same she inhaled with intense pleasure the varied, heavy, penetrating odours which filled the air in the *souk* of the spices; she longed to know what all the different-coloured grains and powders, spread out in shallow oval baskets, were, and sniffed their varied aromas as she passed through.

Bathyadis greeted her with a most disarming appearance of warmth, and again sent his youth hastening to fetch mint tea. Julia told Abdul to wait outside, but the guide interpreted this instruction rather liberally, hanging about the opening of the shop while Julia successfully negotiated the purchase of the delicious little velvet trunk, or coffer, which she had seen the previous day for the equivalent of thirty-seven-and-sixpence. She held it on her knees, gloating over it, as she turned to her real business. A friend had told her, she said, that Mr. Bathyadis might be willing to help her with some information—no, not M. Saint Jonne, though no doubt he would say the same, she added, as a piece of corroborative detail—this was another friend in Tangier. She lowered her voice as she saw that Abdul had now come right into the shop and was hovering within earshot—"Remain outside," she told him curtly. Abdul withdrew. The matter was confidential, Julia explained, and then said quite flatly that she had come from England to make contact with a young Englishman called Monro, who happened to be her cousin; she had reason to believe that he had been, or was, in Fez, and in touch with Mr. Bathyadis.

Almost for the first time since she had started her enquiries the mention of Colin's name produced no reaction at all. Bathyadis looked benevolently blank; apparently Monro meant nothing to him. With one of her intuitions, as Mme La Besse called them, Julia drew a bow at a venture. "I believe," she went on, "that he is in company with another Englishman, very tall, with hair as red as fire."

That *did* register, she saw—Bathyadis looked serious, and suddenly much more alert, too. "My cousin however is very dark, with the face pale," she added, watching the old man closely; and she thought that that description registered too—Bathyadis continued to look serious, and did not answer at once. "He has a curious trick with his right thumb," Julia pursued—what *was* the French for double-jointed? Never mind. "When he is nervous he pushes the joint out, as if it was broken, with a small noise, *plutôt désagréable.*"

At that Bathyadis actually laughed.

"I think I know *le jeune Monsieur* you mean," he said carefully, "but could you perhaps indicate to me why you ask *me* about him?—since you know that he is here, and who he is with?"

Julia could have jumped with excitement at the last words. Her arrow had gone right into the gold—it had quite undoubtedly been Colin that she had seen up in the Kasbah with the red-haired man. But she remained calm outwardly, and told Bathyadis in vague sentences of her urgent need to get in touch with the young man immediately. (She did not, this time, say why—another intuition.) Most unfortunately she had just missed him in Tangier, she added casually, as if she would certainly have seen him had she arrived in time; and she had been sent on to him, M. Bathyadis.

The old man listened, and made a sympathetic reply, but Julia got a curious impression that he was puzzled by something; he kept on glancing at the little trunk, which she still held on her knees. At last he said, slowly and doubtfully—

"But if Mademoiselle is interested in the affair, why does she require the *little* coffer?"

Julia was completely taken aback by this. What affair? And what had velvet coffers to do with it anyhow, little or big? She lit a cigarette before replying, to gain time, and thought quickly. Blowing out smoke she said at last, noncommittally and airily—"A coffer can always come in useful, can it not?—and for all sorts of purposes? And this"—she touched the object on her lap—"is also beautiful."

"Beautiful, yes—but it is so *small*. Would not the larger one be better?"

"I wonder," said Julia, still trying to gain time, and putting on a vague, meditative air. For one thing she couldn't possibly afford the big trunk, that was flat. "You really think so?" she asked, looking at the old Moor confidingly, enquiringly.

"It is usually the larger ones that they buy, and several at a time, Mademoiselle," he replied positively.

This astonished Julia more than ever. Who were "they"? Presumably Colin and the red-haired man—in French Bathyadis' words were perfectly clear: he had said "Ils"—they, not "on"—one, as in "people buy" or "one buys"; in the context he could only be referring to Colin and his red-haired friend. But why in the world should they be buying velvet trunks, and big ones, in bulk, in Fez? Her mind flew to possible reasons—Colin wanting to make a little money on the side, poor darling, in the new curioshops down on the coast? Seething with curiosity, quite at sea, but with his idea in her head she observed, still looking vague—

"I suppose they do business with your son in Casablanca—my cousin and his friend, I mean."

When she said that old Bathyadis bent on her the indulgent look that a kind and wise elder bestows on a peculiarly ignorant or idiotic child.

"But *naturellement*, Mademoiselle. This is how the *expédition* is arranged, as Mademoiselle of course realises."

Julia didn't realise—as she herself would have said, she hadn't a clue. Obviously Bathyadis assumed that she understood all about Colin's activities, whatever they were, whereas in fact she knew nothing. For a moment the word *expédition* held her up—Purcell had said that the red-haired man had bought cases of whisky and gin to take on a journey, therefore on an expedition; but why vast velvet trunks to put the booze in? Then she remembered that in French *expédition* can also mean the despatch of goods: the man who sends one's luggage and furniture from one place to another in France is called an *expéditeur*—so the velvet trunks might conceivably be used for the transport of something, somewhere. Probably that was it. But transport of what and where to? About Morocco? Hardly. Her mind, behind her blank face, raced wildly. Curios at the ports, dealings with the son in Casablanca, a port; *expédition*—oh, she *must* find out. Putting on her most vacant expression she risked another arrow at a venture.

"The export, you wish to say," she asserted, very slowly. And equally slowly a benignant smile showed itself above M. Bathyadis' beard, the smile of one who approves at least one piece of intelligence on the part of the ignorant child. He didn't even nod—but the smile was enough for Julia. She had got it—or got something.

Unluckily, at that precise moment she happened to observe that Abdul had again come into the shop, and had edged his way up close beside them. In her anxiety, her intense concentration, and her bewilderment, this was the last straw; she completely lost her temper. *"Ote-toi de là!"* she fairly shouted at the guide—"Remain outside, as I have already twice bidden you!" As Abdul withdrew she saw another smile—small, shrewd, but still approving—appear in M. Bathyadis' patriarchal beard.

Temper throws one off balance; Julia felt then like an actor who has lost his cue. She returned to the charge, but on another line.

"Is my cousin here just now?"

"Ah no, Mademoiselle—they were here some days ago, but they have gone."

"Where?"

Bathyadis waved a vague hand.

"To the South, as usual, I imagine." Again he spoke as if Julia would know what that meant. This was all inconceivably tantalising: Bathyadis, with his wholly mistaken assumption that she knew all about Colin—though why he should have made that assumption she couldn't for the moment work out—was clearly perfectly willing to talk to her, willing as no one else had yet been, if only she could manage to ask the right questions. She had had extraordinary luck so far, but she must go very warily, and continue to feel her way.

"Ah, yes," she said, nodding her head wisely. Once more she took out her cigarette-case, and this time offered it to the dealer, not realising that devout Moslems (unlike the Berber labourers at the dig) do not smoke; he declined majestically. She lit one herself.

"How soon do you expect them back?" she asked. This seemed a safe question, and it was really more important to contact Colin than to find out what he was expediting abroad in Moroccan trousseau-trunks.

"Probably after the usual interval," the old man replied.

God, what *was* the usual interval? How maddening. She blew out smoke, and then chanced her arm again.

"In a month, perhaps?"

"Ah no, *voyons*, Mademoiselle—it is usually six weeks at least, more often two months, before they return."

"Tiens," said Julia non-committally. *That* was no good. "Two months

is a long time," she said reflectively. "Since my business is so urgent, I think perhaps I had better follow my cousin, and see him."

"Ah *non*, Mademoiselle—that is impossible!" The old man was evidently shocked at this idea. "They work in horrible places" (*vils endroits* was the expression Bathyadis used) "where a young lady like yourself could not possibly go. How could you stay in those cantines?—a young lady alone? And it is a desolate country, terrible!"

Poor Julia groaned inwardly. Where were these *"vils endroits"*? And what on earth, in a Moroccan context, were "cantines"? In England one never *stayed* in canteens—they were places where factory-hands or soldiers ate.

"Then I must have his address, that is all," she said, with a firmness she was far from feeling.

At this Bathyadis recoiled in absolute horror.

"But no, Mademoiselle—no, no, no! To begin with they are naturally constantly moving from one place to another; and as Mademoiselle must very well know, above all one must never *write* anything—least of all the names. A name on a letter, in a *bureau de poste!*—this could be fatal. Mademoiselle does not reflect," the old man said, gently reproving, with a return of his kind benignant manner.

Julia, who had been reflecting till her brain almost cracked, smiled wryly —only no smile ever came out awry on her beautiful mouth, and her eyes remained doves' eyes even when she was frowning above them with worry, as now. Bathyadis smiled benevolently at her, returning a smile which to him merely seemed ravishing.

"Then what do I do?" she asked helplessly.

"Wait till they return, and repose upon the Merciful Goodness of God," said the old man, with a splendid calm confidence.

Those words and the way in which he spoke them did in fact give Julia, suddenly, a strange sense of peace. It might have lasted longer if at that very instant she had not seen, over M. Bathyadis monumental shoulder, the seedy little cross-eyed man from Purcell's bar peeping into the shop from the entrance. Mastering her exasperation she spoke slowly, and very low.

"Please after some instants look round, and tell me if you know who this little man is, who regards through the door. He was here yesterday also."

With elephantine deliberation Bathyadis turned slowly, and moved to a show-case behind him, which he opened, taking out a piece of jewellery; he had a fair view of the entrance before the little man with the cast in his eye bobbed hurriedly out of sight.

"Well?" Julia asked.

"It is a Jew—a German I think by nationality. Mademoiselle says he was here yesterday?"

"Yes—when I went out he was talking with your boy."

"Ah, *méfiez-vous de cet homme-là!* I do not like the little I know of him. Where has Mademoiselle seen him before?"

"Several times in Tangier, and I also thought I saw him at Petit-Jean on the way up—probably it was him, since he is here now."

"Then greatly beware of him. If he is what I think, German, he will be of our enemies," said Bathyadis. He looked troubled. "It is bad, this, very bad, if someone already follows Mademoiselle. They will have been alerted."

Dared she ask who "they" and "our enemies" were, Julia wondered, without giving away how far she was from being what Bathyadis so fortunately imagined her to be? While she pondered this question, looking appropriately serious, a number of American tourists suddenly surged into the little shop, escorted by a replica of Abdul, except for the wart on the nose. That, for the moment, was *that*. She said goodbye, gave Abdul the little coffer to carry—which he instantly passed on to an urchin the moment they reached the street—and returned to her hotel. On the way Lady Tracy's remark about the value of having cover popped up into her mind. Well, perhaps *Yes*.

CHAPTER IX

JULIA SAT eating rolls and drinking coffee in her room next morning, wondering what she should do if Steve Keller didn't come. He was only a stray pick-up in the train, anyhow; but she didn't much care to go out with the inquisitive Abdul again, who anyhow cost a lot, and what else was there to do, except get hold of Mr. St John and see if he would tell her what all the mystery was about? She had lain awake half the night, trying to piece together the various items of fact that the old Moor had let fall, and to make some sense out of them—now, by daylight, she ticked them off on her fingers. Whatever Colin was doing, he was doing it with the red-haired man, who either had that house, or stayed in it, in the Kasbah at Tangier—that was one fixed piece of information. Second, they went at intervals to *vils endroits* in 'the South', remaining from six weeks to two months at a time—but not in one spot, they moved about, and stayed in *cantines*. Probably St John could tell her what *cantines* were, and very likely would, if she asked him without letting on why she wanted to know. (Julia was acquiring a very reasonable distrust of anybody's willingness to tell her anything that they knew to relate to Colin Monro.) Third—she drank some more coffee and buttered another roll; very few things ever interfered with Julia's appetite—they dealt with Bathyadis' son in Casablanca for the *expédition*, or export. But export of *what*? Not of the velvet trunks—munching her roll, Julia now totally rejected this hypothesis. There could not be so much mystery about straight sales of antique Moroccan bridal coffers; moreover the Bank of England would surely never facilitate the financing of such a simple and modest enterprise. Then what was the real enterprise? And why the bigger coffers? Presumably to contain as much as possible of something, but once again, of *what*, in Heaven's name?

Well, she had her three facts, Julia thought with a certain satisfaction as she continued to eat her breakfast; sometime or other they might fall into place and make sense. This really *was* detection!—trying to make the pieces of the puzzle fit. At least the 'export' part of it explained Purcell's getting into such a fuss when she had spoken of the curio-dealers' sons in the ports—yes, oh yes! How much, she wondered, did Purcell really know? *Todo*? Quite a lot, if not all, evidently. But one thing still bothered her: why had old Bathyadis so readily assumed that she knew what Colin's activities, still a complete mystery to her, were? She ran over their conversation in her mind, and decided that the first key point had been her reference to the red-haired man—after she had mentioned him the old Moor had spoken freely; he was obviously the important person in this queer business. And—oh yes, she might have thought of that before—very likely, almost certainly, the fact that Mr. St John had brought her to the shop had pre-disposed the antique-merchant to think she knew about the whole affair, since, according to Purcell, St John himself was also a source of information. And, of course, she had at once tried to buy a trunk. But who were 'they'?—Germans, Bathyadis thought; and 'enemies'. Who *had* talked to her in Morocco about Germans? She still could not remember. And—was it in Tangier or Casablanca? Bother!—why need she have forgotten this?

Her cogitations were interrupted at this point by a rather raggle-taggle Arab servant, who entered to say that a Monsieur demanded Mademoiselle below. Julia said 'I descend', and then did not do so; she paused to reflect while she put on some lip-stick. If it was St John again, what should she ask him? About *cantines*, certainly; but should she risk also asking, flat out, the name of Colin's red-haired companion? That was a thing she needed to know, letters or no letters. It was still so early that the idea of the Monsieur being the airman had never entered her head, but when she at last went downstairs it was Steve Keller who came towards her, in uniform this time, a cheerful grin on his nice plain face.

"Well, here I am! How are you making out?"

"Beautifully, thank you. But where on earth have you come from, at this hour?"

"Meknes. Got there last night, and drove over this morning. Now what do we do? Will I show you Fez?"

"Not unless you have a helicopter and a parachute," said Julia. "Those hills have half killed me already." Then as he looked rather dashed she said quickly—

"There's one place I do very much want to see, if it isn't too far."

"Nowhere's too far! Where is it?"

"Volubilis."

"That's easy—fine. I have the car right here. Don't you want a coat, though?"

Yes, Julia wanted a coat, and thicker shoes too—she went up to put them on, and with the *huilerie* in mind stuffed a note-book, pencils, and a centimetre-tape into the pockets of her short loose leather jacket. This was of a warm reddish-orange shade, and set off the peculiar tawny tones of her hair and complexion wonderfully—Steve stared in open admiration when she re-appeared.

"You look wonderful!"

"Ought we to take some food along?" Julia asked, ignoring this tribute.

"No need to—we'll be back in time for lunch, latish. Let's go."

In the entrance to the hotel they nearly ran into the minute figure of Mr. St John; he greeted Julia gaily. "Good morning! Good morning! Do you feel strong enough for another round of Fez?"

Bunched together in the small entry-way, Julia effected introductions. "Mr. St John, this is Mr. Keller, of the American Air Force."

"American *Naval* Air Force," the airman corrected her. Julia swam over this obstruction—"And this is Mr. St John, who lives in Fez, and knows everything." The two men shook hands, Keller looking slightly damped by the interruption.

"Mr. Keller has just driven over from Meknes," Julia proceeded equably; "we thought of going to Volubilis. I want to look at the Roman oil-mill there."

"Admirable! I did not know that you went in for archaeology. There are several *quite* good examples—" the old gentleman went into details.

Even Steve Keller saw that there was nothing for it but to invite Mr. St John to accompany them, which he did with a good enough grace to win Julia's admiration; for obviously this was not in the least the sort of outing he had intended. Mr. St John was delighted, and they set off, Julia sitting in front gazing about her; a certain packing of Moroccan agriculture would fill out a general article for *The Onlooker*.

She was immediately impressed, in fact, by the excellence of the cultivation. The pruning of the olive-trees was in itself a work of art—their flattened tops were cut so regularly that on level ground a ruler a kilometre long could have been run the length of the rows and hardly shown an inch of variation; new plantings were to be seen everywhere, the white bindings of the fresh grafts standing out sharply in the sun. Under the trees in the almond-orchards Moors were hoeing rows of vegetables, beneath the curious dull greyish pink of African almond-blossom; out in the open fields dwarf peas, barely a foot high and already in flower, spread for miles—the chick-peas now used for canning, Julia imagined—or could you not can chick-peas? She must ask sometime.

Presently they left the main highway to Meknes and Rabat and began to climb up into hilly country; here, though the olives and almonds still persisted, there was less tillage, and flocks of sheep grazed on the open slopes. Up in the hills they passed Berber farms, groups of rough buildings surrounded by high irregular fences of dried camel-thorn, a curious mauve-brown in colour, or the far more spectacular hedges of agaves, brandishing their huge curved saw-toothed leaves like giant pale-blue swords; these lines of great silvery-blue plants, so menacing in form, so startling in colour against the drab tones of the countryside enchanted Julia. They dropped into another valley, where small oil-derricks stood up incongruously here and there—yes, they yielded a little oil, Mr. St John told her, when she leaned back to ask; it went down to Petit-Jean in tankers. They climbed up onto an outlying spur of the Djebel Zerhoun, and dropped on a long slant into the valley to the west of it; here, facing the sun, sheltered from the north and east, the olive-trees grew thickly, and of enormous size—Mr. St John leaned forward to tell Julia that from pre-Roman times this had always been a famous centre for olive-growing; even before the Phoenicians came Volubilis, lying in the valley below, had been a wealthy Berber settlement, and the Romans had developed the oil industry to such a pitch that in and around the city not less than thirty oil-mills were still to be seen.

"Gracious," said Julia, aghast. "One will do for me." Keller laughed.

Volubilis is an exquisite place. The French have carried out the excavation and preservation of the ruins with the same thoughtful skill and competent thoroughness that they invariably display on the spot in Morocco, when the local administration has a free hand. A pleasant building houses a small museum, where the principal treasures are on view; neat paths through pretty plantings of shrubs and flowers lead up to the remains themselves, with unobtrusive sign-posts to indicate the way to the various points of interest. One of these, which the small party came on almost at once, said *Huilerie*, and there they went forthwith; a guide sought to accompany them—Mr. St John brushed him off as easily as he had brushed off the horrid Abdul on Julia's first morning in Fez.

Julia found the *huilerie* rather bothering, since it in no way resembled the one at Mme La Besse's site. There was no circular block of stone with a cemented channel round it: instead they saw a huge flat slab of what Julia took to be granite, with a number of narrow shallow runnels carefully chased out in the stone, leading down into two great oblong tanks, also floored and lined with dressed stone. Julia made measurements and wrote them down, Mr. St John the while explaining that the two tanks were for two different types of oil: the best from the first pressing, the less good from the second. Steve Keller lit a Chesterfield and looked bored—Julia was relieved when she had done her duty, and they were free to wander about the charming ruins of a remote but exquisitely civilised past. Storks, newly returned from the South, were turning over the remains of last year's nests on the top of the triumphal arch and some high columns topped by ornate capitals, with clattering beaks, inquiring claws, and a general expression of disgust—storks have a capacity for looking disgusted almost equal to that of camels. A small mauve wildflower bloomed every-where among fallen marble; the sun shone down, African and hot, on the gay mosaic flooring of rooms nearly two thousand years old, still depicting in brilliant colours the scenes from classical antiquity ordered by interior decorators twenty centuries before Elsie de Wolfe and Sybil Colefax began.

It was the private houses which above all entranced Julia. Mr. St John knew his stuff quite as well at Volubilis as he did in Fez, and led her and the still bored American up beyond the triumphal arch and the Forum into the residential quarter of the city, where Roman citizens had lived, pre-sumably loved, and above all undoubtedly bathed. In many of these houses they came on small round baths, six feet or more across and about the depth of a modern bath, cemented within, their raised rims decorated with designs in mosaic: one of these bore a pattern of gold-fish. Julia was in-stantly reminded of Linda's bath, with the swimming gold-fish in its glass sides, in *The Pursuit of Love*, and was ravished; she drew Mr. St John's attention to this resemblance, and he gave his dry prehistoric chuckle—they had to explain the joke to the airman, who had not read Nancy Mitford, and was less amused.

Walking back towards the entrance the sky was suddenly rent by a high mechanical whine, a piercing and threatening note—it seemed to come from the east, and Julia looked up, but nothing was to be seen there but a trail of white vapour leading across the blue; the American, laughing, took her elbow and turned her towards the west just in time to see a plane vanishing behind the hills, while the noise continued to fill the empty sky.

"That's one of ours," he said. "Great, aren't they?"

Julia thought them appalling, and somehow the more so, standing among the lovely relics of an age which had never been tormented by jet propulsion or atom bombs; but Mr. St John promptly entered on a conversation with Steve Keller about the jets, the air-base at Port Lyautey, the instruction being given to the French air-force at Meknes, and concerning the other great American bases further South, near Casablanca. In this the American showed up well—he was intelligent, keen, and knew the technical side of his subject thoroughly; but presently he got on to the political aspect, and again gave utterance to some vague anti-colonial sentiments. "The poor toads of Moors, why should they live in shanty-towns and work for a silly wage, when the French are living in grand apartments or smart villas?"

"Why, indeed?" Mr. St John asked, with deceptive mildness. "Who brings the Moors to the towns?"

"Why, they just come, I guess."

"Exactly. You don't suggest that the French Administration brings them? They come of their own free will, and constitute a great problem—the eternal problem of the lure of city lights, and the possibility of making money more quickly than by the long monotonous processes of agriculture. What do you suggest that the French should do about it?"

"Well, they could put them in decent houses," the young man said, looking rather surprised.

"Could they? Could they? At a rent they could pay? And would this *check* the flow to the big towns? Would not more come, and still more? What was the result of building the new Medina for the Moorish workers in Casablanca?"

"I don't know."

"No, I supposed not. And have you seen the new *bidonvilles améliorées,* the improved shanty-towns which the French have arranged on empty spaces outside Casablanca with piped water and drains laid, ready for the Moors to use if they persist in coming and putting up their horrible petrol-tin shacks?"

No, the airman hadn't seen them.

"Again, I supposed not. It would seem that you have not seen very *much* of what the French have done here. However, these new sites represent an honest attempt at a solution of an almost insoluble problem. Criti-

cism, to be of value or even admissible, should be based on facts, do you
not think?" said Mr. St John primly.

Julia stole a glance at Steve to see how he took this. As she feared, the
rebuke was too elegantly wrapped up really to register; Steve just felt
vaguely that he was being 'ribbed', and said rather sulkily—"Oh well, one
can't help the way one feels. I just feel anti-colonial."

"Regardless of the facts before your eyes?"

"Facts don't alter feelings," the American said stubbornly. "Anyway, I
just tell all the Moors I come across that they'd be better off without the
French, in my opinion."

"You count your feelings as an opinion, then?" said Mr. St John, with
dry exasperation.

Julia felt it was time to intervene. Poor Steve was utterly hopeless, in
his crass ignorance and his refusal to look facts in the face, but trying to
teach less lettered Americans about the Old World was obviously about as
much use as setting out to empty the Atlantic with a teaspoon—and anyhow they were in his car. She glanced at her watch.

"Is there anything else to see near here?" she asked. "Mr. Keller, how
far are we from Meknes? Didn't you say there was a pretty gate there?"

Keller said there was. Mr. St John however, quick to take a hint, proclaimed that Moulay Idriss, the holy city of Morocco, was only a few
kilometres away—should they not rather see that? As they got into Steve's
roadster again Julia noticed another car waiting on the sandy space outside the museum; an Arab driver lounged over the wheel, and Abdul, her
inquisitive guide of the day before, leant against the wing—the wart on
his handsome nose made him unmistakable. He glanced at her and her
two companions with some interest, and spoke to the driver.

"Look, there's Abdul," she said to Mr. St John.

"Where? Oh yes. He's a pestilential fellow," the old Englishman said.
He seemed rather upset.

The road to Moulay Idriss wound round the contours of the Djebel
Zerhoun among those enormous olive trees, bordered by more hedges of
the savage agaves; silver-green above, silver-blue below—what a landscape,
Julia thought, while Mr. St John was telling them from the back seat
that Moulay Idriss was one of the most purely Islamic cities in existence,
since owing to its great holiness neither Europeans nor Jews were allowed
to settle there. From the road they had a view of the twin bosses of hill,
covered with the white flat-topped cubes of Moorish houses, with a green-
tiled mosque away to the left.

One cannot take a car at all far into Moulay Idriss, because the streets
are mere alleys, and anyhow far too steep, steeper even than those of Fez;

but the party took a rather brief walk through the exquisite little holy city. Now and again they emerged onto terraced paths almost as narrow as goat-tracks, which wound round outside the town, and afforded views of the hilly slopes around them and the valley below, a shimmering sea of olive-groves shaken in the breeze—Mr. St John reiterated that the olives were bigger and thicker to the acre here than anywhere else in the world. Moors as usual constantly offered their services as guides, and were as constantly waved aside by the Englishman with courteous skill; but as the party was descending towards the car again one caught him by the arm and said in French—"Come see Berber oil-mill!"

"Oh yes, do let us see that," said Julia. "It might be interesting."

To Julia, at least, it was. The Moor led them through a dark descending passage to an underground chamber where by the light of an oil lamp a blindfold mule walked round and round in a circle, rotating a large stone wheel set on edge in a hollow mortared channel full of black olives which were in process of being crushed to pulp; two or three men with long-handled shovels kept nipping skilfully in behind the mule and throwing the black strong-smelling oily mush back into the path of the wheel— Steve opined that this was 'a kinda one-horse way' of doing things.

"One-mule way, surely," said Mr. St John. Julia however had espied a second chamber opening out of the first, and went into it. Here pulp, enclosed in flat round bags or nets of coarse rope, was being pressed under a complicated arrangement of a stone slab and a long wooden beam, wound down by a handle on a vast screw of polished wood; the clear oil oozed and dripped in bright beads from between the rough fibres into another mortared channel surrounding a circular stone block, on which the bags of pulp were set. This block, and the channel surrounding it, were in fact exact replicas of the block and channel at Mme La Besse's excavation. Julia exclaimed "Goody!" at the sight.

"What have you found?" Mr. St John asked, tapping his way after her with his stick over the uneven earthen floor.

"Only something that will thrill my employer," the girl answered casually.

When they got back to Fez, late and rather hungry, Mr. St John tactfully insisted on leaving the young people to lunch alone; but before they parted Julia made a point of asking him if they could have "another go at Fez" the next day, as she might be leaving the day after—he at once promised to call for her in the morning. Steve was rather plaintive over lunch—"I saw we had to take your dwarf Methuselah along, and he knows a lot; but he's not quite the girl to go to Venice with, is he?" Julia laughed, and after lunch allowed the American to drive her round the wonderful road along the slopes surrounding the city which the French call the *Route du Tour de Fez*; from it one sees from a score of different angles all that Fez permits to be seen: its walls and its heaped flat rooftops, with a few rather bulky minarets looming over them. The day had turned gloomy and threatening, the mountains were the colour of ink, and below these dark shapes the city seemed to crouch, pallid and hostile—Julia thought it more sinister than ever. Steve extorted from her her address in Tangier, and a promise to let him know if she should come to Port Lyautey.

She did another brisk tour of *madrasahs* and *souks* with Mr. St John next morning, including the Moorish house once lived in by Marshal Lyautey; but the tiny old gentleman seemed a little abstracted, the flow of his carved pronouncements less ready than usual, while his whistling sighs occurred constantly. Another thing struck Julia that morning: in the crowded alleys they constantly came on knots of people which were really congealed, standing so close that it was impossible to filter through them as one can usually filter through a Moorish crowd; edging round was the only way. And in the centre of each knot was an Arab with a newspaper, reading aloud to the grave concentrated faces round him.

"Why are they all so keen on the press today?" Julia asked at last.

"The murder," said Mr. St John soberly.

"Not *more* murders! Who is it this time? Another Moulay?"

"No—a French doctor in Casablanca, a man greatly beloved; his practice was largely among the Moors, to whom he devoted himself. He was shot from behind as he was leaving his clinic in the New Medina."

"How horrible! But why, if he did so much good?"

"Aah!—that is the insane part of it. If a prominent Moor is assassinated, a prominent Frenchman will be assassinated too, to redress the balance; and then another Moor, and another Frenchman—it is as endless as an Albanian feud or a Corsican vendetta." He sighed again. "In this case there is particular concern and bitterness among the Moors, because just as Moroccan elements killed the Moulay for being on too good terms with the French, it is suspected that French elements murdered the doctor for being on too good terms with the Arabs."

"You don't mean it!"

"I do, unhappily."

"But that is simply *hopeless*," said Julia. "That understanding, I mean, that de Foucauld wrote of becomes impossible if it's just the people, on both sides, who *do* understand who get murdered. They can never get together if they go on like that."

"No, they can never get together," the old man said in a tone of unutterable sadness.

Julia mused. "It ought to be prevented," she said presently. "It's ridiculous. If it's the prominent people who get killed, they must be known—couldn't they have guards or police or something, to go about with?"

"That is what the French doctors in Casablanca whose work takes them into the Medina thought," Mr. St John replied with acerbity; "they asked the Municipality to provide them with guards, since their hours at the clinics are known, and they were therefore sitting targets for the thugs."

"And didn't they get them?"

"They were offered them, at a price—which they were to pay themselves."

"Good God! The French and their *ça coûte*," said Julia, with real anger in her voice. "How much, for heaven's sake?"

"In English money it would have come to about twenty pounds a month. That is a good deal for a man who does more than half his work for love. Some of the wealthier ones agreed to pay it; this doctor refused, as a matter of principle."

"'And he's just as dead as though he'd been wrong,'" Julia quoted bitterly. "Do you know, Mr. St John, to me that sort of meanness really *smells*."

"The people in Casablanca agree with you. It is not in the papers yet, but I hear that the Préfet was hissed by the crowd yesterday when he attended the funeral—by Moors as well as Europeans."

"Serve him right."

"Not altogether. He is a good man, sympathetic to the indigenous population, broad-minded; but he is tied by regulations, and above all by matters like the vote for colonial expenses at home. The people who really *'puent'*, to use your so expressive word, are the French politicians—ignorant, self-seeking, eternally manoeuvering for position for their miserable parties, regardless of France's real interests, let alone those of her dependent peoples. Blame them."

"Oh, I do! I've been blaming them for years—ever since I was at school, in fact. France has been the sick woman of Europe for over a century, hasn't she?—and a spoilt invalid at that."

Mr. St John laughed.

"My dear young lady, you have a formidable gift of expression! One which, if I may say so, your appearance would seem to belie," he said.

"No one can help her appearance," said Julia, who knew quite well that she looked the dumbest of blondes, but didn't particularly mind. At the moment she was glad that her so unmatching views on the French had cheered the little old gentleman up, and was delighted by his obvious pleasure when she asked if they couldn't go and sit in the museum garden again.

"Ah, you liked it? So do I—a charming spot. Yes, let us go there."

But Mr. St John was very far from showing pleasure when, once more seated on the curb of the fountain, Julia asked him how she could get hold of Colin Monro at once. He started, dropped his stick, upon which he had been resting his gnarled old hands, picked it up again, and asked quite petulantly—

"Good gracious, what in the world do *you* know about young Monro? And what on earth do you want him for?"

"I want him to come home. But unless I find him, I can't tell him that he's got to."

Mr. St John looked like a very cross tortoise indeed.

"And why should you imagine that he is here?"

Julia, however half-baked she might in Edina's opinion be as a journalist, had at least learned in that profession that to display such facts as she was already in possession of frequently led to the disclosure of yet other facts—and she employed this technique now.

"Oh, I know he isn't here at this moment," she drawled, casually—"he went down to the South just a few days ago, with that red-headed type he goes round with, and a fresh consignment of those pretty velvet trunks, but I want to contact him *quickly*."

This pronouncement created a considerable effect. Mr. St John dropped his stick again, and assumed the appearance of a quite furious tortoise; when he was able to speak—Julia picked up the stick this time—he was almost stuttering with vexation and bewilderment.

"Who—who are you? And how do you come to know all this?"

"I'm Colin's cousin—his mother sent me out here to find him. And as for knowing things, of course one has one's contacts," said Julia, rather grandly, but again with careful casualness.

Mr. St John looked so worried and upset that her heart rather smote her for a moment; but after all she had come all this way for one single purpose, and being thwarted so often had aroused her obstinacy; she must not allow pity, even for this rather darling old man, to deflect her. His next question surprised her, though.

"But Lady Tracy—*she* wrote to me about you." He looked immensely puzzled. "Does she know of this—this quest of yours?"

"But of course. She promised to help me, only then her nephew—the botanist one, I expect you know him—went hooshing away, so she couldn't do much. He seems to be her special link with the outside world."

"Ah!" Mr. St John became a reflective tortoise—Julia got a curious impression of a hitch, that she had lost a point somehow, or given something away; but the old gentleman was still upset, sufficiently so to make a remark which he failed to finish: "Ah, then she cannot know"—He checked himself abruptly.

Julia was dying to ask what Lady Tracy could not know, but checked herself too; she must not let her tongue run away with her, or give anything more away—if indeed she had done so; it was only an impression, and a vague one at that. She remained silent, waiting for Mr. St John to speak again, and meanwhile gazed up at the strange shapes of the trees in the museum garden, silhouetted against the brilliant Moroccan sky.

It was some time before her companion did speak again. When he did, he went off on a fresh tack. "*Why* do you want young Monro to come home?"

Gloomily, like an actor speaking a boring part for the hundredth time, Julia went through the reasons: the estate, Uncle John's death, Edina's rich money-making career. Colin had *got* to come home.

"Well he can't," said Mr. St John very curtly. "For the present he is obliged to stay here. I am sorry to disappoint you, but really you had better give up this search of yours. Moreover, I think I should warn you that it is not very prudent to go round asking for this young man by name."

"Oh, because of those infernal Germans?" Julia felt that it would be as well to learn a little more about "our enemies" if she could, while the poor old gentleman was available, and in this slightly dislocated state. The result was pretty good—Mr. St John gazed at her in absolute stupefaction.

"H–h–*how* do you know that?" he stuttered angrily. "Of course!"—again he checked himself. "I believe you are being un-candid with me—you are not what you pretend to be, a friend of my old friend, just an English girl!" he said bitterly.

"Oh yes, Mr. St John, I am precisely that. Only I happen to know a little more than you expected," said Julia hardily. "Do tell me more about these Germans, won't you?"

"No, I will *not*," said Mr. St John, quite furiously, banging the butt of his stick on the stone pavement which surrounded the fountain. "I will tell you *nothing!* How, I cannot conceive, but you know far too much already."

Julia deployed her eyes at their most dovelike on the angry old man, and laid her long pink-tipped hand caressingly on his sleeve.

"Oh Mr. St John dear, don't be so upset, and horrid to me," she said. "You've been so kind, but now you're really being a pest."

"So are you!" he exploded, actually throwing her hand off his arm.

"I daresay. I expect I often am. But you've been so sweet, and I'm so grateful. Look, won't you at least tell me this—which is it imprudent for, me or Colin, if I go about asking for him?"

"Both!" said Mr. St John. "Imprudent for you, possibly mortally dangerous for him."

A little silence fell after that. Dislocated or not, Mr. St John had remained totally uninformative about the Germans, the enemies, except to confirm their inimical existence. Germans, Germans—*who* had talked to her, in Morocco, about Germans, Julia wondered, trailing the fingers of the hand Mr. St John had so summarily rejected in the cool water of the pool behind her. Twice she had tried to remember, and couldn't; now, with the unaccountability of memory, suddenly it flashed back into her mind—Mr. Bingham, rather lit up at his own cocktail-party in Casablanca, had mentioned as one of two side-lines in Morocco the exploitation of rare minerals, started since the War, by the East Germans! And he had said that everyone kept their mouths pretty tightly shut about it, too. LAWKS! —Could it be some rare mineral that Colin and the red-haired chum were expediting, or exporting, in the velvet trunks? Out of pure curiosity, combined with this new obstinacy born of frustration, Julia once more employed shock tactics on the unhappy Mr. St John.

"I'd hate to do anything to jeopardise Colin, naturally," she said gently —"But they are shipping out some odd mineral, aren't they?"

For a moment she thought the old man was going to have a stroke. He became purple in the face, and looked as if he were going to choke.

"Monstrous!" he exploded. "This is absolutely monstrous! You must be a spy!"

"I'm *not*—I do assure you I'm not," Julia said pleadingly. "I only want to get hold of Colin."

"Well, *I* shall not help you—indeed I shall warn Lady Tracy about you! If you did succeed in contacting your cousin—if he *is* your cousin—he could not possibly go home now; no miserable estate, property, inheritance, is of comparable importance to the work he is engaged on! Oh, you shock me!" The poor old man paused, looked wildly round, and as once before asked helplessly—

"Where was I?"

"You'd said Colin couldn't come home, however urgent it was," Julia said, now really alarmed by his state. "But look, Mr. St John, I think you'd better go home. Let me go and find a taxi."

"There are no taxis here. No, I will go to the Consulate, which is just opposite—if you will accompany me so far?"

Julia, rather penitent, took his arm and accompanied him to the gateway with the superb baroque plaster effigy of the Lion and the Unicorn stuck on the wall outside it; she rang a bell, a Moorish servant appeared, and led her old escort in through a pretty court-yard. But before Mr. St John disappeared he turned back to her and spoke again, with menacing finality.

"Go home. Give this up. Don't try to find him; make some other arrangement for his wretched inheritance."

"I can't give it up, and I won't," said Julia. "Oh, but I am so sorry."

"Never mind that—you have been warned," said Mr. St John, as the door of the Consulate closed behind him.

Julia was rather shaken by the painful termination of this interview. She liked Mr. St John; he had been, as she had told him, very kind to her, and now she had left him upset almost to the point of illness by her questions and assertions—upset moreover to such a degree as to have left her alone and unescorted in the street, in Fez. She made her way back to her small hotel without adventure, wondering on the way why anyone so old, and so easily made to lose his temper and inadvertently let things out should be allowed to be in on anything so secret and so important as Colin's activities appeared to be—indeed as Mr. St John himself declared them to be. For really he had, if only by his rage, let out quite a lot. He had confirmed Bathyadis' implication that the Germans were the enemy—presumably the East Germans, in view of Mr. Bingham's remarks; and his violent reaction to her suggestion that a rare mineral of some sort was the object of the operation was tantamount to a confirmation of that idea, too. One did not turn purple and go completely to pieces about something that *wasn't* true. All rather exciting; and *fun*, really, Julia thought as she sat down to a thoroughly French lunch, nibbling the carved radishes among the *hors d'oeuvres* with appetite, and shovelling in the sliced tomatoes, the hard-boiled eggs in mayonnaise, and the inevitable sardines.

One thing however bothered her—she had completely forgotten to ask Mr. St John about *cantines* before she embarked on the vexed subject of Colin. What a clot she was!—now he would tell her nothing, indeed he would probably never speak to her again. After she had consumed some veal followed by salad—the veal, she learned from the waiter, flown in from France—she asked to see the proprietor, who came to her in the little salon while she drank her coffee, and asked politely if he could be useful to her in anything?

Only to satisfy her curiosity, Julia said—she was in fact *journaliste*, and everything about Morocco was of a great interest for her. The manager bowed, pleased and impressed; for some reason *hôteliers*, unlike the rest of mankind, have a passion for journalists. To what, he asked, was the curiosity of Mademoiselle directed? To something in Fez?

No, Julia said, not in Fez. She desired to know more about the *cantines* in the South of Morocco.

As it turned out, she could not have applied to a better person than the *patron*. The *cantines*, he told her, were the official hostels or rest-houses in small towns strung out along the bus-routes; a network of motor-buses now covered much of the Protectorate, and for the convenience of travellers there were, at the end of each day's stage, these *cantines* where they could spend the night, with bedrooms—yes, sometimes even with showers—a bar and a restaurant. Arab-style, of course—all on one floor, rooms opening on a corridor on one side, usually on the garden on the other. He used to run one at Beni-Issar before he came to this hotel in Fez—ah, that was a fine *cantine*, the garden full of roses! Many were directed by exmembers of the Foreign Legion—he himself was *ancien légionnaire*; oddly enough, said the *patron*, expanding on what was clearly a favourite theme, many of these managers were Germans, who had joined the Legion between the two wars—after completing their term of service they married Arab or Berber wives, and abandoning the Fatherland settled down in Morocco as *cantiniers*.

Julia was greatly pleased by this unexpected bonus, as it were, to her enquiries, which were usually so difficult, if not fruitless; she asked the *hôtelier*, as indifferently as she could, whether these expatriate Germans kept up any links with their homeland? Oh indeed yes; once a German, a German to all eternity, the Frenchman replied rather acidly; the door and the heart always open to never-mind-who of their compatriots! But did many Germans come to Morocco, Julia enquired. Yes, quite a few, especially in the last year or two. Tourists? Yes—and others besides.

Julia was rather nervous of risking any very direct questions about these others, even from the unsuspecting *patron*—she tried a more oblique angle. What sort of travellers went to the South, she wanted to know.

Oh, *colons* going to and from their farms, after shopping or business in Casablanca or Agadir; many Moors—with the advent of the autobus the Moors had become great travellers; then there were the members of the Administration of Indigenous Affairs, who frequented the bars, though they usually had official cars; and finally of course the personnel of the mines.

Julia pricked up her ears again, meanwhile carefully looking as stupid as possible.

"Mines? What mines?"

"For the chrome, principally, naturally. Does Mademoiselle, as a journalist realise—" and out came a piece about Morocco producing so much of the invaluable chrome. *That* was a place to see: the gaunt dressing-plants, the great refuse-heaps, the water-pumps, all in a perpetual haze of dust—

un paysage Dantesque, said the landlord, with a surprising flight of imagination. Julia said that sounded fascinating, and she must try to get down to see it all, if she could arrange an escort. And was anything else mined besides chrome? Oh yes—the cobalt, the molybdenum, strategic minerals of all sorts, so rich was the Protectorate; and new discoveries were being made all the time, as science advanced and the prospectors explored further and further. What a future lay there, for the whole country, if only the *sacrés nationalistes* would cease to make agitations, and recognise the benefits which France was bringing, and if those animals of Communists would desist from stirring up trouble!

The idea of communism in Morocco was new to Julia, and she allowed herself to be deflected into enquiring about that. Mostly in the big cities, she supposed? *Mais non!*—there probably also, but they were everywhere, even down in that desolate country of the mines: talking to these poor ignorant creatures of Berbers, creating discontent, denouncing la France, who had done all, but *all,* for the country—he had seen this going on with his own eyes. Many of them were Spaniards who had fled after the Civil War and now sought only to undermine the well-being of other happier people by playing on nationalist feeling, and exciting the envy of those who, for the first time in their lives earning a regular, a decent wage, instead of being at the mercy of droughts and bad harvests, yet saw that their employers were richer than themselves—most naturally. "For developing mines, for machinery, for paying wages, *capital* is required, Mademoiselle; and what capital can the Berber offer? His she-camel and his ass!" Julia laughed, and asked if the Communists were more dangerous, injurious, than the broadcasts from Cairo, remembering Mr. St John's remarks. The landlord fairly exploded.

"But Mademoiselle, it is one and the same thing! Moscow courts the Arab world today, and fosters, if not finances, Moslem nationalism for her own ends; she desires a pan-Arab North Africa, a single unit from Egypt to Morocco, communist-dominated. Ah, their eyes will be opened, *ces pauvres bougres,* if this ever comes to pass!"

Communism, Julia reflected, was one thing that de Foucauld had not foreseen. But though all this would come in very nicely for an article she had her own fish to fry; and presently she reverted to the matter of the mines. Where were they?

South of the Atlas—but a new area, whose development had only started a year or so ago lay further South still near Tindouf, practically *en plein Sahara;* this was enormously rich, and as it was situated inland from the Spanish territory of the Río de Oro, the construction of a railway to bring the products out onto the French coast was in contemplation. And

how, Julia asked, were the products from the older mines, south of the
Sahara, taken to the coast? (This was a question in the answer to which
she felt the deepest interest.) Was there a railway? Ah no, all went by
camion; the value of the exports, especially of the cobalt, made even the
vast expense involved by lorry transport worth while, especially to such
powerful interests as the *concessionnaires* who were behind the affair.

Hum, Julia thought—lorry-loads of velvet trunks, perhaps? But the word
concessionnaire caught her attention, and she asked about that. Oh, quite
evidently for the exploitation and still more the export of strategic minerals
a concession from the Government was necessary; nothing was possible
without it. Legally, that is to say; of course one heard rumours of underhand doings. The landlord shrugged his shoulders.

Underhand doings by whom? the girl asked.

Oh, but naturally by these detestable Germans!

"But do they not have concessions?" Julia enquired, now easily recalling
what Mr. Bingham had said about the East Germans having actually
started the drive for the rarer minerals.

"Some do, some do not," the landlord answered. "I, I have my friends
down there, my sources of information; and you may believe me when I say
to you that there is plenty of dirty work going on, illicit exploiting and
exporting, to avoid paying the heavy fees for concessions and export
licences."

"But how do they manage it?" Julia asked, genuinely interested—cobalt-
running was still quite a new idea. Was this what lay behind the tip-off
that Mr. Bingham professed to have given her, when he said that a nod was
as good as a wink?

"Oh, these types have their methods—disguises, false pass-ports; heavy
bribes, naturally, to right and left; and the commodity itself concealed in
something else, so that it appears other than what it is," said the landlord
breezily. "And they stick at nothing, *ces messieurs-là*—if anyone becomes
too curious he is liable to have a nasty accident. For my part, I am glad that
I am no longer in the South, things have become so unpleasant down there.
Imagine to yourself that an official was killed, not so long ago, in the bar
of my own *cantine!*"

"Good heavens! How?"

"With a home-made bomb. Several were injured, but they made sure of
the man they wanted, who had been too pertinacious in his enquiries, and
knew too much."

"But weren't they caught?—the ones who threw it, I mean?"

The *patron* gave another shrug.

"Mademoiselle, whenever a bomb is thrown in Morocco it is thrown by a nationalist terrorist, or by a counter-terrorist!—so at least it can always be said, and will always be believed. This affords a wonderful camouflage to murder for quite other motives, such as commercial or international rivalry."

"How beastly," said Julia slowly. She was thinking of Mr. St John's words—"possibly mortally dangerous"—if she persisted in enquiring for Colin. Perhaps this particular piece of detection wasn't going to be quite so much fun, after all.

CHAPTER X

In Julia's favourite books on detection, much time was always spent in reflecting on evidence, checking it over, and summing it up to assess its importance—most detectives, whether professional or amateur, wrote down lists of suspects or telling facts in parallel columns for the help of the active-minded reader. Her two conversations that day had given her so much to chew over that a sheet of paper and a pencil would have been a great help, but she decided against this—who knew but that Abdul or the squinting man might not get into her room, somehow? Seated in that same room, after her very revealing talk with the *patron*, she did the best she could in her head.

What had she got? She counted it out, slowly.

From Mr. St John's intemperate exclamations she now knew pretty positively that it was the Germans who were Bathyadis' "enemies", and from the same indiscreet source she had quite sufficient confirmation of the fact that what Colin and the red-haired man were doing was to ship some mineral out of Morocco. It must be very rare and very important, in view of the poor old gentleman's insistence that Colin must stay where he was, inheritance or no inheritance—and Julia paused for a long time to consider this aspect of the matter. If it would really be impossible, or even wrong, for Colin to come home, was there any point in going on with her search? —especially if it might possibly involve him in danger? The landlord's account of the metal racket certainly sounded as if that could be true, and Julia placed rather more reliance on his statements than on Mr. St. John's angry ejaculations. On the other hand it seemed very silly to have come so far and learned so much, and then give up now, without at least seeing Colin. If she could manage to see him she could anyhow tell him the situation at Glentoran, and then let him decide for himself; he was twenty-three, after all, and quite old enough to make up his own mind where his duty lay.

Moreover—though Julia didn't argue this out very clearly with herself —by a succession of strokes of extraordinary luck, such as Mr. Bingham's indiscretions and Bathyadis' mistake about her, she had found out quite a lot, and she wanted very badly to go on until she had unravelled the whole mystery. That would be one in the eye for Geoffrey—and for the Bank of England too! No, she would go on, for a bit anyhow, and as carefully as possible. Very well—and she returned to her assessment of facts. From Bathyadis she knew that whatever was exported went in the velvet trunks: this was confirmed directly by Mr. St John, and indirectly by the landlord, who had said that the mineral-smugglers sent their commodity out "concealed in something else, so that it appears other than what it is." He was talking of the Germans, but what better concealment for a precious mineral than to put it in velvet trunks and—*yes!* send these down to an-tique-dealers at the ports, who could easily, somehow, ship it out. It must be that or "that-abouts", Julia thought, smiling as the old nursery expression at Glentoran rose of itself in her mind. That of course was where young Bathyadis came in, and there flashed back into her recollection how he had expressed such surprising gratitude to Mr. St John for suggesting that he should start up in business in Casablanca. Aha!—the old boy had been responsible for organising that; no doubt it was because with his immense local knowledge he could arrange such things that he was "in on" the busi-ness, in spite of his age and his indiscreet tongue.

But now, what was the next step towards finding Colin? He was in the South, with the red-haired man, staying in *cantines* and moving about: that was all she knew—except that the landlord had said that metal-runners, if illicit, used false passports and disguise. She didn't of course know for certain that Colin's activities *were* illicit, but if they were completely above-board, why the mystery everywhere, and the velvet trunks, which were a sort of commercial equivalent of false beards? No, for the moment she would assume that their business was *not* above-board. Therefore it was pretty useless to attempt to follow them and find them herself; that would in-volve a lot of arranging, since she spoke no Arabic, and would cost a great deal—besides, she suddenly realised, she didn't know in which of the two areas they were operating, the one south of the Atlas, or the new one *en plein Sahara*, near Mindouf?—Dindouf?—no, Tindouf, that was the name —of which the landlord had spoken.

Very well—following them was out, for the moment anyhow. And if they were not coming back to Fez for six weeks or two months it was senseless to wait there for them. Julia paused at that point for some time, sitting star-

ing in front of her, looking perfectly blank. She was wondering if it would
be any good going to see Bathyadis again, with some other guide than the
nosey Abdul, and trying to arrange with him to let her know when they
did return by telegram or telephone, using some code expression like—oh,
"Carrots received" or "House on fire". She grinned a little at these ideas,
but finally decided against that too. Very likely the old Moor would be
unwilling to do either, with his panic about names in *bureaux de poste*;
he would probably refer her to Mr. St John, which would be quite hopeless. No—really the best thing would be to return to Tangier at once and
try to make Purcell tell her some more, using some of her newly-acquired
knowledge to "bounce" him. What Purcell stood for in the whole business
was another thing to find out, but that he was pretty accurately informed
was certain—he had been right about Bathyadis, right about Mr. St John,
and he certainly knew about the antique-dealers at the ports, because he
had been so startled when she mentioned them. And sooner or later Colin
and friend were pretty certain to come back to that house in the Kasbah.

Right—back to Tangier. In her lethargic-seeming fashion Julia was quite
a fast worker, and she now went leisurely downstairs and informed the
landlord that she had decided to leave the following day. The landlord
expressed regret; so did Julia—there was still so much to see in Fez. She
had decided upstairs to make a false excuse, and now smoothly said that she
thought she ought to go down to Casablanca to investigate the matter of
the doctor's murder. (She already knew that the train from Fez went
direct to Casablanca, but by changing at Petit-Jean she could get back to
Tangier.) While they were talking "Madame" appeared; the landlord had
married a French-woman, not a Moor, and Julia asked her politely how
she liked being in Fez, and whether she preferred it to life at the *cantine?*
Oh, but infinitely! Beni-Issar was so *triste*, so isolated—for shopping, for
instance, nothing was obtainable nearer than Mogador, or at the best
Marrakesh where the shops were *plutôts indigènes;* nothing in the way of
clothes in the least up-to-date, and the price of having one's hair set in the
Mamounia Hotel! Julia smiled her slow smile, and sympathised—Madame
was in fact a surprisingly trim and chic little person. The couple invited her
to take an *apéritif* with them, and they sat in the small hall; Madame
pursued the subject of the discomforts of life in "the South". Ah, if only
these travelling vendors of clothes had been going about when they were
there!

Julia made an enquiring sound.

Yes, just in the last few months travelling salesmen had started making
journeys round the southern regions in *camionnettes*, the landlord said;
mostly clothes for men, of course, but he heard that they had a tolerable

selection of garments for women too: stockings, blouses, even *petites robes*. This was clearly a subject of the highest interest to both husband and wife; they pursued it alternately, in strophe and anti-strophe. Such a boon for the personnel at the mines, who could at least see what they were purchasing when they bought a new shirt, instead of getting it by mail-order from Casablanca, said Monsieur. Yes, and equally for the ladies, when they required new stockings, Madame chimed in—and these Austrians and Swiss brought really good *marques,* her friends informed her, like "Nylons Guy."

Oh, it was not the French who conducted this new enterprise, Julia asked, interested—Mr. Bingham had omitted this particular side-line, but it would all fit in nicely to yet another article.

No, no—Austrians and Swiss. Really they were public benefactors, Madame was saying fervently, when the hall door opened and Steve Keller walked in.

"I have the week-end off, so I came to look you up," he said, when Julia had introduced him to the landlord and his wife, who promptly retired to the bureau.

"*Is* it the week-end?" Julia asked vaguely—so much seemed to be happening in Fez that she had almost lost count of time.

"Well day before yesterday was Thursday, when we went to Volubilis, so I make to-day Saturday," said the airman, grinning.

"So it is."

"How's Methuselah?"

"Not very well, I'm afraid," said Julia, guiltily—it occurred to her that she ought before this to have rung up the Consulate to ask if the poor old creature was all right. Should she, or would that introduce more complications? He might have already denounced her to the Consul as a spy, in his frame of mind when they parted—feeling even guiltier she decided to let it alone.

Mr. Keller took the news of Mr. St John's indisposition very cheerfully.

"Then he won't want to come on any more trips," he said. "Fine. What are you doing tomorrow? Care to come for another drive?"

"But I'm going back to Tangier tomorrow," said Julia, thoughtlessly—and then looked quickly round. No, the *patron* was not in sight. "Or rather to Casablanca," she said, more loudly, in case he had been within earshot all the same.

Steve looked puzzled, and also rather dashed.

"Let's get this straight—" he began, rather crossly.

"No—don't let's; at least, not here," said Julia, almost hurriedly for her— "and don't shout. Come outside."

In the sunny street—"I wasn't shouting," the American said rather sulkily. "What's the mix-up, anyway? Where *are* you going?"

Julia felt foolish. Frankness, at least up to a point, seemed the best course.

"I am really going back to Tangier," she said; "but the people here had expected me to stay longer, and they've been so nice—so as an excuse I said I was going to Casa to write up the murder."

"What murder? Oh, that doctor. But what d'you mean write up? Are you a writer?"

"Well, I'm a journalist."

He stared at her.

"You don't look like one! Well—maybe a bit like Virginia Cowles—she's pretty chic," he said, still staring. "But don't you have to go down and cover this murder?"

"Oh no—I write for weeklies, so I can send what I like."

"Then why do you have to leave tomorrow? Why not come for a drive with me, and go Monday?"

Julia hesitated for a moment, but only for a moment.

"No, I must go," she said. "I have a job in Tangier, and if I get back tomorrow I can start work again on Monday. My employer wasn't very willing to let me come up here at all."

"What kind of a job? You are full of surprises, aren't you?—I thought you were just a rich tourist."

"No English tourists are rich nowadays," said Julia. "We get exactly a hundred pounds, which isn't quite three hundred dollars, to spend abroad in a whole year; so if we want to stay abroad we have to earn abroad— that's all."

"Three hundred dollars *a year!* That's just silly," said the American.

"Silly is the word," Julia replied.

Mr. Keller appeared to reflect.

"Say, are you an early riser?" he asked at length.

"If I have to be. Why?"

"How would it be if I drove you down to Tangier tomorrow, if you absolutely have to go? If we started early, I could get back to Meknes the same night. What do you say?"

Julia said Yes. It would save the fare, she would see more of the country, and it would completely fox the little man with the cast in his eye, unless *nos ennemis* sprang him a car. Steve said, "And you fix one of those raw-food picnics of yours, can you?" in tones of great satisfaction.

Julia did not start worrying about Steve, obvious as his pleasure at spending another day with her already was. It was common form for young men to keep on turning up, once she had met them, and to want to take her for drives, or to the theatre, or sailing in uncomfortably small boats. As for the early start, her train would have left at seven a.m. anyhow. She whispered a reminder to him that their destination was supposed to be Casablanca, and then ordered her breakfast and a picnic lunch for two, and went off to dine with him.

And the next morning, sharp at eight o'clock, they set off, with the picnic basket in the back of the car; the sun struck silver through the olive-groves as they spun through Morocco, down towards the coast and Tangier.

That same Sunday morning, Mrs. Monro, Edina and Mrs. Hathaway were sitting at breakfast in the gloomy dining-room at Glentoran. Olimpia was rather a failure at porridge and even at poached eggs, which she was wont to serve on a bed of fried onion-rings, to the horror of Mrs. Monro and Forbes; but she made a wonderful hispanicised version of kedgeree which Edina and the guest were enjoying; Mrs. Monro, who disliked its strong spicy flavourings, had boiled herself an egg in a little electric boiler. Presently a strong smell of burning bread filled the room, and Edina leapt up and ran to the side-table.

"Damn that machine! Why on earth can't it throw the things out?" she exclaimed, removing two charred and blackened pieces of toast from the shining gadget. She peered at it, and then turned indignantly.

"Mother! Forbes really is unutterable! He'd turned it to *six*. Two is the outside. I can't think why you put up with him," the girl added, adjusting the knob and cutting two more slices of bread—"he really is the *world's* fool."

"No washing-up," Mrs. Hathaway murmured.

"True enough—but Mother might try to make him do what little work he does properly. I can't run the place *and* the house," said Edina impatiently.

Her mother wisely said nothing. The fact was, as Mrs. Hathaway had already observed the previous evening, that Edina was getting thoroughly restive at her enforced stay in Scotland, and the older woman understood now why Mrs. Monro had sent her that muddled and inconclusive appeal to "come up and talk things over," which had brought her to Glentoran the day before. Characteristically, however, Ellen Monro had so far shown no disposition to talk on any but the most trivial subjects, and was presently driven off by a neighbour to attend the Presbyterian church at Duntroon. Presbyterian services held no appeal for either Mrs. Hathaway or Edina, and since the nearest Episcopalian one took place over forty miles away they abandoned all idea of Sabbath observance, and settled down over the fire.

"When did you last hear from Julia?" Edina asked, kicking a labrador out of the way in order to put on more logs from the vast wood-basket. "Just this week."

Julia had in fact written to Mrs. Hathaway within a day or so of writing to Edina, and to much the same effect, except that she had omitted the account of Mr. Reeder, and had suggested that if Mrs. Hathaway "happened" to be in touch with Geoffrey Consett, she might "exert a tiny spot of superior-age pressure, and see if that wretched young man can't be made to spill the odd bean." Mrs. Hathaway, who knew Geoffrey quite well, had promptly asked him round for a drink: the conversation which ensued had left her puzzled and rather ill at ease. Mr. Consett, when she questioned him about Colin, had given a life-like representation of a worm on a pin; but he presently stressed what he had written to Julia at Casablanca, only in even stronger terms—that whatever Julia or anyone else did, or said, or wished, it was quite impossible for young Monro to leave his employment for the moment.

"Oh, he is *employed*, is he?" Mrs. Hathaway had asked, promptly and quietly seizing on that ill-chosen and unfortunate phrase, "Who by? The Bank of England, or the Government?"

Mr. Consett's representation of a writhing worm had become more life-like than ever at that question. He stammered, hedged, contradicted himself, and had finally begged Mrs. Hathaway not to press him on a subject on which he was not free to speak. "In fact I really know no more than I have told you, that he can't leave this work, whatever it is. I was not told what it was."

"Official work, anyhow," Mrs. Hathaway responded smoothly.

"I felt that I ought to warn Julia not to go on poking about," Mr. Consett had said then, rather unhappily—"but she has never answered my letter. Do you know where she is, and what she is up to?"

"She's working at archaeology with an old lady in Tangier," Mrs. Hathaway had replied.

"Oh, with Mme La Besse! Good—that will amuse her, and keep her out of mischief." Mr. Consett had seemed considerably relieved at this news, displaying what Mrs. Hathaway felt to be undue optimism, in Julia's case. But she had merely listened sympathetically to his praises of Julia, promised discretion on the subject of Colin, and sent the young man away comforted.

All this was in her mind now as she sat in the ugly pleasant drawing-room at Glentoran, and answered Edina's question. "Has she written to you?" she asked the girl in her turn.

"Yes—I got this last week," said Edina; she pulled the operative portion of Julia's double letter out of the pocket of her porridge-coloured tweed jacket and handed it across the hearth. Mrs. Hathaway read it, and handed it back.

"She doesn't seem to be getting on very fast, does she?" Edina observed.

"Not very—though I wonder whether anyone else would have got on any faster, supposing there was anyone else available," said Mrs. Hathaway thoughtfully. "It seems a complicated business."

"Did she tell you about the hush job too?"

"Oh yes—and how frightfully frustrated she felt."

"I wonder what on earth it can be. Intelligence or something do you suppose?" Edina speculated. "You'd hardly think they'd take on an ex-smuggler for that!" she said, with a small grin.

"Oh, I don't know. Poachers made such wonderful Commandos," said Mrs. Hathaway blandly.

Edina grinned again—then her face clouded; she put out a long slender leg and stirred the logs on the fire with her foot, restlessly.

"Look, Mrs. H., I expect it is all very difficult for Julia, but it's a month now since she went—and I can't stay up here for ever," the girl said; as she spoke she clicked her right thumb out of joint, making a small, soft, sickening sound. Mrs. Hathaway recognised this family trick as a bad sign, in Edina as in her brother.

"I know you can't, Edina," she said. "Tell me this—how much longer *can* you stay, without jeopardising this special work that was waiting till you get back?"

Edina looked gratefully at her mother's friend. Who but Mrs. Hathaway would have remembered that there was a particular job waiting on her return?

"Another month, at the very outside," she said.

"Then I should advertise for a temporary factor at once—unless you know of someone. If you can pick up a suitable person within the next fortnight you could show him the ropes and get him into the saddle before you go back to London."

Edina gave a startled glance at the older woman.

"Good Lord! Why do you say that?"

"Well, you must go back in a month, and what guarantee can we have that Julia will find Colin, let alone haul him home off this secret mission of his, in four weeks? Surely the estate can stand six months of a junior factor's salary?—especially in view of what you earn yourself."

"Well yes—I suppose it might," said Edina thoughtfully. Suddenly she glanced rather suspiciously at Mrs. Hathaway.

"Why do you suggest that?—not that I'm saying it isn't a good idea. Do you know something I don't know about this?"

"No," Mrs. Hathaway said smoothly, remembering Mr. Consett's ago-nised face, and lying in the grand manner. "I'm simply going on the facts we have. Colin is doing a job so 'hush', as you all call it, that even Julia's friend Mr. Lynch, on the spot, can't find out what it is; we assume that it must be something more or less official, because the transfer of his account to Morocco was allowed. But if—or when—Julia does find him, is it likely that he can or will throw up such a job to come home at a moment's notice? I should hardly have thought so."

"No—I getcher," said Edina vulgarly. "I dare say not." She reflected, no longer looking suspicious, and stopped clicking her thumb-joint in and out, to Mrs. Hathaway's great relief—the older woman loathed this particular inherited trait. "There was that boy who was at Cirencester with Colin, what's this his name was?—who went to the Mackenzies to under-study their old factor and train on, but he chucked it after a time."

"Was he no good?"

"Oh, I wouldn't say that. Burns, the factor, was an appalling old toad in his own right, and I expect put it across poor Struthers—*that* was the name, Jimmy Struthers—good and proper, because one day he was to step into his shoes. I don't really know how much use he was."

"Can you get hold of him?"

"I'll write to Maisie Mackenzie. I think they rather liked him, and I'm sure she'll know his address. I'll ask her to ask Roddy how much good he was, and what they thought of his work, Burns apart. Mrs. H. dear, what a boon you are!"

"Failing him, you might try for Julia's officer with the beard," remarked Mrs. Hathaway lightly. "He sounds very knowledgeable."

"Yes he does, doesn't he? We might have a stab at him if Jimmy's no go," said Edina in the same tone, getting up and going over to sit at her mother's confused writing-table. There she swivelled round in her chair towards the guest.

"There's one other letter I think we might write," she said—"I mean to Colin himself, care of that Bank in Casablanca. You remember we didn't before, when Julia was here, because she was going out and we all thought she would find him quite quickly. But don't you think we might, now?"

"They don't sound very helpful," said Mrs. Hathaway.

"No—very much the contrary! But surely, however tatty they are about *giving* information about a client, a bank can hardly hold up letters to him, can they?"

"I simply don't know. No, I suppose not. Anyhow I think it is quite worth trying, Edina."

"Good so. Right, I'll get going—if you will excuse me? I'd like to get them done before lunch—the Macdonalds are coming."

"With Ronan? Then Olimpia is sure to give us quite superlative food," said Mrs. Hathaway contentedly.

"Oh Lord yes—*ne plus ultra!* God, where *has* Mother put the writing-paper?"

While Mrs. Hathaway, the Monros and the Macdonalds were eating Olimpia's exquisite food at luncheon at Glentoran, the rain as usual beating and streaming on the window-panes, which rattled in frequent savage gusts of wind, Julia and Mr. Keller were sitting in blazing sunshine on a heathy slope above a Moroccan highway, also eating their lunch—Julia, in an unwonted fit of mercifulness, had ordered cold veal this time instead of raw ham, and there were tomatoes and hard-boiled eggs; a bottle of local red wine was propped among the rust-stemmed, dark-green leaves, so neat and small, of a pistachio-bush. Tiny blue scillas starred the reddish earth, and a minute mauve daisy; here and there a cistus, hardily, had opened an odd bloom—the air was warm and fragrant. Steve was a good driver, fast but safe; they were already in the Spanish Zone. And when they resumed their drive he deposited her at the Espagnola soon after two-thirty.

"Come in and have another lunch," she invited him.

"*Now?*" the American exclaimed, glancing at his watch.

"Yes. This is a Spanish place—they'll hardly have begun."

So Steve went in, and Julia watched with amusement his efforts to control his expression of dismay over the abundant oil and garlic of the Espagnola food. He wanted to take her to a movie, but Julia refused, saying that she must unpack and deal with her mail, so as to be ready to start work next morning.

"It still seems silly, you having to work," the American said, looking hard at her.

"Oh no, it's fun. Thank you *so* much for bringing me—it was a lovely drive."

"Thanks nothing!—you know I loved it." He wrung her hand rather hard. "I'll be seeing you again—I know where you are, now. Maybe you'll come up to Meknes some time, to look at that gate."

AFTER THE AMERICAN had driven off Julia did read her letters and unpack, and rang up Mme La Besse to say that she had returned and would be round in the morning. But her real reason for wishing to get rid of Steve was that she wanted to get to the bar early to see Purcell. If he proved to know a good deal more than he had told her, which she thought quite likely, it was important to twiddle it out of him. Watching palm-trees outside her window tossing their heads in Tangier's seawind, she gave a good deal of thought as to the best means of doing this. Try the familiar technique of displaying some of her newly-won information, which had worked so painfully well with Mr. St John? Perhaps—though Purcell was rather a different proposition. Anyhow she promised herself a little fun with the all-knowing Purcell, since she had learned so unexpectedly much.

So, gay and feeling rather "on her day", she walked down across the Gran Socco, where the great plane-trees behind the wall of the Mendoubia gardens stood up golden in the evening light, through the crowded alleys of the Medina, and down the Socco Chico. It was nice to be back in Tangier; even her short absence had increased her sense of being at home there.

At Purcell's Bar this happy mood received a check. Julia had expected the door to be locked, for it was still very early; but when the little Moor opened it he announced that Mr. Purcell was not in, and he did not know when he would return. At this perfectly normal statement Julia had a moment, suddenly, of quite irrational panic. Her dismay revealed to her, rather to her own surprise, how much she had come to rely on that strange personality and how confidently she had been looking forward to this meeting with him. She turned slowly away, realising for the first time how isolated she was in this quest of hers. Lady Tracy up on her cliff-top was full of sympathy and good-will, but had not done anything, and she had fatally alienated poor old Mr. St John. Except for Purcell there was in fact *no one* to help her; if he was going to close his door—like that horrible door in the Kasbah—she might as well give up and go home, as Mr. St John had advised. And at that very moment, as she was about to turn back into the Socco Chico, Purcell's voice said—"Oh, good evening. Were you coming in? I am so sorry I was out—won't you come back?"

No sight could have been more welcome to Julia just then than that odd, half-negro face, no words more welcome than this greeting.

"Yes, I was—and I will," she said, turning and walking beside him. "Mahomet said you were out—but of course I am early."

Purcell let them in with his latchkey and passed straight round behind the bar, hanging up his hat as he went—from there, with his usual courteous formality, he asked her what she would take?

"A Martini, please." But she did not sit down at her usual table in the narrow portion immediately opposite the bar; she walked on in to the inner room and sat in a corner—Purcell brought her drink there.

"Is it permitted to ask how you got on in Fez?" he asked.

"Yes—and it's permitted to sit, too."

He sat, at the next table.

"I got on rather well, really," said Julia very cheerfully. Purcell cocked one of those surprising grey eyes of his at her tone.

"You saw Bathyadis?"

"Yes indeed. I bought one of those velvet trunks of his," said Julia, her own eyes on his face.

He gave her a keen glance.

"Ah." He paused; Julia guessed that he was wondering if she meant more than what she said. "Why did you do that?" he asked at length.

"I'll give you three guesses!" said Julia, laughing—this was the fun she had promised herself. He looked at her, something like concern coming slowly into his face, but he said nothing. "You won't guess?" she went on. "Shall I guess for you? Because it was so pretty?—right. Because Mr. St John helped me to get it cheap?—right again." Purcell looked relieved. "Because I thought it might be useful to take something out of Morocco in, without its being recognised for what it was?" Julia pursued. "What is your answer to that one, Mr. Purcell?"

The man got up and came over to her.

"It would appear that you have not wasted your time in Fez," he said.

"No, I haven't. I'm only teasing—I am really infinitely grateful to you for sending me there."

"Thank you. I should however very much like to hear more."

Yes, and how I found it out, wouldn't you? Julia thought to herself. Aloud she said—"Oh, I have quite a bit to tell you. But I should rather like to begin by asking some questions myself."

He looked faintly amused.

"Ladies first!—though I am not very fond of telling."

Julia hesitated for a moment. There were so many things to ask Purcell that she hardly knew where to begin. She plumped for the display-of-knowledge technique.

"Why did you stall when I asked you about the man with the red hair? Why didn't you tell me that my cousin is working with him?"

Purcell gave a start.

"Did Mr. St John tell you this?" he asked sharply.

"Oh no, poor old thing—at least only indirectly. Bathyadis did."

He stared at her.

"I think you must be a witch," he said slowly. "That is the last thing I should have expected Bathyadis to tell you."

"No, I'm not a witch. Merely lucky, and a little putting two-and-two together. For one thing, Bathyadis' son from Casablanca happened to be in Fez, and I met him, too," Julia pursued.

Purcell started again at this rather equivocal statement—for a moment or so he said nothing, and Julia watched the effect of her insinuation sinking in, contentedly. At last—

"I should very much like to know exactly how much you do know," the half-caste said.

"I'm sure you would. And I should love to tell you, if you will promise to tell me the rest," Julia riposted.

Purcell laughed.

"I think I must ask first a question myself," he said.

"Fire away."

"Have you seen your cousin?"

"Now look, Mr. Purcell, be your age!" Julia expostulated, slowly. "How *could* I have seen him? You know when they left here, with all that gin, as well as I do, and you know how long it takes them to load up the big trunks in Fez—and to fix the rest," said Julia, guessing glibly. "Do you want me to believe that you *don't* know how long they usually spend grubbing out their mineral down in the South? I couldn't have caught up with them without a plane, possibly."

His eyes never left her face during this speech—and Julia watched him, too. Surprise; something like consternation; but also, unmistakably, a hint of amusement.

"You are alarming," he said at length. "But since you know so much, what more can you want to hear from me?"

"Lots. I want to know *where* I can most quickly get hold of them, and see my cousin. For instance, do they go to Casablanca themselves to arrange about exporting the stuff, or do they leave that to young Bathyadis?"

"This, too," Purcell murmured, half to himself. "Would you be willing to tell me from whom you have learned all this? It is quite important to me to know."

"Yes, gladly—when you have told me precisely where and how to contact Colin. It is no use my going off into the blue, trying to locate him at all those German-run *cantines*; I should need a car, which I can't afford, *and* an interpreter—which I can't afford either," said Julia. "So please give me a time and a place. I'm sure you can."

Purcell again stared at her, she noticed, when she spoke of the *cantines* run by Germans.

"I wish I knew your sources of information," he said. "In one week!"

"I'll spill every single bean, once you have told me where I can meet him," Julia replied.

Purcell was silent then for quite a long time. At last with characteristic percipience he said—

"I am sure that at this point I ought to tell you to give up this attempt to find your cousin, and that it will be useless even if you succeed—but I am equally certain that it would be quite fruitless to do this."

"Totally," Julia agreed. She began to feel quite hopeful—though she still did not know where Purcell stood, his last words sounded as if he meant to tell her something.

"Therefore," Purcell pursued, "I suggest that in about a fortnight's time you go to Marrakesh, and—"

A tiny crash, quite close by, made them both look round. The little man with the cast in his eye had entered unnoticed; in stealing round the corner to the inner room and creeping in under a table he had dislodged an ash-tray. Julia fairly exploded with rage.

"Will you *please* tell that loathsome little wretch to clear out! I won't have him hanging round me all the time!"

Purcell had risen, like the unhappy man; he took him by the shoulder and led him out, ignoring his protests "Purthell, I wanted to thee you!" After shutting the door on him Purcell locked it, and knocked on the bar-top; the Moor appeared, looking frightened; Purcell berated him in Arabic —Julia couldn't understand a word, but it was evident that Mahomet was getting a terrific tongue-ing; he cringed and clasped his hands in entreaty before his master returned to Julia's table.

"Mahomet must have let him in by the back entrance," he said, sitting down again. "We should have heard the door. But now, will you please tell me what you mean by this man's hanging round you?"

"He follows me everywhere," said Julia, still indignant. "He was at Petit-Jean when I changed trains, going up, and then he was after me in Fez—I saw him twice."

"Where, may I know? At your hotel?"

"No, I never saw him at the hotel. But he was at Bathyadis' both times that I went there."

Purcell looked grave.

"Have you seen him anywhere else?"

"Yes, up in the Kasbah here, when I went to look for Colin in that red-haired type's house. You still haven't told me why you fibbed and pretended that he was staying at the Minzah," said Julia coolly—"but let that pass. Anyhow he was hanging about up there too. Who is he? And why does he follow me?"

"I may point out that you did not tell me about this visit to the Kasbah," Purcell said. "I *see*. You saw them on the roof, of course, when you went up to watch the Mendoub's procession. It is so unwise to sit out there, but Mr. Tor—" he bit the word off.

"He will do it, will he?" said Julia, trying to think of names which began with Tor—there hardly seemed to be any.

Purcell ignored this question.

"And Moshe was up there? Where?"

"Hanging about in the alley. I didn't get in, of course—otherwise I shouldn't still be in Morocco! But who is this creature, and why does he follow me?"

"He is a miserable little Jew, who earns a living as best he can—usually by rather unsavoury activities."

"So I should suppose," said Julia scornfully.

"Jews have a hard time in Morocco," said Purcell with detachment. "They are not over-popular with the Moslems, especially the new nationalist element; they would like to go to Palestine, but Palestine is already overcrowded, and only a few get permits. I believe there is in Morocco a waiting-list of 250,000 or more would-be emigrants—so be merciful in your judgments."

Julia liked him more than ever for saying that, but she pursued her enquiry.

"But why does he follow *me*?"

"He was probably not following you when you went to that house in the Kasbah; most likely he was just watching it. But having seen you there, no doubt he reported the fact, and was detailed to follow you."

"But—" Julia's head was full of questions, jostling one another to be asked first—and there was the business of Marrakesh to be followed up, too. The winning question popped out.

"How could he have known that I was going to Fez?"

"How did you buy your ticket?"

"The hotel porter got it for me."

"There you are. Hotel porters, too, get a nice little *douceur* for supplying such information."

"Yes but Mr. Purcell, who for? *Who* wants to have me watched, and pays that creature for doing it?"

Purcell's face took on one of its gleaming expressions of amused intelligence; Julia was watching him with happy expectancy when a violent hammering on the door began. The half-caste sprang up, glancing at his watch.

"I left it locked," he murmured; "but of course it is time. Can you come in tomorrow at eleven?"

"No, I can't. I must go to my job."

"In the evening then, early. Five o'clock?"

The hammering was renewed, with re-doubled violence, while Julia wondered whether, if she had to go out to "l'excavation", she could possibly be back by five. She decided that she would, come hell and high water.

"Yes, five tomorrow. I'll pay then." As Purcell opened the door and the bunch, protesting loudly in high voices, surged in, she went out.

It was raining next morning. Julia was glad of the weather, as it meant that there could be no question of going out to the excavation—Mme La Besse was like a cat about the wet. Tangier in rain has a strange, disorientated aspect. The colour-washed flats and houses, so brilliant in sunshine, look stained and shabby, the tossing fronds of the palms fling showers of heavy drops into the air; the usually lively little donkeys patter dolefully along on the wet tarmac with drooping ears, their backs darkened with moisture; as for the Arab women, their sodden white draperies cling dismally round them, making them resemble, now, bundles of washing still dripping from the tub—a most unhappy sight. But dampness accentuates scents and odours, and since residential Tangier is full of flowering gardens, in rain its air is unbelievably fragrant; Julia snuffed it up happily through the open window of her taxi.

She was touched by the pleasure with which the Belgian greeted her. They sat down to con over Julia's measurements and descriptions of the *huilerie* at Volubilis; and when she produced a neatly-typed description of the Berber oil-mill in Moulay Idriss, Mme La Besse's pleasure and excitement knew no bounds.

"But this is wonderful! Evidently, our *huilerie* is of this type. Probably the Berbers still use a Phoenician kind of mill; or possibly the Phoenicians adapted a mill already used by the Berbers." She instantly dictated a long and enthusiastic letter to a fellow archaeologist in Tunis—after typing this Julia drove off to post it and to shop in the Gran Socco, where all the Berber women looked pinched, drops falling from the brims of their vast straw hats. She told Mme La Besse firmly that she could not stay late, and sharp at five she was tapping lightly on the door of Purcell's Bar. To her surprise a new Moor opened it, and ushered her in.

"Have you fired Mahomet?" the girl asked Purcell as she sat down; she meant it jokingly, but he answered in all seriousness.

"Certainly. I cannot employ someone who takes money from others."

"Do you think the Jew paid Mahomet to let him in, then?" Julia asked in surprise.

"I *know* he did. Mahomet was bribed."

This episode sent Julia's thoughts back to her unanswered question of the previous evening, when the bunch had come hammering on the door. She did very much want to know who was having her followed, and why —but it was more important to get Purcell to amplify his hint about Marrakesh, which had been interrupted by the entry of the Jew, and she went for that first.

"Horrid little creature," she said. "But now tell me about going to Marrakesh—in about a fortnight, you said?"

"Yes, about that. I think you might learn a little more—much as you seem to know!—and even see your cousin, possibly. Marrakesh is an *entrepôt* for many wares," said Purcell, looking crafty and amused.

"Oh, *how* good of you! *See* him!" Julia exclaimed, delighted.

"Do not thank me too soon. It is a very speculative venture; I should not suggest it to most people. But you seem to have the knack of success."

"Goody," said Julia. "Well, that will suit me perfectly—I want to see Marrakesh anyhow, and I can get driven there from Casa."

"Excuse me, but driven by whom?"

"An Irishman—that friend of mine I told you about. How do I proceed?—who's the local St John? Not that he was much good," said Julia reflectively. "He really did very little but tell me to call it all off."

Purcell laughed.

"Poor Mr. St John. I can imagine him in your hands! Well, in Marrakesh you will really do best by frequenting the Café de France, on the Djema el F'na, the great square—you should eat all your meals there; the food is delicious."

"Expensive?"

"I am afraid so. But it is the place where most Europeans, except the tourists, eat."

"I see."

"And sometimes go up onto the roof to drink coffee; there is a wonderful view of the Atlas mountains, but also it commands the whole square. Have you a pair of field-glasses?"

"No. Oh dear, and they cost the earth!"

"Possibly I might be able to get you a pair fairly reasonably," said Purcell.

"Ah yes—from Gibraltar, where everything is so cheap, I suppose. What do I want them for?"

"To study the crowds on the Djema el F'na—unless you have exceptionally long sight."

"No, mine is very short. Oh what a worry! Well never mind—do get them," she said resignedly. If she could only find Colin through a pair of field-glasses, field-glasses she would have. "How much shall I have to pay?"

"I think I might get you a really good pair, second-hand, for about twenty-five pounds."

"Right—how kind you are! Will you go ahead and do that? Unless Lady Tracy has a pair, just the sort of thing she would have. I'll let you know tomorrow, shall I?"

"By all means."

"Well when I have them, what do I do? Spot my cousin from the roof of this Café place, and then plunge down and find him?"

"Exactly that; unless you meet him in the bar."

"It sounds rather complicated," said Julia dubiously. "Suppose he's walked on by the time I get down? How many flights up is this roof?"

Purcell laughed outright.

"You are so practical! I am not sure—four or five flights, I think. But there is always the chance that he would not have moved on, but would be standing in the same circle watching dancers, or a juggler, or a snake-charmer."

"Fun!" said Julia. "Right, I've got that. But suppose I don't spot him? Is there a local Bathyadis?"

"More or less, yes. At least there is a house in a garden, where curios are sold, and tea is served à la marocaine; there is a tall blonde woman there, Swiss or Swedish, I don't know which—anyhow she is called Mademoiselle Hortense."

"No surname?"

"If she has one I don't know it. Hortense is enough."

"Is her shop stuffed with velvet trunks?"

Purcell smiled.

"I imagine not. But go there and look at her things, and drink mint tea, and talk, to begin with."

"How often? As often as I came to you before I asked about Colin? Anyhow mint tea is cheaper than gin," said Julia.

Purcell's face crinkled with amusement.

"How long shall you be in Marrakesh?" he asked.

"Only a few days—a long week-end, I should think, unless I stay on alone."

"Then you cannot take too much time. Go and drink tea at once, the first day, and arrange to return next morning to look at some piece again. Then get Hortense alone, and ask if she can help you to find your cousin."

"H'm. Do I ask for Colin by name?"

Purcell reflected.

"No, I think not—it is always better not to use names. Describe him; you could mention that thumb of his." Julia started a little at Purcell's mention of Colin's thumb—*sabe todo* with a vengeance. He smiled one of his fine smiles. "You might perhaps even say that he is an admirer, a follower, of Mademoiselle Astrid."

"Goodness! Does she exist?"

"Very much so!" His smile was finer still.

Oh Lord, Julia thought, was there girl trouble too, to add to the other complications? What a worry!

"Beautiful?" she asked, slowly, but with a certain anxiety.

"No—but very rich!" Purcell replied; at this point his smile had to be seen to be believed, so full was it of some secret enjoyment. Julia watched him, puzzled—as he so evidently meant her to be; there was some catch which was entertaining him. But he certainly meant something, and she thanked him again, and asked for Hortense's address. This he gave in a curious form. No street, no number—but starting from the small garden outside the Post Office in Marrakesh, a series of second, third, or fourth left- or right-hand turns, and then a garden wall with a medlar-tree leaning over it, and the upper part of the house visible above. Julia pulled out her diary and wrote these details down.

"I am not sure that that is wise," Purcell said.

"I haven't written down the starting-point, I can remember that," said Julia—at which the man gave a sanctioning nod.

"I suppose your Irish friend will escort you about Marrakesh?" he asked.

"While he's there, yes; if I have to stay on can I walk about alone?"

"Oh yes—certainly by day. Marrakesh is not Fez. But if you visit the souks take a guide, or you will lose your way."

Remembering Abdul—"I'm not all that keen on Arab guides," Julia said.

"Why not?"

She told him how troublesome her wart-nosed escort had been when he took her to Bathyadis' shop—"and when we went to Volubilis, there he was waiting by another car, wart and all. Perhaps I'm getting suspicious, and it was just a coincidence, but somehow I didn't altogether like it."

"I do not like it either. And this reminds me, what have you done with the velvet coffer that you said you bought?"

"It's at my hotel, of course."

"Did you bring it by train?"

"No, I came back by car, with a friend."

"You went by car to Volubilis, I suppose. In the same car?"

"Yes."

"Then the number will be known." He looked concerned. "Is it open?"

"What, the car?"

"No no, the coffer."

"No."

"Well, *leave* it open—with the lid up," Purcell said, urgently. "No—better not to have it with you at all. It has been there twenty-four hours already; I ought to have seen to this last night, but that wretched Moshe!"—He broke off, and glanced at his watch. "You cannot bring it here tonight, there isn't time—the place will be full. Can you take it to Lady Tracy's?"

"Well I could, as I'm going there. But if it's unwise for me, what about her?"

"Lady Tracy is different," Purcell said brusquely. "Nothing can happen to her."

"Why not?"

"The Moors love her too much. Please take it to her this evening."

"All right," said Julia, slightly puzzled by all this. "In fact I'd better go now"—and after paying for two evenings' drinks she took her departure.

"Take a taxi off the rank when you take the coffer," Purcell said at the door—"Do not let that porter telephone for one."

"Oh very well."

The girl duly picked up a taxi on the *place* at the top of the boulevard on her way home, as before booking it by the hour; when she ran in to collect the little coffer she took the precaution of wrapping it in her old duffle-coat, and so swathed carried it out under the curious gaze of the Espagnola porter. "Drive to the Mountain," she told the taxi-man; only when they were out of earshot did she give the address of the pink-washed house on the cliff.

As the taxi wound up onto the high ground west of the Kasbah the girl felt a certain nervousness, a thing rather foreign to her nature. Suppose Mr. St John had really carried out his threat of writing to Lady Tracy about her, what sort of reception might she expect? It was true that the old lady had not, so far, done anything at all concrete to help her; but Julia recognised suddenly what it would mean to her to lose the affection and friendship of this golden character—as earlier in the afternoon she had realised how lost she would be without that other strange character, Purcell.

Nervously then, on the cliff's edge, in the dark, she bade the chauffeur wait, and shouldered the duffle-coated bundle down the cement path to the door of the pink house.

'Abdeslem opened to her, and insisted on relieving her of her burden, which he carried through into the arched hall where the old lady sat in her corner, beside her cluttered table and the broken and equally cluttered Chippendale chair—at her first words, as she rose in greeting, Julia's fears vanished.

"Oh my dear child, how *delightful* to see you!" A warm embrace. "Sit down and tell me *everything*. 'Abdeslem, have some sherry brought. But what is that?" She indicated the oblong shape wrapped in the duffle-coat.

"Darling Lady Tracy, how good to see you. That isn't a *present*, I'm afraid," said Julia firmly—"it's something I bought in Fez, that I thought perhaps you would house for me; my room is so tiny," she said untruthfully. As she spoke she unwrapped the little coffer.

"Oh, charming! Just like mine, but more beautiful. Of course I will keep it for you. Where did you get it?"

"At Bathyadis'," said Julia, watching Lady Tracy's face. No reaction whatever. "Mr. St John helped me to get it cheap," she pursued, still watching her hostess; and this time there was a slight change in the old lady's expression—a wise, careful look appeared.

"Poor Mr. St John! Oh yes—what did you make of him?"

"Oh, he's tremendously learned, and explained all about Morocco, and these Moulays, and quoted de Foucauld," said Julia, with rather studied vacuity. "He was tremendously kind."

Lady Tracy bent an acute glance on her.

"Did you get on well?"

Now why does she ask that? Julia thought. Instead of replying she in her turn asked—

"Lady Tracy, have you heard from him since I was there?"

"My dear child, *yes*—I have. A mysterious note which someone from the Consulate brought down today. He warns me against you, and thinks you are a spy!" The old lady gave a happy chuckle.

"Is he all right?" Julia asked rather anxiously—"I mean not ill or anything? Did he write from the Consulate, or from his own house?"

There was something peculiarly sweet and benignant about the glance which the very old woman bent on the very young one at that string of questions.

"My dear Miss Probyn, I should love you and trust you if *twenty* people told me that you were a spy! Yes, he wrote from his own home, and he did not speak of being ill, though he was clearly disturbed in mind. Why did you suspect illness?"

"Oh, I thought he was going to have a stroke!" said Julia, much relieved. "He asked me to take him to the Consulate, and I did, but he was terribly upset. I *am* glad he's all right." She paused. "Did he say *why* he thought I was a spy? I'm not really, you know."

"No, he explained nothing. The note was infinitely confused. Perhaps he really *is* getting a little old," said Lady Tracy, detachedly.

Julia, drinking sherry, wondered if she should attempt to explain fully what had so upset Mr. St John. But she decided against this, and instead merely said that some enquiries she made about Colin seemed to have disturbed Mr. St John, and that he got quite cross and told her to go home! —"which I really *can't* do."

Lady Tracy seemed satisfied by this, and said of course not—whereupon Julia asked her friend if she could possibly lend her a pair of field-glasses?

Lady Tracy was desolated—her nephew had asked if he could borrow them for his latest botanical trip. Julia began to hate this unknown nephew: always away when he was most wanted, and now carrying off the field-glasses as well, thereby setting her, Julia, back by some twenty-five pounds. Lady Tracy presently said that she hoped the weather would improve by the time Mme La Besse's expert arrived, so that they could get to work on the Phoenician graves. This was all news to Julia, and she enquired about it.

"Oh yes, my dear child, someone immensely famous, from Cambridge; he wants to open some new graves. She thinks there are some that haven't been rifled on that headland close to the site, so he is coming out to excavate."

"When?"

"In about a fortnight, I fancy. Didn't she tell you?"

"Not a thing." Inwardly Julia was rather dismayed. If the expert came while she was in Marrakesh she would miss the grave-digging, a thing she really wanted to see; and Mme La Besse would make a frightful fuss about her going away again. However there was nothing to be done about it— and presently she rose and kissed Lady Tracy in farewell.

"Goodbye, my dear child. I expect you will find your cousin soon," the old lady called as she went out. Julia was tempted to turn back and go into this rather enigmatic statement, but didn't. Mr. St John must have said something about Colin in his note, but it was no good pressing things. Come to that, she had been rather selective herself in her statements to her aged friend.

JULIA WROTE to Paddy Lynch that same evening after supper, by airmail, asking if she would be welcome for a visit in about a fortnight's time, and if he would be able to take her to Marrakesh—"which is really the object of the operation. I believe I may be onto something, but I won't write, tell you when I see you. Will Nita be back?" She further said that she would be glad of two or three days in Casa as well, if it suited, and added a P.S.—

"*Don't* repeat *don't* ring me up—write your answer, please."

The answer when it came was completely satisfactory: she was always welcome, even though Nita was still at home, and Mr. Lynch had arranged to take from Friday to Wednesday off for the trip to Marrakesh. "As for this fancy business about the telephone, don't let Bruce Lockhart go to your head."

Meanwhile Julia promptly tackled Mme La Besse on the subject of the expert who was coming to dig the Phoenician graves. His name, Professor Carnforth, was one which would have kindled Mr. Consett; to careless Julia it meant nothing, but she was glad to learn that he was arriving exactly a week hence, so that she would be able to see something of his operations, anyhow, before she went down to Marrakesh—a subject on which she continued to preserve a discreet silence to her employer. She did not omit to flit down to the Bar the very day after she had seen Lady Tracy, to ask Purcell to get her second-hand Zeiss glasses; that individual displayed his usual rapid competence, and only three days later handed Julia a parcel and a bill for £23.11.9.

"If you prefer to pay that with a sterling cheque, you can," he said.

"Really? Oh splendid. Of course Gib isn't really abroad, is it?" said Julia, causing the proprietor to laugh. "Are they good? Did you look at them?"

"Naturally, or I should not have accepted them. The field is not particularly large, but the magnification is very high indeed, which is what you want for your purpose. Practise using them as much as you can before you go; there is an art in using Zeiss glasses. Stand above the Gran Socco and learn to sweep them over the crowds, slowly, so that you can see every face in each group clearly."

Julia took her sterling cheque down the next evening, and reported having successfully picked out her Berber flower-woman in the market—"and *not* at her stall; she was walking about talking to her chums."

"Continue," was all Purcell said.

Julia did continue—but not only in the market. She took the field-glasses out to the site with her next day, and walked up onto the high headland to the South of it, where the Phoenician graves soon to be excavated by Professor Carnforth were alleged to be. The headland was a strange place, with vast bronze-coloured blocks of hard smoothish stone, mostly sharply rectangular, and often standing upright, giving the impression of Cyclopean doorways—the spaces between them might have been the entrances to passages or even to graves, Julia supposed. Blown sand filled the interstices between the huge rocks, making walking difficult, but at last she reached the top of the long whalebacked ridge, and could look down on the further side.

To her surprise she found herself looking into a quite different world. Instead of the dark heathy slopes and low hills behind her, the country in front was green and almost flat; a shining lagoon bordered with reeds ran into it, separated from the ocean by a sand-bar on which the Atlantic breakers tumbled and thundered. Julia sat down, unslung her new acquisition from round her neck, and focussing the glasses studied this fresh landscape. The flat ground immediately below her was marshy; flocks of small white egrets were pecking and feeding on it, storks strode slowly and majestically about—it was fascinating how the powerful glasses brought these creatures right up to her eyes. Ranging further, she saw that at the far end of the sand-bar, a narrow channel appeared to lead in from the ocean to the lagoon—and in a moment, as she swung her glasses inland, she saw that this must in fact be the case, for tucked in close under the landward end of the ridge on which she sat was, of all things, a small white yacht. *How* amusing—what a queer place for a yacht to be! Fiddling unskilfully with the lenses, Julia managed to get a close-up of the little vessel. She was manned, not laid up for the winter, for washing flapped from her rigging, and a couple of Arabs in very miscellaneous clothing were padding barefoot about her deck, apparently cooking on some form of stove or brazier for'ard. Out of the most idle curiosity Julia tried to see her name— the gilt letters were there, but it required a lot more of her inexpert twiddling before she got them into a focus where she could read, or nearly read them—*Finetta*, it looked like. Funny—Finetta was the name of one of the Monteith girls; the prettiest, with whom Colin had carried on one of those childish innocent boy-and-girl affairs that last summer when she had been up at Glentoran. How silly she was—she had never done anything about the Monteiths, and contrary to Geoffrey's prediction she hadn't met them.

Still a little curious about the yacht's name, Julia rang up their house in the Kasbah that night when she got home—only to learn that the family had gone off some weeks earlier to South Africa for several months. But her curiosity about the yacht with the familiar and unusual name was still not satisfied, and on her next free day—four days a week was her stipulated contract with Mme La Besse—she strolled round to the Consulate-General and once more saw the young and courteous vice-consul.

Had they a Lloyd's Register? Julia enquired.

"I think so, Miss Probyn. But can I help at all?" the polite young man asked.

"Well, perhaps—I just wondered who the owner of a yacht called the *Finetta* is."

At the name "Finetta" a faint disturbance became evident on the rather ingenuous face of the polite young man.

"The *Finetta*—oh, well, yes, she was here at one time."

"Where is she now?" Julia asked innocently.

"I've no idea."

Whose name had she been registered in, Julia wanted to know.

"Well, she has changed hands since then—she was sold getting on for a year ago." He continued to look uncomfortable.

"Was there some trouble about her?" Julia asked—the young man's disquiet was so manifest that "trouble" of some sort stood out a foot.

"Actually yes—there was."

"What, smuggling or something?"

But the vice-consul would not be drawn any further. If Miss Probyn wanted the owner's name she could probably get it, he said, from Lloyd's representative in Tangier, whose name and address he furnished her with. Julia thanked him, and apologised so charmingly for bothering him that he relented to the point of saying—

"The owner's name was certainly not Monro. Wasn't it a Mr. Monro that you were asking about before?"

"Yes. Anyhow I'll see this Lloyd's functionary—thank you so much." And on she went to the Lloyd's agent.

This individual glanced at her rather curiously when she asked in whose name the *Finetta* had been registered up to a year ago, but turned up some files.

"Mr. John Grove," he read out. Julia got the impression, she couldn't have said why, that the man had known the name all along, and that looking in the files was just a piece of what the theatre calls 'business'. "Do you know him?" he asked, she thought slightly suspiciously.

"No—I never heard that name. I expect there's some mistake. And whose name is she registered under now?"

"Mr. Charles Smith," the man said without troubling to refer to the files again.

"Thank you. I am so sorry to have bothered you. For some reason I thought she might have belonged to one of the Monteiths."

"Good Lord no!" the man exclaimed, taken by surprise—"What an idea! Mr. Monteith! He never had anything to do with *that* outfit!" He paused. "Do you know Mr. Monteith?"

"Well they're neighbours of ours in Scotland, and one of the daughters is called Finetta—that gave me the idea," said Julia, with her usual serene vagueness.

"I assure you all the same that there is no connexion whatever," the Lloyd's man said, very repressively.

"And Mr. Smith?" Julia asked.

"Oh, he's a man who is fond of sailing, and comes out here, so I understand, for his health from time to time."

"Is he here now?"

"Ah, that I couldn't say. The yacht isn't in the harbour at the moment, anyhow, so he may have gone off cruising somewhere."

The devil he may, Julia thought to herself, and not so far off either—but she thanked the Lloyd's man, and wandered back to the Espagnola. She didn't for a moment believe that Mr. Smith was actually on the *Finetta* now—crews, whether Arab or British, don't normally hang out their washing and do their cooking on deck while the owner is aboard. Probably the whole thing wasn't in the least important—it was just a bit funny. She must ask Purcell some time about Mr. Grove—he would be sure to know all the dirt. Or Lady Tracy.

In fact it was Lady Tracy whom she asked about the *Finetta* at that point. She had nothing particular to do for the rest of the afternoon, and decided to go up to the pink house and find out if the old lady had any hints and tips to offer about Marrakesh.

Lady Tracy greeted her with her usual affection, and said that she had some news for Julia—"Though negative, I am afraid. The *Frivolity* is in, and I've learned *all* their names—and none is Monro. But one is a Duke!"

"Oh, lovely!" said Julia. "The Harbour-master said one was a lord—all the same to him no doubt." Nothing but yachts today, she thought, and being now certain that Colin was in the interior she couldn't have cared less about the crew, or passengers or whatever they were on the *Frivolity*.

"I wanted to ask you about another yacht, Lady T. darling," the girl said then. "What was all the scandal about the *Finetta*? Do tell me—I'm sure you know."

"Oh my dear, that was a *horrible* business! There were three or four young men on her, I believe quite nice creatures, just smuggling away perfectly innocently—cameras and things from Gibraltar, and American cigarettes, and perhaps a little currency from here—just what everyone else does," said Lady Tracy serenely. "But suddenly one of them started carrying *drugs!*—quite unbeknownst to the others, I gather; *they* said so, and no one gave a moment's credit to anything *he* said," said the old lady, something approaching harshness appearing most unexpectedly in her voice.

"And what happened?"

"Oh, the Zone Police and Interpol caught him, and he was sent to prison in the end."

"And the others?"

"They disappeared. I heard they were all quite furious with this wretched creature, and it seems they really weren't involved—I know my nephew thought they were not—though I believe Interpol still has its eye open for them. Such a *hideous* brush to be tarred with!" said Lady Tracy, indignantly.

"Goodness *yes*. And the yacht?—the *Finetta?*"

"Oh, I've no idea what happened to her. I suppose someone bought her, or perhaps the others went off in her. Hugh would have known," said Lady Tracy, vaguely.

Julia guessed Hugh to be the tiresome botanical nephew but didn't trouble to confirm the fact. Useless creature!

"How long ago was all this?" she asked.

"Now let me think. It was some time last spring—would it have been April or May? Wait"—the old lady rang the brass handbell. "Feridah will know," she said.

"What, about the drug-running?" Julia was genuinely startled.

Lady Tracy chuckled.

"No no!—though quite a number of the richer Moors do use hashish and things, of course. No, but she will remember when Nilüfer's goat—you remember, the pretty woman who lives down on the slope—had three kids. It all happened at the same time."

Julia was entranced by this rather unusual method of establishing facts about drug-smugglers. She watched with her usual pleasure the graceful movements of the Arab maid as she glided in and hung affectionately over her aged mistress. A prolonged nattering in Arabic ensued.

"It was April the 13th," Lady Tracy pronounced triumphantly, while the lovely Feridah and her veils slid out again. "'Abdeslem brought the third kid up here, and we reared it on a bottle. And that very same evening Hugh came in and told me about this horrible Mr. Glade."

"Grove?" Julia murmured.

"Oh yes, it *was* Grove. So alike, glades and groves—all pure Milton," said the old lady. In fact since Lady Tracy had mentioned the previous April or May, sums had begun to do themselves, almost unbidden, in Julia's head: last April was just nine months from this January, when up at Glentoran she had been shown Colin's last letter, in which he said that one of his chums had left the boat! There might be nothing in it, of course—just one of those coincidences; but it was worth remembering. However for the moment she put that aside and turned to her more immediate preoccupation, which was Marrakesh.

"Lady Tracy, can you keep a secret for about five days? Because if so I want to ask you something."

"Dear child, I once kept a quite *lurid* secret for forty years!—by which time of course it had lost most of its luridness. What is it?"

"Well I don't want Mme La Besse to know too soon, and be upset just with this Cambridge V.I.P. coming," said Julia slowly, "but I'm going to Marrakesh in about ten days."

"Poor Mme La Besse! Yes, she will be terribly fussed. However I suppose it is something to do with your cousin, or you wouldn't leave her just then." Julia nodded. "In that case you must go," the old lady pursued. "Do you think there is really a chance of your seeing him down there?"

"A faint chance. But I have to try."

"Of course. I do hope you succeed."

"Anyhow I shall see Marrakesh," said Julia.

"Oh yes—such an exquisite place. You are going with friends I hope? Do they know it well?"

"I've no idea. They're not madly learned. Is there anything I especially ought not to miss?—that's what I wanted to ask you."

"Oh indeed yes. The Saadian Tombs are unbelievably lovely; you must see them—though even the *least* cultured people would probably take you there."

Julia scribbled in a little book.

"And then you must see the Apartment of the Favourite in that Palace that Marshal Lyautey used as his headquarters. He put Edith Wharton in it!" said Lady Tracy, with antique glee.

"*No!*"

"Yes he did!—*absit omen*, we all said—when she went to stay with him. The Palace itself is nineteenth-century and really nothing except for its vastness—and showing how gay and elegant even quite late buildings can be in Morocco; but the apartment is fascinating, when you think of that *ultra*-American woman living in such surroundings. Wait—I'll get you her book." The old lady struggled to her feet, and with Julia's arm perambulated her book-cases till she found the volume, and handed it to her young guest.

"She saw so *much*—Lyautey thought a good deal of her, and she was on the spot so early, before the interior was really opened up at all. It isn't a *good* book," Lady Tracy mused, "although she was such a good writer—Africa muddled her; it often seems to muddle Americans."

"*And* how!" Julia said, thinking of Steve.

"Ah, you find that? But there are things in it about Morocco that you will find nowhere else. Bring it back—she wrote what they call 'a sentiment' in it for me!"

"I will," said Julia.

With Professor Carnforth's advent imminent, Mme La Besse kept her young secretary on the run practically non-stop, and Julia's conscience about taking leave at this juncture smote her to the extent of causing her to offer to work six days instead of four in the ensuing week, and to work late on all of them—too late for it to be of any use going to the bar to ask Purcell about the *Finetta*, since the place would be full. Indeed she was so busy, and by nightfall so tired, that for the moment she more or less passed the *Finetta* up. Certainly it was an odd affair, and the yacht's unusual name suggested a link with Colin, while the dates undoubtedly fitted in with his last letter—but it was all too indefinite to bother about.

Julia chose the moment for telling her old employer that she wanted to take another fortnight's leave with some care—in fact a few minutes after she had fetched the eminent man in the Chrysler from the airport, and deposited him in Mme La Besse's ugly little house. By mentioning the subject hastily, over drinks, and in a stranger's presence, she hoped to avoid a scene, but she was wrong. Mme La Besse emitted a screech which caused the Professor to jump and drop his cocktail, breaking the glass.

"*Now* you will leave me? Now, NOW? Just when I need you most? Oh, *c'est une saleté!*"

"I'm not going till Monday; that gives us all this week," said Julia mildly. "I am so terribly sorry, but I can't help it—I must go."

"What is a *week*? And why 'must' you go?"

"Because I have to." Professor Carnforth watched with interest how the slow, calm firmness of this pretty young woman—who looked so silly but who drove so uncommonly well—gradually mastered the rage and dismay of the so much older one, by whom (for some reason) she appeared to be employed. Still suffering from suppressed indignation, Mme La Besse at last accepted the inevitable, and even sealed the reconciliation with a bearded kiss. And next day they all drove out to the site and began the examination of the headland.

One of Mme La Besse's great merits was knowing when she was beaten. Of course she was dying to show Professor Carnforth the factory site, in detail and at length; but when he said firmly that though he hoped to see that later, graves he had come for and with graves he would begin, she shook with chuckles and gave way. She also suggested that he and Julia should proceed ahead to the summit of the headland, while Achmet and Abdullah could haul her up after them.

As the advance party toiled upwards through the clogging white sand between those strange bronze-toned rocks—

"You are interested in archaeology?" the Professor asked Julia.

"Oh God no! I don't know the first thing about it."

The Professor had been a surprise to Julia. In her usual total ignorance of matters academic she had expected someone very old and untidy, with moths flying out of his clothes and probably a long beard—whereas Carnforth was relatively young, clean-shaven, rather good-looking, and neat in his dress to the point of nattiness. He had a nice voice and a pleasant laugh, which emerged at this frank statement.

"Then why—?"

"Oh, the travel-allowance. I'm out here about something else, and I have to earn my keep. But I'm a *good* secretary—when I'm there!" said Julia blithely. "I can't be there all the time—I warned poor old Mme La Besse of that. And in fact I hate missing this grave-robbing—I'm dying to see all that gold jewellery! *Do* find some!"

"I'll do my best," said Carnforth, laughing his pleasant laugh again. By now they had reached a point in the ascent where the wind-borne sand ceased, and was replaced by stony reddish earth set with stunted shrubby plants; here the rocks were further apart, and the Professor paused before a low mound rising from the soil.

"This could be a grave," he said. "Where are those Arab creatures with the spades?"

The creatures were far below, pulling up Mme La Besse; so the Professor marked his mound with a minute cairn of small chips of rocks, and proceeded upwards—they found several more promising spots, which he similarly marked. On the top they sat down for a breather, rejoicing in the sun and the keen salty Atlantic air; Julia took her field-glasses out of their holder and established the fact that the *Finetta* was still lying in the lagoon, and her Arab crew still cooking on deck. When the old Belgian and her escort arrived digging began.

The next few days saw feverish activity on the headland. Carnforth insisted firmly that at least six of the Berbers from the site should come up every day as soon as he arrived, to dig under his directions, bringing their mid-day meal with them to avoid loss of time—thus he was able to work on more than one mound at once. There are several peculiar features about

Phoenician graves, in Morocco anyhow. One is that ninety per cent of them have already been opened and rifled—this was the case with the first three or four which the Professor tackled. Another is the troublesome circumstance that once you have started opening a grave you must go on till you have finished—either by establishing that it is empty, or by removing the contents; otherwise the ingenious Berbers from the surrounding villages will swarm up at night, complete your operations, and carry off anything of value. The only way to avoid this is to mount guard over an unfinished excavation during the hours of darkness.

The first grave of all was a beauty and fascinated Julia; it was entered through an elegant little doorway with stone columns and lintel, from which a short flight of steps led down into a chamber walled and roofed with beautifully cut slabs of stone. As the Berbers' spades removed the last of the soil which masked the entrance Carnforth gestured them aside, and did the final clearing himself carefully, with some help from Julia and her trowel. When the doorway was clear it could be seen that earth had fallen down the steps and into the interior; this Carnforth allowed the Berbers to remove under his supervision—he was considerably impressed by the fact that they had brought up rush baskets in which to carry it out.

"Ah, ils ne sont pas mals débrouillards, ces types-là," Mme La Besse commented acidly—"It is not the first time that they uncover a grave!"

Within, by the light of the Professor's torch, they saw along the sides of the tomb narrow stone-cut niches in which the coffins of dead Phoenicians had once been reverently placed, now empty. It was all rather touching, Julia thought—these non-Christian people caring so deeply about an appropriate and beautiful resting-place for their dead.

But however elegant, however touching this particular tomb was, it was now empty. The Professor made notes and measurements—twelve foot long, six foot wide, seven foot from the floor to the peak of the gabled stone ceiling—but that was all it held for him, and he went on to others of his little cairn-marked spots. Julia, though excited by the first tomb, in her bird-witted way soon lost interest, and during the succeeding days pottered idly about the ridge which formed the headland, watching storks and herons in the marshy land below through her glasses, watching the culinary operations of the *Finetta*'s crew on her rather dirty deck. But in the course of her casual wanderings she came on several more of those unmistakable stone-lintelled entrances to empty tombs; with her cigarette-lighter she examined them—empty, vacant, but perfectly cleaned out. She reported these to Carnforth, and he went with her to look at them—yes, well, there you were, he said; the place was stiff with them, but all rifled and from his point of view useless.

On the evening before she left for Casablanca Julia went down to the bar, hoping for a last word with Purcell, but early as it was the place was not empty; a tall man in tinted glasses sat on one of the high bar stools, reading *Le Mensonge de Tanger*. Julia, annoyed, barely glanced at this intruder as she turned towards her table; the tall man however had lowered his paper and got quickly down off his stool crying—"My dear Julia! What in the world are *you* doing here?"—and kissed her warmly.

"Gracious, Angus, I never recognised you in those ghastly glasses," Julia said, returning the Duke of Ross-shire's kiss with temperate affection. "And why are you here? Oh, I know—you're on the *Frivolity*. All the same, what *are* you in fact doing?"

"My dear Julia, what we all have to do—trying to *live*, in spite of the Chancellor of the Exchequer! Look—what will you drink? Oh, what fun this is!"

"*Scotch* with you, dear Angus, I think," said Julia—"but not on one of those pylons. This is my table." She sat at it, and the Duke brought his drink over. Purcell observed this encounter with considerable interest.

"Well tell me"—Julia said, when his Grace had raised his glass to her with the regrettable expression 'Cheers!' "Go on."

"My dear Julia, I simply can't afford to buy bread and cheese, let alone a drink, if I stay more than two months of the year in the U.K.! I have it all worked out; I spend three weeks in London with Mollie in the season; *three* daughters, dear child!—and what their schools cost! Then three weeks in August at Inverglass for the grouse, when I entertain a few of my friends, and a fortnight for the stalking—in *total* and most blessed solitude—at Gartavaigh. And that's the lot."

"It's rather horrid," Julia mused. "Is old Mackenzie still butling and running everything at the Castle?"

"Oh yes, bless his faithful heart; and he's marvellous with the tourists—did you know that we're open now six days a week in the summer? That's what supports Mollie and educates the girls."

"Where on earth do the tourists eat?" Julia asked, remembering the cooking at Inverglass's only hotel, a small one.

"Cafeteria in one of the wings!—and a huge carpark for the charas out where the old rose-garden used to be. All that pays hand-over-fist," said the Duke cheerfully.

"Well, I expect it's all right, and you have to; but I still think it's rather beastly," said Julia. "What *would* your mother have said? However, let that pass. Why do you live on a yacht? Do you smuggle?"

"Good Heavens no!" Angus Ross-shire stared at her in horror. "What an idea! We live on a yacht, dear girl, because the sea is now the only untaxed and untaxable form of 'normal residence'. Neither the avaricious French nor the contemptuous Spaniards nor the affable Portuguese nor the venal Africans can mulct you of income-tax if you only haunt their shores. So that is where, and how, I live. And mostly in agreeable climates." He paused, with a gusty sigh. "Sometimes I have a great nostalgia for my own *disagreeable* climate," he said. "But however—tell me about *you*. What are you doing out here?"

"Odd pieces for my papers. That gives me an extra allowance, of course; and as well I'm working for an archaeologist, as secretary."

"Good God! What like?"

"A beard."

"My *dear* Julia! Since when have you taken to beards? Tell me all about him."

"It isn't a him, it's a her," said Julia with a giggle. "And about seventy."

"Good Heavens! Oh well, we must try to brighten your life, which does sound very drab, poor Julia, and so unlike you. No boy-friend anywhere about?"

"No, worse luck."

"Extraordinary! I thought Tangier was full of men—they must all have cataract," said the Duke meditatively. "Well, come to supper on board tomorrow, I'll fetch you in our gig."

"Angus, I can't. Oh *bother!*—what fun that would have been."

"Why can't you?"

"I'm going to Casablanca tomorrow."

"But Julia, so are *we*—next week. Wait and come with us; cruise down and save the fare! You see how my mind runs on money."

"Oh Angus dear, what a shame! How I wish I could."

"Well once again, why not? We shall be there in a week. What is the hurry?"

Julia hesitated—not over her decision, but as to what to say.

"Everything is fixed up," she said at length. "And I'm going on to Marrakesh."

"Dear Julia, this is all *quite* absurd—we are going to Marrakesh too! You really must come along and make a party of it. My co-tax dodgers are very nice harmless creatures; and one of them, though of my sex, is of the same age as your Bearded Lady—so he can act as chaperon, surely? Purcell, please be most kind and bring Miss Probyn another whisky—it may assist her thoughts."

Julia laughed rather helplessly at Angus's nonsense, but held to her point—everything was arranged, and she couldn't change it now. The Duke looked rather hard at her.

"Julia, you have something up your sleeve, I fancy. I wonder what it is? Does your aged employer go with you to Marrakesh?"

"Angus, don't pester me! You know perfectly well that if I could come with you, I would. But I can't and that's that."

"No boy-friend, and yet she has her secrets! Very well, we will respect them. *Parlez-moi d'autre chose.* How is the very beautiful Edina? She really is such an exquisite creature."

Behind Julia's back the bar door had opened, letting in a puff of cool air; whoever it was that entered sat down at the table by the door, also behind her—she paid no attention.

"She's up at Glentoran," she said, in answer to the question.

"Ah yes. Such a lovely place, in spite of the ghastly house. Didn't old John Monro, the uncle, die the other day?"

"Yes."

"Then who's running it? Not poor old Ellen M.?"

"No, Edina's doing it—and *hating* it."

"Why hating it? Oh yes, she had a *riche* amusing job in London, hadn't she? But where is young Colin? It's his pidgin now, surely."

"My dear Angus, if only we knew! He was last heard of on a yacht somewhere out here—only he *was* smuggling. But we can't trace him." Julia was rather pleased with this answer of hers, which she brought out quite pat—but it caused Angus Ross-shire to look thoughtful.

"You don't mean to say he was one of that crowd on the *Finetta?*" he asked. "Not that anyone but Grove was really involved, I gather, but it was a horrid business."

Julia was startled. "Why do you ask that?" she demanded. As she spoke she glanced across to where Purcell stood behind the bar, and saw his face. It told her, as plainly as any words, that he had heard what her companion said, and that Colin *had* been on the yacht that was now lying in the lagoon behind the headland.

"My dear girl, naturally the whole of *le grand bidet* was ringing with the story, and I thought I remembered the name Monro—but of course I never connected it with Colin. They tried to pull *us* in for it at one point—poor Interpol, they try so hard!—but the Zone Police soon cleared that up." The Duke gave Julia a shrewd amused look.

"You wouldn't be out here *looking* for Master Colin, by any chance, and doing archaeology with your circus sideshow as a supporting bye-line?" he asked.

Julia could not refrain from glancing at Purcell. He had heard again —a veiled discreet delight showed in his face. Bother Angus—he was too intelligent by far.

"You'll be cutting yourself soon if you aren't careful," she said coldly —and to her surprise heard a stifled laugh. It was not Angus, who was merely grinning at her smugly; and it was not Purcell, smooth and correct, carrying a drink to the table behind her, though still carefully enjoying himself, evidently. Her companion now leaned across to her, and spoke in a lowered voice.

"Don't look now, but there's a rather sinister type sitting just behind you who seems to be taking a deep interest in us."

"Was it he who laughed?" Julia asked, in the same tone.

"Yes, damn his impertinence."

"Then I shall look." Slowly and deliberately she turned fully round. At the table behind her sat Reeder.

Julia did rather well, Angus Ross-shire thought. She got up very slowly, and held out her hand.

"Good evening, Mr. Reeder. How nice to see you again. Won't you come and join us, properly?" And as he rose, a little shamefacedly, she made the introductions—"Mr. Reeder, the Duke of Ross-shire. Mr. Reeder was First Officer on the boat I came out on, and was very kind to me," she said equably.

In fact Mr. Reeder also did quite well. He shook hands with the Duke, sat calmly down, and said to Julia very nicely—

"I do apologise for laughing just now. I couldn't help overhearing, but I oughtn't to have laughed."

Julia swam over that.

"I daresay I was talking rather loud. Tell me, what are you doing here? Is the *Vidago* in?"

"Not she. Poor old *Vidago*—Freeman piled her up, going in to Seville to collect sherry."

"No! Is she done for?"

"Well we hope not—but it will be quite a while before she's on the run again, so I'm taking a bit of leave."

"Was anyone hurt? Is the Captain all right?" Julia asked, with an eagerness which rather surprised Angus Ross-shire.

"Oh, Cheery's as right as eight trivets. But you should have heard him swear!—you know he never does as a rule, but he let Freeman have it, superbly."

"I *wish* I'd been there! Precious Captain Blyth!" said Julia, with enthusiasm. She turned to her friend. "The *Vidago*'s the most darling boat, I was so happy on her—and Captain Blyth is an angel. So you're hanging about here for a bit?" she asked Reeder.

"Yes. I thought I'd go inland now I have the chance—see Fez, and Marrakesh, and all that; there's never been time before."

"It looks as though we shall all be 'piling up' at Marrakesh, though let's hope not actually wrecked," said the Duke. "You are going, Miss Probyn is going, I and my party are going. I hope we all meet there and have a drink. Where shall you drink in Marrakesh, Julia? The Mamounia?"

"Mercy, no!" said Julia. "The Café de France."

CHAPTER XIII

"Now WHAT is all this nonsense about not being rung up on the telephone?" Mr. Lynch asked, as he steered his car skilfully through Casablanca's traffic on the way from the station.

"It may be nonsense, as you say, Paddy, only I have been shadowed pretty persistently—even as far as Fez."

"Who on earth by?"

"A seedy little creature who was pretty unsuitable for the job because he had a squint which one simply couldn't mistake."

"And in whose interest is this flatty employed, do you imagine?"

"I don't imagine, and I don't know. I can only guess—and I want you to help me with my guessing. In fact, a car is such a good place to talk in—do you think we could potter about a little instead of going straight home? I've got a lot to tell you."

"God help you, you have got it on your mind," said Mr. Lynch. "O.K.—we'll potter."

Julia had decided on her way down in the train to tell Mr. Lynch everything. He was intelligent, trustworthy, and had lived in Morocco for a considerable time; moreover not being a British subject he would be free from certain inhibitions. Her cogitations about this had been constantly interrupted by what she saw from the train windows—the endless young plantations of eucalyptus inland from Port Lyautey; the curious fact that all the orange-groves, gleaming with fruit in their neat squares, were surrounded by 20-foot hedges of some evergreen thing like a cypress; the large pale-brown winged insects that sprang up in clouds from beside the line in several places as the train passed—could they be locusts? She must ask Paddy about all these things—but also, she managed to decide, she must tell him her whole story. And while they sat drawn up by the curb in the open space near the new Cathedral—that inspired combination of gothic form with the characteristic Moroccan open-cut plaster-work in the windows, creating quite a new sort of beauty in ecclesiastical building—she did tell him. Julia had no great gift for lucid exposition; she began at the end rather than at the beginning, and continued with many parentheses and flash-backs. But from the moment when she said—"Well, I know what Colin is doing: he is digging out some rare mineral somewhere down in the South and shipping it out in velvet trousseau-trunks which they buy from an old Moor in Fez"—she held Mr. Lynch's attention. There was no more mockery; now and again he asked a question, but on the whole, at the end, he accepted her piecing together of facts from so many different sources, including his friend Mr. Bingham.

"Old ruffian," he said cheerfully. "He told you much more than he ever has me! I knew about the chrome and molybdenum of course, and I'd heard vague talk of some rarer things being prospected for, but I'd no idea the East Germans were doing it. I'd better see what I can find out. There are others who know things besides Bingham."

"Oughtn't we to go and see young Bathyadis?" Julia asked.

"Oh we will, by all means—I'd like a good tray as a baby-present for Nita, anyhow. But we shan't get anything from a Moor."

"I did from his father," Julia pointed out.

"Yes—that's the queerest part of the whole business. *Very* odd, his assuming you were in on it, and an amazing stroke of luck; everything else has flowed from that—though I'm not saying you weren't almighty smart, dear Julia. Whoever'd think it, to look at you? Your face really *is* your fortune!"

"Yes, isn't it?" said Julia tranquilly.

Mr. Lynch continued to meditate.

"I wonder if it would be any good having a go at the *Affaires Indigènes*."

"Why?"

"They keep tabs on all travellers: everyone has to have a *fiche*, a sort of *permis de circulation* with their name and so on, which is checked and stamped in each Administration Post. Car-drivers are even asked at one post where they are making for, and the French check by telephone to find if they've clocked in where they said."

"Goodness, do they? They ought to be easy to trace, so, Paddy."

"Not if they're using false names and false passports. And one person may dig a thing out, but there are probably whole echelons of men of straw between him and whoever ships it—in this case presumably young Bathyadis." He reflected. "I'll think about it. Anyhow, come on home now and have a drink."

"There he is!" Julia ejaculated, as Mr. Lynch swung the car swiftly round.

"Who is?"

"My shadower—look, the little man in the bad hat, on that seat. Oh, he's going off."

Mr. Lynch pulled the car sharply back onto the wrong side of the road and overhauled Moshe; springing out, he caught the little Jew by the shoulder, and stared relentlessly in his face.

"I shall know you if I see you again," he said in French—"And if I do see you again you will come to call on the police! Why do you pursue Mademoiselle?"

"I do not, I do not! I take the air only."

"Well, take some other air! Go back to Tangier! Where's your note-book?"

Even as the little Jew said piteously—"Monsieur, I have no *carnet*," one hand flew protectively to the breast pocket of his shabby jacket; Paddy's followed it, and drew out a small book.

"*Très bien!* I keep this. Be off—it is not permitted to pursue young ladies in Casablanca." He returned to the car, tossing the note-book into Julia's lap as they drove off.

They studied it together over their drinks in Paddy's villa. There were various dates: Julia identified the two days when she had called on Bathyadis, with a small "f" in front of them; the number (which she happened to remember) of Steve's car, with the date of her return in it to Tangier, and such a quantity of entries with "P" and a date that Paddy laughed out loud when Julia explained that these must presumably represent her visits to Purcell's Bar.

"No wonder you needed to seek 'gainful employment'—you seem to have lived in that bar!" he said, delightedly. Julia ignored this and went on studying the note-book—in view of what Purcell had said about the Jew's probably having only started following her after he had seen her outside the house in the Kasbah, she was looking for the date when she went up to see the Mendoub. There it was—with "XO1" and "XO2" against it. She showed these to Paddy, with great satisfaction.

"There's a car-number on the next line," he said. "See? Moroccan, by the look of it."

"Goodness, so there is! That might be the car they fetched the gin and whisky in. *Paddy!* Couldn't we trace them with that?"

"Might do. We'll have a fair try, anyhow. Do you want to change?"

In the pretty downstairs bedroom allotted to her Julia found an airmail letter on her dressing-table. "Oh yes—sorry; that came this morning," said

Mr. Lynch, "but with all this Inspector Alleyn stuff I forgot to tell you. Dinner in half-an-hour?"

In spite of unpacking and dressing in a hurry, Julia found time to gobble her letter while she smeared stuff on her face and wiped it off again. It was from Mrs. Hathaway, to whom she had written about her impending stay in Casablanca, and brought news. After describing her visit to Glentoran and her suggestion to Edina about getting in a factor Mrs. Hathaway went on—"And young Struthers *was* free, and is there now; Edina is running him in, and she says he's shaping so well that she hopes to be able to come South next week. She is delighted, of course. And from what your friend Geoffrey said (but don't tell him I told you) it seemed of little use her hanging on indefinitely waiting for Colin."

"Good for you, Mrs. H.!" Julia ejaculated. "But I wonder exactly *what* Geoffrey has been saying." She herself had mentioned confidentially to her old friend that she thought she might be on Colin's track, though it was far from certain that he could or would return even if she found him; but that letter could only have reached Mrs. Hathaway some days after the visit to Glentoran, when she had already suggested getting a factor at once—so Geoffrey certainly had said something.

Mr. Lynch, who had a very sound sense of priorities, called on Casablanca officialdom on his way to the bank next morning; he rang Julia up to say that lunch would have to be pretty late, as he proposed to have "some useful drinks", and would she tell Mahomet? Julia relaxed in the sun on the balcony among the geraniums, still studying Moshe's grubby little note-book. There were various entries of "XO1" and "XO2" prior to the day when she had seen Colin on the roof of the house in the Kasbah, but none after; presumably these figures represented him and the red-haired man, and when they left Tangier some one else had followed that line and Moshe been told off, as Purcell had suggested, to tail her. She smiled slowly when she noted that the last entry of all bore yesterday's date, with a small "c" and a car-number, presumably Paddy's. Would the little Jew also have memorized it?

Mr. Lynch came back in high spirits.

"Well, I've got the name of the owner of that car," he said, throwing a slip of paper to Julia—"English all right, though not Monro." Julia took up the slip—on it was written: "M. Charles Smith."

Her air of stupefaction as she read was so marked that Paddy got up and came over to her.

"What's the matter?"

"Nothing—only I think it means that Colin must have been on the *Finetta*."

"That drug-yacht? Why on earth do you deduce that?"

She told him why, at some length; when Mahomet appeared in the archway leading to the dining-room he was told—"Five minutes more."

"I didn't bother to tell you all this yesterday, because it was just a possibility," Julia said at the end. "The dates fitted all right, and Angus Ross-shire mentioned that *he* thought Monro was one of the *Finetta* names—but I couldn't be positive. I think this ties it in, though."

"So do I. But what on earth is the yacht doing in that lagoon where you say you saw her?"

"What indeed? That will want some thinking about. But isn't the first thing to find out where Mr. Charles Smith's car is now? Won't your *fiche* experts be able to tell that?"

"They should be. It'll take a little working, but I'm pretty *bien* with one of them, luckily. I'll tackle that the moment after lunch—and after tea, what about a call on Master Bathyadis?"

The visit to Bathyadis produced no fresh information, as Mr. Lynch had foretold, except concerning the situation of his shop, which was just outside the Old Medina, the original Moorish quarter, and therefore quite close to the harbour. Young Bathyadis expressed polite pleasure at seeing Julia, but seemed rather reserved otherwise, though he sold Paddy an exquisite old brass tray rather cheap. There were no velvet trousseau-trunks on view, and Julia refrained from asking to see one.

"We'll just call round at the Bureau to see if they've traced that car," Mr. Lynch said as they drove off. Julia waited in the car—her companion presently returned with another slip of paper.

"Garaged, and in *this* town," he said, "I think we'd better check right away." They drove to the garage, where Julia again waited outside.

This time the pause was prolonged. Presently Paddy came out—"Got any money on you?"

"About 20,000 francs."

"I daresay that will do."

She handed over the notes and then waited again. When at last Paddy emerged he drove off very fast.

"*Very* sticky, M. Martin," he said. "The car's there all right—I saw it; a black saloon. But it took most of your good francs, my dear Julia, to elicit what I so badly wanted to know: which is that for his trips to the interior Monsieur Smith leaves his car there and takes a closed *ca-mionnette*."

"Golly! Did you get its number?"

"Yes I did—that was what cost the money. How *are* you off for cash, by the way?"

"Oh, masses. I earn a salary in francs now, you see."

"I don't see—but here we are. Wait again, will you?"

They were once more outside the Administration Offices—and this time the pause was brief before Mr. Lynch returned.

"Mr. Smith has now metamorphosed himself into a Swiss," he said as he drove away. "Herr Nussbaumer. He travels in men's clothing and ladies' dresses, down in the South. What do you make of that? Can it be the party we want?"

"Oh yes—it sounds exactly right to me. I know all about these Swiss and Austrian travellers: they sell shirts to the personnel at the mines, and frocks and nylons to the wives of the cantiniers."

"And how do you know that, my girl? You seem to have plenty up your sleeve."

Julia explained about the hotel patron at Fez and his wife, who had been so informative. "It all seems to me to tie in. Couldn't one put coffers, or sacks of ore, on the floor of the camionnette under the suits and dresses? And they'd have a perfect excuse for cruising about near the mines."

"They would that. Yes, so far so good. I wonder how Mr. Smith gets away with two passports, though."

"Two cars, and a false beard on one passport, do you think?"

"Yes—plus a venal garagiste."

"But what can this ore be?" Julia asked, "to be worth so much fuss?"

"Ah, yes—I never told you about that at lunch, you got so het up about Mr. Smith. It was the East Germans who found it originally—old Bingham was quite right—helped by a Swiss metallurgist who'd been in the Legion, and stayed on here; they went for it bald-headed because it gave them something unique to trade to the Russians, so's they could keep their end up a bit, see? They have some proper concessions, mostly for chrome and molybdenum, but they get this stuff as well, and ship it out along with the other, secretly."

"But Paddy, what is it?"

"Some very queer ore. I had to make the man who told me so tight— hence our late lunch—that I could hardly understand him at the end! But it has some special properties, besides being practically pure uranium, with next to no waste products, so it's worth sending out unprocessed, in those trunks of yours." He swung the car smartly into his drive at this point— Julia got out, and after a minute or two he joined her in the sitting-room and poured out drinks. During those few moments alone Julia had been thinking back—recalling Mr. St John's emphasis that what Colin was doing was too important to be left for any inheritance.

"So I suppose our people want it too," she said. "Oh yes—I'm beginning

to see. It will be the East Germans who are tailing Colin and Mr. Smith
as rivals, and now me—Bathyadis and poor old Mr. St John really agreed
that the Germans were *'nos ennemis'*."

"Could be. Anyhow England would certainly like to be sure of a supply
of this stuff, Astridite or whatever they call it."

Julia sat up. "Say that again," she said quite sharply for her.

"Say what?"

"The name. Did you say *Astridite?*"

"Yes, that's what I gathered through my acquaintance's hiccoughs. Mean
anything to you?"

"Yes, it means a whole lot," said Julia slowly. She was thinking that this
practically answered the question she had never cleared up with Purcell,
as to where he stood; he had spoken of "Mademoiselle Astrid", and if he
knew that name he must be in the whole business up to his neck, surely?

"Did your informant make any fuss about telling you that name?" she
asked.

Paddy looked surprised.

"Actually he did. When I repeated it to him, to be sure I'd got it right,
he crossed himself and said—'Mother of God, did I say that? I must be
drunk.' 'Poor man, you are that,' I said. But why?"

"Just confirmation of another tip I got. Paddy, we couldn't go to Marrakesh a bit sooner, could we?"

"No, my dear. Friday at dawn is the earliest possible! But it seems to me
that we haven't done badly so far, in the time."

"No, indeed, Paddy dear. You've been wonderful." She thought. "Where
shall we put Moshe's book? I'd rather it didn't lie about."

"Where is it now?"

"In my handbag." She gave it to him.

"Well I hope I don't get leprosy," said Mr. Lynch, putting the unsavoury object in an envelope before tucking it into the inner breast
pocket of his jacket. "I'll seal this tomorrow and leave it in the safe."

Julia passed the next two days quite contentedly—she had the use of
Paddy's car in the mornings, and caused Ali to take her first to see the
bidonville, the shanty-town created by the Moors who persisted in pouring
into Casablanca in search of higher wages and a gayer life than were
obtainable in the *bled*, the agricultural country-side. It was nasty enough:
the shacks, crammed together, were constructed of every sort of rubbish—
old sacks, straw mats, decayed fabrics of indeterminate origin; those that
were really made of hammered-out *bidons*, or petrol-tins, were mansions
compared with the rest. And they were minute in size. She commented on
this to Ali, who as usual became informative. They were no smaller, he

said firmly, than the Moroccan country-man's normal habitation, the *nuala,* a sort of tent of straw or rushes, some eight or nine feet across at the base at a maximum; he would take Mademoiselle to see some of these if she wished. Mademoiselle did wish, and they spun out into the country, where Ali led her along a muddy track to a group of three *nualas,* standing within an untidy straggling hedge of camel-thorn. Ali continued to expound—he would have made a splendid P.R.O., Julia thought. The *nualas* were in fact pre-fabs—a newly-married Moor bought one ready made, erected it on his plot, and lived in it; after a year he bought a second, lived in that, and turned the first into a kitchen or store-house; a year later he bought a third to live in, and turned the original one into a stable for his animals. In four years a *nuala* simply fell to bits, so the Moor of the *bled* bought a new one every year, and continued this extraordinary turn-round of differing uses.

It wasn't, Julia thought, a very high or energetic way of life, this huddling on one spot in fragile impermanent dwellings, less solid and elegant by far than the highly mobile tents of the Bedouin which she had once seen in Syria. Next day she made Ali take her to one of the *bidonvilles améliorées.* There, shacks were going up in quantities; there were the stand-pipes, with an occasional ragged woman drawing water at one; but of any use being made of the facilities for sanitation there was no sign— slops were being emptied, and evacuation taking place, on the open ground.

"*Ah, ils ne se fichent pas mal de tout cela, ces autres,*" said Ali, with the high contempt of the already urbanised man for his rural brethren.

Julia set out for Marrakesh with a considerably higher degree of anticipation than she had felt on her journey to Fez. For one thing, any tips of Purcell's were now proved to be reliable, so that she was more curious to meet "Mademoiselle Hortense" than she had been to see Mr. St John; for another, they had found out so much, quite independently of Purcell, that she really felt herself to be fairly hot on Colin's trail. Mr. Lynch had cajoled his acquaintance in the Casablanca Bureau to produce a note of introduction to his opposite number in Marrakesh, and hoped to be able to arrange for notice to be given them if—and when—Herr Nussbaumer's camionnette turned up in the oasis city—this seemed a more hopeful line than studying crowds through field-glasses from the roof of a restaurant. It was a fine sunny morning, and as they left the city for the open country Julia began to hum a little tune.

"Feeling good?" Mr. Lynch asked.

"Quite good."

"We're just coming to the big Yank air-base," her companion said presently. "It's a vast place; they say the run-way is 11,000 feet long."

"*Is* that long?"

"Dear fool, it's immense. The most enormous bombers can use it. Look, the barbed wire's just beginning; on your right."

Julia took a glance at the speedometer and noted the figure of kilometres already run before she turned her attention to the American air-base. There was little to be seen at first behind the high barbed-wire fence but huts and sheds; the run-way and main hangars lay out of sight, in the middle, Paddy explained—but presently they came to a well-guarded entrance, beyond which sanded roads led off among tidy bungalows, with creepers on trellises and flowers in bloom, at which Julia looked with interest; were these the sort of quarters lived in by Steve at Port Lyautey? A large notice said "T.V.A.", and she asked Paddy what it meant.

"Temporary Village Accommodation—that's where the officers and their wives live."

The base was certainly large. When at last they left the barbed wire behind Julia looked at the speedometer again—they had done 25 kilometres, or roughly 15 miles. She pointed this out to Paddy.

"Yes, it's immense—and we're coming to another soon, on the left, that they run in conjunction with the French, like they do at Meknes. And then there's the one at Port Lyautey. These great Yank air-bases are one of *the* dominating factors in North Africa to-day, and come to that, in Southwest Europe too—though very few people seem to realise it. You might do a piece about them for your paper."

Some distance beyond the bases they came into camel-country. Even close round Casablanca an odd camel may be seen, ploughing yoked to an ass or mule, but here they were everywhere—ploughing in pairs, walking in circles at well-heads winding up the water-buckets, or merely grazing on the stony reddish land like cows: some, like cows, with a calf at foot, delicious little creamy creatures. When they stopped to eat their lunch in the shade of a wood of young pines a commotion presently arose on the far side of the road—a troop of sixty or more of the huge beasts was being driven along a track through the spindly trees, headed and followed by a Moor riding a donkey; they threw up their great saurian heads, snarling and hooting, as they plunged along.

"Oh good," said Mr. Lynch. "There must be a fair on in Settat. I'd like you to see that."

Settat is for North and Central Morocco in the matter of camels what Ballinasloe is for horses to-day in Ireland, or the Falkirk Tryst used to be for cattle in Scotland—*the* great mart, where fairs are held frequently, and the animals are driven long distances to be sold. When Julia and Paddy took the road again the resemblance to the outskirts of Ballinasloe on a fair-day became very marked, except for the uncouthness of camels compared with the neatness and grace of Irish horses—in threes or fours, or in bunches of up to a hundred, the earthen track beside the road allocated to four-footed traffic was alive with camels. Mr. Lynch sighed for Ireland; Julia was delighted—something more for *Ebb and Flow.* They pushed slowly through Settat, a rather undistinguished town of white houses, since even the main highway was jammed with the grunting snarling creatures and their brightly-clad buyers and sellers, the latter displaying the same total indifference to the needs of motor traffic as Mr. Lynch's compatriots do; but out in the country beyond the animals were once more confined to the earth track, and the car shot ahead. A range of low mountains rose in front of them: that was the Djebelet, the Small Mountains, her companion informed Julia—"and the French are doing some interesting afforestation work there."

"Oh—why?"

"How pitifully ignorant you are, Julia! Forests bring rain, and also hold the water in the soil instead of letting it pour out over the land below in great scours, smothering what wretched topsoil there is with silt and stones. This country suffers from drought for more than half the year, and from ruinous erosion for the rest of it; the French are spending a fortune trying to correct that—not an enterprise that would occur to an Arab!"

Indeed when they entered the defile by which the road passes through the low range of the Djebelet Julia could see for herself what the French Administration was doing: trenches two or three feet deep following the contours of the hills, with trees planted along their lower edges, thus at the same time securing a supply of water to the roots, and preventing scouring.

In the pass through the hills the camel-track was crammed close up against the high-way; rounding a blind turn Mr. Lynch prudently gave a blast on his horn. This startled the leaders of a troop of laden camels coming round the bend from the opposite direction, and as the car came in sight two or three of them appeared to shy violently, dancing awkwardly at the end of their head-ropes. They were laden with *crin végétal,* the fibre, made from leaves of the palmette, with which Arab mattresses are stuffed; the hairy greenish stuff bulged through the holes of the big rope nets in which it was carried, slung pannier-wise on either side of the hump. Mr. Lynch pulled up: the caravan-men hauled agitatedly at the head-ropes, trying to drag their charges back on to the track, below which a gully ran down to a stream-bed; but one camel got completely out of hand, and plunged so wildly that its load came adrift and fell off onto the road, breaking the net—out from among the hairy mass tumbled a plum-coloured velvet trunk, which also burst open, scattering lumps of stone of a peculiar pinkish orange all over the grey tarmac of the highway.

Julia was out of the car in a flash.

"Paddy! This is *it!*" she cried, and ran towards the mess-up.

"Take care—don't upset them," Mr. Lynch called after her. But Julia never heeded him—here was Astridite itself under her very nose, or she was a Dutchman, and she pounced on two or three of the fallen lumps. That particular camel-man was too busy trying to calm his beast to take any notice, but the Moor in charge of the caravan came over to her gesticulating angrily, obviously demanding his bits of rock back. Mr. Lynch also hastened up.

"Give it back; we don't want any fuss," he said.

"Oh, woe!" But Julia obediently pulled a couple of pieces out of the pocket of her orange suède jacket and gave them to Mr. Lynch, who handed them to the Moor with some pacificatory remarks in Arabic.

"Well, there you have it," said Julia as they drove off. " 'Confirmation strong', as the Victorians used to say. *What* a piece of luck!"

"I'm not so sure. I expect *he's* taken our number now. That was rather stupid, Julia."

"Oh *no*, Paddy dear. I had to have a piece—and how could I know he would be so tatty?" She felt in her pocket again and drew out a lump about the size of a cake of bath soap, worn down to little more than an inch in thickness, and examined it. "It's frightfully *heavy*," she said, balancing it in her hand—"like lead. And it's got funny marks on one side, almost like the bark of a tree. Look"—and she held it out.

"Really, Julia, you are a crazy creature!" said Mr. Lynch, laughing in spite of himself, as he took the piece of rock from her hand. "Golly!—it *is* heavy," he said, handing it back. "But do for goodness sake put it away where it can't be seen."

"Handbag," said Julia, opening that article. "I suppose that consignment is on its way down to Master Bathyadis."

"Undoubtedly, I should think."

There are two ways at least of entering Marrakesh by road. The main highway from Casablanca goes straight into the town, showing nothing of the astonishing oasis with its miles and miles of palms, their dark fronds swinging in gentle restlessness against the sky in the perpetual movement of air from the High Atlas beyond; there is however a détour which leads round into this lovely and peculiar place to enter the city from the South—this Mr. Lynch took. Julia gazed entranced as they passed through grove after grove of the strange plumed trees, rising from creamy sand; this, unlike Casablanca, was wholly Africa—and African too were the long low castellated walls, sandy-pink at all times, rose-pink then in the rich sunset light, through which they passed under a gate-tower into the town, and drove through a relatively modern quarter to their hotel.

The Mamounia is not in the least African, in spite of gallant attempts with rugs and furnishings; it is pure cosmopolitan comfort, plus a splendid view and a delightful garden, in which the wise have breakfast. Julia and Mr. Lynch were among the wise next morning, and ate rolls and drank coffee in air heavy with the scent of stocks in full bloom.

"It's rather a bore to come to a place like this, and then spend one's time doing Scotland Yard stuff," said Mr. Lynch, leaning down to pick a carnation, which he put in his button-hole. "However when you've finished I suppose we'd better hustle off to the Administration and enquire for Mr. Nussbaumer."

"I've been thinking about that. Would he have come through here on his way South from Fez?"

"He needn't, if he was coming direct from Fez and going down to Tagounite or Ouarzazate or Zagora—he could cut through the Atlas by the pass from Azrou to Boua Sidi; the road isn't so good, but the buses use it. But mustn't he have come to Casa to switch from the car to the camionnette?"

"Of course—but *when?* Would he pile all those trousseau-coffers into the saloon? I should have thought they'd be a bit conspicuous. Wouldn't he be more likely to go straight to Casa from Tangier, change machines, go back to Fez and pick up the trunks, and then on South?"

"I think you're right—yes. In which case there's no means of telling whether he'd have come through here or not."

"Except by asking." Julia leisurely poured herself out another cup of coffee. "I hope your friend's friends play. And then to the blonde Hortense." (Julia had told Mr. Lynch about Hortense.) "I shall feel a frightful fool talking about Mademoiselle Astrid, knowing what we know now."

"I should see her all the same. She might give you a line on when to expect them, or even more exactly where they are."

"Yes—especially if I show her this," said Julia, taking the orange-coloured piece of rock from her hand-bag and fondling it. "Look—it exactly matches my jacket!"

"Do put that thing away!" said Mr. Lynch, almost irritably. "I wish you hadn't got it."

At the Administration offices a tall courteous official, looking slightly like General de Gaulle, led them, Paddy's card in his hand, into a typical French office; rather untidy, and reeking of Gaulois cigarettes—excusing himself, he read the note brought from Casablanca. He seemed a little surprised, stepped to the door, and asked someone unseen for files; then he turned to the two English people. "If one might ask why—?"

Mr. Lynch was very ready. Mademoiselle was *journaliste*, and concerned herself with all aspects of life in Le Maroc. Julia, taking the hint, whipped out her Press card and did some patter about her interest, and that of her readers, in conditions of living for *women* in the remoter areas —which, she understood, were ameliorated by activities such as M. Nussbaumer's. The Frenchman smiled; partly no doubt at Julia but, Paddy guessed, a little also at her mission—the French are apt to consider that 'the woman's angle' takes care of itself. Some papers were now brought in, which the official—again saying "You permit?"—studied, occasionally consulting his assistant. Then he turned back to the visitors. Yes, M. Nussbaumer was quite well known; for the past year, or nearly, he had been making regular trips, going South about every two months, though he did not always pass through Marrakesh. He had however gone down five or six weeks ago, and should be back any day. If it would assist Mademoiselle, it might be possible to establish from one of the more southern posts when he was likely to return.

This was an unhoped-for boon; Julia, turning eyes of a loving dove onto the handsome officer, said that this would in effect assist her immensely. She would call again—when should she call again?—to learn the result of M. Le Commandant's so kind enquiries.

If Mademoiselle was at the Mamounia, the officer replied, there was no need to derange herself; he would give her a blow of the telephone.

"I prefer to call—I detest the telephone," said Julia. "Towards six?"

"Yes, towards six. By then I should know."

Outside—"Now to the Post Office," Julia said.

"What for?"

"To find Hortense."

"What do you mean? I thought you had her address."

"So I have—but it begins at the Post Office." She got out her diary, and from that small garden outside the yellow building they turned and twisted through the bright sunny streets, following Purcell's directions, till over an ochre-coloured wall leaned a medlar-tree, with a building much taller than most of the houses in Marrakesh rising behind it. "Here we are," said Julia.

This preliminary visit to Mademoiselle Hortense was of course intended to be inconclusive, and was—but it had side-effects. They went through a small door into an untidy but charming garden, and rang a bell at the door of the tall house; Hortense herself let them in and led them upstairs, to floor after floor, a room or two on each, all full of really beautiful and valuable antiques—the best, Paddy muttered to Julia, that he had seen yet in Morocco. But already Julia's heart was not in this visit, nor in the antiques, though she forced herself to praise a lovely eighteenth-century robe, woven in tones of plum-colour and dull gold. On the top floor of all, mint tea was offered them as they sat in comfortable armchairs.

"Funny place. I must say I'm glad to know of it," said Mr. Lynch while they waited for the tea—"Colin or no Colin. They've got superb stuff."

"I hate it!" said Julia unexpectedly.

"Why on earth?"

"I don't know. It makes me feel nervous, for some reason. Do let's get away as soon as we can."

"Must drink the tea," said Mr. Lynch.

Julia got up and went over to a window, restlessly—suddenly she unslung her field-glasses and put them to her eyes. "Paddy, come here," she said, rather low.

He got up and went over to her. The window commanded the street; there stood his car, and behind it a tall Arab, writing something in a book.

"Take the glasses, and tell me if that man has a wart on his nose," Julia commanded.

"Yes—as pronounced as Cromwell's. Why? Know him?"

"It's Abdul, the guide I had at Fez. Look, Paddy, either Moshe did memorize your car-number, and he's checking, or this place is being watched. Anyway he's taken it now," she said, as the Arab stowed away the notebook in his voluminous robes.

"Come back and sit down," said Mr. Lynch—"don't let it get on your nerves." They regained their armchairs just in time, before an Arab brought in the tea, followed by Mademoiselle Hortense. Julia, sticking rather grimly to Purcell's directions, arranged to come the following morning to have another look at the prune-coloured robe.

As they drove away—"Of course, if these people are known to be contacts for Herr Nussbaumer—or Mr. Smith—I expect the house would be watched as a matter of routine," Mr. Lynch said.

"Yes, I daresay—but why a guide from *Fez*? I don't *like* it, Paddy."

MARRAKESH HAS NONE of the withdrawn, enclosed, secretive quality of Fez. The whole city in its wide plain lies open to the sun, within its low peach-pink walls; the exterior, at least, of every building can be seen, nothing is hidden—one would say that Marrakesh has no secrets. Least of all does it attempt to hide its own highly peculiar life—on the contrary, on the Djema el F'na, the great open *place* in the centre of the town, this life is lived in fullest publicity, but in a strangely absorbed fashion. The dense crowds which fill it all day and till late into the night comprise practically every race from Northern and even Central Africa: sitting in circles on the ground round the professional story-tellers, watching every gesture of the narrator, or standing five or six deep round the dancers—white-clad men ranging from grey-beards to young boys—craning their necks to miss no detail of the beautiful foot-work; eager groups crowd about the vendors of cures, herbal or magical, or even modern proprietory brands from Europe; jolly groups sit outside the open kitchen booths, eating happily; veiled women throng the stalls where sweetmeats and strange foods are sold.

It was the self-containedness, the absorption in their own affairs of this vast mass of exotically-clothed people which chiefly impressed Julia when Mr. Lynch led her through the great Square after leaving Mademoiselle Hortense, judging, quite rightly, that the Djema el F'na is enough to afford distraction to anyone, however nervous. When they pressed into a circle to watch the entertainment going on within it no one paid any particular attention; even the man who took round the collecting-bag seemed to do so at the same regular intervals.

"Yes—it's not done for tourists; this is the playground of Africa," said Mr. Lynch, when she remarked on this. "Now come and have lunch."

The Café de France lies at one end of the Djema el F'na, separated from its crowds by a not very broad street, along which cars pass all the time; that end of the square is closed by a mosque, beyond which a wide passage leads through into the maze of the souks or bazaars; just beyond the café a side-street leaves the main street on the right. The whole front of the café is occupied by a broad verandah filled with small tables and divided in two by a screen of coloured glass; it is raised barely a foot above the level of the street, and since there is no railing, Moors of all ages, from little shoe-shine boys to the sellers of musical instruments freely step up to pester the European patrons—the sedate Arab habitués who sit for hours drinking coffee they leave severely alone. A door at the end furthest from the glass screen opens into the bar, which is indoors; beyond it flights of stone stairs lead up to the coffee-terrace on the roof.

The bar was rather smoky and murky, and Julia opted for having their drinks and lunch on the verandah, where she could watch the coming and going on the great *place*. The casual African tempo prevailed in the Café: the drinks took a long time to come, so did the lunch; various pedlars, with uncanny persistency, sidled up to the table over and over again, stealthily laying on it something that they desired to sell—Julia laughed, Mr. Lynch repelled them good-humouredly. The food when it did come was quite as good as Purcell had said; in particular there was a rich mutton stew over which one had to sprinkle a brown powder as fine as flour, with an unknown and delicious taste—when Julia asked the waiter what it was he said "Cumin".

"*Oh* what fun!—'tithe of mint and anise and cummin' like in the Bible."

Passing through the bar on their way up to the roof for coffee, Julia was greeted by someone—"Good afternoon, Miss Probyn"—peering through the gloom, she saw Mr. Reeder.

"Oh, how do you do? I hardly knew you in those clothes!" the girl said. Indeed the *Vidago*'s mate was curiously altered by civilian dress; in his rather good tweeds he looked like a country squire. He invited them to have a drink. "No, we've eaten; we're having coffee on the roof; come with us,"—which Reeder did.

There are two things which everyone must do on the roof of the Café de France: look at the view of the High Atlas, and eat Cornes de Gazelles, long slender curved cakes of ground almonds, with their coffee. The High Atlas that day was shrouded, a distant blue line with here and there a cold snowy gleam among high clouds; the party were thus able to concentrate on the Cornes de Gazelles, which are too sweet for most tastes.

"Know Toledo?" Mr. Reeder asked. "At that restaurant in the Square there they give you marzipan cakes just like these, only stumpier."

"Yes, I remember," said Julia. "How funny."

"Not really, you know. Did you notice the metal clappers those dancers use down on the square? Just the same principle as castanets. Spain really is practically Africa; down the south-east coast even the butterflies are the same."

Mr. Lynch was rather impressed by the sailor's display of knowledge, but the mention of the dancers drew Julia to the parapet; leaning on it, she tried to use her field-glasses, but found herself completely baffled. The square was so vast that even when she could pick out faces in a particular circle, when she put down the glasses it was hard to be sure which circle she had been looking at. "Hopeless," she said to Paddy, re-seating herself.

"I travelled down from Petit-Jean to Casa with a friend of yours," Reeder said to Julia—"an American called Keller."

"Steve? Goodness, what's he doing there?"

"Looking for you, I fancy. He said he'd gone to call on you in Tangier and heard you were at Casablanca, so he was going there. I told him you were coming here, and he must have followed on; I saw him in the bar this morning." The smile in Mr. Reeder's beard was rather marked.

"I wonder where he's staying," said Julia.

"Here, same as me," Reeder replied.

In the afternoon Julia demanded to be taken to the Bahia Palace to see the Apartment of the Favourite—Reeder came with them. That curious suite of rooms opening out of one another through archways without doors leads off the vast painted and balconied court which once housed three hundred concubines. No one, as Reeder said, can really take any interest in *three hundred* concubines, but both he and Mr. Lynch were highly entertained by this strange setting for an American novelist. In the centre was a tiny courtyard open to the sky, with a tinkling fountain; rooms brilliant with colour from walls and tiled floors opened off it, in one of which stood a huge four-poster bed upholstered in crimson cut velvet— "She could see the fountain as she lay in bed!" Julia breathed. "What a place. I must say I wish I'd known Marshal Lyautey, and been allowed to stay here."

They idled about in the souks after that, watching various craftsmen at work; Julia bought for Edina one of the crocheted cotton caps which every other man on the *Place* wore, and an inlaid cedar-wood travelling-mug for Mrs. Hathaway—then they dropped Reeder on the *Place* and went on to the Bureau, where the goodlooking French officer had accumulated quite a budget of information about M. Nussbaumer and his assistant.

They had been lately at Tinerhir, near the rocky gorges of the Dadès and the Todra—*un drôle d'endroit* for them, since it was rather wild country, though there were cantines there. But he was expected at Ouarzazate tonight, and if he came straight on he should be in this town sometime tomorrow. In which case, "since Mademoiselle dislikes the telephone so much," he, the Commandant, would send a note to her hotel.

"Paddy, this is wonderful!" Julia exclaimed as they drove away. "What sucks for old St John, telling me to give it all up. *Dear* Colin! It will be lovely to see him."

"Don't talk too loud," said Mr. Lynch, using his native idiom for not provoking Providence.

In the hall of the Mamounia they came on the Duke of Ross-shire, seated alone over a beer; he rose and embraced Julia.

"Well, here some of us are, anyhow! My ancient friend, who would have chaperoned you, has gone sick in Casablanca; the others *said* they were staying to succour him, but I think they really wanted a little night-life. So I came on by myself, by the bus."

"What spirit, Angus. Look, this is Mr. Lynch, who's brought me"—the men shook hands, and Paddy ordered drinks—"Beer is very unwholesome in Morocco at sunset; abandon it and have whisky."

"Mr. Reeder's here too," Julia said, as Angus Ross-shire laughed and agreed to whisky.

"What, your nice eavesdropper?"

"Yes, we're all going to dine together on the Djema—you'd better come too."

"Indeed I will, whatever the Djema may be. I need both company and a guide. But what an exquisite place this is."

As they sat talking Steve Keller entered that brightly-coloured hall, and stood staring round at the various groups scattered about it.

"Here!" said Julia, holding up a languid hand; the young man hastened over, and greeted her with a warmth that was innocently obvious.

"How you do get around!" he said, grinning.

"Well yes—I'm seeing Morocco. But you must meet my friends. The Duke of Ross-shire—Mr. Keller, of the American Naval Air Force; and Mr. Lynch, Mr. Keller."

At the first of these introductions a curious expression, compounded of astonishment, embarrassment, and a faint hostility appeared on the ingenuous countenance of the American—Julia saw it.

"Sit down and have a drink, Steve, and talk to the Duke. He was a Pathfinder in the war, though I don't think there were any jets then. Mr. Keller is a jet-fiend, Angus," she said. And in no time at all Mr. Keller, to his amazement, found himself talking with real pleasure to a man who might be that legendary thing, a Duke, but to whom the air was a familiar place, and who possessed a surprising knowledge of technicalities—Julia, with satisfaction, overheard Angus Ross-shire receiving a warm invitation to come and take a look at the base at Meknes.

"Dear Julia, you *said* no boy-friends," Angus murmured in her ear as they stood waiting on the steps while Paddy brought round the car, "but were you being quite candid? What do you call your so delightful mechanical chum?" Julia giggled—"They occur, you know, Angus," she said.

They all dined together at the Café de France, where Reeder awaited them; Steve had borrowed a car from an acquaintance at the Casablanca

base, and came on by himself. Afterwards they all strolled again on the
Djema el F'na. There was a full moon, and the great Koutoubia minaret
—to eyes familiar with the minarets of Turkey, slender as knitting-needles,
so much more like a tower—stood up almost transparent in the moonlight,
in all its immense dignity and beauty. At night, under the naphtha flares,
the tempo of pleasure and entertainment on the great square—the *"place
folle"*, as the French call it—is heightened: the circles round the dancers
are more dense, the grey-bearded performers leap more wildly, while the
metal clappers, the original castanets, rattle like machine-gun fire; the gestures of the story-tellers are more dramatic, the serpents of the snake-
charmers writhe like souls in torment. Public enjoyment for its own sake
here achieves an expression unparalleled elsewhere on earth—it is inde-
scribably stimulating. But it is also exhausting, and presently Julia declared for bed.

Going upstairs Julia said—

"Paddy, it seems *too* silly to waste time going to see that Hortense person again."

"Oh nonsense! Snap out of it, Julia. We've no idea where they'll be
staying, or even if they will stay in Marrakesh at all. You can at least ask
her if Colin will be going to see her."

"As Colin, or as M. Nussbaumer's assistant?"

"Both, I'd say."

"Honestly, I'd rather go to the Saadian Tombs," said Julia.

In fact on the following morning they did go to these before visiting
Hortense, taking Angus Ross-shire with them. The Duke especially was
quite ravished by this exquisite flowering of Hispano-Mauresque architecture: the slender marble columns supporting the high shadowy vaulting
of the roof of carved cedar-wood, whose gilding and delicate colours glowed
richly and dimly in the airy gloom; the lacelike fragility of the incised
plaster-work of the walls, combined with dazzling glazed tiles; and on the
ground the reason for it all—the tombs themselves, of grooved marble,
peaked like a roof and the colour of old ivory, where Ahmed the Golden,
his son, his grandson, and various male and female kinsfolk lie at rest. Julia
was rather disappointed that one no longer, like Edith Wharton, had to
wade through nettles to reach this exquisite place; instead, the Administration has created a neat garden, set with brilliant flowers.

They dropped the Duke off at the Post Office, and then once again took
that complicated set of turnings to the tall house with the medlar-tree;
but Julia absolutely refused to go in alone.

"You *must* come too—I'll say you're my brother."

Hortense—when Julia, fingering the prune-coloured robe again, began to put her questions—was extremely cagey and suspicious.

"Who sent you to me?"

"That I cannot say."

"But I must know *why* you come—*enfin,* I must have some credentials."

Julia, to Paddy's horror, opened her handbag and took out the orange-coloured lump of Astridite.

"There are my credentials," she said.

The woman positively recoiled.

"Put it away! It is dangerous. You are crazy!" She became angry all of a sudden. "And since you come, yesterday, *des mauvais sujets* hang about the place. I do not like it."

Paddy said firmly—"Do not tell me, Mademoiselle, that this is the *first* time your house has been watched." Hortense shifted her ground.

"They took the number of your car—I saw them."

"Yes, so did we," said Julia coolly. "Abdul is always taking car-numbers."

"Ah, you know this man?"

"Yes, damn him!—and I'd like to know why he's taking them here instead of in Fez."

For some reason this remark caused Mademoiselle Hortense to relent slightly—she even smiled a little.

"I also should like to know this, though I fear I can guess; if he had your car-number in Fez he will have traced you here."

"Oh no he won't—not by the number; *that* car has never come nearer to Marrakesh than Port Lyautey."

The blonde woman shrugged her shoulders. "Anyhow you are under suspicion from that quarter—and if I may permit myself the expression, with good reason," she said, with a meaning glance at Julia's handbag.

Julia smiled, slowly.

"Mademoiselle Hortense, I don't want to worry you—I see that it is a bore for you to have us here. Tell me one thing and then we will go, and leave you in peace. Where does M. Nussbaumer eat when he is in Marrakesh?"

"But on the *Place,* naturally."

"In the booths, or at the France?"

"It is uncertain. I think the France, as a rule."

"Thank you very much."

"I told you that would be a waste of time," said Julia as they left.

"Why didn't you ask her where they stay?"

"A., she wouldn't have told me, and B., I wonder very much if they do stay here at all. In their place I should be inclined to blind on to Casa, get

in after dark, park the camionnette with the avaricious but venal M.
Martin, and go and curl up for the night in an outsized coffer chez
Bathyadis."

Paddy laughed.

"Perhaps you have something there. Anyhow it's time *we* ate now—the
others will be waiting." It had been settled the night before that they should
lunch at the Café de France with Reeder, Steve, and the Duke.

"Paddy dear, let's *just* flip round by the Hotel, in case there's a message
from your high-powered acquaintance," said Julia urgently; Mr. Lynch
obediently drove to the Mamounia.

There was in fact a note at the desk for Mademoiselle Probyn; she went
into the hall and sat down to open it. "The Messieurs you seek entered the
city half-an-hour ago," it said, and nothing else, except "12.46 *heures*"
written under the date. Julia folded it up slowly, put it in her handbag,
and went and washed.

"They're here," she said to Paddy as they walked out to the car. "Got in
at 12.15."

Paddy glanced at his watch.

"Ten past one. That's early to eat, by Moroccan hours; still, we'd better
keep an eye open for them at the France."

"Always allowing for those false beards. Damn, if the redhead wears a
wig I'm sunk!"

"We'll take a scout through the bar before we settle down, anyhow," said
Paddy.

Reeder, the Duke and Steve were all in the bar when they arrived. Julia
accepted a drink, and then stood peering round her in that dark smoky
place. It had occurred to her that even with false beards their exceptional
height might give the pair she was looking for away, but she realised immediately that it is not easy to judge the height of a man seated on a bar-
stool. There were eleven people in the bar besides themselves: three young
Moors drinking orange squash, five stumpy elderly Frenchmen, whose little
round pots entirely precluded their being the two she sought, two French
officers in uniform, and the Commandant.

"No beards," Julia muttered to Paddy. "Let's get out of this smog."

Out on the verandah, though the sun poured in, there was a little teasing
breeze; they had two tables pushed together right on the inside and close
up against the glass screen, where it was relatively warm and sheltered,
and sat over another round of drinks while awaiting their lunch. Julia had
carefully seated herself with her back to the screen, facing the door leading
through to the bar, beside which a small French police officer sat sipping a
Pernod—she could thus watch the whole length of the verandah except the

smaller portion behind the glass screen. Just as the *hors d'oeuvres* were being served two tallish men stepped up from the street and began to cross towards the door—one had a scanty and immature black beard, the other a heavy and rather improbable-looking reddish moustache; both wore bérets which practically concealed their hair, and dark glasses, but this time they were so close that even Julia could not be mistaken.

"There they are!—the two in bérets," she murmured to Paddy. "The one with the beard is Colin." She rose as she spoke, and also began to thread her way between the tables towards them. Just as they reached the door she called "Colin!" softly—which caused the Duke, amused and inquisitive, to get up and follow her. The younger man looked round, paused for a second, and then followed his companion into the bar—Julia continued to make her way slowly in that direction between the large forms of the coffee-drinking Moors.

Suddenly there was a bright flash and a loud explosion—Paddy Lynch could never be sure afterwards whether it took place inside the door or out. What he did see, in that first instant, with horror, was that Julia and the Duke both fell. After that all was confusion—French voices within the bar crying "Les Nationalistes! Les Terroristes!", while excited crowds surged across the street from the *place* to see what was going on; there was broken glass everywhere, from the windows and the shattered screen.

Steve was quicker off the mark than either of the others—he fairly shot down the length of the verandah, knocking over Moors and tables impartially; he had reached Julia's prostrate shape and stood pugnaciously over it just in time to prevent her being trodden on in the panic-stricken stampede out of the bar. Mr. Lynch, following him, saw the two tall men in bérets emerge in the wake of this rush, but at a more reasonable pace; the bearded one paused and looked down distressedly at Julia's fallen body —the Irishman noticed that he jerked his right thumb-joint outwards in a sickeningly distorted fashion. But his companion with the red moustache turned and beckoned him on—he followed, and they were instantly engulfed in the swarm of Africans which filled the street. It was impossible to follow them, or even to see which way they went.

A van-full of police arrived almost at once, and with the Commandant began an assessment of damage and casualties; a doctor, summoned by telephone, arrived with commendable promptitude. The *agent de police* who had been sitting at the table by the door was dead; so was a waiter, emerging with a tray of coffees at the instant when the bomb exploded. Julia, who was lifted and laid on the bar, was unconscious, blood pouring from a cut in her big white forehead; the Duke, who had been a little behind her, was able to pick himself up, but sat rather dazed in a chair—

blood was streaming also from a gash in his head from flying glass. The
police began to demand identities—which caused a rapid melting-away of
the indigenous crowd. Paddy during this interrogation happened to glance
round towards their table; he raced back just in time to seize the wrist of
an Arab who had picked up Julia's handbag—the man, he saw, had a wart
on his nose. Furious, Lynch wrenched the bag free, and with his other hand
took a twisted grip of the folds of the man's robe, yelling at the pitch of
his voice to the police—"*Ici!* This is one of them!" Abdul twisted like an
eel, but it is impossible to wriggle *out* of a jellab, with its long sleeves,
and Lynch was very strong; a couple of *agents*, delighted to secure at least
one prisoner after the outrage, seized Abdul and bore him away. The Irishman's one idea now was to get that infernal piece of rock out of the handbag
before the police began looking for papers—turning away, he extracted it
and stowed it in an inner pocket and then returned to the bar.

Here the doctor was taking Julia's pulse and lifting her eyelids—he
diagnosed shock and concussion, while Lynch showed her passport and
fiche to the Commandant. At this point a little French pressman appeared
and also began taking names, by the simple method of looking over the
shoulders of the police while they examined the papers of the casualties.
Steve now cut across officialdom.

"Let's get her hospitalised!" he said. "Isn't Casablanca the best place?—
she said it was good on hospitals. I have a car right here—I can get her in,
fast. This Marrakesh seems a pretty hick town; surely we'd better get her to
Casablanca?"

Paddy Lynch was inclined to agree—"But, Mother of God, there's all
her stuff at the hotel!—she won't want that left after her."

"Well, why don't I drive her in, and you collect her things and bring
them along, when you've done talking to these police guys? She's sick, and
we're wasting time! Give me the *a*ddress, and I'll go."

Both the police and the doctor had by this time got round to the Duke;
the doctor put a temporary dressing on the cut in his head—he had already
done this for Julia—while the little pressman greedily copied down all the
particulars given to the police. Angus, who was coming round gradually,
hearing of Steve's plan said—"I could come along, and hold her head
steady. Perhaps, Lynch, you would be so good as to collect my gear too and
bring it. Oh yes—and pay my bill." He handed a bundle of notes to Paddy.

So Steve fetched his borrowed car and Julia, still unconscious, was placed
along the back seat, her head resting on the Duke's further arm; Mr. Lynch
furnished the address of the appropriate hospital, and the American shot
off in the best film style.

"What about your things?" Paddy shouted to him at the last moment. "I'll be back," the airman shouted in reply.

As sometimes happens, the explosion of that bomb on the Djema el F'na really made more noise in England than in Morocco. Londoners are not so prone to listen to the nine-o'clock news as country-dwellers, since they are usually having dinner, or at the theatre, or attending a "cocktail *prolongé*", so it was poor Mrs. Monro who first heard of it, sitting at Glentoran over her wretched fire with Jimmy Struthers. She was so upset that she tried to ring up Mrs. Hathaway, but that lady was watching a new French film at the Academy Cinema—"Ask her to ring you back," Struthers prompted, and finally did this himself for his agitated employer.

But next morning a selection of banner headlines announced the episode to every breakfast-table or tray in Britain.

"TERRORIST OUTRAGE IN MARRAKESH. TWO BRITISH CASUALTIES" said the sober journals; "SCOTTISH DUKE SERI-OUSLY INJURED—GIRL JOURNALIST NOT EXPECTED TO RECOVER" screamed the more scare-minded prints: in either case, their friends soon learned from the smaller type that both the Duke of Ross-shire and Miss Julia Probyn had been blown up in a restaurant in Marrakesh by a bomb, and rushed to hospital in Casablanca, while two other people (fortunately French) had been killed outright; Miss Probyn had serious injuries to her face.

Ringing up Mrs. Hathaway was a habit with others besides poor Ellen Monro—Edina telephoned before 8.30, asking if she might come in at lunch-time, and was told that she could be given lunch; Mr. Consett, more restrainedly putting his call through from the Treasury at 10, was also bidden to luncheon. They found their hostess very much distressed, though still her usual sensible self.

"What was she doing looking for Colin in Marrakesh? Surely that's right inland," Edina said.

Mrs. Hathaway glanced at Mr. Consett.

"I think she thought he might have gone inland," she said smoothly.

"Was she with that Lynch man, do you suppose?" Consett asked.

"Oh yes—he was taking her to Marrakesh."

"Then he must know something. God, what did I do with his address?"

"I can give it you. But I telegraphed to him this morning to ask for more details."

Edina was turning over the mass of morning papers restlessly, throwing them aside, and jerking her thumb-joint in and out.

"I think I shall go out and see what's happening," she announced suddenly. "After all, she went on our account, and this is pretty rotten for her. One doesn't know what the hospitals are like, or anything."

Mrs. Hathaway looked relieved.

"If you really can get away, that would be splendid," she said. "Geoffrey, can one fly direct to Casablanca?"

Mr. Consett thought B.E.A. to Gibraltar and on would be the best—"Besides, you must have visas for French and Spanish Morocco, and those, as I know to my cost, take ages here, whereas in Tangier you can get them in no time." He added that he had a friend in the Foreign Office who would help to "hurry" the Spanish and International Zone visas.

"All right—I'll go to Tangier. It will take forty-eight hours at least, I suppose, to get all this, and the currency; but I'd better get on to B.E.A. at once. Mrs. H., may I use your telephone?"

"I expect the Consulate General will help you about telephoning to Casablanca even before you get the visas, as Julia is a British subject," said Mrs. Hathaway.

"Yes, and poor Angus Ross-shire too—he's such a sweet. I'd hate him to be badly hurt."

When the Foreign Office tries it can arrange things rather fast, and it was only three days after her sudden decision when Edina set off by air for Tangier. She rang up Mrs. Hathaway triumphantly just before she left.

"I've got my exes! We've thought up an African layout for camel's-hair coats for some rather big clients of ours, and they've jumped at it. It may take some time, so I shan't be rushed, and I can go anywhere."

"That's good. But Edina, be sure to telegraph me the moment you've seen her, and let me know, won't you? And about her face."

"*Dear* Mrs. H., of course I will. What did Paddy Lynch say?"

"Only 'Still in hospital injuries less serious than feared firstly,'" said Mrs. Hathaway, laughing rather weakly.

"What a man! *Firstly!*" said Edina with contempt. "Well I won't cable you in journalese! God bless—and look after poor Mother."

"Oh yes—I've promised to go up to her tomorrow, by the way, so telegraph to Glentoran, please."

In fact if Mr. Lynch had delayed his cable to Mrs. Hathaway for another twenty-four hours he would have been able to send a much more reassuring one. Julia's concussion proved to be slight, and her naturally calm, not to say lethargic nature greatly lessened the effects of the shock; the cut on her forehead, though disfiguring, was not deep enough to require stitches, and was merely strapped up with plaster; on her third day in hospital, when visited by Mr. Lynch, she declared herself "as fit as a flea", and demanded to be taken away. "Dr. Gillebeaud says I can go—wait, let's see if we can get him, if you don't believe me. Go and shout for the nurse."

Dr. Gillebeaud when he appeared showed himself to be helplessly under Julia's spell; he pronounced that yes, if Mademoiselle could have reasonable attention, she might leave.

"You can give me reasonable attention, can't you, Paddy darling? Fatimah is *so* good."

"I shall have to push out either Reeder or Keller— They're both staying with me," said poor Mr. Lynch.

"Well push them out, in God's name! Who's your *old* friend? *Really,* Paddy!"

Keller was pushed out, and Julia returned to her charming ground-floor rooms the same afternoon; Mr. Reeder, whom Paddy rightly judged to be much less flush of foreign cash than the American, remained. The Duke, who had telephoned regularly to the hospital, turned up at the villa almost immediately after Julia's return, to enquire.

"Dear Julia, I would never have believed that anyone could look so lovely with Elastoplast all over her face," he said, kissing her affectionately. "We ought to have you photographed and send a glossy to the advertising Edina; I am sure it would put on sales."

"Well yes, perhaps. How is your scalp, Angus? Oh, lucky you!—only a scalp wound though you seem to be doing quite a bit in the bandage line."

"Yes, my sweet; but under it there are *eight* stitches—and oh the horror of having them tweaked out! I am going back to Tangier for *that* martyrdom; my sickly elderly friend is better, but he is insular enough to put all his faith in the English doctor there. So now that you are better, we shall probably sail tomorrow." He turned to Reeder. "What are your plans? If you are returning to Tangier, would you care to pilot us up?"

Reeder looked towards Julia.

"What are you doing, Miss Probyn? Staying here? If you are going back to Tangier I don't think you ought to travel alone."

"Oh thank you so much, but Steve is going to drive me back to Tangier when I go, the kind creature."

"Then, thank you very much, I should like to come up with you on the yacht," said Reeder to the Duke. "In fact I believe I could take any ship into Tangier harbour blindfold!"

"You'd better come on board with me tonight, then, so that we can sail tomorrow at the hour which the tide, or the moon, or the pilot, or whatever it is dictates," said Angus Ross-shire.

When they had left—

"I don't suppose it will be a ha'porth of use going to see young Bathyadis again, do you?" said Julia.

"No, quite futile. Besides, now that they've gone, I have a bit to tell you. The police are letting it be believed that terrorists threw the bomb, but I think they have a pretty fair idea of what lay behind this particular one."

"Do you mean thrown who *by*, or who *at?*" Julia asked ungrammatically.

"Both. I didn't tell you in the hospital, with all those nurses dodging in and out, but I copped Abdul trying to pinch your bag, and handed him over."

"Goodness, did I leave my bag?"

"Yes, you foolish creature!—and I had to do a nice bit of sleight of hand to get that infernal piece of rock out of it and into my pocket before the police examined your papers. But they grilled Abdul pretty thoroughly, I gather from my friend here, and learned that he was employed by we-know-whom."

"You mean the East Germans?"

"Of course. But Abdul, in a very natural fit of pique—no one *enjoys* being grilled by the French police—seems to have made it abundantly clear to them that others besides his employers were probably exporting strategic minerals without concessions, and that it was the people in this organisation that the Germans were gunning for."

"In fact Colin and the redhaired man?"

"Yes, presumably."

"What did they have to say about that?"

"Not much. The French are always pretty cagey, and out here they've got to be nearly as mute as the Arabs. But unless the British have some top-secret agreement somewhere else, I'm beginning to wonder how much longer the velvet-trunk industry will last."

Julia frowned in thought, as well as she could for the elastoplast.

"It *must* be official, or why the B. of E.?" she said at last. "But it's all rather funny. Anyhow as far as we are concerned I think the only thing now is to watch the *Finetta*—don't you?"

"Yes—and that house in the Kasbah."

"Of course. Well the day after tomorrow, Paddy dear, I think I'd better get Steve to drive me back to Tangier."

"Sure you're fit for it? It's about six hours' run, you know."

"Oh I think so. I do really want to be on the spot, in case they turn up. Maybe Purcell could arrange to have that house in the Kasbah watched for me—I wouldn't put it past him! And I want to go out and see what the Professor has dug up in those graves, if anything."

"You're completely mad, Julia, God help you!" said Mr. Lynch, laughing.

"Well I should think you'd be glad to be quit of me and my chums, flooding your house out! I hope you realise what an angel you've been."

"I like all your chums—the Duke best perhaps, but Reeder's a grand man, and your poor besotted Yank slave is uncommonly nice too. What'll you do about him?"

"Oh, the soft rub-off that turneth away wrath. I thought the drive would be a good opportunity to get that over with."

"May the Lord have mercy on you for a cold-blooded creature! However, I suppose practice makes perfect."

"That's about it," said Julia equably. "But oh Paddy dear, isn't it *sickening* to have missed even speaking to Colin, when he was within *feet* of us, and we'd been so clever?"

CHAPTER XV

IN FACT the long drive from Casablanca to Tangier, plus the anticipated emotional interlude with poor Steve *en route*, tired Julia more than she had expected. The urgent simplicity and sincerity of the American made the soft rub-off not so easy to administer—Julia, the cool and composed, found herself in tears before she could convince him that she would not marry without love, and that she did not love him "in that way". She was too shaken and exhausted when she arrived at the Espagnola to think of going to Purcell's; all she craved was her bed, where she ordered supper to be served. But to her dismayed surprise she found herself a heroine and a centre of interest; the manager wrung her by the hand, praising God for her preservation; the other occupants of the pension crowded round, full of eager questions—Julia escaped to the manager's office, whence she rang up Mme La Besse.

"Ah *dieu merci* that you are back!—what an escape! I will ring up Lady Tracy at once; she has been in anguish about you—as we all have. But I must tell you that we have found an *intact* grave!—at last! We only began on it today, and the Professor guards it tonight."

"How splendid. Shall I come out tomorrow?"

"But yes, if you are able. *Chère enfant,* how glad I am that you are safe! Now I ring Lady Tracy."

Julia was doing a little hasty unpacking when she was summoned to the telephone again—this time it was Lady Tracy.

"Oh my dear child, I won't keep you a moment, I'm sure you ought to be in bed, if not in hospital! But I did just want to hear your voice! How merciful that you were not killed, like that poor French policeman, and the Arab waiter—imagine, he was a cousin of 'Abdeslem's."

Julia, rather faintly, made some suitable response, and asked how Lady Tracy was.

"Oh, quite as well as I need to be. And *Hugh* is back—he arrived today; he says the flowers were marvellous further South. When you are up to it you must come and meet him—in fact I think I shall arrange a small sherry-party."

Julia said that would be lovely, and as soon as she could rang off. It amused her that in spite of their genuine pleasure at her safe return, both her elderly friends felt constrained to tell her about their own concerns, of which the grave interested her much more than the advent of Hugh.

In the hall the manager confronted her with a neat little man who implored "but two small minutes" with Mademoiselle, a reporter from the *Mensonge de Tanger*—behind him loomed a tall individual with a slight air of habitual inebriation, who said he represented *World Press*. Julia protested.

"No, *really*, Señor Huerta; I'm too tired. They must go away. I'm sorry, but I won't see *anyone*. Is that understood?" Indignant, she went upstairs.

As she was eating her supper in bed, eagerly fussed over by Natividad, the chambermaid, the porter came up to say that a Señorita below wished to see the Señorita, urgently. Damning all journalists Julia told him that she would see *no one*, and to say that she was away. She made Natividad lock the door for good measure till she had finished her supper; when the maid went out with the tray she slipped in again after a moment with a bunch of flowers, a mixed posy of the sort made by Julia's Berber flower-woman; on the card was written—

> *"Très respectueusement*
> J. Purcell."

"Heaven Purcell!" Julia muttered as she closed her eyes.

She woke after thirteen hours of the solid sleep of youth feeling perfectly refreshed, and went round to Mme La Besse in time to drive her out to the site; there she hastened up to see the new grave. It was some distance down the slope of the ridge on the farther side, above the lagoon, and Julia's first glance as she topped the rise was for the *Finetta*. Yes, there she lay—but no washing fluttered from her rigging, the cooking apparatus had disappeared from her deck, and the two Arabs were swabbing her paint-work vigorously. Ah!—Mr. Smith had presumably returned, or at least was expected. She must see Purcell tonight and try to fix something about having the house in the Kasbah watched, she thought, as she descended the slope to where Professor Carnforth, rather bleary-eyed, was directing the Berbers' operations—a sleeping-bag and a thermos lay under a rock. Julia had bethought her to bring her own thermos with fresh coffee and some buttered rolls from the Espagnola; the weary man sat down and consumed these gratefully while Julia peered into the partly excavated chamber. In a wall-niche on the left the end of one coffin was already exposed; it appeared to be covered with Egyptian hieroglyphics, and Julia went out into the sun again to ask about this. The Professor expounded, between mouthfuls of *croissant:* yes, certainly; the Phoenicians constantly used Egyptian coffins, which they purchased ready-made—there was a continual passage of vessels to and fro along the whole coast, and what easier than for a quinquereme, coming in ballast to pick up a cargo of wine, oil, and pickled fish at the factory, to bring down a score or so of coffins from the Nile Delta?

They made good progress that day. Three more coffins were quite literally un-earthed, but by the afternoon the Professor was yawning so pitifully that Julia volunteered to take that night's watch. The grave was just at the stage when it would be most tempting to the local Berbers, and Mme La Besse, who had often slept in partly excavated graves in her time, told the Professor that if the old Spanish foreman stayed with her Miss Probyn would be quite all right—he might not resist Berber bribes alone, but he would certainly guard her faithfully. "He can sleep in that empty grave a few yards away, and she can shout to him in need." So it was settled that Julia should take Mme La Besse home early, get a few hours' sleep, and drive out to relieve the Professor at eleven.

This suited Julia perfectly. After dropping Mme La Besse she parked the Chrysler outside the Espagnola, ran swiftly down the familiar route through the Gran Socco and the Medina, and walked into Purcell's Bar—there, at her old table, sat the Duke, Reeder, and Edina.

"Here she is, herself!" Angus Ross-shire exclaimed, rising. "So you've got her at last, Edina."

Edina had risen too, and rather to Julia's surprise kissed her warmly.

"I was beginning to think you'd been kidnapped as well as bombed," she said—"I couldn't find you anywhere."

"But Edina, whatever next? When did you turn up, and why?"

"When, yesterday morning—usual plane hold-up at Gib. Why, to look after you—the papers practically had you dead, and everyone was mad with worry; all our fault too, of course. But you don't look too bad," Edina said, staring rather anxiously at Julia. "Will it show?"

"Far from looking bad, a photograph of her as an ad: for Elastoplast, we thought," said Angus, who had an affection for his own jokes. "Whisky, Julia? Now you're no longer concussed, alk can do no harm."

"Yes, thank you, Angus. But Edina, why couldn't you find me? I'm at the Espagnola."

"My dear Julia, you're *not!* I've been there over and over again, and either you hadn't come, or you'd gone again. I know my French isn't much good, but that manager's is worse! "She has not come"; "she has come, but she has gone"; "she is gone again"—the place is a perfect looney-bin!" said Edina indignantly. Mr. Reeder laughed.

"All very well for you!" Edina said to him, in a tone which rather startled Julia—it was the tart casual note of reproof usually reserved for one's intimates. "And Casablanca was just as bad," she pursued, turning to her cousin again. "I try your chum Lynch—he's at the Bank; by the time I've found out *what* Bank, he's gone to lunch! When I get him after his wretched lunch, he says you've left for the Espagnola! Well I've told you how useful *that* was."

Julia, sipping whisky, laughed rather weakly. A little checking of times made what had happened clear. Edina had first called at the Espagnola just half-an-hour before she and Steve arrived; the second time she, Julia, had refused to see her, thinking that she was a reporter. And today she had been out at the site, when Edina, twice, went again. "Just a second," Julia said when this had finally been elucidated—she left them, went over to the bar, and held out her hand across it to Purcell.

"Thank you for the flowers, very much," she said.

"You are really all right? This will not be too disfiguring?" the half-caste asked, like Edina with an anxious glance at her forehead.

"Usen't women to marry German officers for their duelling scars?" Julia said. "Please don't worry, Mr. Purcell."

"I warned you that it would be speculative, but I never thought anything like this would happen," he said ruefully—then he leant across the bar and lowered his voice. "Did you see him?"

"Not to speak to—the bomb interrupted us! But I have an idea that they'll soon come here—could you keep tabs on that house in the Kasbah for me?"

"Oh, they are back—they arrived yesterday."

"Well look, now I *must* see him"—Julia was beginning, when Angus Ross-shire's arm was slung round her shoulder.

"Precious Julia, come back and drink. And Mr. Purcell, to whom you so naturally want to talk, must for once break all his rules and join us. Purcell, you can't refuse to drink Miss Probyn's health."

Purcell did not refuse. There was no one else in the bar, and he sat with them, saying little but smiling quietly, while Edina expounded to Julia her secondary concern with camel's hair, and hence with camels.

"Oh, for camels you must go to Settat—it's full of them." She explained where Settat was, and Edina said that she should hire a car and drive there from Casablanca—"The sky, thank God, is the limit, where expenses are concerned."

"In that case do go on to Marrakesh—it's so beautiful."

"My *dear* Julia!—and have her blown up too? What a notion!"

"I don't think Edina will be blown up, Angus," said Julia, slanting a glance at Purcell, who gleamed at her in response.

"I remember saying, at this very table, that we should all pile up in Marrakesh, but not, I hoped, be wrecked," said the Duke. "In fact you and I, Julia, damn nearly did pile up there for good."

The cheerful inconsequent talk went on, but Julia noticed presently that Edina and Mr. Reeder returned to what was apparently an unfinished conversation about sheep, marginal land, hill-cattle subsidies, and similar highly technical subjects, while the Duke and Purcell discussed what forms of drink paid best in bars. When other customers, including the bunch, came in Purcell had to leave the party, and Reeder startled Julia by asking them all to dine with him at the Minzah "to celebrate". The Minzah is Tangier's most expensive hotel, and as they walked there through the picturesque crowds and the vivid lamp-lit evening, in twos—Edina and Reeder, Julia and Angus Ross-shire—Julia expressed slight misgivings at this extravagance on the part of the *Vidago's* mate.

"Oh, don't worry about that. I found out about him on the way up. He's one of the Northumberland Reeders; they have a most lovely place in the Cheviots. He took to the sea, I gather, because he can't get on with his father; no wonder, I met him once, and he's a most cantankerous old party. There's an elder brother who'll come into the property, but a remote aunt of Mollie's married one of them, and left all she had to this man—it all came back to me afterwards. He can afford to feed us on caviare, if he wants to! But he's a most splendid fellow—Edina will be lucky indeed if she gets him."

Julia was startled a second time.

"Goodness, do you think there's any question of that?"

"Well, watch them. I should say Yes. They haven't done badly in forty-eight hours."

"How did they meet?"

"She was in Purcell's when Reeder and I went in the morning we arrived."

Julia did watch the pair during dinner—at which in fact they were given caviare—and decided that Angus, sharp old thing, was not so far out. She recalled the mate's interest in Edina, and his questions about her, on board the *Vidago*; in particular what he had said when she told him that her cousin was black-haired and slender—"If I meet her, I'm sunk!" It was plain that Mr. Reeder, if not actually sinking, had already taken a heavy list.

It was easy to escape early from the party on the score of fatigue. The Duke drove her to the Espagnola, where she collected her duffle-coat, torch, a thermos of coffee and some food and wine; at the last moment she snatched a pillow off her bed, threw the lot into the Chrysler, and roared off into the Moroccan night.

The Spanish foreman rose stiffly out of the shadows by the shed at the site, and helped to carry her effects up onto the headland. By night it was a strange, out-of-this-world place: the waning moon cast strong shadows from those fantastic rocks onto the white sand, making it hard to recognise the now familiar way up, and on the further slope they had considerable difficulty in finding the right grave—Julia finally stood and shouted "Professor *Carn*forth," till he emerged and led them to the spot. He then went off; the old foreman crept into a neighbouring tomb, and Julia proceeded to arrange her effects in the one just vacated by the Professor. It amused her to wedge her cup and thermos into one of the coffin-niches, opening like oven-mouths along the walls; indeed the tomb was altogether the strangest sleeping-place imaginable. The light from her torch, propped on the floor, showed the outlines of the sloping slabs of the roof and the dressed stones of the walls through the pale stucco, clean and fresh in the upper part of the small chamber as when it was put on nearly two thousand years before, while in their dark niches along the sides the Phoenician dead lay quiet all round her. She put her pillow at the head of the Professor's sleeping-bag, still comfortably warm from his tenancy and then went and sat outside to smoke a last cigarette. It was perfectly still, and not in the least cold; a faint rumble of snoring indicated old Fernando's resting-place, but otherwise, except for the distant roar of the Atlantic on the sand-bar there was not a sound; below her the lagoon gleamed like dull metal between its dark shores. Hullo, there were lights on the *Finetta*, whose white shape just showed away to her left; the port-holes were not lit up, but small lights moved about her decks, as from torches or lanterns. How tricky the moonlight was!—Julia would have sworn that the yacht was lying closer inshore than yesterday, but in that deceptive illumination it was impossible to be sure. Promising herself to look out often during the night, in case Mr. Smith was up to some funny-business, she turned in, snuggling down in the Professor's flea-bag among corpses nearly two thousand years old.

She had not meant to sleep, but she did. She was awakened by a small noise quite close by; cocking an ear, she decided that it was at the entrance to the tomb. Silently, a little frightened, she groped for her torch, turned it towards the doorway, and switched on. The sharp white light revealed a figure in Berber dress, on all fours at the foot of the short flight of steps; but it was an English voice that ejaculated sharply—"Good God! Who's that?" Under the hood the face was that of Colin, now without his Low beard.

"It's Julia," said Julia calmly, lowering the blinding light a little. "Don't you think you might come in and have a talk, Colin, since you *are* here? I've been looking for you for a long time."

"I know you have, and a nice mess-up you've made of things," the young man growled. "Anyhow, what the devil are you doing here at this time of night?"

"Guarding this tomb from marauding Berbers, like you," said Julia, with a giggle.

Perhaps it was the slow gurgling sound of Julia's giggle, an infectious source of amusement from his earliest childhood, that caused Colin to relax his hostile attitude—anyhow he crawled further in, sat down with his back against the wall, and said—"Why guarding?"

"Tomb's half-excavated—probably that coffin behind your head is full of gold jewellery."

Colin grunted.

"Are you all right?" he asked. "I thought you'd still be in hospital."

"Not too bad—poor face a bit the worse for wear."

"Let's see." Julia turned the torch onto her forehead.

"Golly, that's big," the young man said, leaning across and fingering the long line of plaster—the intimacy of the gesture, and the simplicity with which he made it, carried Julia straight back to Glentoran, and the long happy days there, with Colin, always Colin, as her inseparable and dearest companion. "Will it show permanently?" he asked—like everyone else, Julia reflected.

"'Fraid so. But I don't much mind."

"I *hated* having to go off and leave you on the ground like that," he said unexpectedly. "I didn't even know if you were dead or not. But we simply had to get away at once. Who was that Yank who stood guard over you?"

"Oh, a *frightfully* nice creature called Steve Keller—I mean, I never saw him keeping guard, but he was the only Yank about, so it must have been him."

"*How* nice? Nice enough to marry?" Again Colin Monro's words were unexpected, and his eyes were fixed on her face, in the rather dim glow from the torch, now lying on the earthen floor.

"No—I refused him yesterday." As she spoke Julia felt about among the pile of provisions beside the sleeping-bag for the bottle of wine.

"What about a little drink?" she said, holding it out. "I've got eats too, if you'd like some. Frankly, I'm hungry."

"Greedy, you mean!—you always were greedy, Julia. Yes, we might as well have a mouthful—I'm pretty peckish too. But I mustn't stay long."

Julia produced buttered rolls and slices of her favourite raw ham; the wine they drank from her cup, in turns. It was a happy little meal, eaten in those highly peculiar surroundings; the past came flooding back—other meals they had eaten together, in caves along a Highland shore, or in ruined houses to get out of the wind when out after black-game in January: "Do you remember?" they said to one another. Julia had a curious feeling that Colin was perhaps clinging to the past to avoid the difficulties of the present; but at last he asked—"How has that new salmon-pool on the Toran worked out, that we made just before I came away? Did the logs hold?"

"Oh yes, and the gravel piled up against them splendidly; Uncle John got no end of fish there the last two years." She paused, and then said— "You know he's dead?"

"Of course I know—I see the papers," he said, half sulkily.

"Well, *can* you come home, Colin? That's what I've been trying to get near enough to you to ask for the last two months! Someone's *got* to run it—you can't let Glentoran just go down the drain, and you know Aunt Ellen simply isn't able."

"Why can't Edina do it?"

"Because she's earning £1500 a year, and they need that money—she makes your mother an allowance!"

"Fifteen hundred! Good God! What at?"

"Advertising. And her screw's going up to £2000 this summer, with any luck."

Colin whistled at the figure.

"Two thousand a year for *advertising!*" he said. "Edina always was a great apostle of the phoney."

"That's not fair—she isn't," said Julia hotly. "You're just being a jealous beast, Colin, as you often—not always—were. Anyhow, *can* you come home?" she persisted.

Colin began to jerk his thumb in and out.

"I'm simply not sure," he said. "In the ordinary way this job would have gone on for quite a time, but you've managed to stir up so much dust that we may have to chuck it."

"Whatever dust have *I* stirred up?"

"What haven't you, you mean! First diddling old Bathyadis into spilling the beans to you—though I gather that was mostly St John's fault, silly old man; he really is too old for this job now, only he's so damned good with the Arabs. But what was much worse was your goings-on in Casa and Marrakesh. Affaires Indigènes aren't *quite* blind, and when two foreigners start displaying so much interest in the *camionnette*, they naturally did a bit of checking-up on their own account."

"Did they tie in Monsieur Smith with Herr Nussbaumer from Martin at the garage?" Julia asked, beginning to gurgle again.

"Goodness, *that* was how you found out, was it?" he asked, startled. "But how did you get onto the name of Smith?"

"Seeing the *Finetta* in the lagoon here, when we were digging—so I went and asked Lloyd's man what name she was registered in."

"You infernal diggers!" he growled. "But I still don't see how you traced the car."

Julia explained about Moshe, and the capture of his note-book—"but it cost 20,000 francs to get the number of the *camionnette* out of Martin. I hope Affaires Indigènes got it for less."

"You bet they got it for nothing! But Julia, don't you see that your Jew tailer will have tipped off the lot he was working for that you'd got his book? So you can bet they kept an eye on you both in Casablanca and Marrakesh, and knew you'd gone to the Bureau in both places."

"I see that all right, but—so what?"

"So a bomb, silly! Tried to mop us up before we could be hauled in and spill what we knew about *them*, as they knew we damn well would, of course, if we got into trouble ourselves."

"But Colin"—Julia was trying, not very successfully, to keep all this straight. "Is what you and 'Smith' are doing legal or illegal?" she asked bluntly.

"Illegal here, of course, but perfectly legal in Paris, because—" he broke off.

"But how—?" Julia was beginning, but he interrupted her.

"Leave all that, would you mind? Forget I said it."

"Oh very well." She reflected for a moment while she got out a cigarette, and handed her case to Colin, who took one eagerly. "More wine?"—she held out the bottle again. As they drank in turns—

"You don't half do yourself well, Julia!" the young man said, with an impish grin. "Still the same old greedy-gub, luckily for me! But tell me, why are you mixed up in this archaeological racket?"

"My dear Colin, I had to *live* while I was hanging about after you, so tiresomely elusive!—so I took a job as secretary to an archaeologist."

"Oh, the old La Besse. Well I must say she has a *toupet,* to make you come and sleep in her tombs!"

"She didn't—I offered. But come to that, Colin, what are *you* doing, creeping into our tombs in fancy dress?"

"You mind your own business!" he grumbled, with a return to his familiar youthful surliness when in a difficulty. Julia had smoothed this over a hundred times; now she poured him out a cup of coffee, and as he drank—

"I bet I know!" she said gleefully. "You've got masses of velvet trunks full of Astridite hidden in tombs on this slope, all ready to go on board the yacht, and you just happened to hit the wrong tomb. What sucks for you!"

"Julia, I shall slap you in a minute!"

"No no—don't slap Julia, fresh from the jaws of death! But aren't I right?"

"Damn you, yes, as a matter of fact. I remember I never thought you as stupid as everyone else did, even as a child," he said reflectively—"you always had a way of hopping onto things. Remember the time you spotted the rifle of those deer-poachers, and got Andy Mac to take the contact-breaker out of the distributor of their car, so they couldn't get away?" He laughed and thumped her knee.

"Yes, of course. So you *have* got some stuff here? What a joke!"

"Well, we had to bring the last lot here—we've had to pass up young Bathyadis, with all this fuss. His place is almost certainly being watched." The young man explained how Mr. St John had managed to get word to them down in the South, through trustworthy Arab channels, that Julia was not only on their track, but had also met young Bathyadis; but this information reached them too late to prevent the despatch of a camel-convoy to Casablanca with two-thirds of the fruits of that period of digging.

"Oh, that was the caravan we met in the Djebelet," Julia interrupted blithely. "So handy—a trunk fell off and burst."

"I know it did," the young man said wryly. "You've had the devil's own luck, all along, Julia."

"Well, you silly, it's all your own fault. Why couldn't you at least answer letters, and all those ads? Then no one would have come chasing you."

"In our show we aren't supposed to give our whereabouts away," Colin said, rather pompously.

"And what may 'our show' be? One of these Protean forms of the Secret Service, I suppose, since the Bank of England backs you up."

"Julia, you are a devil! What do you know about the Bank of England?"

"Oh, one has one's contacts," said Julia, airing her favourite tease-phrase. "Never mind, I'll forget that too if you want me to," she added hastily, as he seized her wrist with some violence. "Ow! Don't hurt me, Colin—that's your old nasty trick. Anyhow, how do you get the trunks aboard through all those reed-beds?"

"In the dinghy. There's a good firm track on the east of this ridge that a jeep can come up, and we man-handle the stuff up and into the tombs one night, and get it on board the next."

"And where do you take it when it's on board?"

"Out to sea, where we meet a boat, and trans-ship. But you'd better forget that, too," he said hurriedly.

"Oh, I'll forget anything you like. Who sails the *Finetta* on these jaunts?"

"*Me*. I'm the master now," Colin said, with rather touching pride. "Isn't she a lovely boat, Julia? Very different to the poor old *Thomasina!* Do you remember how you piled her up on Gigha?"

"I *didn't!* You were steering!" said Julia indignantly. "At least, you were holding my arm."

At that, laughing, the young man leant over and held her arm again. "Oh Julia, what fun we've had!"

"Yes, heavenly fun—and please God we'll have more, Colin dear."

At that he edged up the tomb, wriggled in beside her, and sliding an arm round her waist rubbed his cheek against hers, confidingly.

"It's good to see you," he said. "Such a long time away. Julia—" he stopped.

"Yes?"

"Don't you see that one reason why I didn't answer the letters was all that absolute *beastliness* about Grove? I couldn't know how you'd all feel about that. But none of us but him knew a thing about it—I *swear* that."

"Nor did any of us know a thing about it—it never got into the English papers at all."

"Didn't it? How extraordinary. Oh well, I suppose Torrens must have fixed that."

"So *that's* the name that begins with Tor! Good-oh—another point cleared up," said Julia with satisfaction. "He's your boss, is he?"

"Well, he was starting to work up this show out here just about the time that Grove got copped; we others were pretty fed up with smuggling, with *that* label tied on to us, and didn't know what on earth to do with the boat —I had a third share in her, of course. But he thought it might be handy to have a yacht for just this sort of job, with someone who could sail her, and knew the coast, so he bought us out and re-registered her. *How* he got onto me I really can't think, for we were lying pretty doggo."

"Purcell, I should imagine," said Julia.

He turned to stare at her.

"I believe you're right. I never thought of that." He paused. "But how do *you* know Purcell?"

"Oh, just a regular client. It's the nicest bar in Tangier."

"That isn't why you suggested what you did," he said suspiciously. "Nice bars aren't the same thing as—well, contacts."

"Aren't they? I should have thought they made the very best kind of contact," said Julia. "Anyhow, I contacted Edina there this evening."

"Edina? What on earth is *she* doing out here?"

"She flew out to see how I was. Some people quite minded my nearly being killed."

"Julia, don't be idiotic! I told you I hated having to leave you there on the floor. What do you think I should have done?"

"Socked Mr. B. Torrens one over the head and told him to go to hell, and then succoured me," said Julia readily.

"Nonsense! Angus Ross-shire was there to succour you, I saw him—and your Yank. You had plenty of succour, and I had a job to finish. So put a sock in it," the young man said firmly.

Julia was pleased; this stout-heartedness was new in Colin, who used to be unduly nervous and sensitive. She was all the more touched when he pulled her to him and kissed her lightly on the cheek. "Oh darling, there never was anyone like you, for all your monstrousness—and there never will be," he murmured in her ear. Then, in the manner of men, he let her go, reached for the torch, and looked at his watch. "God! It's half-past one! I must go. I wonder where the devil those other tombs can be, with the stuff in."

"I bet you I can find them—there are three or four half-right from this, a bit downhill; but don't make a noise, because of Fernando."

"Who the devil is he?"

"The foreman at the site—my watch-dog! He's asleep in a tomb a bit above this."

"Damnation! He's bound to hear my chaps."

"I tell you what—when we've found the place I'll go up and sit outside his cubby-hole, and if he does hear anything I'll tell him it's me, and keep him occupied. Come on."

They crept out—Julia led the way downhill and to the right, where sure enough the light of her torch presently revealed, in three tombs, the rich gleam of velvet studded with silver, stowed in the niches intended for dead Phoenicians. She began to laugh softly.

"What is it?"

"The whole thing. It's so funny. Never mind—cancel laugh! How do you summon your merry men?"

"Whistle," said Colin, putting two fingers to his lips. She snatched his hand away.

"You can't do that, idiot—or not till I've fixed Fernando; but whatever I do he'll hear a whistle. Try my torch—press the button and flash it."

The young man did so, and an answering wink of light presently appeared below them.

"That seems all right—I expect they'll come up. Now you buzz off and muzzle your infernal watch-dog."

"Yes but how do I see you again? There's masses more to talk about. When do you get back from your cruise?"

"This evening, probably. Where are you staying?"

"The Espagnola."

"Oh I know. Is Edina there too? I'm not all that keen on seeing her just yet, till I know more where we are."

"No, she's at the Minzah—on expense account!"

"God Almighty, what a girl! Well look, J. dear, I'll come round and see you."

"I'll be at the site all day—I'm a wage-slave! But I can be in after supper. No I can't—I'm dining with Angus on the yacht tonight. Oh dear, what can we do?"

"Wait till tomorrow night. I'll leave word with Purcell, one way or the other—how's that?"

"Fine." As she spoke a sound of feet was audible on the slope close below them.

"Here they come! Breeze off!" said Colin hastily.

Julia moved away uphill, and sat down outside Fernando's gîte. A thin veil of cloud was obscuring the moon, but she could just distinguish figures with objects on their shoulders moving down towards the lagoon, and then she heard the splash of oars. Fernando's snores came steadily and undisturbed to her where she sat, and continued to do so while again, and yet again, shadowy figures crept up the slope, and descended it bowed under gleaming burdens. She sat there, happy, quiet—still moved and warmed by the recent presence of Colin, and his evident affection; darling creature, he hadn't changed a bit!—or only for the better. She waited till she saw port and starboard lights run up on the *Finetta*'s rigging, and heard the groan of the winch and the rattle of the chain as the anchor came up; then she went back to her tomb, crept into the Professor's flea-bag, and went to sleep. When she woke in the morning the lagoon was empty.

JULIA SLEPT so well in her tomb—"Like the dead, really," she observed to Professor Carnforth when following her example he came up to her with coffee and rolls—that on hearing that he proposed to open one of the coffins on the spot that afternoon she insisted on returning to the site then, perfectly refreshed after a bath, a couple of hours snoozing, and lunch. By the time she arrived the coffin had been brought down to the shed; Carnforth, ingenious man, had purchased a hammock from one of the ships' chandlers in the port, in which it could be slung down the steep slope between the rocks without injury. It now lay on an improvised table in the little courtyard, and Mme La Besse, Julia and Fernando crowded round, seething with curiosity and pressed from behind by all eight Berbers, who breathed heavily down their necks, as the lid was raised. Carnforth, who was experienced as well as ingenious, had arranged with the archaeological section of the Administration to have two *sergents de ville* of the Zone Police sent out, whom he posted himself at the tomb to mount guard while he was busy with the coffin, lest the well-informed local villagers should attempt a daylight raid. "No one came near you last night?" he had asked Julia when he went up to relieve her. "Not a soul," she told him blandly.

The "funerary furniture", as archaeologists call it, fully came up to Julia's ignorant but eager expectations as the Professor, with infinite care, lifted out object after object and laid them on cotton-wool in a large cardboard dressbox. Two small terra-cotta figurines of deities—one was Ashtaroth, serpent-entwined. A tiny amulet, to ward off evil spirits; a hand-mirror with an exquisite design on the back; a minute delicate cosmetic-box. "Poor love, she used rouge," Julia said, turning it in her hands and noting the faint trace of colour within. At last came the jewellery. Clearly the dust within this coffin was that of a woman, for out came a pair of ear-rings, crescent moons hung on slender chains; a fine gold bracelet, to fit the narrowest of wrists; a couple of rings. Finally, after much blowing into the coffin, and soft sweepings with an old shaving-brush, the Professor lifted out a magnificent necklace.

"Mon Dieu!" exclaimed Mme La Besse. "That was worth the trouble!"

"Do let me try it on," said Julia, opening her flap-jack and propping it against the coffin-lid; she held the jewel round her own throat and peered into the tiny mirror. "Suit me a treat," she said. The Professor laughed.

He decided that all the remaining coffins should be taken back to Tangier that same afternoon, and placed in safety in the Museum. The hammock was called into play again to bring them down, and Julia, accompanied by one of the police sergeants, was kept busy driving the Chrysler in and out with these unwonted passengers, dead Phoenicians, in the back. She tore to and fro at a shameless pace, with dinner on the *Frivolity* in view; besides if possible she wanted a word with Purcell—the rendezvous was to be at the Bar. In the end she had no time to change—clean stockings, fresh sandals, a hurried wash and face-do, and she spun off in a taxi.

Only Purcell was there. "Beaten them to it, thank goodness!" she exclaimed, dropping into a chair.

"You look exhausted," the man said. "I think you should have a whisky."

"Yes, I will. Thank you. But let him get it"—she said, as the new Moor appeared. "I want to speak to you."

Purcell at once came to her table.

"I've seen him!" she said, her face alight.

"Excellent. Where?"

"In a tomb!" she brought out triumphantly. But the gleam in the half-caste's face told its own story. "Oh, you know that too! There's no surprising you," she said, with a *moue*.

"Indeed I am surprised, for how in the world came *you* there, at such an hour?"

"Oh, I was guarding one of our tombs, full of lovely coffins, and he came in by mistake."

"This was rather imprudent, if you will forgive me for saying so—you should surely have been in bed, after your accident."

"No, I slept very well, except while he was there. Oh, such jewellery!—we opened one of the coffins this afternoon."

Purcell ignored the coffins.

"Did you meet the other?"

"Cold-blooded fish Torrens? No, and I don't want to!"

"He is very nice," the half-caste said, smiling.

Julia in her turn ignored this statement.

"Listen, dear Mr. Purcell—tell me something quickly, before the others come. It *was* you who put him onto Colin, after all the stink about Grove, wasn't it?"

"Did your cousin tell you this?" Purcell asked.

"No—I told him! But it's true, isn't it?"

"Yes, it is true."

She looked at him in silence for a moment. Then—

"Well look—now that the whole thing seems to be in process of being broken wide open, can't you indulge me a little, and tell me just *where* you come in?"

He gave one of his rare laughs.

"Since you will quite certainly find it out for yourself if I don't, yes, I will. I have for a considerable time—shall we say acted in concert with?—the British Intelligence people. After all, I am a British subject."

"Really?"

"Yes. I was born in Edinburgh—or rather Leith. And when that most disagreeable character Grove got caught I was sorry for the other three boys, who were perfectly innocent; I guessed most of their capital was in their boat, but the ill-repute round her name made her unusable for ordinary harmless smuggling."

"Was Grove in her from the start?" Julia asked.

"No, he only joined them about two years ago—tools ready to his dirty hand!" Purcell said bitterly—"He bought out one of the others, who was short of cash, and re-registered the yacht in his own name; then he started picking up drugs here or in Ceuta and ran them to Marseilles, where he was spotted somehow—and Interpol and the local Sûreté got to work. He was caught here. But I knew that Major Torrens was starting this new enterprise just then, and was on the look-out for a boat, and someone to sail her who knew the coast; your cousin was far the most competent of the lot, so I recommended him. He's a born sailor."

"How did you know that?" the girl asked.

"I was born in a port, and I have been at sea myself; I heard them talking—and also I made enquiries. That is how it happened, Miss Probyn." He paused, and suddenly laughed again.

"What's funny?" Julia enquired.

"Well, when this was arranged, it was necessary to cause all three of them to disappear rather suddenly. The Major had the other two shipped home, but the Sûreté here, which is headed by an Englishman, are still looking for 'ce jeune brigand Monro', while in fact he is in the pay of the British Government."

Julia's laughter at this revelation was still resounding through the bar when the door opened to admit the Duke, Edina and Mr. Reeder—it was so loud and hearty that it startled them.

"Goodness, Julia, what is it?" Edina asked.

"Mr. Purcell was telling me a funny story," said Julia, dabbing at her eyes. "Angus, I do apologise for not having changed, but I was terrified of being late."

"What have you been doing to make you late, beautiful and dear Julia?"

"Chauffeuring the dead."

"My dear child, what can you mean?" Angus asked.

"Yes, literally. Phoenician corpses. I've brought in six; the dust of ages is in my hair."

"It suits it," said Angus, kissing the top of her head. "Everything suits you—even plaster! But please amplify this extraordinary statement of yours. Why do corpses, even Phoenician ones, require 'carriage-exercise', as my grandmother used to call it?"

Julia's account of the unrifled tomb, the Egyptian coffins, the business of getting them down and the jewellery in the one so far opened kept the party going all through drinks, and during a good part of dinner on the *Frivolity*, to which they chugged across the harbour in a neat fast launch. Angus and his fellow tax-dodgers did themselves quite well, Julia thought, as a smart steward in a white jacket handed round excellent food, and the other dodgers were, as he had said, pleasant harmless people enough; but she could not help recognising in all of them a certain rather pitiful nostalgia for a less comfortable, perhaps, but more *directed* way of life. The one they led was entirely pointless except, in the Duke's case anyhow, to rescue enough money from penal taxation to educate his children and preserve the property on which his family had lived for seven centuries. Beastly war; and beastly social revolution, Julia thought to herself, remembering Murphy and his fellow-dockers and their private plane to Belfast. What values were *they* upholding to compare with the learning, the benevolence, the unpaid public service and the patronage of the arts which even she had seen obtaining at the Castle? "Prizefights", "the pictures", and "the telly"—the very names, so completely ignoring their classical origins, betrayed a sordid lowering of the standards which humanity had held in esteem for centuries past.

In spite of these gloomy sociological reflections, she found time to keep an eye on her cousin and the mate of the *Vidago*. Clearly they were going ahead at a rate of knots—and presently Edina threw out, with elaborate casualness, that she had arranged for Mr. Reeder to accompany her as courier for her journey southward in search of camels. She would have to pick up a photographer in Casablanca, but he would probably be some terrible dago, "or a Moor with sheik tendencies". "One must have a man with one in these Moslem countries, Angus says," Edina pronounced seriously—"and Mr. Reeder speaks Spanish. I had enough of Hispanidad at your pub, Julia, to last me for life." Anyhow, she added airily, it would all go to expense account. Julia shot a glance at Reeder; he raised his thick eyebrows at her with a comical look of resignation—happy resignation. "What did I tell you?" those eyebrows signalled—Julia grinned sympathetically in response.

When the launch took the three guests ashore Julia was struck afresh by the calm, natural manner in which Edina sent Mr. Reeder to fetch a taxi; when it came—"I'm taking Julia home," she said. "Where shall we drop you?" Mr. Reeder said he should walk—"Probably look in at Purcell's."

"Give him my love," said Julia.

In the taxi—"Do you like him?" Edina asked, her thumb beginning to jerk in and out.

"Yes, enormously—but do keep your damned joint quiet, Edina! It makes such a sickening noise!"

Edina laughed, and held her right hand in her left.

"It—it seems to be brewing up a bit," she said, with unwonted hesitation, almost shyness.

"Brewing up! Edina, it's practically on the boil! But how do *you* feel?"

"Well, as a matter of fact, I feel an inclination," Edina said, at which Julia laughed loudly.

"J., don't be coarse," her cousin protested.

"Sorry, dearest. I really do like him terribly."

"And this trip," Edina pursued, with more of her usual firm manner, "will give one an idea of what he's like to work with, and—well, of what he's worth."

"Worth in what way?"

"Well, I've absolutely no use for men who try on extra-marital relations; I know it's done, all the time, but I *despise* it. If he 'propositions' me on this trip, which is a business arrangement, he's out."

Julia pondered.

"A test, in fact?" Edina nodded. "Rather a stiff one, isn't it?"

"I want it to be stiff!" Edina said—there were centuries of Presbyterian ancestors in her voice.

The taxi drew up at the Pension.

"Come in and sit with me while I get into bed—we'll have a cuentra," Julia coaxed.

"Isn't it rather late?"

"Eleven?—they'll only just be sitting down to dinner," said Julia. "We keep *horas españolas* here!"

Upstairs—"But Edina, if you marry, what about your job?" Julia asked, peeling off her clothes and flinging on a nightgown. "Golly, how good it is to be in a bed again!" she exclaimed as she lay back on the pillows.

"Weren't you in bed last night?" her cousin asked in surprise.

"No—in a flea-bag in that tomb! Push the bell, Edina." Natividad appeared on the instant—undoubtedly she had been hovering outside. "Cuentra, Nati—*prontito. La fiasca.*"

"Julia, you're utterly mad! You said you had to leave Philip's party early last night because you were tired."

"Well one has to say something. Anyhow bother me and the tomb—what *about* your job? Ah, *muchas gracias*, Nati. Pour out, Edina, like a kind creature—Thanks. Now go on—your job."

"Being married and having lots of children is an infinitely better job than fooling people into buying things they don't really need," Edina pronounced vigorously. "And besides"—she paused for a moment—"it might be a sort of double job. He—Philip—knows everything there is to know about running a place like Glentoran; so if we can't find Colin, or he won't come home if we do, he could do it perfectly—and what's more I believe he'd like to. Which would put paid to *that* worry. Oh by the way," she went on, with a rapid and (Julia guessed) deliberate switch of subject, "Angus has a story that you thought you spotted Colin in Marrakesh just before the bomb."

Julia hesitated for a moment. No, until Colin was willing to meet Edina she ought not to say anything about him.

"Well yes, actually I thought I did, but just then I got blown up," she said. They both laughed. "So now I'm a bit concussed about it all."

Next day a note arrived from Lady Tracy, bidding Julia to a sherry-party two days hence. "The *Frivolity* party are all coming, and Angus Ross-shire tells me you have a most lovely girl cousin staying with you—do please bring her too. Pray ask her to excuse me for not writing to her, but I have stupidly forgotten her name. Hugh will be there, so you will meet him at last—I am so glad! And he says he is bringing a charming young friend of his, who goes with him on his botanical trips." There was a P.S. "I do hope you are *resting*. Don't let Clémentine work you too hard in her enthusiasm—enthusiasts have no mercy."

In fact Julia was resting that day. She found herself surprisingly tired after her broken night in the grave, and all the driving to and fro on top of it; the coffins were safe in the Museum, and she spent most of the day lying on her bed and writing to Mrs. Hathaway. She had told Edina not to come in the evening, so as to leave the field free for Colin, but he turned up about five. This second meeting was calm and easy; but presently Julia asked why Astridite had marks like the bark of a tree on it?

"How do you know that?" Colin asked.

For answer Julia drew her precious lump, which she had recovered from Paddy Lynch, out of her handbag.

"I say, you oughtn't to cart it round like that! It's radio-active, you know. How long have you had it?"

"Since we met the caravan."

"Oh, only about a fortnight. All the same I shouldn't." He took it from her and tossed it out of the window, where it landed in a bed of freesias under a palm.

"Are you going to leave it there?"

"No—better not." He ran downstairs and Julia saw him stamp it into the freesias with his heel.

"I'm not an expert, but it's stuff to be handled fairly carefully," he said on his return. "I expect that's too small to do any harm, and it was in your bag anyway."

"Oh dear, I did like it! But Colin, if it's bad for me, what about the camels?—and the boat?"

"The camels only carry it for a few days, and it's always taken off them at night—and on board it's stowed well away from the living-quarters. We only handle it at longish intervals, too."

"Still you haven't told me why it had marks on it like the bark of a tree," Julia said.

"Persistent creature, aren't you? Because it *is* a tree—fossilised. They get something like it in America too, a uranium phosphate, found in sand-stones and near phosphate deposits—of course this country is stiff with phosphates."

"But does it look like a tree when it's in the ground?"

"Not very, though you do find a bit of fossil bark now and again. No, it looks more like soft sandstone, so soft that one can chop it out in chunks; usually we bag it because it's so friable—and we bag the rich sand, too."

"What fell on the road in the Djebelet wasn't bagged," Julia observed.

"No—the damn bags got mislaid on that trip."

"How did you get the trousseau-coffers down from Fez to Ouarzazate or Tinerhir or wherever you were going? Surely you couldn't get enough into the camionnette, along with the shirts and nylons—after all you had to have something to sell."

He stared at her.

"How on earth do you know that we were in Ouarzazate and Tinerhir?"

"Well that was Affaires Indigènes, actually."

"And they told you about selling shirts and so forth, I suppose?"

"Did they? Oh yes, M. Nussbaumer! But I'd heard that before, in Fez." She explained about the ex-*cantinier* at her hotel there. "Perfect cover, of course, and taking you right into the area of the mines. Only what I'm still not clear about is how you get the coffers down from Fez, and where you keep them while you're grubbing out your fossil chunks."

"Generally we send them down by lorry direct from Fez to a French *cantinier* who's in the thing."

"Ah, and then pick up one or two at a time and cart them out to your little diggings, hidden under the gents' wear?"

"That's it. Oh Julia, I wish you could see all those places!—it's terrific country. Sometimes you come on huge gorges nearly a thousand feet deep, with a great river raging through, and the little thread of road looking as if it was disappearing into Hell's mouth! And scrambling slowly about among the scrubby herbs and bushes—most of them smell so sweet in the sun!—with the Geiger-counter—at right angles to the strike of the rocks, of course—till you think you've picked up another deposit; and then working round plotting it on a one-metre or five-metre grid to make sure. You'd love it."

"Goodness yes. But Colin, when you've bagged your ore, and crated it in the coffers, where do you assemble it for the caravan? Surely you couldn't keep a mass of it at a cantine?"

"Lord no—there are far too many snoopers—like your Jew. No, that can be a problem. If there's a handy cave—often there is—we use that; if not we use our wits! One can't use the same place twice of course, though old St John's camel-men are very trustworthy as a rule—they'll do anything for him."

"Did he tell you I was a spy?" Julia asked.

"Well he told Torrens so, but he gave your name, and of course I guessed then that you were just after me, and said so. But this job is so secret that it was damned disconcerting to have anyone know as much as you'd obviously found out, you wretch!"

"But where can young Bathyadis stow trunks and trunks-ful of the stuff, till some ship comes in? His shop didn't look very big, and there were at least thirty camels in that caravan, with two trunks apiece, I suppose?"

"Yes, that has been another of the rather tricky things," he agreed. "We try to arrange only to send it down when we know that a suitable ship is due—but ships aren't always very punctual."

"You're telling *me*," said Julia with feeling. "Are camels any better?"

"No—worse! But—you saw his shop?"

"Yes—just under the wall of the Old Medina, nice and handy to the harbour."

"Exactly. And he's had a great hole scooped out in the thickness of that wall where he can stow the trunks quite safely, and if, for any reason, like a ship failing to call, we can't use Casa at all, there are always the tombs," he said grinning.

"And the *Finetta*. I see. By the way, did you get this last lot off all right?"

"Yes—worked like a charm. If we're really stuck I take the yacht down to Casa to relieve young Bathyadis. It's a lovely run."

Julia was still thinking it all out. It was wonderful to get the background to the problems which had been obsessing her for the last two months, but there was still more that she wanted to know.

"Why are you doing something illegally here, if you say it's legal in Paris?" she asked.

"You must ask the boss that—I'm not really in a position to say. These small lots that we've been getting out are only for experimental purposes—if the stuff does all the back-room boys hope, I imagine that there will be a proper international agreement, with concessions, all open and above-board. But everything in Morocco is such a mess-up at the moment, with no one knowing whether the ex-Sultan will come back or not, or where the French will stand if he does, that I imagine *they*," he grinned—"thought it better just to carry on quietly under the rose for a start. Mind you that's only my private guess."

When Colin finally said that he must be getting along—

"When can Edina see you?" Julia asked. "You know what trouble there'll be if she meets you somewhere, and finds I've been keeping you hidden!"

"Why should she meet me anywhere?"

"Why shouldn't she? She goes to Purcell's."

"Yes, but I don't, for the moment."

"She may go up to see the Mendoub, and spot you on the roof of Mr. T's house, like I did," said Julia gaily. The young man put down his béret, turned round, and stared at her.

"*Did* you see me there?"

"Yes. That's how I knew you and he were together. It helped a lot, one way and another."

He appeared to reflect.

"That might explain Bathyadis, of course, if you mentioned Torrens to him. Did you?"

"Naturally—at least I described him."

Colin took up his hat again—and then suddenly gave her a boyish hug. "You must have had a lot of fun!" he said. "Bless you, Julia love. I'll be seeing you. Look after your face."

Lady Tracy's small sherry-party had developed, by the time it took place, into a rather large cocktail-party, as these affairs have a way of doing—if the household is going to be disturbed in any case why not work off as many social debts as possible?—and one can't really leave out the poor So-and-Sos, they would be hurt. So most of Tangier's small *Corps Dip-*

lomatique had been invited, including the young Vice-Consul who had been nice to Julia; the Bunch, who were residents of long standing, and the English head of the Sûreté branch of the Zone Police, a tall dour Highlander called MacNeill; Mme La Besse and the Professor, the Duke and all the *Frivolity* party, and many more. Arrival by car or taxi was a little complicated, since only one machine at a time could perform the difficult manoeuvre of reversing and turning at the edge of the cliff; but it was a fine night, and most people elected to get out some distance down the street on the landward side and walk the rest of the way—Moors in wild dress stood holding lanterns at intervals down the steep cement path to light the feet of the guests. This rather unusual approach to a social function delighted Edina, "*How* Old Testament!" she said, pausing.

"Why?"

"Oh, 'Be Thou a lamp unto my feet and a light unto my path'—that really means something here. And besides, look at their clothes!"

"Yes, but come on—I think we're late," said Julia.

They were rather late. When 'Abdeslem ushered them into the big hall it was quite full of people, though the noise was less deafening than at most cocktail-parties because the voices rose up and lost themselves in the vaulted ceiling, above the high Moorish arches. Julia led Edina through the crowds across to where, as she expected, her hostess sat enthroned in her usual chair, under Jane Digby's picture of the Wilder Shores of Love; she introduced her—"This is my cousin Edina Monro, Lady Tracy."

The old woman gave the two young ones her usual gracious greeting— "But now you must meet Hugh. Hugh!"—she waved a copy of *Ebb and Flow*. "That is my signal. Ah, here he is. Hugh, I want you to meet my dear young friend Miss Probyn." Julia turned and found herself face to face with the red-haired man.

Major Torrens' expression at that moment was not lost on Edina Monro.

"How do you do?" Julia said in her slowest tones, holding out a languid hand. "I am delighted to meet you at last—I have been wanting to for quite a long time."

"Er—the pleasure is mutual," he replied rather stiffly—his well-drilled politeness, as Edina said afterwards, recalled the barrack square.

"Really? Do you know, that surprises me," said Julia coolly. "The last time we saw one another you seemed, I heard, to be in rather a hurry to get away."

He flushed up to the roots of his hair—Lady Tracy looked from one to the other, with raised eye-brows.

"But have you met already?" she was beginning, when another guest claimed her attention.

"Good evening, Lady Tracy. A splendid party! And how are *you?*"

"Oh Captain MacNeill, how nice to see you! Now—Hugh I think you know, but not Miss Probyn"—she indicated Julia—"and her cousin, Miss Monro. Dear Julia, this is Captain MacNeill, of the Sûreté."

This time it was Julia who observed a certain stiffening in the police officer's expression at the name Monro. Edina's likeness to Colin was very marked—the height, the dead-white skin, the black hair and the surprising grey eyes. He shook hands, however, politely enough, and was saying something suitable about hoping they liked Tangier when Edina gave a sudden cry.

"*Colin!*" She darted into the throng and grasped her brother by the arm. "Oh goodness, Colin, you at last! What a place to find you! Come"—she tugged at him—"Here's Julia, poor love—all plaster!"

Heads turned at this little scene; the wretched Colin thought it simplest to follow his sister where she led—which was up to the space near Lady Tracy's chair already occupied by Julia, Major Torrens, and the Head of the Sûreté. "Julia, *here's* Colin!" Edina said triumphantly.

"I've seen Julia," said Colin, shaking off his sister's hand from his arm, and glowering at MacNeill.

"But do you know one another already, too?" Lady Tracy said, beaming at the three beautiful young creatures, who indeed made a group of astonishing splendour as they stood together. "This is Hugh's assistant, dear Julia, whom I wanted you to meet."

"Yes, darling Lady T.—but he's also Edina's brother, and my cousin, and the missing man!" As she said this Julia shot a glance of delighted mischief at the Head of the Sûreté, who stood gnawing his moustache and looking sourly from Colin to Torrens and back again. "Don't you remember, you always promised to help me to find him? Colin Monro?—and here he is!"

Lady Tracy looked a little vague. "Ah yes—I do remember now. Monro—that seems to be everybody's name! And all so handsome!" She rounded smartly on her nephew.

"Hugh, do please bring some drinks! Here are all these beautiful young people dying of thirst, and poor Captain MacNeill too." Her tone was one of brisk authority, and to Julia's secret delight Major Torrens obeyed with the alacrity of a curate.

"I'll come and help—" Colin began, but Edina grasped his arm again. "No you don't—not out of my sight till we've talked a bit!" She turned to her hostess. "Lady Tracy, will you forgive me if I get into a huddle with my prodigal brother? It's so exciting to find him here."

"Oh yes of course—if you go through that archway you will find two or three more rooms, and fewer people. But wait till Hugh brings you something to drink. How amusing this rencontre is, isn't it?" she said to Captain MacNeill. "This poor child has been looking for Mr. Monro for *ages*."

"Er—yes—quite so," the police officer replied rather stiffly, as another guest approached Lady Tracy.

"I'm not the only one, am I?" said Julia, a slow mirth spreading in her calm face.

"I beg your pardon?"

"Looking for Colin, I mean. It seems to be quite a local industry in Tangier."

Captain MacNeill stared at her, incredulously—then his face became blank.

"I'm afraid I don't understand."

"Don't you? Do you know, I really thought you did! Oh well, never mind—anyhow you know now, from Lady Tracy's own mouth, that Colin is Major Torrens' assistant; and he has been, for the last ten or eleven months. That's from mine, but you can take it from me, and confirm it at your leisure."

Captain MacNeill bent his dark Highland gaze, like a gloomy searchlight, on Julia.

"I don't think I caught your name," he said. "Might I know it?"

She laughed out loud.

"Oh, you're in the very best tradition! *Quite* splendid. My name is—"

"Darling Julia, *here* you are!" The Duke of Ross-shire had come up, and enfolded her in one of his usual expansive hugs. "Evening, MacNeill. How's crime? Nothing but Spanish murders and dull smugglers? I see you are cultivating Miss Probyn as a welcome change—how wise. She is more bombed against than bombing!—I was there; I can vouch for it."

"Angus, have you had your stitches out yet?" Julia asked, rightly considering that the Duke had amply answered Captain MacNeill's last question.

"Yes, dear kind child; this morning. *Agony!*—but all over now, thank God. Ah, and here is Hugh with some drinks—thank God for that too!" He took a glass from the tray held by Major Torrens, handed it to Julia, and took another. "MacNeill, how are you. Hugh, I had an idea that I caught a glimpse of you the other day at Marrakesh, in a *highly* improbable moustache, just an instant before Miss Probyn and I were bombed. Or am I wrong?"

"My dear Duke, can even you be wrong sometimes?" Torrens asked—his words were adroit, but his brow was irritable. But both his adroitness and his irritability were lost on Angus Ross-shire, whose glance, straying round, lighted on the two young Monros, standing together in silent and rather angry beauty, waiting for their drinks, as bidden by their hostess.

"Good God! Isn't that young Colin?" he exclaimed. "Torrens, what an *un*-gay deceiver you are, keeping him hidden all this time, and driving our lovely Julia into the jaws of death looking for him—also, I may say, making an almighty quick get-away from those same jaws yourself! I must have a word with him"—and he strode over, glass in hand.

Julia entertained herself with a glance at Captain MacNeill; she found his expression rewarding.

"I find all this rather amusing," she said. "Don't you?"

"It has the merit of the unexpected, if that is a merit," he said slowly, but a little less stiffly.

Major Torrens presently came up to Julia with another drink.

"Oh, thank you. Do you think you and I could talk sometime?"

"Yes, perhaps we had better. Only this crowd—" he looked about him.

"Is there a corner? What about the roof?"

He laughed shortly.

"You seem to know as much about this house as about everything else. Yes, the roof by all means."

Julia led the way up. The air struck cool and sweet on her face as she came out into it; the night was full of stars, the sea was conversing gently with the rocks at the foot of the cliff. Away to one side Tangier threw up a diffused golden glow, set here and there with strings of brilliant lights; on the other, when she went and sat on the parapet, a single very small light shone up from the dark slopes below. "That must be Nilüfer's house," she said, gesturing at it with her cigarette.

"Yes." There was still hostility in the man's tone; slowly, she turned full towards him.

"Look, Major Torrens, I don't think we shall gain anything, either of us, by quarrelling, or even by stalling. I know you are not very pleased with me—but quite frankly, I am not very pleased with you, either."

"Oh really? Why not?"

"Well, presumably you took the trouble to find out something of my cousin's home background before you roped him in for a job of this sort—or not?"

"Yes, naturally I did."

"Well, if you knew that he was the only son of his mother, and she a widow, don't you think it was rather irresponsible of you, not to say merciless, to prevent him from answering any of the letters urging him to come home—or the advertisements?"

"Did he tell you that I prevented him?" Torrens asked.

"Of course not. But I know him, and now I've met you—and I am perfectly confident that he discussed it with you, in his concern, and was acting on your advice when he didn't reply. Are you prepared to swear that I am wrong?"

"I feel a good deal like swearing, but—no, I am not prepared to swear that. I gave him the advice that in the circumstances seemed to me wisest. When I took him on to work for me he also took on certain obligations—including a considerable obligation of secrecy." He paused. "And I covered up a good deal of disagreeable publicity on his account."

"Oh, I know you did. That—oh and taking him on at all—was really a work of mercy, and I'm grateful for it. By the way, was it you who got his last letter posted at Ceuta? A cover-up, was it?"

Torrens laughed—but this time the laugh sounded genuine, almost friendly.

"How detailed you are! Yes, of course."

"Good-oh. That was one of the things I wanted to know."

"Are there others?"

"Yes. If it's really all right in Paris, why have you been getting out this Astridite stuff so secretly here, and running all these risks?"

"I see Colin has been indiscreet," Torrens said.

"Not about the name—I got that elsewhere," said Julia.

"The devil you did!"

"Yes, but never mind how. Do go on."

He proceeded to explain. One Secret Service might have an agreement with another Secret Service, if it was to the ultimate advantage of both; the French in fact preferred these particular underground activities to be carried on by the British—"We are less subject to leaks—as a rule! This time we haven't been quite so successful as usual."

"Meaning me?" Julia asked.

"In fact, yes."

"Oh what a worry! Shall you be able to go on?"

He hesitated for a moment before replying, and walked quickly round the roof; no washing encumbered it on this occasion, and it was easy to establish that no one was lurking behind the two chimney-stacks.

"I think it will probably not be necessary," he said when he returned to where she sat on the parapet. "What we have been sending was really for experimental purposes, and I think they have sufficient for that now."

"What, with this last lot from Bathyadis, and the tombs?"

"Yes." She could almost hear that he was smiling.

"So in fact Colin could come home?"

"If it was absolutely vital I suppose he could, if he wanted to. But it would be a great pity."

"Why?"

"Because he is rather a valuable person for this sort of work. He's clever, he's resourceful, he's energetic, and he has a most unusual gift for languages; he has picked up Arabic, which isn't an easy language, in the most amazing way—he can even imitate rustic dialects."

"He always was a good mimic," said Julia happily. "Go on."

"Well, I have been working with him now for nearly a year, and I think I understand his character to some extent; I believe he could make a career for himself in the service in a way he would hardly be likely to do outside it. He hates routine, being in harness"—

"That's true," Julia interjected.

—"And in this job, though there is discipline, there's very little routine. I should have liked to see him find himself in work for which he is quite peculiarly adapted, where he could make a reasonable living, and be of real use to his country. He's young still, of course, and uncertain of himself—and sometimes unwise"—this time the smile was quite audible—"not unnaturally, perhaps, in the circumstances."

"How well you know him," said Julia; there was warmth in her voice. "I've got fond of the boy. But you think it's his duty to go back to his place and his people?"

"It certainly was at one point—when everyone wrote. But it's just possible that there might be another solution to that problem, now."

"Oh really? It would be quite excellent if that could be arranged. Are you going to organise it? That would relieve me of all anxiety—if I may say so, you seem to have rather unusual gifts too."

Julia turned from the parapet and swept him a curtsey; the distant glow of Tangier's lights on her black-and-gold frock illuminated the graceful movement.

"*Merci!*" she said.

"Well, Miss Probyn, I have to hand it to you," Torrens said. "Reluctantly, I admit! But though I have been on this job for a longish time, and often up against quite powerful organisations, I've never before been brought to a full stop by a single young woman."

"Oh splendid!" said Julia, laughing. "You wouldn't have a job for me too, as a sort of Mata Hari, or something?"

"Not till I have young Colin properly run in and thoroughly stabilised —not on your life!" said the Major. "Apply again three years hence. But will you try to get him released to carry on with me?"

"It doesn't really depend on me—but I'll try to foster it. If Colin stays with you, where will it be?"

"God knows! Wherever we're wanted next."

CHAPTER XVII

JULIA AND MAJOR TORRENS descended from the roof in high good humour, exchanging laughing remarks; at the foot of the stairs they encountered a new arrival coming in from the front door, a very diminutive figure indeed —it was Mr. St John. Hugh greeted him warmly—"Oh, splendid, Sir. I'm so glad you made it; my aunt will be delighted. I believe you know Miss Probyn, don't you?" he added blandly.

"Er—yes, we have met," said Mr. St John stiffly; but he made no movement to shake hands—he stood looking from one to the other with the aspect of an incredulous, resentful, and completely bewildered tortoise. Julia's ready pity awoke.

"Major Torrens and I have made it up," she said gently. "And I have seen Colin at last—in fact he's here tonight! So perhaps you will let me say how sorry I am to have caused you so much anxiety in Fez, when you had been so good to me."

Mr. St John opened his mouth and shut it again two or three times, soundlessly, like a lizard catching flies; then he turned his small reptilian eyes inquiringly to Torrens.

"She's perfectly right, Sir. I'm so glad you're down—we must have a word later on. But I have practically retained Miss Probyn's services as an assistant! I think she may be able to help me very much."

"Miss Probyn's *ability* was never in doubt," the old gentleman enunciated dryly. "Therefore it is almost certainly better to have her as an assistant than as an opponent; and though I confess to surprise at this development, for your sake, Torrens, I welcome it." He turned to Julia, and glanced at the long strip of plaster on her forehead.

"I was sorry to hear of your accident," he said, in his precise tones; "but you may remember that I warned you that your intervention might be dangerous. I hope you are recovered, and that there will be no permanent disfigurement?"

"Oh I don't expect so, thank you so much. But am I forgiven?"

"If Major Torrens has forgiven you, clearly I may also," the old man said, a little smile at last appearing on his withered lips.

A Moorish servant came up with a tray of drinks—several of these creatures, hardly less wild in appearance than the lantern-bearers outside, constantly moved through the rooms; Julia guessed that they were some of the hangers-on who took their toll of Lady Tracy's peas and eggs. Mr. St John took a glass of sherry; Julia and Major Torrens went on with cocktails.

"Look, Sir," Torrens said, after politely raising his glass to the old man —"Before you come and talk to my aunt, have you any news? You can say anything in front of Miss Probyn," he added rather hastily—"she is practically on the strength!" Julia grinned at this statement.

"Yes," said Mr. St John, with his customary deliberation. "Very interesting news, in fact. Of course you left Marrakesh rather hurriedly, and in any case your contacts are on somewhat different lines to mine." He paused, and sipped his sherry.

"Yes, Sir?" Torrens said, with rather studied patience.

"I hear that the Glaoui is changing his mind," the old gentleman pursued. "He recognises, it seems, that resentment at the deposition of the ex-Sultan is stronger than he had reckoned on, and he is considering the idea of his return."

"Good Lord! You don't say so!" Torrens exclaimed. "But the Glaoui took the main part in throwing him out."

"Quite so. He miscalculated—not a usual Arab mistake. But the broadcasts from Cairo have been intensified considerably since he took that decision, something he could not foresee. Anyhow he is now trimming his sails to suit the prevailing wind—it may not emerge for some time, months, perhaps—but it will happen."

"Will that be a good or a bad thing?" Julia asked, putting in her oar. "You told me before that the ex-Sultan was frightfully recalcitrant, and held up all reforms, so that he really had to go."

Hugh Torrens' eyebrows went up at this statement—Mr. St John gave an unexpectedly genial twinkle.

"You see that you are indeed to be congratulated on your new assistant, Torrens! She has quite a grasp; but then she is a disciple of de Foucauld." He turned to Julia.

"Perhaps the ex-Sultan miscalculated too—and it may be that a disagreeable exile has caused him, also, to modify his attitude. As to that I have no information as yet, though I expect it presently. But you can count on the other development. And now I think I must really pay my respects to my hostess."

Hugh was about to go with him when Julia laid a hand on his arm. "Just one second."

"Yes?"

"I forgot to ask you upstairs. If you're closing down partly because Affaires Indigènes have got wise to your goings on, what about the East Germans? As they know now about them too, I mean."

"Why do you suppose that Affaires Indigènes know about them too?"

"Well, don't they?"

He laughed.

"I certainly won't swear that they don't! But how did *you* know?"

"Good contacts. But won't they be cleared up?"

"Probably. It is being discussed, I believe."

"Why not certainly?"

"Oh, because metropolitan France is in such a bloody mess!" said the man, with a sort of cold, weary anger. "Neutralism in high places—the Abomination of Desolation standing where it ought not, in this case in Paris. Has it ever struck you how apocalyptic the world is, today?"

"Yes, often," said Julia. "When one was a child and read all those ghastly goings-on in the Old Testament, dashing children's heads against the stones and all that, one thought it just crazy barbarous rubbish, something the world had grown out of—but in this last war it became completely *à la page,* every bit of it."

"How right," he said, turning onto her a deep intense stare which startled Julia. "I see that you recognise our times for what they are. But then you are a disciple of de Foucauld, St John said?"

"Yes—anyhow, a student." But her words were unimportant; what spoke was the interchange between their eyes—his fixed plunging gaze, the half-reluctant compelled response of Julia's doves' eyes.

"God! I should like to have you to work with," he said at last. "All the root of the matter—and *such* natural camouflage!"

Julia laughed, in slight and quite unwonted embarrassment; but she was aware of a strong desire to respond somehow to this rather back-handed praise—it was of a different order to the tributes she was accustomed to receive. Before she had found any words—

"You were so sweet to the old boy," Hugh Torrens went on, "when he'd been all set to do you down."

"Weren't you, too? You were nearly as nasty as he was when we first met, tonight."

"Was I? Perhaps I was. You weren't very friendly yourself, if I remember rightly! Anyhow I should like to take it all back now."

"Julia, sweet!" Colin Monro, coming up, hooked an arm familiarly through hers. "I've got some good news—at least near-news."

"Yes?" said Julia, with a certain lack of enthusiasm—at that precise moment she could have dispensed with the presence even of her dear Colin. Major Torrens made to move away.

"No, half-a-second, Hugh—this concerns you, too, even if it is a bit of a family secret still."

"Well, what *is* it?" Julia asked impatiently, though beginning to guess.

"Well, I might not have to go home after all—I mean conceivably I might not be needed even if I *could* go—because Edina has mopped up a most delightful type—although he has a beard—and Angus says he knows all about sheep and farming, and moreover is very *rich*, believe it or not! So if they were to get married he could prop up Glentoran indefinitely, as well as run it."

Major Torrens threw a glance of amused enquiry at Julia.

"And exactly how do I come into this, Colin?" he asked the eager young man.

"Well Sir"—belatedly, Colin remembered his official manners in Julia's presence—"you did say something about possibly keeping me on even if our show here has folded up; of course I should like that better than anything, if it didn't mean leaving Mother in the cart, and the place to go down the drain." He paused.

"Yes—so?"

"Well, the position is this: Edina—my sister—has to go South in a day or so on some lunatic business about getting camels photographed for advertisements, and she had laid on this aspirant for her hand," said Colin, with a grin—"to act as courier and so forth, because he speaks Spanish. But she has suggested that I might come along too, as I speak Arabic, to help out with the camel aspect, and—well, to act as chaperon, I suppose. Save any embarrassment, and generally foster the affair. But would that be all right by you?"

"Colin, I think you couldn't be better employed," said Torrens. "Go by all means."

"Thank you very much, Sir. I'll do everything in my power to see that they do get engaged—judicious absences, and all that. I'll go and tell Edina it's O.K."—and he moved gracefully away.

"So it is Colin who is to 'foster' this excellent arrangement, not you," said Hugh Torrens to Julia, looking amused. "I should enjoy seeing him acting Cupid, I must say."

"Lunatic child! But you know he will do it beautifully. He's very percipient and quick," said Julia.

"That seems to run in the family! Well, I do hope he brings it off, or it brings itself off. Meanwhile, would you dine with me tonight, when this show is over, or are you entangled with your relations? My aunt I know will go straight to bed—she loves parties, but they exhaust her completely."

"Yes—what a mercy she has someone like Feridah to take care of her."

"Oh, you know Feridah? Of course you would. But did 'Yes' mean that you will dine?"

"Well, I shouldn't think Edina and her 'aspirant' will want an extra, and I daresay Colin will tag along with Angus Ross-shire," said Julia. "Oh by the way, why do you know him well enough to be called 'Hugh', and Lady T. not know him at all?—Angus, I mean?"

"I was his fag at Winchester, and since he's been in and out of here I have seen him fairly often—my aunt of course lives in a certain isolation, in the sense that she doesn't meet all the casuals. But—forgive my persistence—*are* you going to do me the honour of dining with me?"

"Thank you. Yes, I should like to very much," said Julia. "But not in your house," she added quickly.

He looked at her in surprise.

"It shall be wherever you like, of course. But why not in my house?"

"Because it's the only house in the world where I have given my name, and then had the door shut in my face."

He looked disturbed and astonished. "Please explain," he said.

Julia explained.

"Yes, well Hassan was only obeying orders, up to a point—but he was being a little extra smart," Torrens said at the end. "I dislike its having happened, though." Suddenly he began to smile. "So you saw us on the roof? Well!"

"Purcell says he was always warning you not to sit out there," said Julia; "but it was well for me you did, that day, because it gave me my only clue."

"How did that clue help you?"

"Telling Bathyadis that the jeune Monsieur I was seeking worked with a red-haired man," said Julia. Torrens pounced on this.

"Oh, *that* was what made the old Moor blow the gaff! We've all been wondering how on earth you worked that—whether you slipped a Truth Drug tablet into his mint tea, or what. I hope you will tell me every detail tonight—at the Minzah!"

"Chère enfant, *where* have you hidden yourself all the evening? One has not seen you, and now we leave," said Mme La Besse, coming up with the Professor in tow.

"I got here rather late—I'm so sorry," said Julia.

"You come tomorrow? We shall open some more of the coffins in the Museum."

"Yes, assuredly. *Adieu, Chère Madame*—goodbye, Professor."

Other people were beginning to leave; in the mysterious manner normal to the end of cocktail-parties the hall, so recently densely packed, in a matter of minutes was almost empty. "We must go. I wonder where Edina is?—I must find her," said Julia, who with Torrens had begun to make her way over towards her hostess.

"Oh, good evening, Miss Probyn." This was the young vice-consul. "I expect you know already, but your cousin for whom you were enquiring before is here tonight—I met him just now, with the Duke of Ross-shire."

"Oh thank you so much—yes, he came to see me yesterday. He's been away," said Julia smoothly. "But you have been *so* kind. Goodbye." The young man cast a curious glance at Major Torrens, still at her side, as he moved away.

"*Born* for it!" Hugh exclaimed in delight.

"No, but tell me this—why didn't *he* connect Colin with the *Finetta* business? I went to ask him about that, and though he obviously knew *something*—he wouldn't say what—about the bother with the *Finetta*, he never connected Colin with her."

"That was owing to the efforts of your humble servant."

"At the Consulate-General! They *must* have known."

"Another department," he said blandly.

"Oh I see. Now there are our lovers, in the far room; would you round them up, while I say Goodbye."

"Dear child, must you go?" the old lady said, as Julia bent and kissed her.

"Darling Lady Tracy, *yes*—we've stayed a shameful time, but it was such a lovely party. Thank you and thank you."

"Did you have any talk with Hugh?" Lady Tracy asked, with a bright glance.

"Yes, a splendid talk—all about Colin."

"Ah yes—how *amusing* that it is he who has been helping Hugh all this time. If only I had realised!—I could have helped you so much sooner, and you need not have got your face hurt," said the old lady, putting up a hand and stroking Julia's forehead. "But you will always be beautiful—and a scar is so *interesting*."

Julia, though a little puzzled by the beginning of this speech, was still laughing when Major Torrens came up, shepherding Edina and Mr. Reeder. "Now where's my young aide?" he said, looking round.

" 'Here Sir! Here Sir! Here Sir! Here Sir!'—as they say at the opposition shop," said Colin, emerging from a window-recess. They all made their farewells. "Heavens! We're the very last last! How awful," said Julia, as they crossed the hall. "Major Torrens, oughtn't some one to send Feridah to your aunt? She must be quite worn out."

"Look," was all he said—glancing back Julia saw that lovely veiled figure bending over her aged mistress, in the familiar caressing attitude.

Out on the windy concrete path, where the lantern-bearers still lingered —Moors always know whether the last guest has left a party or not; they probably count them—Hugh Torrens said—

"Now, who's going where? I have a car."

"I'm meeting Angus at Purcell's before I go on to dine on the yacht," said Colin, after a glance at his sister.

"Purcell's will do for us," said Edina. Colin gave a nip to Julia's arm at the "us". So to Purcell's they went—Torrens told Julia, rather abruptly, to sit beside him in front.

"Plenty of room in Mr. Smith's car, Charles!" she murmured in his ear as they drove away down the steep narrow street—he laughed explosively.

It was very late when they reached the bar; except for the Duke it was empty.

"My friends have gone on board to recuperate," he said to Colin. "We will follow them in due course. But do everyone sit down and have a stirrup-cup first—indicate your particular form of stirrup, all of you."

"The Mongols line their stirrups with cork," said Torrens, sitting down beside Julia.

"Quite appropriate to cups, Hugh, corks. But am I right in assuming that we all go on with cocktails? Right—much wiser. Purcell, could we have six Martinis?" He turned to Julia. "And now that you have found your long-lost cousin—you may remember how cross you were when I suggested, in this very room, that that was what your charming presence here was in aid of—what are your plans? Are you going home, or will you come and cruise with us? My sickly friend is going back, so there is a cabin to spare."

Julia was suddenly and unaccountably aware of a tension, at this question, in the man sitting beside her.

"Neither, Angus," she said in her near-drawl. "I shall stay on for a bit. I can't *plaquer* poor old Mme La Besse just now, while her Cambridge expert is here—and besides I want to see all those coffins opened. I'm hoping to filch a pair of Phoenician earrings when no one is looking."

"Devoted girl! I can only applaud, though I found your whiskered female employer *peu séduisante* to a degree. And our lovely Edina is setting out for the South to photograph camels, and make millions out of it, *n'est-ce-pas?* —so she can't come. Colin, are you tired of the sea?—or have you other commitments?"

"It's very good of you, Angus, but I'm going South with Edina."

"But I thought Edina already had an escort," said the Duke.

"Ah, but he can't talk Arabic—I shall cope with the camel-owners for her."

Reeder was saying something inaudible to Edina—she nodded. He cleared his throat.

"I am allowed to say that Miss Monro and I are engaged to be married," he announced. "You might as well all know it now as later."

"No! What a surprise!"

"Angus, you're tight," said Edina bluntly.

"Darling, at least I'm not *quarrelsome* drunk."

Reeder ignored this exchange.

"I realise that a week may seem rather quick work," he pursued, in the very cultivated accents that had first struck Julia on the wet quay-side at the London Docks—"but since it was bound to happen anyhow, it seemed more sensible to settle it at once. It gives me a *locus standi.*"

Julia got up, sliding out with some difficulty past Torrens' knees, and gave her cousin a kiss. "Darling, how *lovely*. Bless you," she said. She turned and took Reeder's hand. "It couldn't be nicer."

"What did I tell you, right at the start?" he said.

"Yes yes—how right you were."

"As head of the family, I should perhaps say that this arrangement has my full approval," Colin pronounced, with a fine display of young male pompousness, as he too shook Reeder by the hand.

"Edina, have you realised that he'll be able to talk Spanish to Olimpia every single day, so you'll always have the most miraculous food at Glentoran?" said Julia gaily.

"Yes. Olimpia is our Spanish cook, and she only functions properly after a dose of her own language," Edina explained to Reeder.

"Oughtn't we to send Aunt Ellen a telegram?" Julia asked presently.

"Do you think so? At once?" Edina said, a little doubtfully.

"Yes I do. There are she and poor Mrs. H. stewing and worrying away, when Colin's found, and you're engaged, and I'm perfectly fit again—as well as Angus—and the factor problem, I rather gather, is solved—or is it?" She glanced at Reeder.

"Yes. The new factor is engaged," he said, grinning broadly in his beard.

"Well, then!—and here we all sit carousing, while they moulder! We *must*, Edina."

"She's quite right," Reeder said to Edina, with a certain brusque firmness.

"It'll have to be a jolly long telegram," Colin observed.

It was fairly long. They compiled it there and then, with a good deal of laughter; everyone except Torrens signed it, and Reeder undertook to get it sent off that night. "Our agents can always make a signal."

"Well, now that filial piety has done its part, and the electric telegraph is about to give its imprimatur to this happy arrangement, I think it should be drunk to in due form," said the Duke. "Purcell, would you have any champagne?"

Purcell had champagne—moreover when it came to the table and was poured out it was obvious that it had been in ice for some considerable time. Across her frosted glass Julia glanced towards Reeder—"*Sabe todo*" she murmured. He laughed.

When the health of the pair had been duly drunk she said—

"I should like to propose another toast."

"Whom to, dear? Me?" the Duke asked.

"*No*, Angus. To Mr. Purcell, who seems to me to have been responsible, one way or another, for most of our happy endings."

"I second that," said Torrens.

"And I," said Reeder.

From the first moment that she set eyes on him Julia had always been fascinated by the play of expression in Purcell's face; but when they all six stood up—Angus Ross-shire and Edina manifestly a little mystified—and raised their glasses to drink his health, that half-negro mask surpassed itself —tears, unbelievably, stood in those surprising grey eyes. He came round from behind the bar, bent over Julia's hand and kissed it, murmuring "*Con permiso*".

Over dinner at the Minzah Hugh Torrens and Julia had a tremendous clearing-up of what, on either side, lay behind the events of the last two months—always such a highly satisfying process to the participants. Hugh for instance learned how she had originally got onto the fact of the transfer of Colin's account to Casablanca, of Mr. Consett's *volteface*, and Mr. Panoukian's highly suspicious behaviour; Julia, in fits of mirth, listened to exactly what poor Mr. St John (in code) had written about her. They got it straight, bit by bit, mightily enjoying themselves; but quite at the end Julia, still puzzled by Lady Tracy's enigmatic remarks as she said Goodbye, quoted them. "*Did* she know all along that Colin was working for you? And does she know what you are doing?"

"One never really knows *what* she knows!—almost always more than one thinks."

"But I told her his name at the very beginning, when she promised to help me."

"Ah yes, but she forgets names—she's ninety-two, remember. Did you tell her about the Bank, and all that?"

"Well no, I didn't." Julia did not feel it necessary to mention the reason for this, her desire to protect Mr. Consett.

"Ah, there you are. I feel pretty sure that if you had told her that it would have rung a bell, and she would have done something about putting you onto Colin, because she's absolutely enchanted with you—not so very surprising!"

"Yes, I'm sure Lady Tracy would always be perfectly straight, if she remembered," said Julia—a little unsteadily under his words and his eyes.

The telegram composed in Purcell's Bar in Tangier reached Glentoran the following afternoon. Mrs. Hathaway and Mrs. Monro had been out calling on old Lady Monteith, and since Forbes was too deaf to hear anything on the telephone, and Olimpia knew no English, the Postmistress flagged the car as it passed through the village, and handed the envelope in at the window. "Grand news for Mistress Monro about Miss Edina," she said, beaming.

Mrs. Monro fingered the envelope, which was unusually fat, as the car turned into the drive.

"Why about Edina? Why not about Colin?" she said, rather fretfully.

"Try opening it to see," said Mrs. Hathaway, displaying her usual patience with her poor friend.

"Oh—well here we are at the house—let's go indoors first," said Mrs. Monro, struggling incompetently to disentangle herself from the rug before the chauffeur could come round to remove it. "Forbes, tea in the morning-room," she said, as the old man appeared on the steps. And indeed it was only in the morning-room, a small apartment next to the dining-room—with faded chintzes and a fire as bad as all the other fires at Glentoran—that at last, putting on her spectacles, she opened the telegram.

"I can't make head or tail of it," she said, still fretfully, having done so. "And why should Angus Ross-shire sign it? You read it, Mary"—and she handed the sheets to Mrs. Hathaway. At last that much-enduring lady read—

COLIN FOUND SAFE WELL HAS GOOD JOB STOP JULIA QUITE RECOVERED
SCAR WON'T BE MUCH STOP NEW PERMANENT FACTOR ENGAGED WHO
SPEAKS SPANISH NAME PHILIP REEDER STOP EDINA IS ENGAGED TO HIM
STOP FIANCES AND JULIA RETURN IN ABOUT A MONTH COLIN'S RETURN IN-
DEFINITE BUT THAT DOESN'T MATTER NOW STOP EVERYTHING PERFECT
ALL VERY HAPPY AND ALL WRITING STOP BEST LOVE FROM COLIN EDINA
JULIA HUMBLE SALUTATIONS PHILIP REEDER STOP ELLEN I ENTIRELY RE-
PEAT ENTIRELY APPROVE

ROSS-SHIRE.

"Can *you* understand it?" Mrs. Monro asked, as her friend turned back to the beginning again.

"Oh yes, Ellen."

"But can Edina be going to marry a factor? What an awful idea."

"That's only a joke," said Mrs. Hathaway. "That tiresome old Sir Robert Reeder of Otterglen had a son called Philip who went away to sea; he was a godson of an old aunt of Mollie Ross-shire's and she left him all her money the other day—no doubt that's why Angus approves so much!" Mrs. Hathaway added, with an amused smile.

"But if he's so rich, why should he take a job as factor, Mary?"

"That's just their nonsense—I expect they all drafted it over drinks," said Mrs. Hathaway astutely. "Don't you see, Ellen, if young Reeder marries Edina *he* can run the place—that's all they mean."

"Then they should have said so. But why isn't Colin coming home? It's him I wanted to see," said poor Mrs. Monro, beginning to hunt in her bag for her handkerchief.

"He's bound to come home for the wedding—he'll have to give Edina away," said Mrs. Hathaway, with compassionate cheerfulness. "And you see they say he has a good job, too. *And* that precious Julia's lovely face won't be spoilt," she added, half to herself. "Look, Ellen, take off your hat and sit down quietly, and let's draft an answer before the Post Office shuts."

"Oh well, if you think we ought to," said Mrs. Monro, putting away her handkerchief—the two ladies were sitting concocting their telegram when Forbes came in wheeling a trolley, surmounted by a vast silver tray, with the tea.

"Forbes, Miss Edina is engaged to be married," said Mrs. Monro.

"Yes, Mistress Monro, so I heard. To a very rich gentleman, who speaks Spanish. Yon cook is highly delighted," said Forbes, with respectful contempt, as he left the room.

Mrs. Hathaway laughed. Then she glanced out of the window. Daffodils in thousands were just coming into flower under the chestnut-trees beyond the rather unkempt lawn, where the ground fell away to the noisy river; great scarlet rhododendrons bloomed above an untidy growth of saplings on the further slope; over all stood the silent outline of the hill. So much beauty, so long neglected—it was good to think that it would be cared for again at last.

She returned, happily, to composing the telegram.

The
Portuguese
Escape

Two YOUNG MEN were sitting under a gaily coloured sun-umbrella on the terrace of a restaurant, overlooking the Tagus between Lisbon and Estoril, a little detached from the crowd of people at the farther end, where a cocktail party was in progress. One was First Secretary at the American Embassy in Lisbon, the other his opposite number in the British Mission, and they were talking with the easy frankness which obtains between diplomats who are also friends.

"So she's really coming?" Richard Atherley, the Englishman, asked.

"She *is*—she's in Madrid at this instant, and arrives here tomorrow morning. I have to support the devoted Mama at the station at 9 A.M."

"We really have to hand it to the Countess for getting her out at last. *How* long has she been at it?"

"Well, it's ten years since she and old Count Páloczy came out themselves," Townsend Waller said, "and I suppose when they found there was no hope of getting back to Hungary they started in trying to get young Hetta out. Say nine years ago."

"Why did they leave her behind in the first place? It seems a mad thing to have done."

"She was down with scarlet fever at her convent school when the Russians came in—it wasn't very practical to move her. And I don't think anyone realised, at that stage, what the Russian occupation was going to amount to, nor how permanent it would be. Anyway it was really urgent to get the old Count out: the Communists had him as a top priority on their liquidation list, because he'd been a main opponent of Michael Károlyi and the Béla Kun Communist revolution in 1919."

"1919! He must have been very young then."

"Not all that young—he was a whole lot older than Dorothée. You never met him, did you?"

"No, he died just before I came."

"Pity. He was so nice, and a real *galant' uomo*," the Bostonian said thoughtfully. "And this child was the light of his eyes; I don't think he was ever *not* thinking of her for half-an-hour together—while he was awake, that is. He spent the last nine years of his life in hell. It was a damned shame, for a man like that."

"A damned shame for any man," Atherley agreed. But he had been doing sums in his head. "How old was the girl when they left?"

"Twelve, I think."

"So she'll be twenty-two now. Good Heavens!—a grown woman, who hasn't seen her mother since she was a child. What a strange situation."

"Strange enough—especially when you consider Dorothée," the American said, causing Atherley to give a short deep laugh rather like the brief bark of a big dog.

"Good God, yes." He continued to think it over. "Where's the girl been all this time?" he asked.

"I don't know—accurately. With the nuns, I suppose."

"I thought all the convents were washed up."

"No one knows that—no one really knows anything about actual conditions in Hungary. The child was traceable, and traced—because the Páloczys tried everything: Red Cross, Quakers, Hungarian Legation in Washington, American Legation in Budapest *and* in Vienna—with just precisely no result. At one point the Hungarian government tried to do a trade, the U.S.A. clamping down on the Voice of America broadcasts to Hungary in exchange for young Hetta: but of course the State Department couldn't agree to that. Then there was a round-about suggestion of money—so many thousand dollars to be made available for purchases of things they wanted. The Countess was advised against that, of course, but she wouldn't listen, and I believe she sprang half-a-million dollars. But still no Hetta."

"You don't say so!"

"It's exactly what I *do* say. Ask for money, get money, and don't carry out the bargain."

Atherley looked thoughtful.

"That is really horrible, when you think what tremendous 'gentlemen,' in the best sense of the word, the Hungarians used to be."

"Did you know them?" Townsend Waller asked.

"A little, yes. I was out there in 1939, shooting—only for a few weeks, but I stayed all the time in Hungarian houses, and got to know some of them rather well. It was a splendid way of life; it's hideous to think of it all being wrecked and ruined."

"Why was it so good? I thought it was pretty feudal."

"Feudalism *is* good—and pretty too!" the Englishman said roundly. "And just as nice for the peasant as for the prince! Don't go all bogus about the Common Man, Townsend; you know better in Boston." Then as his friend laughed, he reverted to the subject of Hetta Páloczy and her exit from Hungary. "Whose idea was the Press Conference? Yours?"

"Not on your life! It was Dorothée's own notion, and I know the Ambassador tried to shelve it; but of course she's an American citizen, and a free agent, and nobody could really stop her. Naturally Perce helped it along, once it was clear that Dorothée was determined to have it, and rounded up a good show of correspondents; but no one expected it to resound the way it did. I never remember anything like it, and nor does Perce; and he's been a Press Attaché for a long while, and a pressman for longer."

"Yes, it did resound," said Atherley. "I should rather like to have been there."

"Dorothée did it awfully well; I have to give her that. She's nobody's fool, whatever one may think of her social efforts, and she didn't overplay her hand at all; she kept very quiet, just gave all the facts, and what had been done, and promised, and the broken promises—and threw in the old Count's death with quite a neat quiet little implication that he'd died of a broken heart. I daresay he did, even if it was technically a grippe—I would imagine he felt he just couldn't go on living in that agony about the girl any more. Anyhow the world press the conference got must have shaken up Moscow quite considerably, for it was just forty-eight hours before the telegram came to say that the Countess Hetta Páloczy was being shipped out."

"A telegram from Moscow?"

"No, Budapest—but we all know where they take their orders from."

"Stinkers!" said the Englishman, without heat. "And what does your Ambassador say now?"

"Oh, he's as pleased as a dog with two tails!" said the American, with a wide agreeable grin.

"Well, here's to the poor little Countess." Raising his glass, he saw that it was empty. "*Mais dois*," he said to a hovering waiter, who swept away their glasses, and returned almost instantly with two more. Atherley gave the toast again. When they had drunk it, "I suppose no one has any idea what the girl is like?" he said thoughtfully.

"I asked Johnson that, when he called me from Madrid to advise us that she was coming—all he said was 'Silent.'"

"Then she must be plain. Dorothée won't like that."

"She wouldn't like it so very much if she was a beauty," said the American.

"No. What the Countess would like is something in between—passably pretty, and chic. Can a woman from behind the Curtain be chic?"

"I wouldn't think so, by what I hear from our people in Moscow."

"Poor girl! It really *is* a situation," said Atherley thoughtfully—he never minded repeating himself. "You know, after all those years to come now, a grown woman, quite *fresh* to Dorothée—"

"Look out! Here she comes!" his friend adjured him hastily. The table at which they sat was just at the top of the flight of steps leading down from the restaurant to the broad roadway which runs along the north bank of the Tagus, now bordered with the dark shining shapes of parked cars, so that anyone descending the steps had to pass close by the two young men. Atherley glanced round. A tall woman, obviously middle-aged but still slender, was moving with rather deliberate gracefulness towards them, accompanied by a man whose black garments, and still more the peculiar combination of urbanity, experience, and astuteness of his expression un- mistakably indicated a dignitary of the Roman Catholic Church.

"With her familiar spirit!" Atherley muttered irrepressibly.

"*Will* you shut up!" his companion repeated anxiously.

When she reached their table the Countess Páloczy paused.

"Are you two not at the party, or are you contracting out?" she asked, with a little smile.

The two young men sprang up.

"A little of both, Countess," Townsend Waller said. "We are at the party, but we had business to discuss."

"Practically in conference!" she said, with slight mockery. "You know Monsignor Subercaseaux, don't you?"

They both bowed.

"But naturally—I hope rather well," said Atherley, holding out his hand to the priest. In fact Atherley always enjoyed the company of the Monsi- gnor—his high degree of intelligence, his subtlety, and his remarkably un- inhibited freedom of speech were all most entertaining and refreshing, the young man felt, in the stereotyped and conventional society in which they both moved.

The Countess was speaking to Waller.

"You will be at the Rossio tomorrow morning? I—well, I shall be glad of support. It is so sad to be meeting the child alone." There was a slight stress on the last word.

"Yes indeed, Countess—I'll be there. I'm afraid your daughter will have an awful night, in those little coffins of sleepers they've put on now from Madrid."

"Are they bad?"

"Oh, ghastly! They've almost doubled the number of sleepers to a coach; you can hardly turn round, the washbowl's the size of a tea-cup, and there's no room for luggage—you can't fit in a hat-box!"

"I don't suppose Hetta has much luggage," the Countess said measuredly. "Very well—till tomorrow morning. Goodbye. Goodbye, Mr. Atherley." She moved away, still accompanied by the priest.

"I like Subercaseaux," Atherley said when the Countess Páloczy's Rolls-Royce, gliding noiselessly to the foot of the steps, had borne the pair off. "He can be such fun."

"He's entertaining all right; but do you think, Richard, that he's really a man of God?" the Bostonian asked, turning deep-set, suddenly serious eyes onto his friend. Atherley laughed out loud.

"You dear old Pilgrim Father! I don't know. If he is, it's too heavily over-laid with the wisdom of the serpent to be very obvious; but I don't exclude it. Nothing is ever obvious about R.C. priests, not even holiness—and there have been some very holy ones. Why does it worry you?"

"I don't think ministers of religion should get mixed up in politics," Waller said slowly.

"But Townsend, does he?"

"Oh Richard, be your age! None of these foreign royals and politicos here stir a foot without consulting him. I bet you he arranged this marriage between the King of Calabria's daughter and the Comte de Bretagne's son; and I shouldn't be a bit surprised to learn that it was he who tipped the Countess off to hold that press conference."

"He did a good job, if so. But if he does give advice—and I'm sure his would be good—it's as un-obvious as everything else about him."

Townsend Waller stared earnestly at his friend.

"Richard—forgive my asking—but you aren't thinking of becoming a Catholic, are you?"

At that question Mr. Atherley's laughter became like the baying of sev-eral bloodhounds, causing heads to turn at the more populated end of the terrace.

"Oh Townsend, you'll be the death of me," the young man said when he could speak. "NO! I'm only saying that a wise man, trained all his life to wisdom and self-abnegation—as well as being as clever as a sackful of monkeys anyhow—probably gives advice worth listening to when, if, he's asked for it. What's the worry?"

"I don't like Catholics," the American said slowly. "You mightn't, either, if you lived in Boston."

"Why not?"

"They run the city, and rackets—and anyway they're mostly Irish."

Atherley laughed again, but less loudly.

"Subercaseaux isn't Irish, whatever other sins you may lay at his door," he said. "I don't know what his nationality is, as a matter of fact. But look, Townsend, I must leave in ten minutes—I'm dining with H.E., who keeps English time—and I think I had better mingle a little before I go. In fact you ought to mingle too." He rose, threw a note on the table, and walked off towards the throng of guests at the farther end of the terrace.

The Rossio Station is a curious place. In some ways it resembles the entrance to a rabbit-burrow, for the railway, tunnelling through one of Lisbon's seven hills, only emerges in the station itself, which is practically scooped out of the cliff of houses that overhangs it; it is cramped, gloomy, and awkward of access for cars.

Here, on the following morning, Townsend Waller stood beside Countess Páloczy on the platform, reluctantly inhaling the sulphurous fumes which always hang round the mouths of tunnels; these were also being inhaled by a group of reporters, several press-photographers, and a man with a television apparatus, who all stood as close to the two principals—Waller hated the realisation that he was, inescapably, a principal—as even press decency permitted, which was about seven feet away. The Countess was nervous; she tapped her foot on the ground, constantly uttered rather disconnected remarks, and snapped at one of the cameramen, who asked if he could take a picture of her "awaiting re-union with a beloved child"—he couldn't, she told him curtly. The train was late, it often is; the strain increased. Turning to her companion the Countess at last made a perfectly natural utterance, a thing not common with her—"Townsend, shall I *know* her? She was only a child when I saw her last."

Mr. Waller reassured her hastily. He had got Countess Hetta's coach and sleeper numbers from Madrid, and had caused the Wagons-Lits man to be instructed to contact the Station-Master as soon as the train arrived. This worthy was already on the platform, and Townsend went and spoke to him, glad to escape for a moment from the atmosphere of emotional disturbance generated by the Countess; a moment or so later the train steamed in, propelling fresh clouds of smoke and sulphur in front of it. Everything was managed with the unobtrusive skill and smoothness characteristic of the Portuguese. The Station-Master went over to stand beside Countess Páloczy, nodded at the Wagons-Lits attendant, standing by his half-open door, and when the train came to a halt said—"*That* is the young lady, Minha Senhora," as a dark pale girl, short but slender, climbed down out of the sleeping car.

Countess Páloczy went forward and put her arms round her daughter. While the cameras clicked, and the TV man cursed a correspondent and several porters who got in his way, Townsend stood by, assessing the new arrival. She too was clearly very nervous—her small ungloved hands were shaking. She was shabbily dressed—well, what could you expect?—and wore no make-up, and her hair was all wrong. But she had a pair of huge,

splendid dark eyes under decisive brows, and that amusing and unmistakable structure of Central European faces, both lips and cheek-bones much
more prominent than in western ones, and rather flaring nostrils; the whole
thing was clean-cut, a good *strong* face—and her complexion was perfectly clear, pale but not dead. His instant private conclusion was that the
Countess might have her hands full with this new acquisition; certainly
she would not have the walk-over that she was accustomed to.

When he was introduced the girl spoke in good English, though with
the pretty, rather full and plummy Hungarian accent. For something to
say he complimented her on her English—"There used to be a nun from
England at the convent," she answered, with what he noted as admirable
self-possession.

The American Press Attaché now came up. Would she have just two
words for the correspondents?—they were all keyed up, it would be very
much appreciated. Before anyone else could speak Townsend intervened.
"Perce, I fancy the little Countess is starving—there's no restaurant-car
on this wretched train. Let her get home and rest—the Press can go out to
Estoril tomorrow." Perce Nixon tried to press it, while the correspondents
crowded round. Townsend was prepared for a glance of enquiry from the
girl to her mother, but nothing of the sort happened; courteously but quite
decidedly, Hetta Páloczy said—"Not this morning. I am tired and, as Mr.
Waller says, hungry; and not recollected. At another time." Mr. Nixon, his
jaw dropping at this display of firmness, could do nothing but drive off
his press-men, while the girl turned unconcernedly to the Countess.

"Mama, where is the car? Can we not go home? I should so much like
to have breakfast."

"*Well!*" Nixon said, as he and Townsend drove off to the Chancery together, the ruffled feelings of the Press having been soothed by the promise
of an interview the following day in the Countess's suite at the Castelo-
Imperial in Estoril. "*Well!*" he repeated—he seemed unable to say anything
else.

"That's some girl," said Townsend, with his gloomy chuckle. "She was
one too many for you, Perce."

"I don't see why *you* had to put in your two-cents' worth," Mr. Nixon
replied, not without irritation. "You gave her the tip—she might have
talked, otherwise."

"I don't believe that young woman stands in any need of tips from anyone," said Townsend, thoughtfully.

"The Countess wouldn't have objected; in fact I know she wanted it."

"The Countess is a hard-baked, publicity-minded old So-and-So, with
about as much consideration for other people as a sack of dried beans!"

Townsend responded vigorously. "That train leaves Madrid at 10 P.M. and it's now"—he shot out his left wrist—"10:10. That unfortunate girl can't have had anything to eat for over twelve hours; she's coming into an unknown world, and you want to let these damned vultures drop on her with a lot of phoney questions! I'm ashamed of you, Perce."

"I don't see what difference two minutes would have made. You exaggerate, Townsend," Nixon said discontentedly. "You generally do. Anyway what did she mean by saying she 'wasn't recollected'? To recollect means to remember, but you can't remember yourself."

"I never heard the word used that way before," said Townsend, who had also been struck by the phrase. "I assume it's a Hungarian expression for not having pulled yourself together—if so, it makes sense." As the car pulled up outside one of the large bright modern buildings of which the newer parts of Lisbon are full—"Here we are," he said. "For mercy's sake leave the girl in peace till tomorrow, Perce. Will you?"

"All het up, aren't you?" his colleague said sourly, getting out of the car. "Yeah—I've fixed tomorrow morning for the boys. Don't you butt in on that!" he added, menacingly. "Don't forget it was the Press that got her out!"

In the other car, spinning over the grey-blue tarmac surface of the speed-way which leads along the estuary of the Tagus from Lisbon to Estoril, more reprehension of Hetta's refusal to speak to the Press was going on. The girl sat gazing out of the window, delighted by all she saw; the stately houses and black-and-white pavements in the Rossio Square and its adjoining streets—re-built by Pombal after the earthquake of 1755 had reduced most of Lisbon to rubble; then the shining river on her left, and to the right the heaped white houses with their coral-pink roofs, rising up against the brilliant blue sky. "Oh, but it is beautiful!" she exclaimed. "Lisbon is much more beautiful than Madrid, Mama."

"Lisbon is one of the most beautiful cities in the world," said her mother, rather repressively. "But listen, Hetti—of course you have everything to learn about life in the ordinary world, so I shall not hold it against you; but you should not have refused to speak to the correspondents. It was not gracious—they had all come to meet you, and waited a long time."

"Mama, how could I? I was quite unprepared for this request."

"You should have consulted me, instead of taking your own decision. I know the importance of these things."

The girl turned and looked at her mother.

"But you could not have told me what to say—and surely that was the important thing? I mean, that was what they wanted to hear?"

The Countess made a small rapid movement of impatience, quickly controlled.

"Dear child, you have a great deal to learn. Probably you don't realise that getting you out at all took some doing. *I* had to give a Press Conference."

"Did you, Mama? How good of you. But today I assure you that I am not equal to it. One should always be sure of saying the *right* thing, should one not? And this morning I am too tired and also too hungry, as this kind Mr. Waller understood."

It was the Countess's turn to stare at the pale face beside her in the Rolls-Royce—serious, calm, assured. Was that last remark, with its rather damaging implications, made innocently? Innocence gazed back at her from the immense dark eyes, but there was also that troubling assurance, that complete composure.

"Oh well, we'll leave it," she said rather shortly.

"Yes; and today when I have eaten, and rested, I will recollect myself, so that tomorrow I may be able to satisfy these journalists—and to please you, dear Mama, I hope." She turned to the window again. "Oh, how beautiful those white waves are, below that big round tower standing in the sea. What is it? I suppose that *is* the sea? Do you know that I have never seen it?"

"Why Hetti, you *have!* We went to Brioni, when you were little."

"How little?"

"Four or five, I suppose."

"Ah, well then I have forgotten. But what *is* the tower?"

"A lighthouse—it flashes at night," said the Countess rather absently. She was wondering which was likely to prove the more disconcerting— Hetta's tendency to take her own decisions, or her dutiful-daughter attitude. "Attitude" was the word she used in her own mind—she was not very familiar with spontaneity, in herself or in others; she did not, by choice, move in very spontaneous circles.

"And why do the waves break white just there?" Hetta asked. "Not above, not below—just at that point?"

"I have no idea."

It was a fact that Countess Páloczy had lived for ten years on the Tagus estuary without ever realising that a sand-bar stretches across it, and that the *raison d'être* of the two lighthouses, one on the great fort of São Julião da Barra, is to draw the attention of ships to this obstruction. How tiresome it was going to be if Hetti was always asking questions and demanding facts, she thought. Oh well, she would have to turn her over to the Monsignor, who knew everything.

The car presently turned inland past a public garden brilliant with flowers, and drew up before a large modern hotel. Porters and pages in uniform swarmed round the door; more porters and more pages stood bowing as they passed in through the big glass doors. The interior of the Castelo-Imperial is like that of any other super-luxury hotel, except that it is in rather better taste than most, the deep carpets and brocade upholstery of the hall and salons being mainly in a warm grey, with touches of soft pinks and soft blues; the rooms of course vast, but with the undignified low ceilings which hotel architects, forgetting the noise that human voices in bulk make, always seem to design. Hetta's eyes grew round as she glanced about her on the way to the lift—the enormous spaces of floor, the masses of flowers, the numbers of people and still more of those inclining uniformed attendants, who seemed to have no other occupation. "Do they keep so many, just to bow to people?" she murmured to her mother. The Countess gave a little laugh, not displeased; if Hetta could do an observant ingénue act it would not be at all out of place. But here was the manager, washing his hands and also bowing; she introduced him to Hetta, and he made an elegant little speech of welcome and congratulation before they entered the lift and were borne aloft. In fact, though Hetta did not realise it, most of the occupants of the hotel and as many as possible of the staff had assembled in the hall simply in order to catch a glimpse of the young lady who had just come out, so romantically, from behind the Iron Curtain.

Countess Páloczy had a large suite in an upper corner of the big building, looking out on one side over the flowerbeds of the public garden, on the other onto the sparkling estuary—it was even fuller of flowers than the public rooms, and Hetta exclaimed at them in delight. "I like flowers —I am glad you do too," her mother vouchsafed. The apartment contained a dining-room and a salon, but they took breakfast in a small pretty morning-room; Hetta tucked in thankfully to the omelette which the Countess ordered for her, in addition to the normal coffee and rolls. Then she was led to her own room, where a Portuguese maid had already unpacked her few possessions, and was putting a hot-water bottle into the bed.

"I have ordered a cheval-glass for you, and a proper dressing-table at which you can *sit* to do your face," said the Countess; the only mirror, a small one, stood on a high chest of drawers. "This was your father's room, so it is rather austere."

"Pappi's room? Oh then do leave it as it is—I should prefer it so. *Darling* Pappi—how I wish he was not dead!" And to her mother's dismay Hetta Páloczy burst into tears.

HETTA AWOKE from a long sleep to see Esperanza, her mother's Portuguese maid, setting down a huge vase of carnations on the businesslike writing-desk which stood under one of the windows. When she sat up and stretched the maid detached a small envelope from the flowers and brought it to the bed. On the card inside, below Townsend Waller's name, a few lines were scribbled—"I shall look in this evening about six-thirty to see how you are, if you are not too tired to see anyone. T.W."

"Oh, how kind! Please bring the flowers here," she said to the maid. Esperanza, who had been with the Countess for some years and had learned a modicum of English in the course of them, brought over the vase, and the girl smelled the strong scent. "Thank you. What is the time?" she asked. Like most dwellers behind the Iron Curtain she had no watch; the Russian troops, who had arrived in Europe with no watches either, had seen to that. The Portuguese servant, however, had a neat wrist-watch—"Five less a quarter," she said.

"So late! Can I have a bath?" She could, in a bathroom next door to her bedroom. "Only for the Menina," Esperanza explained; "the Condessa has her own"—from which Hetta guessed rightly that she herself was the Menina. While the bath was running she fingered the immense bath-towel and the fine linen face-towels, all with her mother's monogram, with astonishment—they seemed to her almost too beautiful to use. Esperanza meanwhile ran to and fro, bringing in freshly ironed underclothes—Hetta had only two sets, and neither had come up to the maid's standards of smoothness and cleanliness. Turning off the taps and dashing in bath essence—"And will the Menina wear her little suit, or the black dress? The dress is pressed." Hetta said she would wear the dress—this was in fact her only alternative to the suit. "I should like tea after my bath," she added.

"*Muito bem*. In the Menina's own room?"

"Yes please."

Bathed refreshingly in sweet-scented water, dressed in clean undergarments, Hetta, back in her room, lay on the freshly-made bed while she consumed a hearty tea of rusks, *marmelada*—a sort of quince cheese—and some very rich chocolatey creamy cakes. She was still hungry, and enjoyed it all hugely. As she was finishing the last cake her mother came in.

"Did you have a good sleep?" she asked kindly.

While Hetta slept the Countess had persuaded Monsignor Subercaseaux to come round to luncheon, and had poured out her disappoint-

ment over Hetta's refusal to say "even one word" to the journalists at the
station, and her general concern about their future relationship. "She is
so—so *independent,*" she said, in tones of dissatisfaction.

"But my dear Countess, how naturally! For ten years she has been without parents—how should she at once show a child's dependence on *your*
judgment, when for so long she has been thrown on her own resources?
You will have to be very patient, and let time, and your own affection
and kindness, gradually develop what is usually a normal growth." Then
he had asked what Hetta was like?

"Oh, small—small, and not pretty," the tall once-beautiful woman had
replied. "But I think she *could* be made chic."

"You must be patient also with her lack of height and of beauty," the
priest said, smiling. "Beginning *now.* These first days and weeks are
crucial." Dorothée—whose real name was Dorothy, but who preferred to
sign herself like a Frenchwoman—promised to be patient.

"Show affection," the priest further enjoined. "Neither of you can have
much genuine affection for the other at present, since you are in effect
strangers, and both grown women—but you can show it. Affection, after all,
is one aspect of charity."

The Countess had agreed to all this with suitable humility; later she
asked Monsignor Subercaseaux if he had any news of "the invitation."

"Not so far. I understand that the lists are extremely long already—
and as I told you before, dear lady, the Bretagnes are very anxious to keep
it as far as possible a family affair—indeed so is the King."

"The Fonte Negras are going, and the Ericeiras."

"Ah, but Countess de Fonte Negra was a Lencastre, so in a way a
relation; and in the case of the Duke of Ericeira there is his position in
the Order of Malta—quite apart from the fact that he puts up so many
of the guests, here and in his house in Lisbon. Last time I believe he ac-
commodated forty!" said the priest, laughing cheerfully. "You will agree,
Countess, that this gives him a certain claim!—though he is not doing so
this year; his sister has not been well."

"Well, I rely on you to do what you can, Monsignor. You know that it
means a great deal to me—and I am devoted to little Princess Maxine—
she will make a charming bride."

However, sitting on a chair in her daughter's bedroom three hours later,
the Countess was concentrating on showing affection, as her confessor
had bidden her.

"I have made an appointment for you for 6:30 this evening with Alfred,
the coiffeur," she said. "Esperanza will show you the way." Thoughtfully she studied her daughter's hair, which was dark, thick, straight, and

at the moment merely a heavy mane. "Not a permanent wave, I think; but shaped to a rouleau at the back. I wish I could come with you, but I must go to a cocktail at the Belgian Embassy, so I shall have to leave soon after six. But Alfred is very clever about styling, and he will do you himself— so leave yourself entirely in his hands." She considered again. "Should you like a fringe?"

"Should *you* like me to have one, Mama?" Hetta also was anxious to be accommodating, up to a point.

"I am not sure—I should ask Alfred. He is a very good judge. And then we must see about getting you some clothes—of course you can't go anywhere until you have something to put on. But fortunately there is one really good tailor here, who was with Lanvin for years, and a wonderful woman for blouses; and for *petites robes* we can get you a few things off the hook in the Chiado."

For Countess Páloczy providing pretty clothes was one of the most genuine demonstrations of affection imaginable; Hetta, vaguely recognising this, took her mother's words in the spirit in which they were meant.

"That will be lovely, Mama. A person from the Government took me to get my suit and the black dress, but of course there was no time to get them altered and they are rather big and bunchy on me."

Dorothée opened her eyes wide.

"A person from the *Government* bought your clothes? What can you mean?"

"Oh yes—they wished me to look nice when I came out, so this woman came and took me to a shop, and bought the suit and jersey, and the dress. But it was all done in a great hurry; and the clothes are not as pretty as yours. I see that," said Hetta simply, little realising that her parent's exquisitely plain grey frock came from Balenciaga. Oh goodness, why couldn't she have told the Press that this morning, Dorothy Páloczy thought—*what* a story! Look *nice* indeed!—she must get that publicised somehow. But mindful of the Monsignor's exhortations, she said nothing for the moment.

"Well, we'll have fun together, getting you fitted out," she said.

"Oh yes, indeed. Mama, do you think I could have a watch or a clock? It is so tiresome not to know the time."

"Of course. But what became of the little Rolex your father gave you?"

"The Russians took it."

"Good gracious! Yes, we will get you one tomorrow—and for now"— she went to her own room and returned with a little travelling-clock. Glancing at it—"I must be off," the Countess said. "And you'll go along to Alfred this evening."

But at that point Hetta's spirit of accommodation stopped short. She was determined not to miss the nice American.

"No, Mama. I am too tired tonight. I will go to the coiffeur tomorrow, as early as you wish—but not today."

The Countess did her best not to show her vexation.

"You are sure? It is all arranged, and it is not so easy to get Monsieur Alfred himself."

"I am sorry, Mama, but I am quite sure." Oddly enough Hetta's conscience did not trouble her in the least about this white lie; people who live under Communist régimes soon develop callosities on the conscience.

The Countess, resignedly, took up the telephone beside Hetta's bed, cancelled the appointment in fluent French, and made one for the following afternoon. Then she kissed her daughter and went off to her party.

The moment she had gone Hetta sprang up, put on the government-provided black dress, which was indeed very bunchy, dragged a small cheap comb remorselessly through her thick mop of hair—hair-brushes are of rare occurrence in the People's Democracies—and then, standing in front of the small looking-glass on her father's tall chest of drawers, unskilfully applied a little powder to her pale face. The powder was of a rather tawny shade, and as cheap as the comb; like the black dress it had been provided by the female emissary of the Hungarian Government. About 1943 Moscow started a drive for cosmetics, but the quality was poor—Hetta, after looking at her face covered with Soviet powder ran to the bathroom for a towel, and rubbed it all off again. "It does not *match* me!" she muttered disgustedly.

So it was unpowdered and in all her Communist inelegance that she went through into the drawing-room. Besides the flowers, mostly hothouse white lilac, it was full of signed photographs of celebrities in silver frames, newspapers, and French, English, American and Spanish illustrated weeklies—there were no books. She had only been sniffing the cold delicate scent of the lilac for a few moments, and wondering vaguely about her father in such surroundings—as she remembered him he was always knee-deep in books, with a gun somewhere close at hand—when Esperanza ushered in Townsend Waller.

"Well!" he said, shaking her warmly by the hand—"You look better. Are you fed, and rested?"

"Yes—both, wonderfully. You were so *kind* this morning," she said, with an earnest sincerity which struck the young man as almost frightening in a girl of her age. "And the flowers are lovely—thank you so much." She paused.

"Mama is not here," she went on; "she had to go to a party."

"I know—the Belgians' cocktail. I cut it; I wanted to see how you were making out."

"Please?" "Making out" quite defeated Hetta.

"Well, getting along," he said laughing—in fact not helping her much. But the mention of the word cocktail caused him to glance round the room. The usual tray with bottles was not there.

"Don't you want a drink?" he asked.

"Thank you, I am not thirsty. I had tea not long ago."

He looked at her with incredulous amusement.

"I didn't mean tea, or real thirst; I meant *drinks*, what one has at this time of day."

"What does one have? You see I do not know. Do you want something?"

"Yes please. One has sherry, or cocktails, or whisky, before dinner, here," he said.

"Oh, I am sorry." She too looked round the room, rather helplessly. "I wish you could have what you like, but there does not seem to be anything here."

"One rings the bell for it," he said, doing so.

When Esperanza appeared he told her that the young Countess desired *as bebidas*—the maid smiled, said "Immediately, Minho Senhor," and disappeared in the direction of the dining-room. Waller looked at Hetta thoughtfully.

"Don't you have drinks before meals in Hungary?" he asked.

"I did not. You must forgive me for entertaining you so badly, but I have never drunk a cocktail in my life."

"Well, try one now," Townsend said, as Esperanza reappeared with the tray. He mixed two Martinis. "Only take a little—we mustn't make you tight!" he said.

"Please?"

Oh God, what will become of her? Townsend thought. He explained.

"But not *women*?" Hetta said, now as incredulous as he.

"Not often, no; and never nice women, unless they are inexperienced, and it happens by mistake. Do you like that?"

Hetta sipped, then wrinkled up her nose in a funny grimace.

"No. It has rather a disagreeable taste, I think; curious, but not agreeable. Wine is nicer."

"Then you'd better have some sherry." He poured her out a glass of Manzanilla.

Townsend, well-brought-up in the high Bostonian sense of the phrase, nevertheless had few or no qualms about thus organising drinks for himself in Countess Páloczy's apartment. She was always liberal with them, and would have hated a compatriot, or anyone else, to sit dry and miserable in her rooms; she was fundamentally quite a kind person, he reflected, if she did tend to attach a rather exaggerated importance to social success.

"So you do drink wine?" he said to Hetta, who was not making any faces over the sherry.

"At Detvan we did, even I—it was always on the table at meals. Our own wine—we made it at home. Pappi loved his vineyards, and was so proud of his wine."

"I bet it was good." The young man followed up this promising line; he asked questions, and listened with interest to the answers, which on this familiar and obviously well-loved subject came in an eager flow. He got a clear, even a vivid picture of a happy country childhood in patriarchal surroundings—the vast flat fields, intensively cultivated; the enormous herds of cows and oxen, the droves of pigs, the flocks of geese and turkeys being brought back to the village at night by the swineherds and goose-girls. "Of course the pigs and geese belonged mostly to the peasants, and when they came down the village street in the evening it was so funny, how each small flock knew its own homestead, and of its own accord turned in at the right gate—the geese stepping so sedately, the cows walking, the calves perhaps jumping a little, but the pigs *galloping*, kicking up their heels and squealing!" Her face was alight.

"But why were the pigs and the cows all mixed up together, so they had to find their own gates?" Townsend asked, rather puzzled.

"Oh, but of course the animals from the whole village went out to feed together; Pappi gave the grazing, and paid the wages of the cowherd and swineherd. It is always so—I mean it *was*," the girl said, rather sadly.

"Didn't the peasants have any land of their own, then?"

"Each house half a hectare, to grow what they liked—and of course the garden round the house. But one cannot graze five cows on half a hectare, especially with calves too."

"Did each peasant have five cows, then? For goodness sake! And how many peasants in the village?"

"In Detvan there were a hundred-and-fifty houses; in the other two villages perhaps a little fewer; about a hundred in each, I think. But each peasant could keep up to five cows, and as many as forty pigs—not more."

Townsend did sums in his head.

"And your father gave free grazing to sixteen hundred cows, *and* their calves? And paid the cowherds' wages with it? It's fantastic!"

"Why?" Hetta asked flatly. "With us it was always so."

"Fourteen thousand pigs too," Townsend mused. "Don't know what *they* eat. And your father just *gave* the people all this?"

"But naturally."

"Doesn't seem at all natural to me, in the twentieth century."

"I cannot see what the century has to do with it. They were our people; they worked for us."

"Did they get any wages?"

Hetta laughed at such ignorance.

"Of *course* they received wages—and some of the produce of the estate: maize, and wheat, and wine for each family."

"I begin to see what Atherley meant about feudalism," Townsend said thoughtfully, really to himself. "Yes—on those lines it *is* pretty good for the peasants too. He's quite right."

"Who is Atherley?" the girl asked, catching hold of something concrete in these rather puzzling utterances.

"A friend of mine in the British Embassy here—you must meet him; he's a grand person. And he knows Hungary."

"No! Oh, I should so much like to meet someone who knows Hungary."

"You'll meet him all right—your mother likes him. But tell me—I say, might I call you Hetta?"

"I had rather you called me Hetti—that is what friends used to call me."

"Fine—though I like Hetta better than Hetti. Anyway, what's become of all this free grazing and everything since the Russians came in? Weren't all the big estates broken up?"

"Yes, indeed; everything was taken, and the land divided up among the peasants—at first."

"Did they like that?"

"How should they like it?" the girl exclaimed vigorously. "Each family was given four-and-a-half hectares, and a pair of horses or oxen to plough. But what is this, compared with what they had? You cannot feed two cows, and make hay for them, on four-and-a-half hectares, and where were the bread-grains to come from?—and the land for the pigs to feed? Concerning the pigs, this was soon settled"—she gave an angry little laugh—"because the Russians took them nearly all away."

"Took them away?"

"Yes. Over five million pigs they sent to Russia in the first year, and nearly all the turkeys. The women loved their turkeys; they fed in the fields after the harvest, and so grew fat; when they were sold the money was for the housewife—the birds were hers."

Townsend was doing more mental arithmetic—American career diplomats are very well-informed.

"The hectare is nearly two-and-a-half acres," he said, thinking aloud.
"No, you couldn't do even subsistence farming on eleven-and-a-quarter
acres. But why was there enough for everyone before?"

Hetta had her answer pat.

"Because on a big estate, with huge fields and no divisions—fences, do
you call them?—and with good manuring, much more was produced than
simple peasants can do, on these silly little plots. Also everyone worked then
together at the harvest, as my father and his—do you say manager?—
directed; whereas now, except in the collectives, each man works alone,
or tries to get his neighbours to help; and there are arguments and
quarrels—all is without organisation."

In spite of the curious phrases she used, Townsend got a clear picture
of the two different epochs; so clear that it rather surprised him. "How do
you come to know so much?" he asked.

"Oh, before my parents went away I used to go with Pappi when he
drove about the estate to overlook everything; the harvest, especially, was
in the holidays, so that I was at home, and he liked to have someone with
him. Mama did not care so much for the country things, she liked Pest
better; so it was I who went."

I bet she liked Pest better, Townsend thought. Aloud he only said—
"But how do you know what it's like now—were you in the country? Didn't
you stay in your convent in Budapest?"

"Till the end of 1948, yes; then the Communists forced all convents to
close. It became a crime to be a nun!" Hetta said, her dark eyes huge.
"All had to put on civilian dress; they looked so strange without the habit!
—in fact in ordinary clothes they looked *awful*."

Her tone made Townsend laugh. "Awful in what way?" he asked.

"Silly!" Hetta said crisply. "In the habit, and living their own life of
work and prayer they looked as they felt—calm and full of purpose; therefore dignified. But thrown out into the world, which they had given up
and forgotten, they felt utterly lost; and again they looked as they felt—
lost, and very silly."

This time the young man did not laugh. Some strange ring, of a
strangely objective compassion, in the young girl's voice as she pronounced
the last four words precluded laughter.

"Were they always silly? One hears nuns get so," he said.

"But not in the least! Living the life they had vowed themselves to, of
prayer and works of charity—or of education, like my nuns—they are
perfectly competent; noble, heroic even. But suddenly obliged to take jobs

as servants, or as waitresses in factory canteens, which is what most of them did, can you wonder if they were at a loss, and seemed foolish? *Oldish* women, please reflect. No Mass to begin the day, and Holy Communion; no times of meditation before the Blessed Sacrament. Instead, hustle and bustle among pots and pans, or handing plates of food to young Communists! This they willingly did for the love of our Lord, who blessed even a cup of cold water given in His name; but how should they be good cooks, or quick waitresses? Of course they seemed silly."

As Hetta poured this out—"She looks like a sybil"—the young man thought to himself. It was all surprisingly reasoned, too; she was no fool, if she did seem a bit ultra-religious.

"Yes, I get all that," he said. "Well, go on—where did you go when your convent broke up? You were—let's see—fifteen then, I suppose?"

"Nearly sixteen. Mother Scholastica—she was one of the nuns, who taught us Latin—took me with her; she went first to the house of a friend in Pest, as a cook, and I helped her. To strangers we had to pretend that I was her daughter—*imagine*, for a nun!—but I was accustomed to calling her 'Ma mère,' so it was not too difficult. Then after a time the deportations began, and the lady we were working for was threatened, so we had to leave."

"What deportations? To Russia?"

"No no—from Pest to the country; the May deportations. All who were not 'workers,' in industry or something the Communists thought useful were sent away, to make room, so they said, for the workers; but really it was just"—she hesitated—"animus. Should I say spite, or malice, perhaps?"

"Animus will do," Townsend, who had received a classical education, said smiling a little. "Where did these deportees go, in the country?"

"To peasants' houses—in a *good* room, if the peasants were friendly, as usually they were; but then often the village Commissars came, and said that they were 'enemies of the people,' and must sleep in the barn, on straw. Oh, the wickedness and cruelty! Shall I tell you what I have seen with my own eyes?"

"Please do," Townsend said, unable to repress a secret wish that Perce's press correspondents could hear what he was hearing.

"There was an old lady—over seventy—the widow of a former Prime Minister, the Countess X; this is a great name in Hungary, and he had done much for the people, and was beloved. She was sent to the same village where Mother Scholastica and I went, and naturally the peasants treated her like a queen, and gave her the best of whatever they had. But the Commissars came and said she must work for the nation, and since she was far too old to do any real work they took her out into the cornfields, and tied branches to her head and hands, and made her stand there in the burning sun, waving her hands to frighten the birds from the grain—she was to be a bird-scare."

"Scare-crow," Townsend muttered automatically. "Good God! You *saw* that?"

"Certainly I did. As often as I could, when no one was about, I went and changed places with her, so that she could go and rest in the shade—I put on her old hat with the branches, and she tied the other boughs to my hands, and so I stood, hour after hour. The heat is unbearable, in the Alföld in harvest time."

"Good for you. What's the Alföld?"

"The central plain of Hungary, down to the east of the Danube—the black-earth country, they call it; the soil is very rich. Detvan was on the edge of the Alföld," the girl said, that bright look again illuminating her face as she mentioned her home.

"And what did you and the learned Mother What's-her-name do when you went to the Alföld, as I take it you did?"

"Oh, we were so fortunate! The lady we had worked for in Pest somehow arranged for Mother Scholastica to take a position as housekeeper and cook to a *wonderful* man, Father Antal, who had gone to be a village priest down there."

"Why was he wonderful?" Townsend asked—he was rather allergic to priests.

"Because he was holy, and learned, and wise, and also very brave," Hetta replied with her usual clarity. "He managed to say Mass almost daily, in spite of the Commissars; the peasants hid bottles of their wine for the Mass in the thatch. He went quite often to see Cardinal Mindszenty in his prison—"

"Goodness, was he allowed to do that?" the American interjected.

"Of course not—not allowed; he went disguised as a peasant, bringing in wood for the fires, or some such thing. It was a fearful risk."

"Did you hear how the Cardinal was?"

"Not much—it was better not to speak of such things. I gained the impression that he was not really ill, but not well; the confinement and the distress about his people were *eating* him," she said—"and the loneliness too, of course. It did him so much good when Father Antal went to see him; they were friends, they had studied at the same seminary—and it was a chance for him to hear a little truth, for a change. Lies, lies, lies, every day and all day long; these are suffocation. I think without the Father's visits he might have died. This is partly why I would do anything for Father Antal. I loved cooking for him."

"But were you the cook? I thought you said the nun was?"

"So she was supposed to be, but she was a terrible cook! First, she had no idea how, and further, she was always leaving the saucepans in order to recite the Office!" Hetta said, with an honest girlish giggle. "So, one cannot cook! No, I did most of it."

"And can you cook? How did you learn?"

"As a child at Detvan I was often in the kitchen with Margit, our old cook, who had been with us for ever; I used to watch her, and afterwards remembered, and did as she had done. Father Antal liked the food I made."

"Sounds as if the priest had been just as fortunate as you and the scholastic mother," Townsend said. He poured himself out another drink, gave Hetta a second sherry, and returned to his chair. He was impressed by what she told him, although all the stress on saying Mass and so on passed him by completely, indeed rather alienated him. But he could not help realising that here was a first-hand behind-the-curtain story, from a person who had the power to make it vivid; he began to see all sorts of possibilities. He asked more questions—about the deportations, how much luggage people might take, and so forth; and also about how the village commissars were organised. Her replies were satisfyingly detailed and lucid, especially about the commissars. "Everywhere are there not sometimes young men who are failures, and therefore dissatisfied?—and such turn often into *mauvais sujets*, small criminals; without conscience, and angry with a world in which they have no success. But give them the chance of *power* over other people, and they are delighted; they take this to be the success the disagreeable world has denied them, out of malice! Such were the commissars; sometimes from the villages themselves, or from some small town near by. Where we were, one was actually the village idiot— a lumping youth, with one eye squinting, his mouth hanging open always, his nose dirty! It was he who had the idea of sending the old Countess to stand in the fields to frighten the birds."

For a moment or two Townsend was fairly silenced by the horror of this. At length, pulling himself together, he said with an effort at lightness—

"I see that your nuns gave you a course in psychology, among other things!"

"Please?"

"Oh Hetta, you must learn not to say 'Please'! Say 'I beg your pardon?' or 'Would you repeat that?'—anything but 'please'!"

"Very well. Thank you for telling me. In German one says *bitte?* when one does not understand, but in English this is wrong?" she asked.

"Yes. It's—well somehow it's tiresome," he said, feeling ashamed. "I'm sorry."

"Do not be. This helps me—I have so much to learn. Will you tell me again what I should say when I have not understood?"

"Well, I think 'would you repeat that' is about the best," Townsend said, quite abashed by her humility.

"Thank you."

"Shall you feel up to meeting the Press tomorrow?" he asked presently.

"Oh yes—I have told Mama I would."

"Fine. I'll tell Perce—our Press Attaché, you met him this morning—that I think it ought to be as full-dress as he can make it. It will be a big thing."

"Can you tell me *why* one must speak to journalists?" the girl asked. "You and my mother both think so, but I do not really see why."

"But—" he paused, staggered by such ignorance. Then he began to expound the importance of publicity, the propaganda value of her story, so unique and fresh. Warming to his theme—"I'm certain Radio Free Europe would love a recording of a talk by you," he said—"You could do it in Hungarian, if you'd rather. And some articles, too—they'd be syndicated all over the States."

"Pl—I mean what does 'syndicated' mean?"

"Printed in about seventy papers. It's such a story!—the Press will eat it up."

She considered all this for a little while in silence; her first look of surprise changed then to one of mild and lightly charitable disdain.

"You mean, tell newspaper men, or write for newspapers, what I have told you?"

"Yes—exactly that."

"No," Hetta said—and the single syllable again had a ring. "I told you because you have been kind, and saw that I was tired and hungry. But I will not make this 'story,' as you call it, for journalists and the radio. What business is it of theirs?"

"I've just told you"—and again he tried to hammer home the importance of publicity and propaganda. But Hetta would have none of it.

"I feel all this to be quite false. If such things must be done, they should be done by people who know a great deal, and have importance. I am quite unimportant, and know nothing but what I have seen."

"That's the point—you *have* seen; you can tell the world." But Hetta would not give way; he was surprised both by her toughness, and at her reasons.

"If the world is to be told, it must be told by those who can speak with authority. The recollections of an ignorant girl are mere gossips."

The phrase made him laugh, but when he tried to press her further she quietly shut him up, saying—"If I could help my country in any proper way, I would; but this—please forgive me—is to my mind foolish, and almost indecent."

"Then you won't see them?"

"Of course I will see them—have I not said so?—because my mother wishes it. And I will describe my journey, and speak of small things. But I will not do what you suggest, and make 'a story.'"

"You're making a great mistake," the American observed, gloomily.

"Possibly. But I shall make it," Hetta said.

CHAPTER III

IF THE MEETING with the Press next morning was not exactly a failure it was mainly owing to the Countess, who herself did a good deal of the talking, and compèred her daughter as far as she could, leading her on to describe the expedition to buy those dismal clothes, and so on—it was perhaps just as well really, she reflected, that Hetta hadn't felt up to going to M. Alfred the previous evening, for her shock-headed-Peter aspect fitted in very well with her ill-fitting ugly dress. Hetta, caught between her desire not to vex her mother, and her distaste for the whole idea as Townsend Waller had revealed it to her, did her best within her self-imposed limits, confining herself as far as possible to dates and generalities. "Looks to me as if she'd been brain-washed before she came out, so she'd give nothing away," one correspondent muttered to a colleague, going down in the lift.

"Maybe she's just born dumb, though she doesn't altogether look it," the colleague responded. "Anyway those clothes are a story in themselves!" They both laughed.

Townsend lunched that day with Atherley in the latter's small house up in the Lapa quarter of Lisbon, not far from the British Embassy. Richard Atherley disliked flats, and had been delighted to get hold of the little house: it was thoroughly Portuguese, with azulejos (coloured tiles) running in a bright cold 3-foot dado round the walls of the narrow hall and the small rooms, and rather sketchy plumbing; the furniture was distinctly sketchy too, except for a big sofa and some comfortable armchairs which

the young Englishman, who was by no means poor, had brought out
from home. But the house was perched on the lip of what was practically
a ravine—although its broad bed was floored with small one-storey houses,
their back-yards full of rabbits and washing, set in cramped little gardens
equally full of onions, fig-trees, and vines trained over trellises, under
which the owners cleaned their shoes, ironed their clothes, and ate their
meals—and commanded a spectacular view across that end of Lisbon, white-
walled and pink-roofed, to the great stretch of the Tagus and the green
hills of the Outra Banda, the southern shore. It was very up-and-down,
really like a small house in Chelsea except for the tiles and the view—
and the food; unless the hostess cooks it, very few houses in Chelsea enjoy
food like that which Atherley's elderly Portuguese servant habitually produced.

"Well, how did the arrival go?" Atherley asked at once, over drinks in
the little upstairs drawing-room—and Townsend described the scene, and
Hetta's instant and spontaneous refusal to talk. "But I went to see her
yesterday evening—I knew Dorothée would be at the Belgians'."

"You never! What did you get out of her? Anything?"

Townsend's account of what he had got out of Hetta lasted through
most of the meal—towards the end he recounted her unaccountable attitude towards propaganda and publicity. "Does that make sense to you?"
he asked.

"What happened this morning? Did she meet them, or not?"

"Oh yes, she met them all right; but Perce says you'd have thought it
was Dorothée who'd been in Hungary all this time!—she did most of the
talking. I think they *just* got by. But can you understand why the girl
won't tell a story like that?"

"Yes, I think I can," said Richard thoughtfully. "But she sounds interesting. I must meet her."

"Oh, you'll meet her all right! I'm sure Dorothée still means to cash
in on her—though hoping for the best, poor woman, I expect after this
morning!" said Townsend, with a rueful grin.

But in fact it was well over a week before Hetta Páloczy next appeared
in public, and Atherley had the chance of meeting her. The interval was
filled with endless visits to M. Lilas, the French-trained tailor, to Mme
Azevedo, who produced blouses fine as cobwebs covered with what
the French call *travail,* most delicate openwork and embroidery; to
"Hélène" in the Chiado, one of the best shoe-shops in the world, for elegant confections in lizard and alligator-skin, and to Le Petit Paris, also
in the Chiado, for simple becoming frocks. The Chiado (whose real name
is the Rua Garrett) must be the steepest shopping street in the world; one

pants going up, and is apt to slip going down on the tiny polished cobbles of the pavement—the shops are minute, yet produce superb craftsmanship. It is all very Portuguese; they are the most unobtrusive of races, preferring performance to advertisement. All this amused Hetta; and as she was dutifully anxious to please her mother she tried also to be interested in her new clothes—she ended, quite naturally and girlishly, in enjoying her pretty outfits.

She eventually made her début at a cocktail party at the hotel, for which her mother had sent out the invitations on the same day that Hetta met the journalists. In theory it was a purely social affair; in fact the Countess had invited Mr. Nixon, some of the better-known correspondents, and a pretty clever girl representing Radio Free Europe, hoping that on a less formal occasion they might contrive to "draw" her daughter. She therefore responded favourably when Mr. Atherley rang up in the morning to ask if she would perhaps allow him to bring a young Englishwoman who had just arrived in Lisbon to "cover" the royal wedding for an English newspaper.

"Of course I shall be delighted to see her, Mr. Atherley. What is her name?"

"Miss Julia Probyn, Countess. That's very good of you."

"Where is she staying? I might get a card to her."

"Oh please don't bother—I'll bring her. She's staying with some Portuguese friends." Atherley astutely refrained from mentioning that these friends were the Ericeiras; he knew that they were among the members of the *sociedade* of Portugal whose acquaintance Countess Páloczy had long sought in vain. Julia Probyn had spent some months teaching English to the Duke of Ericeira's only child, Luzia, and had become intimate with the family, and slightly acquainted with Atherley himself.

Hetta was about as inexperienced in social matters as a European young woman of twenty-two could possibly be, but perhaps just because of this she had the sharpened perceptions of a child or a clever dog. As she stood beside her mother, in a pretty and highly becoming cherry-red frock which exactly matched her new lipstick, and accentuated her clear pallor and the darkness both of her eyes and her now beautifully-arranged hair, she registered with considerable acuity which people her parent considered important, and to which she, Hetta, was supposed presently to talk. The young lady from Radio Free Europe began asking questions at once; Hetta was wise enough to leave her mother to indicate to the girl that she should do this later on—"When the receiving is over, my daughter will enjoy talking to you."

There were some other very concrete indications which Hetta did not

miss. A short, brisk, cheerful Portuguese lady, greeted by the Countess
as Mme de Fonte Negra, said as she shook hands, rather late—"Well,
my dear friend, so this is the daughter! You must send her to lunch with
me one day; I should like to talk to her." She glanced round the rooms.
"I see the Regent is not here."

"No. They go out *so* little, as you know"—but Hetta recognised from
long ago a sign of annoyance in the slight fluttering of her mother's eyelids. Later another guest said—"I've not seen the Archduke; are they here?"

"Oh poor dears, she is so lame, and it is such a long way for them to
come, with no car," the Countess replied, again with that rapid fluttering
—and Hetta at once seized on the situation. Oh, poor Mama! If the Archduke would have come, her mother's car would undoubtedly have been
sent for him, however far away he lived. There was a lot of talk about
the impending royal wedding, too, both while she stood beside her mother,
and later when, as directed, she moved about among the guests: who
was going and who was not was clearly the burning question at the moment, and she overheard enough of the jockeying for position, the
intrigues for invitations suggested or boasted of, to cause her a rather painful astonishment. So much effort, so much emotion merely about being
at any wedding struck her as unworthy, unreal. But she kept her ideas
to herself. All through the innumerable introductions and the stereotyped
questions she was actively recording in her mind—this was now to be
her world, and however little she might like it, she must get to know
it. In one way Hetta was rather well equipped for this particular task,
since she had already had to come to terms with a world quite strange
to her when she emerged from her convent school into a Communist
Hungary, and she quickly marked down a few people as likeable and
trustworthy among so many whom she found distasteful.

In particular she was delighted by a little old crook-backed Hungarian,
an *émigré* journalist, who spoke to her in perfect idiomatic English. Instead of the stock questions he surprised her by saying at once—"Are they
bothering you to talk, and write? If so, don't do it—tell them all to go to
Hell!"

"I have, more or less," Hetta replied laughing. She had just been firm
with the pretty girl from Radio Free Europe and with Mr. Carrow, whose
name in American journalism, Perce Nixon had told her, stood "right
at the top."

"Well, go on. They will tell you it's for Hungary, or for freedom and
democracy—but in fact as to fifty per cent at least, it's either to line their
own pockets or boost their own egos, or to gratify a vulgar curiosity which
has no moral or political importance whatever. Of the readers or listeners

on whose behalf they are pestering you, how many would lift a hand, give a penny, or even cast a vote for Hungary or for freedom? Perhaps one per cent!"

The old journalist spoke the last words loudly and emphatically; they were overheard by Mme de Fonte Negra, who laughed, tapped his arm, and protested—"Monsieur de Polnay, do I hear you traducing the public of the free world?"

"No, Madame," he replied quickly, kissing the hand that tapped him —"for really it is hardly susceptible of being traduced! I am telling this young lady, who as yet knows nothing of our western monstrousness, the truth—which you really know as well as I."

"I hope we are a little better in Portugal—but, enfin, I am afraid I must agree with you on the whole." She turned her strongly-marked elderly aristocratic face to Hetta.

"I should like it very much if you would lunch with me one day. I promise you that no one but I will ask you questions, if you come! Your mother and I know each other well."

Hetta had taken to this frank lady, and accepted with pleasure.

"Very well—next Sunday, at 1:30. Your mother usually has people to luncheon on Sundays, so she can easily spare the car to bring you in to me."

As Mme de Fonte Negra moved away Richard came up.

"Good afternoon, Monsieur de Polnay. I hope I see you well?"

"My dear Richard, you know perfectly that nobody ever sees me *well*. As Maurice Baring once said—'I'm always worse, and *never* better!' However, thank you for the little phrase."

Atherley laughed.

"Moreover, your intention in greeting me is not in the least single-minded," the Hungarian went on. "You simply wish to be introduced to Countess Hetta Páloczy. Very well—Countess Hetta, allow me to introduce Mr. Richard Atherley, First Secretary at the British Embassy, who in spite of this lamentable exhibition of double-talk is really my very good friend."

Hetta, laughing, held out her hand. Richard Atherley was very good-looking in a rather neutral English way: that is to say that although he was very tall he had hazel, not blue eyes, and mouse-coloured hair, and his skin, though clear and healthy, was by no means pink. But his face was intelligent and expressive, something one noticed long before the excellent modelling of the features and the brilliance of the hazel eyes; he looked gay and amusing and pleasant. He was all three. He bowed over Hetta's hand and kissed it, surprising her.

"*Tiens!* We are going all Hungarian, are we?" said M. de Polnay. "Well, *je m'absente*—which in American means 'I'll leave you to it.'" He, too, kissed Hetta's hand, and hobbled away.

"What a very nice man this is," Hetta said, looking after him. When coaching her daughter for her first appearance in society Countess Páloczy's main injunction had been "Talk!"—she was now endeavouring to carry it out.

"Yes, he's an absolute darling, and as clever as paint, too."

To his immense surprise Hetta said—

"Would you repeat that?"

"Repeat what?"

"This that you said about his being clever."

"I said he was as clever as paint, didn't I?"

"Yes. Would you tell me what this means?"

"Oh, just that he's very clever—it's an expression one uses. But why did you want it repeated?"

"Mr. Waller told me I should say 'Would you repeat that?' when I have not understood, instead of saying 'Please?' It seems that 'Please' has a disagreeable sound in English."

Atherley gave his big laugh.

"Oh, Townsend! What a man! You go on saying 'Please?' as much as you like. Do you know, I believe I went to your house in Hungary once?" he went on.

"Did you really? When? Mr. Waller said you knew Hungary."

"It was in 1939—I was staying with the Talmassys at Bula, and they took me over to lunch at Detvan."

"1939—oh, then I was only six, so I could not have seen you! Did you like it?"

"Yes, I thought it a most charming place—dignified and yet so homely, with that great courtyard, and the farm buildings. And full of sun."

"Was it not? Oh, you have completely *seen* it!—this is evident."

"I liked the new chapel your father had just built, too. Of course it wasn't as perfect as the little old rococo one, but like that it was a part of the house, as well as being big enough for all the peasants to come to Mass in on Sundays, instead of trailing over to Bula."

"Oh, yes; that meant so much to them. Did you see the telegram?" the girl asked eagerly.

"You mean the one from Cardinal Pacelli that hangs up in the porch, framed, giving the building his blessing? Yes, of course I did—your father showed me that at once. It seems they were friends."

"Indeed yes—he was often at Detvan; they were close friends. And now one is the Holy Father, and the other is dead," Hetta said, on an elegiac fall of voice which struck Atherley with curious force.

"I'd forgotten—of course Pacelli is Pope now," he said, conscious of a certain lameness in his words after hers. What a strange being she was!— that smart hair-do and pretty frock, and the eyes and voice of a priestess at some Delphic shrine. Feeling his own inadequacy in a way most unusual with him, Mr. Atherley decided to call up his reserves.

"There's someone I want you to meet," he said. "May I bring her over? I think you might like her."

"But please do." Hetta was prepared to like any friend of the man who had been to Detvan and noticed how that long low house with its wide courtyard used to be full of sun—it was one of her own most vivid memories. She was still thinking how clever it was of him to have noticed the sun-filled quality of her home when Mr. Atherley returned with Julia Probyn, and introduced them.

Young women have mental antennae longer than lobsters', and as delicately fine as those of butterflies. Hetta's and Julia's antennae reached out and did whatever the lobster-butterfly equivalent of clicking is—in human terms, they took to one another immediately. There was a moment's check when Julia mentioned that she was a journalist, but Hetta's sudden expression of dismay was so obvious that it made the others laugh.

"Don't worry—Miss Probyn won't bother you. She's only concerned with the royalties," Atherley said.

"Oh, this wedding." Hetta's distaste for the whole subject of the wedding was so audible in her voice that Julia laughed again; as Hetta listened to that long slow gurgle a happy reassured expression came into her face.

"You, too, think it funny that people should care so much, whether they go or not?" she asked.

"Oh no—perfectly normal. There's surely more social snobbery in the Century of the Common Man than ever before in the world's history," Julia said. "I *have* to go—it's my bread-and-butter."

The party was thinning, and Atherley murmured to Julia that they ought to leave. He turned to Hetta.

"Will you lunch with me on Thursday? So that we can talk about Detvan?"

"With Mama?"

"Of course if you say so—but Miss Probyn will tell you that in the free world young ladies do lunch with young men without their parents."

"So? This too I do not know."

"Ask the Monsignor—he's your mother's spiritual adviser, so if he approves, she can't object," said Atherley smiling. "Anyhow Miss Probyn will be there."

"If Mama has no other plans for me, I shall be happy to come. Thank you," Hetta said, with the composed decision that somehow had so much distinction.

"She *is* out of the top drawer, isn't she?" Julia remarked to Atherley as they drove back to Lisbon.

"Who, the young Countess? Yes. It's so curious, really, that little aristocratic air of hers, when she's been a convent school-girl for nearly two-thirds of her life, and cook to a rustic priest in Hungary for the rest."

"Oh, was she?"

"Yes." He repeated what Townsend Waller had passed on to him of Hetta's experiences.

"Mmm," said Julia, reflectively. "*She* can't be the frightfully important Hunk who was going to be got out to tell the world about conditions there, can she?"

"What important Hunk?"

"Oh well, I heard ages ago that one was to be got out, if it could be fixed."

"Who from?"

"Just a friend, who does those sort of things," said Julia airily, while the slight blush which always enraged her appeared. "But this girl would hardly be high-powered enough, would she?"

"She seems fairly high-powered, but I gather the one thing she *won't* do is tell anyone anything," said Atherley, "so I shouldn't say telling the world was really her line. Anyhow she came out quite openly, as the result of a piece of perfectly honest blackmail—didn't you read about Countess Páloczy's Press Conference?"

"Oh, that—yes, of course I did, but I thought that was some poor little tot."

"Really, Julia, you are too vague to live! Well, now you've met the little tot."

"Yes. She's certainly small, but so is an atom bomb, I believe."

"Is that your impression of her?"

"Oh well, I think all this convent life and cooking for country priests may simply have been smothering some sort of dynamite. Or developing it—did your American chum establish whether life was safe and easy for her in the People's Democracy, or risky and dangerous?"

"Not for her, I don't think. The priest she cooked for took risks, he said."

"Oh," said Julia. After a pause—"Well I hope I *am* coming to lunch

on Thursday, or whichever day it proves to be. I'd like to have a go at
her myself."

"Of course you're coming."

Two days later Mr. Atherley was sitting in his room in the Chancery,
which looked out, not onto the Rua S. Domingos à Lapa, where the trams
rattle up and down over the steep cobbles, but onto the green tree-filled
space of garden behind, memorizing phrases in that famous Portuguese
lesson-book, a "must" for students of the language, *A Familia Magalhães*.
(These seem to have been a family rather like the Dales, and presumably
descendants of the gentleman who gave his name to the Straits of Ma-
gellan.) Atherley's studies were interrupted by the rather brusque entrance
of a small man who bore the title of assistant Military Attaché.

"Atherley, I've got one of our chaps downstairs—Torrens, from Morocco. I wonder if you'd see him?"

"Good morning, Melplash. Why does the man from Morocco want
to see *me?*" Atherley asked rather repressively, putting a finger in the
Magalhães family to keep his place.

"He seems to think he may want backing-up at a higher level than
mine," Mr. Melplash replied, grinning cheerfully—"so he wants to put
you in the picture. D'you mind?"

"What's it all about?" Atherley asked.

"Some top-secret, top-priority Central European who's been got out,
and's coming here," Melplash said, in his usual hurried gabble.

"Not a Hungarian, by any chance?"

"Yes, I rather think it is—but he'll tell you all about it. May I bring
him up?"

"Very well," said Atherley resignedly, putting the Magalhães family
away in a drawer. H'm. That pretty Julia Probyn, whom he had met a
good deal when she was with the Ericeiras, and had liked enough to
take her along to Countess Páloczy's party two days ago—was she rather
well-informed, or what?

Melplash reappeared with a tall red-haired man. Having introduced
him he said—"Well, I'll leave you to it," and scuttled away.

"Now, what can I do for you?—or what do you hope I can do?" Atherley asked, pushing a gay Alentejo box of cigarettes across the table to
his visitor.

"Thanks. We might not want you to do anything—but then again we
might," said Major Torrens, grinning rather more subtly than his intro-
ducer had done. "May I hold forth?"

"Please." As he said the word Atherley was reminded of Hetta, and
smiled a little.

"We have just got someone rather important out of Hungary—" Torrens began.

"How?" Atherley interjected.

"He came out as part of the Hungarian film unit which arrived a few days ago for the Film Festival at Cannes; they're showing two films this year—both rather good, I hear. And as you know, some of the stars and so on usually go too, for prestige purposes."

"Is this individual a film-star?"

Torrens laughed.

"Good God no! But he came out disguised as a technical director; one of the real stars is pro-West, and arranged with our man in Hungary to bring him along."

"Where is he now? In Cannes?"

"No. Our people have got him out. Not too easy—the opposition were watching them all the time like lynxes; but the star organised *five* different parties on the same day; to La Turbie, Vence, Grasse, and what-have-you; that rather foxed the sleuths, and our man got down to the Vieux Port and on board a little yacht, and sailed away to Port Vendres."

"Where is that?"

"The last port in France before the Spanish frontier—a tiny place. He's in Spain now, on his way here."

"May I know why he's coming here? To live?"

"No, he's going on to the States; primarily I suppose to boost the morale of the Hungarians there—you know there are something like 100,000 of them in and around Pittsburgh alone—and of course to give up-to-date information to the Free Hungary Committee, or whatever it's called. But I think the 'Voice of America' people have their eye on him too, for broadcasts."

"Then why is he coming here? Just to take a plane? If so, I hardly see where the Embassy comes in, if his papers are in order—and I'm sure your people have seen to it that they are," Richard said, in rather chilling tones.

"Oh yes, his papers are all right—a German technician with a specialised knowledge of printing processes and types! I'm told he speaks faultless German."

"Does he know anything about printing processes?"

"Seemingly he does, a great deal; but he isn't coming here for typography," Torrens said, looking a little amused. "He has to make an important contact, which may take some time. If all goes well there will be no need to bother anyone—but if we run into any trouble it might be necessary for the Embassy to step in."

"The Ambassador would hate that," Richard said, continuing to display the regular diplomatist's reasoned and wholesome distaste for any involvement in under-cover activities. "Have you any reason to expect trouble?"

For the first time his visitor hesitated. "Well?" Atherley pressed him.

"I'm not sure, really. There was no difficulty whatever at Cerbère—that's the Spanish frontier post near Port Vendres; but on the way to Barcelona, by car of course, there was what *might* have been an incident, at a little pub where they stopped to eat. Another car drew up, several men came in, apparently tipsy, ordered wine, and contrived to start a general fracas, in the course of which our men got the impression that there was an attempt to slug the Hungarian. We had three people with him, and two of them were middle-weight boxers, so they slugged the sluggers, and got clear. But of course he would have been missed in Cannes well before that, and presumably spotters spotted him as he crossed the frontier, and followed him."

Richard frowned.

"Probably—that's common form, of course. Anything since?"

"Not so far—but I only heard that this morning. We're holding him over in Barcelona for forty-eight hours before he flies to Madrid. We have a fairly thug-proof hide-out for him there."

"And from Madrid he comes here?"

"Yes, and stays a bit to meet his contact before flying on to America."

"I see." Atherley brooded. "You have an equally thug-proof hide-out for him here, I hope?"

"I think so. Melplash has it in hand."

Atherley restrained a groan—he had never been inspired with much confidence by Mr. Melplash. But he let it pass.

"Do you by any chance know a Miss Julia Probyn?" he now asked.

Torrens stared a little, surprised at the question.

"Yes, I do." He gave a sudden confidential grin. "She stood me up once, completely, out in Morocco."

"Oh, really? How amusing. When was that?"

"Year before last."

"And you haven't seen her since?"

Torrens looked still more surprised.

"Yes—I met her here in January, on my way home to report. But why?"

"No reason on earth," Atherley lied easily, pleased with the information he had picked up. "Except that I wondered if you would come to lunch on Thursday to meet her."

Torrens was caught off guard.

"Is she still here? I thought she went back to England in March."

Then they *are* in touch, Atherley thought to himself, but not in very close touch.

"She did, but she came back five days ago, to cover the wedding for some paper. So I hope you are free on Thursday. Little Countess Hetta Páloczy will be there too."

"Oh, really? The one who's just got out? Yes—thank you, I should like to come very much."

"Good—that will be very pleasant. Just the four of us, I thought—it will be easier for Countess Hetta. She seems a little inclined to find the West the *Wild* West," Atherley said. "Not really so surprising, in a way." He gave Torrens a card with the address of his house, and scribbled the hour on it. "Goodbye for the moment," he said, rising to terminate the interview.

When his visitor had gone Atherley sat for a little while, reflecting on what he had heard. Torrens himself impressed him favourably: he was in quite a different class to so many of these S.I.S. types—like poor little Melplash, for instance. He rang up the Military Attaché—the Embassy had a private exchange, unconnected with the Lisbon telephone system except for outside calls—and asked a few questions. The M.A. did not know very much, but the little he did was satisfactory: a sound man, thoroughly reliable, and with a high reputation. "He was in the Scots Guards to begin with," he said, with a certain finality.

"That won't make H.E. like it any better if he drags us into some mix-up over a Central European," Atherley said rather sourly—and Colonel Campbell laughed down the telephone. "Let's hope he won't," he said.

Atherley continued to reflect. Quite clearly it must have been from Major Torrens that the lovely Julia had picked up her rumour about the important Hungarian, presumably when he passed through Lisbon in January. Both his own impression of the man, and the Military Attaché's account of his record led Atherley to decide that his visitor was not a person to talk recklessly about service matters; he would only do so to someone with whom he was involved in some way, usually emotionally. But not necessarily emotionally, of course, he thought; they might be working together. Press assignments sometimes covered other activities. H'm. Perhaps he had better try to find out from Miss Probyn a little more about her relations with the Major, past *and* present. When dealing with these Secret Service people—or indeed with almost anyone—it was impossible to know too much. He had actually reached out his hand to the telephone on his desk when the instrument gave its low discreet buzz— he lifted the receiver.

"Atherley," he said.

"Good morning, Richard." It was the Ambassador's voice.

"Oh, good morning, Sir. How is her Ladyship?"

"Splendid, thank you—and the baby is putting on weight like any-thing! She gets up today, and I think we ought to have a cocktail party next week; we seem to have been more or less *incomunicado* for some time. I thought of Friday—Helen should be thoroughly strong by then. But we should like you to be there. Are you free?"

"Of course, Sir," Atherley said dutifully, even while he felt in his breast-pocket for his engagement book, and thumbed it awkwardly with his left hand to find next Friday's page. Before he had found it—and his con-scious mind told him that it was merely to gain time—he added—"Shall you be asking Countess Hetta Páloczy? You know she's arrived?"

"Oh yes, so she has. How interesting—I expect Helen would like to meet her. Must the mother come too? Yes, I suppose she must. Very well—I'll ask Miss Cuthbertson to send cards to them both. *What* is the girl called?"

"Countess Hetta"—he spelt it out.

"Yes. The surname is the trouble; but I expect Miss Cuthbertson knows how to spell it. I never can be certain whether Polish or Hungarian names are the worst! Well, we shall count on you on Friday."

"I shall look forward to it, Sir. And I'll see that Miss Cuthbertson gets the name right! Countess Hetta is an interesting girl—unusual," Richard added; and then wondered why he had said that.

"I imagine that she has led a rather unusual life, by our standards," said the Ambassador a little drily, and rang off.

After a moment or two Richard lifted his receiver again and asked the bi-lingual telephone operator—the Portuguese wife of one of the Eng-lish-born Chancery messengers—to ring up the Duke of Ericeira's house and get Miss Probyn for him. He then replaced the receiver, opened the drawer in his desk, and resumed his study of the life of the domesticated but so informative Magalhães family. When that discreet buzz came again he once more took up the instrument as before, saying "Atherley."

"Really, Richard," Julia's voice said indignantly—"what a way to speak! Atherley indeed! Have you become a Duke, or something?"

"No, it's simply common form—it avoids confusion," Richard said. "Can you come round to my house for a drink this evening?"

"Party?"

"No, you and me. Yes—No?"

"Yes"—rather hesitantly. "Yes, I think probably. Could I call you back presently and let you know? What time?"

"By all means. Sevenish—or whatever suits you." As he put back the receiver he added aloud—"According to what time your dinner with Major Torrens is, dear Julia!" The Major, he decided, had been uncommonly quick off the mark after learning that Miss Probyn was in Lisbon; indeed, unless he had telephoned from the Embassy he could hardly have done it in the time—he had left Atherley's room under half-an-hour earlier. Curiosity prompted Richard to find out about this.

"Mrs. Tomlinson, did a Major Torrens put a call through from the Chancery this morning?" he asked the operator.

"Yes, Mr. Atherley, he did—about twenty minutes ago, from Mr. Melplash's room. Mr. Melplash spoke to me first."

"Quite all right, Mrs. Tomlinson. It was to the Duke of Ericeira's, wasn't it?"

"Yes, Mr. Atherley. To the same young lady that you spoke to just now." There was a certain smugness, Richard thought, about the operator's voice. "Thank you," he said.

Julia rang back later to say that she would be with Richard at 6:45—"I've a dinner engagement."

"Do you want fetching?" the young man asked.

"No no—I have my own car; got it yesterday."

"I'm glad the firm's so rich," he mocked.

Julia was looking very lovely when she came into his drawing-room that evening, in a short full-skirted sub-evening dress of very rich dark-green brocaded silk.

"Goodness, Julia, what a frock!"

"It's my wedding dress. Do you really like it?"

"It's *quite* beautiful," Richard said. "But I am afraid you have probably put it on more for Major Torrens than for me."

The detested blush dyed Julia's cheeks to the tone of a fully-ripened apricot set against a sunny wall.

"What do *you* know of Major Torrens, pray?" she asked rather tartly.

"He came to see me this morning, and I very kindly told him that you were here, which he didn't know. You owe this dinner to *me*, dear Julia."

She laughed. "Oh well."

"Poor liaison, I thought," Richard pursued. "You didn't know he was here either, till he rang you up at 11:15 A.M., or as near as no matter."

"Richard, how *do* you know all this?"

"Never mind that, for the moment. But as a reward for my valuable services, will you now tell me exactly how you stalled him in Morocco last year? Come on—I have a feeling that it's a good story."

It was rather a good story—how she had gone to Tangier to look for her missing cousin Colin Monro, and in the course of her search for him had stumbled on Major Torrens' current activity of shipping a new and rare radioactive mineral out of Morocco; how her enquiries, quite without her intention, had raised so much dust that the operation had to be closed down. However, they had got all they needed for tests by that time, Julia said airily, so it didn't matter—"and now Morocco is such a muck-up that nobody can do anything there anyhow. I was blown up by a bomb!" she added, rather proudly.

"Good Heavens! Not that affair at Marrakesh? Wasn't some Duke blown up too?" Richard asked, quite driven off his usual careful-casual line.

"Yes, Angus Ross-shire. But nothing like as bad as me—here's my scar." She lifted her lion-gold hair to display a narrow white line running down her forehead.

"Golly! And did you ever find your cousin?"

"Oh yes; he was working for Hugh—for Major Torrens," she corrected herself hastily—"running the stuff on his little smugglers' yacht."

"Is he still with Torrens?—though I expect I shall soon be calling him Hugh myself," Richard said.

"Oh, rather—though he isn't here just now."

No, dear girl—I expect he and his little yacht have been scooting from Cannes to Port Vendres with a Hungarian passenger on board, Richard thought to himself. He gave his beautiful guest another drink, and when they parted it was on terms of greater intimacy and liking than before—Julia even, finally, vouchsafed laughing that at one point Major Torrens had suggested employing her.

"Oh, you would do them a treat—I can't think why they hesitate for a moment," Richard said, standing at his door, while she climbed into her rather large hired car. The bright Lisbon evening was soft and full of stars; lights from houses shone, warm and yellow, along the built-up sides of the ravine. "See you Thursday," he called as the girl drove off.

CHAPTER IV

THAT WAS on a Tuesday. On Wednesday evening, just as he was locking the drawers in his desk prior to leaving the Chancery Richard's telephone buzzed. It was Major Torrens, who asked if he could come round to see him.

"How soon?" Richard asked without much enthusiasm—he was dining out.

"Immediately."

"How soon is that? Where are you?"

"Oh, where I am! But I can be with you in eight minutes."

"Very well," the Head of Chancery said resignedly; he unlocked one of his drawers and took out the *Familia Magalhães*, who kept him company till Torrens arrived.

"Any trouble?" Richard asked.

"A little. The opposition seem to be rather active in Spain."

"Really? They haven't copped your man?"

"No—but it was only by accident that they didn't. I told you about the little hold-up between Cerbère and Barcelona—owing to that he missed the plane he was to have taken to Madrid. But *that* plane had engine failure and made a forced landing right out in the country somewhere on the upper Ebro—and the moment it landed a number of murky-looking types, who certainly weren't all innocent peasants, swarmed round it and made a rather thorough inspection of the passengers."

"Um. Cause of engine-failure known?"

"Yes. Sugar in the petrol-tanks—the Iberia people are quite solid on that."

"Did Iberia report the murky types?"

"No. One of our people from Madrid was on board, and mentioned them—he'd gone to Barcelona to meet our party, but had to get back at once."

"And where is your man now?"

"On his way to Madrid by train, I hope."

Richard considered. "Have you any idea who 'they' are, in Spain?— the actual operators? Spaniards?"

"I fancy so; leave-overs from the Civil War. Funny how little people in England realise what a Communist-dominated affair that was! A lot of them fled to North Africa—Morocco was full of them when I was there; but I suppose they are sent back to Spain as required. They would be more suitable than anyone else for the job. I gather some East Germans are in it too—Spain is full of German business men just now, doing an export drive, and nothing is easier than for an East German to masquerade as a West German."

"Well, that's all most interesting," Atherley said, glancing furtively at his desk clock. "But where do we come in?"

Torrens laughed.

"You don't, yet. I really only wanted to warn you that if they are as busy here as they seem to be in Spain, we might have to call on you. But I hope not."

"So do I, I assure you!" Richard said with considerable fervour. "Well, I shall see you tomorrow."

The cards for the cocktail party at the British Embassy arrived the day before Hetta set out for Mr. Atherley's luncheon. Hetta was always up early—lying late, let alone breakfast in bed, formed no part of her pattern of living; she usually went to Mass at half-past seven in the big church just across the gardens, and then ran on down to the sandy *plage* for a quick swim before walking back, glowing and contented, to breakfast— the water was still very cold, but she liked that. On this particular morn- ing a letter lay beside her plate—apart from the note which Townsend Waller had sent with his flowers, it was the first that she had received since she arrived in Portugal. "Who should write to me?" she muttered, as she tore open the stiff envelope.

The formal card, with the Lion and the Unicorn embossed in gold, impressed her a good deal—and why, she asked herself, should Lady Loseley, who appeared to live at the British Embassy, ask her, Hetta, to a cocktail party? Hetta knew by now what cocktail parties were, her mother had taken her to several since her clothes arrived; but she knew no one at the British Embassy except Mr. Atherley. When she had finished her coffee and rolls she went to her mother's bedroom—the Countess always breakfasted in bed. After the good-morning kiss Hetta held out the card.

"Mama, I am invited to a party at the English Embassy."

"So am I," said her mother; she looked very pleased, Hetta noticed. "But is it not rather strange, since I don't know them?"

"Not very strange—people are interested to meet you. The Loseleys are charming," she went on, "and of course as we know Mr. Atherley, and he is on the staff there, it is quite reasonable that we should be asked." Hetta realised then that this was her mother's first invitation to the British Em- bassy, and that it was a source of satisfaction to her. How peculiar!

Hetta set off in the Countess's car for her luncheon with Richard Atherley with sensations which were rather mixed. She was pleased to be going to see again, and in his own house, the man who remembered Detvan and the sun there; on the other hand she was a little nervous about this, the first social engagement that she had attended alone, though that big beautiful English girl whom she liked so much would be there— evidently a great friend of Mr. Atherley's. Bowling smoothly up the Tagus estuary, her thoughts were occupied with this new world of hers. She had asked Mgr Subercaseaux, at confession, about going to lunch with young men, and had received full sanction; later he had been to see her at the hotel when her mother was out, and spent an hour with her. He was kind, genial even, and clearly anxious to help her and to smooth her path in this unfamiliar life; but she did not like his kind of help, and she did not like him. The fact was that Hetta Páloczy found herself rather up against the Western world as presented to her at Estoril in many of its aspects, of which the social ease, the urbane worldly wisdom of her mother's confessor was most definitely one. The richly-dressed congregation at Mass on Sundays, with shiny cars waiting outside, the interior richness of the churches themselves, with all their treasures displayed, not hidden away in the deep reed thatch of some peasant's house for security—the very safety of it all jarred on her, after the passionate devotion of the people at home, holding with such stubborn intensity to the practice of their religion in the face of persecution and danger. She remembered the skilful, wary sermons preached—only very rarely—by Father Antal, when he knew full well that there would be several "Spitzel" (Communist spies) posted among the congregation, waiting to lay information against him if anything he said could possibly be twisted into an anti-Communist utterance. Here, priests were safe, and could preach as they pleased—and then go on to eat of delicate dishes at luncheon, bow to rich ladies, and make graceful little jokes. "Pfui!" said Hetta (who spoke German as well as she did French, English, and Hungarian) to herself.

Of course she was unjust. The young often are, and with less reason than Hetta, who had grown up in an unusually hard school; born courageous and tough, she had become intolerant. But as the car pulled up outside Atherley's little white house she forgot her criticisms in a warm feeling of happy anticipation.

A pretty smiling maid in a frilly apron and white cotton gloves led her up the narrow staircase and ushered her into the long narrow drawing-room; Atherley turned from the window at the far end as she entered, came over and kissed her hand.

"Here you are—how nice. Your chauffeur found his way to my slum all right?"

"How do you do. Please, what is slum?" she asked.

"Slums are where poor people live; I am not so very poor, but I live in one because I like it. Come and see my neighbours"—and he led her to the window, below which the family life and daily activities of the inhabitants of the ravine were spread out like a diagram, or a child's toy farm on the floor. Hetta studied them all, thoughtfully.

"This looks nice," she said at length. "So we lived in the Alföld, cooking

and washing out of doors when it was warm weather. But this is 'slum'?"
She pronounced the word with full Hungarian plumminess.

"No, it isn't really a slum at all," Richard said, forced into accuracy by
her literalness. "I was being affected. Slums are degraded places in big
cities, like London or New York, where people have no gardens, and no
chance to live with decency or dignity. If there are gardens there is never
degradation, and therefore no slums. That is Dr. Salazar's idea too," he
went on—"When he lays out a new working-class suburb he insists that
each house shall have a *bout de terre*, a small garden-plot where the husband can grow onions and saladings to bring in to his wife, instead of
wasting his evenings and his money in drinking. He says that sociologically
this is a fundamental principle, and he's quite right."

Some of this was rather too difficult for Hetta's command of English—
she seized on Dr. Salazar.

"He dictates this country, no?"

"NO, and no twenty times!" Richard exploded. "He guides it." He went
on for some time about Dr. Salazar, for whom he had a well-founded
admiration.

"You must forgive me—I am still learning," Hetta said. She turned away
from the window to the room. "But where is Miss Probeen? She does not
come?"

"Yes, she's coming all right; she's only late, as usual. Come and have a
drink. Townsend tells me you like sherry better than cocktails."

"He remembers this? How *nice* he is," Hetta said warmly.

Atherley, having given her a glass of sherry, was busy with the cocktail-
shaker. "Oh yes, Townsend is nice," he said, without much enthusiasm—
why should young Hetta think Townsend so very nice? "Tell me," he
said as he filled his own glass, "did the Monsignor say that you might
go out alone to lunch with young men? Did you ask him?"

"Yes, I did—and he said yes, certainly. He explained many things," said
Hetta; a certain lack of enthusiasm was evident in her tones.

"Don't you like him?" the young man asked, slightly surprised.

"No—I do not. He—"

The door was opened by the befrilled maid to usher in Julia and Major
Torrens. There were greetings, one introduction, drinks—then they went
down to the little dining-room on the ground floor.

It was a pleasant meal. The other three bestirred themselves to draw
Hetta out, and in this congenial company they found little difficulty in doing so. The food, which as always in Atherley's house was delicious,
caused her to volunteer her most spontaneous observations: she ate care-

fully, consideringly, Atherley noticed with approval, and occasionally commented on a dish.

"There is something—yes, it is *fenouil*—how do you say that in English? —in this sauce," she said at one point. "*So* good."

"We call *fenouil* fennel," said Atherley—"but how smart of you to spot it. I always tell Joaquina to put very little of any flavouring in things, so that people shall wonder why they taste good, but not know why."

"This is so *right*—and she does it beautifully. I should not have known if I were not a cook myself."

"You a cook!" Torrens exclaimed. "What do you mean?"

"I have been a cook for six years in Hungary," Hetta replied airily—"to a priest. A nun whom I was with was supposed to be his cook, but she was *so* bad, therefore I did it. I love cooking."

"Do you really?" the Major asked, fixing her with a startled eye.

"Oh yes—also I love food," the girl said frankly. "And is it not a form of blasphemy to abuse the gifts of God by bringing them badly cooked, and therefore *horrible,* to the table?"

"Amen to that," Richard said, while the others laughed.

There was only one rough patch, and it was Hetta's fault. Inevitably the subject of the royal wedding came up, and Julia mentioned in all innocence the extreme desire of a certain highly-placed official's wife to attend it—through the Ericeiras she was *au courant* with all the social and political gossip of Lisbon.

"Well, if Madame de X. wants to see Princess Maxine married, X. will have to stop his opposition to the new ferry scheme," Richard said, equally innocently. "He's been making a perfect nuisance of himself to the Government about that."

"Oh, he will—I understand that he went round to the Ministry this morning in a plain van, carrying a small ladder to climb down by," Julia said gaily, causing everyone to laugh. Except Hetta, who leant across the table, gazing at the young Englishwoman with what Torrens later described as a basilisk's eye.

"May I know?—this Monsieur de X. attached importance to opposing the ferry scheme, whatever this may be?"

"Certainly he did"—Richard, rather negligently, answered for Julia.

"And withdraws his opposition at his wife's wish, because she will see a princess married?"

"Just that. Men are often rather at the mercy of their wives."

"But for this man, this Minister, it was a matter of principle to oppose?"

"One imagines so, or he would hardly have made so much fuss for so long," Richard said frankly. "But why, Countess? Does it matter?" He was astonished at her persistence.

"To me such a thing is infamous," Hetta Páloczy said, once again with that ring in her voice. "To sacrifice a principle for a social occasion! Where I come from people *die* for a principle!"

Of course that led to an awkward little pause. It was broken by Julia Probyn, who said gently—"I expect we all lead frightfully low, unworthy lives by comparison with the people you have been accustomed to live among. I'm sorry. That's the way we are—we have been too safe, and had it too easy, for too long. You'll have to be patient with us—I hope you will be."

"Oh, *you* are nice—you are *true!* I knew this at once! Please forgive me—everything here is so strange!" She looked ready to burst into tears.

"Of course it's strange to you—and in fact we are probably a lot of miserable bastards, as Miss Probyn says," Richard said comfortingly. "Don't worry, Hetta—if I may call you that?"

"Hetti, please," she said, the tears now falling.

"Very well. Dear Hetti, go upstairs with Julia and powder your nose, and then come and have coffee in the garden."

The garden was really only a small flagged terrace at the back of the house, shaded by a vine trained over a trellis, with two or three narrow flowerbeds; its low walls were both faced and topped with glossy blue-and-yellow *azulejos*. There was an azulejo-topped table too, and some garden-chairs with cushions, but when the two girls came out Torrens and Atherley were sitting on the wall, enjoying the view.

"Oh, how pretty!" Hetta said with her little *grande dame* air, to Richard's relief entirely ignoring the scene she had created only a few minutes before. "But this is perfectly charming." She went to the wall and looked over. "Another garden—is this yours also?" she asked him.

"No, that belongs to one of my neighbours," he said. In fact the gardens of the little houses below came right up to the foot of the wall; the nearest was full of ancient and enormous medlar-trees with grey leathery leaves, vegetables growing among them; similar gardens, divided from one another by the frailest of fences draped in runner beans, spread right down to the houses at the bottom. Torrens turned to examine them, standing with a foot on the wall.

"Where does that track between the houses go to?" he asked.

"It leads out into a maze of little streets, down towards the river, and that level-crossing where the goods trains hoot so frightfully at 2 A.M. Lady Loseley is always grumbling to the Commandant of the City about it; she says the noise comes right in at the Embassy windows," Atherley said.

"Perfect get-away if you wanted one—drop off the wall and down through those shrubs and creepers," Torrens pursued.

"Ah, but I enjoy diplomatic immunity, so I don't have to think of those things, Torrens. Hetti, have some coffee?"

"Richard, I think I've persuaded Countess Hetta to come out and have supper at the Guincho on Tuesday," Julia said—"Will you come too? Hugh, of course, goes without saying."

"Julia, I don't go *anywhere* without saying. What is the Guincho?"

"A place along the coast beyond Cascais, all sand and rocks, with one or two little shacks of restaurants where one gets the most delicious seafood."

"Thank you, I shall love to come," said Atherley. "I like the Guincho."

"Good. Perhaps you'll bring Hugh, and I will take the Countess."

"If Mama has nothing else arranged for me—but I can let you know, if you will give me your address."

"Oh, I'll keep you in touch with one another," said Richard rather hastily. "Don't bother, Julia." He made a face at her over Hetta's head, and Julia obediently put away her card-case—she had become accustomed to the use of visiting-cards during her stay in Portugal.

Richard drove Hetta back to Estoril. The moment they were in the car she apologised for her behaviour at lunch. "To be so angry, and to cry! I am very sorry; I was silly—as silly as a nun!"

"Are nuns silly?"

"Only when they come out into the world, and everything is strange. Not in convents."

Richard had been startled, and rather upset, by Hetta's outburst. He was considerably taken with her, little dark thing that she was, with her splendid eyes and her remarkable voice—and he found her freshness of outlook interesting. But Atherley liked a certain ease and smoothness in social intercourse, and he had remembered Julia's uncomfortable remark about Hetta's conventual life possibly "smothering dynamite."

"Oh well, I don't think you are silly, only a little inexperienced, and perhaps rather too fierce," he said, turning and smiling at her. "You will have to learn to take people as they come. Tell me," he went on, "why you don't like Subercaseaux? You were just going to when the others came."

"He is part of it all," Hetta said slowly, looking straight in front of her.

"Part of all what?"

"This life here. So much is false, I think—the importance of attending the marriage of a King's child, of being invited to an Embassy—or that politician who sacrifices his principles to gratify his wife's snobbism! I cannot help it—I have said I am sorry that I burst out at your table—but to me all this is incomprehensible, *despicable*. And for a priest to accept it all, take part in it!"

"Oh, that's your quarrel with the Monsignor, is it? Well yes, he does take part, I agree. But can't he perhaps do good by doing so?"

"Possibly. Back there, where I come from, compromise is not possible; our priests live in hourly danger. If you knew the risks Father Antal runs!"

"Is he the priest you cooked for?" She nodded. "What special risks did he run?"

"Going to see the Cardinal—" and she told him more of what she had told Townsend, ending up—"But he at least does not compromise with evil."

"But Hetti, *are* royal weddings and Embassy parties evil? Don't you exaggerate?"

"Oh, there are those lovely ships!" the girl exclaimed, forgetting the argument as the car came in sight of thirty or more big schooners, lying at anchor out in the Tagus. "These are the ones which go to catch the salt fish, no?"

"Yes; all the way to Newfoundland"—and Richard told her about the annual voyage of the Portuguese cod-fishing fleet to the foggy waters of the New World, to catch, salt on board, and bring home *bacalhau,* the dried fish which is a main part of the staple food of the nation, in town and country alike; at the next place they came to he made a detour through side streets to show her the flat triangular bodies hanging up in a grocer's shop. They were as hard as boards, and Hetta fingered one doubtfully. "Is it not very nasty?" she asked.

"Yes, if it's badly cooked it's quite horrible, but properly prepared it can be delicious. Next time you come to lunch with me you shall have it; Joaquina does it wonderfully, especially with braised fried onions, buttered rice, and a very mild mustard sauce."

"You speak like a cook yourself!" said Hetta laughing, as they drove on.

"Yes, I'm interested in food. I completely agreed with what you said at lunch about the blasphemous nature of bad cooking—I liked you for that," Richard said, again turning to smile at her. "But do you know"—and he went on to tell her how every spring before the bacalhau fleet sailed the Cardinal-Patriarch of Lisbon said a special Mass for all the men of it, out on the quay-side if it was fine, in the great Jeronimos church at Belém if it was wet.

"Oh, how I should like to see this," Hetta said.

"Get the Monsignor to take you—he always goes, and he'll get you a good seat."

"This he would *certainly* do!" the girl said ironically.

"Hetti, I think you're taking Subercaseaux up all wrong," Richard said. "Don't make up your mind in too much of a hurry. I think he's a splendid person."

"You are fond of him?" She sounded incredulous.

"Yes, and I admire him. He adapts himself to his world, of course—which you will have to do, sooner or later—but he *does* do good in it, for that very reason." He spoke with unusual earnestness; Hetta was silent.

Between the small towns strung out along the Tagus there are still open spaces of waste land, for the most part dry and sandy, where occasionally small flocks of sheep or goats, with tinkling bells, crop such scanty herbage as they can find—it is one of the charms of the environs of Lisbon, this artless penetration of the life of the country into the life of the town. In spring these waste spaces are misted over with the flowers of a minute dwarf iris, drifts of blue against the background of yellowish soil. A few moments after Atherley's last remarks about the Monsignor, which still remained unanswered, the car drew abreast of one such open space—"Oh, *could* we stop?" Hetta asked.

He pulled in to the side at once, by no means unwilling to prolong this tête-à-tête. "Of course—what is it?" he asked.

"The little lilies—for days I have wanted to pick them, but Mama is always in too much hurry for us to stop." She began to get out of the car.

"They die in five minutes," he told her, thinking—How she runs away from a subject! But he did not believe that it was from cowardice—why was it?

The girl came back after a moment or so with her hands full of the lovely little things; in the car she sat looking at them in silent delight.

"They aren't lilies really, they're irises," he told her as they drove on.

"So? The iris is the rainbow, isn't it?"

"I believe so; but it's this kind of flower too."

In a few minutes the small blossoms did indeed begin to wilt and shrivel together, as Richard had foretold; it is a fact that this particular species cannot endure separation from the soil.

"Oh!—oh! they *do* fade," Hetta lamented. "But it is so few minutes."

"I told you so," Richard said, slowing down again; he looked at her as she sat beside him, ruefully contemplating the flowers in her hands, noticing for the first time how strong and shapely those hands were, but also—in spite of nail-varnish and other evidences of careful manicuring—that the skin on the inside of the fingers was still cracked and roughened from, no doubt, hard kitchen work. They were strange hands to be associated with that pretty dress, the elegant shoes and hat, the careful make-up—somehow they moved him rather surprisingly.

"They say that if flowers fade quickly on a person it means a warm heart," he said. "But these anyhow fade the moment they are picked, so they tell me nothing about your heart."

"Do you want to know about my heart?" she asked, with a readiness that rather startled him. "Why? It is a most ordinary one."

Why indeed?—if he did; and to his immense astonishment he found that he did in fact want to know if Hetta Páloczy's heart was or was not warm.

"I think perhaps I might want to," he said, starting the car again. "People's hearts are interesting, don't you think?"

"I have never thought whether they are warm or not—if it is important, surely one knows this," Hetta said casually. "Mr. Atherley, I believe we should hurry a little—Mama is taking me to tea with some people at Colares this afternoon. Tell me," she went on, with one of her abrupt switches of subject—"This Major Torrens and Miss Probeen: are they fiancés?"

"I don't know. They could be. They have known one another for some time, but for most of it he has been in Morocco and she here. What do you think?"

"I think there is some sort of relationship between them, but I am not sure if it is this one," said Hetta, as Richard swung the car round into the road alongside the public garden which led to the hotel. "Mr. Atherley, thank you so much—I have enjoyed my luncheon, and it was very good of you to bring me home."

"If I am allowed to call you Hetti, shouldn't you equalise it by calling me Richard?" he said, drawing up before the door of the hotel.

"Possibly. I will ask your friend Monsignor Subercaseaux about this!" she said in a sudden laughing flash. "Goodbye." She sprang out of the car and vanished into the hotel.

"Lumme! Is she a coquette as well as all the rest?" the young man asked himself as he drove off. "That would be odd, in a convent-bred cook!"

At the same moment Hetta, going up in the lift, was also asking herself a question. When Atherley brought Miss Probyn to her mother's party, in her innocence she had assumed automatically that they were engaged; having seen Julia and Major Torrens together, and having just heard Atherley's detached assessment of the situation, she saw clearly that this, at least, was not the case. But why was she glad?

Mme de Fonte Negra's luncheon on Sunday was a very different affair from Richard's little party. She rang up in the morning to stress the fact that Hetta must be there "at 1:20—very precisely, please."

"How curious!—who can be coming?" Countess Páloczy said, when Hetta mentioned this. "All right, I will tell Oliveira." Oliveira was the chauffeur. "She didn't say why?"

"No—just what I told you."

In fact the party included the Duke of Ericeira and his sister—both elderly and rather silent, though when they did speak to Hetta it was in excellent English; but also the Comte de Bretagne, the Pretender to the throne of Armorica, and his tall splendid wife. Her hostess warned Hetta of their advent the moment she arrived, and kindly informed her as to the drill. "They are of the blood royal, but as he does not occupy the throne you merely sketch a curtsey to each; and you address him as Monseigneur, not Sire."

Hetta was rather vexed, partly because she was to meet these royalties behind her mother's back, as it were—and was it not all rather what she called "false," this business of the degree of curtseying, and whether to say *Sire* or *Monseigneur*? While they waited she expressed this view in an undertone to Mgr Subercaseaux, the only person she knew among the company.

"But why?" he said, raising his rather bushy iron-grey eyebrows. "It is exactly like Bridge."

"Bridge?"

"Yes, Contract Bridge—possibly you have never played it. But in this card-game there are certain 'conventions,' as they are called—rules, if you like; and unless all the players observe them it spoils the game."

"So one's life is to be as a game of cards!" said Hetta, rather contemptuously.

"Precisely. In effect, human life, particularly in its social aspects, is very like a game of cards! But the point of my observation, my dear young lady, is that it is as unfair to one's fellow-humans as to one's fellow-card-players not to observe the rules, and so to cause confusion or embarrassment. Did your Director at the Sacré-Cœur never tell you that courtesy is a part of charity?"

"Of course he did," Hetta said, flaring up. "But—"

"There is no 'but' in this case," said Mgr Subercaseaux, still urbanely. "Courtesy, and therefore charity, are to be applied to all human contacts. Our Blessed Lord never stated that one should be rude to Kings—on the contrary, He was rather specific about rendering the proper dues to Caesar, you may remember. Ah, here they are," he said, getting up.

The Comte and Comtesse de Bretagne in fact entered with very little fuss or ceremony, except that all the women made tiny bobs to them; they seemed to know nearly everybody, took cocktails, and stood about chatting

easily. Presently the Comte came over, glass in hand, to where Hetta and
Subercaseaux still stood together.

"Now, Monsignor, I am going to rob you of this young lady's company
for a little while," he said; "I want to talk to her. Countess, will you
indulge me by sitting on this charming canapé? I hope it will bear us both"
—as he sat down on a fragile gilt settee, patting the shining brocade beside him. "I am heavier than I look."

"You do not look at all heavy, Monseigneur," Hetta said, remembering
her instructions—her companion, though fairly tall, was far from stout.

"No, but I have heavy bones. There, now we are comfortable, well
arranged, *n'est-ce pas?* Now tell me—"

Hetta's prejudices about royal personages melted rapidly in the next
few minutes. Her companion asked innumerable questions, but all extremely sensible ones, and apparently based on a degree of knowledge of
conditions in Hungary that astonished her. Could the peasants make any
sort of living on four-and-a-half hectares? How were the collective farms
going?—were they at all popular, and was their population increasing or
diminishing? What proportion, if any, of the people had a real enthusiasm for Communism? Who directed it in the villages?—and what class
of person provided the Commissars—Russians, or Hungarians? How about
religion? Could Mass be said freely?—and freely attended? What had become of the monks and nuns when they had to leave their Communities?
—how did they manage? And what about the Cardinal?

Hetta was soon answering eagerly, warmed by the intelligent quality
of these enquiries; as usual she was lucid and categorical, and her replies
provoked further questions—at the lively frankness of some of her statements the Comte de Bretagne laughed out loud, causing heads to turn
in the direction of the flimsy settee. Their hostess was finally obliged to
come and separate them, very deferentially, in order that the company
might go in to luncheon.

"But this is a wonderful girl!" the Pretender said to Mme de Fonte
Negra as he sat down at the head of her table—royalty, entertained, always takes the head of the table, and the hostess sits at his right hand.
"She is so observant and so uninhibited. Imagine her cooking for a *curé de
campagne!*"

"Monseigneur, you have betrayed me!" said Mme de Fonte Negra. "I
promised that if she came to my house she would be asked no questions."

"Oh, that is too bad! Why did you not warn me? Here, I will question
her no more, but I shall ask her to come to our house, and there she shall
talk to my family. She is immensely interesting."

"Her mother will not like that."

"*Pourquoi pas?* Do I know the mother?"

"No, Monseigneur, you do not. She is that enormously rich Countess Páloczy who lives in the hotel at Estoril."

"Ah, yes." He looked vague for a moment, a rather studied vagueness—then he turned to his hostess, his eyes twinkling.

"And you snatched away the daughter, alone, so that we might meet her?"

"*Je croyais vous procurer un plaisir, Monseigneur.*"

"Oh, you have, you have!—a genuine pleasure. She is thoroughly intelligent, and yet so naïve; it is as if she had just been born, at the age of—what, twenty?"

"Twenty-two." (That was the sort of thing Mme de Fonte Negra always knew.) "But I did not wish to involve Monseigneur in any *embêtements.*"

"Oh, I shall not let myself be *embêté!*—but I should very much like my wife and my children to hear her talk. If she comes alone to you, will she not perhaps come alone to us?"

"Monseigneur, you are a more serious proposition than I!" Mme de Fonte Negra said, laughing her stout jolly laugh. "And there is this complication, that Madame la Mère is dying to come to the wedding."

"Ah, *ça!*" His lively face became vague again, all of a sudden. "Too many wish to come to the wedding, which is after all an affair of the family! There is hardly place for a mouse." He twinkled again. "Is this an indispensable condition? I did not get the impression that the young lady is likely to be tied to anyone's apron-strings."

"I also think she is not—but she may have her own *embêtements*, poor child, with her mother."

"Do *you* know her?—the mother, I mean?"

"Oh yes, quite well. She is a kind woman, really, and spends much in charity—through Monsignor Subercaseaux, therefore it is well dispensed. But she has a certain *folie de la grandeur;* she lives for social success."

"I shall talk to the Monsignor about it," said the Pretender with decision.

"Do. He is her confessor, and can make her do anything."

The Comte de Bretagne did talk to Mgr Subercaseaux after lunch, while Hetta, summoned to sit on a larger sofa beside his wife, talked with her; again the girl had a small success, caused laughter. When the Bretagnes left, the Comtesse said warmly—"I hope you will come and visit us. I shall write to you."

Mgr Subercaseaux asked Hetta to give him a lift back to Estoril in the car, which had been sent to fetch her.

"The Comte and Comtesse de Bretagne wish you to lunch with them next week," he said when they were twisting down through steep narrow streets towards the speed-way along the Tagus.

"They are nice—I should like to go," said Hetta. "But does Mama know them?—visit there?"

The Monsignor was a little taken aback by this question—he hemmed. "In fact, no," he said at length.

"Then I shall not go."

He was surprised by her decisiveness.

"I think your mother might like it if you did," he said.

"I should not. Some other people gave me invitations today, but they seem not to know Mama; at least they did not come to her party. I will not go to such, just because they are curious to hear what I have to say."

She is really quite astute, the priest thought. He did not quite know how to tackle this new attitude; while he was considering what to say Hetta spoke again.

"Mama wishes very much to attend this wedding, does she not?"

"Yes, that is the case."

"Very well. If they invite her, I will lunch with the Comte and Comtesse de Bretagne with the utmost pleasure—but if they do not, I will not go."

At that he burst out laughing. This waif from the wilds of Hungary, issuing her ultimatum to a prince of the blood!

"I thought you considered any desire to attend royal ceremonies—unimportant," he said. He had seen Richard Atherley since that little luncheon, and been told of Hetta's outburst. But she was ready for him.

"My *ideas* on this must be quite unimportant, since I am so ignorant. But I do not wish to be entertained by people who do not know Mama." She paused. "I am sure Pappi would not have wished it," she said, her face suddenly quivering.

Mgr Subercaseaux leant over and patted her hand.

"My child, you are perfectly right," he said, in an unwonted burst of sincerity. "Leave it to me—your mother shall attend the wedding."

CHAPTER V

JULIA PROBYN's party at the Guincho took place on one of those soft warm spring evenings which can make April in Portugal a heavenly thing. The two girls drove through Cascais and on into open country, a broken shore of pale rocks and Atlantic rollers on their left, to the right the landscape swelling up towards the seaward end of the Serra da Cintra—ahead the blunt bulk of Cabo da Roca, the western-most cape on the mainland of Europe, stood up with its lighthouse. They parked the car and strolled down through sand to the restaurant, past outcrops of rock studded with small bright flowers, and big silver clumps of sea-holly growing in the creamy sand. The restaurant was certainly shack-like, as Julia had said; it was built of wood, and approached by a wooden outside staircase—but passing in from the balcony, set with a few small tables, one entered a pleasant room gay with bright cotton table-cloths, and on each table an array of bottles, and bunches of the yellow flowers of the sea-holly. It was all simple, homely, and rather quaint—Hetta was delighted.

"Oh, what a nice place! Our country csardas at home are like this." She fingered one of the check table-cloths almost lovingly. "I did not know that there were such places here."

"Oh yes, lots of them, in almost all countries," said Julia. "Look, the men haven't come yet, I can't think why they're so late—but you and I might start on our drinks. Inside or outside?"

"Oh, can we be outside? There, please."

Julia had learned from Richard Atherley that Hetta had an aversion to cocktails, and it was a fine, dry Portuguese champagne that she caused to be brought out to the small table on the balcony. "I think cocktails before sea-food are a mistake," she said—"and here one eats nothing else."

"Sea-food? What is this?"

"Oh, it's an American expression, but rather a good one—whatever comes out of the sea. Tonight we're having bisque of langouste—well that doesn't come out of the sea, it's a sort of fresh-water lobster—and then crab, cold, and sole, hot, and cheese and salad to finish off with. But the cooking is rather good in this funny little place; I shall be interested to know what you think of it, as a professional."

Hetta laughed.

"Do not make fun! Me a professional! And as we have no 'sea-food' in Hungary, I shall not be able to judge of it very well."

"I'm sure you *will*, Hetti. By the way, Townsend Waller is coming; he heard somehow that we were dining here, and he's dying to meet you again, so I asked him."

"I am glad. He is so *nice*." But Hetta's gaze was constantly straying sea-wards, where big breakers surged in to fall on a narrow stretch of sand between two points of rock. "Yulia, I wish so much to swim!" she exclaimed. "Can I not? This water is so much more *alive* than at Estoril—I would love to swim in it."

"Have you brought bathing-things?"

"No—but I can swim in my petticoat! I often swam in my nightdress in the Tisza."

"It's frightfully cold, and pretty rough," said Julia doubtfully.

"I swim strongly!" Hetta pronounced firmly; "and at Estoril I swim every day—for the first time, here, I swim in the sea. Oh, I do wish to! Where can I undress?"

Rather unwillingly, Julia arranged for Hetta to undress in the bedroom of the proprietor's wife; the girl emerged in a crêpe de chine slip under her pale tweed overcoat and ran gleefully down to the little sandy bay. But instead of plunging thence into the breaking waves she nipped up onto one of the rocky points, threw off her long coat, and entered the Atlantic in a clean dive just as Atherley, Townsend Waller, and Major Torrens arrived on the balcony.

"Good God, who on earth is that diving in?" Torrens exclaimed.

"Hetta Páloczy."

Atherley swung sharply round, and like the others stared towards the sea, where Hetta's black head promptly reappeared.

"What on earth did you let her do that for, Julia?" he said brusquely. "It's not a bit safe bathing here, in water as rough as this, except for very strong swimmers. Surely you know that?"

"She says she *is* a strong swimmer," said Julia coolly—with a second's wonder as to why Richard should be so cross. Anyhow, she was not going to excuse herself to him.

"And *how!*—just look at her!" Townsend exclaimed enthusiastically, watching that black head smoothly surmounting the great crests of the incoming waves. Indeed she seemed to be an eel, a fish, and the water her natural element—as she got further out the watchers noticed that she took to turning onto her back to slide down feet foremost into the trough behind a wave, swinging over as the next approached to cross it with her powerful breast-stroke.

"She seems thoroughly in control," said Torrens.

"Yes. Have a drink," said Julia turning to the table, and filling their glasses with the delicate wine.

"Just the same, I think we ought to yell to her to come back now," Townsend said after a few moments; "she may get into a current—she's going pretty far out."

"Well, yell," Julia said. "She may pay attention to you—she wouldn't to me."

Townsend cupped his hands round his mouth and bellowed "Hetta!"
The black head turned on the summit of a green crest.

"Come on in!" Townsend roared. "We're hungry!"

They could see her laughing face as she turned round and started to
swim towards the shore. But it is much easier to swim out through big
waves than to swim back with them; each one bears you forward, but
after it has passed there is a strong suck-back in the trough until the next
carries you on again. Atherley could see Hetta frowning as she encountered this phenomenon—glass in hand, they all stood at the rickety rail of
the balcony, watching her progress with some anxiety. But she soon learned
the trick of it, swimming vigorously with each overtaking wave, then relaxing till the next came along.

"God, she is a good swimmer!" Townsend said, watching appreciatively. "Half the people who get drowned in swimming do it coming back
in water like this. She must have had a lot of practice."

"No, she says she never swam in the sea in her life till she came to
Estoril," said Julia.

"Well, really, Julia, I must say—" Atherley was beginning angrily when
Townsend exclaimed—"Oh, watch out!"

The one thing that Hetta was not prepared for, strong and resourceful
as she was in the water, was the merciless force of a breaking wave. The
tumbling crest picks the swimmer up and flings him forward like a piece
of wreckage, rolling him over and over till sand and water fill eyes, ears,
and mouth; the only way to prevent this is to turn and dive backwards
through each following wave till the water is so shallow that one can
stand, and even then it is not easy to keep one's feet. But all this the girl
from the heart of Central Europe could not know. Even as the American
shouted the watchers on the balcony saw Hetta picked up, thrown onto
the sand, and tumbled over and over, helplessly, in the creamy surf—
when the water dragged back again she did not rise, but was sucked back
with it.

"She's stunned!" Atherley exclaimed. He was down the wooden steps
in a flash, and raced across the beach, flinging off his jacket as he went;
by the time the next wave threw Hetta forward again he had waded in
waist deep, to snatch her up and carry her to the land. On the sand he
set her down, for she was wriggling in his arms like a captive fish.

"Ow!" the girl said, spitting out sand and sea-water, and rubbing at
her eyes with her fingers. "This is horrible!"

"Are you all right?" the young man asked.

"Yes, except for this sand!" But she was in fact shaking slightly all over, with cold and shock. "I must wash my face," she said, starting back towards the sea.

"No, do that at the pub," he said, catching her by the arm. As they passed up the beach he picked up his jacket and threw it round her shoulders.

"Thank you—oh, now you are all wet!" Hetta said, glancing at his soaked trousers. "I am so sorry. I do not know what happened; I—I was taken by surprise. These waves are so strong, when they come to the shore."

"They are. There's a trick about getting back through them—I'll teach it you some day."

"Will you? That I should like. But could you fetch my coat? It is up on those rocks." She waited while he brought it and then, modestly muffled, went up with him to the little inn.

Julia's dinner was rather late that evening. Hetta had to be sponged down, her hair dried, and dressed—minus her petticoat; a pair of the proprietor's trousers had to be borrowed for Atherley while his own were hung up to dry in the kitchen. Torrens and Townsend Waller, left to themselves on the balcony while Julia ministered to Hetta, became hungry, and in Torrens' case rather impatient.

"She's a beautiful swimmer, our little Countess, but not very considerate," he said, glancing at his watch. "It's nearly a quarter to nine."

"We started late ourselves, anyway," said Townsend, still rather resentfully conscious of having waited in Atherley's room at the Chancery for nearly half an hour for Torrens to appear; he had asked Richard why he didn't call his friend up and tell him to come along, but Richard had been evasive, merely saying—"No; he'll be here presently." Anyhow he, Townsend, disliked any criticism of Hetta.

"Yes, I was late—I couldn't help it," the Englishman said readily. "Sorry. Do you feel like a whisky?—I do. I wonder if they have it here?"

But just as Townsend was explaining that rum or Pheysey gin were all that could be hoped for in the way of spirits at the Guincho first Atherley, and a moment later the two girls reappeared, followed by the proprietor's wife with a second bottle of the local version of champagne. They had another glass, Hetta was dosed with hot rum-and-water, and then Julia hustled them indoors to dine. "Goodness, I do hope the soles aren't ruined," she said.

Nothing was ruined. The bisque was divine, the crab cold anyhow; and the resourceful proprietor—who was also the chef—on finding that the gentlemen were very late and one of the ladies determined to swim had not started cooking his lovely soles till he saw how things were shaping—they, too, were perfect. They had the restaurant to themselves, always a pleasant thing, and two courses of food—Guincho food at that—restored Major Torrens' equanimity; while the excitement of her swim (possibly aided by the rum) had put Hetta Páloczy into higher spirits than any of the others had so far thought her capable of. She sat between Torrens and Townsend Waller, her black hair hanging in damp elf-locks round her curious vivid face above her pretty cherry-coloured dress; she had already made profuse apologies, on returning to the balcony, for "keeping everyone hungry," but now, in response to Townsend's questions as to where she had learned to swim like that, she recounted her father teaching her to dive in the lake at Detvan, and later her solitary bathes in the Tisza on long hot summer afternoons, when for an hour or so quiet reigned on the Alföld. But she made it all natural, simple, and rather funny, told in her curious but expressive English—Townsend, it was evident, had fallen completely under her spell.

It was Hetta who urged that they should have coffee on the balcony, and when they went out from the small, rather steamy room to see whether it would be too chilly there, it was at once clear that she was right. The air was still warm, great stars and a young slip of moon hung in the sky, the Atlantic made a gentle thunder on the shore below.

"Atherley, do you feel like a stroll?" Major Torrens asked. "If Miss Probyn will excuse us?" He directed a glance at Miss Probyn as he spoke which did not escape Hetta—she thought there was complicity in it.

"Oh, very well," Richard replied. It had already occurred to him that there was probably some reason for Torrens having been half an hour late at the Chancery, and whatever it was he would have to hear it sooner or later. "May we leave you, Julia?"

"Of course—but come back for a cuentra."

The two men climbed down the rickety wooden stair. "Don't let's attempt to stroll in this hellish sand," Richard said.

"Don't let's stroll at all—we can sit on that lump of rock over there," Torrens replied, walking towards one of the flower-set out-crops. As they approached it a figure sprang up out of a dark crevice at the foot and raced away towards the road—when it passed through the broad bands of light cast on the sand from the restaurant windows they saw that it was a youth, wearing one of the loud tartan shirts affected by Portuguese fishermen.

"Hullo! Are we being watched?" Torrens said.

"Not at the Guincho, I shouldn't imagine."

"I think I'll just go and check on the cars," said Torrens, and strode up towards the road—before he reached it a third car, parked facing towards Lisbon, started its engine and roared off into the night, its head-lights twisting and swooping till it disappeared.

"That's curious," Richard said, contemplating his and Julia's cars, still standing by the roadside. "There was no one but ourselves in this place, and the others aren't open yet."

"Have the people here a car?" Torrens asked.

"I don't know, but we'll soon find out." They went back to the res-taurant, where Richard walked into the kitchen and put a question in his rather moderate Portuguese. Yes, the proprietor had an *automóvel*, a small van for bringing out supplies; but it had been in Lisbon all the afternoon, and had not yet returned.

"Um," said Torrens, when this was reported to him. "That wasn't a van—it was a rather big open car. Ask if they know whose it was?"

The proprietor and his family knew nothing of any car having come; busy with preparing the dinner, and getting the Menina washed and dried, they had not even heard it drive up.

"Looks as though we *are* observed," Richard said—"or you, rather. Now, where shall we talk?"

"In one of the cars, I think." He drove Julia's large machine out into the middle of the road, well away from the scrubby growth of heath and cistus on both sides, and switched off; Richard got in too. "Well?" he said.

"Things are getting rather hot in Madrid—we must get our man out as soon as we can."

"How hot?"

"They've tumbled to at least two of our people; they're followed the whole time. Two flat tires in traffic-blocks, and so on—a stiletto stuck into them, by the look of the marks. We think our passenger must either have been followed from Barcelona, or waited for when he was met at the station. Anyhow, the whole show there is compromised."

"Awkward," Richard commented.

"It is, damned awkward. He's got to come on here *prontito*."

"How?"

"By plane. But he'll have to travel alone, and board the plane alone, the way things are."

"Well, I suppose he's capable of that."

"Of course he is!" Torrens said, rather impatiently. "But the point is that neither I nor anyone else here knows him by sight; and as you know, one of our friends' favourite tricks is to abstract the person who's expected, and plant one of their own agents on us instead—that's why we usually try to have anyone like this escorted and handed over by a man we do know."

"Well, I don't see how *I* can help you," Richard said, frowning in the darkness. It sounded as if this affair was going to be quite as troublesome as he had foreseen.

"Oh, can't you come off that line for a bit, Atherley? After all, we're in the same show really—we work for the same country. And I need your help."

"All right—but how do you imagine I can help you?"

"Estoril is stiff with Hungarian refugees, and I expect you know a lot of them, and how reliable they are," Torrens said. "It occurred to me that you might be able to get hold of someone who would be certain to recognise this type and would be willing to come to the airport and point him out—one of these Archdukes, or Counts, or someone."

"Is he the sort of person Archdukes would know by sight?" Richard asked.

"Oh, probably."

Atherley was silent for a moment.

"Look here, Torrens," he said at length—"hadn't I, at last, better be told who your mystery man is? I can't, even if I were willing to, do anything till I know that."

"Yes, of course. He's a Dr. Horvath; a considerable theologian, I'm told."

"Christian name? I'd better have the whole works."

"Antal."

Richard started a little.

"Where has he been in Hungary before he came out? In Budapest?"

"No, down in the country somewhere, doing duty as a parish priest."

"Is he a friend of Mindszenty's? Been in touch with him recently?"

"Yes," Torrens said, surprise in his voice. "That's rather the point, as a matter of fact. Why do you ask?"

Richard burst out laughing, his great resounding laugh.

"What's the joke?" Torrens asked, slightly annoyed by this mirth.

"Only that he's the man that Countess Hetta has been cooking for for the last six years!"

"You don't say so!"

"Yes, it must be the one. She only calls him 'Father Antal,' but she told Townsend that he was immensely learned, and she told us *both* that he constantly went in disguise to see the Cardinal. Anyhow I expect she knows his surname—if it's whatever you said, there you are."

"Ye-es," Torrens said, rather slowly. "Yes," he repeated more firmly—"and I imagine she'd be reliable."

"Look, Torrens! Who would be more so?" Richard expostulated.

"Sorry—you see you know her and I don't. Well, we'd better talk to her

—or you had," he said, opening the car door. "I ought to let them have a signal in Madrid tonight—the sooner they get him off the better." He paused, standing in the road beside the car. "I'm sorry I was so late this evening, but all this was just coming in, and I had to wait to help decode it."

"I don't quite see how we're to talk to her tonight," Richard objected.

"Oh, Julia's as safe as houses—Miss Probyn, I mean."

"Yes, but there's Waller. Or is he in on this?"

"Good Lord no. The Americans want this man out, but they have left it to us to do it—we know Europe better, after all. But couldn't you and I drive the little Countess back, and let Julia take the Yank?"

"I expect so. Anyhow do let's go and have that cuentra—any contact with secret service activities always leaves me feeling distinctly weak," Richard said, starting down towards the restaurant; Torrens followed him laughing.

"You'd better suggest it; you know her best," he said.

"Oh yes—I'll be cover."

Richard did it quite well, as the other readily admitted to himself. Sipping a second cuentra he said, very casually—"Julia, I've got to get back rather early, and so has the Major. And I'm sure the sooner Hetti is between the sheets the better, after all that swimming. How would it be if we three went off and left you and Townsend to make a night of it? He likes to drink till 1 A.M., I know."

"Richard, may you be forgiven!" Mr. Waller protested, while Hetta looked from one to the other of the faces about her; the phrase "make a night of it" left her completely at a loss, but once again she surprised a fleeting glance between Julia and Major Torrens, and her sixth sense—the particular sixth sense which becomes so strongly developed in countries where speech is never free, and spies always at one's elbow—caused her, together with this sudden change of plan, to think to herself: those two are up to something! But why, in that case, was it *she* who was being taken away?

She learned very soon. After goodnights and thanks the three of them got into Atherley's car and drove off. To her surprise he did not switch on his headlights—"You forget the lights," she said to him.

"No I don't. I can see by this moon and the starshine—and there's nothing on the road at this time of night." He spoke over his shoulder to Torrens. "No need to advertise ourselves, don't you think?"

"Undoubtedly not."

After a mile or so Atherley slowed down, and began to drive at a snail's pace. "Here we are," he said, suddenly swinging the car into a small side track; this wound inland between high heathy banks, and after some seventy yards a bend concealed the car from the road behind them—Richard stopped and switched off. "There," he said—"I think that's all right. You'll have to con me out later, Torrens. Now, will you talk to the Countess, or shall I?"

"You might begin, I think."

"Very well. Hetti, what was your Father Antal's surname? Do you know?"

"I *do* know—but it was not mentioned as a rule."

"I thought not. But would you tell it to me and Major Torrens?"

She hesitated. "I should like to know why you ask," she said—and Torrens, at least, recognised the ingrained caution of dwellers beyond the Curtain. He decided to speak himself.

"Countess, we need to know it because we may want you to help us, and him. I am in the British Secret Service," he added.

"No! Oh how nice. Yulia too?"

This question caused Richard to laugh out loud.

"Not altogether, no," Torrens replied, ignoring the laugh. "But will you tell me?"

Still she hesitated—for so long that Torrens finally said, rather brusquely —"Is he not really Doctor Antal Horvath, the theologian?"

"Of course he is—since you know it. But why then do you ask?"

"Because we have to be certain—just as you do, back there. Good. Now please listen carefully—would you know him by sight, even if he wore a beard?"

"He does not wear a beard."

"No, I know he doesn't—but would you know him if he were wearing one as a disguise?"

"His *eyes* I should know anywhere—but why?"

"You'd better tell her what it's all about, Torrens," Richard interjected. "You're only muddling her."

He thought that Torrens didn't manage his explanation very well when he did embark on it.

"He's in Madrid just now," the Major began.

"Impossible!"

"Yes he is."

"But how can he come to Madrid?"

"He was got out by our people—he's going to America, to do propaganda work."

"Talking to journalists? This also I do not believe!" Hetta said with energy.

"Suppose I have a go, Torrens?" Richard said. "Listen, Hetti—there are thousands of Hungarians in the United States who are all longing to know how everything is at home, as well as a sort of committee which acts almost like a free government, to look after the interests of Hungarians everywhere. Those are the people the Father is going to see in the first place. He's got as far as Madrid, and quite soon he's coming on here to fly to the States."

"Here? He comes *here?* Oh!" Her voice had that ring again. "Shall I see him?"

"That's exactly what we want you to do—see him, and recognise him," Torrens said, from the back seat.

Hetta ignored him completely.

"Richard, please explain more," she said.

Richard—curiously pleased by her unexpected use of his name—proceeded to tell her both how the priest had been got out, and that it was essential that someone who knew him by sight should be at the airport to meet him.

"Oh, of course I will go. Only what time? For me the morning is the best, because Mama does nothing in the morning—and of course it is best that she does not know of all this, isn't it? In such cases, the fewer who know the better, I think."

"Perfectly right," Torrens said approvingly. "Don't speak of it to anyone."

"Then when?"

"We shall have to let you know that. I'll make a signal to Madrid tonight, and tell them to arrange for him to come on a morning plane—then I can ring you up."

"If you ring up you should be most careful. Ought we not to arrange a form of words for the message, so that others do not understand?"

"Good girl!" Torrens said. "Yes, I think all we need do is to tell you which day. One of us will drive you out to the airport."

"I'll do that," said Richard. "If you let me know the day and time, Torrens, I'll bring the Countess out to Portela."

"You can invite me for 'drinks' when you telephone," Hetta said, with a sudden small laugh.

When this was settled Atherley reversed out onto the main road, Torrens walking to guide him; he continued to drive without lights till they were just entering Cascais, when he switched them on to pass through the town. Presently he was startled by some small strangled sounds beside him—they sounded like sobs. "Hetti, what on earth is the matter?" Atherley asked.

"Nothing. I am simply silly again. But to see *him,* after all these people here!—you cannot know what this is."

"Yes, I'm very glad. But cheer up now," Richard said—moved, and therefore embarrassed, he patted her shoulder rather awkwardly with his left hand.

"Hullo, there seems to have been a smash," Torrens said. "Had we better stop and see if the people are all right?"

Richard, who had begun to drive rather fast once he was on the Tagus speedway, braked; a little way ahead a car was tilted up against a bank hideous with the puce-and-white-wash flowers of mesembryanthemum, a revolting plant beloved of Portuguese road-planners. A man and a woman stood by it.

"It is Yulia!" Hetta exclaimed, as they came to a halt.

"By God, so it is!" Torrens said, jumping out. "Julia, what on earth has happened? Are you all right?"

"Some bastards quite deliberately crowded us into the bank," Townsend Waller said. "Forced us in. Don't know if they meant to tip us over, but they meant to stop us, because they pulled up just in front."

"They caught our wing," said Julia. "But Townsend's quite right—they overhauled us after we got through Cascais, and crowded us in—they weren't drunk, it was done on purpose. They came back and gave us the once-over, and swore in Spanish and drove away."

Torrens and Atherley exchanged glances—the latter walked quickly back to his own car and switched off the headlights; then he returned to the group.

"Was it an open tourer?" Torrens was asking Julia.

"Yes, it was—with three men in it."

"Was one of them a fisher-lad in a check shirt?" Richard asked.

"Oh, let's leave all that, Atherley," Torrens said hastily. "Julia, I expect you got the number of the car?"

"Naturally," she said, in her slow tones. "But I can't read it to you, since Richard has plunged us all in darkness."

"No, don't bother—you can give it to me later. I think we'd better get home. Have you got your things out, Julia—bag and coat and so forth?"

"Oh no—I forgot my bag." She went and groped for it in the tilted car; then Torrens hustled them all into Richard's Bentley.

"I'll sit in front, if you'll forgive me," the Major said.

"Richard, can you cope with the wreckage?" Julia asked from the back seat as they drove off—again without headlights.

"Oh yes—I'll see that someone goes over tonight. Don't worry."

"I'm not. Do you realise that you're driving without lights?"

"Oh, so I am. Well I don't really need them here with these arc-lights," Richard said easily.

It was only about a mile-and-a-half farther on that they came on an open
touring car drawn up, also without lights, at the side of the great road.
"Slow down," Torrens muttered to Richard. "Julia, is that the car?" he
asked, leaning back.

"Yes, that's it," said Julia surprised. "Goody! Shall we ram *them?*"

"No. Step on it, Atherley."

Richard pressed hard on the accelerator—the Bentley roared forward.
"They'll never catch this car—that's only a Vanguard," he said.

In Monte Estoril he swung up to the left, and began to twiddle his way
through the maze of small tree-shaded residential roads which link it to
Estoril proper, switching on his sidelights as he did so.

"Where are you going?" Torrens asked in a low voice.

"I thought we'd drop the little Countess, and perhaps Townsend too,"
Richard answered in the same tone.

"A good idea."

Atherley knew the two Estorils well, and presently pulled up outside the
Casino, which overlooks the public garden—scores of cars were parked
there.

"Townsend, I wonder if you would take the Countess home; it's only a
few steps," he said, getting out and holding open the rear door.

"Why of course—I shall be delighted."

"Will you not all come in and have drinks?" Hetta, who was learning
western ways, said as she got out.

"Not tonight, Hetti, thank you so much. We had better get on." While
Hetta was thanking Julia, Richard drew Townsend a little aside.

"Take her right up to the apartment, and see that Dorothée or the maid
is there before you leave her," he muttered.

"But why," Townsend began—Richard interrupted him.

"I'll explain tomorrow. Do what I say now, there's a good fellow. Would
you mind making your own way home? So sorry, but I don't want to hang
about tonight. I should take the train if I were you."

"That's pretty slow—I can get a taxi."

"All the same I should take the train. And don't *talk* to anyone about this,
whatever you do."

"All right. I shall look forward to the explanation!" said Townsend, with
his usual good-nature. Richard turned back to Hetta.

"Good-night. Sleep well."

"Thank you." Then she reached up to whisper in his ear.

"No, he doesn't—you're quite right. And not a word to anyone else,"
Richard muttered.

"But naturally."

When the pair had walked off towards the Castelo-Imperial Richard turned the car and drove back on his tracks into Monte Estoril.

"Where now?" Julia asked.

"Home, but via São Pedro da Cintra, I thought."

The car was climbing a hill; it passed through a small square with a bus-stop sign, and in a few moments was out in open country.

"It's *miles* round," Julia protested.

"It won't take us long," Richard replied, opening the throttle and at last switching on his headlights; the great car roared through the night.

"Well now perhaps one of you will explain," Julia said, in slow resigned tones. "You seem to know quite a bit about these types who ditched us. What goes on?"

"We'd better tell her everything, Atherley," Torrens said. "She'll find out for herself if we don't!—and she's completely reliable. Anyhow it looks as if we may need to make use of her before we're through, if things here are as hot as this already."

"Very well—you go ahead and tell her. The priest is your export drive, not mine," said Richard coolly.

Torrens proceeded to tell Julia the whole business of Father Antal; then of the watcher they had surprised among the rocks at the Guincho, and the car that had driven off.

"*I see*," she said slowly. "That's how you knew about the tartan shirt. I suppose they took Mr. Waller and me for you, Hugh."

"I imagine they were waiting for both cars—first ditch one and then the other," he replied rather sombrely. "Only Atherley was too quick for them— in every sense of the word. You're sure they swore in Spanish when they found you weren't what they were looking for?"

"Certain. *Carajo* and plenty more in the same strain. Quite like old times in Morocco, isn't it?"

"A good deal too like to please me."

"Well, what's the next move?"

He told her of the plan for Hetta Páloczy to meet the plane, so that some-one might recognise, indubitably, the Hungarian.

"I don't much like little Hetti getting mixed up in this," Julia objected. "Can't you get someone else? Some of all these Hunks here are bound to know him by sight."

"We might use Dorothée!" Richard put in, with his loud short laugh.

"My dear Julia, she's mixed up in it already," Torrens said. "Their spotter at the Guincho will certainly have seen her—she was sitting right by the rail of that balcony in a blaze of light. And besides, doesn't it occur to you that they must know perfectly well that she's here, after the roaring pub-

licity of her getting out? If I know anything of them they will also know—
nobody better—that she's been living in his house in Hungary for the last
six years. Your little Hetti is involved up to the neck, whatever we do or
don't do."

"Then you ought to warn her, Torrens," Richard said abruptly. He was
disturbed—all these implications had not occurred to him.

"Oh, she'll know. These behind-the-curtain people can make rings round
us," Torrens said—and Richard, remembering Hetta's whisper to him about
Townsend Waller, realised that the Secret Service man might be right.
"No, she's the person to do the plane job—it can't make things any worse
for her. But you might suggest that she wears a veil, Atherley. Pity she's so
short; it makes her terribly recognisable."

"Not here," said Julia. "No Portuguese women are tall. Oh, here we are
at São Pedro—sharp right, Richard."

They sat in silence for a little as Atherley drove down the familiar road
towards the distant lights of Lisbon—all slightly uncomfortable. Torrens
was reflecting that he would need to satisfy himself pretty thoroughly as to
the hide-out arranged by Mr. Melplash; to be of any use it would have to be
thug-proof indeed. Richard was worrying about Hetta. He recognised that
what Torrens had said about her being already deeply involved was obviously true, but he didn't like it any the better for that—and what on earth
would the Ambassador say if he himself got still more mixed up in this
affair? Julia was also worrying about Hetta—and about her press car. "How
will you get my chariot mended?" she asked presently.

"Oh, I'm glad you reminded me—we'll go to a garage on the way home
and see about it. Where do you keep it?"

"At the Ericeiras—in the stables. They're vast."

"Yes, I've always understood that that establishment is like a small town
in itself, for all it's in the middle of the city," Richard said.

"Atherley," Torrens put in, "might it be a good plan if you got that car
number from Julia, and mentioned it to the police? They might haul them
in, or lay them a stymie, anyhow."

"I can't have them hauled in simply for tonight's performance, Torrens
—that would be quite impossible, and particularly bad from your point of
view, I should have thought."

"I didn't mean that, naturally—that *must* be kept quiet. But couldn't they
be had up for something else?"

"I'll see. I daresay Colonel Marques of the Special Police could fix it;
he's very resourceful." He pulled up. "Give me that number," he said, and
wrote it among the telephone numbers in his diary by the faint dash-board
light—then he drove on through Bemfica, with its lights and tram-lines, and

into the city itself, where he presently drew up outside a large garage. "Give me *your* car number," he said.

Julia gave it—XL61-91-91. Richard turned the figures into Portuguese aloud—"X.L. *seis um nove um nove um.*" He went in, and returned after a moment or two.

"They're sending the breakdown van at once. I gave no name, just told them to report to me at the Chancery. They do most of the Chancery work, so they'll fix it properly and ask no questions." He got in. "Now Julia, we'd better drop you next—" he stuck his wrist out towards the dashboard, and looked at his watch. "Good Lord, it's after midnight! Have you got a latch-key?"

"Heavens no—that's not at all in the tradition," Julia said, with her slow giggle. "But I shall get in all right. An old old night-watchman sits just inside the front door, in one of those leather chairs with a high hooded back with brass nails in it—do you know?—to let in late-comers."

"Good God!" Torrens said.

When they reached the Ericeira town mansion, with its barred windows in the vast baroque frontage giving on a high narrow street, Julia proved to be correct. She got out, lifted a huge bronze knocker on the great panelled double door, and gave two gentle taps; a sound of shuffling feet was heard inside, the door opened a crack, and the aged retainer appeared in the aperture.

"*Boa noite*, Manoel," Julia said cheerfully.

"*Boa noite, Minha Menina,*" the ancient responded, with a happy tooth-less grin.

Richard had got out to see her in.

"Julia, do let me look at the chair."

"Oh, all right. O Manoel, this Senhor wants to see your chair. He comes from the *Embaixada Inglesa. Pode ser?*"

"*Pode, pode,*" Manoel replied—Richard stepped into the immense shadowy hall, and admired the chair. "Marvellous—just the place to park Hugh's priest!" he said. "Good-night, Julia—thank you for the party. I'll ring you up about your wreckage."

"Now, where do you want to go?" he asked Major Torrens, getting in and shutting the car door.

"I'm not quite sure," the Major replied. "We're so late that I doubt if I can get hold of Melplash tonight anyhow. Would it be a nuisance just to drive past my place, and see if there are any signs of our friends? They seem so unexpectedly well-informed."

"No trouble whatever. Where is your place?"

"Off the Praça José Fontana—I'll show you the street."

The Praça José Fontana is a long narrowish square with a rather modest garden in it. Richard drove in from the northern side and swung round the end of the garden, keeping his eyes open; at the mouth of a side street an open touring car was parked—he flashed on his headlights for a second, and read the number.

"That's them," he said, accelerating. "You'd better come home with me for tonight, hadn't you? I should say that you won't be able to function very usefully until the police have done something about that car and its occupants."

"I'm afraid I agree. Yes, if it won't be a bore I should be glad of a bed. It's very good of you, Atherley."

"The Queen's government must go on!" Richard said, as he shot through the midnight streets. He eventually pulled up, not at his own little house, but outside the British Embassy. The Ambassador's residence in Lisbon is quite separate from the Chancery, and stands in an angle between two streets, one sloping and one level—Atherley left his car in the level one, the Rua Arriaga.

"I hope you don't mind walking a little way," he said, as he pocketed the key and slammed the door—"usually I leave her outside my house, but I don't really want any stilettos in my tires, and your friends are so attentive."

"Is this any safer?" Torrens asked, glancing round him—he did not at once realise where he was.

"Oh very much so—patrolled day and night, as you see," Richard said, acknowledging the salute of a neat Portuguese policeman with a cheerful *"Boa noite,"* and walking off up the steep street.

"Yes, I see now," Torrens said, as they passed the front door of the Embassy. "I've only been here once, to write my name, so I didn't recognise it." He laughed. "Very convenient, to have a guard for your car."

"I told you I enjoyed diplomatic immunity," said Atherley.

CHAPTER VI

"JULIA'S CAR's done for," Richard Atherley told his guest the following morning as they sat down to breakfast on the small vine-shaded terrace. "The chassis's fractured. I've been on to Julia and told her she'll have to hire a new car—she didn't seem to mind. She said everything was covered."

"It's the other car I'm worrying about," Torrens said.

"Naturally. I've arranged to see Colonel Marques about that—someone is having us both in for drinks before lunch."

"Oh, is that how you do it here?"

"Obviously. This is really your people's pidgin, so if for any reason I intervene myself, it is always on a very social plane. Could you look in at the Chancery about 1:30? I might know something by then."

Major Torrens said he would look in. "You seem to have been working rather fast," he said.

"Oh, the Portuguese get up quite early, however lethargic they may be when they have got up. Colonel Marques as a matter of fact is always on call—he's immensely efficient."

"Good." But Major Torrens looked rather abstracted.

"Have you any idea where your man is to be parked when you get him here?" Richard asked.

"No—I left that to Melplash. I must see him about it this morning; the way things are it will have to be cast-iron, a hundred per cent safe."

"Oh, Melplash!" Richard permitted himself that expression at this rather crucial point.

"Precisely. 'Oh, Melplash!' is the word for it," the Major said, with a rather wry smile. "But we have an *homme de confiance* of our own here, so if necessary I can lay him on."

"You'll have to settle that of course before you have your theologian come. You'd better let me know about that, so that I can get the little Countess a veil."

"Get her a veil today—we may have to move pretty fast when the time comes," Torrens said. He got up. "Well, if you will excuse me, I think I will go off. Thank you immensely for the 'bed and breakfast,' Atherley."

"It has been, as they say, a pleasure," Richard replied. "See you presently."

They met again four hours later in Richard's room in the Chancery.

"What a nice place you work in," Torrens said, leaning back in a comfortable leather armchair and glancing appreciatively out of the high windows at the green expanse of garden and trees.

"Yes. Lisbon is one of the more elegantly sited posts. Did you ever see those awful war-time hutments in Washington?—really the most sordid Embassy accommodation ever known, I should think."

Torrens laughed a little—he was beginning to like Atherley.

"Well?" he asked.

"That car was stolen. I told the little Colonel that we were interested in it, and gave him the number—he rang up his people there and then, and in less than half an hour they rang back and informed him that it belonged to a Mr. da Silva, who had advised the city police of its loss soon after tea-time yesterday. The police will soon get it, of course."

"Anything else?"

"Well, I told him as much as I judged necessary—an English journalist's car crowded into the ditch and so on—but he pricked up his ears considerably when I mentioned that the worthies in it had spoken Spanish. He quite properly has his knife into Spanish thugs operating in Portugal—*'les Espagnols à l'étranger seront certainement des communistes!'*—and he wants a description of the men in the car."

"Julia will be able to give that—she's very observant."

"So I should imagine. I'll get it from her and pass it on, today. Have you organised something for your man?"

"Yes—but through my own chap. The other, the local plan, was quite childish."

"That doesn't surprise me at all! Anyhow, when does he arrive?"

"Tomorrow morning, 9:40, at Portela. We thought an early plane would be best, perhaps. Can you marshal your young lady at that hour?"

"As she always goes to Mass at 7:30 A.M. it should be quite easy," Richard said—and then regretted having spoken so energetically. But Torrens appeared to take no notice.

"You won't forget to get that veil for her, will you?" was all he said—words which warmed Richard towards him. "Oh by the way, what about the Yank?" he added.

"The Yank?"

"Yes—the one who was there last night."

"Oh, Townsend." (Richard, having lived in the States, never thought of Bostonians as Yanks.) "Yes—he rang up to report having delivered his charge into her mother's hands."

"Was he curious?"

"Yes, of course, but I stalled him for the moment—he'll be at the Embassy on Friday anyhow. I told him the whole affair was classified," Richard said, grinning a little, "but that I'd give him a sanitary version when I saw him."

"Did he understand that? I confess I don't."

"Oh yes, perfectly. It's the new American jargon: 'classified' information is highly secret, and a 'sanitary' version is what one tells the press. Townsend won't give any trouble; he's very sensible and discreet, as well as extraordinarily nice."

"Good. Well, I expect you want to eat," the Major was saying when the telephone buzzed.

"That was the Colonel. The city police have picked up the car in a side street, *without* the ignition key," Richard said, having spoken into the instrument. "They're towing it back to Mr. da Silva's; luckily for him he has a spare key. But I think I shall have to go off now, if you will forgive me; I must see these young ladies—and buy a veil!—and be here again by five at latest. Unluckily H.E. *isn't* playing golf this afternoon."

Atherley left Mrs. Tomlinson to make his two appointments, and asked her to tell him the results at his house. There he sat down to, first, meltingly tender young french beans, then cold veal with salad followed by a delicious local cheese—all washed down with good red wine from a *garrafão*, the big wicker-covered glass carboy, holding five litres, in which the wise in Portugal buy their wine for household use; it works out at about twopence-halfpenny the half pint. While he was taking coffee on the little terrace Mrs. Tomlinson rang up to say that Miss Probyn could see him at "the palace" at any time after 2:30, and that Countess Hetta Páloczy would be in at four.

Richard was rather interested to penetrate into the Duke of Ericeira's town mansion. Though he knew the elderly brother and sister slightly he had never crossed their threshold till the previous night, when he went in to look at old Manoel's hooded chair; they lived much in the country, and in Lisbon entertained very little, and then mostly their contemporaries—except when they opened the house to accommodate floods of Bourbons for royal weddings. How typical of Julia Probyn to have inserted herself as a familiar into these legendary precincts!—and how rightly the Portuguese referred to the place as a palace, he thought, as he followed an elderly manservant in rich but rather threadbare livery up the immense staircase and along several wide corridors, all lined with treasures of furniture, pictures, ivories and porcelain which fairly made his mouth water with the desire to stop and examine them. In a broad upstairs lobby almost the size of a billiard-room the man handed him over to a pleasant-faced middle-aged woman, wearing a black silk apron over a tweed skirt and a silk blouse.

"I'm Luzia's Nanny," said this individual, in a pleasant Leicestershire accent—"Will you come this way? Miss Probyn is in the schoolroom."

The schoolroom was large and sunny, and looked out onto a big garden; with its bareness, shabby comfortable armchairs and sofa, and bookshelves full of tattered classics it was exactly like an English schoolroom, except for a magnificent ivory crucifix over the fireplace—which had a completely Victorian brass-topped fender standing in front of it—and a lovely polychrome sculpture group of St. Anne and Our Lady as a child on top of the bookshelves; both these holy personages were dressed in the height of 18th-century fashion.

"Here's Mr. Atherley, Miss Probyn," Nanny said comfortably. "Now, Luzia, you'd better come with me and feed the bantams."

Julia was sitting at a large round walnut table in the middle of the room beside a tall coltish girl of sixteen or thereabouts, studying, Richard noticed, a map of Morocco in the *Times* Atlas—she got up, as did the young girl.

"Hullo, Richard," Julia said holding out her hand. "Luzia, this is Mr. Atherley. Nanny, unless the bantams are *starving*, Luzia can stay—she won't be in the way."

"Oh Nanny, do let me! I have never met a diplomatist before! *Please!*" the girl said, imploringly. Richard, surprised and amused by this very Anglo-Portuguese little scene, noticed that Luzia had remarkable grey eyes under her dark hair, and a face which would presently be beautiful—from its unusual vividness of expression as well as from the fine structure of the bones.

"Oh very well, Miss Probyn, if you say so," said Nanny, compressing her lips in the expression of disapproving acquiescence which has been classical among English children's nurses for over a century.

"Thank you, Nanny," Richard said as she left the room.

"Don't let her be a nuisance, Mr. Atherley," Nanny replied, closing the door.

Julia had not been in the least surprised to get Mrs. Tomlinson's message, in fact she had been waiting rather impatiently for some word from Richard all the morning. "Well?" she now asked, sitting down again at the table, and pushing the atlas across to Luzia. "See if you can find Tindouf," she told the child.

"Have you organised another car? When do you get it?" the young man asked.

"Tomorrow."

"Good."

"Oh, Miss Probyn, did you have an accident? I *do* wish you would drive me out in your car!" Luzia said. Completely ignoring the map of Morocco, she kept her surprising grey eyes steadily fixed on Atherley.

"Luzia, if you interrupt you will have to go and feed the bantams with Nanny," Julia said with cool firmness.

"I am sorry—I will be silent." But she did not relax that steady inquiring stare—Richard had difficulty in refraining from laughing. He had seated himself on the big shabby sofa, and as he did so he could feel that the springs were broken—this, combined with Nanny's behaviour, took him straight back to his own nursery days. But what a strange set-up to find in Lisbon!

"Julia, I want you to write down a description, as full as you can make it, of the people in the other car," he now said. "Can you do it at once?"

"Yes of course." She took a block out of a curved drawer in the round table as she spoke, and felt in her bag for her fountain pen. "Who wants it? —besides you?"

"How unflattering you are!" Richard said—Luzia giggled audibly.

"Luzia! Not another sound out of you, or off you go," Julia said crushingly. "Sorry, Richard—I was only enquiring."

"I saw the Colonel we spoke of on the way home, this morning, and it's he who wants it. The other car was stolen—but it was waiting for Hugh outside his diggings last night, so he came and slept in my house."

"Not really?"

"Yes. So do get down to it. May Luzia talk to me while you do your home-work?"

"Yes, but somewhere else. Luzia, take Mr. Atherley to see the *Blanc de Chine* on the top corridor—you know, the white vases and things in those Chippendale cupboards."

Nothing could have suited Richard better than this arrangement, nor could anything have been more satisfactory to Luzia than to have a live diplomat all to herself. "For how long?" she asked earnestly.

"Oh, about ten minutes."

The collection of *Blanc de Chine* porcelain was magnificent, though not more so than the immense glass-fronted Chippendale cabinets in which it was housed. Goodness what wealth!—and what taste!—the young man thought. But on their way to it he had caught a glimpse of an equally spectacular display of the armorial porcelain known as *Compagnie des Indes,* the Portuguese equivalent of "Chinese Lowestoft"; this was really more in Richard's line than antique Chinese stuff, which was beyond the reach even of his rather ample purse, and presently he asked to be taken to it.

"This is quite marvellous!" he exclaimed, gazing at the vast dishes, the exquisite plates, and the tureens great and small. "It's even better than what they have at the Janelas Verdes." ("The Green Windows" is the name habitually used for the Lisbon Art Gallery, once Pombal's palace.)

"But naturally," Luzia replied. "For the Museum they had to buy, here and there; but this was all made for my great-great—well I don't know how many greats!" the young girl said, laughing, "but he was some sort of grandfather, and he was Governor of the Indies, like Albuquerque. These are our arms"—she indicated the coat so decoratively applied to all the larger pieces.

"It's fantastic. What treasures you live among! Do you like them?" he asked, a little curious.

"Yes—quite. I like the chapel better. Have you seen the chapel?"

"No."

"Oh, it is down on the next floor—I don't suppose we have time. There is a wonderful Zurbarán, and some really good sculptures—a Pietà from Viseu which I think marvellous! We say the Rosary there every night after dinner."

"Do you indeed!" For some reason this casual statement of a daily fact increased his curiosity about Julia Probyn's pupil. "Why are your eyes grey?" he asked, suddenly rounding on her.

"Because one of my grandmothers—I think my father's mother—came from the Minho, up in the North; there were many Celtic people there, and also Visigoths—and both, it would appear, had grey eyes. I do not know from which race my grandmother had them."

"From the Celts, undoubtedly—yours are Irish eyes," he said carelessly, amused by this display of ethnographic knowledge in someone as young as the girl beside him. But she blushed so deeply at his words that he began to wonder if she were really so young, after all; he was rather relieved to hear Julia's matter-of-fact voice calling—"Luzia! Where on earth have you got to?"

"Mr. Atherley wanted to see the *Compagnie des Indes;* he likes it better than the *Blanc de Chine*," Luzia explained when Julia joined them. Back in the schoolroom he studied the paper which Miss Probyn handed to him.

"Yes, that will do perfectly. It's very detailed. Did the imperial look genuine, or gummed on?"

"My dear Richard, one really can't see if a beard is put on with gummastic at night, by headlights, when you've just been tipped out of your car!" Julia said indignantly—Luzia, all eyes, nevertheless giggled again.

"Well never mind—thank you very much, Julia. That flat back to his head and the rolls of fat above the collar should be useful pointers, whether his beard is permanent or transitory—no one but Charles Laughton gums rolls of fat onto his neck, and that only for a film."

Julia as well as Luzia giggled at this remark—Richard, rather upset, took Julia by the arm and drew her to one of the windows.

"I say, is she all right? Little pitchers have long ears. Why on earth didn't you let Nanny take her away?" he muttered.

"Oh, Luzia's as safe as houses—she's a wonderful child. And she was so longing to meet a diplomat! You've *quite* come up to her expectations," Julia said, with her slow gurgle of pleasure—"I can see that."

"Julia, I do wish you'd grow up! What Torrens sees in you I can't

think," Richard said irritably, pocketing the paper. "Now, will you please
get me out of this museum? Am I allowed to walk downstairs alone?"

"Goodness no!" Julia replied, ringing the bell. "I'll start you, and Elidio
will meet us on the way up."

"Goodbye, Luzia," the young man said, shaking hands with the girl
who was so soon to be beautiful—his vexation faded as those astonishing
grey eyes, so eager, so candid, were once again fixed on his face.

"Oh, goodbye. This has been a pleasure. Will you not come again, and
look at more of the china? We have a great deal of celadon," the child
said.

"Yes, I will, if your aunt will let me," Richard replied.

"Nanny likes you, and that is what matters," said Luzia. "Oh—oh, but
we go to the country on Saturday!" she exclaimed dolefully: her mouth
on the "oh" was a rounded sculpture of woe. Where was that head of
the Medusa that it reminded him of, Richard wondered—and why should
a Portuguese schoolgirl have a face moulded on the splendours of classical
antiquity? Oh well, the Romans had colonised Portugal, so she might
easily possess Roman as well as Celtic blood, he thought, as Julia and
Elidio between them took him downstairs and out of that labyrinthine
house.

He dropped Julia's paper at Colonel Marques' office, and then drove
quickly to the Chiado and bought a charming veil set with black velvet
stars; it was no good to try and make Hetta look like a widow, and anyhow, he found himself thinking, this was his first present to her, and he
wanted it to be a pretty and an expensive one. (It was certainly expensive.)
Afterwards he dropped down to the Tagus, and raced out along the road
to Estoril.

Experienced drivers like Richard Atherley are apt to find speeding
rather conducive to reflection. The pace, the automatic reactions to the
need to brake, or accelerate, or avoid other vehicles produce something
faintly resembling the effect of fingering the beads of the rosary, also
automatic—one thinks almost involuntarily. Richard, afraid of being late
for his interview with Hetta Páloczy and therefore driving extremely fast,
was soon thinking about her with an unexpected and almost unwanted
clarity. He had not been wholly unaffected by having carried her in his
arms the evening before, in that clinging garment; her shape, so revealed,
was as sturdily slender as a sapling willow, and had a willow's resilience—
in the night he had found himself, almost with dismay, recalling the very
feel of her small supple muscular body twisting and wriggling in his grasp
to free herself. All the subsequent events—the watcher in the rocks, Julia's
car, and Torrens' pursuers had pushed these impressions to the back of his

mind at the time; but in the small hours, when the mind is peculiarly de-
fenceless, they had returned on him with troubling force. And the splendour of her swimming, and the vivid gaiety of her face and her talk at
supper! She was rather marvellous. Atherley, outwardly so much the conventional Englishman, and in addition heavily veneered with the watchful
coolness of diplomacy, in his secret heart adored recklessness and *panache*
—and this little creature, this convent schoolgirl turned cook, obviously
possessed both to a high degree. But then her inexperience, her intolerance, the gaucherie which her prejudices engendered—how troublesome
these were!

Hetta was in the little morning-room, alone; she was wearing a simple
sleeveless cotton frock closely patterned in flame-colour and white, and
white sandals; she looked as fresh as sunrise, and very pretty indeed.

"How do you do? When does he come, do you know now?" she asked
at once. This neutral coolness should have put Richard at his ease; in fact,
since his heart turned over at the sight of her, it suddenly irritated him.
"She can think of nothing but her wretched priest," he told himself angrily. But he proceeded to the business in hand.

"His plane gets in tomorrow morning at 9:40. I will call for you here at
8:30, and take you out to the airport. There are some railings there where
a little crowd always collects—the public, who are not allowed onto the
apron; you will stand among them and watch all the people who get off
the Madrid plane, and when you recognise Father Antal you will point
him out."

"But do I not speak with him?" There was something like desolation in
her face, her voice.

"Not there, no; it would not be prudent. Every plane from Madrid will
probably be watched when it arrives here."

"Oh, by the Spitzel, of course—yes, I understand. But I shall see him
properly later?"

"Yes, you shall," Richard promised recklessly, moved in spite of his irritation by the urgency of her tone. Damn it, Torrens could surely contrive
that much, when she was so ready to help?

And so intelligently ready, as her next question showed.

"And whom do I point him out to?" Hetta Páloczy asked. "To you?"

This quite flummoxed Atherley—somehow or other he and Torrens had
entirely overlooked that particular point when laying their plans. To whom
was Hetta to indicate which of the passengers was the priest? Not to himself, if it was in any way avoidable—he thought gloomily of the Ambassador's justifiable reprobation if a member of his staff were to be involved in
an affair like this, and anyhow he would not be having anything to do

with the subsequent proceedings. It would have to be Torrens, or Melplash, or Julia—Torrens and Julia were of course both known by sight to "the opposition," after last night, but that couldn't be helped. He thought rapidly. One person would have to be in the long hall at the airport through which the passengers entered, and where the customs examination took place; a second must stand at the railings with Hetta to be given the identification, and nip round to contact whoever was in the hall. It was perfectly possible.

"I'll tell you that tomorrow morning," he said. "We haven't decided yet. But someone will be with you, and when you have pointed out Father Antal, he will go round and meet him." He pulled the little parcel with the veil out of his pocket, and said as he gave it to her—"And you are to wear this."

She undid the pretty flowered paper, drew out the veil, and shook it open.

"Oh, how pretty! But why? I never wear veils—they are for older women, with bad complexions, are they not?"

Richard had to laugh. "Yes, as a rule. But tomorrow you must wear this. And put on some dark, inconspicuous clothes—something shabby, if you have such a thing!"

"Oh, I have my *terrible* Hungarian suit; this is as ugly and shabby as possible! But please tell me why?"

He explained to her what Major Torrens had first made clear to him the night before—that she herself might well be in some danger, since her previous association with Dr. Horvath must certainly be known, and therefore she must not be recognised at the airport, if possible. Hetta jumped up, ran to a mirror, and held the velvet-starred veil before her face.

"Oh, it *is* pretty! I think I look very nice! Do you know me?" she asked, wheeling round on him.

"I should know you anywhere, I think, you silly little creature!" Richard said, restraining a strong desire to get up and hug her. "But Hetti, this is serious—it isn't a game. You must be very careful for the next little while. Don't go out alone, except in the car."

"I do not."

"I thought you went swimming before breakfast."

"Oh, this—yes."

"Well you positively mustn't do that, for the present." He spoke urgently—how appallingly easy it would be for her to be pounced on down on the beach, at an hour when nobody in lethargic Estoril was about. "Promise me," he said.

"I must go to Mass!"

"No, you mustn't do that either, unless your mother's maid or someone can go too." Then, as she looked mutinous, he was inspired to say—"Not till the Father is safe out of the country, anyhow."

The mutiny died in her face. "Oh, if it is for *him*. Very well—I promise. But *you* promise that I shall speak with him before he goes away?"

"Yes, I have promised you that. You shall."

They fell silent—a silence which to Richard became uncomfortable because of his own emotions. Hetta broke it with one of her characteristic switches to a fresh subject.

"I believe that Yulia really works with Major Torrens. Doesn't she? You remember I told you when you drove me back from your luncheon that I think they are involved together in some way—now I think it is in espionage, not as fiancés. What do you think?"

"I don't think about them at all," the young man said, getting up. He had got to catch Torrens and organise the arrangements for the morning, as well as clearing up his work in the Chancery, and he had no desire whatever to discuss Miss Probyn's relations with the Major with Hetti—his own relations with her threatened to become of overmastering interest.

"Goodbye, my dear," he said, taking her hand and kissing it. "Remember what I've said, and be ready tomorrow morning at 8:30. Down in the hall."

The airport of Portela lies some distance outside Lisbon, farther up the Tagus; the drive to it is partly through suburbs, partly through open country now becoming increasingly studded with Dr. Salazar's new housing estates—these are rather straggling, since each house must have its *bout de terre*. Richard took Hetti there in a taxi, rather to her surprise; he thought it wiser not to take his own car with its red-and-white C.D. number-plate on this expedition. He had seen Torrens the evening before and they had settled that Mr. Melplash, who was small and suitably inconspicuous, should stand with Hetta at the railings, and then go round and tell the Major, who would be in the entrance-hall, which of the passengers was his man.

"What did you tell your mother?" Richard asked Hetta on the way out.

"Nothing. She will think that I went to a later Mass, or spent long in the sea—she is not interested in what I do before midday."

Torrens was there before them; Mr. Melplash was there too, and was introduced to Hetta; they went off to stand at the rails, where, early as it was, a small crowd had already gathered. Who these people are who have leisure to stand interminably watching the arrival and departure of aeroplanes is one of the standing mysteries of Lisbon life.

"I'll wait in my taxi," Richard said to Torrens—"I've told her to come back to me there."

"Yes, whisk her away. I hope to goodness Melplash doesn't perpetrate some clottery!" Richard recognised one of Miss Probyn's favourite phrases, and grinned. "I don't see anyone with rolls of fat at the back of his head, do you? Perhaps they haven't got anyone here for this plane."

Hetta Páloczy stood at the railings in the bright morning sunshine with Mr. Melplash. Beyond the white surface of the airfield olive trees stood out, shapely, silvered by the morning breeze, against a background of reddish soil shot over with the delicate green of growing corn; in a homely yet rich way the landscape had a certain beauty. But her mind was in a turmoil of excitement and anxiety. Mr. Melplash, eager to be helpful and thoroughly enjoying the situation, promptly pointed out to her the little motor affair, with its trailer for luggage, waiting out on the tarmac; there, he explained, the plane would come down. To Hetta it seemed appallingly far away; if Father Antal was really wearing a beard could she possibly recognise him at that distance? "Where do they go then?" she asked anxiously.

"In at that door, just to our right, where you see the police standing."

The police were reassuringly close at hand. There, surely, she would know his face and his eyes—though how hard it was to visualise that beloved stocky figure in anything but a dusty black soutane rather green with age, and either with his thinly-covered silver head bare or with an equally ancient and dusty biretta perched, rather askew, on it.

A faint hum sounded and grew in the blue bowl of the sky, above the red earth, the rising crops, the sculptured silver of the olives—grew till it filled the bowl, the air, and hummed in the ears of the watchers. "There she is," said Mr. Melplash, tilting his head, as a silver shape crossed overhead.

"But it's going away!" Hetta said astonished.

"No, only going out to turn over the Tagus—look, now she's coming in to land." And in a moment or two more the great machine touched down, gently, with one or two easy bounces, taxied along the run-way, and came to rest by the luggage-trailer.

Hetta leaned forward, straining her eyes to see through the stars on her veil, as the door in the aeroplane's silver side opened and the mobile steps were run up to it. A figure in uniform appeared, then withdrew again into the machine; some officials stood by the steps. Now, at last, the passengers began to descend. Three men with brief-cases, all too tall to be the priest; four ladies in mourning, heavily veiled; a man and a woman, apparently together, for she turned on the steps and spoke to him; three girls whose neat suits, clever shoes, and beautifully-dressed hair betokened Americans, followed by a tall man, also by the shape of his hat an American; two nuns. Then, one after the other, half a dozen men—all of medium height, all carrying the distended brief-cases which will hold pyjamas as well as papers, all wearing the light-weight slate-coloured rain-cloth overcoats which are practically a uniform among continental men travelling by air, brown trilby hats and sun-glasses! Hetta's heart sank as she watched them crossing the apron towards her, in the bright sun; the stars on Richard's veil were maddening, she pushed it up, impatiently, and studied the faces, panting a little. None wore a beard, she noticed with thankfulness, but how could she ever make this Mr. Melplash know which one she meant, when all were so alike, even if she managed in spite of their goggles to recognise Father Antal herself?

That, however, she *must* do, and as these stereotyped specimens of *Homo sapiens europaeus* came nearer, their eyes concealed by the tinted glasses, she was inspired to study the backs of their heads under the trilby hats. Yes—all but one had hair, and darkish hair at that; as the colourless stubble on the sixth head approached the group of police, she recognised—she could not fail to—the blunt ugly nose, the stubborn chin, the wide, wise mouth that she knew so well. She pinched Mr. Melplash's arm.

"That is he—the one whose hair is without colour."

"The bald-pate, d'you mean?"

"What is bald-pate?" Hetta asked, angrily—was this man's stupidity, or her lack of English, to spoil everything at the last moment?

"Well, he is nearly bald, isn't he? Is that the chap?"

"Yes! I said so. All the others have dark hair. Now *go!*" Hetta said, managing to speak in an undertone in spite of her fury with this silly little man.

"All right, all right," Melplash said, rather miffily. "There's no rush—they'll be ages in the hall." What a tartar this Hungarian secret agent was, he thought, for all she looked rather pretty—what you could see of her through that veil. (Major Torrens had thus promoted Hetta into the ranks of counter-espionage; he preferred not to reveal her identity to his local colleague.)

The little secret agent, left to herself, stood for a moment longer at the rails. She was trembling a little from reaction; a few tears fell behind her veil. He was *there,* in that building within fifty yards of her!—and yet she must not approach him or speak to him. It was almost more than she could bear; she clenched her hands round the rails, as if to clamp herself in position, to control the ferociously strong impulse to follow the detestable Melplash round into the building. But the crowd was thinning on either side of her, as it does after a plane has arrived; noticing this she sniffed, blew her nose, dabbed at her eyes, drew her veil down again, and walked back, very deliberately, to where the taxi waited on the parking-place.

"Well?" Richard asked as she got in. "All right?"

"Yes—but what a *stupid* person this Melplash is!"

The taxi-man started his engine.

"Oh, can't we wait just one minute? We might see him again!"

Richard himself would have liked to wait, but he remembered Torrens' injunction to whisk his young companion away at once, and he was going to be appallingly late at the Chancery as it was.

"No, Hetti—better not. Now, tell me what happened."

She told him about the six short men in sun-glasses and rain-coats, her terror lest she should fail to recognise the priest, and her final solution of the problem. "And then this *creature* used a word I cannot know! What is 'bald-pate,' if you please?" she asked indignantly.

"Poor Melplash—he isn't exactly a ball of fire," Richard said laughing. "You've done splendidly, Hetti. Those five or six ghastly little men in overcoats are always on every plane from Madrid. Anyhow," he added easily, "now everything is all right."

But in this he was unduly optimistic.

CHAPTER VII

THE BRITISH EMBASSY in Lisbon is in various ways an inconvenient place for entertaining, not least because the main entrance is in a rather narrow and extremely steep street; moreover, the house is built on the slope of the hill, so that to reach the principal rooms all visitors must climb a quite considerable flight of stairs, broad and dignified as these are. However, once on the main floor, dignity takes over entirely. A splendid portrait of Marshal Beresford looks down on the guests even as they pant up the stairs to the wide hall; the long drawing-room is noble, with splendid views from its six windows; a glazed-in passage leads round a half-square to the great ball-room with its vast gilt mirrors, used for large receptions, and out into a small flagged court from which a flight of stone steps, overhung by the delicate sharply-cut foliage of a big pepper-tree, mounts up into the garden—immensely large for a town house—with its expanse of lawns, shady trees, and brilliant flower-beds. It is, in spite of its inconveniences, one of the most beautiful embassies in the world.

The drawing-room, fine as it is, is too long and narrow to receive in with any comfort—people fail to find their way out by the doors at the farther end, and get jammed in a solid block. Lady Loseley, who was as practical as she was short, neat, and pretty, therefore always awaited her guests in a smaller room, also with two doors, opening off the glass passage; this had a marble floor and marble tables, like mortuary slabs, against the walls—one of her predecessors had christened it "the morgue"; but it is too square for anyone to get jammed in it, and only a few steps from the long buffet in the great ball-room. Here the following afternoon Countess Páloczy, with Hetta in tow and deep satisfaction filling her heart, was for the first time received by the Ambassadress; Richard—looking very peculiar, Hetta thought, in morning coat and striped trousers, a uniform with which she was unfamiliar—stood at Lady Loseley's elbow and introduced them.

"So this is the young lady who is such a good cook!" Lady Loseley said smiling, as she shook hands with the girl; Hetta liked her immediately for this sensible frankness but the Countess's eyelids began to flutter—what a reputation for her daughter. "Henry, I don't think you know Countess Páloczy—and this is her girl who has been in Hungary for so long," Lady Loseley went on; the Ambassador turned away from a conversation with the Papal Nuncio to greet the two ladies. He was not tall, with gay blue eyes in a deceptively cheerful and open face; he had also a trick of picking at one thumb with the nail of the other, and did so as he said to Hetta— "I wish you would do me a *real* favour."

"What is that?" Hetta asked bluntly, entirely forgetting to say Your Excellency, as she had been told to do.

"Teach my idiot of a chef how to make *Hasen-pastete*. We used to have it for breakfast at the Budays—I never ate anything so good. Can you?"

"Yes—but hares will not be in season till September," said Hetta seriously.

"No more they will—though I doubt if that cretin in the kitchen would know a thing like that! All right—you'll come and make one in September." He turned back to the Nuncio.

"Countess, the buffet is round the corner, on your right," Atherley said. "This house is such a jig-saw! Ah, M. le Duc, *quel plaisir!*"

Hetta and her mother perforce moved on as the Duke of Ericeira and his old sister approached their hostess.

Hetta was rather upset by seeing Richard in this formal role—she felt that he was cold, distant; not at all the person she knew. And she had wanted to talk to him, and ask him if he had any more news of Father

Antal, and when she was to see him. She followed her mother out of the morgue in a slightly gloomy frame of mind.

It was a fine warm afternoon, and all the glass doors had been thrown open onto the courtyard, making it almost an extension of the house; most of the many guests were congregated there, and the Countess and Hetta drifted out with the rest—a footman in livery brought up a tray of cocktails.

"*Je préfère le Xérès,*" Hetta told the man, as her mother took a glass.

"*Immédiatement, Mademoiselle.*"

"*Really,* Hetti—" the Countess was beginning, when Mgr Subercaseaux came up and kissed her hand.

"Good afternoon, Countess. What a lovely day! So you still prefer sherry, Hetta?"

"Yes—I do not like cocktails."

"Wise child. Countess, isn't this a charming house? Have you seen the *azulejos* with the coats of arms of the former Ministers and Ambassadors? Oh, but you must—the whole diplomatic history of the English in Lisbon is here; it is unique! Permit me to act as cicerone."

This particular feature of the Embassy in Lisbon is indeed unique, and rather decorative. Since the Moors, seven or eight centuries ago, taught them the art, the making of coloured pictorial tiles has become a Portuguese speciality; and some diplomatic genius initiated the idea of having the arms, crest, and name of each Minister—later of each Ambassador— emblazoned and set in the walls round the courtyard and up the steps leading to the garden. These the Monsignor now proceeded to point out to Countess Páloczy and her daughter. But the Countess was only slightly interested; living notabilities meant more to her than dead ones, and her attention strayed to the people about her. Not so Hetta.

"Oh, look—this Legate was here under *three* Kings!" she exclaimed, as she read the Latin inscription on one plaque.

M. de la Tour, the French Ambassador, who was talking to the Monsignor and the Countess, overheard her.

"*Tiens!*" he said, going up and poking his pince-nez over her shoulder towards the decorative panel—"So he was. Do all young ladies in Communist countries learn so much Latin?"

Poor Hetta had quite forgotten who this busy friendly little man was.

"Communists, Monsieur," she said coldly, "know nothing and learn nothing." She looked round, seeking an escape, and was delighted to be greeted by the old Ericeiras—she remembered them from Mme de Fonte Negra's party, and elderly as they were she liked them. She thus escaped for the time being her mother's vexation that she should have addressed an ambassador as "Monsieur"; the Countess, however, apologised on her behalf to His Excellency—"She has had *no* advantages, poor child."

"Countess, if I were as well pleased with everyone's daughter as I am with yours I should be a happier man and a far happier priest," Subercaseaux said emphatically; he bent a peculiarly benign glance on Hetta, who was working her way round the plaques with the Duke of Ericeira, pouring out Latin and lively comments. The Countess was startled by the priest's tone, and rather upset—she was not wholly pleased, either, to see her gauche daughter on such easy terms with someone whom she herself had never managed to meet. The priest gave her a fine, ironical smile as he moved away; he passed through the crowd, smiling and Dear-lady-ing right and left—Hetta, her tour of the diplomatic *azulejos* with the old Duke completed, observed him with distaste. Then she was fastened on by Townsend Waller.

"Oh hul*lo!* How nice to find you here. Isn't this a fascinating house?"

"I like this outside part," Hetta said, temperately.

"I saw you reading Latin aloud to the old Duque. What a lot you know —thanks to Mother Scholastica! Have you been round the garden?"

"No."

"Oh, come on. Wait—I'll get you another sherry."

Glasses in hand, they went up the steps under the pepper-tree, and out onto the broad lawns between their gay borders. Hetta was delighted. "Such a *huge* garden, in the heart of a city!"

"Have *you* any idea what was really going on the other night?" Townsend presently asked her, as they strolled about.

"No. I only heard what you heard," the girl lied blandly. "Do you not think these Spaniards were drunk, and came back to see if they had killed you and Yulia?"

"No, I don't," the American said bluntly. "I think it was something else, though I still don't know what. Who is Major Torrens, anyhow, and why is he here? Have you any idea?" They were approaching the top of the steps again, and could look down on the throng in the little courtyard. "Oh, there's Atherley," the Bostonian said. "Do you mind if I leave you, Hetta? I want to catch him."

"But of course. In any case I must find Mama—I expect we should go soon." She did not, however, at once leave her coign of vantage, but stood by the low parapet which overlooked the courtyard and watched what was going on below. She saw that Lady Loseley, the receiving over, had come out to talk to her friends and get a breath of fresh air; the Ambassador had done likewise, and so had Richard, released from his official duties; her mother was in a little group which included Mme de Fonte Negra. Hetta

watched Townsend Waller forging his way through the crowd in Atherley's
direction, but before he reached him Monsignor Subercaseaux was suddenly at Richard's side, and speaking in his ear; the young man made
laughing excuses to the people he was with and began to move towards
the steps, the priest beside him. They encountered Townsend—the
summary friendly decision with which Richard dismissed him was dia-
grammatically clear; Hetta laughed softly to herself at the American's
disconcerted face. But how tiresome this was—she, too, would have liked
to speak to Richard. Vexed, she watched them climb the stone steps, pass
her, and move away across the garden. What *could* Richard and the ultra-
social Monsignor want to talk about in private?

In fact they talked at first about her. As they strolled across the lawn
Subercaseaux surprised Richard by saying, "What a delightful child Hetta
Páloczy is."

The young man could only agree.

"I am glad that you see something of her—you do, do you not?—for I
think she feels herself rather at a loss here; all her surroundings are strange
to her, and I fancy there is a good deal that she finds uncongenial."

"That isn't altogether surprising, is it?" Richard said—he never beat about
the bush with Subercaseaux, and certainly didn't intend to in this connection, if he was twenty times Dorothée's confessor.

The priest laughed gently.

"No—indeed it is almost inevitable. Her 'formation' "—he used that un-
translatable French expression for the exterior forces which mould a person—"has been so unusual, and so different."

Richard was really quite glad to discuss Hetta's *formation* with the
Monsignor, since it was one of his main preoccupations at the moment.

"Quite so. But though she is right about many things, she has some
rather unreasonable prejudices," he said slowly.

"She has. I personally feel her prejudice against me not *wholly* reasonable," Subercaseaux said, with the ecclesiastical equivalent of a grin.
Goodness, how sharp the old boy was, Richard thought, even while he
laughed. "But it is quite understandable, in view of her background. And
about certain things she is, as you say, entirely right. Did she tell you that
the Bretagnes wished her to go to luncheon with them, and that she refused?"

"No. Why wouldn't she go? They're such very nice people, and I should
have thought poor Dorothée would have loved it."

"She made it a condition—the invitation was transmitted through me—
that her mother should be invited to the wedding, which is of course the
poor lady's heart's desire."

The young man stood still for a moment—then he burst out laughing. "Oh, well done, Hetti! How splendid! And what happened?"

"It has been arranged," Mgr Subercaseaux said, smiling a satisfied smile. "The Pretender is so anxious to secure little Hetta's acquaintance for his children that he has agreed. The poor Countess will get that so coveted card this evening."

"Well, I hope, Monsignor, that you will make sure that Dorothée knows to whom she owes it!" Richard said. "Hetti never says a word, but I don't think she has too easy a time with her mother—or with herself, poor child," he added, with something like a sigh.

"You are right. But she suffers more from the difficulty 'herself' gives her than from any external cause," the priest said, bending his iron-grey eyebrows thoughtfully on the young man. "The defects of her qualities— that is her trouble. In fact she has few defects; but even her qualities at the moment are like a coat put on the wrong way out, and the lining is not becoming! We must help her to put this garment on the right way out." Richard regarded him steadily.

"Who are 'we,' Monsignor?" he asked.

"You and I, at present. I endeavour to do what a priest can; you, I hope and believe, are doing what a young man can do for a young woman— which is something rather different! But equally important."

Richard was not really ready for anything so direct as this. He hesitated for a moment.

"Monsignor, what are you driving at?" he asked at length.

"At a whole host of things!" Nothing could disconcert Mgr Subercaseaux, and he spoke easily. "But she has special qualities which it is good for her to *use*, and which, here, have so far lain fallow. I think you did well to employ her at Portela yesterday morning."

"I beg your pardon?" Richard said, looking at the priest with a face completely devoid of expression.

"I said that I thought you did well to employ her at Portela yesterday morning—if I am to dot the *i*'s and cross the *t*'s, to identify Father Antal Horvath."

Atherley's face remained stony.

"May I ask how you know this?"

"Major Torrens told me when he brought me in yesterday afternoon to have my first meeting with his—protégé, shall we say?"

Richard stared at the ecclesiastic for a moment longer—then his huge laughter resounded all over the Embassy garden.

"Good Lord, Monsignor! You don't mean to say that *you* are the famous contact?"

"In fact I am," Subercaseaux replied, with a modest smirk. "My dear Richard, can it be that you underestimate me as much as the little Countess does? My vanity is wounded!—so useful for me really, of course."

"But why *you?*—and here? Do forgive me, but I'm all at sea."

"The Vatican. Naturally it is essential that they should hear, as directly as possible, all that this eminent, saintly, and heroic man has to tell of conditions in Hungary, and about the Cardinal—but there were too many practical difficulties about getting Dr. Horvath to Rome himself, so it was arranged that he should come here and see me, and that I should act as intermediary. When he is safely out of the country I can go and report— I was in Rome, you may remember, a few weeks ago."

"Getting briefed?"

"Exactly."

"I'm surprised," Richard said reflectively, "that Torrens should have taken you to see him the very day the Father arrived—I should have expected him to wait till he saw if everything was quiet."

"That was his intention, but he had to summon me to resolve a little difficulty."

"What? May I know?"

"Something the Major found it very hard to understand," Subercaseaux said with a small smile. "The Father wanted to say his Mass this morning; Torrens had forbidden him to leave his room, so I had to intervene."

"Goodness! Oh well, I suppose it's all right for him," Richard said, trying to be charitable. "But with all that's at stake, and the risks other people are taking! What did you arrange?"

"I took him very early to a little church in the Alfama where I often say Mass on week-days; I take an interest in one of those parishes, and by Countess Páloczy's bounty am able to relieve much want, much suffering."

Richard knew the Alfama, that very ancient and very poor quarter of Lisbon huddled below the Citadel; built on rock, the houses there were not destroyed in the great earthquake of 1755, and thus it escaped Pombal's town planning; its streets remain crooked, very steep, and almost too narrow for wheeled traffic—no car can pass another in most of them. It surprised him to learn that the Monsignor should have any connection with such a part.

"Does Dorothée go in for charity? You don't say so!" he said.

"My dear Richard, you should avoid hasty judgements. She does."

"How extraordinary! Well never mind—was it all right?"

"No," Monsignor Subercaseaux said, frowning. "It was not all right. I served his Mass, he served mine, in that dark shabby little building, so touching and so aged; we went just before six o'clock, and the street outside was empty then. But when we came out—it was not yet seven—a lorry was drawn up across the bottom of the *ruelle,* and a group of men stood round it; they were strangers, not people from the parish, in hats and smart rain-coats. This seemed to me rather peculiar, and I decided to go the other way; but even as we turned up-hill a taxi stopped at the top of the street, blocking the way there also, and more of these men, who certainly did not belong in the Alfama, got out of it and stood about."

"How *very* nasty. What did you do?"

"We went back into the church, which has an exit through the sacristy into the priest's house; we got out that way into a different street, and I took Father Horvath back to his lodgings."

"Safely, I presume?"

"Yes. But not unobserved, I am afraid—in fact they must be known, and an agent has been on the watch as early as 6 A.M., who traced us to São Braz and sent those men to entrap him as he came out."

"How did *you* get away?"

"Oh, your Major Torrens is very clever! He has hidden the Father in rooms above a small curio-shop, built right against the slope of one of the hills, and like São Braz it has a back entrance, not far from one of those extraordinary lifts. When I wished to leave I went down into the shop and examined some old prints under the window for half-an-hour, and was able to observe two men constantly appearing and reappearing on the pavement opposite. So I went out by the back way, got into the lift, shot up a couple of hundred feet, and took a taxi back to Estoril."

Richard, though he seldom used them himself, was familiar with that highly peculiar feature of Lisbon, the huge lifts which so conveniently take pedestrians from one level of the tip-tilted city to another. The ingenuity of the priest, and his self-satisfied expression as he recounted it made him laugh a little, but in fact he recognised well enough that this was no laughing matter. He didn't, being a diplomatist, at once say so; what he said was—

"I don't know why you call him 'my' Major Torrens."

"No—you are quite right; it was a slip of the tongue. In fact you are *his* Mr. Atherley."

"I'm nothing of the sort!" the young man protested.

"Oh yes you are—if only because the little Countess is involved in this. But my friend, something else must be arranged; the present situation is impossible. It is hopelessly compromised."

"I'm thinking about that, of course," Atherley said, ignoring the remark about Hetta. "He must be moved at once. It isn't really safe for you to try to see him in those rooms any more."

"Have you any ideas?"

"How you do go on dragging me into it, Monsignor!" Richard said, very good-naturedly. "Yes, I have had one, a quite wild one."

"Well?"

"To park him with the old Ericeiras. Private chapel in the house for saying Mass, and all."

"Do you know this idea came to me also just now, as I watched the little Countess airing her Latin to the old Duke while they studied those plaques together."

"Oh, was she?" Richard was pleased, and his pleasure did not escape the priest.

"Very much so. I thought him quite enslaved—as that young lady enslaves, and will continue to enslave, so many. Could it be arranged through her?"

"I shouldn't think so—he may have been enslaved today, but she barely knows them, and it's asking quite a lot, isn't it? Anyhow they go to the country tomorrow," Richard added, remembering Luzia's Medusa face when she had announced this.

"But better still! To this wonderful house up near São Pedro do Sul? Nothing could be more suitable for the purpose. Do you know them well enough to propose it?"

"NO, Monsignor, I don't!—and I wouldn't if I did," Richard said with vigour. "Why don't you ask them yourself?—you know everyone."

"The Ericeiras only very slightly. And to tell you the truth, Dona Maria Francisca is rather too holy for my taste!" Subercaseaux said, with a sudden boyish gleam of mischief.

Richard laughed.

"Well, in any case this is Major Torrens' pidgin, so let him arrange it— I won't."

"But how can he? He is a stranger here."

"I know that; but his friend Miss Probyn—how far she works with him I don't know, nor if they are fiancés—but in any case she is a close friend of his, and she's practically part of the Ericeira family; she was governess or something to Luzia, that lovely girl of the Duque's, for most of last year —she's staying there now."

"*Tiens!*" Mgr Subercaseaux said. "Ah, then through her no doubt all can be arranged. I think you will be seeing Major Torrens—will you suggest it to him?"

"I hope to goodness I *don't* see the Major!" Richard exploded; "and if I do I'd rather leave it alone. Once for all, Monsignor, I am a regular member of a law-abiding diplomatic mission, not one of your cloak-and-dagger men, and I do beg you to remember it."

Subercaseaux made no reply whatever to this except to smile his fine, rather subtly secretive smile as they strolled back towards the steps.

Their prolonged colloquy had not been entirely unobserved. When Hetta went down into the crowded courtyard she had found her mother by no means in a hurry to leave; she hung about, rather at a loose end, and was pleased to be accosted by M. de Polnay, the old Hungarian journalist whom she had met, and liked, at the Countess's cocktail party. "I hope no one is making you *do* anything?" was his greeting—Hetta laughed and said No.

M. de Polnay always knew everything, and had his private sources of amusement. "Come and let me show you something else," he said, after Hetta had expressed her pleasure in the *azulejo* coats of arms—he led her, hobbling up the steps, to the garden, and across to a small stone seat set in an embrasure in the parapet overlooking the Rua Arriaga, where a little tablet stated that King Edward VII had sat there on Palm Sunday, 1903.

"Such a pity they have not put up another one to say that Edward VIII sat here on Bank Holiday, 1936," he chuckled. But as they walked back towards the steps his sharp eye noticed Atherley and the Monsignor patrolling the lawn at the farther end of the garden. He stood still to watch them.

"I wonder what plot Richard Atherley and this old serpent Subercaseaux are hatching," he observed. "They are together for a long time. Do *you* know?" he asked, wheeling round on her.

"No—I have wondered myself," Hetta said, laughing.

"But is he not in your pocket?"

"No; in my mother's if in anyone's—which I doubt," the girl said. M. de Polnay pinched her arm gaily.

"I see you are learning—you are very ready. Well done—*mes félicitations!* But you know quite well which of them I meant."

"Of their plots, in any case, I am quite ignorant," Hetta said lightly—she thought, rather uncomfortably, that there had been a certain intention behind the journalist's question.

Her drive back to Estoril was uncomfortable too. The Countess was tired, and fatigue with her was apt to take the form of irritability, as it does with so many of us. She had not managed to meet the Ericeiras—something Hetti could so easily have brought off, if she had any tact and social sense at all!—and altogether she was thoroughly disgruntled, and took it out on her child. She was still scolding Hetta for her gaucherie with the French Ambassador when they reached the hotel; in the lift she was perforce silent, but as they went into the apartment she completed a long tirade by saying—"If you *will* perpetrate these gaffes in society, you will never make the most of your opportunities." She was thinking of Hetta's meeting the Pretender and his wife at Mme de Fonte Negra's, a thing which had rankled in her mind ever since.

Letters in the Countess's flat were always placed on a fine old chest in the lobby off which the main rooms opened—Countess Páloczy went at once to examine her mail. There was a note which she passed to Hetta and several, including a stiff white envelope, for herself—she carried them through into the salon and began to open them. After a moment or two she broke into joyful exclamations. "Oh, how wonderful! At last!" Hetta was reading her own note for the second time, and made no reply; but Dorothy Páloczy was one of those people who have to get a response to their own feelings of the moment, whatever they may be, and no matter from whom—forgetting her vexation with her daughter she got up, a little heavily, and went over to her holding out a large card.

"Look! Here is my invitation to the wedding!" she said. "How splendid of Monsignor Subercaseaux—I'm sure he arranged it, though he said he couldn't."

"How nice, Mama. I am very glad," Hetta said pleasantly—of her own part in the affair it never occurred to her to utter a word, but a tiny rather wry smile, which she could not help, played about her wide decided mouth.

"And what is *your* letter?" her mother asked, now all benignity.

"The Comtesse de Bretagne asks me to lunch on Sunday. But we are going to those American friends of yours at the Avix, are we not?"

"Oh, what nonsense! Of course you must go. A royal invitation is like a royal command; one cannot refuse. Let me see it." Hetta handed her the note in silence. "Very pleasant—delightfully expressed. The sudden visit of the Archduke of course fully accounts for the shortness of the invitation, but it is courteous of her to apologise for it. Write at once and accept—I will send Oliveira with the note this evening."

"Oliveira has been out all day," Hetta observed. "Can we not post it?"

"Certainly not—it must go tonight."

"Then what about the Salzbergers?"

"Oh, they don't matter in the least! I will ring up and explain to them. Write your note, Hetti," the Countess said, pushing the bell.

Richard Atherley, too, was slightly tired after the party. He did not dislike the social side of his duties, which came easily to him, but he took them seriously and did them well; and to spend two-and-a-half hours remembering faces and names, and thinking of something polite, and if possible not wholly meaningless to say to several hundred people is in fact quite tiring.

When the last guest had gone and he had had a whisky-and-soda with the Loseleys—the Ambassador always liked such little relaxed post-mortems on these occasions—he had still to go back to the Chancery to sign letters and take a look at his tray. He walked round there—uphill, downhill, uphill again; the Lapa quarter is very *accidenté*—thinking longingly of the supper Joaquina would have ready for him, and of his armchair, his novel— a new Waugh, thank God—his slippers, and his small bright log fire. But when he pushed open the high heavy baroque doors of the Chancery and walked across the hall Tomlinson, the messenger, started up from behind the sort of counter at which he received messengers from other Chanceries, and similar lesser orders of creation.

"There's a gentleman to see you in the waiting-room, Sir."

"God Almighty! I really can't, at this time of night," Richard broke out.

"Gentleman's been there nearly two hours, Sir. I told him you was at the party and it was no good phoning, and that you'd be in a hurry when you did come in—but he said he'd wait."

"Who is it, Tomlinson?"

"That tall gentleman with red hair; Mr. Melplash's contact, Sir, isn't he?"

Richard groaned—and then with difficulty restrained laughter. Trust Chancery messengers to know everything!—especially if their wives, as they so often are, were Embassy telephone operators. He wasted a moment on a crazy speculation as to what Tomlinson would say if he were there and then to ask him—"Where shall we put Father Antal, this Hungarian?" Tomlinson, he felt sure, would not be taken by surprise; probably he would have some extremely sensible suggestion.

"All right, Tomlinson. I'll just go and clear up, and ring down when I'm ready."

"Very good, Sir. I hope the party went well, Sir?"

"Splendidly, thank you, Tomlinson." He went upstairs.

There was, mercifully, very little to do—Richard did it, then rang his bell; a moment or two later Tomlinson ushered in Major Torrens.

"I'm sorry to bother you so late," that gentleman said as he sat down, "but matters have become a little crucial."

Richard pushed the Alentejo cigarette-box across the table.

"I know—I've heard it all," he said rather brusquely. "And I want my supper! Of course Father A. can't stay where he is; he's got to be put somewhere else—*really* safe, this time. You'd better get Julia to take him to the Ericeiras' country place, hadn't you?"

The Major gaped at him in such complete astonishment that again Richard nearly laughed. "How on earth do you know about this?" he asked.

"The Monsignor has just been pouring it all out to me at the party."
Torrens looked vexed.

"Why should he tell *you?*"

"Why indeed? Why you *all* go on pestering me about what is no concern
of mine I can't think! But since you have waited nearly two hours to tell
me yourself, I suppose Subercaseaux felt the same about it," Richard replied, unanswerably.

"What did the old boy want to go out and say Mass for?" Torrens said
with irritation. "He was safe enough indoors."

"Oh rubbish, Torrens. If the opposition hadn't known something about
your famous *homme de confiance's* hide-out already, they would never have
spotted Father Antal creeping round to the Alfama at 6 A.M. Anyhow, it
seems to me that the answer is quite clear—send him to the Ericeiras."

"But they're in Lisbon—Julia's staying there."

"I know she is—but they go to São Pedro do Sul tomorrow."

"Where's that?"

"Miles away, up towards the North. They have a vast baroque mansion
there—complete with private chapel, so there need be no running *out* to
say Mass," Richard said, grinning.

The Major reflected.

"Would they have him? And the Monsignor too? He'll have to go as well,
as I daresay you've realised, since you seem to know so much!"

"There's plenty of *room* for him in that house, anyhow! But why don't
you see Julia? She's the person to organise all this—the Ericeiras eat out
of her hand. Rather a godsend for you, I should have thought." He got up,
glancing at his wrist-watch. "I'm so sorry, Torrens, but I really must go."

The Major remained seated.

"Atherley, do let your supper wait for another ten minutes," he said,
imperturbably. "This is quite important."

"I realise that, but fortunately for you you have the answer—Julia. Why
don't you go to her and settle it at once?"

"But how is he to *get* there? That's a point, even if these people agree
to take him in, about which you sound so uncommonly certain."

"I only know Julia—I thought you knew her even better than I do," Richard said smoothly; he observed with rather malicious pleasure a certain
reddening of the Major's face. "As to how he gets there, I'm sure they will
have a domestic chaplain, like all Portuguese of that class; borrow a clerical
outfit from the Monsignor, and let him go up in the car, or the ox-wagon,
or whatever chaplains travel in in this country! The real chaplain can follow on by train—if the thugs catch him they'll soon let him go when they

find they've got nothing on their hands but a dumb antiquated priest, who can't speak a word of anything but Latin and Portuguese."

Major Torrens emitted a rather reluctant laugh.

"How detailed and knowledgeable you are! Why should you be surprised that we all apply to you?"

"Well, apply to Julia now—I'm going home," Richard said. "Come on; clear out—I want to lock my door." He spoke with a friendly firmness that made Torrens laugh again. "And *don't*, repeat don't, go ringing me up tonight to tell me in guarded language how you've got on, because I'm going to bed," he added, as they walked in single file along the absurdly narrow corridor and down the wide stairs to the hall. Tomlinson, behind his counter, heard them laughing, and reflected that Mr. Atherley would always have his joke.

CHAPTER VIII

WHEN IN LISBON the Ericeiras usually dined at eight-forty-five—if they were alone both Nanny and the chaplain dined with them; he did so at all times, to say grace. On that Friday evening Elidio, the elderly manservant, after a muttered colloquy at the dining-room door with someone unseen sidled up to Nanny and whispered something. Luzia, whose ears were still sharp enough to hear the squeak of a bat on the wing, caught the words "Um Senhor Inglês" and "Menina Juli": she said at once, and out loud— "Who is it, Elidio? I wonder if it could be Atherley."

"*Mr.* Atherley, if you please, Luzia," Nanny said repressively. Asking permission from Dona Maria Francisca she got up and left the room; Julia went on eating her dinner in silence, with her usual relish. After a few moments Nanny returned and resumed her seat and her meal, also without saying anything.

"*Nanny!*" Luzia said after a moment, fuming—"who *is* it?"

"All in good time, Luzia. Go on with your dinner." She turned to Dona Maria Francisca with the announcement that she now had a full clutch of twelve bantams' eggs ready to set; could she have one of the grey hens to hatch them, if there was a broody?—the cook's wife had promised to look after them. (This in fluent Portuguese.)

"Better take the eggs up to Gralheira with you, Nanny; then you can look after them yourself," the Duke said, also in Portuguese. "You are a witch with those absurd little birds."

At last the meal in the great room came to an end; Dom Pedro, the chaplain, said grace a second time, they crossed themselves, and the little party filed out. The Duke asked for coffee to be served to him in his study, as he had work to do, but his sister said, as she always did—"Do you take coffee with us, Miss Probyn?"

Julia was speaking aside with Nanny.

"May I come presently, Dona Maria Francisca? It appears that there is someone who wishes to see me."

"Very well. Luzia, you can come with me," the older lady said, slightly compressing her lips; much as she liked and respected Miss Probyn she could not wholly approve of people who paid calls during dinner—or indeed called at all so late in the evening.

Julia Probyn, while exercising to the full the rather remarkable degree of freedom accorded by custom to a "Miss" in Spain and Portugal, had equally respected the privacy of her employers when she was Luzia's governess; indeed, until Richard Atherley had come to see her two days before no friend of hers had ever crossed the Ericeiras' threshold, apart from Richard's midnight peep at old Manoel's hooded chair, and she was not best pleased to learn from Nanny that Major Torrens was waiting to see her in the schoolroom.

"What a time to come!" she said, as Dona Maria Francisca and the reluctant Luzia disappeared in the direction of the drawing-room. "How boring."

"He's a magnificent-looking man, isn't he?" Nanny observed, suspecting the veracity of Julia's last words. "If Luzia saw him I daresay she wouldn't keep on so about Mr. Atherley." Julia laughed as she went upstairs.

"My dear Hugh, what on earth is this in aid of?" she asked as she entered that bare English-looking schoolroom. "Dona Maria Francisca doesn't allow 'followers,' and nor do I."

The Major, justly provoked, replied by enveloping her in a vigorous and rather stifling embrace.

"Hugh!" Julia protested, when she could speak—"What on earth has come over you?"

"Only you, my dear, as usual—except that I'm not usually as weak as I am at this moment."

"Why are you weak?" Julia asked, sitting down in one of the shabby armchairs.

"Because I'm starving; because I've been waiting to see Atherley in that revolting Chancery for two mortal hours; and because I'm in a jam which I think only you can get me out of."

Julia got up slowly, opened a cupboard, and drew out a tin of Huntley and Palmers biscuits, which she handed to him.

"That's all I can do about the starvation," she said—"Now tell me about the jam."

"Oh, wonderful!" Torrens said, cramming Petits Beurres into his mouth.

"Well?" Julia asked, after a few moments.

"Do you suppose—I expect you'll think me quite crazy—but do you imagine that your employers could conceivably be persuaded to put Father Horvath up for a few days?"

"Are you talking about the Ericeiras?—because they're not my employers any more."

"Damn you, Julia, don't be so pernickety! Yes, I do mean your *ex*-employers, the Ericeiras, as you know quite well."

"And who is Father Horvath? Hetta's priest, I suppose. I thought she called him something else."

"What does it matter what she called him?" Torrens asked, with all the irritation of a hungry and worried man. "Yes. But do you think they would put him up?"

"They're going away to the country tomorrow."

"I know. That's rather the idea."

"What's gone wrong?" Julia enquired. "I thought you'd poked him away somewhere here in Lisbon, to have meetings with a contact."

"So we had, but that's all compromised—don't ask me how! I thought it was cast-iron, but it isn't. They can't meet safely in Lisbon any more."

"So has the contact got to come to Gralheira too?"

"Well that would be the ideal thing, of course; but I daresay he could put up somewhere close by."

"There's nothing 'close by' at Gralheira; it's miles from everywhere. Look, Hugh," the girl said, frowning a little as she thought it out—"this is quite a large order, isn't it? Suppose you tell me a bit more. For one thing, who is the contact?—and why has Father What-not got to meet him?"

Torrens told her a great deal more, including the episode outside São Braz in the Alfama that very morning. When Julia heard that Monsignor Subercaseaux was the "contact" she hooted with irreverent laughter—"Him! Goodness, Hetti simply *hates* him." But she registered with satisfaction the fact that the Monsignor was representing the Vatican—"Of course that could mean a lot. You're *sure* about that?"

"Quite sure."

Julia continued to reflect.

"I think I'd better talk to Nanny first," she said. "Ring the bell, Hugh —by the fire-place." Torrens got up, and gazed about for an electric button, in vain. "No, pull that trace thing," Julia said, laughing a little—the Major obediently tugged on a broad strap of cut velvet which depended on the right of the grate.

"Whose idea is this?" she asked, as he came back and sat down in the other armchair.

"Atherley's really. But it seems that young Hetta rather mopped up the Duque at the Embassy this afternoon, according to him."

"Well, that may help. But the Vatican is the trump card." A footman entered. "O Francisco, I desire to speak with Miss Brown," Julia said. The use of the vocative is still current in Portugal, one of the many pretty archaisms in which the country abounds; it is really rather impolite *not* to say "O Manoel" or "O Francisco" when speaking to a servant.

Nanny, whose private apartments were on the same upper floor as the schoolroom, appeared almost at once.

"Nanny, you saw Major Torrens while we were at dinner—Hugh, you'd better meet Nanny properly; and until she gives you leave she's Miss Brown to you!" Nanny smirked; Torrens got up and shook hands. "Now listen, Nanny," Julia pursued—"The Major is in the English Secret Service." Nanny looked wise. "And he's in a difficulty, and he wants us to help him."

"Well, if it's in any manner possible, Miss Probyn, we ought to, of course," Nanny said, visibly if primly thrilled. "What is the trouble?"

Julia explained briefly what the trouble was: Nanny, a devout Catholic —there are quite a lot of them in Leicestershire—was even more thrilled when she learned that what was at stake was nothing less than to promote a meeting between an important foreign divine and an emissary of the Vatican. "This Father Thingumy-jig has seen Cardinal Mindszenty quite lately," Julia added at the end.

"Not really? Well, I must say I should like to meet him. And it would be an honour to have a person like that in the house. I think I'd better speak to His Grace about it first," Nanny said—"he won't get upset." Julia grinned—Dona Maria Francisca did get upset by anything unusual. "I'd better go at once; it's nearly time for the Rosary," Nanny went on. "When would the priest want to come, Miss Probyn?" She got up as she spoke.

"Well, that's rather the thing, Nanny. He ought to come *with* us tomorrow, with you in the second car—pretending to be Dom Pedro, you see. Everyone knows that we travel with a chaplain, so it would be a complete disguise."

Nanny gave a discreet giggle.

"And how is Dom Pedro to get up? Oh well, he can take his chance on the railway like another, can't he?—if he takes the slow train and gets off at Aveiro they can send the Land-Rover for him, and one of these other two priests can say Mass for us on Sunday morning, if he should be delayed. Is the gentleman from the Vatican to drive up with us too?"

Julia looked enquiringly at Torrens. The Napoleonic thoroughness of Nanny's strategy had taken her unawares.

"If the Monsignor could drive up with you and Father Horvath in the second car, Miss Brown, it would simplify matters very much," Torrens said at once.

"Nanny to you, Major."

"Oh, thank you. Well, when you have spoken to the Duke, and if he agrees, let me know what time you start, and I will have them both here."

"We start at ten-thirty. But I had better see His Grace at once—you wait here." She bustled out.

"That's a remarkable woman," Torrens said, taking another biscuit. He glanced at his watch—it was already after ten.

"Poor Hugh! When will you eat?" Julia said. "I wish I could give you a bite, but that isn't so easy."

"Oh, I'll eat when the job's done. I'm quite accustomed to Spanish hours, from Morocco," Torrens said cheerfully. "I wish I could get onto the Monsignor, though, to make sure of his being in—if they really would take him up with them it would be a great simplification. Those thugs outside the church this morning will have registered his appearance in detail— probably taken his photograph. Anyhow no one could miss his eyebrows!"

"Elidio can get onto him for you," Julia said, getting up and tugging at the huge velvet bell-pull. "There's an extension outside the chapel. I practically forced the Duke to put that in when I came to teach Luzia; I really couldn't go right down to the bottom of the house and scream in the pantry whenever I wanted to talk to my friends!"

Torrens laughed. "What an extraordinary set-up the whole ménage is! I wonder if there's anything like it left anywhere else in the world."

"Richard's description of Hungary sounded much the same, but I suppose that's all finished now," Julia was saying, when Francisco appeared. "What's the Monsignor's number?" she asked—she dashed it down on a half-sheet torn from one of Luzia's exercise books.

"O Francisco, take this number to Elidio. The Senhor Inglês desires to speak with the Senhor there—*um senhor eclesiástico.*"

"*Muito bem, Minha Menina.*"

"Have you got a car?" Julia asked. "I suppose you'll have to flash out to Estoril to settle this—you'll hardly want to do it on the telephone."

"No, I can't do that. I haven't a car; I'm using taxis at the moment—less conspicuous."

"A taxi to Estoril will take aeons. I'll run you out when it's all fixed—if Nanny manages to fix it."

"Why did you leave it to her?" Hugh Torrens asked, rather curiously. "I thought they were so devoted to you."

"Devoted is a strong word," Julia said slowly. "They are quite fond of me, I think, but Nanny has been here twenty years; she came for the little boy who died—such a tragedy—and stayed on to take over Luzia. Then the Duchess died too—poor Duque, he has had it hard!—and of course ever since Nanny has been an irreplaceable fixture. Dona Maria Francisca's a good old thing, but she's a bit of a *beata*," the girl went on, using the admirable Spanish expression for an ultra-religious woman; "with all her limitations, Nanny has been the salvation of that child."

"Yes, I can imagine that. She's a remarkable woman," Torrens said again —as he spoke the door opened, and the remarkable woman reappeared.

"Everything's going to be quite all right," Nanny said comfortably. "But His Grace would just like to have a word with the Major himself."

"All right for *both*, Nanny?" Torrens enquired.

"Yes, Sir. Miss Probyn, you might as well come along too, and do the introducing; Dom Pedro's been in the chapel this last ten minutes, and Dona Maria Francisca will fret if I don't go."

"Half a second, Nanny, while I get a coat," Julia said. "I must take the Major out to Estoril to fix up with the Monsignor." She hurried away and was back in an instant, a loose tango suède jacket slung over her shoulders.

"Bless you for this, Nanny," Torrens said, as they proceeded along the endless corridors towards the big staircase.

"We should be thankful to Almighty God if He gives us the chance to do a work of mercy, shouldn't we?" Nanny responded briskly. "And someone from the *Vatican!*"

Down in the shadowy hall, so vast that it was only faintly lit by the superb 18th-century chandelier which hung in the middle, Elidio stood waiting to inform Julia that he had got *"o número"* for the Senhor Co-mandante—Julia told Torrens to go with the man and take the call in the pantry, and sat down to wait on a high-backed chair of Dutch marquetry upholstered in magnificent but rather threadbare brocade; a dozen of these stood round the walls, and even one would have added lustre to most museums. When Torrens returned Elidio led them into the Duke's study.

This apartment, which opened off the hall, was not only very large, but stuffed quite full of original Chippendale furniture: enormous glass-fronted bookcases along the walls, with cabriolet-legged chairs standing between them; "occasional" tables, delicate and graceful; also two magnificent twin tall-boys, and a drop-front writing-desk from behind which the Duke rose to receive Torrens and Julia as they entered. Major Torrens was furniture-minded in the English way, that is to say he knew and admired English period furniture, and was blind to any other—but he fairly gaped at the contents of that room. Being new to Portugal he of course could not know that when the English wine-shippers in Oporto built, in the year 1785, the Factory House there, in which to dine and entertain their friends, they caused Mr. Chippendale to fabricate their two colossal dinner-tables, and the lovely chairs which still stand round them, each bearing the hidden "C.," the master's hall-mark. Presumably the Ericeira of that day had profited by the presence of these marvellous foreign craftsmen to furnish his own study; anyhow there it was, a room to stagger anyone.

There was nothing staggering about the Duke of Ericeira, except that he looked so very like a Scotsman. He was rather tall, with the same grey eyes as Luzia, iron-grey hair, and a deeply-lined rugged face which some-how also looked grey; he wore grey suits in Lisbon and greyish tweeds in the country—all made in London, and all with that indefinable appearance of being comfortably old from the moment they are first put on which is the special knack of London tailors. He greeted Torrens in perfect English, drew forward a chair for Julia, and then turned at once to the business in hand.

"I am delighted, naturally, to receive these divines," he said, speaking slowly, with a certain formal precision which was also rather Scottish. "I am familiar with some of Dr. Horvath's writings—in translation, of course. A very great man. Tell me, do you wish to bring them here tonight?"

Torrens was as much taken aback by the Duke's promptitude as Julia had been by Nanny's.

"Well, upon my word, I hadn't thought of that, Sir," he said.

"Might it not be better? It is dark now, which always creates difficulties for watchers; and it will be unexpected. Then they can both leave with us in the morning quite naturally; Dr. Horvath can travel in the car with my sister and myself—and my daughter, of course—and Monsignor Suber-caseaux can follow in the second car with my secretary and Miss Brown, taking Dom Pedro's place."

"Dear Duke, don't tell me that Nanny remembered the Monsignor's name?" Julia put in irrepressibly.

The Duke smiled.

"No, Miss Probyn. But she did tell me that the second party was act-ing as the Vatican's representative in this affair, and that could only be Monsignor Subercaseaux." He turned to Torrens. "Well?"

"Yes, Sir. I will bring them both here tonight. That is much the best plan, if it won't be putting you about too much to have guests arriving so late."

"My household is never put about by anything that is my wish," the Duke said, pressing a bell on his desk. "For one thing they are paid to do whatever is required of them, and for another, there still obtains here in Portugal that happy sense of *unity* in a household between employer and employed. Do you know the Portuguese word for the domestic staff of a house?"

"No, I'm afraid I don't."

"It is *'a familia,'* the family."

At this point a representative of the family appeared in the person of Elidio.

"O Elidio," the Duke said, "cause two rooms to be prepared for two guests; let *borachas* (hot-water bottles) be placed in the beds, for the gentlemen are old, and the night is chilly. You will wait upon them yourself, and will enquire if they desire any refreshment—tell the chef to have hot consommé and biscuits ready."

"*Muito bem,* His Excellency. And at what hour does His Excellency expect His Excellency's guests?"

The Duke glanced at the Empire clock on the chimney-place—it was twenty minutes to eleven.

"About midnight, or perhaps a little later."

"*Muito bem, Sua Excelência.*"

"And when the Senhora Condessa has finished the Rosary, tell her that I will come up and speak with her, and also with Dom Pedro—let him not go to bed," the Duke said firmly. Bowing, with another *Muito bem,* Elidio withdrew.

"Well, I think I'd better get going," Torrens said; he too had noticed the time.

"Duke, could Major Torrens have some of the consommé and biscuits when he brings his people along? He's had no dinner yet."

"Of course—how distressing." He pressed the bell again. "You must forgive my lack of hospitality," he said gravely to the Major—"I had no idea of this. Will you take something now?"

"Thank you very much, Sir, but I would rather get them safely here first."

"Very right. Do you come up to Gralheira with your charges? That would, of course, be a pleasure."

"I think not, Sir, thank you so much—there may be things for me to see to here."

"I understand—though I am sorry. Will consommé and an omelette, and some cold turkey, be sufficient when you return?—a poor meal, I am afraid."

"Ample, Sir. Don't bother with the omelette." He rose—"I really think we had better start."

"By all means. Does Miss Probyn go with you?" the Duke asked, suddenly noticing Julia's jacket, as she also got up.

"She is very kindly driving me; her car is faster than a taxi."

"Ah yes—she drives well. I will say goodnight, for I trust you and my other guests will excuse me if I should not be here to receive you when you return."

"Duke, there is one thing we ought perhaps to settle," Julia put in. "What names are they to go by?—their own, or should we make some up? I'm not thinking so much of the staff—it's things like the postman, and all the swarms of people who come and go at Gralheira."

The Duke, who had risen, sat down again behind his Chippendale escritoire.

"Elidio, tell the chef to be ready to serve an omelette and some cold *peru* and a salad, as well as the consommé, when the Senhor Comandante returns with the other guests," he said, when the man re-appeared. As the servant left the room he turned to Torrens. "I think that is a good point of Miss Probyn's, as regards Dr. Horvath; the Monsignor must, of course, come under his own name—my chaplain, my secretary, my steward, in fact everyone knows him by sight. What do you say?"

"Yes, Miss Probyn is right—I ought to have thought of it myself. It would certainly be wiser for Father Antal not to use his own name."

The Duke doodled on his blotting-paper. "One can never think of names when one wants them," he said, drawing his eyebrows together.

"Why not Père Antoine for Father Antal?" Julia suggested. "A French name, as he's a foreigner."

"You are very ready, Miss Probyn! Will that do, Major Torrens?"

"No, Sir, not Antoine—too like Antal."

"Then what?"

"Oh, Père François—they'll call him Dom Francisco anyhow," Julia said abruptly; she was anxious to get off. Torrens agreed to this, and the Duke jotted down the name methodically in a little note-book—"I will tell Elidio and the steward," he said.

As this was settled Torrens gave a fleeting grin, which to Julia's surprise was repeated in the Duke's grey lined face. She registered suddenly that her late employer was enjoying the whole business considerably, and decided to waste two more minutes on increasing his pleasure.

"Duke, you realise that Countess Hetta Páloczy was cook to *Père François*"—she stressed the words, smiling—"in Hungary for six years?"

"Impossible! This young lady who knows so much Latin, a cook?"

"Indeed *yes*. I'll tell you about that when we get to Gralheira, and aren't in a hurry."

"Ought she to come up too?" the Duke asked—nothing, Julia felt, was beyond him that night.

"Not for the moment."

"But *you* come, of course?"

"Yes, rather—only I shall have to get back for the wedding."

"Oh, this wedding!" the Duke said. "That is not for another week, anyhow."

A groom swung back the great doors of the cobbled courtyard of the Ericeira stables to let Julia's car drive out.

"O Fausto, be here to let me in again—in an hour, or perhaps in two hours—but I must not be caused to wait," the girl said urgently. "I shall hoot three times, when I return." As she turned out into the street the gates clanged to behind them.

"Which first?" Julia asked.

"Oh, Estoril. They probably won't be watching Subercaseaux at this time of night—though you never know. How often have you had this new car out since you got it, by the way?"

"Once. It only came yesterday morning, and I took Nanny and Luzia to the Zoo in the afternoon."

"See anyone hanging about?"

"No—though I confess I wasn't looking."

"Well I *was* looking when we came out just now, and I swear that street was bone empty," Torrens said, as Julia twisted down towards the river. "There isn't cover for a cat along those huge house-fronts. We ought to be all right." There was a nervousness in his voice and manner that Julia had never met before—he's tired and hungry, she thought, as they raced along beside the Tagus. The young moon was fuller now than it had been three nights ago, and its light etched the Torre de Belém, the Manueline tower built on the spot whence the great Basque Vasco da Gama set sail to discover the Indies, in black and silver as they shot past it—a black-and-silver tower outlined against the broad black-and-silver river. Julia observed this with pleasure, but she was thinking of the task in hand in all its aspects. It was wonderful how the old Duque had played up, and there came into her mind Atherley's remark—was it really only three nights ago? —when she had taken him to see the night-watchman's chair: "Just the place to park Hugh's priest." Well, now Hugh's priest was going to be parked there—and at the thought she gave her slow giggle.

"What is it?" Torrens asked—she told him, and he laughed shortly.

"Yes, we're almighty lucky—having you there, and the old man being so splendid about it all. What a charmer he is—and so superbly off-hand about having people arrive in the middle of the night. I must say I'm looking forward to that omelette and consommé!"

"There's one thing," Julia said; the omelette had reminded her of it. "Do we pick up Father Antal on our way back or drop the Monsignor first and then go and fetch him?"

"I was thinking about that. It's between not putting all your eggs in one basket, and making as few calls as possible at the Duke's. On balance, I think the second is more important; anyhow I'll risk it. You know that big lift that goes up from near the Rossio—do you know your way to the top of it?"

"Yes."

"Well you can wait there, and I'll go down, collect Hetta's late employer, and bring him up in it."

"That's all right except for one thing, Hugh," Julia said.

"What?" He sounded impatient; she realised that the slightest check or hindrance played on his nerves tonight.

"It's easily got round," she said tranquilly. "That stub of street that leads down to the lift is a blind alley, and a car could block it; all I'm thinking is that it might be better for me to wait in the square near the other end, where I can't be blocked. It's barely a hundred yards from the lift."

"Yes. Yes, you're right. But don't just *sit* in the square, drive round a bit."

"I will. Don't worry, Hugh—I won't bog it." She reached out a hand to his.

"Bless you, I know you won't."

Mgr Subercaseaux lived in a small house with a garden in one of the shady streets between Estoril and Monte Estoril—the road was empty under the lamps as they turned into it; a light shone in one of the lower windows of the house. Torrens sprang out almost before the car stopped, and went up the little path to the door—at that moment the light in the window was quenched, and ten minutes later the two men appeared with a typewriter and a couple of suit-cases; the latter Torrens pitched into the boot, while the priest, clutching his machine, got into the back of the car.

"See anything?" Torrens asked as he got in beside Julia.

"Not a thing," the girl replied as she shot off down the road.

Cruising back along the Tagus speedway towards Lisbon, a small thought came into Julia's mind and nagged and fretted there. It was more a picture than a thought, really—a picture of a long line of goods trucks clanking slowly over that level crossing leading from the docks (whence the engine-whistles so troubled Lady Loseley at night) and of cars held up and standing stationary on either side of it, for as much as five minutes on end. She had a curious, insistent feeling that it would be better *not* to be immobilised for five minutes on the road tonight.

"Hugh, I'm going to turn up at Ajuda, onto the by-pass that goes out past the Stadium, and get into Lisbon from the top," she said.

"Why?" Again he sounded irritated.

"There's a level crossing if we don't, and at this time of night we might be held up by a train," she said, swinging sharply left as she spoke; the car climbed a hill, past the great Palace of Ajuda, past one of Dr. Salazar's new garden suburbs, and emerged onto the by-pass; this led into the city near the great aqueduct, whose gothic arches were as sharply defined in black and silver as the Tower of Belém had been. Torrens quite lost his bearings; he was surprised when Julia suddenly pulled up and said—"There. The lift's at the end of that short street."

He got out, glanced round sharply, looked at his watch.

"All right. Give me nine minutes. If I'm not back then go on cruising about, but close by. Keep moving." He was gone.

Julia too looked at her watch; it was ten minutes past twelve. As she drove away, Mgr Subercaseaux, for the first time, spoke from the back seat.

"Had you any particular reason for wishing to avoid the level crossing tonight?"

"Not what you could call a reason—except that there often *are* trains there as late as this. I just had a hunch that I'd rather not wait there, like a sitting duck, tonight." She was driving at considerable speed through the lamplit, almost empty streets; they came out by the Estrela Gardens, went up past the parsonage of St. George's, the English church, where among cypresses and judas-trees the novelist Fielding lies buried, and fetched a compass round; on the return journey they crossed the end of a long street filled on either side with the lofty frontages of baroque mansions—Julia slowed down as she passed it, and peered up its empty length.

"Nothing there," Subercaseaux said.

"No car, anyhow," Julia replied, accelerating again—it was the street in which the Ericeira palace stood.

"Is this your profession? You seem very good at it," the priest said, clutching the back of the front seat as the car swung sharply round a corner.

"Oh Lord no—I'm a journalist. I'm just helping Major Torrens out. I was governess for some time to the Duke's child, Luzia, so I know them."

"Do you come with us to the country, then?"

"For a few days—I've got to come back to cover this wedding."

"Ah. Do you know Countess Hetta Páloczy?"

"Indeed yes. She's a splendid girl."

"Splendid is the right word," Subercaseaux was beginning, when the car swung round another corner. "Don't talk now—do you mind?" the girl said, as they passed across the end of a square. She turned down one side of it, driving slowly now, and almost halted at the end of a short street. There was not a soul in it. Julia held her wrist-watch out towards the dash-board light. "Nine and a half," she muttered—"Drive round the block!" Rather slowly, now, she made the circuit of the square, and for a second time slowed down at the street. At that moment two figures appeared at the farther end, one carrying a small case. "Here they are—good-oh," she said.

Torrens and a small man got into the car, Torrens in front—Julia had kept the engine running, and even as the door slammed she shot off up the square.

"That's right—drive like hell," Torrens muttered. He was panting like a man who has been running. "I heard a car pull up outside the shop in a hurry, brakes squealing, as we left by the back way; and two men came racing up the passage to the lift just as it got moving. They yelled like mad, but I showed the man a huge note, and he kept on, thank God. I heard them swear—in Spanish, of course—before they ran back down the passage, and then I saw a car flash past along the bottom. They're after us all right."

"They've got to go all round by the Chiado," Julia said—she was driving very fast indeed, taking her turns with careful skill; nevertheless the two priests in the back were constantly ricochetting off one another. "We ought to be all right," she said, in her slow, tranquillising tones.

"Yes, but they were after us, damn them! They must have been keeping a round-the-clock watch on the Monsignor's house. I can't think how they missed us—six minutes sooner, and we were done."

"The level crossing, I expect," Julia said.

"Oh, *that's* why you came round by the by-pass! You thrice-blessed girl!" Hugh Torrens said, slapping his hand down hard on her knee, shining silken close beside his in the faint light from the dashboard.

Julia made no response. She was fully engaged in slinging her rather large car safely round a last corner—they passed now along a street which Torrens recognised. She pulled up on the left, hooted three times, leapt out and ran across to the great double gates of the Duke of Ericeira's stables; even as she reached them there came the dull clanking sound of heavy bolts being withdrawn, and one of the massive portals began to swing open. Julia nipped back and got into the car; she had placed it skilfully, and as the second big leaf of the high doors swung back the machine shot into the huge cobbled stable-yard. She switched off lights and engine instantly and ran over to the great gates, adjuring Fausto as she went—"Come—close everything. But softly, softly; do not make a clamour with your bolts." Noiselessly they eased the immense irons home into place; Fausto fastened a gigantic padlock, pocketed the key, and began a cheerful remark to Julia—"The Menina sees that I did not keep her waiting."

"*Não falar,*" Julia hissed at him—"*Por favor,* silence, Fausto. You did very well," she whispered to him then; "but silence for a few moments." She tiptoed back across the cobbles towards the others, who had got out of the car and were standing by it; Torrens had removed the suitcases from the boot, which he closed, like the car doors, without a sound. Then they all stood in that open court, so strangely large in the middle of a city, listening. Julia stole a glance at Father Antal, but the moon was almost down, and a solitary electric bulb burning over the servants' entrance at the back of the house only cast a faint light immediately below it; all she saw was the silhouette of a small man in an overcoat, clutching an outsize brief-case. There was complete silence in the street outside, at that hour. They stood so for two minutes, three, four.

"We've diddled them," Julia murmured. "Let's go in."

"No, wait; isn't that a car?" Torrens said—listening again. Julia too heard, faint and some distance away, a car's engine. The note altered, then grew louder—"Changing down at the corner," Julia whispered. The sound approached very gradually—a car was evidently being driven extremely slowly along the street. But it did not stop, and presently the noise of the engine died away altogether.

"They must have spotted you at the Zoo and followed you home, or put two and two together somehow," Torrens said—"and so they were just taking a look at this place."

"Well they've drawn a blank," Julia said. "Now let's come in and you get something to eat; it's five-and-twenty to one!"

Torrens never forgot that meal in the Ericeira palace in the small hours. Fausto was horrified at the bare idea of guests coming in at the back door, and wished to send them all out into the street again to make a proper entrance, but Julia over-ruled him in rapid friendly Portuguese; as a compromise she sent him in to fetch old Manoel, the night-watchman, to escort them through into the front part of the house. While he was gone she greeted the Monsignor and Father Antal in French—"I have treated you very brusquely so far, I am afraid, but chauffeurs are not really expected to talk!"

"Chauffeurs as good as you, Miss Probyn, do better than talk—your driving is a poem in itself," Subercaseaux replied at once; the Hungarian bowed, but said nothing. Then Manoel came shuffling out and led them in, through stone-flagged passages with *azulejos* on the walls: they caught glimpses of vaulted recesses piled high with wine barrels, with billets of chopped wood, with *mata*, the fragrant heathy prickly undershrub always used in Lisbon for kindling fires, with masses of the deep green lopped-off boughs of *Pinus pinaster*, throughout Portugal the fuel habitually used for baking bread. They passed the open door of the vast kitchen, where a chef in a high white cap stood before an enormous range; oval *azulejo* plaques of hams, fish, and game—hares, partridges, wild duck, quail—stared down, astonishingly life-like, from its walls. At last through a final door they emerged into the hall, where Elidio, bowing, awaited them—he almost gasped with horror at the sight of Major Torrens carrying the Monsignor's suitcases, and fairly snatched them from his hands; an underling bore them away, while Elidio grumbled at Manoel in Portuguese for having let such a thing occur.

Then they were seated in the vast dining-room at one end of the long table. Elidio held out a chair for Julia, and a footman brought cups of hot consommé, and a big rack of Melba toast. The chef had obviously decided that he might as well be hung for a sheep as a lamb, so there were omelettes all round, followed by an enormous *whole* cold turkey, which Elidio displayed to Julia before taking it to carve at the sideboard—also Chippendale, Torrens noticed, and at least fourteen feet in length. Only Julia and the Major partook of the turkey, since it was Friday; but there was salad, and red wine and white wine; both light, flowery, delicious. No one spoke much at first; in the soft light from the three big silver candelabras on the shining table Julia studied the face of the Hungarian. It was square-set, with the usual Central European prominence of lips and cheek-bones, but what she noticed was how rugged it was—the brow channelled with thought, round the mouth lines begotten of determination or courage, over all a strong expression of calm and benevolence. He really did look to be a splendid person; worthy even of Hetta's unbounded admiration, the girl thought. And at that moment Father Antal raised his deep-set eyes to hers, smiled at her, and said in French—

"This is very good. *Merci*, Mademoiselle."

"Does Hetta make omelettes as well as the chef does?" Julia asked, smiling.

"Oh, you know my little Hetta? Yes, she makes wonderful omelettes—though not often at one o'clock in the morning! How is she getting on, here?"

"Beginning to swim," Julia said—the priest smiled.

"I must see her before I leave," he said—he turned to Torrens. "This can be arranged?"

"Well, really, I don't know—" he was beginning, when Julia intervened.

"Oh yes, Father, easily. The Duke, your host, is a great admirer of hers—in fact he has already suggested that she should join us at Gralheira."

"Is our host a Duke? Which?" Father Antal asked calmly—and Julia was struck suddenly by his complete tranquillity and incuriosity on being whisked off in the middle of the night without having the faintest idea, obviously, of where he was going, or to whom.

"The Duke of Ericeira," she said.

"Ah yes. A great supporter of Catholic Action." Father Antal, it seemed, could place Dukes all right—Catholic ones anyhow.

But Torrens, having been set worrying again, apparently could not stop.

"Julia, we ought to tell the Duke about this," he said in a lowered tone, leaning towards her.

"About what?"

"All this business tonight, and that car coming past the house. It means that there's a certain element of risk about his having them."

"Well it's too late now," Julia said flatly. "They're here—and if you think the Duke will change his mind because of a vague risk, or *any* risk, you're greatly mistaken. Stop fussing, Hugh, and eat your turkey. Do you want coffee?"

"My God, no!"

"Oh, very well." She put the same question to the two priests, but they did not want coffee either—"No coffee," she told Elidio. The manservant, looking disappointed that he might not serve coffee at one-thirty A.M. when most of the household was leaving at ten that same morning, muttered a question in Julia's ear.

"Hugh, Elidio wants to know if you're sleeping here too, or if you want a taxi fetched?"

"Good God!" Major Torrens exploded—"What a place! A taxi, please." And in a taxi he presently drove away, while Julia and the two priests, the latter escorted by Elidio, climbed the shadowy staircase and betook themselves to bed.

CHAPTER IX

THE MAIN ROAD from São Pedro do Sul, like all Portuguese main roads nowadays, is broad, and faultlessly surfaced with tarmac. Where it passes

through a cutting the banks are planted with the horrible mesembryanthemum; elsewhere it is often bordered with neat little hedges, just high
enough to obscure the view—every few kilometres a trim house stands
back from it, built to accommodate the road-menders. But after several
miles a small side-road turns up a valley to the north-east, through pinewoods which could make one imagine oneself in Scotland—especially when
the mists from the Serra behind hang low over them—were it not for the
fact that the banks, sandy like the road itself, are here draped with the
dark foliage and brilliant blue flowers of *Lithospermum,* which English
enthusiasts grow laboriously in their rock-gardens. In spring, if you were
to leave the road and wander through the woods towards one of the many
streams coming down off the Serra, the chances are that you would come
on clumps of *Narcissus cyclamineus,* the exquisite little wild daffodil
whose pale petals turn back and upwards like those of a cyclamen.

Presently, however, the pinewoods cease and cultivation begins: fields
of arable, well-tended olive-orchards, terraced vineyards on south-facing
slopes; the whole, as the road climbs, with an ever-increasing aspect of the
tidiness that wealth and good husbandry bring: the motorist in England
entering the Dukeries gets much the same impression. At last, on the right,
one encounters a high demesne wall of grey stone with the formal, grey-
green, plumed shapes of great cypresses rising behind it, and finally an
enormous house, more formal even than the cypresses—rich with pediments
over the windows, with sculptured swags, with all the splendour and glory
of a baroque mansion of the best period in northern Portugal. A tall
wrought-iron gate, between stone pillars bearing armorial shields, opens
from the countrified little road onto a driveway which, skirting a court-yard
surrounded by less ornamental buildings, leads up to the big front door,
approached by a flight of wide shallow stone steps; beyond, open to the
south and the sun, extends the great knot-garden of geometrical patterns
of dwarf clipped box hedges with gravel walks between.

Strangely enough, this is the Portuguese idea of the sort of garden
appropriate to a great house. It involves almost as much work as lawns
and herbaceous borders, and is not nearly so pretty, but it is the local con-
ception, and is practically inevitable as an adjunct to houses of a certain
period and status. In fact the knot-garden at Gralheira had an added
attraction: the house stood so high that its low parapet commanded a
remarkable view over the rolling country of Beira Alta—small fertile fields,
pink-and-white villages, patches of pinewood—stretching away farther and
farther, fainter and fainter, to the dusty pallor of the sand-dunes along the
coast near Aveiro, and the dim, barely visible blue line of the Atlantic.

Up this small road, to this house, there passed in the course of that

Saturday a considerable number of cars, from the station-wagon with the
chef and a selection of servants to the two Daimlers with the Duke, Dona
Maria Francisca, Luzia and Father Antal in one and Nanny, the secretary,
and Mgr Subercaseaux in the other, Elidio sitting beside the chauffeur.
Very much later Julia also drove up it; later still, long after dark, the unhappy Dom Pedro, chilly and cross, bounced along it in the Land-Rover.

Julia had asked to see the Duke early that morning; she knew that he
always took his coffee and rolls well before nine o'clock. In his study she
reported to him the events of the night before—as she expected, they left
him quite unmoved. *"Raison de plus* for taking them away," he said
calmly; while she was still in the room he rang up the police of the
quarter and arranged for a couple of men to be on duty in the street that
morning, to check on any cars parked there. This done, he turned to her.

"Had you not better drive up with us?"

"Duke, if you don't mind I'd rather follow you later in my own car—I've
got several things to see to this morning. I've packed, and I can leave this
house while the police are still about; if I find I'm being followed I shall
garage my car and come on some other way."

The Duke smiled.

"How shall you ascertain whether you are being followed or not?"

"Oh, pull up beside the point policeman in Alcobaça or Leiria or somewhere and fiddle with my engine," Julia said airily. "I shall soon see if
another car stops and hangs about."

"You are very resourceful!" the Duke said. "Very well—I am sure you are
perfectly able to take care of yourself, but do *take* care."

"Indeed I will—I don't want to cause you any extra bother. It is so
frightfully good of you to take all this on anyhow."

"On the contrary, it is at once a privilege and a pleasure," said the Duke
in his measured tones, and Julia knew that he meant what he said.

Her main reason for wishing to be independent and drive up to Gralheira alone was that she wanted to see Torrens and find out how he was,
and whether he had slept—she had never seen him in such a nervous state
as the night before, and she was worried on his account. Moreover, on her
way downstairs to see the Duke a servant had intercepted her to take a
telephone call on the extension outside the chapel—this was from Atherley,
who asked if she wouldn't come round to the Chancery and tell him "how
everything was going," before she went away to bury herself "in your ducal
province." Julia, remembering Father Antal's expressed wish to see Hetta,
and thinking that Atherley could probably arrange this, promised to look
in at the Rua São Domingos à Lapa before she left. Richard told her that
the Major had intimated that he might be coming along too. "Oh well,

I suppose there's some ghastly waiting-room full of *Punches* and *The Illustrated London News* where he and I can talk quietly, isn't there?" she said.

"You can go into the garden, Maud—much nicer," the young man responded.

"Cheek!—all right. Soon after eleven."

Soon after eleven Julia pulled the inner wheels of her new car well up onto the pavement under the barred windows of the Chancery, out of the way of the trams—this being the recognised method in that inconveniently narrow street, where so many cars are of necessity parked for much of the day—and went in and asked for Mr. Atherley.

"Hugh hasn't come?" she asked, up in Richard's room.

"No, but I expect he'll be here soon. Patience is a virtue!" Richard said with a mocking grin. "Meanwhile, tell me what's happened. Did the Duque play? Is Father Antal going to Gralheira?"

"They've gone."

"What, the Monsignor too? Splendid. No wonder Torrens is late, if he's been tearing out to Estoril to collect the contact! I say, what is it?" the young man asked, suddenly struck by something in Julia's expression.

"We fetched them both last night," Julia said. "It was the Duke's idea, and like all his ideas, it was a good one."

"Did he put them up here in Lisbon as well?"

"Yes—three-course supper at 1 A.M.!" Julia said, with a wry fleeting smile. "But it was all rather disconcerting."

"Why, what happened?"

She told him, in her slow casual voice and with her usual tendency to understatement; even so Richard Atherley frowned.

"Nasty," he said. "But how can they have tied the Monsignor in with the Duke's house?"

"They may have been watching him, and I suppose they bribed the car-hire people and got the number of my new car, *and* my address," Julia said sourly.

"Give me the name of the car-hire people, will you? Campbell must see the Colonel about this," Richard said, drawing a block towards him. "Are you driving up alone?"

"Yes."

"Look here, Julia, I think you'd better take my car. That can outpace anything on the road. Can you drive a Bentley?"

"Drive any make!" Julia replied—"but don't bother, Richard. It's *frightfully* kind of you, but I should be terrified of someone else's car, especially a Bentley."

"No, you'd better. I shall feel easier. What's your hireling?"

"Oh, an old Packard."

"Well give me your key—here's mine." He tossed it onto the table.

Julia was considerably touched by this gesture of Atherley's. Indeed it is not nothing for a man to hand over his car—especially if that car is a Bentley—to a woman with whom he is not in love. She picked up Richard's key slowly, and gave him her own.

"By the way," she said, "Father Antal wants to see Hetta. Can you organise that?"

"Yes—in fact, I must. I promised her she should see him before he goes, and she's certainly going to. How long is he staying?"

"I've no idea. Personally, I feel that the sooner he's out of Portugal the healthier it will be for all of us," Julia said, with some feeling. "Look, Richard, why don't you bring her up to Gralheira tonight for the week-end? Then it would be over with. Are you free?"

"I am, as a matter of fact—the de Freitases have got measles, and have had to cancel. But what about the Duke, and Dona Maria Francisca?"

"Oh, the Duke has invited Hetta already! That's to say, when we were arranging it all last night I told him that Hetta had been the Father's cook, and he asked at once if she was to come along?—but Hugh stood him off. There'll be no trouble about that, if she's free."

"But how can we catch them?" Richard objected. He was at once strongly tempted by the prospect of a country week-end with Hetta, and hesitant at the idea of inviting himself to people like the Ericeiras.

"They always lunch at the 'Lis' in Leiria on the way up, to give the staff a bit of a start—too easy!" Julia replied. "Ring Hetti up—go on. It would be such fun."

Still rather doubtfully, Richard asked Mrs. Tomlinson to get him Countess Hetta Páloczy. While they waited for the call Julia walked over to the window and looked out.

"Nice garden for Maud," she observed. Turning round—"I can't *think* what's happened to Hugh," she said. "When did he say he was coming?"

"About eleven—the same as you."

"It's after half-past now," she said, with a glance at her watch. "Did he sound all right?"

Richard's telephone buzzed.

Hetta Páloczy soon killed the week-end idea.

"Oh Richard, I am so sorry, but it is impossible that I should go away tomorrow," her clear voice told him. "I must go out to luncheon."

"Must you really? I was going to take you to see your late employer."

"Please?"

"The person you used to cook for."

"Oh!" A pause—then "Oh!" again, followed by silence.

"Hullo?" Richard said.

"I am thinking!" Hetta said curtly. "Please wait a little." After another pause—"No, even to see him, I do not think that I can alter this," her voice pronounced rather sadly.

"Who on earth is this luncheon tomorrow with?" the young man asked, slightly annoyed.

"With the de Bretagnes. You see—I am so *sorry*, Richard—I said that I would not go to them unless they asked Mama to the wedding, and now they have. So I think that I must go to déjeuner with them. What a pity!— for otherwise I am quite disengaged. Please do not mention this," she added.

"God Almighty!" Richard ejaculated—then his voice changed. "Hetti, you're a darling and a wonder! God bless you—I'm sure He will, for this."

"I can see—him—some other time, can I not?" the voice on the telephone asked, now very small. "You did promise it."

"Yes, and I'll damn well perform my promise. Don't worry, Hetti darling —I'll see to it. You really can trust me."

"Oh, I do." She rang off quickly.

"What in the world was all that?" Julia asked, full of curiosity, as Richard put down the receiver. "Who *is* she lunching with tomorrow?"

"The Bretagnes." Richard's battle with his conscience was brief, and soon lost.

"Don't pass this on," he pursued, "but the little thing absolutely refused to go to their house unless they invited Dorothée to the wedding."

"And have they?"

"*Yes*; so now Hetti is paying Mama's debts, when she would give her right hand, this minute, to see that priest. You've no idea what it means to her."

Julia was struck by the fact that Richard apparently had such a very good idea of what it meant; that affair must be coming along faster than she had realised. But she only said—

"All arranged by old pussy-cat Monsignor, I suppose?"

Richard gave a rather unwilling laugh. "Well yes," he was beginning when Tomlinson tapped on the door and ushered in Major Torrens.

The Major was far from presenting his usual neat and slightly military appearance. His clothes were crumpled and his shoes dusty; he was unshaven, and there were dark circles under his eyes.

"Gracious, Hugh, you *are* a sight!" Julia said. "What's the matter?"

"Been spending the night on the tiles, Torrens?" Richard enquired.

"No—in the British Hospital."

"Good Heavens! You aren't hurt, are you?" Julia asked, now rather anxiously.

"Not in the least—but it seemed a good place to pass the little that was left of the night in. There was rather excessive thug activity ouside my rooms when I got there, and no answer to the unutterable Melplash's bell, so I thought the hospital would be a good quiet place, and went there."

"I'm surprised they let you in, at that hour," Julia said.

"Night-sister is a charmer, and she remembered me: I often went in to see Campbell in January, when he had tonsilitis."

"Torrens, exactly *what* thug activity was going on outside your pub?" Richard asked.

"Oh, the usual half-dozen men, in the usual grey rain-coats, standing about in the street. I'm beginning to think that some, at least, of the ones who bothered the little Countess so at Portela on Thursday when she was trying to spot our man may have flown in with him from Madrid."

"You didn't see a club beard, or rolls of fat on any neck?" Julia enquired.

"Can't be sure. When I saw them I made my taxi-man step on it, and we shot through them—the fact was I rather wanted to get to bed, somewhere or other. May I have a cigarette, Atherley? I ran out several hours ago."

"Oh, I'm so sorry." He held out the Alentejo box. "Fill your case." He thought for a moment. "Julia, don't you think the Major had better go up to Gralheira with you, as things are?"

"Yes."

"I think I'd better stay here," said Torrens. "I ought to see Colonel Marques myself, and try to get those people cleared up."

"Campbell can do that," Richard said. "Julia's going to take my car, so it should all be quite smooth."

"I can't go like this," the Major protested—"and I've no clothes, or kit."

"*You* could fetch those in your car before we start, couldn't you, Richard?" Julia suggested.

"Yes of course." He glanced at his watch, dialled an interior Embassy number, and spoke. "Oh Campbell, could you ring up the Colonel's Office, *now*, and ask him to have a couple of men outside No. 35 Rua Dr. Antonio Pereira in ten minutes' time? I've got to make a call there, and I don't want any knives in my tires! What? Yes there was a little trouble there last night—I'll tell you later. No, he's all right; going to the country for a quiet week-end, which I may say I think he needs. I'll see you before lunch; can't stop now." He turned to Torrens. "Give me your key."

Torrens next objected that he couldn't go to the Duke's without at least letting him know in advance—"and they're on the road now. It's impossible."

"No it isn't." Julia explained again about the "Lis." "And the Duke did ask you."

"Yes, I'll do that when you've gone. Come on, your key, Torrens. In fact I am an excellent packer," Richard continued, "and you can shave at the Bau in Alcobaça when you stop for lunch."

The drive from Lisbon to São Pedro do Sul is long but attractive. Up the Tagus valley, rather industrialised; past the lovely red-and-white town of Alenquer, looking as Moorish as its name, piled up above the shallow river bordered with long brick-built factories of a Georgian and quite astonishing elegance; through Alcobaça, where the great church is gold flecked with grey; past the even greater abbatial church of Batalha, Portugal's Battle Abbey, grey lightly washed with gold—on and on through the charming *smallness* of Estremadura: little hills, little fields, patches of pine-wood, patches of vineyard or of blue field cabbage, all jumbled up together and studded with snug white-washed villages and elegant small towns—nothing large, nothing grandiose (except the bronze-coated slow-moving oxen, drawing carts laden with dung or country produce at a majestic snail's pace) but all serene, all delightful to a degree.

Through all this, in Atherley's Bentley, Julia drove Major Torrens on that Saturday. They lunched—and the Major shaved—at the Hotel Bau in Alcobaça, as Richard had suggested, but Julia firmly refused to allow her companion to so much as glance into the church—"Do it on the way back," she said. "I don't want to get in after dark." There was a trim little policeman on the wide sunfilled square, who saluted Julia, or rather the Corps Diplomatique number-plate, when she drew up beside him, and instantly undertook to watch over her car while she was taking *almoço* in the hotel, and to send in and report to her if any other car stopped close by and appeared to be taking an interest in hers.

"What nice people they are," Torrens said as he sat down to lunch, having been led by a beaming chambermaid with a jug of hot water to a clean bathroom in which to shave.

"Wait till you get to Gralheira, and you'll begin to see *how* nice," Julia responded.

The food at the Bau is simple and thoroughly Portuguese, but very good; the same applies to the wine. Restored by this, by driving through lovely country, and with a return of self-respect after he had shaved, Torrens began to recover his normal equable spirits, which were increased by the little policeman's report to Julia that no other car had approached the Bentley—"nor even cast an eye upon it." They drove on again, through Leiria and the long stretch of pine-forest beyond it; at Coimbra, a university city as old as Oxford and more spectacular, they crossed the Mondego, the river south of which one cannot, according to the Portuguese, drink *vinho verde*, the astringent, stimulating, prickling wine of the Minho, so rightly delighted in by the inhabitants, so wrongly alleged to be deadly to the foreigner. (Intoxicating it is; indigestible it is not.) At Mealhada they branched right towards Viseu, still through this rich, gentle, happy countryside; in Santa Comba Dão Julia slowed down to point out to her companion the little house where Dr. Salazar was born and where he still spends his rare holidays—a simple low building with a tiled roof, sitting modestly beside the road like the other houses in the village. But once again she would not allow sight-seeing. It was getting late; the light grew rich as the gold of evening deepened it, the air blowing in at the car windows was chill with the approach of nightfall—and it was in the glare of the Bentley's headlights that Torrens at last saw those tall cypresses overhanging the grey demesne wall, the great gateway, and the baroque façade above the front door of Gralheira.

The first stay in a Portuguese country-house usually produces a certain impact on English visitors. There is the unwonted size and splendour of the rooms and their furnishings, to say nothing of the wealth of objects of art strewn about; the even more unwonted numbers of servants; the colossal quantity of wonderful if unusual food and, by way of contrast, a quite astonishing absence of those modern conveniences which most of us have come to take for granted, even in our cramped flats. At Gralheira all these things—the splendour, the service, the food and the lack of modernity were present to a high degree, and did not fail of their impact on Hugh Torrens, though to Julia they had become second nature. Atherley had caught the Ericeira party in Leiria with the message from Julia, and the Major was expected; the Duke emerged from his study to greet him in the hall, already in a dinner-jacket. "I am so glad that you were able to come after all," he said. "Dinner will be in twenty-five minutes; Antonio will show you to your room."

Escorted by Antonio, a countrified-looking man in spite of his livery, Torrens mounted long stairs—on a landing he caught a glimpse of Julia gossiping with Nanny and being hugged by a tall beautiful girl. What first struck him about his room when he entered it was that no attempt had been made to unpack his luggage, though this had preceded him upstairs—nor did the worthy Antonio make any move to do so; he bowed and retired. This surprised the Major, who was familiar with one or two ducal households in England: there, if there *was* a footman at all, he unpacked. The second thing to surprise him was the washing arrangements. He looked round for a fitted basin; there was only a huge marble-topped washstand of Victorian aspect, with an equally Victorian ewer and basin adorned with immense crimson carnations. As he opened his suit-cases and began to fling his effects onto the bed, which had a high pointed wooden headpiece ornamented with faded paint and gilding, an even more countrified youth in a pantry-jacket appeared bearing a white enamelled can of hot water, which he set on the washstand and carefully draped in a colossal bath-towel before he, too, bowed and retired. Torrens, hurriedly but methodically placing his brushes on the high chest of drawers which served for a dressing-table, and emptying the contents of his sponge-bag onto the black marble of the washstand, swore at the immense spaces he had to traverse between each piece of furniture, even while he noticed with envious admiration the superb Arroiolos carpet across which he walked, and with amusement the carnations repeated on the lids of the soap-dish and the long receptacle for a tooth-brush. "Perfect, down to the last detail," he muttered, as he peered under the bed and observed that the china object there also bore red carnations.

There was a tap on the door; at his "Come in!" Nanny entered.

"Good evening, Major. I'm glad you've come. Now you haven't much time, His Grace is always so punctual, but I don't suppose Antonio thought of it, so will you excuse me if *I* show you the geography?"

"Oh yes, Nanny, do—thank you," Torrens said, shaking her hand.

"This way—and don't lose yourself! This is such a house-and-a-half," Nanny said, bustling ahead of him down three long corridors and round as many corners, while Torrens tried frantically to memorize his route. "There —that's the gentlemen's bathroom," she said at last, throwing open the door of an apartment the size of the back drawing-room in the average London house, which contained a bath with a sort of sentry-box at one end of it; the whole was encased in mahogany, and stood out in the middle of the room like a cenotaph; there was also a fitted basin and what should have been a hot towel rail—involuntarily Torrens went and laid his hand on it; it was cold.

"The water isn't always *very* hot in here," Nanny said, observing this gesture. "Dona Maria Francisca always has a hip-bath."

"Could I have one too? I love hip-baths."

"Certainly—I'll tell Antonio. In the morning? And you'd like morning tea, I expect."

"Yes please."

Nanny, leaving the bathroom, indicated a door across the passage. "And that's the other," she said. "Now I'll leave you. Don't lose your way going back!"

"The other," the lavatory, was also Victorian to a degree which highly amused Torrens; it took him back to his earliest childhood, and visits to his grandparents. The pan, set in a mahogany seat five feet wide, was covered all over with blue flowers, as was the little china bowl, let down in the wood, into which a brass handle shaped like a stirrup returned after being pulled up. "Marvellous," he said to himself, as he made his complicated way back to his room.

He just managed to get dressed in time for dinner. Julia was waiting for him at the stairhead, and led him down and into the drawing-room, where the rest of the party were already assembled; the Duke introduced him to Dona Maria Francisca and Luzia, who was in animated conversation with Father Antal—he was offered a very small glass of white port, and downed it hastily; then they all proceeded into the dining-room, which was large, and as gloomy as dining-rooms so often contrive to be, whether in England or in Portugal.

"Monsignor, as my chaplain has not yet arrived, will you say grace for us?" the Duke asked—Subercaseaux obliged with a brief grace in Latin, everyone crossed themselves, and they sat down.

Torrens found himself seated on his hostess's left, with the Hungarian on his other side and Subercaseaux opposite; Julia and Luzia sat on either side of the Duke, with Nanny beside Luzia, and that end of the table was soon gay with the lively chatter of the two girls and the amused benevolent comments of the grey-faced man between them. At Torrens' end there was considerably less animation. Dona Maria Francisca de Lencastre-Pereira was a small, pinched-looking woman in the fifties, who did her still-dark hair in the fashion of thirty years before, and wore clothes—invariably black—to match; she was sincere, kind, and truly good, but her only interests, apart from running her brother's household and rather vaguely supervising the life of her young niece, were religion and the welfare of young girls, for whom she organised schools and rescue-homes, according to their degree of innocence or the reverse. Torrens essayed one or two remarks to her, but with little success; the good lady concentrated her attention almost entirely on the Vatican emissary, who was much more in her line. A holy Venus, *toute entière à sa proie attachée,* the Major thought to himself with a sour little grin, and turned his attention to Father Antal.

He found the Hungarian good company: interested in everything he had seen on his drive up from Lisbon, and full of questions about the local methods of agriculture and so on which Torrens, himself new to Portugal, could not answer—Luzia, from across the table, stepped into the breach.

"They put those clappers or whistles onto the sails of the windmills so that they can hear at once if the wind changes, Père François," she said. Torrens was momentarily startled by the name; it took him a few seconds to remember that they had settled on it in the Duke's study in Lisbon only the night before. "You see most of the millers have a piece of land to till," the girl pursued, "and in this manner they can work at it without turning round to look all the time, because you can hear that noise more than half a kilometre away."

"And what does the miller do if the wind does change?" the priest asked, smiling across the table.

"Oh, of course he goes and adjusts the sails, so that they shall catch the air to the best advantage. There is such a nice old miller close by here—they call him 'The Blacksmith,' though he is a miller, because once when the real smith was ill he shoed a horse."

Père François beamed at her. "I should like to meet him," he said.

"Oh, you shall—I will take you to visit him tomorrow," Luzia said. It was clear to Torrens that the refugee priest and the very young girl with the remarkable grey eyes were delighted with one another—but at her last remark the Duke intervened.

"No, Luzia."

"Why not, Papa?"

"Because I say so. We will speak of it later." He turned and addressed a remark to Julia. And afterwards, when the party had adjourned to the drawing-room and drunk some rather weak coffee, he asked the two priests and Luzia to accompany him into his study—"You will excuse us for two minutes, *ma chère*, will you not?" he said to his sister.

"Provided you let them come back in time for the Rosary. I want the Monsignor to see the chapel."

The Duke of Ericeira's study at Gralheira was something completely unexpected and in startling contrast to the baroque splendour of the rest of the house. Apart from the inevitable crucifix over the mantel-piece—in this case a fine piece of Flemish work—it was as severely up-to-date as the business-room of a progressive Scottish landlord. Filing-cabinets and book-shelves full of works on agriculture, wine-production, and archaeology lined the walls; on the very large desk which occupied the middle of the room there were no less than eight telephones. A few leather armchairs stood about, to which the Duke waved his daughter and the two priests; he himself sat down in a workman-like chair in front of the telephones.

"I am naturally very reluctant to impose any sort of restrictions on guests in my house," he said; "and it is in your own interest that I am impelled to do so now. You have come here, in effect, to seek sanctuary; and within the walls of my estate you will, I trust, find it. But I must request you both, formally, not to go outside those walls without my knowledge or sanction. And there are two places within those walls which you must not visit—the kitchen, and the courtyard." He turned to Luzia, with an indulgent smile. "So if you wish Père François to meet 'The Blacksmith' you must bring him here. But in fact the fewer people outside who know that foreign priests are staying here, and see these priests, the better. Do you understand? It is not necessary for you to know the reason."

"Very well, Papa. I understand," Luzia said—something in her tone made Father Antal look at her rather keenly, but he said nothing.

Subercaseaux however was greatly intrigued by one of these prohibitions.

"My dear Duke, it is not my custom to visit the *kitchen* in houses where I stay, but I am intensely curious to know why I may not visit yours."

"Luzia, you can go now," the Duke said.

"Oh pouff, Papa! Really I know what this is all about; it is so that the man with an odd beard and the rolls of fat on his neck, who seeks Père François, shall not find him—and of course if he were clever he might come to eat in the kitchen one night, with all the others, and ask questions of the servants."

The Duke frowned; he looked greatly disconcerted.

"How do you know this? Can Miss Probyn have been indiscreet?"

"Not she—of course not. It was Atherley."

"Do you mean *Mister* Atherley, of the British Embassy? How did you meet him?"

"He came to see Miss Probyn about the accident to her car, and I heard what he said; she had to write down a description of the men who ran into her, and when he read it he was funny about the man with the fat neck, and Charles Laughton."

"What had Charles Laughton to do with it?" her father asked, in understandable bewilderment.

"*Nothing*, Papa!—I repeat, Monsieur Atherley was being funny. Then at dinner last night this red-haired Commandant comes asking for Julia, and sees you, and she takes her car and goes off with him. And soon after half-past twelve the car came back—I was awake, and as you know Tia Maria Francisca *will* make me sleep in this nasty little room which overlooks the stable-yard," Luzia said, clearly voicing a long-standing grievance—"so when I heard it I looked out and saw them all: Messieurs les prêtres and Julia and the Commandant, and Fausto, all standing like statues, *frozen*, listening to the sound of a car in the street; the luggage on the ground, no one moving or coming into the house till the other car had gone. And today these gentlemen drive up here with us, and *you* tell them that they have found sanctuary. So I have drawn certain conclusions. In any case, Tia Maria Francisca told me herself that the Monsignor is an emmissary of the Vatican—she is quite *exaltée* about it!" the girl ended, a surprising gleam of irony lighting up her young face.

Father Antal laughed out loud.

"Monsieur le Duc, I think you would be well advised to take your daughter into your confidence! Any attempt at concealment from her will obviously be time wasted."

Rather reluctantly, the Duke laughed too.

"I am afraid I agree. In due course I will tell this inexcusably acute child of mine the little that she has not heard, or guessed."

But the Monsignor returned to his enquiry about the kitchen being out of bounds—he was not easily deflected from any point which had aroused his curiosity.

"Duke, do pray tell me who all these people are who invade your kitchen at night, and *why* they should come there?"

"They come to eat," the Duke said briefly. "It has always been the custom in this country that poor people, wayfarers, should be able to stop at houses like this and be given a meal at night, somewhere to sleep, and breakfast before they go on their way in the morning." His long, rather gnarled fingers tapped reflectively on the broad polished expanse of his desk.

"Here in Portugal," he pursued, "we have not as yet established very thorough 'social services' in the modern sense; we still hold to something which I myself regard as valuable, because it is more direct, more intimate—the personal responsibility of those who have wealth to supply some, at least, of the needs of those who have not. That is why my house is open to the traveller; and in fact Luzia is right—someone who was acquainted with this custom could easily enter the kitchen with the rest, and a silly maid-servant might answer his questions."

"But in the *kitchen!*" Subercaseaux was still inquisitive. "Is there room for them? How many come?"

"Tonight there are fifteen," the Duke said, smiling. "Elidio always tells me the numbers, but this evening before dinner I went out, as I often do, to see them and bid them welcome. And there is in fact plenty of room."

"At any price I must see this kitchen, which can accommodate fifteen guests while a dinner such as we have just enjoyed is being cooked!" Subercaseaux exclaimed.

"You shall see it tomorrow morning," the Duke said, rather pleased. But the Monsignor's curiosity was not yet exhausted. His gaze moved to the telephones ranged on that enormous desk.

"My dear Duke, I have, as you will have observed, a prying disposition. May I ask, why *eight* telephones?"

Ericeira laughed.

"A measure of economy! It costs me less to install eight instruments than to pay the wages of someone to operate—almost certainly extremely inefficiently—a switch-board." He leaned forward, and tapped the machines one by one. "This is to the bailiff's office, and this to his house; that to the oil-mill, that to the stables; this one is to the farm, and this to the *lagare*, where the wine is made—of course it is only used during the vintage; this is to the garage, and finally, here is the one which connects me with the outside world."

"This same system used to operate in the big country houses in Hungary," Father Antal put in, "and for the same reason. Rustic people find these complicated mechanical contrivances difficult to manage."

There was a tap on the door, and Nanny's neat head, veiled in black lace, appeared round it.

"I'm sorry to interrupt, Your Grace, but Dona Maria Francisca wants to know if the Monsignor is ready to come to the chapel for the Rosary?"

"Oh yes," the Duke said rising, with a rather resigned expression. "They will come immediately." He kissed Luzia—"Goodnight, my child" —and turned to the two priests. "I must ask you to excuse me—I have things to attend to. I wish you a very good night. Make my excuses to the Senhora Condessa, Nanny," he said urbanely. When they had all gone off to say the Rosary he settled down in an armchair and began to read *The Farmer and Stockbreeder*.

CHAPTER X

"You aren't by any chance poaching just a little on my preserves, are you?" the Military Attaché said to the First Secretary on the morning of that same Saturday, when after Julia and Major Torrens had driven off Richard Atherley went and asked Colonel Campbell to get Colonel Marques to come round to the Chancery.

"If I am it's most unwillingly, I assure you, my dear Campbell," Richard said heartily. "Your miserable clients are pestering the life out of me—

even the Monsignor! However, thank you for organising police protection for me at No. 35."

"What on earth were you doing at Torrens' diggings?"

"Packing his clothes for his visit, under Miss Probyn's wing, to the Duke of Ericeira's country-seat."

"Oh, he's gone up there, has he? I think he might have told me."

"Between ourselves, I think he was a little distraught."

"Hardly too distraught to pack his own bags before he came away, I should have thought."

"He didn't know he was going, and anyhow he wasn't at home last night."

"Where was he, then?"

"In the British Hospital," Atherley said blandly, with enjoyment.

"Why? Is he ill?"

"No. He just thought it would be a good place to sleep in."

"Well, perhaps you'll explain all this," the Colonel said, leaning back and looking resigned.

Atherley explained at some length what had taken place the night before, and how he had dispatched Torrens and Miss Probyn in his own car, not twenty minutes ago.

"Good God, do you mean to say you're letting that girl use your Bentley?" Colonel Campbell asked—this fact seemed to impress him more than all the rest of his colleague's recital.

"Yes—in *your* interest, Campbell, I may say! But you realise, don't you, that her car is already compromised, though she's only had it two days; the car-hire firm she got it from must have sold the number, and her Lisbon address, to the opposition. That's what I want you to see Marques about."

"Well he'll be along in a few minutes. Yes, he ought to get after those car people. Where's Miss Probyn's car now?"

"Under your window. Here's the key"—he threw it on the table. "Over to you, Campbell—you can be your own game-keeper for a bit," Richard said, with an amicable grin. "By the way, what are you doing this afternoon?"

"Playing golf. Why?"

"I wondered if you would lend me your car? I want to take someone for a drive, and I don't particularly want to use Julia Probyn's, and be mobbed by Spanish Communists in rain-coats."

"Yes, of course take it—that's the least I can do, though as you know it isn't a Bentley! I can use one of the Chancery cars. Why, has the Countess turned up?"

Richard stared in incomprehension. His mind was on Hetta: she had said that she was free for the whole week-end, and he had conceived the idea of taking her out for a drive that afternoon; her self-abnegation over the luncheon with the Armorican Pretender on Sunday had moved him a good deal. "She hasn't left Estoril since she got out, so far as I know," he said, taken by surprise by Campbell's question.

"Oh, sorry—you're talking about little Countess Páloczy. I meant the Countess de Vermeil," Colonel Campbell said, looking slightly embarrassed.

Richard looked embarrassed too, and rather annoyed. Naturally he had not reached the age of thirty-five or thereabouts without having been "subjected to other influences" as the French so elegantly call it, and one of the foremost among these influences was a certain Countess de Vermeil; she had been very much in the ascendant during his time in Washington, and Colonel Campbell, there on some war-time mission or other, had met them both; when Atherley was at the Embassy in Paris before coming to Lisbon, he had in fact seemed quite dominated by her, and Colonel Campbell, then assistant Military Attaché there, had again registered the fact. She was a widow, older than Atherley; ultra-*mondaine*, skilful, witty, and well-dressed to a French degree of perfection which was like a sort of lacquer over her whole person—she was also tall, blonde, and sufficiently beautiful *just* to be visible herself through her wonderful clothes. (There are women who dress so well as to render their actual selves practically invisible, but Fanny Vermeil contrived to avoid that.) Lately Richard, absorbed by Hetta, had given very little thought to this enchantress, and the young man in his present mood felt his colleague's well-meant question peculiarly ill-timed.

"As far as I know, Madame de Vermeil is not expected here," he said coldly.

At that moment Tomlinson ushered in Colonel Marques. Both men, their minds fully occupied in giving the latest facts to the head of the Portuguese Security Service, forgot about any Countesses, young or less young. Colonel Marques was, as always, practical, brief, and shrewd: he noted down the address of the firm from which Julia had hired both her machines, and on learning that she had driven up to Gralheira in Richard's C.D. car nodded approval, and asked where the young lady's car was at that moment?

"Under this window," Richard said for the second time.

Colonel Marques asked who had the key. Campbell showed it to him.

"It would be convenient if I might borrow the key, and the car, for a day or two," Colonel Marques said—"If it is not required?"

"You can do anything you like with it, provided you take it away from under my window," Colonel Campbell replied. "We don't in the least want it standing about in the street!"

"Very well. Thank you. Leave it in my hands, Monsieur le Colonel."

"I'll leave you now," Richard said, rising, and went back to his room to ring up Hetta Páloczy.

After some thought as to what would please her most, he took her to Obidos, the little walled city lying between the main Lisbon-Alcobaça road and the sea, one of the most beautiful walled towns in Europe. In its smallness and completeness it compares with Gruyère, and like Gruyère a mediaeval castle dominates it from one end, but in some ways it is even more beautiful; the golden tone of its castle and walls is warmer and richer than the slate-grey of the Swiss town.

Hetta was delighted by it. They left Colonel Campbell's car outside the big fortified entrance, incongruously lined with blue-and-white *azulejos,* and inside climbed a flight of stone steps up onto the top of the western wall; a narrow path, originally a firing-parapet for bowmen, runs along the whole length of this to the massive block of the Castelo at the farther end. Neither the steps nor the firing-walk have any form of hand-rail, and people with a bad head for heights find them alarming, but to Richard's relief Hetta tripped up the steps and along the walk with complete unconcern—he had once had the disconcerting experience of taking a V.I.P. to Obidos, and finding that he could only negotiate the path along the wall on his hands and knees. The girl looked out through the loop-holes at the bright multi-coloured countryside, pink and green with plough-land and springing wheat; the dim blue of the Atlantic bounded the horizon, and nearer at hand was the brilliant blue of the great sand-enclosed lagoon, the Lagoa de Obidos, in which enterprising bathers can catch grey mullet in their hands. On the other side they looked down, very intimately, into the back gardens of the inhabitants, where shapely grey-green medlar-trees stand up among hen-houses, rabbit-hutches, and beds of vegetables. Hetta, inveterately practical, commented on the fact that these back-yards contained almost no lines of washing.

"No, they spread it out on those slabs of rock with the agaves on them, below the Castelo. Look." He took her elbow, and pointed to the open slope, gay with white and parti-coloured linen drying in the sun.

"Oh I see—how nice."

They were both very happy. In fact many people do experience an unexpected happiness in Obidos; it is a quality of the place. Moreover, this was Hetta's first expedition into the Portuguese countryside, and she was loving every moment. The Castelo has been turned into a *pousada,* a government-run hostelry, but when they descended from the battlements by another of those dizzy flights of steps just below it he did not take her there, but led her instead a few yards along one of the two streets, which are all that Obidos boasts, and into a tiny room barely ten feet square, with narrow benches along the walls and a broad wooden counter with wine-barrels below it. Richard knocked on this, and a bright-faced young woman with a flowered kerchief on her head came running in from the next room, and greeted him with cries of pleasure—these brought in a much older man, wearing the regular Portuguese country-townsman's rig of an open waistcoat, shirt-sleeves with floral stripes, and a black felt hat crammed down on his round head. He, too, showed the utmost satisfaction at the sight of Richard, and wrung him by the hand; he spoke to the young woman, who went out and reappeared after a moment with a big earthenware jug brimming with wine, which she poured into two thick tumblers and handed to the guests.

"This is their better wine," Richard said to Hetta—she sniffed, sipped, and then nodded her head.

"It is good," she pronounced. "This is such a nice place, Richard; it is like a Kis-Kocsma in Hungary."

"And what does Kis-Kocsma mean, pray?"

"A small wine-room. They are a little bigger, as a rule, but like this." She drank again. "Do you know, this is excellent."

"The Menina approves of your wine," Richard told the man—"And she knows of what she speaks; her father had his own vineyards."

"In what part of Portugal?"

"Not in Portugal at all—the Menina is Húngara."

This statement produced some rather surprisingly on-the-spot remarks.

"From Hungary, eh? Where they have put a Cardinal in prison? I thought the Húngaros were all Communists. Is the Menina a Communist?"

"No, she is a Condessa," Richard said laughing. "She has come to Portugal to escape from the Communists." But as he spoke he was seized with a sudden pang of the anxiety that had tormented him before on Hetta's behalf. "You don't go swimming alone in the mornings any more, do you?" he asked.

"Not since you told me I should not. Why?"

"I just wanted to be sure. Have some more wine."

"Yes please. But would he mind if we took it outside and sat in that square? It is so beautiful, this town—I cannot see it enough."

"There's nowhere to sit in the *largo*."

"Richard, do not be English, and diplomatic! We can sit on the steps."

On the steps they sat, their refilled glasses in their hands, looking up at the great bulk of the Castelo high above them.

"I'm glad you like Obidos; it's a place I love," Richard said. He felt warmed towards her, towards the whole world, as he sat drinking his wine, watching her face tilted up to gaze at the castle's golden crenellations profiled against the blue sky overhead. "Tell me why you like it?"

"Because it is happy, and simple. Much nicer than Estoril!" she said, with one of her sudden flashes of contempt. "I should like to live here—perhaps in one of those houses."

Below the *largo* stood a short row of houses considerably more elaborate than most of the town, with green shutters folded back from their windows, creepers on the walls, and in front of them neat little gardens with paved paths leading up to the doors; they had a sort of homely elegance.

"That one with the notice on it is to let," he said. "Would you like to live there with me, Hetti?"

He spoke on an impulse, born of his immediate happiness, his romantic love for Obidos, and his half-recognised love for the girl beside him. She turned her face towards him at his words, and studied him for some time before she spoke.

"Richard, I should like to live with you anywhere where you would be happy," she said at length. "But I am not sure that you would really be happy living in Obidos. Or indeed living with me," she added.

"Hetti, I really believe I should be happy with you anywhere," he said, taking her hand. This was really all he could do in the way of demonstration, since the square immediately in front of them had suddenly become filled with small boys, kicking a rather desiccated football about. The Portuguese have of late years developed an obsession for Association Football, which they call *futebol*; as professionals they play it extremely well, but the entire male population of the country, from the age of seven upwards, spends most of its spare time kicking some sort of ball about any available open space.

"I know you believe it," Hetta said, returning the pressure of his hand with the small firm clasp of her own. "But I am not sure, dear Richard, that—that your belief is true. I mean, I think that perhaps you do not know yourself. You would soon begin to think me too young for you, and in social ways of course I am—though in more real ways I think I am much older, because of how I have lived. Your reality has been easy, mine has been hard; and so a lot of the things you think important are to me quite unimportant. Looks, dress, *savoir-faire!*" the girl exclaimed, with a ring of contempt in her voice—"for you these are all-important;

they fill your sky! But to me they are little, little, *little!* My mother has them all!" she ended, and sprang to her feet and walked away.

Richard, too, rose, and followed her slowly. He was rather disturbed —and startled by her perspicacity. She had sized him up with an accuracy which plenty of older women had *not* shown in regard to him, he thought ruefully. How clever she was! No, it was more than cleverness; she was wise. For a young man of his antecedents, living the life he did, Richard Atherley was rather unusually honest; he accepted Hetta's evaluation of himself as true, and did not resent it. But could one live beside such acuity? The remark about her mother—she would never have said that if she had not realised his own contempt for poor Dorothée, careful as he thought he had been to conceal it.

Hetta meanwhile was sauntering slowly along the lower of the two streets, her dark head sleek in the sun, that orange-patterned cotton frock of hers, that he liked so much, turning a deeper shade as she passed from sun to shadow—she walked beautifully, even in her silly white sandals and on that rough paving: she had that particular quality. He came up with her just as she had reached the spot where a church stood below the road; he laid a hand on her bare arm and said "Hetti!"—he could not find words for anything he wanted to say; he did not know, he was all at sea. She turned at once, with her wide gentle smile, and said with the blandest unconcern—"Should we not go into this church? I believe there are remarkable paintings in it, by a woman."

It again struck Richard, rather forcibly, that many women of the world could hardly have bettered her self-possession, immediately after receiving what practically amounted to a proposal; it was so completely incongruous with her clear-sighted statement that he would feel her "too young" for him that he burst out laughing, with his great laughter that resounded up and down the little street. But her knowledge took him by surprise too.

"What do *you* know about Josefa of Obidos?" he asked.

"Oh, she had a school of painting here—such an extraordinary thing for a woman, in the 17th century! And she was an etcher as well, and a silversmith, and modelled in terra-cotta. Do let us go in—I should like to see her paintings."

"How on earth do you know all this?"

"The Monsignor lent me that book about Portugal. I have read it twice, but, of course, I cannot easily go about to see all these buildings and pictures because the car is needed for other things."

Richard's heart smote him. He doted on Hetta, for his own pleasure he saw her whenever he could; but until today it had never occurred to him to do that quite elementary thing, show her Portugal—nor indeed that she would want, and want rather intelligently, to see its artistic riches.

"Look," he said, as they stood outside the door of the church, "if you can keep your week-ends fairly free I'll drive you out on Saturdays and Sundays, and show you anything that's within reach."

"That would be lovely," the girl said.

The parish church of Sta Maria in Obidos is in fact too dark for the visitor to see much of the versatile Josefa's pictures, particularly since these are skyed right up under the painted ceiling, above the decorative *azulejos* which adorn the walls. Hetta was disappointed. "Since we cannot see them, her pictures tell us nothing of her," she said. "How sad." Out in the sun again, she swung round on Richard.

"Our glasses! Did we not leave them in the square? We must take them back, those nice people will want them—poor people cannot afford to lose two glasses."

"Hetti, do you know that you are very kind and very good?" he exclaimed.

"*Niet!* It is only that you know nothing about poverty, and I know a great deal," the girl replied. "You are simply ignorant, not bad; I *know,* but I am not therefore good. Really, Richard, you are very ingenuous for a diplomat!"

"How censorious you are!" But he laughed and took her elbow as they went back to the *largo* below the castle. Their tumblers had gone; some of the youthful *futebol*-players, seeing them abandoned on the steps, had taken them back to the "small wine-room," as they at once explained to Richard when he began to peer about.

"What are you doing for dinner tonight?" the young man asked, as they drove back towards Lisbon.

It appeared that Hetta was doing nothing for dinner; her mother was dining out.

"Then come and dine with me," Richard said. He was in a divided mood. On the one hand he acknowledged the truth of her diagnosis of his own attitude towards her; on the other, the mere fact that she was shrewd enough to make it, and her subsequent lively uppishness about diplomats drew him to her more strongly than ever—and he had a sudden desire to push the thing further, if only to find out more about his own feelings, and hers.

She made no answer to his invitation.

"Well? Yes—no?" he asked.

"No," the girl said, turning to him—"It is No, please, Richard."

"Why on earth not?"

"Because we are not ready—I am not, you are not. You want me to come tonight so that you may make a little love to me, and see if that is nice. Oh, of course it would be nice!" she exclaimed—"lovely, delicious, *fun!* But you and I are not people to live just by fun; you have perhaps been a little spoilt, but you need *truth* in your love, and you do not know yet where the truth is, I think. I told you that on those steps. We have done enough for today about what is between you and me. Let us leave it—take me home."

Again her honesty and clear-sightedness took him by surprise; he felt something like reverence for her just then, mixed with admiration for the cool fearlessness with which she had spoken of love between them. Oh yes, she was right about him: he *had* wanted to try it out on the physical plane, leaving everything else in a warm happy fuzz; and Hetta, uncompromising as ever, wouldn't have that.

"Whatever *has* been done about us today, it's you that have done it," he said, putting his hand over hers.

"Because I am so old!" she said lightly.

As they approached Estoril—"Richard, will you let me know when I am to see Father Antal quite *soon?*" she asked. "I would excuse myself from almost any engagement, except just this one with the Bretagnes, for that. Where is this place in the country to which he has gone? Is it far away?"

"Yes—the better part of a day's drive. He's at Gralheira, the Duke of Ericeira's house near São Pedro do Sul, right up in the North." Richard had no scruples about telling Hetta this; she was in the whole affair up to her neck. "It would mean staying a night," he went on, "but I don't suppose your mother would object to your going to the Ericeiras. What about next week-end? I have something on, but I would cut it for that— for *you,* Hetti."

Hetta ignored his final words.

"So long?" she said dismally. "Could we not go sooner? You see, he may be going on to America. Do *you* know when?"

"No, I don't. But I'll find out. Don't worry, Hetti—I've promised, and I will keep my promise. Goodbye, my dear one. You will come and dine with me sometime, won't you?"

"Yes—at the *right* time!" she said, as they drew up at the hotel. "Thank you, dear Richard, for the lovely expedition. I have been so happy."

Hetta enjoyed her luncheon at the Bretagnes the following day. It was a homely, family affair. Innumerable Bretagne children, of all ages down to a seven-year-old, sat round the long table gazing at her, and occasionally firing off questions in her direction; the only guests beside herself were the young Archduke, a lively fair-haired youth whose questions about Hungary poured out like machine-gun fire, and a big, tall, lusciously beautiful woman who had, it seemed, only arrived by plane that morning, and having telephoned was bidden to this very unsocial meal—her name Hetta, too often absent-minded, failed to catch, though she realised clearly enough that this was a last-minute addition to the party. In this pleasant atmosphere the girl expanded, answered the Archduke briskly, and laughed heartily at the innocent question of one very youthful princeling—"Did you give the priest you cooked for soup? I *hate* soup!"

"You would not hate my soups; they are delicious," she told the child.

"Then I wish you would come and speak with our cook. He gives us *bouillon de légumes*, which is altogether horrible," the little boy pronounced.

"Countess, it looks as though I shall have to employ you to nourish my family!" the Pretender said laughing—"or are you tired of cooking?"

"I shall never be tired of cooking, Monseigneur—I love it."

"What a lucky man your husband will be! Well children, until she marries, shall we engage Countess Hetta to make your soups?"

"Yes!" the younger ones chorused.

"Monseigneur, I am not sure that I shall be able to enter your employment at once," Hetta said with a mock-grave face. "The English Ambassador has already engaged me to go and teach his chef how to make *Hasen-pastete*."

"*Jésus Gott!* Can you really make *Hasen-pastete*? I haven't eaten it for years!" the Archduke exclaimed. "Would you make one for me?"

"If Your Highness can bring himself to shoot three hares and two partridges out of season, I can make one for you at any time," she replied.

This was rather Hetta's hour, though a small hour. The talk soon turned back from food to Hungary, but presently the girl registered the fact that the beautiful golden-haired lady—a Frenchwoman, it seemed—looked on and listened with a detachment which seemed to contain an element of contempt; whether for Hungary and its affairs, or for a person who cooked, she could not be sure.

Towards the end of the meal the Pretender asked Hetta, who sat on his left, if she had seen much of Portugal?

"Very little so far, Monseigneur—but yesterday someone from the English Embassy took me to Obidos."

"Oh, this exquisite place! I am sure you liked it."

"I loved it. In fact I almost decided to live there!"

"You might do much worse." He turned to the Frenchwoman, who sat on his right. "Obidos is a most perfect little gem of a mediaeval city;

you should visit it," he said, courteously drawing her into the conversation. Then he turned back to Hetta. "And did your English escort wish
to settle there too?" he enquired teasingly.

"He played with the idea, but I did not think it would suit him!" Hetta
replied—her small success had made her a little reckless.

"And may we know who this English diplomat is, who would like to
live in Obidos?" the Pretender asked.

"It was Monsieur Atherley," Hetta said, still reckless. "But the life of
a *petite ville de campagne* would not really do for him."

"No, I agree; he is a charming person, but *plutôt mondain*." He looked
rather keenly at Hetta, as if he found something amusing—but the girl
was much more sharply aware that the big Frenchwoman had somehow
stiffened at the mention of Atherley's name, and was staring at her in
cold surprise. "Do you know Monsieur Atherley, Madame de Vermeil?"
the Comte de Bretagne asked, once again courteously bringing his other
guest into the conversation.

"*Very* well—and for many years," the lady said, with emphasis. "Certainly I imagine that *petites villes de campagne* and love in a cottage
are not at all what would suit him—Mademoiselle is quite right."

"Yes—the *Countess* Hetta Páloczy has excellent judgement," the Pretender replied, in an urbane but rather unusually direct royal reproof.

The Comtesse de Bretagne, slightly preoccupied with making her
younger family eat tidily, had missed this interchange, and when the
three guests were about to leave she asked Hetta if she could drop the
Archduke in Monte Estoril, and the Comtesse de Vermeil at the Castelo-
Imperial—"where you are staying yourself." Hetta, making her semi-
curtsey, of course agreed, and Oliveira bore them all away in the Rolls.
The Archduke continued his flow of enquiries about Hungary till the
very moment when he was set down before the small villa where he was
staying—Archdukes, in the modern world, never put up in places like
the Castelo-Imperial, they can't afford to; they leave them to the occupation of ship-owners and international financiers from the Middle East.
He kissed the hands of both ladies, but it was to Hetta that he said—"Do
please let us meet again. There is so much to talk about! Do you come
to the wedding?"

"No, but my mother does," Hetta said, wishing that he were not getting out—she had no desire for a tête-à-tête with this big beautiful woman
who professed to know Richard so well. *How* well, she wondered, as the
car purred smoothly on again—every part of her went onto the defensive.

"You know Monsieur Atherley for long?" Mme de Vermeil asked at
once, in an almost caressing tone.

"But naturally not, Madame la Comtesse, since I have been in Hungary until a few weeks ago," Hetta said casually. "He is quite a recent acquaintance—*du reste*, like everyone else in Western Europe, as far as I am concerned."

"Ah." The Frenchwoman appeared to reflect. "You must pardon my ignorance of your movements—but at luncheon I thought that you seemed to profess to a certain knowledge of Monsieur Atherley's character; this misled me."

"Some characters one can assess more rapidly than others, do you not think?" Hetta responded, trying to keep cool—she wished fervently that Oliveira would drive faster, and bring this conversation to an end.

"Possibly. Though not perhaps that of the person in question, who is, believe me, a rather more complicated character than he may appear." She spoke with an appearance of kindly indulgence. "Rapid assessments can be, also, mistaken ones," Mme de Vermeil added, with a fine air of detachment.

Hetta inclined her head politely in response to this observation, but said nothing.

"Has it occurred to you that *Richard*"—the Countess stressed the name —"is rather *volage*, as well as being very mature?"

"Indeed yes," Hetta said curtly. "That is why, as you doubtless heard me tell the Comte de Bretagne at luncheon, I said only yesterday to Monsieur Atherley that it would not suit him to live in Obidos." To her great relief she saw that the car had at last reached the public garden; in a few seconds this encounter would be over. But Mme de Vermeil had not finished with her.

"Did he propose to live in Obidos alone?" she asked.

"Madame la Comtesse, since you know him so well, why do you not ask Monsieur Atherley *himself* with whom he wished to live there!" the girl flashed, driven beyond all endurance by this final impertinence, as the car drew up before the hotel. She sprang out, not waiting for the swarming pages to open the door. "You will excuse me—my mother awaits me. I am happy to have been of service to you," Hetta Páloczy said, with an impeccable last word, and ran in through the revolving glass doors.

Up in the flat her mother, mercifully, was by no means waiting for her; after lunching with the Salzbergers at the Avis—where she had greatly enjoyed making elaborate apologies for Hetta's absence because the Pretender had summoned her to lunch with him—Dorothée had betaken herself to bed with two aspirins and *Time* magazine. So Hetta was free to run to her room, fling off her coat and hat, and then walk about, raging. What an insupportable woman!—and what unendurable

insolence! *"Stupid,* too!" the girl muttered furiously—"As if I had not told
him myself all, and more than all, than she told me!" But what lay behind
all this? Could Richard really care for a person like that? Oh yes—alas,
he could; Mme de Vermeil possessed, to an extreme degree, all the things
which she, Hetta, had so ruthlessly belittled to him only yesterday in
the *largo* at Obidos: looks, dress, *savoir-faire.* No, not complete *savoir-
faire;* the Frenchwoman's good manners had failed her twice—at luncheon, when the Pretender, however elegantly, had corrected her, and again
in the car, no doubt provoked by her, Hetta's, attitude. This must mean
something—Hetta studied what it meant, and reached a not inaccurate
conclusion. "Whether he loves *her* or not, she is in love with him, and
means to keep him for herself!" the little cook from the presbytery in
the Alföld said to herself, sizing up the beautiful Parisienne; having decided this, she burst into angry tears.

Hetta's distress was easy enough to understand. In this strange and
difficult world into which she had so suddenly been plunged Atherley
had been to her, from their first meeting, a link with home: a person
who had been to Detvan and known and liked Pappi, the one adored
and stable figure throughout her childhood, till he was swept away on
the inrushing Communist flood, and she was left alone with the good
nuns. In fact that loneliness had been extreme to the eager, positive, impulsive child, accustomed to the most expansive intimacy with so many
people at home; the deliberate, carefully inculcated detachment and im-
partiality of the convent, easily endurable for three terms a year, had become a terrible thing to bear when there was *no* let-up, no times-off to
be loved and spoiled and petted at Detvan.

Atherley, therefore, had come trailing clouds of all sorts of glory to
her first cocktail party, when he had at once spoken of the Alföld; and
he had been *kind* to her, patient with her when she made a fool of herself
at his luncheon, interested in her even, she told herself with frank humility, before he began to be a little in love with her. And as she had
said of Julia Probyn, she felt that *he* was nice, *he* was true; she trusted
him and felt at home with him. The bare idea of being loved by, even
possibly marrying such a person had made a sort of opening, however
distant and uncertain, in a future which otherwise seemed to her dark
and blank indeed—to lose him would be a desolating loss.

She soon dried her eyes—Hetta very seldom cried, and was ashamed
of herself when she did; tears had not been approved of in the convent—
but she continued to walk to and fro across her bedroom, thinking. This
antagonist of hers, she recognised, was a powerful and dangerous one—
in spite of being so old! (Mme de Vermeil was in fact thirty-eight, but to

twenty-two thirty-eight is practically antique.) Hetta had begun to realise the sheer *power* of perfect clothes and social skill, even while she despised them; and certainly this full-blown rose of a Frenchwoman—the contemptuous phrase came of itself into her mind—had them to the last, the supreme degree. A smaller person might have entertained the foolish notion of trying to acquire a rivalling degree of elegance herself; this has often been done by young girls in her situation, with conspicuous ill-success. But Hetta Páloczy was too intelligent and too uncompromising to waste time on such ideas. She had no intention of remaining passive while her hopes and her future were drowned in a flood of perfect make-up and marvellous clothes, but she needed help, advice, reinforcement—and for these she absolutely *must* see Father Antal. She decided, rather reluctantly, to ring up Richard and ask him to help her to get to—what was the place called?—Gral something—as soon as possible. There was really no one else to whom she could turn—Yulia and her red-headed Major were already up there, and Hetta with the ingrained caution born of long years of living under Communism hesitated to suggest such a trip to anyone else.

If she had rung up there and then things would probably have turned out differently, for Atherley at that moment was sitting with his feet up in front of his little log fire, reading Evelyn Waugh and intermittently thinking, with a good deal of affection and a slightly worried admiration, about Hetta herself. But just as she was about to ask for his number Esperanza came in to say that the Senhora Condessa was going to take *chá*, and wished the Menina to join her. So Hetta went and drank tea in her mother's room, and good-temperedly underwent a detailed cross-examination about her luncheon at the Pretender's, and who had been there and what had passed. Dorothée was at once slightly annoyed and rather comforted that it had been, the Archduke apart, such a very family party.

"And this Frenchwoman who came at the last moment—what was her name?"

Hetta couldn't tell her name, she had never caught it. "She was a Countess, a great huge woman, very blonde and very well-dressed—I brought her back; she is staying here."

"Oh, then it must be Fanny de Vermeil. How nice that you have met her, and were able to give her a lift—I suppose her car is coming by road. Has she come for the wedding? I expect so; she and the Comtesse de Bretagne were at school together." Now that she was sure of a place at the wedding herself, Dorothy Páloczy could talk quite cheerfully about others who were to attend it.

Hetta could not say whether Mme de Vermeil had come for the wedding or not.

"Oh, you may be sure she has. She goes to everything! Didn't you find her charming? And her clothes are so wonderful."

Hetta, readily agreeing to the wonderfulness of Mme de Vermeil's clothes, managed with relief to avoid any reply about her degree of charm. But this conversation, which went on and on, increased her sense of desperation, and the urgency of her desire to see Father Antal at once. Jésus Maria!—if she was to be cooped up in this dreadful hotel (how *could* Pappi have borne it?) with that ageing French siren as well as her mother, what would become of her? The animosity of one, the contempt of both— it was impossible! And where was charity, in such a strait? When her mother at last went to take a bath the poor child, instead of ringing up Richard, flung a scarf over her head and ran across the garden through the sweet-smelling dusk to the church, where she knelt and prayed for pardon for her angers, for help, and for the man she loved.

She came back more leisurely, calmed and soothed; changed her dress so as to be ready for dinner, and then, at last, rang up Atherley. But by then the fortunate moment had passed—Mme de Vermeil had for the last half-hour been sitting in Richard's little drawing-room, and they were in the middle of a rather awkward conversation, largely concerning Hetta herself.

"Atherley," Richard said into the telephone. "Oh, it's you"—when she spoke. "Could you ring up a bit later on, or tomorrow? I'm busy just now." In his embarrassment he spoke more coldly than he intended, and his tone chilled Hetta—it also roused her temper.

"No, I would rather speak now—I will not keep you a moment."

"Oh, very well," he said resignedly. "What is it?"

The resigned tone angered the girl more than ever, even while it filled her with a vague terror.

"It is that I need to see Father Antal at once," she said, almost as coldly as he. "Tomorrow, perhaps?—or on Tuesday? It is necessary that I should see him quickly."

Richard had already heard enough from Mme de Vermeil to guess why Hetta felt it necessary to see Father Antal so urgently. He had, of course, been given a skilfully distorted account of what had passed at luncheon. "In your own interest, my dear Richard," the lady had said languidly, "I think you should try to prevent her from boasting that you suggested living with her in some country town." But though he had said "Oh don't be a fool, Fanny; I'm certain she never did any such thing. How disagreeable you can be when you try!" he was left wondering uncomfortably exactly what Hetta *had* said—she was so guileless, so unworldly, liable to be so indiscreet.

"I'm not sure that that will be possible," he said now, speaking carefully. "But let me telephone to you later tonight, will you?"

Hetta, at her end of the telephone, was making her own guesses; she might be unworldly, but it had occurred to her before she rang up that the French lady would lose no time in seeking Richard out and getting him into her toils again—no doubt she had done so.

"No," the girl said abruptly. "I need to know at once. *Will* you take me to see him? You made a promise, you may remember."

Richard in his turn was dismayed by the icy edge on her voice, but he was angered too—no man likes to be reminded of a promise that it is not at the moment convenient to fulfil.

"I did—and I will keep it. But I am not a free agent, as you know; I have my work to do. I will ring you up later tonight."

"No, do not trouble to telephone," Hetta said, trying to control her voice, which sobs now threatened to invade—was this the Richard who had told her yesterday that she was "very kind and very good," and that he could be happy with her anywhere? "I will make other arrangements—please do not concern yourself," she said, and rang off. After a moment she lifted the receiver again and told the hotel exchange to get her Mr. Townsend Waller, of the American Embassy. Also, she added, apart from the American Senhor, she would take no more calls that night.

CHAPTER XI

"Now, Monsignor Subercaseaux," the Duke of Ericeira said, coming in on Monday morning to the sitting-room overlooking the knot-garden which had been placed at the disposal of the two priests—"would you care to come and visit the kitchen, which interests you so much? Or do I disturb you? You both appear very studious!"

The two ecclesiastics did look rather studious. At the Duke's entrance Father Antal closed an atlas, while the Monsignor put an elastic band round a small leather notebook in which he had been making microscopic scribbles, and tucked it away in his soutane.

"On the contrary, my dear Duke, I shall be delighted," he said.

"May I come too?" Father Antal asked.

"Dom Francisco, I hoped you would." The Duke, not alone among the occupants of Gralheira, had begun to make comparisons between the blunt simplicity of the Hungarian and the florid politenesses of the Monsignor.

The kitchen at Gralheira was really something to see. It was roughly the size of two billiard-rooms placed end to end; the part nearest the entrance from the house was used for all cooking operations, the farther end for eating; another door led from this into the courtyard. Two great chimney-hoods descended over a pair of Briffault ranges, their bright-steel surfaces polished till they shone like silver, from a ceiling as lofty as the roof of a mediaeval tithe barn; a low brick-built shelf, with ovens set in it and open cooking-spaces on the top ran for several yards round the wall— an old crone knelt on the floor before one of these last, fanning the charcoal under a copper casserole to a glow with a palm-leaf fan. Down the opposite side of the great room several yellow marble sinks, with brass taps above them, projected from the wall; in these kitchen-maids were rinsing out crockery and copper pans, and washing vegetables. But the most remarkable sight of all was the tables. There were two, each fully twenty feet long; their solid tops were made of the same yellow marble as the sinks, and rested on carved marble trestles. The farther one was already being set for the mid-day meal by two more kerchiefed girls, who plumped down gay country-made earthenware plates, thick soup-bowls, and heavy tumblers for wine in some forty places; a cheerful array of bottles, and huge wicker platters of *broa*, the maize bread beloved of the Portuguese country-people, were already in position down the centre.

On the other table, nearer the two ranges, various culinary operations were in progress. (If you have a kitchen table seven feet wide and twenty feet long quite a number of different jobs can be done on it at the same time.) The chef himself stood, immaculate in his white coat and high pleated hat, rolling out delicate pastry; next him a youth was pounding *bacalhau* in a mortar; farther on two more boys were chopping parsley and slicing onions respectively, and another old woman was beating eggs in a bowl.

"Yes, you could practically feed an army here," Subercaseaux said. "Wonderful!"

"Where is the bread baked?" Father Antal asked.

"I will show you." The Duke led them out through the door at the farther end into the courtyard and to the bakery, fragrant with the resinous scent of the pine-boughs which stoked the ovens; here he sent a man, white with flour, back to the kitchen to fetch a key—"You might care to see the store-house."

This was on the same generous scale as the kitchen. Cheeses in scores were ranged on shelves round the walls; below stood vast wooden bins of dried peas and beans, and barrels of pork pickled in brine and garlic; from the raftered ceiling hung endless rings of sausages, hams in dozens, and white loops of lard. The Portuguese, so cleverly, do not preserve lard (which they call *banha*) awkwardly in a sheep's or pig's stomach, forming a clumsy oval lump, as the English do—or did; instead they pour it into the animal's large intestine, and tie the ends, so that Portuguese lard can be cut off in convenient lengths as required.

This magnificent demonstration of country self-sufficiency surprised Subercaseaux, who commented and exclaimed. To Father Antal it was nostalgically familiar—"So it used to be in Hungary," he said. "Ah, the good life! I am glad there is somewhere in the world where it is still led— *still* led."

The Monsignor wanted to see where the wayfarers slept, and the Duke led the way up an outside stone staircase to a great loft, fragrant from the mass of hay which filled the farther end; immediately inside, blankets lay tidily folded on a score of neat mattresses of hay, with coloured cotton pillows.

"*Tiens!* Whoever sleeps here is well lodged," Subercaseaux exclaimed, while the Duke was telling Father Antal that women travellers, who were rather rare, slept in a dormitory adjoining the house, supervised by one of the old kitchen-women—"This Maria do Carmo, who was fanning the charcoal. She is not only very sage, but also a *tigress*," he said.

At luncheon the previous day Subercaseaux had praised the delicious odourless oil on the salad, contrasting it with the rank smell which defaces almost all salads in Portugal—now, as they descended into the courtyard, the Duke asked him if he would care to see the oil-mill? "It is not working now, of course; that occurs only in late autumn, when the fruit ripens. It is a short walk, and the day is pleasant."

The day was very pleasant indeed. The three men walked through the high delicate sunshine of spring in northern Portugal, which seems to throw a clear, an almost classical light, like the lambency of Latin prose, over a landscape in itself Virgilian—vines, white flocks of sheep and lambs grazing, olive orchards shimmering silver in the breeze, great oxen with coats like polished bronze turning up the rich red-brown earth. Behind, blue and immense, the great range of the Serra shouldered up into the sky. The oil-mill was one of a group of yellow-washed farm buildings, a large airy shed lighted by high windows; in the centre, now clean and at rest, stood the granite wheel which pounded the olives to pulp in a cemented basin, and at one side were ranged the metal butts in which the oil stood, mixed with water, to purify it. The Duke became enthusiastic as he expounded how one made *good* olive oil.

"First, the olives must be *fresh*. My rule is, two hours from tree to mill! Second, the oil must be drawn off in *cold* water; if hot water is used you get a slightly greater yield, but the smell of the pulp is transferred to the oil; with cold water this does not happen. But on most estates in Portugal there persists the lamentable habit of carting in the olives and leaving them in a heap for a week or more; naturally corruption sets in, creating a most unpleasant smell, and on top of that *hot* water is used in the butts, thus ensuring that the maximum of this foetid odour accompanies the oil to the table."

Both the priests had to laugh at the vigour with which their host expressed his view. They walked back to the house another way, which brought them by a flight of stone steps up into the knot-garden, where they came on Miss Probyn and Major Torrens, deep in conversation, on the most remarkable seat Father Antal had ever seen. A circular bench, curved in like a shell below with a high ornate back; the seat, the panelled back and curved support were all covered in blue, pink and white tiling, with lively 18th-century representations of hunting-scenes. One of these beautiful seats adorned each of the four corners of the knot-garden.

The two young people rose at their approach; Father Antal, with his usual lively curiosity, peered at the *azulejos*.

"Really, this is quite beautiful, though so strange," he said. He studied every detail. "Duke, here a bear pursues the hunter up a tree. Is this based on fact?"

Ericeira laughed.

"Yes. My great-great-grandfather was chased up a tree by a bear in the Serra, but when he gave the order for these *azulejo* seats he did not contemplate being immortalised in that situation! However, it had become a local legend, and the artist could not resist it." He turned to Torrens and Julia. "You come in with us? Luncheon will be in twenty minutes."

Of course they all went in together. Punctuality was one of the Duke of Ericeira's little manias; he could really only enjoy a meal if all those who were to eat it were safely marshalled in one of the great salons at least eight minutes before Elidio came in to announce that the Senhora Condessa was served.

Adept and skilful in worldly affairs, where his life's work lay, Subercaseaux naturally cultivated the art of making himself agreeable in his current surroundings, whatever they were; but at luncheon he rather overdid it. Seated as usual beside his hostess, he talked mostly to her; and Nanny's subsequent expression, "smarminess," described his conversation with painful accuracy. He praised the food, the oil-mill, Dona Maria Francisca's charities; there was a good deal of talk about royalties in connection with the impending wedding; there were remarks to and about Luzia—"this young lady who will have such immense opportunities." It was not sufficiently well done; Julia closed her immense eyes, Luzia became openly restive, and upstairs in the school-room later, she burst out.

"Truly, the Monsignor is too detestable! 'This young lady'!"

Nanny reproved her. "But really, Miss Probyn, if one didn't know, I must say you would think Dom Francisco was the person from the Vatican, wouldn't you?"

Downstairs, in the sitting-room overlooking the knot-garden, the two priests prepared to resume their interrupted task. But Subercaseaux had not finished the excellent cigar provided by the Duke, and walked up and down—Father Antal, seated before the atlas, asked him a question prompted by the conversation at lunch.

"You said that Countess Páloczy was to attend the wedding—is that the mother, or the daughter?"

"Oh, the mother—though the Pretender would greatly have preferred that it should be the daughter!" And he told the Hungarian how Hetta had refused to lunch with the de Bretagnes unless her parent received the invitation she craved.

"This *good* child!" Father Antal exclaimed. "For really the Countess cannot be at all *comfortable* as a mother."

"Oh no, she isn't. She's a most difficult subject, poor creature," Subercaseaux said frankly. "Poor little Hetta could not have entered a more trying milieu for her introduction to the West."

"How is she getting on?" the other asked, turning an earnest gaze on his companion.

"In some ways quite well." The Monsignor continued to patrol the room, drawing appreciatively at his cigar. "There is a young man in the British Embassy, an admirable fellow, who has had the good taste to fall in love with her, and this is helping her in her adjustments." He gave his abrupt barking laugh—then he frowned. "But now I am afraid even this may go wrong."

"Why?" Father Antal asked—his eyes never left the other's face.

"Oh, the old story. The mistress of long standing is about to re-appear— of course for the wedding."

"Does the young man not appreciate Countess Hetta sufficiently to pre- serve him from the mistress?" Father Antal asked, severity in his tone.

"Oh my dear Dr. Horvath, *yes*, of course he does, or he would not have fallen in love with the child—who has, one must admit, the defects of her qualities to a degree which is rather marked in diplomatic society! *Voyons*," the Monsignor said, throwing the end of his cigar into the fire and spread- ing out his hands—"this young girl has done a wonderful thing—do not think that I fail to recognise it. With her world as she knew it in ruins she has managed to construct for herself a moral fabric of her own, and one of great integrity. But apart from her contact with you, the materials to her hand were very limited: a convent school, and the life of a servant! Now she is plunged into an international society—royalty, diplomacy, urbanity *in excelsis!* Naturally her formula is inadequate; she makes mistakes. But her admirer is born into this world, and he finds her mistakes embarrassing —whereas the old flame makes none! Surely you can comprehend the position?"

Father Antal continued to follow the Monsignor with an intense, unrelenting gaze.

"Of what sort is the mistress?" he asked.

"Well-born, and exceedingly clever. She has never allowed her reputation to become tarnished, for she is skilful, and her high social standing protects her. A stupider woman, or one less highly placed, would have little reputation left! Young Atherley is by no means her only lover—or was."

"And she is in Portugal now?"

"Is, or comes immediately." This was the sort of thing Subercaseaux always knew.

Father Antal got up, a little heavily, and also began to walk to and fro. "I am troubled," he said at length. "I am greatly troubled," he went on after a pause. "My little Hetti!" He rounded on his companion. "I must see her," he said—"quickly. Can she not come here?"

"For that we must consult Major Torrens—he is responsible for the security side. And Countess Hetta, you see, is already compromised."

"Compromised?—by whom? By the young Englishman?" Father Antal asked, with sudden anger.

Subercaseaux laughed gently.

"No no—by *you,* dear Dr. Horvath! Please!" he said, holding up a hand as if to ward off the Hungarian's furious glare—"I speak the language of counter-espionage now! In that sense only, Hetta Páloczy is what the Secret Service calls 'compromised,' since of course the fact that she worked in your house in Hungary is well known to the Communists."

"So." Father Antal expelled a deep breath, and stopped glaring. "Well, let us now speak with Torrens."

There ensued a whole series of consultations. Torrens, walking in the grounds with Julia, once again found his conversation with her interrupted by an active footman despatched in search of him by Elidio. When he came in, looking rather sulky, he said that if Countess Hetta was to come to Gralheira Miss Probyn would have to arrange it with the family. Julia was sent for, and walked, cool and beautiful, into the study; on hear-

ing what was at issue she said, as usual, that she would talk to Nanny.
"It'll be all right," she said comfortably to Father Antal. Julia then talked
to Nanny, who talked to Dona Maria Francisca: in the end the Duke
himself, looking more Scotch than ever in his grey country tweeds, appeared in the priests' sitting-room. He addressed himself to Torrens.

"I gather that there is some question of an addition to our party here."

"Yes, Sir. Father Antal wants to see Countess Hetta Páloczy," Torrens
said glumly.

"Oh, but by all means let her come! I should like my daughter to know
her. Telephone at once, and see if she cannot be persuaded to pay us a
visit."

"There is just one catch about it, Duke, which you may not have
realised," Torrens said, more glumly than ever.

"Which is?"

"Simply the fact that the Countess was employed in Father Antal's
household in Hungary—which is, of course, well known to the agents of
the other side. So she is certainly under observation—in fact you may call
her something of a security risk."

The Duke smiled largely.

"What fascinating phrases the modern world coins!" he said genially.
"A security risk!—it sounds quite American. Well, let us take this 'security
risk'"—his tone made a mockery of the words—"and ask the little Countess
to visit us. Who shall telephone?"

"I'd better," Julia said—"she knows me best."

"Will you come and do it from my study, Miss Probyn?"

Torrens again intervened.

"Excuse me, Duke, but before we ring Countess Hetta up we should
arrange how she is to get here."

"Will she not come by car?"

Subercaseaux put in his oar.

"It is not certain, my dear Duke, that her mother will be able to spare
her car for a whole day, at such short notice."

"And in any case she oughtn't to travel alone—we have asked her not
to go out unaccompanied," said Torrens.

"Here, in Portugal?" the Duke said, looking bewildered.

"Duke dear, in a Portugal at this moment *full* of Communist thugs,"
Julia said, turning her immense eyes on him disarmingly. "No—I think *I'd*
better drive down and bring her up; I've got Atherley's C.D. car, and she
can either wear a veil, or crouch down in the back. Better the veil, I think
—crouching makes one so stiff, and she won't be able to see the lovely
darling country! Isn't that best?" she asked Torrens.

"Yes, I think it is. The diplomatic number-plate is a great safe-guard," the Secret Service man said, rather grudgingly.

"Very well—that's settled. So shall we go and telephone?" Julia said to her host.

But when they repaired to the study and the eight telephones, and eventually got through to the Castelo-Imperial at Estoril, it was only to be told that the Countess Hetta Páloczy had left.

"Left? When does she return?" Julia asked. The clerk said he would enquire.

"Where *can* they have gone? I should have thought wild horses wouldn't have dragged Mama Páloczy away just now," Julia speculated aloud, the receiver half at her ear. "The wedding's on Saturday. Unless she's flown to Paris to get a new frock."

The Duke laughed—in his private and rather silent fashion he derived a good deal of pleasure from Miss Probyn's uninhibited speech.

"Possibly that is the explanation," he was beginning, when Julia said "*Sing?*" sharply into the telephone. (Improbable as it may seem, this syllable in Portuguese, spelt *sim*, means "Yes.") "Sing, sing," Julia pursued, and went on saying "Sing" at intervals for some moments—"*Muito obrigada*" she said finally, and rang off.

"That's rather odd," she said. "Hetta left at ten o'clock this morning, with a suitcase, in a *diplomático* car, with a Senhor; she told the porter, who of course asked her, that she might not return for two or three days. The receptionist rang up her mother's apartment and the maid said that *they* had no idea where she had gone, nor who the diplomatic Senhor was! I don't think it can be Atherley, because I've got his car here."

"Does she know any other diplomats?" the Duke asked.

"Yes. That nice Townsend Waller, in the American Embassy. He's really her slave," Julia said, looking calmly amused.

"Then should we not ring up the American Chancery and ask, discreetly, if they know where this gentleman has gone? Or not?" The Duke looked a little bothered—running off in cars with *diplomáticos* rather upset his previous impression of Hetta as a desirable acquaintance for his daughter.

"Not," said Julia. "I think we ought to talk to Major Torrens before we do any more telephoning."

"Very well—let us speak with him."

The Major, who had been waiting with the two priests, flatly vetoed ringing up the American Embassy.

"They aren't in on this at all," he said, "except for my opposite number. They might start asking all sorts of questions." He looked put out, and gnawed at his small red moustache; the loss of one of the characters in this ill-assorted cast worried him. "I'll ring up Atherley; I can talk to him so that no one else understands, and he's pretty sure to know all about young Hetta's movements—they seem pretty thick. May we do that at once, Sir?"

Richard Atherley was sitting at his desk in the Chancery, staring out over the green garden, trying to make up his mind whether to have another shot at ringing up Hetta, when his telephone buzzed. Three times the evening before he had been infuriated by the smugness of the hotel operator's voice saying "The Countess Hetta Páloczy is not available tonight." What a remorseless little savage she was! He snatched off the receiver, hoping that she might have relented.

"A call for you from São Pedro do Sul, Mr. Atherley," Mrs. Tomlinson said. And then came Hugh's voice on the line.

"That you?"

"Of course." Richard's voice was cold with disappointment. "What is it?"

"I should be grateful if you could make some enquiries for me, unless you happen to know the answer yourself. Listen carefully, will you?—and don't use any names. Can you hear me?"

"Perfectly. What's the question?"

"You remember that you took a lady for a drive one day last week," Torrens' voice went on, with maddening deliberation.

"Well, what of it?" How the devil did Torrens know about Obidos, Richard thought, stiffening.

"In a taxi," Torrens pursued, ignoring the interruption—"and wearing a veil. Do you know who I mean?"

Richard relaxed a little.

"Yes, of course. Well?"

"We want to establish her whereabouts today, but we think it simpler for you to do that. Will you?—and call me back? You know where I am; you can look up the number."

Richard was embarrassed by this application in a way the Major could not of course have foreseen.

"I presume she's at home—I mean, where she lives," he said rather coldly.

"Ah, we don't want presumptions, we want facts," Torrens rejoined, dispassionately. "Your presumption is a little out of date. She left the place where she lives this morning, in a C.D. car, driven by a man, taking a suit-case with her, and said she might not be back for two or three days."

"Good God!" Richard could not control the exclamation.

"Quite so," Torrens said calmly. "You can probably make as good a guess as we can as to the identity of the owner of that car—since it obviously isn't you! You remember we all dined together not so long ago, outside Lisbon. We thought you might ring up his place of business and learn anything that is known of his movements, and then report back."

Every word Torrens said increased the fear, jealousy, anger and remorse that had begun to seethe in Richard, joined with a lively and positive hatred of Mme de Vermeil.

"The editorial 'we' including Julia, I suppose?" he asked waspishly.

"Of course. But don't use names." Torrens was quite untroubled. "How soon do you think you'll be able to ring back?"

"Damn it, why should *I* make your enquiries for you?" the young man exploded. "Haven't you got your own machinery?"

"Yes. Certainly I will do it through them, if you prefer it so. Can you have this call transferred to the little man we both despise?—I'll put him onto it at once. I have got to find out, you see."

Richard had been trained to think fast; clouded as his mind was by conflicting emotions, he instantly saw that anything was better than to have the ineffable Melplash prying into Hetta's movements.

"No, I'll do it," he said. "I shall get more out of them than your ghastly employee. I'll ring you up when I've got something—I can't say when." He rang off.

Sitting back in his chair he reflected, miserably, on his last conversation with Hetta. "I will make other arrangements; please do not concern yourself." Yes, of course she would have turned to Townsend, her faithful and uncomplicated slave, to get her up to Gralheira. But what a thing to do, to drive off with a man in a car, from the very door of the hotel. She really was too innocent to live!

The person he decided to ring up was the Counsellor at the American Embassy, a kind shrewd man with a passion for music.

"Townsend?" said this individual. "Oh yes, he called me last night to ask if he could take two or three days' leave. No, I didn't ask any questions —I thought maybe he just wanted to bury his grandmother! People do, you know, now and then. Why? Does it matter?"

"Not very much. Could you give me the number of his car?"

"Listen, Richard, do you mean you want to have him *traced?*"

"Arthur, I just want to know where he *is*—there's nothing to panic about. Someone's with him," Atherley said, unwillingly.

"Well so I supposed! All right—I'll get that number. But don't do anything embarrassing, will you? What in hell is all this about?"

"I'll tell you that some other time. Just let me have that number, there's a good fellow."

While he waited for the call from the American Chancery Richard relieved his feelings by ringing up Mme de Vermeil.

"*C'est toi? Bonjour,*" the lady said blithely.

"Good morning," the young man said. "I find I shall not be able to dine with you tomorrow night. I must ask you to excuse me." He spoke with an icy politeness which was not lost on the Frenchwoman.

"*Quel dommage!* Your Ambassador makes difficulties, or *la petite?*"

"It is out of my power to come," Atherley repeated stiffly, ignoring both questions.

"*Tiens!* So some other night? Which?" Mme de Vermeil still sounded blithe.

"I cannot say. Possibly never." He rang off before she could reply.

When the American Counsellor came through again he first gave Atherley the car number. "I happened to meet Perce while I was checking," he went on—"he's sort of a buddy of Townsend's, so I just asked casually if he knew what he was up to."

"And did he know?"

"Nothing very definite. Townsend told him, all in a hurry, that he had to take someone who was in trouble up to the North, and might not be back for two or three days. So then I had a word with our telephone operator."

"Well?" Richard asked.

"She says Townsend booked two rooms, on *different* floors, at one of the hotels at that spa place near São Pedro do Sul, the Bela Vista. It's the best hotel anywhere up there except that British place at Canas da Senhorim, so I imagine the trouble is in or near São Pedro do Sul."

"Oh bless you, Arthur! Thank you very much," Richard said.

"That tell you anything?" the American asked curiously.

"Only what I wanted to know. Goodbye."

When Mrs. Tomlinson got the Gralheira number the Duke of Ericeira himself answered. Richard recognised his voice, and instead of pronouncing the name "Atherley," as usual, said—"Oh, how do you do, Duke. Could I speak to your red-haired visitor?"

He heard Ericeira chuckle before he replied.

"Certainly. He is here"—and then Torrens said "Richard?"

"Himself. *O Richard, o mon roi!* Here's the dope. Spending two or three nights at the Belle Vue at the spa near St. Peter of the Sun. Can you translate that? If not you'd better get Julia."

"Julia's here. Perhaps you had better tell her—I'm not so hot on all these names. Hold on."

Julia was much hotter.

"Oh yes, I know," she said, when Atherley repeated his Anglo-French version of the address. "Splendid—how clever you are! With the person we thought?"

"Precisely. His car number is"—he gave it. "His employers charitably assume that he is busy burying his grandmother," Richard said, rather sourly trying to conceal his own malaise under the borrowed crack.

Julia gurgled; then she said—

"Oh nonsense! You know perfectly well she adores you. I expect she just wanted to see the little man we all love, only she more than any. But why didn't she ask *you* to bring her up this way?"

"Damn you, Julia!—have you got second sight?"

"Oh yes—Highland blood! I see—and for some protocol reason you couldn't make it, so she turned to the boy-friend from Massachusetts! Well never mind—we'll get her all right now. 'Bye."

Julia was over-optimistic. After a consideration of time and mileage in the Duke's study—slightly hampered by the fact that none of them knew what make of car Mr. Townsend Waller drove—they decided that at the best Hetta and her escort were not likely to reach the Bela Vista before half-past four. It was now three-thirty.

"So we telephone then?" the Duke said. As in Lisbon that Friday night, Julia realised that he was rather enjoying the whole business.

"Oh, do we?" she asked, with a doubtful glance at Torrens. "I should have thought drive over and see them."

"Certainly," Torrens said. "There has been a most unfortunate amount of telephoning already."

"But surely this can have done no harm? You have all been so clever—it has been an entertainment to listen to you!"

"Unfortunately the people we are up against are quite clever too," the Major said wryly. "No, we had certainly better drive over."

"And bring her here?—I see. And the American also? There is plenty of room, of course."

"No, dear Duke. Boundless as your hospitality is, I think poor Mr. Waller had better stay at the Bela Vista tonight and scoot back alone to Lisbon tomorrow. Miserable for him of course, but we don't want an *un-ceasing* stream of C.D. cars up your by-road—don't you think, Hugh?"

"I *do* think. So good of you," he said to his host, "but Miss Probyn is right; it is much safer that Waller's car shouldn't come here."

Ericeira, in spite of the novelty to him of these goings-on was quite quick-witted.

"I understand," he said. "Then had you not better drive to São Pedro do Sul in one of my cars? They are a familiar sight there."

"That would be admirable, Sir. Thank you." Torrens glanced at his watch. "How long does it take to get in?"

"Twenty-six minutes to the town; to go on to the watering-place, another four-and-a-half." Times were one of the things about which the Duke was quite unfailing. He lifted the receiver of one of the eight telephones and ordered a car to come round to the house at once. "You will do it comfortably," he said. "Who goes?"

"I think we'll both go," said Julia. "Better for Hetta if I'm there. I'll just get a coat." She went out.

The post at Gralheira only arrived in the afternoon—on her way through the hall Julia took a look at the long walnut table on which letters were always laid out. The post was in, and there was a letter for her from her old and beloved friend, Mrs. Hathaway, forwarded from Lisbon on the very day she left; she read it hurriedly on her way to her room.

It announced Mrs. Hathaway's arrival in Lisbon that very day. "This will only give you very short notice of my advent," the good lady wrote, "but it was a last-minute decision. Since you left England I have been somewhat tied to the bed-side of an old friend who was lingering with cancer; but in the end he died very suddenly—it has been rather a shock, and I feel like the change. I have managed to get a plane passage on Monday; if you aren't at the airport—and *don't* bother; I know how many claims there are on your time—I shall go straight to the Hotel Lucrezia in Lisbon, which your Treasury friend Geoffrey Consett says is a very nice moderate hotel, near the main shopping street. I do apologise for this short notice, and you must not let me be a bother. But it will be blessed to see you." There was a P.S. "I have bought a Portuguese phrase-book, with instructions for pronunciation. How very odd that O should be pronounced OO, and OU O! And S as SH! Why have an alphabet?"

Julia laughed, and then frowned, over this missive. Damn! Of course it would have to happen that her precious Mrs. Hathaway must needs arrive in Lisbon in her absence, and while she was so tied up with Hugh's affairs that she couldn't race back to look after her old friend. However, once they had got Hetta safely tucked in at Gralheira she might get away tomorrow; anyhow she would ring Mrs. H. up tonight. She slung the orange suède jacket, which so delightfully matched her tawny-blonde hair and apricot complexion, over her shoulders and left her room.

In the corridor she encountered Luzia.

"Oh Miss Probyn, you are going out! I saw the car coming up to the door—I thought so. *Can't* I come too? I am so dull; and I *hate* cutting out aprons for Tia Maria Francisca's wretched lost girls to sew, which is what she will make me do if I am at home. I have hardly seen you today—you have been all the time with Torrens, or the priests! *Do* say Yes," the girl implored, twining an arm cajolingly through that of her ex-governess.

Julia, laughing and releasing her arm, decided instantly that she would say Yes. To drive into São Pedro do Sul, not only in the Duke's car but accompanied by the Duke's daughter was an excellent bit of cover for their errand.

"All right, you can come," she said. "Go and get a coat—but hurry."

CHAPTER XII

TORRENS, who had only come that way when it was practically dark, was especially pleased to see the countryside. Passing through the pinewoods clothing the slopes of the Serra they crossed ravine after ravine, each of which was spanned by small curved terraces on which spring crops were growing—they looked like whole strings of bright-green horse-shoes, suspended on silver threads of water between the dark pines.

"They don't waste an inch, do they, these people?" he said.

São Pedro do Sul is a pleasant unpretentious little town, lying, as its name implies, on a southern slope facing the sun. As the car drove into the curious raised square immediately below the Igreja Matriz, the Parish Church, Torrens' eye was caught by two things: the spectacular front of the Reriz Palace, with its huge impending cornice and innumerable balconies of wrought-ironwork, and the exquisite little façade of the Misericordia Church, whose baroque window-frames of dark granite are set, not as usual in pale plaster, but in aqueous blue-and-white *azulejos* which cover the whole surface of the building.

"Julia, do for goodness sake let us stop for five minutes and look at all this!" he exclaimed. "We're well on time, and some of these things are fantastically lovely."

"Oh very well"—Julia tapped on the glass and told the chauffeur to pull up.

Torrens sprang out at once, and strode off across the square towards the Misericordia, followed much more leisurely by Julia; Luzia got out too, but with her adolescent acuity decided to leave her companions to themselves— they get few enough chances in our house, she thought. She pottered contentedly about the little square in the warm sunshine, taking note of the various cars parked round its edges. Her eye was caught suddenly by the red-and-white number-plate with "C.D." and six figures, which in Portugal makes diplomatic cars unmistakable—she walked over to it. The car was American; it was empty.

"*Tiens!*" Luzia said to herself. Diplomatic cars were not a very common sight in São Pedro do Sul, especially out of season. She looked about her. As always in Portugal one or two beggars were sitting sunning themselves outside the parish church and she went up to them, feeling in her purse for small coins as she did so—at her approach they held out dirty hands and began their customary gabble.

"There, O Santinha! There, O Santinho!" the girl said, dropping money into the outstretched palms of a very old woman and a crippled man. In northern Portugal it is the delightful custom to honour poverty by addressing beggars as "Little Saint"; moreover, the giver thanks the beggar for affording him the opportunity of an alms-deed. Automatically Luzia did so now—"*Muitissimo obrigada*" (most greatly obliged) she said; then she briskly addressed the cripple, who looked the more intelligent of the two.

"What quality of persons came in this *carro diplomático?*" she asked. "Did you see them?"

"*Sim, sim, Minha Menina,*" the old man said. "There was a Senhor, who appeared to be an Americano, and a Menina—very dark, she was."

"And where have they gone?"

"The Menina went into the Igreja—she gave me *silver!*" the beggar quavered excitedly.

"And the Senhor?"

"He went to drink wine in that small shop across the *praça*. While he was within another big *carro* drove up, with four Senhores; they looked at the *carro diplomático*, and as the Menina has done one of them asked us where the *pessoas* in it were. So I told him; but he gave me no money!" the old man said angrily.

"And then?" Luzia asked.

"Then they drove the car close up to the entrance of the Igreja Matriz, and three went in, while one waited at the driving-wheel; and presently they came out with the Menina."

"Well?" Luzia pressed him.

"They put her into the car, and drove away all together."

"Without the Americano?"

"*Sim*—without him. Curious, was it not?" the cripple said detachedly.

Julia had not bothered to mention to Luzia the reason for their drive to São Pedro do Sul—for one thing she was confident that the girl would have heard of Hetta's impending arrival from Nanny anyhow, and she had a firm trust in her pupil's tact and discretion. Her confidence was well-founded: Nanny had of course told Luzia that "we" were expecting a young lady—"Hungarian; a Countess it seems, and a great friend of Dom Francisco's. She's driving up from Lisbon today." It had not taken Luzia long to connect this fascinating fact with their expedition that afternoon, and when she saw the car with a diplomatic number-plate it took her exactly one second to leap to the conclusion that it had probably brought the Hungarian young lady to their remote district—hence her questions to the beggar. But she had heard, and guessed, enough of what was going on to be thoroughly disturbed by what the cripple said.

"How did the four Senhores look?" she asked, as casually as she could.

"Foreign—the one who talked with me spoke Portuguese very badly!" the old man said.

Luzia reflected quickly, then tried a further question.

"Had one of them a beard, and rolls of fat at the back of his neck?"

"*Sim, sim!* They wore grey," the beggar added.

The grey conveyed nothing to Luzia, though her mind recorded the fact, but the beard and the fat neck frightened her very much.

"And did the Menina go willingly with these Senhores?" she asked.

"*Não, não!* She struggled, and the bearded one put his hand over her mouth before they thrust her into the car. Was this not also curious?"

To Luzia it was not so much curious as horrifying. She gave the creature another coin, to stimulate his wits, and asked what the *carro* of the four foreign Senhores was like?

Black, large, shining, and closed, she was told.

"And by which road did it leave?"

São Pedro do Sul is the junction for four main roads: north to the valley of the Douro, south-east to Viseu and Guarda, but also to Coimbra and Lisbon; due west to Aveiro and the Atlantic; north-west—a poorish road —to Vale de Cambra and Oporto. But about this the cripple was less clear. The car had driven away very fast; and precisely at that moment a rich, a charitable lady had come up to him, and in speaking with her he had failed to notice which road the big black car took.

"Did you see its *número?*" Luzia asked, without much hope.

"Ah no, Minha Menina—I cannot read numbers."

"Is the Americano still in the wine-shop?"

"*Não, não*—when the big car has left he comes out, he goes into the church, no Menina!—he comes out again, he runs here and there looking for her; I think he is gone to the *Policia.*"

Luzia wasted no more time on the beggar except to thank him politely —she ran like a deer to the Misericordia Church, outside which Julia and Major Torrens now stood, admiring the delicious little narrow balcony—

such a curious feature for a church front—immediately above the copper-green door. The girl caught Julia by the arm.

"They've got her! They've taken her away," she said.

"Who's got whom?" the Major asked. Julia was quicker.

"D'you mean Hetta Páloczy? How do you know?"

"It must be her. Come this way," she said, propelling Julia a few steps towards the square. "Do you see that diplomatic car? A dark girl came in that, with an American man; she went into the Matriz Church, he went to drink. And then"—she repeated the beggar's story of the men in grey pushing Hetta into the car. "One put his hand over her *mouth*," she said, staring at Julia, her eyes immense with horror. "It can only be her."

"How did you learn all this?" Torrens asked.

"From a beggar by the church. Beggars watch everything—what else have they to do? But do not waste time on him; I have sucked him as dry as a lemon! What must we do?" the young girl asked urgently.

"Ring up the Colonel, don't you think?" Julia said to Torrens. "They're pretty certain to make for Spain, and he can have the frontier watched—closed, if need be, can't he?"

"I suppose so." He looked worried. "Did your observant beggar get the number of the car?" he asked Luzia.

"No. He can't read. But it was a big black saloon. Oh, and I didn't tell you—one of the men had a beard, and rolls of fat at the back of his neck. Surely this is the person who smashed your car?" Luzia said to Julia, causing Torrens to gape at her—Julia nodded briefly.

"Well, that sounds like it," the Major said, rather slowly, to Julia. "But of course we're not certain it is the little Countess at all—Luzia doesn't know her by sight. Or do you?" he asked the girl.

"No—but who else would be forced, struggling, into a car? To me, it all fits. Do telephone!" she urged Julia.

"We'd better do that from the *Policia*," Julia said. "Where is it, Luzia?"

As Luzia led them towards the police-station a frantic figure came hurrying from that direction, staring about him as he ran; his hat and the cut of his overcoat blazoned him as American, in that European setting.

"Oh, there's Townsend," Julia said calmly. "Let's ask him about this. Oy! Townsend," she yelled—the Bostonian heard her, and raced towards them across the open space.

"Have you seen Countess Hetta?" he panted as he came up. "Julia, it's good to see you! D'you know where she is? She went into a church to pray, and I went to have a drink, and now I can't find her!"

"Relax, Townsend. We're looking after this," Julia said kindly. "Come along with us."

"But where *is* she?" the American asked.

"We think she's been abducted," Torrens said brutally. "By Communist agents. Why on earth did you let her out of your sight?"

"Oh shut up, Hugh," Julia said. "It's all our fault for keeping him in the dark."

"Communist agents?" the Bostonian asked, aghast. "Were they at the bottom of that business of crashing your car after the Guincho, Miss Probyn?"

To the surprise of the others, Luzia answered. "One man, at least, was the same both times," she said. Townsend, for the first time, noticed her.

"This is Luzia Ericeira, Townsend," Julia said, using the customary Portuguese form of identification. "But come back to the *Policia*—we want to telephone about this at once."

As they walked on Townsend's distress was painful to see. "Shouldn't we go after her?" he asked. "Communists do frightful things to girls!"

"We might, if we knew where they'd gone," Torrens replied. "But we don't know the number of the car." He took Julia by the elbow and muttered in her ear. "For God's sake detach him somehow! We don't want him fretting round while we're telephoning to the Colonel."

"There—that is the *Policia*," Luzia said. She turned to the American. "I think you are quite right—we should go after her. Will you come with me while they are telephoning? I want to arrange something."

Julia didn't know whether Luzia's extraordinarily sharp ears had overheard Torrens' aside to her, or whether the girl was simply using her customary astuteness and tact, but she was thankful to be relieved so painlessly of poor Townsend's presence.

They got through to Lisbon rather fast—Colonel Marques' name and telephone-number seemed to act as a talisman. The local police, deeply impressed and much excited, stood round while one of them sat at the telephone; meanwhile Julia and Torrens examined a large map of northern Portugal which hung on the wall—she showed him the various routes from São Pedro do Sul into Spain.

"It just depends whether they choose a fast road, with a big, efficiently-manned frontier post on it, or a slower route to some dud little place where they might get through more easily—I don't suppose Hetta has her passport with her," she said. "Look—Fuentes de Onoro is fairly small; it's"—she worked out the distances with a pink-tipped finger—"nearly 200 kilometres, via Viseu and Guarda; the road's good all the way, but it's frightfully curly. Then, going north, there's Barca d'Alva—that's only just over 140 kilometres, and it's a *tiny* place, but the road's appalling; they'd have to turn off the Guarda road at Celorico, and trickle through Pinhel and Figueira de Castelo Rodrigo. And I don't know whether the bridge has been re-built yet." She turned and questioned the policemen. "They're not sure," she told Torrens. "So I think we can count that out."

The Major nodded. "Yes, I see," he said, though he saw little but the map before his eyes; he was bewildered by the flow of difficult names, and amazed at Julia's apparently inexhaustible fund of information about Portu-guese roads.

"Well that only leaves Vila Nova de Foscoa and Chaves. Vila Nova's a long way too, about 180, though it's a fair road almost all the way—and it's not a very big place. But the fastest of all would be—"

"Minha Menina, I have the connection!" the policeman at the telephone called out.

"Muito bem—I will speak." Leisurely, she went over and took the re-ceiver. "No," she said in Portuguese—"I must speak with the Chief himself. A name Inglês—Probeen." And in a moment the Colonel was on the line, and she handed the instrument to Torrens.

Colonel Marques' admirable command of English was an enormous asset on an occasion like this; so was his quickness at the uptake. Torrens did his part quite well—"We suspect an abduction of a little foreign lady—do you know who I mean?" he began at once.

"The identifier? Certainly. What do you know? Speak openly, but fast—English is difficult for these others, if spoken quickly."

Torrens told him, speaking rapidly, the little they knew. "But we have failed to get the number of the car."

"Oh, I have that," the Colonel said cheerfully. "I sent some stooges" —he pronounced the word with a certain relish—"out in a certain car over the week-end, and as I anticipated, it was followed! How long ago did this abduction take place?"

"Hold on." Torrens consulted Julia, his hand over the mouthpiece; they both looked at their watches—it was five o'clock.

"We've been here at least half an hour—no, more," Julia said—"but of course we've no idea how long Townsend was drinking and Hetta praying. Say about four."

Obediently, Major Torrens said, "About an hour ago," down the tele-phone. "We imagine, of course, that they are making for another country," he added.

"So I also imagine. From where do you speak? The house, or the town?"

"From the town."

"Muito bem! Excuse me if I ring off now—I want to close the frontier to this car. Wait! Where can I contact you later?"

Once more Torrens consulted Julia.

"Tell him to try the house—we may be there, or we may not, but we certainly shan't be *here*."

"Well that's something—he'll stop all the exits now," Julia said, when Torrens had rung off.

"If he's in time. I wish we knew how fast that car is."

"I think he's bound to be in time—the shortest route, the one with the dubious bridge, is eighty-five miles, and that's an appalling road; they'd have to *crawl*."

"Which was the one you were saying was the fastest, just when we got through to him?" Torrens was beginning, when Luzia and Townsend Waller walked in. All the police greeted the young girl with a combination of affection and deference which amused the Englishman.

"You have got him?" Luzia asked. Julia nodded. "But look, pipe down a moment, Luzia," she added. "Mr. Waller, you don't mind waiting a second or two, do you? I want to explain something to Hugh." She turned again to the map on the wall, and traced a line with one finger.

"Much the fastest is to blind straight north to Chaves, crossing the Douro at Regua—see?—and on through Vila Real; it's the main route north into Spain, and a good road all the way. But it's over a hundred miles, and a major frontier post, of course. Could they do it in the time?"

"Touch and go," Torrens said, looking at his watch—it now said 5:10. "No, they would hardly do it, even on an auto-strada, in under an hour-and-a-half—unless the black saloon is a super-charged Mercedes-Benz or something like that." He thought, frowning. "It all depends, really, on how quickly our friend gets the frontier alerted. Very fast, I imagine—he is so enormously efficient."

Luzia suddenly spoke up.

"If they were well-informed, and clever, they might not cross the frontier on the main road at all. In Chaves they could turn left to Montalegre, in the Terras de Barroso; and from Montalegre there are two little, small roads into Spain—so tiny, I doubt if the frontier posts have telephones at all. One goes to Baltar, and one to Lucenza; both in Spain."

"How do you know all this?" Torrens asked, staring at her doubtfully.

"Papa has a small house—do you call it a shooting-box?—near Montalegre, where he goes to shoot wild goats; so I know the roads there."

"Luzia, is there a telephone at the shooting-lodge?" Julia asked, while Torrens digested this information.

"Of course."

"And they're sensible people, discreet?—the keepers, I mean?"

"Martinez is wonderful—he is a *Gallego* Spaniard."

"Could he do something about having the car stopped? How far is the lodge from Montalegre?"

"Only eight kilometres. But let us start to telephone now; there is no car up there, and Maria-Rosa at the exchange at Montalegre is not very prompt!" She turned to one of the police and gave a number. "Expressly for the Senhor Duque, tell them," she added brusquely, "and *urgente!*" —grinning, the policeman did as he was told.

"How will your keeper stop the car?" Torrens asked, lighting a cigarette.

"Oh, leave all that to Martinez!" Luzia said cheerfully—pushing aside some dusty and faded files she had perched herself on the office table, and sat there swinging her long thin legs, the legs of a very young but thorough-bred colt. "He will stop it by some means or another, if he is told to."

"I think we ought to ring up the Duke and say we may be delayed," Julia said presently, also seating herself on the table beside Luzia.

"I've done that," Luzia said. "Mr. Waller and I went and did it from the Câmara, while you were telephoning to Lisbon."

The Câmara is the name used in Portugal for the municipal offices of any town. In São Pedro do Sul this rather uninspiring organisation is most splendidly housed, behind superb baroque façades, in what was formerly the Convent of the Frades; along corridors where once religious walked in stately meditation, little clerks now scurry to and fro on errands concerned with street lighting and sewerage disposal. It is something when these noble buildings, left vacant when the religious orders were driven out in the 19th century, are used as Câmaras or barracks, for then at least the fabric is preserved; all too many are simply abandoned to the ravages of the elements and the tender mercies of squatters, who crouch in one corner of some vast ground-floor room—probably with a magnificent painted ceiling, now rather damp-stained—along with their skinny fowls and their stinking goats. Julia grinned a little at her pupil's resourcefulness. But just as she was about to speak the telephone rang; Luzia leapt off the table, and gabbled into the instrument in Portuguese.

"That is arranged," the girl said, as she put down the receiver. "Now, do we go after her?"

Poor Mr. Waller, who had perforce remained a rather passive spectator since he and Luzia returned to the *Policia*, now spoke up.

"Of course we do. We have to! We can't just leave her in their hands!"

"Just a moment"—Julia spoke very calmly. "Luzia, who did you speak to at Gralheira?"

"Elidio—Papa was out."

"And what did you say?"

"That there was a contretemps, and we should not be back in time for dinner; we might be very late, and they were to keep food hot for us. I was *exceedingly* discreet!" the girl said.

"That all sounds in order," Townsend said to Julia. "Let's go. What are we waiting for?"

"Let's go and talk about it in the open, anyhow," Julia said. "I think these polite policemen must have had about enough of us." She spoke courteous farewells and thanks, which were received with a perfect ballet of smiles and bows and a chorus of *um muito grande prazer!* (a great pleasure). "I told you you'd see up here what nice people they were," Julia said to Torrens as they walked towards the square. "Well now, had we better go after her?"

"I think some of us must, anyhow. I wish to God we knew which road to try, though."

"I think Chaves is much the best bet. The others are all far slower," Julia began, when a piercing whistle just behind them made both her and the Major jump.

"Oh, I am sorry! But there it *is*," Luzia said; once more she put two fingers in her mouth and emitted that frightful sound, usually a shepherd's secret, and waved vigorously. The Gralheira Land-Rover, driving slowly into the square, swung round in their direction.

"Good gracious, what's this doing here?" Julia said astonished.

"I had it sent. For these bad, small roads in the Terras de Barroso it is *much* better than the Daimler, and on a good road it can do a hundred kilometres an hour easily," the girl said earnestly. "So I told Elidio to send it in."

Torrens burst out laughing.

"Splendid! Send back the other car, and we'll go in this. Waller, have you locked yours?"

Townsend had. But Julia began to feel some slight qualms about her pupil.

"Luzia, you'd better go home in the Daimler," she said.

As Luzia opened her Medusa mouth in a bitter protest, Torrens broke in.

"Damn it, Julia, you can't do that! The child has had the wits to produce the right machine for the job, and she may be very useful in dealing with all these types on the spot. For pity's sake let her come along."

Julia glanced at him in surprise. "Oh, very well," she said—Luzia, in her thankfulness for this mercy, swallowed the Major's use of the humiliating word "child." The Daimler was despatched to Gralheira, and the four of them piled into the Land-Rover and roared off towards the north. From habit Torrens glanced at his watch—it was a quarter to six.

From São Pedro do Sul to the frontier, a few kilometres beyond Chaves, is about 106 miles. The Land-Rover did it in two-and-a-quarter hours, battering its occupants almost to jelly in the process; for the road goes up hill and down dale, descending to cross the deep golden-schist valley of the Douro at Regua, and then climbing up onto and over the wild high-lying country of Trás-os-Montes, the most remote province of Portugal. Exactly at 8 P.M. they drew up in front of the wire barrier closing the road, climbed down, and went to interview the frontier officials. By common consent Julia did the talking. She showed the man at the barrier Torrens' "white card," an invaluable document issued by the Security Police only to senior members of diplomatic missions and to Portuguese Cabinet Ministers; Torrens had, of course, been furnished with one of these coveted objects, which enable their fortunate possessors to go practically anywhere, and—most useful of all—to park their cars in places where parking is normally forbidden. (In fact they do confer *carte blanche* on their owners.) The frontier guard recognised this portentous document when he examined it by the Land-Rover's headlights; he pushed the long slender barrier back a little way, beckoned the party through the gap, and led them to where his superiors were smoking cigarettes and drinking red wine in a small office.

Here Julia introduced the Senhor Comandante Inglês as a friend and colleague of Colonel Marques, and then began her questions about a large black car. Yes, such a car had driven up about 6 P.M., but it did not bear the number advised telephonically by the Colonel, so the occupants had not been held; however, the Colonel had closed the frontier tonight, so it was not allowed to pass—it turned round, and drove back towards Chaves. Was there a Menina in it? Ah, that they could not say; since it did not bear the specified number it was not examined—it came, and it went.

"Well that gets us exactly nowhere," Torrens said gloomily when Julia passed on this information.

"Shall I ask if the men wore grey overcoats?"

"Might as well."

Julia did so. Yes, in effect the Senhores had worn grey top-coats— "like most travellers who are not Ingleses," the customs officer said, with a side-long glance at Torrens' rather vivid tweed. Luzia laughed.

"That really tells us nothing either," Torrens said, as they walked back towards the barrier. "I wonder what our next move is?" Luzia, however, was speaking to the frontier guard in his own tongue; she rounded briskly on the Secret Service man.

"They consulted a map when they got back to the car!—he *saw* them. They might have seen these little roads on it. Oh, do let us go to Montalegre and see if Martinez (she pronounced it Marteensh) has done something!"

On to Montalegre they went. The young chauffeur in the Land-Rover was new, and Luzia sat with Torrens beside him on the front seat to show the way. As they drove through that wild upland country they met nothing but one rather broken-down old car, with weak and wavering headlights; Luzia, however, drew the Englishman's attention to one of the most peculiar features of the place—the stone walls dividing one field from another, almost as frequent as the walls which turn Connemara into a chessboard. But whereas the Irish walls are loosely made of shapeless lumps of the local lime-stone or marble, these Portuguese ones, also dry-stone built, are of a most elaborate, even elegant construction—between upright slabs of silvery granite nearly two feet across, slender and much smaller flakes of dusty-gold schist are piled slant-wise, producing a quite extraordinary effect of golden hammocks or curtains, slung between broad silver pillars. Seldom can peasants merely in search of utility have created anything so beautiful.

"Are they not strange, and pretty?" the girl said. "I wish you could see them by day; the colours are beautiful."

Montalegre is a very small town indeed, and so remote that the cheerful friendly people who live in the little houses of its narrow primitive streets often only see a stranger once in two months; so, as Luzia explained to Hugh Torrens, it was an easy place in which to make enquiries. As they drove in, the enormous mediaeval castle, looming high above the town clustered at its foot, was beginning to be illuminated by the rising moon— "Goodness! That is quite magical," Torrens exclaimed. Luzia ignored the remark; she had just told the young chauffeur to drive slowly, and was peering out through the wind-screen. "There is Francisco—stop!" she said. The Land-Rover pulled up before Montalegre's nearest approach to an inn; outside it stood a little group of people. Luzia bounced down out of the high seat and spoke with a handsome dark youth who leant across a bicycle —Torrens climbed down after her and saw, close in front of them, a large black saloon car drawn up. He walked quickly to it and looked inside; it was empty; moreover, he then observed that all its four tires were flat! He went back to where Luzia was talking to the young man with the bicycle, the inn-keeper, and the town policeman; an attentive audience hung on every word.

"They *did* come here!" Luzia said to him excitedly as he came up. "Did I not tell you they would? And they went into this house to drink wine, and ate an omelette, and bought some bread and cheese, and made enquiries about the roads to Lucenza and Baltar. *She* was with them! While they were within—they got here just before seven o'clock—Francisco put a knife in all their tires! Martinez has sprained his ankle, that is why he sent Francisco; if he had come himself he would not have let them go."

"Oh, they've gone, have they? Where to, and how?"

"Back to Chaves. There is a sort of taxi in the town, and when they found their tires flat, they took it; Senhor Antonio here"—she indicated the tubby figure of the inn-keeper—"got it for them."

"That must be that ghastly old rattle-trap we met on the road," said Julia, who with Mr. Waller had now joined the group. "How maddening! —I wish we'd ditched it! Then we should have got her by now." She turned to the inn-keeper. "*Que pena* that you ordered the *carro* for these people. They are Communistas!"

"*Minha Senhora,* I did not know! How could I know? And they offered poor Pedro such a magnificent price to drive them to Chaves—he with all those children, and for weeks now not a single person requiring his machine! I thought I did well." The little man was pitiably distressed— Luzia cheered him up.

"Do not fret, Senhor Antonio—as you truly say, you could not know. But tell me the *número* of Pedro's machine."

Twenty voices gave her the number of Montalegre's one hire-car—"In any event, everyone in Chaves knows it by sight," said an enormous man, the local butcher. "*Sim, sim,*" said Luzia, "naturally." She turned to the others. "We should follow them back to Chaves, should we not?"

The Montalegre policeman now spoke.

"My Countess, what shall be done about the strange *carro*? Does it remain?"

"Of course it remains—since its tires are flat, it cannot move," Luzia said laughing.

"An outrage was committed upon it," the policeman said rather anxiously, casting a baleful eye upon young Francisco, who still leaned, now visibly wilting, across his bicycle.

"This was done by the orders of the *Chefe* of the *Policia* in Lisbon," Luzia said majestically. "*I* transmitted them. But if you are in doubt, telephone to Lisbon yourself." The policeman subsided; Julia spoke up.

"Hadn't we better search the car?"

They did—but their hasty examination revealed nothing. "You'd better tell the bobby man to seal it up, and leave it where it is," Torrens said to Luzia. "The Colonel can send someone to search it properly." Luzia passed on these instructions to the policeman, who was clearly inflated by this idea—"Certainly the priest will have sealing-wax," he observed hopefully.

"Oh, how is Dom Gil's rheumatism? No better? Ah, *pena!*—please give him my love." She went on with local enquiries, as about the inn-keeper's

wife's new baby, and replied to similar questions concerning the health of
the Senhor Duque and the Senhora Condessa. All this drove poor Townsend Waller nearly distracted; he stood in a fever of anxiety.

"Look, Miss Luzia," he broke in at last in desperation—"Shouldn't we
get going? You say they left here at 7:15; well it's nine now, so they have
nearly two hours start."

"All right—yes."

It was just after 9:30 when they drove across the splendid Roman bridge
of sixteen arches which in the 20th century still carries all traffic from the
South into Chaves. They had arranged on the way that Julia and Torrens
should be dropped at the *Policia* to ring up Colonel Marques, while Luzia
and Townsend were to rout round the few garages and try to ascertain the
number of the car which Hetta's captors had taken—assuming reasonably
that no one would try to go very far in the Montalegre taxi.

When Torrens reported to the Colonel he gave the number of the car
which they had found, and left, at Montalegre.

"But this is not the one!" the Colonel exclaimed.

"No. We found that out at the frontier; that was why they didn't hold
it."

"These *fools* of mine!" Colonel Marques said angrily. "They must needs
have a puncture just before Coimbra, and of course lost sight of the car!
It will be in Coimbra that these others changed to a different one, no
doubt." His voice ceased for a moment—"Hullo?" Torrens said.

"Do you know the number of the car they have taken in Chaves?" the
Colonel asked then.

"We're trying to find out. I'll let you know if we get it."

"*Très bien.* In any case I will now ensure that *no* car passes the frontier
anywhere for the next twenty-four hours—this is troublesome, but it cannot
be helped. They may of course try to take the girl away by sea or by air;
I will have the ports and air-fields watched."

There was no sign of Luzia and the American when Julia and Torrens
emerged from the police-station, so they walked by moonlight to the hotel
where they had all agreed to meet for dinner. Chaves is now a thriving spa;
in past centuries, owing to its proximity to the frontier, it was a favourite
meeting-place for diplomatic missions between Spain and Portugal, and
even the scene of dynastic intermarriages—probably its hot springs, which
are alleged to cure everything from rheumatism to syphilis, pay better. Anyhow it has two really rather good hotels with excellent food; Julia and
Torrens sat down in the one recommended by Luzia and ordered dinner
for four with a certain enthusiasm—it was now just on ten o'clock, and they
had eaten nothing since lunch at 1:30. The waiter produced gin and

French Vermouth; after a deep preliminary gulp the Major sank back in
his chair, relaxed and thankful.

"Feeling better?" Julia asked.

"Yes, much. But this is a ghastly show—I've never touched anything so
hopeless."

"Hugh, *why*? It seems to me that you've been getting no end of help—
thanks to Luzia of course."

"Oh yes—she's a wonder-child! But where are we now? At a dead end,
as far as I can see—and that poor little creature in the hands of those bastards at this moment."

Julia, woman-like, poured him out another drink.

"Sup that—I'm going to ring up Gralheira," she said, and went out.
The Duke himself answered.

"From where do you speak, Miss Probyn?"

"From Chaves. *La petite Hongroise* has been abducted—that's why we
came here. It was Luzia's idea, and it was a good one, but we just missed
them."

The Duke sounded grave.

"This is a terrible thing! How could it happen?"

"Oh, her poor Yank boy-friend left her alone in a church, and they
pinched her," Julia said, deliberately using these slangy expressions in case
of line-tapping. "It was our fault; he didn't know. I'm sorry we shall be so
late; do please apologise for me to Dona Maria Francisca. We're just going
to dine now; I suppose we shall get back about one. Don't keep any
food."

"You abandon the pursuit?"

"We've lost the trail—there's nothing more we can do tonight. And Luzia
ought to get to bed. Oh, can we bring the American with us? I don't like
leaving him alone, he's in a terrible state."

"Of course."

"You *are* kind."

"By the way, the British Embassy constantly telephones, asking for you
—three times, so far."

"Oh, let them wait!—say I'm dead!" Who *could* have told Atherley what
was going on, Julia speculated—it could only be he who was ringing up.
She said Good-night and rang off.

When she returned to the hall where she had left Torrens she found
Luzia and Townsend Waller; the latter was drinking gin too.

"Miss Probyn, could I have a *porto branco*? I *feel* like one!" the girl
said.

"She'd much better have a brandy," Torrens interposed—Luzia's pearl-pale face was now white with fatigue.

"Yes—order one, will you?"

While Luzia sipped brandy-and-water, Townsend recounted their fruitless endeavours to trace the car to which Hetta had been transferred from the Montalegre taxi. "They were seen at at least three garages, but the people just weren't talking."

"Not even to *me!*" Luzia added, with a naïve indignation which amused Torrens. "They must have given *huge* bribes!"

"We'd better let the Colonel know about this—he can have the heat turned on them," the Major said rather reluctantly—he wanted his dinner. "Back to the police-station, I suppose."

"Oh nonsense! Let's do it from here; the whole town will be buzzing with it by now," said Julia, and put the call through for him.

Over their much-needed dinner they discussed what further moves they could make.

"My own bet is that they'll go back to Lisbon and think again," Torrens said. "It's clear that they have quite an organisation there."

"I agree," said Julia.

"I don't see how you can talk about it so calmly," Townsend burst out. "What will they do to her in the meantime?" He was in a pitiable state, only playing with the good food in front of him.

"As to that, for the present you can only pray," Luzia told him, rather severely. "That is why I took you into the Igreja Matriz; but I think you did not pray—you only looked at those lovely carved angels which stand on top of the organ, and the two golden deformities of dwarfs that hold it up!"

Julia and Torrens burst out laughing.

"Well, that organ *is* extraordinary," the Bostonian said defensively. "It's so beautiful, although it's so queer."

They did not linger over the meal; they climbed into the Land-Rover just before eleven, and set off on the two-and-a-half hours of pounding and shaking back to Gralheira. Luzia fell asleep, and toppled off onto the floor —Torrens picked her up and took her in his arms, arranging her long thorough-bred legs across Julia's knees.

"It's all right, sweetie—just you go to sleep," he said when she opened her eyes—"You've done a splendid job." Luzia closed her eyes again and relaxed like a baby, her head on his shoulder; Julia slid one arm out of her suède jacket and spread part of it over those long legs. Then she too closed her eyes, in silent endurance of the prolonged battering. But several times during the next two hours she opened them to glance at the Major, holding her pupil so tenderly in his arms, with an indefinable expression.

CHAPTER XIII

JULIA WAS SURPRISED and touched, when they reached Gralheira a little after one, to find the Duke still up and waiting for them in his study, with a blazing wood fire and a tray with whisky. Nanny was hovering in the background; she pounced on the sleepy Luzia and bore her off to bed—over her shoulder she threw Julia an indignant "Well, Miss Probyn!" Julia apologised to their host—"I really am so very sorry. It seemed the only thing to do, to go on and try to get hold of her."

"Of course you could do nothing else. But now you must all drink something."

Julia was touched afresh by the degree of the Duke's concern for Hetta, when over their drinks they told him their adventures. "This *poor* young girl! What happens to her at this moment?"

"I daresay they won't dare to do anything very much—they just want to hold her to ransom, and worry us," she said as convincingly as she could, for Townsend's benefit. At that moment a telephone bell rang sharply.

"This is doubtless your friend at the Embassy!" the Duke said, selecting one of the eight machines, and lifting the receiver. "Yes," he said in English—and handed it to Julia with a smile.

It was Atherley—and Julia handled him rather roughly. "My good friend, do you realise that it's going on for *two*? You really can't ring people up at this time of night! And I gather you've been pestering this house the whole evening. What is it?"

"Have you got her back?" Julia hardly recognised his voice, it was so strained and toneless.

"No, we haven't, I'm sorry to say. But how did you know she was missing?"

"From Hugh's Colonel. After I'd spoken to Hugh this morning I thought I might as well let him know where she'd gone, by way of no harm; so when you told him what was going on this afternoon, he told me. But what happened? Weren't they stopped? He said he had their car number."

Guardedly, Julia told him why that car number had been of no use, and of their fruitless pursuit right up into the North-West.

"So you have absolutely no means of tracing her?"

"No—except that we've alerted you-know-who, so they can't leave the country by road. But otherwise, we're completely at a dead end." Between fatigue and distress Julia's own voice fell away on the last words. She was tired out, she was tormented about Hetta; but she was also irritated by Richard's ringing up at such an hour. She felt—more rightly than she knew—that it was really all his fault for not bringing his girl-friend up to Beira Alta himself. "Well, goodnight," she said.

"No, wait! This is too frightful! We *must* do something. I'll come up."

Julia managed not to utter the words that came into her head—What good do you think *that* will do? Too exhausted to protest, really at the end of her tether, she merely said resignedly—"Oh very well. Come early, come all, and vote for Eisenhower!" and banged down the receiver.

"Duke, I fear we may anticipate a visit some time tomorrow from the First Secretary at the British Embassy," she said, as she returned to the fire.

"This is your friend who telephones so persistently? Atherley? An agreeable young man," the Duke said, very courteously, in view of the hour at which the call had been made.

"Well I suppose I may call him a friend, but he's little Countess Páloczy's young man, and that's what all the telephoning has been about," said Julia thoughtlessly and indignantly. "Personally, I think he has probably perpetrated a *total* clottery of some sort! Silly ass!" She emptied her glass and added—

"Duke dear, I'm dead. I simply must go to bed. You've been an angel," —and left the study. In less than two minutes the others followed her, Elidio escorting Townsend Waller to his room.

Nothing is more tiring than distress and anxiety; and however she might preserve her outward composure, Julia Probyn was in fact deeply distressed and cruelly anxious about Hetta, and had been for the whole of the eight hours that she had spent bucketing about North Portugal in the Land-Rover. Never had she so much craved a solid twelve hours' sleep; but before settling into bed she took steps both for and against this. *For,* she swallowed some Seconal with a gulp of water from the Victorian tumbler, exquisitely engraved with vine-leaves, on her washstand—which like the Major's had a marble top; *against,* she set her little American folding alarm-clock on the bed-side table to ring its pretty but persistent chime for 7:30. "Good God! Only five hours!" she muttered with a glance at the tiny luminous face, as she snuggled down to sleep.

At Gralheira Father Antal had taken to saying Mass in the chapel at 8:30, just after Dom Pedro, the chaplain; the Monsignor said his rather later. Julia, roused by her little Travalarm, pealed her bell for Manoela, the housemaid who attended on her, demanded her morning tea *pronto*, drank it thankfully, and was dressed and waiting on the landing outside the chapel in time to catch the Hungarian priest before he went into the little sacristy, with its carved rococo vestment-cupboards, to vest himself for Mass.

"Dom Francisco, just one moment," she said, gesturing away one of the men-servants, who took it in turns, eagerly, to serve Mass for these eminent foreign divines.

"Oh, good morning, Miss Probyn. You are up early! Is there anything I can do for you?"

"Yes, Father, there is. I want you to pray like *mad* for Hetta Páloczy!"

He looked troubled.

"Why, please?"

"Come here." She led him a little way along the landing, out of earshot of the hovering footmen, and told him hurriedly of Hetta's disappearance and their fruitless pursuit. "So now we've completely lost track of her, and so have the Security Police; there's absolutely nothing we can do—God simply *must* take a hand," she said, with a direct earnestness which made the words far from irreverent.

"Thank you for telling me, my daughter. I will offer the Mass for her release. Pray yourself," he added as he went away.

"Oh, I will—for what *that's* worth," said Julia. She drew from her pocket a little black lace scarf, such as all women in Portugal carry in their handbags for use in church, twined it round her tawny-gold hair, and went and knelt down in the chapel. A moment later Dona Maria Francisca sidled in and knelt also, followed by Nanny and some of the maid-servants, among them the old kitchen crone, Maria do Carmo, whom the Duke had described as a tigress; several shabby-looking men with broken boots crept in too, escorted by Antonio, and knelt on the opposite side of the aisle—these Julia recognised, without surprise, to be some of the Duke's wayfaring guests who had passed the night in the hay-loft above the courtyard. At Gralheira not only food and lodgement, but Mass itself were available to the poorest traveller who desired it. How lovely that was, the girl thought, most unwonted tears suddenly filling her eyes. She glanced round at the pictures and small statues that made the chapel a treasure-house: the Grão Vasco Crucifixion over the main altar, and an enchanting Nativity by the same hand in the Lady-chapel on the right, the faces in both vividly alive; everywhere delicious polychrome sculptures of Our Lady and various saints, mostly dressed in the height of 18th-century fashion, but nevertheless possessing an unmistakable devotional tone that is all their own. The odd thought struck her: how idolatrous, how papistical, this beautiful rococo building and its rich ornaments would seem to thousands of people—to her low-church Aunt Ellen in Scotland for instance. But Aunt Ellen would not ever see those shabby poor men, with their cracked boots and their stubby chins, fingering their rosaries so devoutly just across the aisle from her. No, this was *real*, a reality that the normal Protestant world would never understand unless, like her, they could come and live with it.

The thought of Aunt Ellen reminded her of Mrs. Hathaway, always her poor aunt's mentor and stand-by in any emergency—she *must* ring her up the moment after breakfast.

A tiny silvery chime of bells, jangled by the footman-server kneeling at the altar steps, announced that Mass had begun; Father Antal in a wonderful faded chasuble of silvery rose brocade was saying the *Judica me*. Like everyone else Julia crossed herself, recalled her wandering thoughts, and began to pray. She was not a Catholic, she was just a very usual type of casual Anglican, who went to Church when she felt like it—because she was in Durham and the Cathedral was so beautiful or, elsewhere, because the singing would be good or the preacher interesting. She made her Communion at Christmas and Easter, because she always had; she lived a kind and generous life partly because she had a kind and generous nature, but even more because she was unconsciously drawing on an enormous bank-balance, so to speak, of inherited Christian traditions of living. But during her long sojourn with the Ericeiras she had got into the habit of attending Mass, and going up to the chapel after dinner to say the Rosary with Dona Maria Francisca, Nanny and Luzia—partly, again, out of a generous impulse not to separate herself from her pupil in anything; so this morning's proceedings were all perfectly familiar, and in her present distress on Hetta's account she found them deeply comforting.

When Father Antal went up to the altar to say the Introit there was a slight rustle and a tiny push beside Julia—Luzia had slipped into the pew. The Mass pursued its brief, majestic course—so stately, so impersonal, so overwhelming in its implications. After the dismissal Father Antal left the altar, and at the foot of the steps began the prayers "for the conversion of Russia"; Julia said them with unwonted fervour, realising as never before that under "Russia" were comprised all Communists, everywhere. As the priest left the chapel Luzia whispered to her—"It is frightful! I was too late to ask Dom Francisco to offer his Mass for Hetta. This idiotic Anna let me sleep. Now I suppose I must ask the Monsignor."

"Dom Francisco *did* offer it for her—I asked him to," Julia whispered back; she felt a curious gladness and relief as she told Luzia this. The girl's great grey eyes glowed under the black mantilla that shadowed her pale face.

"You did? Wonderful! How thankful I am!"

Emerging from the chapel with Luzia, out on the broad landing Julia heard a voice she knew coming up from the hall below—Richard's voice, talking his rather peculiar brand of Portuguese to someone; looking down over the carved walnut banisters she saw him in conversation with Elidio. Luzia saw him too, and shot down the three right-angled sections of the wide staircase like a rocket.

"Oh Atherley, she is lost! She is lost! We followed her, we tried to save her, but we failed!" She clung to his arm, her face more Medusa-like than ever, and more beautiful.

"Luzia! Luzia!" Dona Maria Francisca and Nanny, on the landing above, hissed vainly in reprobation, without producing the smallest effect; Julia was reminded irresistibly of geese by the roadside hissing at a high-powered car—laughing a little, she walked down the broad shallow stairs. Just as she reached the hall the Duke, disturbed by his daughter's high-pitched lamentations, came out from his study to see what was going on.

"Ah, Atherley, it is you. This is very pleasant—welcome to Gralheira! I hope you stay with us?" He turned to his daughter. "My child, must your greeting to a guest be to wail like an Irish peasant or a Chinese woman at a funeral? You make a most lamentable noise. I think you had better go and have your breakfast."

"Papa, I was only telling him"—Luzia began, when Townsend Waller walked in at the front door, and simultaneously Major Torrens appeared from the direction of the smoking-room. Meanwhile Father Antal, having divested himself, was proceeding calmly down the stairs in search of breakfast, which was normally served to him on a tray in the priests' study.

"Hullo, Atherley, you're very early!" Major Torrens said. "You must have been driving all night. Well don't accuse *me* any more of involving you in our affairs! You've bought it this time, coming up—" He broke off suddenly at the sight of Richard's stricken face; but not soon enough to forestall Luzia, who said brusquely—"Major! You are being tactless!" While the Duke stared in amazement at this unwonted behaviour on the part of his offspring, and Julia stifled unseasonable laughter—even as she tried to think of some remark to tide over the awkward little pause which followed Luzia's words—yet another figure appeared in the hall: the rather portly soutaned shape of Monsignor Subercaseaux.

"Good morning, good morning! My dear Duke, good morning to you!" He glanced about him. "Quite an assembly—*both* our young ladies! And Atherley! *Mon cher*, this is an unexpected pleasure! When did you arrive?"

Then his eye lighted on the American. "Monsieur Waller, too!—how very pleasant." He shook hands. "My dear Duke, are you giving a breakfast-party, or what?"

The Duke of Ericeira was exceptionally well able to deal with such situations. "Come into my study a moment, Monsignor," he said. There he explained the events of the evening before. Subercaseaux, who like Father Antal and everyone else had only been told that Luzia and her companions had been "delayed," was horrified.

"This child in the hands of the Communists! But this is frightful. What is being done? Does Colonel Marques know?"

"Colonel Marques?"

"The Head of the Security Police. Oh yes, Major Torrens will certainly have told him. But this is an appalling thing! How could it happen?"

"Major Torrens will be able to tell you that," the Duke said. "But it seems that Monsieur Atherley is greatly attached to the young lady, and his feelings need to be spared. The American, too, is apparently devoted to her, and feels to blame. And now I think I must rejoin my guests."

"And I will go and say my Mass." Chastened in a way most unusual for him, Mgr Subercaseaux left the study and went slowly up the staircase towards the chapel.

His rather unfortunate little joke about a breakfast-party had inspired Julia to more drastic action than she usually took in the Ericeira household. Nanny and Dona Maria had stopped hissing like geese on the upper landing, and vanished; she sent Luzia up after them, then rang the bell and gave some orders to Elidio. When her host re-appeared she muttered to him in an aside—"Duke, I hope I haven't done wrong, but I told Elidio to order breakfast for all these people, to save time. Poor Atherley must be starving, he's been driving all night; and I'm sure Mr. Waller usually eats a steak in the morning! All right?"

The Duke laughed, with his usual appreciation of this lively sensible young woman.

"Perfectly right. What a comfort you always are, Miss Probyn! But I am not sure that there is beef-steak, properly hung, in the house," he added seriously.

"Oh, hang his steak!—I mean bother it!" Julia said briskly. "I said tomato omelettes all round, in the morning-room; then we shan't interfere with all Elidio's fusses over flowers and polishing in the dining-room."

To her great surprise the middle-aged man bent and kissed her hand.

"No congratulations will be sufficient for the man who becomes your husband!" he pronounced.

"Dear Duke, you really are a poppet!" said Julia, touched by this praise.

(Several hours later the Duke, in his study, consulted an Anglo-French and an Anglo-Portuguese dictionary for the meaning of the word "poppet"; since both described it as some form of doll, he was left mystified.)

Richard Atherley was in torture over the whole business. Ever since Torrens had telephoned to him the morning before he had recognised that he was responsible for Hetta's having gone off with the American—he, and he alone; and the quite hideous outcome, though it could not have been foreseen, was his fault. On the long drive up, first through waning moonshine, then through the sweet-smelling Portuguese dark, the young man had spent those hours of solitude doing what Housman has perhaps described better than anyone else:

> I took my question to the shrine
> that has not ceased from speaking,
> The heart within that tells the truth,
> and tells it twice as plain.

—and his heart had told him, with loud and piercing distinctness, that whatever her mistakes and her gaucheries, for him henceforward it was Hetta, only and always; and that unless she was somehow restored to them he would have lost the person who meant more to him than anything else in the world. A frantic impulse of remorse had sent him off in the middle of the night in one of the Chancery cars, leaving a cryptic and abjectly apologetic note for the Ambassador with the night-watchman; by daylight, over breakfast at Gralheira, he realised plainly enough that he had made a fool of himself. What could he hope to achieve that would not be better done by Colonel Marques or Torrens?—or indeed, it seemed, by Luzia? These reflections left him with an extreme consciousness of his own folly and misery, and a great desire to unburden himself to someone. For this last purpose who could be more desirable than Mgr Subercaseaux?—and the instant they rose from the table he asked the priest if he could spare him a few minutes?

"But of course, my dear young friend. Shall we walk in the garden?—the sun shines."

French windows led from several of the groundfloor rooms into the knot-garden; stepping out, they walked there. For years afterwards any sense of shame or embarrassment would bring back to Atherley, quite unbidden, a picture of dark geometrical patterns on a pale ground, so deeply were the close-clipped shapes of the tiny box hedges burnt into his mind that morning during his talk with the priest.

"Monsignor, I want to tell you—I—in fact this is all my fault," the young man began, with none of his usual aplomb.

"You wish to explain to me why Countess Hetta made this journey with Monsieur Waller rather than with you?" Subercaseaux asked as Richard paused.

The young man stared.

"You know, then?"

"No, I deduce. Did she ask you to bring her here?"

"Yes, and really I wished nothing more than to do so; but she happened to suggest it at—at an awkward moment. I said I would telephone to her later, but when I tried she was not taking any calls."

"This was when?"

"Sunday evening."

"Had Madame de Vermeil arrived?"

Richard stared again—then, in spite of his distress, he gave one of his baying laughs.

"Monsignor, there is no end to you! Yes, she had; in fact they met at the Pretender's, at luncheon."

"Ah, that explains much. I expect this detestable Fanny—I am sorry, my dear Richard, but to be honest with you I do really regard this person as one of the most pernicious of creatures!—did or said something perfectly hideous to that poor child. And then she asked you to bring her up here, and you temporised? Is that it?"

"Yes, that was it." He kept his eyes on the box hedges. "She said she would make her own arrangements," he said wretchedly. "Well we know what those were, and what they have led to! I would give *anything* that it hadn't happened; I could kill myself!"

"More practical is to decide, finally and definitively, which of these two ladies you now propose to pursue," Subercaseaux said, with elegant severity.

"Hetta! I've broken with Fanny. She doesn't believe it yet, but it's true."

"She will find plenty of consolations, believe me," the priest said sardonically. "But if—when—" he sighed and looked distressed. "If and when you are able to renew your addresses to Countess Hetta," he went on, "I think you should realise that there must be no sentimental harking back, in fact no outside flirtations at all. This young girl is not the sort of person either to understand that kind of thing, or to tolerate it."

"I know she isn't," Richard said humbly. "And honestly, Monsignor, I didn't start it this time. I had no idea, even, that Madame de Vermeil was coming to Lisbon till she turned up at my house on Sunday evening. That was the damnable part of it."

"Damnable is indeed the word, especially for this poor child, in the event," the Monsignor said. He could guess at the details of the "awkward moment." "But can you explain one thing to me—how came the American to let her out of his sight?"

"That was my fault too," Richard said miserably. "He was with us the night Miss Probyn's car was crashed, and I promised to tell him what it was all about—or at least enough to make him careful; but what with one thing and another I never did. He isn't in the least to blame."

"I see—no."

A little silence fell, as they walked to and fro in the strong sunlight.

"If only there were something one could *do!*" Richard broke out.

"You could pray, of course, if you have that habit." Richard shook his head. The priest looked at him quizzically.

"Of course if you were a Catholic I could give you a swingeing penance," he said. "That would do you all the good in the world. But for a Protestant penitent, who doesn't even pray, I hardly know what to prescribe! I suggest that you go and do something to distract poor Mr. Waller —play billiards with him, or take him for a walk. Not in the least as a penance, he is too nice. And when you are alone—" he paused.

"Yes?"

"Reflect long and carefully on what your relations are to be with Countess Hetta, if by God's mercy she is restored to her friends, and to you. If you were to marry her, both her integrity and her naïveté would irritate you twenty times a week! Spend this time of suspense and distress in asking your heart whether you can school yourself to abide that with patience, and with *sweetness;* if you cannot, leave her alone."

He turned away and went into the house.

When the breakfast-party broke up Julia had gone first to find Dona Maria Francisca, and make her apologies both for returning so late, and for keeping Luzia out. Then, at last, the girl felt free to do what had been at the back of her mind all the morning, namely to ring up Mrs. Hathaway in Lisbon. They had so tormented the Duke with all their telephoning the previous day that she went straight to that inconvenient instrument by the pantry, and put through a call to the Hotel Lucrezia; she lit a cigarette and waited, perched on a case of wine. When the call came through she demanded Mrs. Hathaway, and presently heard that familiar voice.

"Darling Mrs. H., there you are at last! I only got your letter up here yesterday afternoon, just as I was going out; I meant to ring you up last night, but we didn't get back till one o'clock this morning. I am so sorry. How are you? Is the pub all right? I do wish I hadn't been away."

Mrs. Hathaway replied, cheerfully, that she was quite all right, and the hotel charming; also she had been astonished to see how *red* Portugal looked from the air—"like Devon—quite extraordinary!" Then as usual she brushed aside her own concerns to enquire into Julia's. "Dearest child, what *were* you doing, out till 1 a.m.? A ball? Was it fun?"

"No, it wasn't a ball, and it wasn't fun," Julia said sombrely. "I can't tell you properly now, but a quite darling girl has been carried off by perfectly *deadly* people, and we were chasing after her. You can probably guess for yourself who the deadliest people in the world are today!—well it's them, and we're all in agony till we get her back. I don't know when I can come down, Mrs. H. dear, with this going on."

"Was she carried off in a car?" Mrs. Hathaway asked sharply.

"Yes," Julia said a little surprised. "Why?" It wasn't like Mrs. Hathaway to ask futile questions.

"She isn't short and dark?—and her initials P.H. or H.P.?" Mrs. Hathaway pursued very briskly.

Julia was utterly amazed.

"Yes—yes to both. But how on earth do *you* know this?"

"I've got her here in my room in the hotel, at least I think it must be her. *Exquisite* H. and P. monograms on all her underclothes! The Doctor thinks she's been drugged, but he gave her an injection, and we've *poured* black coffee into her, and now she seems to be sleeping it off fairly naturally. There's a policeman outside my door, too, and another at the front door; they seem quite concerned about it."

"But why is she with you?" Julia asked weakly.

"Because when the car she was in rammed my taxi and we all got out, I saw her lying in the back, with a gag in her mouth, and I was worried. I *peeped*, you see," said Mrs. Hathaway, in a satisfied voice. "So I got them to let me have her carried up to my room in the hotel, and made that nice police official, who speaks such *good* English, get a doctor. I really couldn't let her be left to the police."

"Well!" said Julia—all other words failed her.

"Oh, here's the police officer again—I think I must ring off," Mrs. Hathaway said. "I'll ring you up later."

"No, *wait*, for goodness sake!" Julia protested. "I must—"

But Mrs. Hathaway, implacably, had rung off.

Julia sank down again on the wine-case. After a moment she got up. "Hugh must hear this," she murmured as she walked towards the hall; and then, "How *like* Mrs. H.!" She was all astray, between relief, astonishment, and uncertainty; but Colonel Marques could soon settle whether it *was* or was not Hetta Páloczy whom Mrs. Hathaway was, so improbably, nursing in her room in the Lucrezia.

"Anyhow if it *is* her, that's Father Antal's Mass," Julia said out loud, as she stepped into the hall.

CHAPTER XIV

Mrs. Hathaway, descending from the sky at Portela airport on that Monday afternoon, soon registered that her young friend Julia Probyn, at whose instance she had decided to visit Portugal at all, was not there to meet her. Resigned and calm, she submitted quietly to the inquisitions of the Portuguese Customs, and presently, by air-line bus and taxi, found herself at the hotel recommended by Mr. Consett. There she lay down and rested in the double-bedded room which the management, untruthfully, said was all they had free; later she took a bath, and went down and had a very good dinner. Afterwards she caused the hall-porter to ring up the Ericeira Palace—which created a great impression—and learned that the Duke with all his party had left for Gralheira two days before. Still resigned, she decided to start looking at Lisbon by herself, and told the porter to order a taxi to be at the hotel at 9:15 next morning to take her to Belém to see the Tower, the Jeronimos Church, and the Museum of the Coaches; she also ordered *petit déjeuner* for half-past eight. Then she went to bed, and slept the sleep of the just and the sensible.

The taxi was a little late, and Mrs. Hathaway first bought a camellia from a man on the pavement with a tray of them for what seemed to her nothing, and then stood at the door of the hotel watching with interest the brisk morning bustle of traffic in the street: cars and taxis shooting by in the bright sunshine, women in black mantillas returning from Mass, and, what completely charmed her, the *varinhas*, the women fish-sellers, striding up barefoot from the river-side markets with shallow oval baskets of fish balanced on their heads, their shoes perched casually on top of the fish. The Lisbon City Fathers wage an unequal contest with the *varinhas* over this matter of shoes: they hold that barefooted women in the streets of a capital create an impression of poverty and backwardness, and insist on shoes; the fishwives, who have always walked barefoot and prefer it—and anyhow how much more economical!—conform to the point of having shoes with them; but they habitually carry these objects not on their feet but on the fish, a charming piece of individualism in our regimented modern world.

When the taxi finally arrived the hall-porter handed Mrs. Hathaway into it with the deference due to someone who telephoned to the Duke of Ericeira's, gave the requisite instructions to the driver, and slammed the door; Mrs. Hathaway drove off, full of the happy anticipation of the intelligent sightseer in a strange city on a fine morning.

She did not get very far. Less than a hundred yards from the door of the hotel a large grey car, shooting out of a side turning, collided with her taxi; both vehicles were slewed round sideways by the force of the impact and came to a halt, partly blocking the steep and crowded street. Three men in grey overcoats leapt out of the car, cursing and gesticulating at their driver—their fury surprised Mrs. Hathaway; her taxi-man got out too and examined the damage, shrugging his shoulders phlegmatically. Cars started to hoot angrily; a little crowd gathered round the accident, and a small, neatly-uniformed policeman came up and began to ask questions.

It was at this point that Mrs. Hathaway, realising that she would certainly not reach Belém in this particular taxi, got out of it. The calm demeanour of the little policeman impressed her, but she was struck afresh by the fury, almost desperation, of the three men when the policeman produced a note-book and began, obviously, to demand names and addresses, while two more of his colleagues appeared from nowhere. It was probably this curious display of emotion, combined with her natural curiosity, which caused the good lady to "peep" into the other car; there to her immense astonishment she saw, lying across the back seat, what she at first took to be the corpse of a young girl, white and motionless.

After that there was of course no holding Mrs. Hathaway. She opened the door to examine this corpse more closely; took a wrist and felt a very faint pulse—moreover, she then noticed, projecting from one corner of the pallid lips, a piece of material. Rather gingerly she pulled at it; the lax jaws allowed her to draw out a sizeable piece of some rough, coarse, rather dirty rag, sodden and disgusting. Mrs. Hathaway stared at it incredulously; then quietly put it in her handbag, from which at the same time she drew out her Portuguese phrase-book, and stood for a moment ruffling the pages, looking for words which would enable her to say— "There is a young lady who has been gagged in this *automóvel*." Unfortunately phrase-books seldom contain information of that sort, and after a few seconds of fruitless search Mrs. Hathaway decided to rely on English and on herself, and went to tackle the policeman.

By now the crowd had concentrated round this worthy, his colleagues, and the three furious men in the grey overcoats; the group was joined by an elegant slender man in a green uniform at the very moment when Mrs. Hathaway, tall, grey-haired and imposing, lifted up her voice and said— "Does anyone here speak English?"

"I do, Madame," said the man in green. "Can I help you? Or you have information to offer?"

"Yes, a little information. But I think you should put those three men under control immediately—the ones in grey."

Police in all countries, but especially in the Latin ones, make a regular practice of stalling in any emergency; as she spoke Mrs. Hathaway saw incredulity appear on the face of the official in green.

"Oh very well; never mind. Just come here"—and taking the elegant man by his green elbow she propelled him firmly towards the grey car and opened the door. "Look there." While he stared in at the helpless form on the back seat Mrs. Hathaway opened her handbag and drew out the piece of rag. "Please look at this, too," she said—"I myself pulled it out of her mouth not two minutes ago."

The official in green picked the horrid object up in gloved fingers, and examined it.

"You say this was in her mouth?"

"Yes. I saw it and pulled it out. My taxi was run into by this car," Mrs. Hathaway stated in explanation, "and I thought the behaviour of the men in it so very odd that I looked and found this girl—gagged. To *me* it seems rather abnormal; but of course I am a stranger to Portugal."

The man threw her a shrewd glance.

"This is abnormal in Portugal also, Madame, believe me," he said.

"Well, what are you going to do? Oughtn't she to have attention? She's alive, I felt her pulse; but I think she's very ill. Can't I take her into my hotel and look after her while you make your enquiries? I think a doctor should see her."

Mrs. Hathaway saw the expression of official obstructiveness reappear in the man's face.

"Where is your hotel, Madame?" he asked.

"The Lucrezia—it's just up there."

"This young lady is known to you?"

"Not in the least! I've just found her. But she's ill, and needs help. Isn't that sufficient?"

"Your charity does you credit, Madame," the man in green said smoothly, still stalling. "But this is obviously a case for police enquiries and the utmost caution; and frankly, I have no idea who you are."

"Of course not," Mrs. Hathaway replied, as smoothly as he. She took her passport from her bag and handed it to him. "Naturally this tells you nothing but that I am an English visitor," she pursued, still smoothly. "If you want further credentials I suggest that you ring up Gralheira, the Duke of Ericeira's country-house; my friend Miss Probyn, who is staying there at present, can tell you all about me—I have come to Portugal at her invitation."

This told, Mrs. Hathaway saw the green-clad official prick up his ears at the mention of the Duke's name, though he said nothing except to ask how to spell PROBYN while he jotted down notes in a pocket-book.

"Thank you, Madame," he said politely. "This shall be done."

"Yes, but what about this poor girl? You can't just leave her lying in a car in the street while you telephone; it's monstrous! Do let us get her into bed, and call a doctor. I certainly shall not run away, and she *can't*."

Mrs. Hathaway's mixture of common sense and imperiousness might have prevailed anyhow; combined with the Ericeira connection they did —though slowly. The official summoned yet another policeman to watch over the grey car, and invited Mrs. Hathaway to wait in it, which she did; he asked for her room-number at the hotel, and went away. From the car window Mrs. Hathaway saw the three men in grey being led off in custody; then she waited. At last a stretcher was brought and the uncon- scious girl placed on it and carried to the Lucrezia, accompanied by the man in the green uniform and Mrs. Hathaway; she noticed that a police- man now stood at the entrance to the hotel, and when they reached her bedroom another was standing outside the door.

"Oh, excellent," Mrs. Hathaway said. "Will he stay?"

"Yes, he will stay," the official replied, with the hint of a smile.

Mrs. Hathaway had the unknown girl placed on her own bed. "I *know* this is aired," she said. "Can you arrange to have a doctor sent immedi- ately?"

"I will. And will you, Madame, be on the look out for any marks or labels which might identify this young lady?—and if she speaks note down what she says?"

"Of course. The Doctor must speak *French*," Mrs. Hathaway added firmly. "I know no Portuguese."

"He shall," the official said, now smiling openly. "Au revoir, Madame; I shall return soon."

One of the Portuguese words Mrs. Hathaway had carefully memorized on the plane was *boracha*, which means hot-water bottle; she used it freely now, while she took off the girl's overcoat and suit and removed her shoes, stockings, and suspender-belt; and soon several *borachas*, carefully wrapped in towels, had been disposed all round the figure in the bed. It was during these operations that Mrs. Hathaway's attention was caught by the beauty of the monograms with H.P. on the delicate underclothes. She had only just finished when the doctor arrived, a tall man with an intelligent square face who spoke, not French, but extremely good English. He felt the pulse, lifted the eyelids, put a stethoscope to the heart, and turned to Mrs. Hathaway.

"Drugged!" he pronounced.

"What with?"

"I don't know." He drew back the bed-clothes again, examined the bare arms, and showed a tiny pink spot to Mrs. Hathaway. "An injection here, do you see?"

"Well, what do I do?"

"You order black coffee, very strong, and when it comes make her drink it. I will give an injection; I am guessing, but it is probably a barbiturate."

While the doctor prepared his injection Mrs. Hathaway rang the bell; when a servant appeared she said, "Doctor, will you order the coffee? They may not understand me." The doctor gabbled vigorously in Portuguese, and then asked Mrs. Hathaway to turn the helpless body onto its side—she did so, and he jabbed a needle into the buttock; then he turned the girl back onto the pillows and washed his instruments. As he was finishing the coffee appeared, brought by a waiter. Mrs. Hathaway tasted it.

"Yes, that's quite strong, but I shall want someone to hold her up while I get it down," she said. "Will you have a chambermaid sent, please?"

Like the police official, the doctor smiled.

"Madame, you are a hospital in yourself! Perhaps you have nursing training?"

"Certainly not—just common sense," said Mrs. Hathaway rather repressively, as she pushed the bell. When it was answered the doctor demanded the manager, and on his appearing, nervous and troubled by all these goings-on, the doctor asked him to send "a strong and discreet" chambermaid, to assist the Senhora Inglesa in carrying out his treatment. "Let her bring a small basin," he added. Then he bowed over Mrs. Hathaway's hand.

"I shall return in an hour or two, but continue with the coffee; give it over and over again," he said. "It is the best of all antidotes. If she is sick, so much the better—that will help to clear off the poison."

Only those who have actually undergone the experience of trying to restore a drugged person to life—fortunately they are few—can realise what Mrs. Hathaway now went through. To begin with it was all quite new to her—far more than the doctor she was "guessing"—and moreover she had to carry out this unwonted task labouring under the terrible sense

of helplessness engendered by being in a country where one cannot speak
the language, a thing quite extraordinarily defeating. When an elderly
chambermaid with a severe and rather negroid face appeared, carrying a
small enamel bowl, Mrs. Hathaway had to indicate to her by signs that
they must lift the inert figure up to drink the coffee, which she had already
cooled in the wash-basin; but an unconscious person is astonishingly heavy
and clumsy to handle, and though when Mrs. Hathaway pushed the
flaccid lips open and held the cup to them the girl gulped and swallowed
automatically, a lot was spilt—the maid clucked in dismay at the dirtied
sheets.

"Bring the bath-towel," Mrs. Hathaway said, but of course the woman
didn't understand; she went and fetched it herself, but by the time she
returned to the bed the flabby body had collapsed again. Patiently Mrs.
Hathaway heaved it up once more and placed the maid's hands under the
clammy armpits—"Hold her *so,*" she said, with an emphasis which tran-
scended language, while she spread the bath-towel in front of the girl and
placed a soft shawl over her bare shoulders. Then she applied the cup
again.

They kept on at it for what seemed like an eternity to Mrs. Hathaway.
Before the first lot of coffee was exhausted she sent for another; halfway
through the second brew the girl was sick—Mrs. Hathaway held out the
basin almost in time, but not quite; the maid clucked again, but very
intelligently hustled out and returned with fresh bath-towels, shortly followed by a waiter with yet more coffee. So they went on: the girl gulping
down, being sick, gulping down again. At last the vomiting ceased, and
it seemed to Mrs. Hathaway that the swallowing was performed more
consciously; still guessing, she decided that they had done enough for
the moment, and shook her head when the chambermaid held out the
coffee-tray questioningly. The pulse seemed to her stronger; quite definitely
the hands were getting warm, and that chilly perspiration had stopped.
She put another blanket over the girl, and drawing an armchair up to the
bed sat down in it; she suddenly felt extraordinarily tired.

But she had only been resting for five minutes when she was summoned
by a page to the telephone. The Hotel Lucrezia has one of these on each
landing, and edging out past the small policeman Mrs. Hathaway took the
call from Julia Probyn already recorded; in the middle of it the official in
green re-appeared, and Mrs. Hathaway, ignoring Julia's protests, rang off.

"How is she?" he asked.

"Better, I think. Come in," Mrs. Hathaway said, once more by-passing
the policeman, who raised his hand in salute to the officer.

"She has not spoken?" the man said, after glancing at the figure on the bed.

"No—and as she seems to be sleeping fairly naturally I think she should be left alone. But I rather *think*, from what I heard on the telephone just now, that she was abducted by Communists."

The official suddenly became very alert.

"May I know to whom you were telephoning?"

"I wasn't, at all. My friend Miss Probyn rang me up from Gralheira. But she said that they had been out half the night chasing after a girl who had been carried off by Communists; so I asked if she was short and dark, and whether her initials were H. and P.? And Miss Probyn said she was, and they were," Mrs. Hathaway said, not very lucidly.

"These are the initials, H.P.?"

"Yes, they're on all her underclothes."

"No papers in her pockets?"

"Oh really, Senhor, I didn't look," Mrs. Hathaway protested. "I have been trying to revive her! I'm not a detective! Do by all means search her clothes yourself."

The official slid a practised hand into the pockets of M. Lilas's trim little suit and the pretty matching overcoat, and drew out a rather grubby handkerchief, and a tiny copy of St. Thomas à Kempis; the hanky bore the monogram H.P., and on the fly-leaf of *The Imitation of Christ* was written—"P.H. from H.A., Easter, 1953."

"So!" the green-clad official said, thoughtfully. "H.A.—or A.H., perhaps. The other initials are reversed also." He put the little book in his pocket. "Please excuse me if I leave you now. I must make a report."

"*No,*" Mrs. Hathaway said firmly. "I see you have learned something. Do *you* think that this is the girl Miss Probyn was hunting for last night? If so I think you ought to tell me what you found out?"

At this the green-clad official laughed out loud.

"Madame, you are *impayable!* In strict confidence I may tell you that we believe the three men we hold to be what you suspect."

"And my patient? What does H.A. or A.H. tell you? Something, I can see."

But here the man in green was firm.

"Madame, I am sorry that I can really tell you no more at present. But I am most grateful for what you have done. If the young lady becomes sufficiently conscious to speak, please ask her her name and anything she can tell you of what happened to her—especially as to whether she was questioned, and revealed any facts under pressure. This could be of the

utmost importance, and the sooner we know it the better." He drew out a
small card on which was printed—

"T. Soubrinho de Almeida." On this he scribbled a telephone number,
and handed it to Mrs. Hathaway.

"If you will have this number rung up and mention my name, I or
another officer who speaks English will come round immediately. But I
cannot impress on you sufficiently that the very greatest discretion is essential. As you see, I am reposing great confidence in you," he ended, and
bowed and went away.

Mrs. Hathaway returned to her chair by the bed. She asked the grim
chambermaid her name—most unsuitably, it was Flora—and indicated by
signs that she would ring four times if she wanted any more assistance;
the woman departed, and Mrs. Hathaway sat reflecting on what she had
just heard. The man in the green uniform certainly knew more than he
was willing to say. Well quite soon she must ring Julia up again—she had
promised to—and then she might learn more; but she would rest a little
first. That struggle to get the coffee down had been quite exhausting; it
was so *tiresome,* how fatigue got the better of one as one grew older. Thinking how tiresome old age and fatigue were, Mrs. Hathaway, in her armchair, fell into a doze.

When Julia Probyn got up off the wine-case outside the pantry at Gralheira her first intention had been to tell Major Torrens what she had
heard, but in the hall she changed her mind and went along the corridor
to the priests' study. To relieve Father Antal's anxiety was more important
than anything else; if the girl in Mrs. Hathaway's room *was* Hetta she was
safe anyhow, with the indomitable Mrs. H. in charge, and English-
speaking police officers—damn the man, turning up just then!—popping in
and out.

Father Antal was alone. The Monsignor was still giving Atherley the
treatment out in the knot-garden; beyond the high windows their figures
could be seen passing to and fro. The old Hungarian was sitting at the
table, his head sunk in his hands; he raised it as Julia came in.

"Dom Francisco, I think it's *almost* certain that she's safe!" Julia said,
going over to him.

He got up, slowly.

"Why 'almost,' my child?" he asked, rather heavily.

Julia told him all that Mrs. Hathaway had said, and asked, and how
their conversation had been interrupted.

"Drugged, and cannot speak!—poor soul, whoever she is. And who is
this lady who so charitably took her in?"

"The best person in the world! She's been all the mother I've had since my own mother died."

He considered. "Still, it is not sure," he said at length.

"Dear Dom Francisco" (Julia automatically used the agreed name) "don't you think it *is* pretty sure? Granted that there might easily be two, or even three short dark girls in Portugal who have H.P. embroidered on their underclothes, would any of them but Hetti be likely to be found drugged and gagged in a car? I don't see how it *can* be anyone but her."

He smiled at her conviction.

"You have made a good point. Yes, I believe I agree. Let us give thanks to God."

"Oh, I do!—or rather I will in a minute, when I've told Major Torrens. I just wanted to let you know, Father dear." She hurried away.

The smoking-room at Gralheira was an apartment seldom used except on the rare occasions when the Duke entertained a shooting-party, and Torrens had more or less appropriated it to his own use. As Julia went in at the door Atherley was in the act of entering by the French window; in obedience to the Monsignor's instructions he had come in search of Townsend Waller. Townsend was not there. "He went out," the Major told Richard.

"All right, I'll go and find him."

"No, wait, Richard—you'd better hear this too," Julia said.

"Don't say you have some news?" Torrens asked.

"Well, near-news, anyhow." She recounted what she had heard on the telephone. Richard said, "Oh, thank God!"—the Major, like Father Antal, asked who on earth Mrs. Hathaway was?

"Oh, a darling—and just the sort of person who *would* go and look in the other car when she'd been crashed in an accident!" Julia said.

"Well, whatever it's worth, I think the Colonel ought to hear it," Torrens said temperately.

"Let's find out first if the poor Duque is in his study." Julia rang the bell as she spoke. Elidio, who answered it, said that His Excellency was gone out to the vineyards to examine the vines.

"*Muito bem, Elidio—muito obrigada*. All right; he's out," she said.

"*Which* of these accursed machines gets the exchange?" Torrens asked gloomily, surveying the array of telephones on the Duke's desk with distaste.

"Well really, Hugh, by now you ought to remember that much!" Julia said laughing—her own conviction that Hetta was safe had put her into the highest spirits. "Second from the right."

It was getting on for noon when Major Torrens got through to Colonel

Marques. He made a guarded beginning: "I think perhaps we have some news of the lost lady." The Colonel interrupted him.

"Oh, the little identifier! Yes, I know," he said breezily. "She is in the care of this admirable lady, who nevertheless did not think to look in her pockets! One of my men did so, however; he found a book with an inscription which I think makes the matter certain—but to leave nothing to chance I have sent a car to fetch the maid-servant from a certain place, to make the identification absolute."

Torrens asked about the men who were with "the identifier" when the so lucky accident took place. The Colonel was still breezy.

"Just the ones we wanted, and expected!—three. We are holding them; their papers are not quite in order!" Torrens could hear the pleasure in the Colonel's tones. "But one is missing; the principal, I am afraid. I must ask you not to relax *any* precautions; after all, the little person in question was only a means to an end, and the *end* is still with you. I will ring you up again when the identification is confirmed; in the meantime I must ask you to be very watchful." He rang off.

Torrens had just begun to retail all this to Atherley and Julia when the Duke walked in with Luzia. He was delighted at the news of Hetta Páloczy's almost certain safety, and fascinated by Julia's account of her rescue. "But this must be a most remarkable lady!"

"Oh, she is!" Julia responded. Torrens however was particularly concerned to impress on his hearers what Colonel Marques had said about the escape of "the principal," and the importance of relaxing no precautions; he did so at some length. Atherley saw Luzia listening to this intently, her grey eyes very wide.

"Yes yes, of course we will continue to observe all our rules," the Duke was saying a little impatiently when Dona Maria Francisca sidled in—her manner of entering a room always gave the impression that she felt it immodest to walk straight forwards. "Yes, *ma chère?*" her brother asked.

"I only came to enquire—I hear there has been telephoning—whether we are to expect the young Countess today?"

"No, not today, my dear sister. I will advise you of her advent in good time."

Dona Maria Francisca looked disapproving; she muttered something about the notice yesterday having been very short, and when the room was prepared, after all no one came.

"Yes, the American came," Luzia piped up. "And now also Atherley!" —looking with great satisfaction at Richard, who grinned back at her. Luzia was a source of endless pleasure to him.

When Dona Maria Francisca sidled out again she took the reluctant girl with her. Before the door closed they heard Luzia's voice from the hall—"Go in, go in; there is good news; she is safe!"—and Townsend Waller appeared.

"Is it really all right to come in, Duke?" he asked apologetically. "And it is true that the little Countess is safe?"

Torrens told him that it was almost certainly true, and how it had come about.

"But it's not a hundred per cent certain yet?" the American asked doubtfully.

"Yes, Townsend, it really is a hundred per cent," Julia assured him. "It's only a police fuss, sending for the maid. Don't worry."

The Duke was pursuing a train of thought of his own.

"As soon as the young lady is well enough to travel, should she not come here?"

Before anyone else could answer, Atherley said, "Yes, Sir; she ought to come as soon as possible." He was still acutely conscious of his own responsibility for Hetta's misadventure. "The whole reason for her making this expedition at all was to see Father A."—he checked himself.

Townsend stared at him in bewilderment.

"Father A.? Who's he? She never said a word about any Father; she just said she was upset about something, and to take her mind off it she wanted to see the North, and to call on some friends."

Julia intervened.

"She was only being discreet, Townsend," she said with kindness. "People get to be, you know, when they live under the Communists. But the friend she most wanted to visit up here was one of the two priests you saw at breakfast."

"Not Subercaseaux, for goodness sake!" the Bostonian exploded incredulously.

"No, the other one," Julia said. She turned to the Duke.

"When Hetta is better, since you are so kind, we can arrange for her to come up. Now we'll stop invading your study! Come on," she said to the three men. "Let's go and put Townsend properly in the picture—it's high time."

This briefing was conducted in the smoking-room. Julia took upon herself to expound to Mr. Waller how Father Antal had been got out of Hungary, and the necessity for his having ample opportunity to report to Rome through Mgr Subercaseaux—"he's the Vatican contact, you see. Then Father Antal will go on to the States and do things there, broadcasting and so on." The mere name of the Vatican was slightly repugnant to Townsend Waller, who belonged to the straitest sect of the Unitarian Pharisees of New England, but he took the point all right.

"I remember seeing a cable about some high-powered agent who was to be got out of here by plane; our Security people were to send someone over to meet him, but I didn't register exactly when."

"Well the priest we're calling Dom Francisco *is* the high-powered agent," Torrens said; "and the escort will fly over to meet him when I tell my opposite number in your outfit that we're ready—he'll cable for him, and your Security man will be here in thirty-six hours."

Waller reflected for a moment or two.

"What I don't quite see is why you British are handling this here, if he's coming to the States, and being flown across by our people," he said then, looking rather straight at Torrens.

"I think I can tell you why, Townsend," Richard put in before the Major could answer. "This is a small, but a very explosive operation where Europe is concerned, and one that has had to be organised hand-in-hand with the Catholic net-work over here. And though your Catholic net-work is much wider than ours, it's looser mesh!" He smiled very pleasantly at his friend. "As one Protestant to another, I expect you'd agree that European Catholics during these last years have become admirably security-minded—they've had to; the English ones of course have been ever since the days of Good Queen Bess! And security was Word Number One, in this."

Townsend looked a little uncertain.

"But is *he* a Catholic?" he asked, glancing at Torrens.

"No," Richard said, laughing. "But he's been working in with them now for a long time, and they know him. It was just a case of how to get the job done in the safest way. Maclean or no Maclean," he added with a grin.

Townsend, who was far from a fool, and moreover had the admirable quality of great honesty, took the point.

"I see," he said. "Yes, that makes sense." Suddenly he too grinned, ruefully and disarmingly. "Well seeing I was stupid enough to lose Countess Hetta, I suppose I must let you say what you like about wide mesh! But you never told me what it was all about, Richard, as you promised to; if you had, I wouldn't have been so careless."

"I know. I've told you I'm sorry about that," Richard said.

A gong boomed, the preliminary summons to luncheon. "Goodness, where's the morning gone?" Julia exclaimed, and went upstairs to attend to her face.

It was shortly after lunch that Mrs. Hathaway, as promised, rang up again; Julia took the call outside the pantry—"Oh, the inconvenience!"

she muttered bitterly. The girl was now conscious, Mrs. Hathaway said; the doctor had been again, and said that she was quite all right.

"And has the servant been?—is she really who we thought?" Julia asked.

"Oh yes, there's no doubt about that; she *is* your friend."

"Is she fit to travel?"

"Oh, do you want her? The little fat man thought perhaps you might." (By the little fat man Julia guessed that Colonel Marques was meant.) "Not today, but tomorrow I think she could."

"Is she going back to her mother, or staying with you?"

"She will stay with me tonight anyhow. The fat man seemed to think it better, and of course I like having her; now she's awake, she's charming. But she seems very troubled about something she's said, or done—I wish I could get her mind off it."

This is it, Julia thought; she *has* given something away, poor little wretch. Down the telephone—"I couldn't speak to her, could I?" she asked. "Is she still in bed?"

"Oh no, she's up and dressed. I'll see. But this isn't a very *convenient* place—it's out on the landing, and there's that man at the door, and people going up and downstairs all the time. Wait a minute."

Even more inconvenient than here, Julia thought, grinning to herself, as she sat down again on the wine-case, the receiver at the full stretch of the flex held to her ear. There was a long pause. At last—

"Here she is," said Mrs. Hathaway's voice. "I'm sorry to have been so long, but the bobby—I'm sure you understand me—didn't want her to leave the room, or use the telephone. I got the manager to overpersuade him, but it took some time. I've told her not to use any names. Now!"

And then Julia heard Hetti's rather deep voice saying—"Is it you?"

"Yes, darling. How good to hear you! Are you all right again?"

"Yes yes, quite all right. But oh Yulia, I am so miserable! I have done a terrible thing. Only I cannot tell you about it on the telephone."

"No no—for goodness sake don't try!" Julia said hastily. "I shall be seeing you very soon; either I'll come down, or you will come up. Do you understand?"

"Yes, I do. Is *he* still with you?"

"Of course. Tell Mrs. H. she will be rung up later about plans."

"Please? Mrs. Who?"

"Oh, the lady you're with, silly! Ask *her* her name!" Julia said impatiently —to her relief she heard Hetta laugh.

"She is an *angel!*" the girl said fervently.

"I know she is. Goodbye. Do exactly what she tells you, and don't worry."

"Yulia, I *must* worry! And please be so careful, because of what I have done."

"All right. Now you do what you're told! Bless you. Goodbye."

After ringing off Julia went at once in pursuit of Major Torrens. She had some difficulty in finding him. Richard, still anxious to implement the Monsignor's recommendation to do something to distract Townsend Waller had offered to take the American round that remarkable house, and Torrens had gone with them. She ran the party to earth at last in one of the huge salons, full of Boulle and Empire furniture; as she went in the Major was commenting in some astonishment on the fact that though the room contained seventeen armchairs there were only two table lamps, both heavily veiled in grey crêpe-de-chine. "How on earth do they *read?*" he asked.

"Oh, the women don't much; anyhow no one ever sits in here," Julia told him. "Listen, Hugh—Hetta's all right again, quite fit to come up to-morrow, so we must settle how to get her here. Should I go down in Richard's car?—if I might?"—glancing at Atherley.

The two young men broke into eager enquiries, which Julia answered rather brusquely. "Yes, *perfectly* all right; I spoke to her. But for goodness sake be quiet for a minute and let me settle this with Hugh." She pursued the thing with Torrens. "She's given something away, I gather."

"What?"

"Of course I wouldn't let her tell me. I presume simply that Father Antal is here—she begged me to be very careful. And I imagine, too, that by now the pavement outside the Lucrezia is stiff with Commie agents, disguised as camellia-sellers!" Julia ended, with vigour.

Torrens laughed. "We'd better consult the Colonel," he said. "Where's the Duke? Out, please God."

The Duke was out.

"Spilt some beans, has she?" the Colonel said, displaying his usual pleasure in using English slang. "Well no wonder. Was she tortured?" Torrens couldn't say. "In any case, you and her friends are much more likely than I am to find out what she *has* said, and it would be useful to know—*precisely*, please, if she can remember. But people under torture are apt to forget what they have said; it is part of the psychological blotting-out of distress."

Those words, so casually uttered, caused Major Torrens to shiver a little. He knew that Communists do use such methods, and merely said—

"The thing is how to get the person in question up here. Miss P. thought of going down to fetch her, in the car in which she brought me up."

"Oh, do not let her go to this trouble! Why not allow this admirable

Englishwoman who succours her—and to whom we owe the fact that the young person was discovered so soon—to bring her up? I can supply a car and chauffeur, which will be closely followed by another car with my own men. No one knows the old lady by sight, and *la petite* can wear a veil, as she did at Portela. Can Miss P. arrange this at your end? I gather she is the contact for the Englishwoman."

"Hold on," Torrens said, and spoke to Julia.

"Of course. Lovely! The Duque will adore Mrs. H.—and so will you. Say *Yes*."

CHAPTER XV

MAJOR TORRENS thankfully left it to Julia to organise the reception of these extra guests. How on earth, without her, could all this have been managed? A perfect hide-out, too, with those high walls all round the place. In the circumstances he did not worry over-much about what the poor wretched little Countess might have given away.

Julia took no immediate steps. The Duke was out on the farm, and Nanny usually had a shut-eye in the afternoon. She observed with amusement that both Hetta's admirers showed every sign of remaining where they were—"Oh very well!" she muttered to herself, as she went in search of Father Antal.

She found the dear old man in the priests' study, just about to set out for a walk; he looked rather like Hilaire Belloc, arrayed in an extraordinary cloak with a shoulder-cape and a broad-brimmed hat, produced by the Monsignor as chaplain-disguise; he had a breviary in his hand.

"Oh, you are going out?"

"Yes—will you not come too? It is a most beautiful day," he said, smiling on her.

"Well, just a little way—I have some good news for you," she said, stepping through the open French window. The sun stood high and hot over the knot-garden, bringing out the aromatic woody scent of the tiny box-bushes; men with rakes were smoothing the walks between them. "Let's go into the park," Julia suggested.

They descended by the flight of steps near the corner seat with the *azulejo* picture of the hunter being treed by a bear; as they walked over short pastures, where sheep were grazing, Julia told Father Antal that the girl at the Lucrezia was undoubtedly Hetta, that she was nearly recovered, and was coming up to Gralheira tomorrow. His delight at this news moved her a good deal. "Tell me more about Hetti, Father," she said.

He told her, obviously happy to be asked, how Hetta had come to his country presbytery as the protégée of the poor incompetent old nun, and how promptly and energetically the girl of sixteen had taken over the running of the house, the cooking, and all the dealings with people who came for help or advice when he was out. "This poor Mother Scholastica could seldom get a message right!—but Hetta always had everything clear for me. In no time at all it was the old religieuse who was really *her* protégée; but she never failed in showing her all deference and respect. This dear child followed so completely the example of our Blessed Lord—she 'took on her the form of a servant.' And so happily, and with obedience."

"That's funny—I can't see Hetti very obedient," Julia said.

"In one thing she was *not*," the priest replied, smiling reminiscently. "I could not stop her, in summer, from going to swim in the Tisza—in her night-dress! She went in the afternoons, when in the great heat there was no one about in the fields, but it was unsuitable; however, in this she would not be controlled. She had the passion for water of a little fish!"

Julia had begun to tell him of Hetta's swimming at the Guincho when suddenly Father Antal stood still and held up his hand, enjoining silence. "What is this sound?" he asked.

Julia listened too. "Oh, that's from the windmill," she said, now hearing the "clock, clock, clock, clock" that filled the sunny air. "Look, there it is, just over the wall."

They had reached the eastern boundary wall of the demesne; a narrow iron gate, heavily padlocked, led through into the open country outside, where the four blunt-ended sails of a whitewashed windmill revolved rhythmically, clock-ing at each revolution. Father Antal went and stared through the iron bars.

"Is this the mill of the miller whom they call The Blacksmith?" he asked.

"Yes," Julia said. "How on earth do you know that?"

"Luzia told me." He continued to peer through the bars. "Is this he, this old man who digs?" he asked.

Julia also looked through the gate. A rather bent figure, using the outsize hoe which in Portugal takes the place of a spade, was diligently turning up the reddish-brown soil. Europe is divided into the races which dig *away* from themselves, as in France and England, and those who dig *towards* themselves, as in Portugal.

"Yes, that's him."

"It is true—he does not look round as he digs," Father Antal said. "Luzia was quite right."

"She's usually right, about country things especially," Julia replied.

The sound of their voices did cause the miller to look round, not at his mill, but towards the gate; seeing Julia he waved.

"*Boas tardes!* (Good afternoon) *Minha Menina,*" he called.

"*Como estai, O Ferreiro?*" Julia called back. *Ferreiro* is the Portuguese word for blacksmith; the old man, grinning at this greeting, shouldered his heavy tool and walked over to the small gate, quite ready to break his toil with a little gossip. He asked who the priest was?

One of the Duke's chaplains from the house, Julia told him promptly, but foreign—he spoke no Portuguese. The miller expressed regret. "I could have wished to speak with him; he has the countenance of a saint." Not being able to converse with the saint he asked after Luzia, and then broke into a paean of her praises. "Ah, there is one who has all the loving-kindness of *a mãe* and the intelligence of *o pai*. A noble child!"

Julia translated this for Father Antal as they turned homewards: loving as her mother, intelligent as her father; she knew it would please him.

"Yes, she is a noble child," he said. After a moment's silence he asked suddenly—"How well do you know my little Hetta? Have you seen much of her?"

His train of thought was obvious to Julia—for him Hetta was another noble child.

"I haven't seen as much of her as I should have liked," she said. "What I have seen I like very much." This sounded cold and inadequate, and she added quickly—"I think she's intelligent, and brave, and very honest; perhaps too honest for her own comfort, let alone that of the people about her."

He laughed. "You are very right! How often I have seen this in my own house. She would give me, as I told you, a perfectly clear message from some peasant; but when I asked what she had said in reply, nine times out of ten her answer would be—"I told him not to be a fool, and not to bother you!"

Julia could hear Hetta saying it.

"And this young Englishman?" Father Antal pursued—"What is he like? Is he serious, good? You must know him well—I notice that you call him Richard."

"That means nothing. Everyone calls everyone Richard or whatever their name is, if they don't call them 'darling,'" Julia said rather impatiently. "I don't know him particularly well, though I've known him for some time. He's intelligent too, as you can see, and rather unusually open-minded for a diplomat, but I've no idea whether he's 'serious' or not; in fact I'm not sure that I know what you mean by serious. 'Sérieux,' in the French sense?"

"Yes."

"Well no, I shouldn't have thought he was; rather *volage*, really. But I do think he's seriously in love with Hetta—I suspect for the first time in his life! Funny, isn't it? Because I imagine his other affairs have been with middle-aged married women who never put a foot wrong socially."

The priest stared at her.

"You know of Madame de Vermeil, then?" he asked in surprise.

"No—who's she? One of the middle-aged mistresses?"

Julia had merely been guessing, rather shrewdly, at the component parts of Atherley's love-life hitherto—she gurgled with pleasure when Father Antal burst out laughing at her last question.

"Miss Probyn, I think you must be a witch!" he said.

"The last person who thought I was a witch was a half-caste barkeeper in Tangier!" she exclaimed gaily. "But one needn't to be a witch to spot the normal line of a person like Atherley. All the same, I do think he's really nice, underneath all the diplomatic stuff; if he were to marry Hetta, though they'd have a rough passage at first, I think she might be the making of him."

"You answer my questions before I put them," the old man said, bending a benignant smile on her. "Witches I believe wait to be asked; so probably you are something better than a witch—wise! I speak openly to you. While this child lived in my house I came to love her dearly; now she has left my care and my world, and I know as little of her new world, and the people in it, as I know of the great geographical New World to which I soon go, and of the people in that—though I confess that I dread this experience! So I seek to learn all I can about her surroundings."

"Well of course her mother is a perfectly *pestilential* woman, in my opinion," Julia said flatly. "Anything to get Hetta away from old Dorothée."

"You mean, even take something of a risk in marrying this young man? Is he, in your opinion, *fundamentally* able to love her and value her?"

Julia reflected before answering.

"He *loves* her, anyhow," she said. "You'd only to watch his face this morning to see that. I fancy he did something frightfully stupid which made her come rushing up here with Townsend—the American; and he's been in agony over it. But as for being capable of valuing her—honestly, Father, one has to take some risks in any marriage; you can't expect safety on a plate! If she's in love with him—and I think she is—I should say they'd better marry as soon as possible, take a *long* honeymoon, and Richard get himself transferred to some other post in the meantime, out of the way of the old Countess."

He smiled at this blue-print for Hetta's future. "Thank you. I believe I agree with you," he said.

"Good." She paused for a moment and then added—"As Hetta's Father in God, couldn't you tip her off to be a little less uncompromising herself, and bottle up her prejudices? It really won't do in diplomacy for her to tell her husband's visitors not to be fools!"

"I had it in mind to do this," the priest said smiling. "So much I see."

On their way back to the house they encountered the Duke deep in conversation with his head shepherd and the bailiff about some new rams from England, who were nibbling away in a small hurdled enclosure in the pastures; he joined them.

"Duke, there's good news," Julia told him.

"Is she found?"

"Yes, found and safe. And with your consent she will be coming up here tomorrow."

"Of course I consent! To whom do I say so?"

"Well in fact as you were out, and as you *had* asked her already, I gave your consent myself," Julia said. The Duke laughed.

"Miss Probyn, I think you must never leave us again! You manage my affairs better than I do. I am delighted."

"Yes, but there's just one thing," Julia pursued. "She'll have to come with an escort."

He looked alarmed.

"Not the mother?"

"Oh Lord no—heaven forfend! With that English lady who found her. Would you mind? You see, no one in Portugal knows *her* by sight, so she's good cover."

"Indeed I do not mind! I should like to meet this spirited lady, and as a friend of yours she is doubly welcome. Have you given my consent to this also?" he asked slyly.

"Well yes, I have," Julia admitted.

"Excellent! I will tell my sister. Really, how interesting it makes one's existence to be involved in these matters! Usually here at Gralheira we lead a life which is tranquil almost to the point of being a little dull," he said to Father Antal. "But since you and the Monsignor came we have the house full of handsome young men, we have alarms and excursions, the telephone ringing at all hours—and now a rescued heroine and her duenna! So amusing."

"You are all goodness; and so is this young lady," Father Antal said, with a benevolent glance at Julia.

"There you are right!" But the Duke raised a question which had not occurred to Julia.

"Who pacifies the formidable Mama, whose daughter ran away from her yesterday morning with this so well-mannered young American? Has she been told?"

"Good gracious, I never thought of that. Well whatever happens, don't let *us* do the pacifying!" Julia exclaimed. "I'll talk to Major Torrens, but personally I think all that had much better be left to Colonel Marques; he's on the spot, and after all he can cancel her residence permit tomorrow, if he wants to. Then she'd miss the wedding!" Julia added cattily.

"Ah yes—the wedding! Dear me, I had quite forgotten it, with all these other affairs. We shall have to go down on Friday, I suppose," the Duke said ruefully, "And you also, Miss Probyn?"

"Yes, I must. I'd forgotten all about it too."

The Duke turned to Father Antal, with careful courtesy.

"You will remain here, of course. The absence of my sister and myself will make no difference, and in any case we shall only be away for forty-eight hours; we return on Sunday."

"You are more than kind," Father Antal said, measuredly. "In fact I think I have almost completed my work with Monsignor Subercaseaux; my movements are in the hands of Major Torrens after that."

"Let us both leave it all to Miss Probyn, then," the Duke said, again slyly.

At the house she promptly put the point about Dorothée to the Major. "We simply can't have her coming storming up here, when the Duque is being such an angel; but he's quite right—she's got to be sorted somehow," Julia said, using the West Highland expression for dealing with a person. "Ring the Colonel, don't you think?"

Torrens did think; and the Duke being now in possession of his own study, he gloomily telephoned from outside the pantry, while Julia as usual sat on the case of wine.

"Oh this mother!" Colonel Marques barked angrily. "*Well* may you be worried about her; for two centavos I would send her out of the country tomorrow! I went myself to see her, to relieve her anxiety: she is playing Bridge with Madame la Comtesse de Vermeil, she can see no one! When I send word that I desire to examine her *permis de séjour*, out she comes flying! But she made great difficulties about the daughter: threatened to go to the American Embassy, and Heaven knows what! Since I cannot and will not tell her where her daughter *is*, or where she goes, this is very troublesome."

"What *did* you say?" Torrens asked.

"That her Father Confessor—you know who I mean—would come to explain matters to her; meanwhile, that her daughter was in his care. After all she will be tomorrow, so what difference does it make?"

"Oh, none," Torrens said cheerfully. This Dunne-like treatment of time did not worry him in the least. "But have we got to send the old holiness down?"

"Yes, *mon cher*, I am afraid you must do this. Brief him first, of course; but that one needs little briefing!—merely *no* indication of where *la petite* is or will be, and of what has happened. He is the one person who can keep her quiet. How soon can you send him?"

Torrens, after consulting Julia, repeated her airy assurance of—"Oh, Richard can drive him down first thing tomorrow; they can be there by lunch-time, in that car."

"*Très bien.* Then I inform *Madame la mère* that she may expect her Director for luncheon tomorrow, and that he will explain everything."

When Marques had rung off Julia and Torrens went back to the smoking-room.

"I suppose it's all right letting him go," the Secret Service man said. "After all, they were watching his house on Friday night."

"Only to try and catch Father Antal," Julia said. "And he'll be in a C.D. car. Let's go and tell him, and the wretched Richard. How furious he'll be at being sent off, just when Hetta's coming!"

Neither the ecclesiastic nor the diplomat were in the least pleased at their assignment. The Monsignor took it best. "Yes, I understand," he said resignedly. "Of course maternal feelings must be placated, but how one wishes that in Americans they were not so pronounced! Very well—at what hour do we start tomorrow?"

"At eight sharp," Julia told him firmly.

"*Miséricorde!* That means saying Mass at seven!"

"I'll see that Antonio calls you in good time," Julia assured him, not without malice.

Richard was much more recalcitrant.

"But it's tomorrow that she comes up here!" he exclaimed unguardedly. "Why do *I* have to drive him down? Can't he go in one of the Duque's endless cars?"

"No. It's much wiser that he goes in a C.D. car," Torrens told him.

"Well, Townsend has his car sitting in the *praça* at São Pedro: can't he do it?"

"*No*, Richard," Julia said firmly. "We've had quite enough of Townsend driving people about!—and his car's nothing like as fast as yours. Anyhow, whose fault is all this Hetta thing?"

The young man stared at her.

"Why do you say that?"

"I'll give you three guesses!" she said. "No, Richard; you take him down." Atherley capitulated.

"Oh, very well. Must I stay down there to bring him back, or just dump him?"

"Well oughtn't you to get back to your Chancery? Of course that's between you and your Ambassador," Julia said remorselessly. "I shouldn't think the Monsignor will want to come up here again before the wedding; that's on Saturday, and tomorrow is Wednesday. By the time he's flattened Dorothée there'll only be forty-eight hours before he has to put on his war-paint and assist at the Nuptial High Mass."

"Oh Lord, yes!" Richard groaned. "I'd forgotten that infernal wedding. Haven't you got to come down for it too?" he asked rather sourly of Julia.

"Of course. But I don't really mind!" she replied with a grin. "The Duke and Dona Maria Francisca are going, of course; I shall take a lift off them, in one of their endless cars."

"Damn you, Julia!"

Torrens weighed in.

"You're going rather too fast, Julia. The Monsignor has got to come back here to finish off with Father A., and anyhow Marques has already told Countess Páloczy that he is looking after Hetta. That's in the future conditional tense, but we're bound to run into trouble if Subercaseaux stays in Estoril; he's sure to be seen, and she's sure to be told."

"Oh, ah, yes; I see your point," Julia said blandly. "Very well, let Richard bring him back tomorrow night. And the Monsignor can go down again on Friday with the Duque and me and all. Old Dorothée won't make any fuss *at* the wedding—she'll be much too excited! But I wish I could be a fly on the wall when he tackles her tomorrow."

"He'll win—you can bet on that," Richard said.

Monsignor Subercaseaux did win, although he was playing on a bad wicket and the Countess on a good one. When he walked into the apartment at half-past one he saw at once that she was all set to give him a rough passage; but the Monsignor was not at all inclined to submit to rough passages, and did not on this occasion.

"Well, Monsignor, I hope now you will have the goodness to explain to me what goes on about Hetta?" she began. "That quite *insufferable* Colonel Marques said you would."

"You dislike him?" the priest said, raising his bushy eyebrows. "I find him so intelligent, and invariably *courteous*." He glanced towards the tray of drinks under the window; after being driven at nerve-wracking speed by

Atherley for five and a half hours he felt like a glass of sherry. The Countess saw his glance, and interpreted it; already a little cowed, she moved towards the tray.

"A glass of Tio Pepe, Monsignor?"

"Thank you, my daughter." The last words put her back in her place as his spiritual child. He sipped, gently, and sniffed appreciatively at a bowl of roses.

"Well?" the Countess asked sharply. "Why did she rush off like that? And was it with Townsend Waller or with Atherley? I know she went with a man—right from the door here! She has *no* sense."

"Do you remember a conversation we had about her, just after she arrived?" the Monsignor asked tranquilly. "You complained then of her independence, and I made certain recommendations as to your own course of behaviour. I am beginning to wonder if you have carried them out."

"Now look here, Monsignor, you're trying to put me in the dock, and I don't like it," the angry woman said. "Are you really suggesting that this performance of hers is *my* fault?"

"I am not sure. Your treatment of her might have been a contributing factor, let us say."

"No, let's not say that, or anything like it! I've been doing everything in the *world* for that child, gauche and difficult as she is, since she came." In her anger the Countess's voice took on the rasping accents of the Middle West, and she reverted to her native idiom. "Quit stalling, Monsignor, and tell me where my daughter *is?*"

"She is in my care," he said, in tones of studied moderation. "She is well, and she will return to you presently; but I am not going to tell you her address, I am not going to send her back till I think fit, and I am, above all, not going to enter into explanations as to why she left, or with whom, at this stage. Later I may do so; but the present is not the moment."

The calm authority in his voice checked Dorothy Páloczy momentarily; then her resentment flamed up afresh.

"In fact you're taking my own child out of my hands? Is that it?"

"No. Your child left your hands of her own free will and without my knowledge; you may ask yourself why. But now, I repeat, she is in *my* care."

"It's—it's absolutely outrageous!" the Countess said fuming, walking up and down the pretty flower-filled room. It was, of course, and no one knew it better than Mgr Subercaseaux. But security demanded that the wretched woman should be kept in the dark—to say nothing of their obligations to the Duke, to Father Antal, and to Hetta herself. The Monsignor had no qualms at all about the line he was taking. He drank some more sherry, and sat relaxed in his chair, waiting for the storm to blow itself out.

"Well, when *is* Hetta coming back?"

"Oh, soon after the wedding, I think. You do not want her to come before that, do you? Will you not be very much involved in your own preparations, till then?" There was a hint of irony in his tone, and Dorothée, who was not altogether a fool, realised that he was thinking—quite rightly—of all she would be having done to her clothes, her feet, her hands, her hair, her face. She gave an angry laugh. "Oh very well—you win! But when what you call 'the moment' for explanations comes I shall want a full one, remember!"

"I shall not forget." He pulled out a thin gold watch in a Cartier case from somewhere in his soutane, and glanced at it. "My dear Countess, I have to leave at three. Will you do me the honour of lunching with me downstairs?"

"No, I won't!" the Countess said flatly. "We're lunching here, in the apartment, where the chef will send us something fit to eat."

"You are very kind. Do you wish me to ring?"

Dorothy Páloczy had been slower than most American women married to Europeans about learning to let things be done *for* her; after twenty-five years she was still liable to do them herself, especially when her nerves were out of order. She moved now to the telephone and ordered luncheon to be served immediately; then she poured out another glass of sherry for her guest. Subercaseaux was relieved by this promptitude. He had undertaken to walk up and meet Atherley outside the Casino sharp at three, but he was exceedingly hungry, and did not at all want to cut his meal short.

Atherley lunched more briefly, and rather less well. After dropping the Monsignor he raced in to Lisbon and from the Chancery rang up the Ambassador's residence to ask how soon he could see him? Sir Henry was in, and luckily had no luncheon-party; he sent a message to say that his First Secretary could come at two-fifteen.

"Tomlinson, what can you get me to eat, *here,* in five minutes?" Richard asked, sitting at his desk, and groaning inwardly at the sight of three laden "In" trays.

"Well in five minutes, Mr. Atherley, that isn't so easy; there aren't any restaurants close round here. Must it really be *five* minutes?"

"Yes, Tomlinson, it must."

The messenger reflected, wrinkling his pale forehead.

"Well Mr. Atherley, I hardly like to suggest it, but Mrs. Tomlinson and I often bring along some of her meat pies if we're liable to be busy; I could bring you up some of those at once, if you would fancy them. They're fresh-baked; she did them last night."

"That's very good of you, Tomlinson—the meat pies by all means. But what will *you* do?"

"Oh, I can go out, Sir. We're not so rushed as we expected; the Messenger's plane was held up, so the bag isn't in. Would you like some wine, Sir? We can get that just round the corner, and it isn't too bad either—though not what you're accustomed to, of course."

No district in Lisbon is without its small wine-shops, however lacking it may be in the matter of restaurants, and the Lapa quarter is no exception; in less than five minutes a tray was placed on Atherley's desk with a china jug of wine, tomatoes, and a plate of Mrs. Tomlinson's meat pies. These were the most English food the young man had eaten since he came to Portugal—stodgy, wholesome, and the pastry in fact rather good; he was ravenous, and helped down by the tomatoes and the rough cheap wine they made quite an adequate meal. Richard grinned as he ate, amused by this side-light on the domestic arrangements of the messenger and the telephonist—imagine that little thing going home, after her day's work in the head-phones, to roll out pastry and bake meat pies!

Punctually at a quarter past two he was waiting in the Embassy drawing-room, where a coffee-tray stood before the fireplace at one end of the long room; in a moment Sir Henry and Lady Loseley came in by the door at the farther end—Lady Loseley, after a pleasant greeting, took a cup of coffee and said that she must go and see the baby, and tactfully went out.

"Well Richard, does this visit mean that you contemplate returning to us?" the Ambassador asked, turning a quizzical blue eye on his Head of Chancery.

"Not if you can spare me for another forty-eight hours, Sir. I came to beg you to do that"—he spoke with an earnestness so unusual that it rather impressed his chief. "And to apologise for rushing off the night before last."

"Oh! Have you really driven all the way down from Beira Alta just to say that?"

His shrewdness embarrassed Atherley.

"Well no, Sir. I brought Monsignor Subercaseaux down, and I'm afraid I must take him back. But I can be in the Chancery by nine tomorrow morning if you wish it," he said rather stiffly.

The Ambassador chuckled.

"Had to bring him down to tranquillise the troublesome Countess, eh? I'm not surprised; she's been making a terrible commotion. And where *is* that nice little daughter who cooks? Up at Gralheira? I don't wonder she ran away."

"She's on her way there," Richard said. "But she didn't go off just to escape from her mother; she had a more valid reason than that."

"Oh, ah." The Ambassador, his eyes always gay and shrewd, picked at his thumb-nail. "Am I to be told the more valid reason?"

"Well really, Sir, at this stage I think you had better know the whole thing," the young man said rather desperately. "I tried hard to avoid getting involved in this, but that infernal Secret Service man simply dragged me into it. You see—" and then he poured out the whole tale of Father Antal.

"Oh yes, I know about that," the Ambassador said airily, still picking at his thumb, his eyes still amused. "The Duke of Ericeira really is a *galant' uomo* to take on the whole boiling like that, though of course all these ecclesiasticos are just his sister's cup of tea! But why do you say the little lady is on her way to Gralheira? Didn't she go there on Monday with her *cavaliere servente?*"

"No Sir; she never got there." Seeing how much the Ambassador already knew—probably from Campbell, Richard reflected sourly—he decided to tell the rest of the story. "At São Pedro do Sul the wretched American went to have a drink while she went to say her prayers, and in his absence she was pinched by some Communist agents and carried off."

"Good God! What a frightful thing!" The Ambassador was startled by this development. "But how on earth was she recovered? I should have thought they'd have swept her straight off into Spain."

"They would have but for Luzia, that beautiful little girl of the Duke's —do you know her, Sir?"

"No, alas."

"Well, she prevented it. Everyone in São Pedro do Sul eats out of her hand, of course: she got an eye-witness account of the kidnapping, so Torrens rang up Colonel Marques and had the frontier closed."

"What a wonderful story!" the Ambassador interjected, his blue eyes gleaming. "Do go on. Did the remarkable Luzia go after them and catch them?"

"They went after them all right, and Luzia telephoned and caused some thug to give their car four flats before it crossed the frontier! But they got away in the local taxi."

"Ah, she probably rang up Martinez at the shooting-box," the Ambassador said reflectively. "Lovely country up there; and those wild goats give one some very sporting shots. But how was the little Hungarian recovered in the end? Where is she on her way to Gralheira *from?*"

"Here, Sir. When the agents found all exits blocked they hived back to Lisbon; by God's mercy their car was involved in a street crash yesterday morning, and Countess Hetta was found, and saved."

"It sounds as if there was another story there," the Ambassador said. "However, I won't delay you by going into that now, since you have got to get out to Estoril and drive the Monsignor back to Gralheira. I know that the Duke likes to dine punctually! Just tell me this—how much did the little Countess give away?"

Richard blinked slightly at this further instance of the all-knowingness of his gay, bland chief.

"Something, Sir, but we don't yet know what. I'm sure we shall find all that out this evening; she will tell Miss Probyn—she trusts her."

"I think I really must meet this Miss Probyn; she seems to be a sort of lynch-pin in this whole business," the Ambassador said. "Very well, Richard; take your extra forty-eight hours of leave—let boy meet girl! You know your way out. Goodbye."

And with this final shattering display of omniscience the Ambassador walked up the long room and went out by the farther door, leaving Atherley blinking after him.

CHAPTER XVI

MRS. HATHAWAY and Hetta, with their police escort, reached Gralheira soon after five. Dona Maria Francisca was dispensing prizes for needle-work at a local "Instituto Bom Pastor," i.e., a rescue-home; the Duke, with Townsend Waller and Torrens, was off at the far end of the estate inspecting his forestry plantations, but Julia and Luzia, the latter bursting with curiosity, were out on the steps to greet the new arrivals. Hetta looked pale, Julia thought; she consigned her to Luzia's care—"I'll see you later, Hetti." She turned to Mrs. Hathaway. "I thought you and I would have tea up in your room. Dona Maria Francisca was so sorry—" She led her guest upstairs.

"My dear child, what a wonderful house!" Mrs. Hathaway said, her eye travelling round as she went. "And what a beautiful room!" she exclaimed a moment later, taking in the carpet, the period furniture, the space and dignity, and the view from the two high windows.

"Yes. We'll have tea in here while Marta unpacks," Julia said, opening another door into a sitting-room. "This is yours too; you have a suite, all but the bath-room!" While Mrs. Hathaway took off her hat and coat Julia explained about the only two Gralheira bath-rooms. Mrs. Hathaway was as amused as Major Torrens had been by these Victorian dispositions. Lying on a brocaded chaise-longue in the boudoir, drinking tea, she gave a little sigh of pleasure.

"How nice this is! Really I am wonderfully lucky to be here, however it came about."

"Tell me every word," Julia said—and so Mrs. Hathaway did; to Julia she even admitted the agonising helplessness and distress of that first hour or two of her efforts to bring Hetta round. "But who is the little fat man who sent the car to bring us up here? He wouldn't let me pay a penny! Is he something to do with the police?"

"Yes, he's the head of the Security Police."

"Well now Julia my dear, I should like it so much if you were to tell me what all this is *about*," Mrs. Hathaway said. "You call this girl Hetti, but who is she?"

"She's Hetta Páloczy; a Hungarian." Julia told the whole story, ending up with Father Antal's escape.

"You'll meet him at dinner; he's the dearest old creature you can imagine."

"That is all quite fascinating," said Mrs. Hathaway. "But, Julia, I feel that you ought to go and see that poor child; she's on thorns about something, and I know it's you she wants to talk to."

"All right, I will. Just tell me how Edina is."

"Splendid, when I last heard. But do go to your Hetta. If I could just have a *boracha* I think I would lie down for a little. At what time do we dine?"

Julia laughed and kissed her old friend. "*Boracha!* You know the words already! Dinner is usually at eight-thirty; tonight it may be a little later because the Vatican contact has to get back from Lisbon. But Marta shall call you, and I will come and take you downstairs to meet them all. Oh, what fun this is!"

She found Hetta in Nanny's sitting-room, lingering over an ample English tea and actually laughing at some nonsense of Luzia's; at the sight of Julia, however, the gaiety left her face, and she sprang up, saying —"At last there you are! Now, please, I *must* speak to you." She turned to thank Nanny and Luzia for "so delicious a tea," and looked anxiously at Julia.

"Come along to my room. Countess Hetta is next to me, isn't she, Nanny?"

"Yes, Miss Probyn. It's rather *small*, really only the dressing-room, but

I thought the Countess would put up with that for the sake of the communicating door."

"Perfect, Nanny," said Julia, who had in fact herself asked her hostess to put Hetta there. She glanced round as they passed through to see that Manoela had unpacked properly, and led Hetta on into her own room, which was big, and as much a sitting-room as a bedroom; Julia had organised this for herself during her spell as Luzia's governess. The two girls sat down on a comfortable English sofa under one of the windows. "Now, Hetti, tell me what the trouble is," Julia said.

Hetta's account was rather confused, to begin with.

"Yulia, first I must tell you that when Richard would not say that he could bring me here when I asked, though he had promised, I was angry. There was a reason for that, but it does not matter," Hetta said, on a falling note of the voice.

Aha and oho, Julia thought to herself—enter Mme de Whatnot!

"Well never mind; go on," she said.

"So then I asked Townsend instead, and he drove me up to this beautiful little town—but how beautiful *all* Portugal is! He wanted to drink wine; I did not, so I went into a church. That is always a nice way to spend time, and this is a beautiful church; I grew more happy. Then these horrible men come in, though how they can know I am there I cannot imagine!—they drag me out and put me in a car and drive away; a *long* way. At last we stop, and I see it is a frontier; I try to get out, and shout; but they pulled me back and held my mouth, and tied something over my eyes so that I should not see. Then the car is turned; I could feel it going backwards and forwards, so I knew that it had not crossed the frontier, and this was *something*."

"Indeed it was! And then?"

"We drove, not for so long now, and presently stop while one of the men asks questions; then they bring me into a *very* small inn, first taking the bandage off my eyes. In this place *they* ate, bread and butter, and an omelette, and drank wine, but to me they gave nothing; I must sit and watch them eat!" Hetta said indignantly. "And I was now very hungry, for Waller and I had taken lunch at one. But I would not ask for food!"

Julia sat listening, with a sort of pang at the strangeness of it, to Hetta's blindfold account of the journey that they had so painstakingly traced out only two days before—one story, but from two how different angles.

"And after that?" she prompted.

"They take me out again, but there is some trouble about the car; one takes me back into the inn, swearing! And presently we get into another

most *terrible* old car, and again they tie my eyes; but even through the
bandage, just once I could see the lights of another car that met us, and
I tried to put my hand out of the window to wave—but they snatched my
hand away, and struck me."

Julia was shaken by this, realising that it was the lights of the Land-
Rover that had pierced the bandage over Hetta's eyes; that it was to her
own friends that she had tried to beckon. But all she said was—"Well,
after that?"

"We stop several times, and there is more talking with people; at last
we get into another car, much better, with a chauffeur, and drive again."

"I wonder where to?" Julia speculated.

"To the frontier, I think. Is there a place with the word honour in it?
I thought I heard 'Onoro' several times."

"Yes, there is. Fuentes de Onoro."

"*That* was it. And again the car is stopped; they cannot pass, but turn
round and drive away. Then they got out a map, I heard the paper crackle,
and one says, 'No no, Lissabon!' Now this is how *Germans* say Lisbon,"
Hetta said, opening her eyes at Julia—"so I begin to think that though
they speak Spanish, one or two are perhaps really German. We drive a long
time, very fast, and then stop; it seems the driver does not know the way.
They swear and swear; it is dark, the road is empty—no people, no houses;
the chauffeur speaks only Portuguese. One of them speaks that, a rather
fattish man, with a short beard; I can see this when he gets out to look
for which road they shall take, because after we leave this Onoro place,
by bending down and rubbing my face against my knees I managed to
push the bandage off my eyes."

"Why didn't you use your hands?" Julia interrupted, making a horrified guess at the reason.

"After I tried to wave to that car we met they tied my hands behind
my back, so tight that it hurt; it was most disagreeable, because now I
cannot lean back, and I am *so* tired."

Julia wondered whether to ask for more details about the fattish man
with the beard, but decided that it was better to let Hetta get her story
out in her own way.

"You must have been—*poor* Hetti! Do go on."

"So presently we drive again, the man with the beard always telling
the chauffeur to go faster; but in their anger two speak now altogether
in German, and one says—'*Eine verfluchte Geschichte!* It is nearly four,
we shall not reach Lissabon before it is daylight!' And the bearded man
says he will get out when we pass through a town called Santa something, and '*allein arbeiten*'—this means work by himself," Hetta explained.

"At Santarém, I expect," Julia said. In her mind she was tracing the route of the car after leaving Fuentes de Onoro: down through Beira Baixa on the farther side of the Serra da Estrêla to hit the Tagus valley at Abrantes, and on to Santarém. "Well?" she asked.

"Then another man says, 'So had we not better stop and do the questioning of the little one now, that you may profit by what she knows?' Oh Yulia, when I heard that I was so much afraid!"

"Darling Hetti, I don't wonder! But do tell me everything. You'll feel better when you've got it all out, and we must know because of Father Antal." She was full of nervous distress herself, dreading what might be coming.

"Him! That is just the thing! But I must ask you to try to understand," Hetta said, speaking with a curious quietness. "I am very tired, and I am also very hungry; it is now four in the morning, and I had last eaten with Waller at one o'clock the day before. Also these men do not allow me to go to the lavatory in that small inn where they ate, nor to leave the car; so for *fourteen* hours I do not go, and I am quite *miserable!*"

"Hetta, I do understand. Frightful!"

"Then the car stops," Hetta said, speaking slowly now, "and in bad French they ask me, 'Would you like to get out, and go to the side of the road?'—grinning most vulgarly! They have switched on the light inside the car. 'Yes,' I answer. 'You shall,' they say, 'when you have answered one quite small question: where is now Dr. Antal Horvath?' At that I shut my mouth; I think No, better endure shame, stain my clothes, be disgusting, than do this! When I shake my head the one with the beard strikes me across the face with the palm of his hand, first one side, then the other—five, six times! This is a horrible thing," Hetta said flatly, "but I do not speak, except to say No. Then they untie my arms, and twist them so hard that it hurts very much, and the bearded man slaps my face again, but still I do not speak. Then he looks at his watch, and says, quite furiously—'We cannot lose any more time; it is dangerous. She *must* speak.' And they whisper together, and I am more afraid than ever! Another says, aloud—'Let us search her first; we have not done that yet.' And they begin to feel me all over, in my pockets and inside my clothes, also touching me in a very disgusting way. But one takes my handbag and looks in that, and suddenly he gives a shout—'I have it! Give yourselves no more trouble; here is what we want!'"

"What had he found?" Julia asked.

"This is what is awful of me! I had written a note to Father Antal, and put the name Gralheira on it. I thought I would make Townsend drive by the house, and that we could send it in by a servant, and then the Father could get someone, you perhaps, to telephone to me at this hotel where we were to stay. It was quite *id-yot*, I should have known better; in Hungary I should never have put a name and a place on paper. But that is what I did, and what they found. After I was taken from the church I ought of course to have eaten the letter," Hetta said matter-of-factly, "but I was confused at first, and by the time I thought of this, my hands were tied. So now they are all quite cheerful, and say 'Very well; now you can get out.' But one stands near and flicks the torch on me; it may be in order that I should not escape, but I think also to humiliate me! For where could I escape to, in the night, in Portugal? And I am so—Yulia, I cannot express it properly, but *weak* with relief—that I just go back afterwards to the car, like a silly person!" Hetta said, with an expression of profound distaste.

"I don't see what else you could have done, Hetti dear; if you *had* tried to run away they would simply have caught you," Julia said. "What happened after that?"

"They offered me wine and bread, but I would not take them!" Hetta said, with a lift of the head. "Accept anything from such animals?—no! Those two go on talking in German—so stupid, this, to think that I should not understand German, brought up in Hungary!—and I heard one say: 'We must be careful as we enter Lissabon; she must not make a *Geschrei*.' Then they push some piece of stuff into my mouth, so that I cannot speak; this dries the mouth quite up; my mouth is still sore. But he with the beard says, 'If we do not tie her hands again she may pull it out, and shout, and we cannot drive her through the streets with bound hands; it could be seen. Better to make her *ohnmächtig*.' And he turns on the inside light of the car again, and tells the chauffeur to stop, and takes out a little case and fills a syringe from an ampoule. I *see* all this, while the others hold me!" Hetta said, in a tone which brought that moment vividly before Julia. "Then he pulls off my coat and jacket, and pushes up my sleeve, and gives me the *piqûre*. I remember them putting on my jacket and coat, and the car starting, and after that *nothing*, till I wake in bed in Mrs. Hattaway's room."

It seemed to Julia that Hetta had very little to reproach herself with. (The idea of *eating* compromising letters she had only encountered up to now in books about the *maquis*.) Still, Torrens must be apprised of the fact that the bearded man knew, and had known for thirty-six hours, that Father Antal was at Gralheira. She kissed and consoled Hetta, told her to lie down till she was called to dress for dinner, and then went off to see if the Major had returned. Elidio informed her that he had, and was in His Excellency's study; Julia betook herself there, and poked her leonine-golden head round the door.

"Oh, but come in," the Duke said, rising.

"Please, no—I've just come to snatch away the Major, thank you so much." She gestured with her head at Torrens.

"Our new guests arrived safely, I hear," her host said.

"Yes. They adore Gralheira already! Do excuse us"—and she swept the obedient Torrens out of the room.

In the smoking-room she told him, without any details, what the Communists had found in Hetta's handbag, and how the "bearded man" had proposed to leave the car at Santarém.

"Yes, Marques said they'd only pinched three of them," Torrens said. "Well, we'd better let him know at once. That ghastly telephone in the passage, I suppose?"

Even heads of Security Police must, one imagines, sometimes eat; anyhow on this occasion Colonel Marques was not to be got on the telephone. They tried for Colonel Campbell, but he too was out.

"Well don't attempt to get Melplash," Julia said. "Stupid clot, he'd only make a muddle. Let's try the Colonel again after dinner. Nothing much can happen between now and then."

Dinner that night was rather late. The Bentley only crackled over the raked gravel to the front door at eight-thirty, and Gralheira was not a house where people were told not to bother to change for dinner; Atherley and the Monsignor hurried away to their rooms. Julia had warned the Duke that they would almost certainly be late, so he was not fussing acutely when the rest of the company assembled in the drawing-room, Julia shepherding Mrs. Hathaway and Hetta. The Duke greeted Hetta with warm kindness, his sister with her usual rather pinched courtesy; Townsend was duly presented to Mrs. Hathaway, and wrung Hetta's hand in almost speechless relief and apology. The girl spoke gently to him, but her eyes were straying round the enormous room; this actually contained as many as five lamps, but it was nevertheless out of a certain degree of shadow that Father Antal's voice came, saying—"My child?"

They all heard it; for a moment they all watched her as she flew to him and kissed his hand. Then in the blessed half-dark the pair spoke together in that impossible language, Hungarian, which no one else could understand. The Duke with his impeccable courtesy began a conversation with Mrs. Hathaway, Julia did the same with Dona Maria Francisca. Presently Elidio appeared to announce that Os Senhores had returned, and that in mais dez minutos (ten minutes more) they would come down. The Duke nodded and looked at his watch; then he glanced round the room and observed that two of the company, who should have been there, were missing.

"My sister, where are Luzia and Miss Brown? They do not seem to be present."

They were not—and they were still not present when Atherley and the Monsignor came in, followed by Elidio, who whispered in his master's ear that the young Condessa and Meess Brown begged to be excused from dining; they would eat upstairs. The Duke frowned—this was unheard-of—and muttered a question to Elidio; he was answered by the ineffably evasive shrug of the old and privileged Portuguese servant. "My sister, we will not wait for Nanny and Luzia," Ericeira said authoritatively, and they all trooped into the great dining-room, where the Duke, as Julia had foreseen, was quickly beguiled by the cheerful astringent quality of Mrs. Hathaway's conversation. Hetta, of course, sat beside Father Antal, and neither had eyes or ears for anyone else; but Atherley, seated next to Julia, asked uncompromisingly—"Where on earth *are* Luzia and Nanny? I thought everyone simply had to show up for meals, here."

"I haven't a clue," Julia said airily, though in fact she was quite as curious as Atherley could be about the reason for their absence. Atherley was not a very lively companion that evening; his eyes strayed constantly across the table to where Hetta, her face pale, but alight with happiness, talked eagerly and incomprehensibly with the old priest. "Have you found out if she had a bad time?" he asked anxiously.

"Uncomfortable, but nothing serious," Julia told him. "They found a note in her bag addressed to Dom Francisco, *here,* before they resorted to extreme measures; and as that was all they wanted, they just drugged her and took her on to Lisbon."

Atherley was much relieved.

"Does Marques know they know he's here?" he asked.

"No. We couldn't get him before dinner; Hugh's going to ring him up afterwards. That will give him something to think about!" Julia said, with what Atherley thought misplaced levity.

But when Major Torrens did eventually ring up Colonel Marques he had something rather unexpected to tell the Chief of the Security Police. In the drawing-room after dinner Elidio, holding out a silver tray with small cups of weak coffee to Julia, murmured that Meess Brown desired to speak with Meess Probyn in the schoolroom. Julia drank the cheerless coffee hastily, made her excuses to her hostess, and hastened upstairs.

In the schoolroom she found Nanny and Luzia tucking into cold chicken and salad, on both their faces a remarkable expression of smug triumph, as of two cats who have each swallowed an out-size canary.

"Well Miss Probyn, I hope His Grace isn't too much upset, but really there seemed to be nothing else to do," Nanny began, in a busy sort of voice.

"Nanny, please!" Luzia interjected. "Do let *me* tell Miss Probyn. Did I find him or did you?"

"Tell away, tell away," Nanny replied cheerfully. "Blow your own trumpet!—I will say this time you have the right to."

"Oh do get down to it, Luzia!" Julia said impatiently. "Who have you found?"

"Him! This 'principal' of whom Torrens spoke, the one with the beard, who was not taken in Lisbon with the others," Luzia announced triumphantly.

"Where, for goodness sake?" Julia asked, half incredulous.

"In the kitchen. You see after I heard Torrens yesterday telling Papa in the study that he had escaped, and that we must continue to take all precautions, I went out last night to the kitchen to look at the travellers who were eating there, to see if any looked suspicious. None did; just poor Portuguese working-people. Tonight I went again, and there at the table, eating with the rest, sat a man with a beard, in poor clothes, but they do not fit him very well; and moreover, he had rolls of fat on the back of his neck!" said Luzia, her eyes like saucers.

"Gracious! Well?"

"So I went round the table greeting all the people, there were only six or seven tonight, and at last I came to him, and he spoke *very* bad Portuguese, just as the beggars said of the man at São Pedro do Sul. I said nothing then, but went to find Nanny."

"Well Miss, of course I went down at once," Nanny said, taking up the tale with evident pleasure. "Luzia was quite right not to say anything in front of the servants, but to come to me. And I find my gentleman talking to one of the kitchen-maids as she served his food, asking if there weren't foreign *eclesiásticos* staying in the house? The cheek of it!" said Nanny indignantly.

"Goodness! What on earth did you do?"

"Well, I felt sure you and the Major would wish to see this person, but the chef was just about to send dinner in, and I knew I couldn't get you then. So I spoke to the man myself, and said, if he wanted to see the foreign priests I could arrange it, if he would make it worth my while, and come with me."

"And did he?" Julia asked.

"Indeed he did; he got up at once and came along as meek as a lamb. I gave a sort of wink to the chef and old Maria do Carmo, so they made no trouble—for as you know, Miss, those people never come through into the house, except for Mass. And I just caught Elidio in the passage, and sent the message to His Grace. But then I had to think where to put him."

"Heavens, yes! Well, where *did* you put him?" Julia was beginning to gurgle with laughter; this performance on the part of Nanny and Luzia was too superb, if it really was "the principal" whom they had got.

"Out in the old night-nurseries, Miss Probyn. You see there are bars on the windows, so he can't get out. His Grace had them put in for the little Count, God rest his soul!" Nanny said, sadness for her long-dead baby boy for a moment eclipsing the satisfaction in her sensible time-worn face. "And those rooms are right at the far end of the East corridor, and give onto the garden, so he can scream his head off, and no one will hear!" the good woman pursued, triumph again returning to her expression.

"And he's there now?"

"Yes. I told him the priests were just about to sit down to dinner, and it would be an hour or more before he could see them; but that he *should* see one of them, if he made it worth my while. I repeated that, so as to lull his suspicions, as you might say," Nanny concluded, looking smugger than ever.

Julia laughed loudly. "Nanny, how marvellous! *Did* he make it worth your while?"

"Indeed he did, Miss Probyn. He gave me a conto." (A conto is a thousand escudos, worth about £12 : 10 : 0 in English money, but a small fortune in Portugal.) As she spoke Nanny drew a bundle of notes out of her bodice. "I shall give it to Dona Maria Francisca for her poor girls, of course. Then I told him that all this was very irregular, and I should get into terrible trouble if he was found, and I was going to lock the door so that none of the servants could get in and find him. He didn't seem to mind that; in fact he looked quite pleased, and settled down in my old armchair as cool as a cucumber! So I locked the door on him, and rang and ordered our supper—and there he is, and here's the key." She laid it on the table.

"Nanny, that is splendid. And Luzia, *how* well you did!"

"I expect you'll want to tell the Major," Nanny observed, falling to once more on her cold chicken.

"Yes, I must. Don't go near him again till I've seen you, Nanny." She got up.

"*Can't* I be with you when you tell Torrens?" Luzia implored, getting up too. "I *did* find him!"

"*Major* Torrens, Luzia. And you haven't finished your supper!"

"Bother my supper! Miss Probyn, *please!*"

"All right, come on," Julia said.

Down in the hall she summoned Elidio and told him to fetch the Senhor Comandante out to her. "But discreetly, you understand—so as not to attract attention."

Major Torrens did not really relish the long formal evenings in that huge, inadequately-lit room, and was relieved at the chance of escape. "What goes on?" he asked Julia in the hall.

"Come into the smoking-room and hear."

When he had heard what Julia had to tell he considered for a little. "You haven't seen him yourself?" he asked. She shook her head. "So we don't know for certain that it is the man we want."

"Oh Hugh, would any *other* man with a club beard and a German back to his neck show up here in the kitchen, and ask about foreign priests? We know that the 'principal' knows that Father Antal is here, and now we have this person arriving. If you won't ring Marques, I shall."

"I was going to ring Marques anyhow," the Major said calmly. "Of course I shall tell him what's happened. I suppose we can do it from the study this time? I hope to goodness he's in now."

Colonel Marques was in. Torrens told him first, very guardedly, what the Communists had found in Hetta's handbag, and went on to relate how someone "corresponding to the description of the fourth man" had been found in the house, making enquiries about "divines from other countries."

"Where is he now?" the Colonel asked.

"Under lock and key upstairs. He was promised an interview with one of the divines, and has paid a large bribe to secure it. Should we afford him any interview?"

"*Ah non, mon cher!* That would be too great a risk. I will come up at once; this is certainly worth investigation. You have not seen him yourself? Nor your lady colleague?"

Neither, Torrens told him; only a very youthful member of the family, and an old member of the staff, a foreigner.

"*Bon!* Now listen closely, *mon ami.* It would be highly desirable that this inquisitive individual should pass the time till I arrive in a deep and restful sleep; the old servant might perhaps offer him a glass of wine, or a cup of coffee. Can this be arranged? Have you what is necessary?"

"Of course I have the stuff. But not *coffee,* here; it wouldn't disguise the taste of barley-water!" the Major exclaimed hastily, causing Miss Probyn to laugh. "Hold on," he added, and turned to his ribald lady colleague, his hand over the receiver.

"Can Nanny administer a drug to the beard? I've got the dope."

"Yes, I'm sure she'd love to," Julia responded heartily.

"That can be done," Torrens said into the telephone.

"Excellent. And please arrange for us to be let in when we arrive: in about six hours from now. An awkward time, I am afraid."

Torrens glanced at his watch—it was just after ten.

"I'm sure that will be all right," he said, remembering his entry into the palace in Lisbon with the two priests in the small hours. "See you then." He rang off.

"So Nanny is to drug him. Oh, what fun for her!" Luzia exclaimed. "I *wish* I could do it!"

"Let's go up and see Nanny," Julia said, ignoring her. "You get your drug, Hugh, while I get something from Elidio to put it in. Vintage port, don't you think? Oddly enough the Duke has some, and that should mask the taste of your stuff as well as anything, though mind you it isn't really *good*. Port simply won't hold in this climate—the summers are too hot."

It is a curious fact that the Portuguese themselves have small taste for their country's supreme product, vintage port; they greatly prefer lighter wines. The Duke of Ericeira, however, with his wide circle of English friends, kept a small stock of some of the more noted vintages; only, as Miss Probyn had truly remarked, owing to the very hot summers and the lack of adequate cellerage they were seldom at their best.

"All right," Torrens said. "Only how am I to find Nanny? This house is like the maze at Hampton Court!"

"I go with you, and bring you to Nanny," Luzia said eagerly.

"Yes, you do that, Luzia," her ex-governess said. "Take Major Torrens up. I'll meet you there."

It gave the measure of Miss Probyn's standing in the Ericeira household that she had little difficulty in causing Elidio to decant a bottle of Graham's 1945 port; this, with a rather large glass, she took from the old servant.

"*Minha Menina*, let *me* bring this to wherever you desire it," the butler said earnestly. Julia shook her head.

"On this one occasion, Elidio, I will take it myself," she said smiling; an answering smile, coupled with an expression of ineffable intelligence, overspread the rather monkeyfied visage of the Portuguese. "*Muito bem, Minha Menina*," he said, and let her depart. Elidio had not failed to draw his own conclusions from the arrival of two priests in Lisbon after 1 A.M. the previous Friday; nor from "Meess Brown's" escorting, tonight, a *pessoa* from the traveller's table in the kitchen into the house.

Torrens, Luzia, and Nanny were waiting in the latter's sitting-room when Julia arrived with her salver.

"Well, Nanny, has the Major told you what he wants?" she asked.

"Yes, Miss Probyn. Quite an unusual request!"

"Do you think he'll take a glass of port?"

"I'll see that he does. I shall stay and talk about the foreign priests to him while he drinks it, and ask for more money. Asking for money always sort of carries conviction," Nanny stated, making Torrens laugh.

"Let's taste that wine, Julia," he said.

"I did. It's quite strong. I'd say it would mask most flavours."

The Major took out the stopper of the decanter, and sniffed. "Wonderful! What is it?"

"Graham's '45. I asked for that because it's still fairly young. Are you going to put your dope into the whole decanter, or pour out a glass?"

"I am certainly *not* going to ruin a whole bottle of Graham's '45!" the Major said emphatically. "I see you've brought a fairly large glass—good." He filled it; then before the fascinated gaze of the others he drew a small ampoule from his pocket, sawed off the neck, and emptied the contents into the glass of port. He stirred the fluid, carefully, with his little finger, then sucked the finger.

"Perfect," he pronounced. "This particular thing has very little taste." He replaced the glass on the silver tray. "There you are, Nanny; go and do your stuff. I'll come along behind you, just in case he smells a rat and tries something on." He picked up the poker from the grate and followed her as she took the tray and went out.

He reappeared in about five minutes. "It all seems to be going all right," he observed. "He's drinking it, and talking to her, quite jolly. This acts very gently and gradually, you know." He looked at the table. "Pity we haven't some port-glasses! We could use some of this decanter."

"*I* shall get them!" Luzia flew from the room before anyone could stop her.

"This really is the most extraordinary set-up," Torrens said when she had gone.

"Rather fun, don't you think?" Julia said contentedly, lighting a cigarette.

"Put that out, Julia, if you're going to drink port," Torrens said peremptorily. "It's desecration to smoke before stuff like this."

"Oh, very well." Always good-natured, Julia flung her cigarette into the fireplace—the Major looked on her with love.

"Darling, do you know that you really are an *absolute* darling?" he said, getting up as he spoke.

"Hugh dear, cut it out! Luzia will be back any minute, and you remember that we agreed to cut all this out till the Hetta-Antal business was finished, only the other day in the knot-garden, when the Duque and the holies interrupted us."

"It isn't easy to cut it out when you're so sweet," the Major was beginning, when Luzia flew in.

"There you are! Nanny *loves* port," the young girl said, banging four exquisite Marinha Grande port-glasses down on the table. Like port, the beautiful glass of Marinha Grande is a product which Portugal owes to English enterprise; as long ago as 1748 a factory was started there by John Beare, and carried on by the Stephens brothers, who prudently secured from the great Pombal the right to buy wood for their furnaces in the neighbouring forest of Leiria, the oldest man-controlled forest in the world; since the 13th century this has been felled, re-planted, and thinned under human direction. Julia was telling the Major about this when Nanny came in.

"Gone down?" Torrens asked.

"Yes, Major; he quite enjoyed it. I *hinted* about some more money, so he gave me another conto!—and he was half-asleep when I left."

"Splendid, Nanny!"

"Hugh, hadn't we better go and have a look at him presently, to see if he really is the man I saw on the road outside Cascais?" Julia asked.

"Give him another quarter of an hour," Torrens said, looking at his watch. "He'll have passed clean out by then. And meanwhile, I think we might drink Nanny's and Luzia's health."

After fifteen minutes pleasantly spent drinking admirable port they proceeded along the East corridor to the old night-nurseries, where Nanny unlocked the door. There, slackly sunk down in an old-fashioned nursery armchair, upholstered in faded cretonne patterned with turkey-cocks, lay Nanny's captive, snoring gently, his mouth half-open. Major Torrens went over to him and lifted an eye-lid; getting no response he briskly felt him all over, and from a pocket extracted a small revolver, which he pocketed himself. Then he turned to Julia.

"Is that your man?" he asked.

"The beard's all right. Let me see the back of his head."

The Major heaved the inert figure upwards and forwards, out of the comfortable cup-shaped back of the old chair.

"Yes, rolls of fat! I'm sure that's him."

The Major replaced the man in the chair and they all went out, Nanny locking the door.

"Nanny, I'd better have that key," Torrens said. "The head of the Security Police will be here about 4 A.M. to collect this person, and I don't want to dig you out of bed at that hour."

"Very well, Major. Does His Grace know? Elidio will have to wait up."

"No, I must see His Grace now." He looked at his watch. "We'd better get hold of him at once."

"Yes. And you're for bed, Miss!" Nanny said firmly to Luzia, and swept her off.

CHAPTER XVII

THE DRAWING-ROOM PARTY was just breaking up when Torrens and Julia got downstairs. The girl shepherded Hetta and Mrs. Hathaway to their rooms, while in the study Torrens, over a whisky, was about to inform his host of the events upstairs when Mgr Subercaseaux poked his head round the door. "Do I intrude?" he asked; the Monsignor liked a nightcap. Torrens frowned, involuntarily.

"Yes, I see that I do. Goodnight, my dear Duke."

"No, Monsignor—come in, come in!" his host said. Then he, too, noticed Torrens' face. "You did not wish to speak to me *privately?*" he asked, recalling that the Major had rather formally requested a few minutes with him.

"Well, as a matter of fact I did, Sir; but I don't suppose it much matters the Monsignor hearing what I have to say."

"Then shut the door and come and sit down, Monsignor. Say when."

Torrens told his tale. The Duke listened with half-incredulous delight. "Incredible!" he ejaculated. "And you mean that man is in the house now?"

"Yes Sir; in some disused rooms upstairs."

"Do let us see him!" Subercaseaux exclaimed. "A spy spotted by a *jeune fille* and drugged by a *bonne* is really something worth looking at!"

The Duke was also quite anxious to see his daughter's prize.

"I hope I can find the room," Torrens said rather doubtfully as they went upstairs; however, on the landing they encountered Miss Probyn, who had just said Goodnight to Mrs. Hathaway. "Ah good, Julia. You can conduct us to that creature. The Duke and the Monsignor want to see him."

In the old night-nursery the Duke did not at first so much as look at the man lying slackly in Nanny Brown's armchair by the fire-place; instead his glance strayed to a little cot in one corner, a tiny chair and a low table, miniatures for a child's use. Julia knew why. He was thinking back to the little son who had not lived to carry on his name and care for his estates. When at last he did examine the drugged figure—"He looks like a Baltic German," he observed. "How strange."

Julia and Torrens exchanged glances. But Torrens wanted above all to get the business in hand organised.

"Quite so, Sir," he said briskly. "Now, Colonel Marques and his men are coming to fetch him about 4 A.M. Can someone stay up to let them in? And do you agree to his staying here till then; locked in, of course?"

The Duke pondered—Julia saw him glance again at the cot in the corner, and guessed at his distaste.

"Yes, of course," he said then with a shrug, as if shaking off his private thoughts. "Elidio shall let these people in and bring them up by the back stairs, so that they will not be heard."

"Thank you, Sir. I shall wait up myself, of course."

"In that case you had better use my study. I will tell Elidio to keep the fire in. Now let us return to our drinks. Miss Probyn, will you not join us?"

In the study Mgr Subercaseaux suddenly put a question.

"Major Torrens, I think you said that this creature upstairs is probably the principal in the organisation?" Torrens nodded. "That being so," Subercaseaux proceeded, "and at least three of his associates being also laid by the heels, might not this be a good opportunity to get Dr. Horvath out of the country, before they have a chance to reorganise?"

"That was my idea. Have you done with him?"

"Substantially, yes; we could finish in a couple of hours. And since His Grace will be driving back to Lisbon on Friday for the wedding, it occurs to me that Dr. Horvath could travel down as he came up—if you agree, Duke?"

"Of course. Strange how one keeps on forgetting this wedding!" the Duke said. "It had quite passed from my mind again."

Subercaseaux turned to Torrens.

"You would, of course, have to make your transatlantic arrangements," he said. "How quickly could you do it?"

Torrens considered.

"Do you know, Sir," he said, "I think I had better go down with Colonel Marques when he comes to collect the body—a *corpus vile* if ever there was one!"

"Leave at four in the morning?" The Duke looked horrified.

"Yes, Sir. Of course I must hear whether Marques agrees with the Monsignor's estimate of the situation; if he does, I think we should go ahead. Could Father Antal spend just the Friday night in your Lisbon house again? You have been so good already that I hesitate to ask it, but it would save a lot of complicated arrangements."

"I am vexed that you should hesitate to ask!" the Duke said warmly. "I think you must know what a privilege it has been to have so great a man as Dr. Horvath under my roof."

Major Torrens was rather crushed by this. He had never realised that Father Antal was in any sense a "great" man in his own right; he regarded him as a little priest—a bit of a theologian, apparently, and as nice as you like, of course—whose special knowledge of conditions in Hungary made the Americans covet him for broadcasting on the Voice of America. As for the Vatican, God knew *whom* they attached importance to, or why: though one had to admit that the Roman Catholic Church was one of the few things that really seemed to worry the Kremlin, so good luck to it! He was relieved when the Monsignor put another question.

"You think you can get the agent from America over by Saturday to take him back? That seems rather quick work."

"Oh, no. This is only Wednesday—well it will be Thursday in half an hour!" he said, glancing at the clock. "But if Marques is on time we should be in Lisbon by ten-thirty tomorrow morning, and I ought to get through to Washington in an hour at most."

"That is only seven-thirty there," the Monsignor observed.

"Yes, but that office works round the clock. I don't know how long they'll take to lay on the special plane, but even their smaller jets do the trip in nine or ten hours."

"You will telephone to Washington?" the Duke put in, much interested.

"Radio-telephone, Sir. With a scrambler, of course: that is how Roosevelt and Churchill used to have those long heart-to-hearts during the war."

"They will come to Portela?" Subercaseaux asked.

"I shouldn't think so—much more likely Montijo. But Marques will have to arrange all that. He can have the plane advised which airport to use when it stops at the Azores to re-fuel. Then they can take Father Antal off some time on Saturday."

Julia spoke.

"Is all this rush really necessary?" she said coolly to Torrens. "It's a little hard on Hetta, don't you think? She'll hardly have any time with Father A. at this rate; only tomorrow, and I gather the Monsignor proposes to mop up most of that. Considering what she's been through for the sake of seeing him, I think it's rather tough."

Torrens looked annoyed and hurt; the Monsignor gave his barking laugh.

"Dear Miss Probyn, you remind us of the human element, so rightly the woman's role! But in this case perhaps there are over-riding considerations."

The Duke did not laugh.

"Miss Probyn, could not Countess Hetta come down with us to Lisbon on Friday? Then she could spend a quiet evening with Dr. Horvath, and possibly Saturday morning also. It is easy to take a third car if we need it."

"Duke dear, you're an angel! Yes, that's perfect. But I don't think you'll need to take a third car; Mr. Atherley has to get back to Lisbon on Friday, so *he* could drive Hetta down."

Subercaseaux threw her an enquiring glance, but he said nothing.

"Of course all this is subject to Colonel Marques approving of the plan," Torrens said. "Duke, if you will excuse me I think I'll go and put my things together now, so that there will be no delay when he comes."

"Certainly, my dear Torrens. Ring when you are ready, and Elidio will have your luggage brought down." He rose as he spoke. "I am afraid that this is Goodbye," he said, "but I hope only for the present. We shall see you in Lisbon, of course. Your visit has been a great pleasure."

Once again Major Torrens was abashed by his host's words; he spoke almost haltingly as he tried to express his own thanks. "You've been unbelievably good to us, Sir." Then, hastily, he made his escape.

"I think I'll go up too, Duke," Julia said, observing that her host was still on his feet—that was the sort of thing the darling Duque managed so well, she reflected amusedly, as she watched the Monsignor reluctantly heaving himself up out of his comfortable armchair.

Miss Probyn once again set her little Travalarm, and appeared in the study a few minutes after 4 A.M., in a highly becoming black velvet housecoat.

"Good heavens, Julia!" the Major exclaimed, surprised and glowing. "What on earth are you doing down here?"

"I just thought I'd come and see the coffin carried out, and hear what the Colonel has to say."

"*Darling!*" But the embrace on which Torrens was just embarking was forestalled by a sound of car-wheels on the gravel outside the windows; he stood back, and listened.

"Coming in with his engine shut off—good man," Julia commented.

"He's early," Torrens said resentfully; a moment later Elidio ushered in the Colonel.

"Well, our man is still fast asleep, I hope?" Marques said, shaking hands. "An excellent piece of work, this."

"You'd better come up and see if it *is* your man, Colonel. He should be quiet enough still."

"Oh, I know it's our man," Marques said. "Our people traced him to São Pedro do Sul this evening, but there was an inexcusable delay about getting the report through. However, the counter-espionage in this house is so good that it didn't matter! If you will just give me the key of the room, Major, my men will carry him down."

"We'd better go up with them; no one in the house knows where he is," said Torrens.

"Oh yes, the Duke gave instructions to his butler." Indeed at that moment Elidio appeared at the door and asked the Colonel for *a chave*; Torrens, amused, handed over the key.

"There; now we need not disturb ourselves," the Colonel said, going across to the fire and holding out his hands to the blaze. "Do I see whisky? That would be very welcome—the night is quite chilly." And soon the Chief of the Security Police, glass in hand, was listening very contentedly while the Major outlined his plans.

"Admirable. Yes, by all means come down with me; I have two cars. And this is an excellent moment to get Horvath out; their organisation here is disrupted for the time being—there were note-books on the three we caught, so we were able to land several others as well."

"*Did* any of them come in on the plane with Father Antal?" Julia put in unexpectedly. Marques glanced at her with amusement.

"Yes; four. How much you know, Mademoiselle!"

Presently Elidio, perfectly impassive, appeared at the door and announced that *este homem*, the agents, and the luggage of the Senhor Comandante were all now in the cars.

"Oh, but look here—*momentinho*, Elidio—they must have some coffee or something before they start off again!" the girl exclaimed. She spoke to the servant; Elidio said smugly that the policemen had already partaken of coffee and bread.

"Are you sure *you* don't want coffee or something?" she asked Colonel Marques.

"*Au contraire*, whisky was much better. So, *en route*." He bowed over Julia's hand, Torrens gripped it hard; a moment later she heard the cars crunch over the gravel and hum away up the drive.

When Julia told the Duke in the morning that Torrens was gone, and that the Colonel had given his blessing to the plan for getting Father Antal out of Portugal at the weekend, her host drew a pad towards him and began one of his careful computations, jotting down names as he spoke.

"So you go, and I, and my sister—the wedding party; also both our divines; five." He drummed with his fingers on the desk. "I think if pos-

sible we must take Dom Pedro by car; he was miserable coming up. He
dislikes riding in the Land-Rover, it seems."

"I don't wonder!" Julia exclaimed bluntly. The Duke laughed.

"But you say Monsieur Atherley is driving down, and could take the
little Countess; could he not take Dom Pedro too?"

"No, Duke; not on any account!"

"Oh?" He raised an eyebrow at her. "You have some combination in
your head?" he asked.

"Yes—'a consummation devoutly to be wished,' and you really *mustn't*
spoil it. Let Townsend Waller drive Dom Pedro down; if he does mislay
him it won't matter," said Julia coolly. "The Communists wouldn't hold
that poor old creature for twelve hours! Townsend can't stay here for ever,
either."

Ericeira burst out laughing.

"Miss Probyn, I sometimes envy your remorselessness! It simplifies many
problems. Very well: Dom Pedro either with us or with the American,
Atherley and the Countess." He made more notes, and looked up at her
again.

"But your delightful friend, Mrs. Hathaway! We are forgetting her.
Presumably she will wish to return to Lisbon also. How vexatious that
we must leave just now! I should have liked her to pay us a much
longer visit; she is interested in agriculture."

"Why shouldn't she stay here, then? We shall all three be back on
Sunday evening—if I may come back?"

"Of course you come back! But you think Mrs. Hathaway would not
mind this, being left for two days in the company of a child and a nurse?"

"Judging by a talk I overheard between her and Nanny this morning I
think she'd love it. They were getting on like a house on fire."

"Very well; so it shall be. You are the best judge. I must say," the Duke
said thoughtfully, "that it would give me great pleasure to show your
friend something of the estate, and of my plantations. She appears to have a
considerable knowledge of forestry."

Julia, who knew Mrs. Hathaway's knowledge of forestry to be confined
to conducting acrimonious disputes on her Aunt Ellen's behalf with the
Forestry Commission about "dedicating" some of the woods at Glentoran,
was delighted, though not surprised, that her old friend should have spent
the previous evening to such good purpose, and hastened off to open the
plan to her.

In the hall, however, she was intercepted by Atherley.

"Julia, be a good friend! Can you somehow break through the sort of
harem system that seems to operate in this house? I really do want to talk

to Hetti, but the women apparently never appear downstairs except at meals, or in a covey."

Julia laughed. Richard's picturesque description of Portuguese country-house life was in fact extremely apt.

"I'll do what I can," she said. "But of course you realise that the really important thing is for her to get as much time as possible with Father Antal, since he's flying to America at the week-end."

"*Is* he? When was that settled?"

"With Colonel Marques, early this morning. Oh, of course you don't know—it's *such* a performance!" And she told him about Luzia's and Nanny's exploits. Atherley bayed with delight.

"That *glorious* girl! Really she is a wonder." But then he pressed his request about Hetta.

"Well have a little *patience*, Richard!" Miss Probyn said, her voice displaying a marked absence of that quality. "Anyhow on the Duque's car-and-passenger schedule for returning to Lisbon tomorrow you are billed to drive Hetti down, *alone*."

"You've arranged that? Oh bless you."

"Yes. He wanted to plant you with Dom Pedro as well, but I suppressed it. So even if you don't get much time with her today, you'll have all tomorrow."

"Do I have to take her back to Dorothée?" Richard asked apprehensively.

"Oh Lord no! To the Palace; she's staying there till after the wedding, anyhow."

Julia had made up her mind that it was important that Father Antal should have an opportunity to give Hetta his guidance in what lay ahead of her—life in the Western world, probably a diplomatic marriage—before Atherley started on the poor child. But on her way to the priests' study she was caught by Hetta's other admirer.

"Oh Miss Probyn, *there* you are!" Townsend Waller said. "I was wondering—do you know where Countess Hetta is? I never had a chance to speak to her last night, and I really *would* like a talk with her."

"Townsend, I know you would, and I expect it can be fixed presently. But just now I'm trying to arrange for her to have a long, *quiet* talk with Father Antal; you see he's probably flying to the States on Saturday, so she and he won't have much time together; and honestly I think you young men can wait!"

"Leaving on *Saturday*!" the Bostonian exclaimed.

"Yes. I'll tell you the story later—it is quite a story! But Townsend, I must go now." She felt ready to shake both these greedy grasping creatures, thinking so much more of their own desires than of Hetta's real needs, and walked into the priests' study in a mood of strong impatience.

Subercaseaux had been sufficiently impressed by Miss Probyn's *démarche* in the study the previous evening to raise no objections when she stated that *now* would be a very good time for Father Antal and Hetta to have a little talk, alone. "If I don't arrange it no one else will," the girl said. "There are all these wretched suitors clamouring for her all over the house—she might be Penelope! Can't the Vatican take your infernal revisions as read, Monsignor?"

Both men laughed; Father Antal rose at once. "I am at your disposition." "Splendid. Come along."

Julia had decided that the knot-garden or anywhere out of doors was too liable to interruption, and led the priest to one of the huge deserted salons; there she looked round for an ash-tray, another rarity in Portuguese country-houses, and ruthlessly grabbed a small celadon dish off the chimney-piece.

"There you are—now smoke away! I'll bring her down."

She looked in on her way to see if Mrs. Hathaway was all right; she found Nanny seated with that lady in the latter's boudoir, deep in conversation, and both mending stockings—Mrs. Hathaway's stockings. "Oh, the young Countess is in my sitting-room, helping Luzia with her puzzle," Nanny said. Julia found Hetta, and bore her off with "Father Antal wants to talk to you."

Will it work? she asked herself as they went downstairs; these arranged things sometimes didn't. But unless this *was* arranged they would get no chance. She pushed Hetta into the great room, and left them to it.

"This is nice," Hetta said happily, pulling a brocaded tabouret over to the rather severe upright Louis XV armchair in which Father Antal, regardless of his own comfort, had settled down, and seating herself at his feet. "How did Yulia get this tedious Monsignor to release you? For I am sure she *did*. It seems he never lets you out of his sight!"

"Who told you this?" the priest asked, non-committally.

"Luzia; there is nothing she doesn't know. I find her—but *quite* enchanting!"

"She is. Now tell me why you describe Mgr Subercaseaux as tedious?" He was still perfectly non-committal.

"Oh but really, Father, surely you can see this for yourself! Flattering this poor old *beata* Dona Maria Francisca last night, being agreeable to the Duke, to everyone; enjoying his wine and his cigar!" Hetta said contemptuously. "And he is always the same: with my mother, with the Comte de Bretagne, with anyone who is rich or great! I dislike it. He is so—so *utterly* different to you!"

Father Antal made no direct reply to this outburst.

"Do you know about your mother's charities in the Alfama?" he asked quietly.

"Charities of *Mama's?*" She sounded incredulous. "No, I never heard of them. And where is the Alfama?"

"It is one of the districts of Lisbon where only quite poor people live, and money for the necessary charities is therefore hard to come by. But for the last few years the parish priest has received practically all he needs—from your mother."

"This is *very* odd! At home it was always Pappi who took an interest in poor people, and charities. That parish priest must be a most persuasive person, if he has succeeded in interesting Mama!"

"She has never met him," Father Antal said. "It is the Monsignor, whom you so despise, who has tapped this source of wealth to help the poor. Also he goes and says early Mass there at least twice a week, to give the parish priest a chance to rest and say his Mass later. As you know, working people must hear Mass early, or not at all."

Hetta pondered.

"He drives in from Estoril to say Mass? At what time?"

"At seven."

"Then he must leave his house soon after six. Well, that is something for him!" She pondered again. "Father, you mean some particular thing by telling me all this—what is it? Do not leave me to guess; you know that I am stupid at guessing!"

He patted her head gently.

"My child, I think you are in a certain confusion. Partly it is due to ignorance and inexperience, partly to the natural intolerance of youth; what is unfamiliar to you is necessarily wrong! This is a mistaken idea, believe me. What I wish you to recognise, and accept, is that there are other ways of serving God than those which obtained in the Alföld! God's plan for the world, and His wisdom, are not limited by your personal experience; He uses other means, other men, and it is presumption not to recognise the fact."

She was silent, troubled.

"I fancy this is, in you, a certain spiritual pride," he went on. "That, as you know, is a sin. You have only seen certain aspects of Monsignor Subercaseaux's activities, and in a certain milieu which, since it is unfamiliar, you take upon yourself to disapprove of—you, an ignorant girl of twenty-two! Who are you to judge?"

Hetta was deeply disturbed. In all their years together her beloved Father Antal had never spoken so severely to her before.

"But Father—he is so different to you," she repeated lamely.

"And am I the only model for God's servants? Must they all be cast in the mould which Hetta Páloczy approves? The Monsignor is quite as efficient as I am in achieving God's ends, and as uncompromising; and those ends are always worth achieving, even if it should be done by associating with the great or the rich."

Hetta burst into tears.

"Oh, it is all so difficult!" she exclaimed, between sobs. "To me, nearly everything here is a muddle! Compromise, compromise!—dress well, say always the right thing, whether it is true or not, and you are safe, you are accepted! But how can I live so? It is not my nature, and I have never learned it."

Father Antal let her cry for some time; then he put out a hand and raised her tear-stained face to look at him.

"This is what you must now learn," he said. "What made you a good little cook in a country presbytery, and a dutiful helper to Mother Scholastica will not suffice here. You must learn tolerance, and control, and moderation—but tolerance above all. Listen," he said, as she shook her head rebelliously, scattering tear-drops on his knees and her lap, "God has some particular work for each of us to do—yes, even for His little ignorant obstinate Hetta! But we must accept the place, and the conditions, which He chooses to set; if we do not accept them we are useless. And part of our acceptance must be a willingness, a *humble* willingness, to learn the appropriate technique. This for the present is your duty, since you have been set down by Almighty God in the free world, and in rather *mondain* surroundings. I shall be distressed," he ended rather sternly, "if you do not accept these terms."

This time Hetta did not cry. She shook back her hair and frowned, concentrating on his words; it was some moments before she spoke.

"I *have* tried to accept Mama," she said at last. "And truly I have tried to be docile: to go forever to the coiffeur, to put stuff on my face, to wear the right clothes. But—just lately—other things have come in, too; they make me wonder what I must do. Oh, I don't know whether I *can* live out here!"

"Are you thinking of M. Atherley?" Father Antal asked.

She stared at him. It was a strange expression that came over her strong face just then: surprise, hauteur, uncertainty—but, he would have sworn, also joy.

"But—why—I know that he is here; has he spoken?" the girl asked. Her words were confused, but there was no confusion in her manner; as always it was perfectly direct.

"Not to me. Has he to you? My child, I do not wish to force your confidence but before I leave I should like to know how this affair stands."

"Asked me to marry him—no," Hetta said thoughtfully. "I think he has become attached to me, in a rather unthinking way; he did once say to me that he thought he could be happy with me anywhere."

"And what did you say?"

"That he had not given the matter any thought; that I should drive him mad by—by my lack of control and tolerance and moderation!" the girl said explosively. "All the things you wish me to learn." She paused. "In any case, he is not a Catholic, and that is difficult," she ended in a different voice.

"Might he become one?"

"Well, at least he very much admires the Monsignor!" Hetta exclaimed. "We have arguments about him. Perhaps this is the road to Rome!"

Father Antal burst out laughing.

"This is a hopeful sign!—though it may only mean that Monsieur Atherley has more experience, and therefore more tolerance, than my late cook! One would expect this of a diplomat, of course."

Hetta laughed too, then became grave.

"Father"—she hesitated.

"Yes, my child?"

"Supposing he—Richard—did not wish to become a Catholic at once, should you approve of my getting married to him all the same?"

The priest took his time over replying. The question itself told him much. Clearly Hetta was anticipating a proposal; and his mind returned to what that so excellent young Englishwoman had said to him only yesterday about the importance of getting the child away from her mother. But there was the official Catholic view on this matter. At last, with deliberation, he spoke.

"My child, as you know the Church does not approve of mixed marriages. But Mother Church also takes particular circumstances into consideration; and in your case I should not oppose your marriage to this Englishman, provided that you love him, and are prepared to try to fit yourself to be his wife. Do you love him?" the old man asked bluntly.

"Oh yes—very, *very* much!" Hetta said in ringing tones. There was no bashful hiding of the face; she threw up her head as she announced her love for Richard Atherley. "Only I think we might have fights! But not *so* many if I practise these things you have told me of. And—" She stopped, her face clouding, as if the sun of her love had gone in.

"Yes?"

Hetta, too, delayed her reply, frowning in thought.

"Look, Father dear," she said at last, "I am young, and as you say without experience, unsophisticated"—there was a note of contempt on the word. "So it is hard for me to know if this, I mean to marry me, would be right for *him*. He *is* sophisticated, and the other day I met a person, a"— she faltered—"well, to me a most *disagreeable* person, who claimed to know him very well; and she made it plain that in her opinion I should make him miserable. This I have so much wanted to ask you about, for me it is important—in quite a different way to how it is important to her!" the girl said, with sudden anger. "She is an old woman who wants to keep a young lover; I am young, and I think of a husband, and having children, and a life together!"

He stroked her dark savage little head; he could not help smiling, though he was moved.

"Monsieur Atherley has broken with Madame de Vermeil. That affair is finished," he said.

"*You* know about this? How extraordinary!"

"No, personally I could not know. But Monsignor Subercaseaux, owing to this worldliness which you so contemn, knows all about the lady in question. And only two days ago young Atherley told him that the thing is over, and that he will never willingly meet this person again."

"So," Hetta Páloczy said thoughtfully. "So," she repeated slowly. She was considering this information. It must mean that the two priests had discussed her and her relation to Atherley; almost certainly it must mean as well that the Monsignor and Richard had also spoken of her relation to him. Now, no young girl whose heart is engaged before her hand really relishes the idea of her relations with the man of her choice being discussed by other people, but in Hetta's realistic Central European make-up there was no room for the quivering sensibility of the Nordic races over matters of romance. If they had all talked her and Richard over, well they had, and that was that; at least she had learned one really most precious fact—that this hitherto redoubtable enemy, the Frenchwoman, was no longer to be feared. She got up off the tabouret.

"Father, I do thank you. You have helped me so much: cleared my mind and my conscience. Now I see my way, if it should turn out so." Her deep voice hung suspended on the last words. "And now I am sure the Monsignor wants you!" She knelt on the Aubusson carpet. "Father, will you give me your blessing?"

His hands on her head, he did so, tears at last running down his face.

CHAPTER XVIII

ON THE FRIDAY MORNING preceding the nuptials of the son of the Comte de Bretagne another procession of cars passed down the by-road from Gralheira to São Pedro do Sul. In the twenty-four hours before an event of this sort one might have expected a certain degree of fuss to prevail; in fact there was none. For such occasions Dona Maria Francisca invariably donned a slightly richer version of her usual out-of-date black, and unlike Countess Páloczy gave no thought whatever to her hair or her face, let alone her feet; as for Julia, she had left the green brocade dress, which had so *épaté* Atherley, in a cupboard in the Ericeira Palace in Lisbon, all ready to put on.

The Duke had apologised deeply to Mrs. Hathaway for his own absence, and for taking away Elidio.

"This poor Antonio! I hope that he will wait on you well; but on the telephone he is hopeless, and there may be many calls in Lisbon. In any event we shall be back on Sunday evening, and you have only to ask Nanny for anything you want."

"Oh, Nanny and Luzia and I are going to enjoy ourselves thoroughly," Mrs. Hathaway said. "It is so good of you to keep me. Please don't worry. Nanny is a host in herself."

Nanny, for her part, expressed similar sentiments to Julia.

"Well really, Miss Probyn, it's quite a privilege to meet someone like your friend. It's not often I come across anyone that I could have such an esteem for."

"Yes, Nanny, she's grand, isn't she?" Julia said.

"A great advantage for Luzia, too, the company of a person like that," Nanny observed rather patronisingly; Julia went away laughing, realising how little of Mrs. Hathaway's advantageous company Nanny was likely to allow her charge.

So down the sandy road between the pines the cars poured that morning: a station-wagon containing Elidio and other servants, then Atherley's Bentley with Hetta and a rather gloomy Townsend Waller, who with Dom Pedro was to be dropped in São Pedro to pick up his car. Poor Townsend had not achieved a talk with Hetta—for which, rightly, he blamed Julia. Some time after the Bentley came two of the Daimlers with the rest of the party.

Atherley had made his own dispositions about this drive. He, too, had not yet succeeded in talking to Hetta; therefore he asked Elidio the day

before to provide *lanche* for two—*lanche* being the Portuguese word for
any form of meal carried in a basket to be eaten out of doors. After dropping
the chaplain and Mr. Waller in São Pedro do Sul he shot on to Aveiro, the
so-called Venice of Portugal. Here the flat coast-line is broken up into a
maze of lagoons, and a net-work of canals brings the brine of the Atlantic
into shallow salt-pans, divided by low earthen banks; these are filled
through small sluices and then left to be evaporated by the strong sun; the
good resulting salt is scraped off the floor and the pans re-flooded. This
process goes on all through the summer, and by early autumn conical
mounds of snow-white salt cover this peculiar landscape, like ranges of
miniature Alps. Richard had seen this once, and he wanted Hetta to see
it too, but in his urban ignorance he had ignored the seasons; this was
Spring, and hardly any salt had accumulated; there were no snowy
mounds.

"Oh well never mind, we'll go and see the Convent of Jesus instead,"
he said. "That's there all the year round." And he drove Hetta to that
amazing place, where the interior of the chapel gives the visitor the impression of standing inside a golden box, covered all over with the richest
possible gilded carving. Hetta was more surprised than pleased by this—
"Must one have so much gold about to worship God?" she asked, causing
the young man to laugh. But she stood long before the portrait of Santa
Joanna, the King's daughter who became a nun, with her plain melancholy
face, her heavy jowl, and her exceedingly long nose.

"Yes, that one could really have been a Saint," she said. "About some
one wonders, but not her. It must be a true portrait. Who was the artist?"

"Nuno Gonçalves, who painted the triptych with Prince Henry the
Navigator in it. Have you seen that yet?"

"Oh, *that* painter! Yes; no wonder," Hetta said, turning back to stare
at the sainted Princess again.

"Who took you to see the triptych?" Richard asked, slightly annoyed; he
would have liked to do that himself.

"Waller. He is very *gebildet*; he comes from Boston, where it seems that
all are extremely cultivated," Hetta said, again provoking Richard to
laughter. The priest's cook was coming on if she had already registered
the Boston passion for culture!

The Bentley's speed was so great, on the almost empty Portuguese
roads, that in spite of their détour they overtook the stately convoy of the
ducal Daimlers, proceeding at a majestic pace, several miles short of Leiria;
Hetta waved gaily to Julia and Father Antal, in the second car.

"Now we are ahead!" she said.

"Yes, but we're not going to eat with them all at the Lis; you and I are going to have a picnic by ourselves," he pronounced; the arrogant happiness in his voice sent a vibration through the girl. A mile or so farther on he swung the car sharply to the right down a small road which led through pinewoods to the village of Pinheiros, already on the edge of green open country with a river running through it, all brilliant as enamel in the spring sunshine, and the great church of Milagres standing up across the valley, a lonely wonder of baroque. Richard carried the lunch-baskets up a path to the fringe of the pinewoods, where he spread a rug on the clean mixture of silvery sand and fragrant needles; there, the dusky shadow of the trees behind, the shining river with its crumbling bridge in front, they had their lunch.

Portuguese servants have rather exalted ideas about picnic food. The *lanche* provided by Elidio included a bottle of sherry and another of red wine, with their appropriate glasses, thermoses of soup and coffee, and a jar of cream; these were merely adjuncts to a boned stuffed chicken already cut up and slices of *paio*, loin of pork spiced, salted, and rolled into a sausage; there were also buttered French rolls, a dish of dressed salad, and a box of chocolate éclairs. Richard ground the bottles and flasks into the shining sand to keep them upright, and poured out the sherry.

"Well, darling Hetti, here's to your future happiness!" He raised his glass.

"Prost," she said, and drank to him.

"You don't drink to *my* happiness, I notice," he said.

"Prost means 'to your well-being.' Isn't that enough?" she countered.

Her readiness pleased him. And she looked so *right*, there on the sandy edge of the forest, in her unobtrusive suit, open-necked blouse, low-heeled shoes and heavy-weight nylons. That a woman should look right in the country is always very important to Englishmen; another thing to which they often attach considerable importance is legs. Richard Atherley now observed that Hetta's legs, stuck out carelessly in front of her on the sand, though strong and shapely were rather thick, as Central European legs are apt to be; they were not in the least like Julia Probyn's long lovely ones. And with a sort of pang of surprised emotion the young man realised that in this girl, at any rate, he could even love thick legs.

"No—my well-being, like patriotism, is not enough," was all he said. "I would like you to drink to my happiness, Hetta. Do you know the one thing necessary for it?"

Again that vibration shook her, but she spoke deliberately.

"Richard, I am not certain that I do, truthfully. If your happiness requires two women, and I am to be one, I am afraid that you will have to go without it."

"Meaning?"

"That if I were to marry, I cannot share my husband with anyone—least of all *you* with this Frenchwoman! If I am married my husband must be mine!" she exclaimed.

He put down his glass so quickly and carelessly that it fell over; the sherry seeped away into the white sand as he took her in his arms.

"Darling, you won't have to share me with *anyone!*" he said, between kisses. "That nonsense is all over." He paused. "I learned the other night, when I thought I'd lost you, what I really want—you, and to spend my life with you. But in fact I had that idea before; do you remember what I told you at Obidos? Anyhow, will you marry me? This is a formal proposal, and requires an unequivocal answer," he said, giving her another kiss and then holding her away from him so that he could watch her face.

To his infinite delight she gave a tiny laugh; then she put up her hand and stroked his cheek. It was a very small gesture, but combined with the laugh to him it seemed to demonstrate comprehension, humour, and great love.

"Yes, Richard, I will marry you," she said. "On these terms that you have just stated—I hope, unequivocally also!"

He shook her shoulders. "Oh, you are a proud piece! Yes, unequivocally! And now, my fiancée, please give *me* a kiss. This affair mustn't be altogether one-sided, you know."

The kiss Hetta gave him was so satisfactory that it demanded a rather protracted response; it was some time before they returned to the normal world and the business of drinking and eating.

"See, you have upset my glass as well as your own—what waste!" Hetta said. "How shall I live with a husband who is so careless? Hungarians are thrifty."

"Oh, go ahead with your thrift, my saucy darling! We shall need it; diplomacy is a ruinous career. I never knew an English Minister or Ambassador who didn't end up several thousand pounds down out of his private pocket."

"But you are not an Ambassador."

"No, sweetheart, but it is quite inevitable that I shall become one—unless the demands of your love extinguish me before my time!"

She gave him a little slap.

"Do not be id-*yot!* I am hungry. Do you allow your wife, or your wives, sometimes to eat?"

In such a mood Elidio's *lanche* went down very well: the soup was drunk, the French rolls munched; between them the two young people demolished the whole of the boned chicken, the salad, and the spiced pork, to the accompaniment of the Duke's good red wine. Seeing Richard take up a final slice of *paio* before he vulgarly wiped out the salad-dish with the last roll, Hetta asked rather anxiously, "Do you like *l'ail*? I think the English call it something else."

"Garlic. Yes, I do."

"That is well. I should find it almost impossible to cook *good* food without it, though one should not always recognise quite so clearly that it is there as one does in this curious *Schinken*." (*Paio* in fact reeks of garlic.)

"Sweet, you won't have to be *my* cook, as well as the old priest's," Richard said. "We shall have a cook, please God."

"I shall be much in the kitchen, nevertheless," Hetta averred firmly. "A good *maîtresse de maison* is constantly there, taking counsel with the cook, as my Grandmother did at Detvan. And so I shall do with our cook."

Those two very ordinary words, "our cook," were astonishingly sweet in her mouth to Richard's ears. His fears, the inevitable hesitations of a lively handsome young man finally and definitely confronted with matrimony, began to fall away as another picture opened on his imagination: of a home with a wife in it, who would "take counsel" with his cook about his food, and never allow dead or dying flowers, one of his particular phobias; of a hundred homely domestic intimacies—perhaps even children. Richard Atherley had never hitherto contemplated any picture of the sort; now he did, in a wondering silence, and found it strangely delightful. He was silent for so long that at last Hetta touched his hand. "I have said something stupid?" she asked.

"No, you've said something very nice indeed. Look"—he held her hand —"how do you feel about having children?"

"*Feel* about it? What should I feel? I hope we have many; one child is not a good thing." She paused and looked at him, uncertainty coming into her face. "Do *you* not want children? Richard, I cannot marry without."

"No, I do. Darling, this is all so new—don't be impatient with me." It was he who was anxious now. "We'll have lots of children! Well say four; they cost the earth to educate! Will four do you? But I do want *some*; I'd like to have a son, I must say."

Hetta laughed at him.

"And what shall you do if you only have a daughter, like the Duque? And my poor Pappi," she added, no longer laughing.

He caught her to him. "Try, try, try again!"

They arrived in Lisbon rather late, because Richard had insisted on giving her at least a glimpse of Batalha and Alcobaça; and then they felt that they must drive out to Obidos and have another glass of wine in the tiny room that Richard so idiotically called "The Ritz," and look again at the house in which he had first suggested living with her. During those hours of driving through the sun-drenched countryside, laughing and touching hands, there grew in them both, strongly, the extraordinary sense of *security* that becoming engaged brings, and the quite irrational self-satisfaction at having achieved this security, this feeling of being anchored. Richard told the man in the flowered shirt-sleeves who poured out their wine in the Ritz that they were going to be married, whereupon a surprising number of relations crammed into the minute space to laugh and drink their healths.

As they drove on again Hetta asked a question.

"So do we tell everyone, now, that we shall marry?"

Richard reflected, but only for a moment. Thinking of Fanny—

"Yes, immediately," he replied. If everyone in the Ericeira Palace knew of their engagement tonight it would ring all round the wedding reception tomorrow, and could not fail to reach Fanny's ears, and Fanny would always accept a *fait accompli* that was publicly proclaimed, however unpalatable; she was much too clever to make a fuss which might jeopardise her position in the eyes of the world. But even as he reached this reassuring conclusion another quite fresh idea struck him: how low and calculating such considerations were—his, and Fanny's—compared with Hetta's spontaneous and unself-seeking honesty. Even loving and desiring her, he had thought patronisingly of her lack of sophistication; now, startled, he saw that there was such a thing as moral sophistication, that fierce delicate rectitude in relationships, regardless of one's own position. And Hetti had it, and he and Mme de Vermeil had not. Oh, once she had mastered a little of the technique of tact and discretion she would be able to make rings round all the Fannys in the world!—as Maggie Verver had made rings round Charlotte Stant in *The Golden Bowl*, in the end of all.

Hetta was silent for some time.

"If we tell others, I should tell Mama," she said at length.

"Yes, you must of course. But may I give you a piece of advice?" She nodded.

"I shouldn't do it tonight. She's not worrying about you; you know I took the Monsignor down to see her, and he straightened all that out, and if you telephone to her this evening she'll only get in a fuss, just when she ought to be resting, to be at her best for the wedding tomorrow." Feeling slightly like Judas, he added, "You should know how much that means to her."

"This is true." She frowned a little, thinking. "But if she hears it from others at the wedding, she might be hurt."

"She's not likely to hear it from the Ericeiras," Richard said bluntly. "Why don't you leave it to the Monsignor? He's made himself responsible for you to her."

"Yes, Yulia told me. He has been kind, in this. All the same, that someone else should tell a mother that her daughter is engaged: this is not very nice, do you think?"

He reflected. "I suggest that you write a note to your mother tonight—after all, we've only got engaged today—and let the Monsignor give it to her tomorrow. Then she will hear it from you, and at once."

Again Hetta considered.

"Yes, I will do that. It is—*just* adequate."

Julia and the Monsignor were down in the hall when they reached the palace; Subercaseaux at once asked Richard if he was staying to dinner? "If not, perhaps you could take me out to Estoril. The telephone has ceased to function, so there is some difficulty about a taxi; and the chauffeurs appear to be at supper."

"I shall be delighted," said Atherley unwillingly. He turned to Julia. "Hetti and I are engaged to be married."

Julia gave Hetti a warm hug. Still with an arm round her—"I hope, Richard, that you realise exactly *how* lucky you are," she said.

"Truly, Julia, I believe I do."

"Well don't go forgetting it later on!" Miss Probyn said crisply.

The Monsignor also made appropriate congratulations. "I think this match will be welcome to your mother," he added to Hetta.

"My note!" Hetta exclaimed. "I must write to Mama, so that you can give it to her the *moment* you see her, Monsignor, please. Yulia, *where* can I write?"

While Julia took Hetta away to write her note Richard explained the advice that he had given the girl about telling her mother; Subercaseaux nodded approval.

"Yes, for the Countess to telephone tonight might create complications. For the moment the instrument is out of action, but that cannot last long." He looked shrewdly at Richard. "You will have many things to learn from this child," he added.

"Monsignor, I've realised that." He liked and trusted Subercaseaux enough to expound his sudden enlightenment about moral sophistication.

"Precisely—that is what I mean. She needs to acquire the lower forms of this necessary but uninspiring quality, sophistication; but you, my dear Richard, would do well to master the higher ones! Ah, there they are!" he said, as Julia and Hetta cascaded down the great staircase; he took Hetta's note, and they drove off.

Too many descriptions of royal weddings can be tedious. This particular marriage was both exclusive and brilliant; it was followed by a reception, in the course of which the British Ambassador found himself practically pushed into the rounded front portion of Mgr Subercaseaux. "Oh, how are you, Monsignor? Everything going well? Tell me, is that Miss Probyn here? If she is I should like to meet her."

The Monsignor threw a practised eye over the throng. Not far off he saw Miss Probyn, whose height made her conspicuous; he and Sir Henry slowly made their way towards her between the jammed, richly-dressed bodies. Julia, in the green brocade dress, with a close-fitting toque of cock's feathers which continued down one side of her white neck to curl over her left shoulder, was really a very splendid sight; the Ambassador's blue eyes rested on her with pleasure.

"At last," he said. "I've been wanting to meet you for some time."

"Oh. Why?" Julia asked, in her near-drawl.

"You seem to be a sort of key to all these doings in which my First Secretary has been involved. Tell me, is he going to marry the little Countess?"

"Yes, they got engaged yesterday. Do you think it's a good idea?"

"It's always a good idea to marry a woman who can cook," Sir Henry said. "Especially nowadays. He will be comfortable when he retires, which is more than I shall; my good wife can't boil an egg."

"Oh how sad!—poor you!" Sir Henry chuckled. Few people say "poor you" to Ambassadors.

"A marriage with a foreigner won't *help* his career, of course," this one said, "but I expect he will surmount that. He's very able, and she is such a charmer. *Good,* too; you know lots of diplomatic wives seem to lose practically all ethical sense—if they ever had any."

Julia laughed. But she was thinking more of the present than of Richard's retirement some thirty years hence.

"Look, dear Sir Henry," she said coaxingly, "can't you push him off now somewhere else, out of reach of Mama?"

Sir Henry threw her a glance of half-comic outrage.

"So you want to rob me of the best Head of Chancery I've ever had, in any post?"

"Certainly I do. What do Chanceries matter compared with love and marriage? And for two such unusually nice people, in this case. I think they come even before the convenience of Ambassadors."

He laughed, and picked at his thumb.

"Miss Probyn, you fully come up to my expectations! No wonder everything hangs on you." He considered. "In fact I know that the Office wants someone of about his seniority for Rome."

"Then do get them to send him there, for goodness sake! Rome would be perfect for Hetta—it's full of expatriate Hunks, isn't it? And, of course, the Holy Father as well."

The Ambassador laughed again.

"I promise you that I will try—against my own interests." He gave her a shrewd glance. "Wasn't that exceedingly nice American, Waller, one of her admirers too?"

"Oh yes, but that didn't work. Hetta likes him, he was kind to her when she came; but—well, these things happen in one way and not in another." He mused.

"Yes; yes, of course." He went on picking at his thumb. "Thirty-five years ago, no, more, when I was a Second Secretary in Washington I often met Emily Waller; his mother, you know. She was a very forceful woman. And their toffee doesn't always set."

Julia laughed so loudly that heads turned in their direction.

"Ah, but that isn't confined to America," the Ambassador said. "My dear Miss Probyn, London is full of such men."

At this point the Duke of Ericeira appeared beside them.

"Duke, you are the other person I wanted to see," Sir Henry said. "Miss Probyn I have, at last, met." Julia took this rather broad hint, and drifted off. "You have been unspeakably good to our people over all this," he went on. "I do thank you."

"Your Excellency, I cannot tell you the pleasure it has been to have them all in my house. I have long been a student of Dr. Horvath's writings, but I never hoped for the privilege of meeting him, let alone to have him as my guest. And the good Torrens: an admirable person, especially when galvanised into life by our dear Miss Probyn; and Atherley and the nice American, to say nothing of the enchanting little Countess. I assure you, my friend, it is long since Gralheira was so full of life."

"You like the little Countess? Good. I hear she and Master Atherley are going to make a match of it."

"Yes, so Miss Probyn tells me. From the little I have seen of her I should count him fortunate, for she seems to have real *fonds de caractère*. Would you agree?"

"Well, yes and no," Sir Henry said. "I think the girl is a good girl, with plenty of individuality; but the Service still takes a curiously *static* view about our diplomats not marrying Englishwomen, you know, and this girl comes from a Curtain country. Her father had a great reputation, of course,

as an anti-Communist, back in 1919. But the poor boy will be saddled
with a rather dreadful mother-in-law."

The Duke agreed. "Look out, *mon cher!*" Sir Henry suddenly exclaimed
—"We are going to be *coincés par la mère!* Can we get away?"

They couldn't; the crowd was now too thick. Only someone of Dorothy
Páloczy's ruthless determination could have forced a way through it just
then; she succeeded, and appeared beside the two men, a formidable ap-
parition in all her war-paint—the clothes, the hair, the make-up. Mme
de Vermeil was at her elbow. After greeting the Ambassador, "I don't know
the Duke of Ericeira except by sight!" the Countess said gaily.

Sir Henry was both firm and adroit.

"My dear lady, I am in precisely the same situation in regard to Madame
de Vermeil," he said promptly. "Do please present me." This introduction
was followed up by a flow of questions from Sir Henry about people in
Paris, during which the Duke, thankfully, contrived to edge away.

"Oh, he's gone!" the Ambassador exclaimed, after a final earnest enquiry concerning *"cette chère Violette."* "What a pity! Well, some other
time. Now tell me—are you happy about your little daughter's engagement
to my admirable Head of Chancery? I do hope so, because I am very fond
of him. Moreover, he's extremely able; he has a great future before him."

"I'm very glad to hear that. Yes; I haven't seen a great deal of Richard,
but I like what I have seen," Dorothée said. A certain sharpness came
into her voice. "Did Monsignor Subercaseaux fix this up?"

Sir Henry looked shocked.

"Oh my dear lady, NO. What an idea! Richard has been head over ears
about your daughter ever since they first met; and when she—well, disappeared—" the Ambassador said carefully, "he was quite distracted. My good
young man, my right hand, you might say, deserts both his chief and his
job, and rushes off in the middle of the night to look for his lost love!
Personally I regard this as practically a *crime passionnel,*" the Ambassador
observed, chuckling. While he spoke he had kept one shrewd blue eye on
Mme de Vermeil; she took it as he had expected she would, unblenchingly,
but he decided to rub the thing in thoroughly.

"This really *is* Love's Young Dream," he went on; "I can assure you of
that. The Monsignor I know is delighted—as well he may be, since he is
extremely fond of Richard too. All this young man's friends can only rejoice at his great good fortune."

Dorothée was rather swamped by these complimentary phrases. Thrown
off her balance—"I still don't know where she is," she said. "Do *you* know,
Sir Henry?"

"No notion! Mustn't we both leave all that to the Monsignor? I gather he's in charge. Au revoir, chère Comtesse; au revoir, Madame de Vermeil. I see the Cardinal Patriarch over there; I must have a word with him." The crowd was beginning to thin a little; skilfully, the Ambassador, too, escaped.

At that very moment Hetta Páloczy was standing out on the apron of Montijo airport, seeing Father Antal off. Thanks to the kindly planning of Julia and the Duke she had had a long quiet evening with the old priest the night before, and another blessed two hours with him this morning. She had told him of her happiness, he had given her his final blessing as she knelt devoutly in front of him, pressing his hands strongly on her little black head. Afterwards, "But do not forget what I told you at Gralheira," Father Antal said. "Now you enter upon a life in which your husband will be among those who wield power and influence. See to it that you do not diminish his influence by any mistakes of yours, any roughness or clumsiness. Be humble; be gentle. Do you remember what Ruysbroeck said? 'Be kind, be kind, and you will be saints.' I think, my Hetti, that you are not always kind in your judgements, as for instance concerning the Monsignor! And you must be good to your mother, too. She is very much alone, now." With tears, Hetta had promised to obey these injunctions.

That was her real farewell, but all the same she could have hugged Major Torrens for saying, off-handedly, that she might as well come along to the airport. Now, in the blinding sunshine, she stood in a little group which included Colonel Marques, the Major, and the Military Attaché, forcing herself to talk politely to the agent from America, a quiet, soft-voiced Southerner; at any other time he might well have charmed her, but now all her eyes and half her ears were concentrated on the stocky little figure of the priest. Once more he was wearing his European disguise of the grey overcoat and sun-glasses; the silver stubble on his head was half-concealed under the incongruous Trilby hat. The mouth and that cropped hair were really all she could see—she looked and looked, trying to force into her mind a picture that might have to last her for the rest of her life.

"And you cooked for him?" the Southerner said. He had heard enough of Hetta's story to be interested in her.

"Yes. I like cooking. Oh, but where does he go now?" Hetta exclaimed, as Marques, Torrens and Father Antal moved away. The man from Louisiana glanced at her with compassionate understanding.

"You go after him; you don't have to worry about me." Hetta followed the others.

"She loves that old man, the poor child," the American muttered to himself, as he moved after her.

On military airports like Montijo there is none of the civilian vulgarity of loud-speakers braying commands, only a brief discreet summons to the official passengers by word of mouth. This had just been given: the American followed Hetta slowly towards the great silvery bird-like shape poised for flight on the tarmac. He saw his special cargo, the freight he had to deliver safely to his employers in America, pause and look round; saw the pretty girl with whom he had just been talking break into a run, seize the old man's hand and cover it with kisses; when she turned back towards him Captain Glenny averted his eyes from the pain in her face. But he took her hand, saying, "Countess, I'll look after him; please don't worry."

Hetta made no reply. She stood stock still, watching, while Father Antal and the American climbed into the plane; watched while it rose, circled, and hummed away in flight over the red earth and the silver olive-groves, till it disappeared, seawards, behind the Serra da Arrabida.

It was just about then that Richard Atherley and Townsend Waller were sitting down to cocktails on the terrace of that restaurant above the Tagus. Richard had asked Townsend to lunch; one way and another he had rather a bad conscience about his friend, and he particularly did not want the Bostonian to hear of his engagement from any outside source.

"We've not been here since the day before Hetta arrived," Townsend said, tilting the Martini round in his glass thoughtfully.

"No. It's warmer now," Richard said, idiotically; he felt nervous. He pulled himself together. "Townsend, Hetta and I are engaged. I proposed to her yesterday on the way home, and she has accepted me."

"I was really expecting that, I think," Townsend said, after a moment's pause. He drank half his cocktail at a gulp, and set down his glass. Then he lifted it again.

"I don't have to wish you good fortune, Richard, because you have it! But I do wish you every conceivable happiness; you and her"—and he drained the glass.

Richard was touched by this. But there was nothing more to be said, really, and all through their meal they rather carefully talked diplomatic shop. Presently cars returning from the wedding reception began to stream along the broad road immediately below the terrace, and they amused themselves by noting the occupants. The Duke and his sister in one of the Ericeira Daimlers were among the first, shortly followed by the Loseleys in the Embassy Humber: on this highly official occasion the tiny Union Jack, usually discreetly furled in its black case, fluttered from the right wing.

"Oh good, H.E. will be back early. I shall have to go and see him," Richard said. A little later—"Goodness! There's the Monsignor, in Dorothée's car," he exclaimed. "What on earth is *he* hiving into Lisbon for, do you suppose? Father Antal must be gone by now; one would have expected Subercaseaux to be sleeping it off."

Mr. Waller laughed. But the sight of Mgr Subercaseaux had aroused another train of thought in his mind; he looked earnestly at his companion.

"Richard, please forgive my asking this, but are you going to become a Catholic when you marry?"

This time Richard did not laugh at the question, as he had done on an earlier occasion.

"Townsend, I don't think so; not at once, anyhow. I don't suppose they'd have me, come to that—I'm not at all religious."

"Oh, they'll have anyone! And they'll *condition* you so that you get religious!" the Unitarian said bitterly. "Almost everyone that marries a Catholic ends up by becoming a Catholic themselves! Don't, *please*, do that, Richard."

"Townsend, it's too soon to promise anything," the Englishman said. "Every marriage calls for endless adjustments, and I suppose one makes them as they come along." Suddenly he felt irritated by this pressure; he spoke almost harshly. "If you were to marry her what would *you* do, if she wanted you to become a Catholic? You'd be wax in her hands, and you know it!"

"Not wax to that extent, Richard—no. But let's not quarrel about it. I'm sorry."

The Monsignor, half-asleep in Countess Páloczy's Rolls-Royce, was going to Lisbon, most reluctantly, to bring back Countess Páloczy's daughter. He had warned Miss Probyn at the reception that Dorothée was insisting on this, and that resourceful young woman had contrived to put through a call from back regions overflowing with caterers' men to poor Hetta, warning her to pack and be ready; the palace telephone was working again. "Oh yes, I shall not make him wait; he will be tired," Hetta said. "Is it a nice wedding?"

"Yes, lovely—the greatest fun; Princess Maxine looks entrancing. The Comte de Bretagne has been asking after you, and the Archduke too; he's frightfully disappointed that you aren't here! If I don't see you before you leave I'll come out tomorrow," Julia added. "Did Father A. get off all right? Good."

Hence there was no delay for the Monsignor when he called for Hetta;

she was waiting in the hall, Elidio carried out her single suit-case, and they were off. The Monsignor asked if Father Antal were safely gone?

"Yes. I went with him to the plane; Major Torrens was so kind. But you must be quite exhausted, Monsignor; do not trouble to talk with me. Could you not sleep a little, even in the car?"

Subercaseaux glanced at her in surprise.

"Yes, my child, I will. I am in fact very tired." He studied her face. "You are a good girl; you will do your Richard credit." He leaned back and closed his eyes.

Up to the day before Hetta had been dreading her return to the Castelo-Imperial. She hated hotel life anyhow; and her mother, to her never a congenial or sympathetic person, would not only be angry with her, but would be reinforced by the detestable presence of Mme de Vermeil, her rival with Richard. The high-bred ease and pleasantness of life as it was led at Gralheira had, even in those two days, increased her reluctance and distaste. But *now*, everything was altered; she was engaged, secure; she need fear nobody, since Richard stood behind her.

Esperanza took her at once to her mother's room. Dorothée was on her bed, the lowered sun-blinds only admitting a dim light; she had taken several aspirins to counteract the royal champagne and lay somnolent, triumphant, but more than a little cross.

"So *there* you are! Well later on you can tell me *what* you've been up to, and where—but now I really have to rest. The wedding was *marvellous,* but these big functions are quite exhausting."

"I am so glad you enjoyed it, Mama. You got my note?"

"Yes of course, but we must talk about all that later on. I really am too tired now."

Hetta was hurt, with good reason, that this should be her mother's sole reaction to the engagement of her only child. A sharp sentence came into her mind; she bit it back, remembering Father Antal's words—"Be kind, be kind," and bent over the bed to give her difficult parent a kiss.

"Naturally, Mama. Rest well; I am sure you need it." As she stood up Esperanza came in.

"A Senhor from the British Embassy asks for the Menina on the telephone. Shall I put the call through here?"

"Yes, yes!" Dorothy Páloczy said irritably. "Here, of course." Esperanza went out, and Hetta eagerly lifted the receiver of the bedside telephone; in a moment she heard Richard's voice, to her full of reassurance.

"Darling! Are you all right? I rang up the old holy, and found that he'd carted you back."

"Yes, quite all right," Hetta said.

"The Major tells me that your private holy got away according to plan, and that you saw him off. I'm so glad."

"Yes; he was *very* kind to arrange this."

"Well I'm sure that has made you feel rather sad, sweetheart, and I'm having a quite hideous time here, trying to clear off my back-log of work. I suggest that presently we both call it a day, and cheer ourselves up by going out to have supper at the Guincho. What do you say?"

"This is where I swam?"

"Yes, my love, you did indeed!"

"And the cooking was *so* good! Yes, Richard; I will come."

"Excellent. I'll call for you soon after seven. Till then, dearest Hetti."

The girl put down the receiver and addressed the rather collapsed figure on the bed.

"Mama, that was Richard. He asked me to dine with him this evening. I have said Yes."

"Well really, I should have thought that tonight, at least, you might have dinner with me, and explain everything," the Countess said crossly. "Anyhow I don't want you to do any more running around with young men, after this week's escapade. You'd better call him back and say No."

Hetta was silent for a moment.

"I cannot do that," she said then, quite gently—"at least, I shall not. To-night, dear Mama, I dine with my *Verlobte*." (In the stress of this first moment of deliberate independence she could not remember the English word for "betrothed.") She stooped down and gave her mother a second kiss. "Rest well. Why not have something to eat in bed? You must be so tired." She went out closing the door as gently as she had spoken. Alone in the darkened room Countess Páloczy burst into angry tears, interrupted by hiccoughs—in five minutes she was asleep.

CHAPTER XIX

BEFORE DRIVING OUT to Estoril to take Hetta to dine Mr. Atherley carried out his intention of going to see the Ambassador; as he left the Chancery he was accosted by Tomlinson.

"May I offer my congratulations, Sir? I understand that you are engaged to be married."

Richard was highly entertained—oh the delightful diplomatic grapevine! Who would know about his engagement sooner than the messenger and the telephonist?

"Thank you very much, Tomlinson," he said, holding out his hand. "I may say that my wife-to-be, like yours, is a very good cook!"

"Yes Sir; so I understand. She cooked for quite some time for this Hungarian agent who was flown out today, didn't she?"

Richard shouted with laughter.

"Tomlinson, I believe you're employed by Colonel Marques on the side!" He went out through the walnut-wood and wrought-iron doors, while Tomlinson slipped into the telephone-room to report the Head of Chancery's latest crack to his wife. "Mr. Atherley looks ever so happy."

"He's nice—I hope she is," Mrs. Tomlinson replied. "*Esta?*" she said into the mouthpiece of her head-phones, and went on with her work.

Richard was looking more thoughtful than happy as he set out on that short up-and-downhill walk from the Chancery to the Embassy, through the cheerful inconsequent architecture of the Lapa quarter, brilliantly pink and white in the rich sunshine of late afternoon. During the night—and the day as well, for the few moments when his mind had been disengaged —he had been suffering from the back-thoughts inevitable to sensitive people after they become engaged. For Atherley these doubts were rather more acute than is usually the case, since he was perfectly well aware of the attitude of the Office towards foreign marriages; and while he was not inordinately ambitious, he did care a great deal about his work, and his career in connection with it. And he was not only marrying a foreigner, but one who had just come from behind the Iron Curtain; the vitriol press would undoubtedly seize on this, barely disguising malice as romance or sensation—there would be references to Burgess and Maclean. As he turned the last corner into the steep street leading down to the Embassy (in whose lower reaches washing, propped out on cords from the windows, flapped with a pleasant domesticity in the river-breeze blowing in from the Tagus) he threw up his head and drew a deep breath of the soft salty air that ruffled his bare head. Hetta was worth it, whatever happened!—and anyhow he could always retire to farm and shoot on his mother's place in Herefordshire if the Office got really bloody-minded, and tried to send him to Bogotá.

The Ambassador always kept open house for his staff at the end of the day, with a choice of Scotch or Irish whisky, in a big downstairs room whose windows gave onto the Rua Arriaga, known as his study; he greeted Richard there. "It's so warm, shall we go up and sit in the garden?"

They sat in that small paved courtyard where Hetta had read out the Latin inscriptions and armigerous mottoes of former envoys to the Duke of Ericeira. Richard realised that Sir Henry had suggested this arrangement in order that they should not be interrupted; down in the study the most junior of secretaries, under this accessible chief, could pop in through the Arriaga entrance un-announced, but up here in the private apartments permission must be asked. He was rather touched by this thoughtfulness; H.E. really *was* a kind old boy. It was pleasant in the courtyard: the delicate formal foliage of the great pepper-tree overhanging the steps cut a fine tracery against the blue sky, the scent of flowers came down from the beds fostered by Lady Loseley; from a cage outside the glazed passage her doves cooed gently.

"Those doves!" Sir Henry said. "Comical birds—they're very knowing. They laugh, you know, when anything amuses them. I remember in 1938 listening on the wireless to the speech of one of our masters after Munich; it was chilly, so we had the doves indoors, and when he began to talk about 'peace with honour' you should have heard them—'Hoo-hoo-hoo-hoo-hoo!' We had to laugh ourselves, though it was no laughing matter."

"No animals seem to have cared much for that individual," Richard said, delighted by this reminiscence. "Did you ever hear, Sir, about Miss Stark's little alligator, or lizard, that some Sheik had given her, complete with a golden collar and chain? It rather liked music on the wireless, but one evening in Italy when they were listening to him too, the little creature got so furious that it broke its chain and ran away, and they spent two whole days hunting all through Asolo for it before they got it back."

The Ambassador laughed loudly.

"Your story is rather taller than mine, Richard, but I like it."

"What I really came for, Sir, was to thank you for those two extra days' leave," the young man said. This was true, but he felt such confidence in his friendly superior that he was hoping for an opportunity to air his doubts and problems. He was not disappointed.

"It worked out all right, did it? I gather you're engaged."

"Yes. I don't suppose the Office will like it much, but that can't be helped—one really can't marry merely to please the Private Secretaries and the Chief Clerk!" Richard said somewhat acidly.

"Well in the first place, Richard, I congratulate you most warmly. I think your little Countess is a splendid girl—pretty, intelligent, and learned." He threw a glance at the plaques. "*And* a good cook! I think you've done remarkably well for yourself." He cocked an eye at his Head of Chancery. "Now I'm going to make myself unpopular, and give some unasked-for advice."

"Please do."

"Don't patronise her, Richard. Of course she's got a good deal to learn superficially, but I suspect that her real knowledge begins where that of most diplomatic wives leaves off."

"I realise that, I think." Richard spoke slowly; he hesitated, and then said—

"How much do you think this will affect—well, what I do?"

"Anyhow you can obviously never be sent to any Curtain countries!" Sir Henry said cheerfully. "That's an enormous let-off in itself. Think of those poor devils in our Missions in Moscow and Prague and Warsaw—what a life! You'll escape that." He eyed Richard. "Are you worrying about it?"

"Just a little."

"I shouldn't. It may prevent your being sent to Washington, at least for some time; but Washington is so infernally hot, *and* so infernally expensive!—that's really a let-off too. The fact is, my dear Richard, I think your little lady will soon turn into such a winner—if you don't cow her and make her nervous—that she will be a raging success anywhere."

All this was nectar and ambrosia to Atherley, of course.

"How would you like Rome?" the Ambassador asked suddenly.

"Rome? Why, am I being shifted?"

"Not that I know of. But I think they may want someone for Rome quite soon, and I could slip in a word. If, of course, it would suit you to be shifted. I should be exceedingly sorry to lose you," Sir Henry said—"but possibly you might prefer another post, now."

"Really I should be most grateful if you would slip in that word," Atherley said. "In fact 'grateful' is silly; I should hardly know how to thank you—sorry as I shall be to leave. But—well, I think a change might make things easier for Hetta."

"I think so too," the Ambassador said drily. "Very well—I'll do what I can. And now how about telling me that story we hadn't time for the other day?—of the rescue. Didn't you say the Duke's little girl had played some sort of a lone hand? Another whisky?"

While Richard Atherley—keeping a furtive eye on his watch—was telling Sir Henry Loseley, with considerable relish, the full tale of Hetta's rescue in the Embassy courtyard in Lisbon, the news of the engagement reached Gralheira. Mrs. Hathaway was with Nanny and Luzia when Antonio summoned her to the telephone; on her return she said—

"That was Miss Probyn. It seems the wedding was quite splendid; she says she's busy writing up her despatch about it, but they'll all be back tomorrow afternoon, so we shall hear everything then. And Mr. Atherley is engaged to little Countess Páloczy. They settled it yesterday, on the drive down."

"Well, I call that very suitable," Nanny said. "It's time he settled down, and she's a very nice young lady; well-connected, I understand, too, in her own country."

Mrs. Hathaway glanced at Luzia. The girl's strange Celtic-classical face had taken on its Medusa look; it startled the Englishwoman—she watched that face, suddenly, with the sort of anxiety with which a disposal squad might look at an unexploded bomb.

"Hetta is lucky," Luzia said at last—and Mrs. Hathaway let out the breath which, quite unconsciously, she had been holding. "Atherley's wife will be very happy."

"*Mister* Atherley, Luzia," Nanny said mechanically, as so often before. But on this occasion Luzia was recalcitrant.

"Atherley's wife," she repeated; "or *Richard's*. She is lucky," she said again—"and I hope they will both be most happy." She sprang up from her chair and ran out of the room.

Mrs. Hathaway looked questioningly at Nanny.

"Oh, ever since he came to the house to talk to Miss Probyn about the accident to her car, and all this business of the priests began, the child has been quite mad about Mr. Atherley," Nanny said. "I'm sure you know how young girls are, Madam—at about sixteen their heads are full of poetry and beauty, and absolutely nothing else. They're just waiting for love, only they don't know it; and the first man they see they fall for. Well that's rather a vulgar expression," Nanny said apologetically. "These girlish fancies, they're as fine-spun as cobwebs with the dew on them! But they can be very upsetting, all the same."

Mrs. Hathaway was struck by Nanny's percipience, and still more by the manner in which she expressed it. The neat elderly woman in the navy-blue suit and white silk blouse must at some point in her undiscoverable past life have been impressed by the silver gauze, spangled with dewdrops, spread out on autumn pastures in Leicestershire—to the point of using it for a comparison with the lyric love of sixteen, as she had observed it. Or had she experienced it, too? Almost awestruck by this idea, Mrs. Hathaway gazed at her companion. But Nanny soon brought her down to earth.

"Personally, I think the Major much the more attractive of the two," she said. "But, of course, it's been obvious all along that he has no eyes for anyone but Miss Probyn; whereas this business of the Countess and Mr. Atherley has been what you might call short and sharp."

"Ye-es," Mrs. Hathaway said thoughtfully. She had encountered Major Torrens with deep interest, and was still wondering how that affair stood, and whether he was really the person for her beloved Julia. She would have been rather glad to hear Nanny on this point, but could not quite bring herself to ask. Nanny, however, obligingly volunteered her views.

"I don't know, I'm sure, whether Miss Probyn will take him or not. And I find it hard to make up my mind whether she'd be wise to. He's a splendid gentleman, but he's *solid,* and she's so quick—it mightn't work."

"You're very fond of her, aren't you?" Mrs. Hathaway temporised.

"Of course—what's more, I *admire* her. Who wouldn't, that had lived and worked with her?"

Mrs. Hathaway's discretion was melted by this tribute.

"Nanny, you think she—well, might blow him sky-high?"

"She might; or he might pull her down. It wouldn't hurt *him* to be given a bit of a lift, but I should hate to see her wings clipped," Nanny pronounced—and Mrs. Hathaway, deeply agreeing, could have embraced her for those words.

While this conversation was taking place the subjects of it were standing together at the window of the schoolroom in the Ericeira Palace in Lisbon, occupied with the same problem. The round table behind them was strewn with sheets of typescript; when the Major arrived Julia had been busy finishing her account of the wedding, which she intended to take out to Portela by car to catch the late plane for London—Julia was rather good at wheedling pilots or bribing stewards into doing this sort of job for her. Torrens' arrival threatened to upset her time-table, but the moment he entered the room she realised that he was in a state of emotional urgency; she greeted him kindly, looked at her watch, and decided that he could have twenty-five minutes for whatever was eating him. She could guess all too well what it was.

"Well, that job's done," she said easily, after hearing his account of Father Antal's departure.

"Yes, thank God. It has been a teaser, too. And but for you I should have mucked it—they would have nabbed us at the level crossing coming out from Estoril that night. In fact really you've done it all." He looked at her. "The last time our lines crossed on a job you were against me, and you beat me; this time you were on my side. I—I very much prefer it that way."

"Well anyhow bless you, Hugh, for having taken Hetti out to the airport to see him off," Julia said, still lightly and without stress. "That was a real kindness."

"You say 'Bless you' so easily," he said irritably. "But you know quite well that there is only one blessing I really want, and you go on and on withholding it. When are you going to make up your mind?"

The girl continued to stare out of the window onto the garden, where one corner of the lawn was rendered countrified by a coop in which a hen still sat on Nanny's bantam eggs—that good woman had decided against taking the clutch up to Gralheira lest the drive should spoil them. She found it hard to answer the man beside her—moreover, she had a slight sense of guilt on his account. When she had first met him in Tangier, just over a year before, he had seemed determined and masterful, almost aggressive—up to a point that was something she approved of, and she had rather fallen for him. She did still like him very much; physically he could easily stir her. But—oh, what was it? Somehow in this Portuguese context he had shown himself as *less* than he had in Morocco; occasionally he had been at a loss, or out of key. All that was natural enough: he had found himself plunged into a totally strange environment, to her deeply familiar —it was no wonder that he had had to rely on her for a great deal. And to be just to him he freely admitted his debt. But—again—it was no good marrying someone whom you had to be *just* to! Perhaps later on it might all come right; in other circumstances, or elsewhere. She was angry with herself that at this moment there should arise in her mind, quite unbidden, the picture of Hugh sitting in the Land-Rover holding Luzia in his arms: that was irrelevant and unworthy—but having arisen, it stuck like a burr. Well he would have to wait, till she saw her way; no, *felt* her way, in a fashion which would make justice as irrelevant as his merciful care of that exhausted child.

"Hugh, I can't make up my mind now," she said gently. "If I did, it would have to be No—and I don't want that to be the answer, any more than you do. But you must leave it yet-a-while."

Of course he argued, protested.

"No!" she said at last, sharply—"I won't be rushed. If you try that on, it's No for keeps! I expect I've been vague and daffy-ish, and I apologise, if so—but don't try to bounce me. I won't stand for it."

"If you don't want it to be No ultimately, I don't see why you can't make it Yes now," he urged. "What *is* it, Julia?—what's in your mind?"

"I don't know—Portugal, perhaps. But please leave it for now, Hugh."

"I believe you're in love with the Duque!" he said angrily.

"No, I'm not—though I can't think *why* not; he's such a charmer. Of course the person he ought to marry is Mrs. Hathaway," she said. "That would be so marvellous for Luzia." She turned to him. "Hugh, when do you leave?"

"Day after tomorrow."

"Where for?"

"London, in the first place."

"And where's Colin?"

"Back at Gibraltar—I heard this morning. He did that business at Cannes very well."

"May I tell Edina? Discreetly?"

"Yes, I think so. Wait till it breaks in the press, though."

The mention of the press reminded Julia of her despatch; she looked at her watch.

"Hugh, you'll have to go now; at least I shall. I must get this thing off to my paper." She moved to the table as she spoke, and began pushing the sheets of typescript together; then she left them, and turned to him. "Don't be angry with me, whatever you do. Drop me if you think I'm too much trouble to be worth while; otherwise just forgive me for wanting to be certain." She pulled the velvet strap of the bell. "Goodbye."

"No, damn you, au revoir," he said; and picked up his hat and went out.

The run out to Portela was a relief to Julia after this scene, which left her dissatisfied with herself, sorry for Hugh, but implacably determined not to marry him till her heart and mind should give the word together. The evening air came in at the windows and cooled her flushed cheeks; the horizon over the Tagus was a soft green and rose, and out in the open land the olive-trees detached themselves, dark and shapely, from the green and rosy fields. At the airport she handed over her package of script to one of the air crew, and then drove leisurely back into Lisbon. At this hour, just before nightfall, there was a wonderful quality in the light—the pale tones of the buildings glowed, street lamps burned like great stars through trees whose green had a depth and richness unknown by day; in the blocks of flats the windows were oblongs of soft light. Back at the house, after parking her car in the courtyard she rang up the Castelo-Imperial; but Hetta of course was out, dining with Richard at the Guincho. Oh well, never mind—tomorrow she would recover her car from Colonel Marques and flip out to see the child before driving herself to Gralheira.

She went up to the schoolroom. Her typewriter still stood, open, on the table; mechanically she clipped on the cover and set it in its place on the bookshelf, emptied an ash-tray, patted the faded cushions on the old sofa—there! But still the room, now tidy, was somehow full of poor Hugh and his distress. With an impatient shrug the girl went over to the window and leaned her elbows on the sill. And at once Hugh and his troubles fell away; Portugal and its beauty enfolded her once more. The light was almost gone—the white shapes of the two swans who circled, cold and detached, in the pool on the lawn gleamed in the gathering dusk: she could barely distinguish the humble grey oblong of Nanny's hen-coop. To think of Nanny was to think of Luzia, and her mind lingered on that lovely child—Julia had guessed what Nanny had guessed, and she remained for some time wondering just how hard her pupil would be taking the news of Atherley's engagement. About that engagement itself she had no doubts—Hetta was as tough as Hell, she would learn what she needed to learn, and be the making of Richard, once that old poppet of an Ambassador had pushed him off to Rome. But what a funny, *rapid* business it had all been! The last thing she expected when she came out to cover the wedding for the *Northern Post* was to find herself involved in the escape of a little Hungarian priest and in Hetta Páloczy and her affairs; all the same these episodes, Julia Probyn decided, as she leaned from an upper window in Lisbon, were intrinsically much more important and exciting than the royal marriage which tomorrow would fill the headlines of the world's press.

Tomorrow!—tomorrow would see her back at beloved Gralheira, sunk in the country life of Portugal, with its ageless calm and beauty. As she turned away from the window there came a knock on the door, and Francisco the footman entered.

"*Minha Menina*, the Senhora Condessa desires to know if the Menina is coming down to say the Rosary?"

"*Sim*, Francisco—I come." And twining her black lace mantilla round her golden head, Julia Probyn went down to the Chapel to join her hostess.

The
Numbered
Account

CHAPTER I

GLENTORAN

THE RED-FUNNELED *Flora Macdonald* sidled skillfully alongside the grey wet quay of the small west Highland port, watched by Edina Reeder, who also scanned the passengers waiting above the gangway; when she saw among them a tall, elegant figure with a tawny-gold head she smiled and waved. Presently a porter in a seaman's jersey carried the luggage out and stowed it in a brand-new Land Rover, while the two cousins kissed and exchanged greetings.

"Philip and I thought you were never coming back to Glentoran," Mrs. Reeder said. "You haven't been up since our wedding, and that's nearly two years ago."

"I know. I was such ages in Portugal—both times. But it's heavenly to be back now."

Julia Probyn was a young woman of independent fortune; an only child, with both parents dead, she had few family ties except with her Scottish cousins. To occupy herself she worked, rather intermittently, as a free-lance journalist for some English weeklies, and even a quite important provincial daily paper; she was a good linguist who enjoyed foreign travel, and in the second of her two visits to Portugal she had incidentally become involved in work for the British Secret Service—to which Colin Monro, Mrs. Reeder's younger brother, belonged.

As the car shot off from the harbor—"This is a terrific machine," Julia said. "Philip, I suppose?"

"Oh yes, everything is Philip. You won't know Glentoran!" Edina replied. "When we got married Mother, in her most Early-Christian-Martyr way, suggested withdrawing to the little dower house, but of course we didn't allow that—she's in the west wing. Philip has turned it into a self-contained flat, with a subflat for Forbes, horrid old creature!"

"I thought the west wing used to be damp," Julia said.

"Ah, but not any more. Central heating throughout! I expect it's very bad for one, softening, and all that, but I must say it's exceedingly comfortable to be warm everywhere, after those awful wood fires. Colin's here," Mrs. Reeder then said. "He was delighted when you rang up to say that you were coming, because he's going off again fairly soon to the Middle East, or one of those troublesome places."

"Oh I am glad. What luck! Dear Colin." Miss Probyn was devoted to her other cousin. "How is he?"

"I fancy he's got something on his mind," Edina said, slinging the Land Rover round the curves of a steep hill under huge overhanging beeches, "but he hasn't uttered. I daresay he'll tell *you*." As they reached the top of the hill and emerged into open country—

"Goodness! You've ploughed that slope above Laggan-na-Geoich!" Miss Probyn exclaimed. "It used to be all rushes. What *can* grow there?"

"Winter wheat. It's all been drained—with the Government grant, of course—and fenced, as you see."

Indeed as they now entered on the Glentoran estate, evidences of prosperity and good husbandry appeared on all sides: strong pig-wire fences, Dutch barns, new iron gates painted red; so different from the beloved but rather derelict Glentoran that she had known all her life that Julia fairly gasped. "I can't think how you've got it all done in the time," she said, after being shown three or four silage pits, and a herd of pedigree Ayrshire cows.

"Oh, Philip works all day and most of the night, and adores it. But I must say it's very nice to have some money to come and go on, and be able to treat the land properly."

Julia presently returned to the subject of her cousin Colin.

"What makes you think he has something on his mind?"

"He mopes, and jerks his thumb."

Many of the Monro family had the hereditary peculiarity of double-jointed thumbs, enabling them to turn that member downwards in a spectacular and quite horrible fashion; the operation made an audible creaking sound which was curiously sickening. Edina used this peculiar gift sparingly, being a calm person; but Julia was intensely familiar with it in Colin, as a symptom of nervousness or worry.

However he showed no sign of either at luncheon, which took place rather late. In spite of all the external improvements, Glentoran, within, was its old shabby self, rather to Julia's relief—except for the genial all-pervading warmth from the central heating, and a newly installed fitted basin with scalding hot water in her bedroom. Clearly Philip Reeder believed in spending his good money on useful, practical things rather than on aesthetic amenities; the drawing room, to which she presently went down, had its old worn and hideous carpet, and the familiar faded cretonne covers. Here Philip gave her a stiff gin, and here also she encountered her cousin Colin and old Mrs. Monro, his and Edina's mother.

"How nice to see you, Aunt Ellen," Julia said, kissing her, and holding out a long casual hand to Colin.

"I can't think why you haven't been near us for so long," Mrs. Monro said fretfully.

"I've been abroad, you know."

"Everyone *will* go abroad—I can't think why. Mary Hathaway has gone abroad, when she might just as well have been here," Mrs. Monro pursued, in a complaining tone. "She's gone to Switzerland, of all places."

"To stay with an old flame," Edina put in. "*Really* old—about eighty. He lives in Gersau, wherever that is."

"On the Lake of Lucerne," Colin said.

"Oh, you know-all! Mother, if you've finished your sherry let's go in, shall we? Julia, bring in your drink."

Julia, instead, downed it. She hated spirits at table.

Over the meal Mrs. Monro resumed her grumbles.

"I can't think why Mary should have wanted to go to Switzerland. I went there once, and I thought it a most horrid place—all mountains, really there's nowhere to walk on the flat. They took me into an ice grotto, in some glacier, and it dripped down my neck. I think all that ice and snow about is most unhealthy."

Philip Reeder, laughing, reminded his mother-in-law that large parts of Switzerland were far from any ice or snow, and really not much more mountainous than Argyll; round Lake Neuchatel, for instance. Julia noticed a certain preoccupation in Colin's expression while the talk was of Switzerland, which left it when they turned to discussing local affairs; presently he addressed her in Gaelic, still spoken here and there in the district; they had both picked it up as children from the keepers and the boatmen, and he gave his rather high-pitched giggle of pleasure when, after a second's hesitation, she replied in the same archaic tongue. After that they talked in Gaelic across the table; this irritated old Mrs. Monro, who eventually protested—"I was brought up to think it very ill-bred to talk in a language that others present cannot understand."

"They're not ill-bred, Mother; they're merely good linguists," Edina told her mother. "So was Father, he spoke Gaelic perfectly, the old people always tell me—'He had the Gahlic,' is their phrase. You and I aren't linguists, worse luck for us; if we were, we could have learned it."

"My dear, I never *wished* to learn such a useless language," said old Mrs. Monro, with the complete finality of the rather stupid person.

After lunch Colin determinedly took Julia out to stroll in the garden; Philip went off to the farm and Edina, after returning her mother to the west-wing flat, settled down to some overdue correspondence about Girl Guides. Julia was struck afresh by what a little money—Philip's money— was doing to Glentoran: the lawns closely mown; the strangling brambles

cut down from the immense species rhododendrons (brought back as seeds
by Hooker himself from the Himalayas) along the banks of the burn; all
the deadly growth of sycamore seedlings cleared out from between the rare
shrubs along the upper avenue.

"Goodness, it is lovely to see this place being put to rights again," she
said.

"Yes, I suppose so." Colin sounded *distrait*, as though the improvement
in what was really his own estate meant very little to him. Since his work
constantly took him abroad, he was glad to let his sister and his wealthy
brother-in-law live in and run Glentoran. Presently he stood still.

"Julia—" he paused.

"Yes?"

"I know it's none of my business, but I'm so fond of him that it worries
me—" he paused again, in obvious embarrassment.

"Well?" Julia asked, guessing what was coming.

"Well, how *do* things stand between you and Hugh?"

"They don't stand at all," Julia said, quite unembarrassed. "He asked me
to marry him in Portugal, and I said No."

"Why on earth? He's such a splendid person."

"I just couldn't feel it the right thing to do—somehow he didn't seem the
same in Portugal as he did in Tangier."

"What do you mean?"

"What I say—and more than that I won't say, because I couldn't explain
properly. I'm sorry about it, very, but there it is."

"Don't you think it's about time you stopped amusing yourself with men,
and then turning them down?" Colin said crossly. "First it was that
wretched Consett, though I admit he was a bit of a wet, and now it's
Hugh—who certainly *isn't* wet."

"No, of course he isn't," Julia said, with perfect good-temper. "But I
can't marry him because he's your boss, and you're fond of him. I must
want *badly* to marry the person I do marry; it wouldn't be fair to them,
otherwise—in fact much more unfair than rubbing them off in good time."

Colin laughed, rather unwillingly, at the flat way in which Julia brought
out this piece of wisdom. Suddenly he gave her a kiss.

"Oh well, you're not actually a *hag* yet," he said, "even if you are rather
a monster! I daresay you'll find a man you badly want to marry one of
these days. Don't leave it too late, though."

"Try not to, darling," Julia said, returning his kiss.

Julia wondered after this conversation whether Colin's gloom had been
about her and Hugh Torrens, his chief in the Secret Service, and hoped

that having said his piece, the young man might feel better. But he continued abstracted that evening and the next day.

The whole party forgathered for tea in the dining room which, Julia had already observed with nostalgic satisfaction, was as gloomy, shabby, and ugly as ever—wood lice still crawled, and died, between the outer panes and the hideous stained glass which defaced the upper half of the windows; the log fire still spat and fizzled ineffectually—though, thanks to the central heating, this made no difference to anyone's comfort. Halfway through the deleteriously ample Scottish meal of two kinds of scone, four different cakes, assorted jams and jellies and honey in the comb, the telephone rang. Philip Reeder had installed an extension in every sitting room in the house, as well as in his own and Edina's bedroom, instead of the single inconveniently placed instrument in the chilly cloakroom near the front door; he rose from the table and answered the call.

"Telegram for you, Julia," he said, and held out the receiver.

Julia went over to the table under the woodlice-laden window, listened, wrote on the pad, questioned, scribbled again—finally she tore the top sheet off the block and returned to the table.

"So sorry, Edina. It's from Mrs. H."

"Why does Mary Hathaway need to send you such a huge long telegram?" old Mrs. Monro asked.

"She's ill, Aunt Ellen, and she wants Watkins to go out and look after her; she's afraid of being a trouble to this old Mr. Waechter and his servants."

"I'm sorry to hear that," Philip Reeder said—he had soon come to share the Monro family's affection for Mrs. Hathaway, always their prop and stay in any trouble. To Julia Mary Hathaway meant even more than this; since her own mother's death, when she was quite little, Mrs. Hathaway represented all she had ever known of motherhood.

"What's wrong with her?" Philip went on.

"Congestion of the lungs."

"There! What did I say?" old Mrs. Monro exclaimed triumphantly. "Switzerland is unhealthy. I expect poor Mary went into an ice grotto!"

"There are no glaciers within forty miles of Gersau, Mother," Colin put in.

"Then I expect old Mr. Waechter, who I believe is extremely rich, drove her to one," his mother said obstinately. Philip put a more practical question to his guest.

"Why does she wire to you, Julia? Can't Watkins just take a ticket, and go?"

"Oh no," his wife hastily told him. "Watkins can't bear traveling abroad

—that's why Mrs. H. didn't take her along. Julia, I suppose this means that you've got to drag that spoiled old creature out in person, doesn't it? Oh what misery!—when you've only just come. I can't think why anyone has a lady's maid!"

"My dear, when they existed they were a great convenience," her husband told her—"though this Watkins person sounds rather an unsuitable type, I must say."

"Watkins has been with Mary Hathaway for twenty-five years, Philip," his mother-in-law pronounced—"and she is a most faithful and excellent servant."

"Well *have* you got to go out and take her, Julia?" Colin asked—rather to his cousin's surprise.

"Yes, I'm afraid I must do just that," Julia said. For her, to do anything her beloved "Mrs. H." asked was an absolute imperative—and now the darling was *ill*. "Edina, I am so sorry. Philip, may I send a telegram? I ought to do it after tea."

"Of course. But send it N.L.T., at half the day price," her host said, with his usual practicality.

"Fine. I must wire to old Watkins too, and tell her to pack her traps and be ready to start when I come. Oh yes, and I must book a flight from Renfrew. *What* a bore! I was so happy to be up here again!"

"I suppose you'll fly?" her host said. "Shouldn't you book plane seats to Switzerland too?"

"Oh no; Watkins will never fly—we must go by train. Yes, of course we must get sleepers."

"Where to?" Reeder asked.

"Berne," Colin pronounced suddenly. "You change there for Lucerne, and then take a steamer on to Gersau."

"How *do* you know all this?" his sister asked him. The young man jerked his thumb out of joint as he replied—"I just *do* know."

"Next assignment Switzerland?" his brother-in-law asked. "Sounds as if you'd been mugging it up."

"It's coming in very handy for me," Julia said, as Colin merely shook his head, frowning at this attempt at humor.

After tea much telephoning and sending of telegrams took place: a flight was booked from Renfrew for the following afternoon; Cook's promised sleepers from Calais to Berne two days later; Julia just caught her bank manager and organized traveler's checks. During all this fuss, Colin hung about, silent and preoccupied; when Julia said, "Well, that's that—" after talking to the bank, he put in a word.

"What about Watkins' passport?"

"Oh Lord!—I never thought of that. I don't for a moment suppose she's got one. Will they be shut now? What are we to do? We shan't have much time to rake up a minister of religion or a justice of the peace to vouch for her."

"I think I'd better ring up the office. They will probably be able to fix it."

"*Could* you? *Would* they?" Julia said, immensely relieved. She was also happily surprised by Colin's helpfulness; for a junior official to suggest taking such action was something quite out of the way.

"I expect so. What's her Christian name?"

"No idea," and "May," Julia and Edina said simultaneously.

"Just May? May Watkins? What a name for that old dragoon."

"Yes, May," Edina repeated firmly. "Her mother doted on old Queen Mary. Endless girls in Watkins' generation were called after 'Princess May.'"

"All right—though it sounds pretty silly to me. Now you girls can clear out. I'll tell you what happens."

Julia and Edina obediently removed themselves; they sat on a new teak seat on the terrace, in the westering sun, looking out over the drifts of daffodils in the rough grass round the lawn. On the great horse chestnut, the pink candles were just coming into flame—its lower boughs drooped down to the ground.

"How funny that Colin should lend a hand like this," Edina said, "after being so sour when Philip ragged him about Switzerland."

"I was just thinking the same thing," Julia replied. "But anyhow, what a boon! That office of his can fix anything. Still, I do wonder what's behind it—it isn't a bit like him." (She was soon to learn what was behind it.)

A window was thrown up in the house.

"Where shall May's passport be sent?" Colin's voice inquired.

"My flat. No, my club; of course the flat's shut."

"That grisly place in Grosvenor Street?"

"Yes." The window was slammed down again.

"Good for him," Julia said.

Presently Colin appeared on the terrace.

"All fixed, darling?" Julia asked.

"Yes, darling darling."

This was another piece of youthful nonsense, dating from the long happy holiday summers when Colin was at Eton, and Julia at a finishing school in Paris; they used the word "darling" then as a sort of call-note, like a bird's special note of alarm, for any secret thing between them. This had irritated old Mrs. Monro even more than their speaking Gaelic at meals, but it warmed Julia to hear Colin use the old silly reduplication now. And when he said, "Come up to the azalea glen—they're all out, and you haven't been yet," she agreed at once.

"She ought to pack," Edina said.

"Oh, I'll pack tonight." The two young people went off up the avenue, arm in arm.

The azalea glen at Glentoran in flower is something to see. The banks of a narrow ravine, down which a small burn runs, were planted long ago with azaleas which have grown to an immense size; the great rounded bushes overhang the water, sprawl above the path, below the path, and even encumber the small wooden bridges which here and there span the glen—fallen blossoms are carried away by the clear noisy water. It is a most beautiful place, full of all shades of color from cream to coral; the scent, with its hint of incense, is almost overpowering. And here, on a rather decrepit wooden seat—Philip Reeder had not yet extended his new teak benches as far as the glen—Colin and Julia sat and talked; and what Julia privately expressed as "the nub" emerged.

"If you're really going to Switzerland anyhow, darling, I thought you mightn't mind doing something."

"For you?"

"Well yes, in a way." His horrible thumb shot out.

"Tell," Julia said comfortably.

"Yes, I will. It's about Aglaia Armitage. Her father's dead and her mother's no good—she ran off to the Argentine with a Dago tenor even before poor Armitage died, four years ago."

"Is Aglaia in Switzerland?" Julia had visions of a girls' school near Lausanne or Ouchy.

"Oh no. But her grandfather died the other day."

"Was he looking after her?"

"Not much, no—she lived with an aunt in London, her father's sister. But"—Colin paused, and his thumb jerked out again. "He left her quite a lot of money, and she ought to be sure of getting it," he said.

"Well can't the will simply be proved, if he left it to her?" Julia asked, puzzled by Colin's obvious anxiety.

"The money isn't in a will. It's in Switzerland." He stuck again.

"Darling, do be a little more clear. Why no will?"

"Oh, there's a will all right, and she's his heir. But—did you ever hear of numbered accounts?"

"No. What are they?"

"Well, people all over the world, if they want to have some of their funds safe and sure, put them in Swiss banks."

"Oh, funk-money. Yes, very sensible. I expect masses of Jews and Armenians and rich ones from those unreliable South American republics have millions stowed away there. But what are these numbered accounts?"

"Accounts with a number, but no name. Anonymous, you see."

"No I don't, quite. Unless somebody in the bank knows which name is attached to what number, how does Mr. Sophocles Euripides or Senhor Vasco da Gama get his money out when he wants it?"

Colin laughed.

"I don't know the exact mechanism, but there's some sort of secret record, or code, and the owner *can* touch his cash in need. Only it's not quite so easy when the person who made the deposit is dead, and that's the case with Aglaia's fortune."

"What was her grandfather's name? Armitage? The English do this too, do they?"

"I wouldn't know. He wasn't English, and his name wasn't Armitage; that was her father."

"Then what was the grandfather's name?"

Colin hesitated; he gave a curious youthful giggle of embarrassment before he said—"Thalassides; Orestes Thalassides."

"Oh Lord, not the old shipowner? He must have been worth a packet."

"Yes he was. And he did make a will all right, with proper legacies— don't you remember, half a million to Cambridge alone for science fellowships, and more to various Redbricks? But although the papers called her a great heiress, all that didn't leave an awful lot for Aglaia except this Swiss money. And"—again he checked—"you see he *may* not have told the Swiss bank that she is his heiress."

"Won't the will show that?"

"We hope so, but it isn't dead certain."

"If the will makes her his residuary legatee, or whatever they call it, surely she's on velvet?—except for death duties."

"That's just the point. The lawyers seem to think that the will may have been left a bit vague for that very reason."

"Oh, these smart foreigners! Here are all our own dukes and peers selling their family portraits to pay those revolting death duties, and Mr. What's-it-ides puts his dough in a foreign bank to escape paying!"

"Don't be nasty, J.," the young man said, mildly and rather sadly.

"Sorry—no, I won't." She considered. "But Aglaia knows this money has been left to her?"

"Yes."

"And told you?"

"Yes," Colin said again, blushing.

Julia pounced, so to speak, on the blush.

"Colin, are you engaged to Aglaia?"

"M'm'm—after a fashion."

"Is she sweet?" Julia asked, with warm interest.

"Yes, incredibly sweet. I want to marry her, if only to get her away from this dim aunt she lives with since her mother ran away. Well, not 'if only'— I long to marry her."

"Where did you meet her?"

"Oh, in London, like one does. She knows some cousins of the Macdonalds." He paused. "But you see I've really nothing to marry *on*."

"Well I suppose you really have Glentoran—though of course you don't want to call that in, with Philip and Edina so blissfully happy here, and making such a go of it."

"No, of course I don't, and anyhow I want to go on working. But that doesn't bring in much."

"Does that matter, if Aglaia's got plenty?"

"Only that everyone will think I'm marrying her for her money—which I'm *not*. I'd marry her if she hadn't a single Swiss centime, if I could support her! And she wants to marry *me*," Colin added guilelessly, "so she might just as well have her own cash, since it's there. But you do see, darling, that all that is just why I should like someone like you to go and *aborder* the Swiss bank. I mean, you know I'm not after her money."

"Of course, darling." Julia reflected for a moment, sniffing at a spray of azalea which she had picked off the nearest bush. "What I don't quite see," she said then, "is why your Aglaia can't simply go out with a copy of the will in her hand, walk into the bank, give the secret number, and get the cash. How much is it, by the way?"

"About half a billion dollars, I believe."

"That says nothing to me," Julia stated airily. "I never can remember if a billion is a hundred million, or a thousand million, or a million million. And anyhow I can't really think in dollars—'divide by three' is what I say when I place an article in America. But it sounds quite a nice little lump sum, whichever it is! Well, why can't she do what I say?—just go and collect, herself?"

"Well for one thing she's a minor, under twenty-one; and for another, she doesn't know the account number."

"How ridiculous! Who does? Don't the lawyers or the executors?"

"No. It seems these things are kept pretty dark—no one in London has the faintest idea. But there is someone out there who quite certainly *does* know; her godfather, a Swiss pastor who is also her guardian."

"Why a *Swiss* godfather? Oh well, never mind; no odder than a Greek grandfather—all international! Well, can't she go and get it from him?"

"Not at the moment, no. For one thing her mother has just sent for her to go and pay a dutiful visit in the Argentine—she's sailing this week."

"Colin, what nonsense! *Why* must she go to her unpleasant mother?"

Colin hesitated. "Well, it might be a wise move. The lawyers think her mother may have an idea that the numbered account exists—Aglaia has told *them*, of course—and that if she goes out there it might put the mother and her Dago husband off the scent, and prevent *them* from trying to get hold of the money. The lawyers have been wondering, and so has Aglaia, how to set things in train in Switzerland in the meantime, very discreetly and quietly, of course—now that you're actually going to be out there, it struck me at once that you could have a try. Your lovely silly face is such a help!"

"Beastly child!"

"Well would you?"

"I don't see why not, when I've got Mrs. H. all settled. It might be rather fun, really—and in Morocco I seemed to have quite a light hand with bankers, like some women have for pastry. Have you got the guardian's address, who has the essential number?"

"I can get that for you."

A huge sound of a distant bell resounded through the glen. Julia sprang up.

"The dressing bell! We must fly."

"We don't dress," Colin said, following her down the path between the mountains of blossom.

"No, but we clean ourselves! And Ronan and his Mamma are coming to supper, so I must tidy up a bit." She ran on.

Out in the avenue—"I shall have to have a copy of the will, you know, Colin, or the bank certainly won't play; and some *pièces justificatives* for the godfather, or he won't either," Julia said.

"Yes, of course. I'll get you all that—I shall have to come South and see that you're properly briefed, now that you've agreed to take it on. Darling, I *am* glad that you will." He gave her a quick light kiss. "I needn't tell you to keep it all utterly dark."

"Hardly!" Julia said, with good-tempered sarcasm.

Colin's remarks the previous day about her throwing men over had rather upset Julia—until all the business about Mrs. Hathaway broke they had been wriggling about at the back of her mind like small ugly worms; she had remembered poor Steve in Morocco, whom Colin didn't know about. He made a third. While she quickly changed into a short dress for dinner she thought with discomfort about Ronan Macdonald, and wished he weren't coming; on some earlier visits to Glentoran he had obviously been attracted by her, and she had flirted with him a little, gaily and unseriously. She hoped he wouldn't start all that up again, under Colin's very nose.

He did, however. Julia Probyn's unusual lion-tawny blondness and great grey eyes were something men readily fell for, and did not soon forget—after nearly two years Ronan Macdonald had evidently not forgotten them, and tried to begin again where, he hoped, they had left off, when he found himself sitting beside her at dinner. Julia was markedly cool to him, both then, and afterwards in the drawing-room—he finally withdrew, hurt, and devoted his attention to his hostess. After the guests had gone Julia stated her intention of going upstairs at once and breaking the back of her packing before she went to bed; Glentoran is a long way from Renfrew, and she would have to make an early start. However she was extremely disconcerted when Edina, who had come up with her, and sat in an armchair while Julia rapidly and skillfully folded suits and dresses and stowed them in suitcases, tackled her on the subject. After accusing her of being "beastly" to Ronan all the evening she said— "You and he had such a carry-on round the time of our wedding that I thought *he* might be the reason why you turned that Torrens person down—Colin's boss."

"Colin shouldn't gossip," Julia said vexedly, snapping a suitcase to and laying it on the floor. "Certainly that had nothing to do with Ronan."

"I've sometimes wondered if you cared for Colin," Colin's sister pursued.

"Wrong again!" Julia said, putting another suitcase on the bed, on which she had carefully spread her bath towel to protect the quilt. "I adore Colin, but there never has been, and never *will* be, any question of our marrying. Really, *you* might have realized that, Edina—you're his sister."

"I'm sorry—I expect I've been sticking my neck out. But you do rather go on and on, don't you?"

"All you young married women think of nothing but making matches for your friends!" Julia said, not without justice. "However, I won't hold it against you—I know you can't help it!" Edina laughed, and kissed her Good night.

But flying South from Renfrew next day, in between thinking about Colin and his Aglaia, and the general danger of marrying too much money, the worms—added to by Edina—wriggled in Julia's mind more actively than ever. Was there really something wrong with her and her behavior? Was she a *belle bitch sans merci?* She laughed her gurgling laugh at her own phrase, but she was troubled all the same. Ought she, next time, to let the thing rip, whatever happened? She continued to brood on this idea till rage at the behavior of the staff at London Airport mastered all other feelings.

"THERE," JULIA SAID, returning from the bookstall at Victoria to the carriage where she and Watkins were installed, and throwing a batch of illustrated weeklies and the livelier dailies down on the seat. "Now we shall have something to read. I know you like *The Queen*, Watkins."

"Oh, thank you, Miss. I do indeed. But I'll save that for a bit later on. Do you want the *Mirror*?"

Julia didn't; but before starting on the *Times* she glanced through the *Express* and the *Daily Sketch*. She was a little startled to find in both numbers of photographs of Aglaia Armitage, with flaring headlines: "Millionaire's Heiress Goes to Join her Mother"—"Richest Girl in Europe Sails for South America"; the *Mirror* too, she saw, struck a characteristic note—"So Beautiful, So Small, and So RICH!" She examined all the pictures of Colin's girl with the deepest interest. Aglaia Armitage was indeed *tiny*, seen in relation to gangways, police, and bystanders; she could hardly be much over five feet. But she was beautifully made, with lovely feet and ankles, and her face in the studio photographs was attractive and intelligent, as well as undeniably pretty. Fascinated on Colin's account, Julia read the reporter's descriptions—things which normally she execrated. Miss Armitage, she learned, besides being "petite," was ash-blonde, but with dark eyes—"an unusual combination." True enough—and on the whole she liked the look of the girl her dear Colin loved.

Her study of the papers was interrupted by Watkins.

"Do look at that man, Miss—the tall one, talking to the inspector on the platform. Do you think he can be a detective? He keeps walking up and down, up and down, watching the passengers."

Julia and Watkins had arrived early, and so had plenty of time for staring out of the carriage window, as everyone does at Victoria, besides reading the papers. Julia now looked obediently where Watkins directed. She saw a tall man, lightly built, with a curious sharply-chiseled face (the word "gothic" sprang into her mind) which besides intelligence showed an amusing quizzical quality; she thought he looked what she called "fun." He was strolling up and down beside the inspector, casting rather sardonic glances at the passengers for the Golden Arrow who passed, accompanied by porters wheeling their luggage.

"Don't you think he *must* be one, Miss?" Watkins pursued. "He's been doing that for ever so long."

"Shall I ask him if he is?" Julia said, on a gay impulse—going abroad always went to her head far more directly than any alcohol.

"Well why not, Miss?" Watkins said, with a discreet giggle.

Julia slipped along the corridor, stepped down from the train, and went over to the tall man; the inspector tactfully moved away.

"I beg your pardon, but are you a detective?" she asked, hardily.

The man put a finger to his lip.

"No. On business," he said with a faint smile—his voice and accent were as attractive as his appearance; the small episode seemed to amuse him.

"Oh I see. You behave so like one! Please excuse me for asking."

"A pleasure," the man said, smiling more broadly; Julia, feeling a little foolish, went back into the train. "He says he isn't," she told Watkins, and started on the *Times*. But soon she was again interrupted by the maid.

"Do look at that young lady coming along, Miss! Isn't she the proper ditto of that girl in the papers? Can she be going to South America *this* way?"

"No, not possibly; she sailed yesterday, you know," Julia said, before she even looked out of the window. When she did she was startled. Walking along the platform between two men was a girl whose resemblance to the photographs she had just been studying was quite astonishing. She was minute, her hair was the palest blonde possible, and when she turned her head in their direction to speak to one of the men with her, Julia could see that she had dark eyes and eyebrows. How *very* peculiar! The occurrence was so surprising as to cause Julia a sudden faint sense of unease. She looked carefully at the girl's two companions. One was a tall, dark, handsome young man, slender but athletically built, and distinctly un-English in appearance; the other was shorter, broadly built with grey hair and a bushy grey beard—he too didn't look entirely English, nor did he walk like an old man. Julia glanced round to see what had become of the detective—she still thought of him as that, in spite of his denial. Yes, there he was, chatting to the inspector, and apparently paying no attention to these late arrivals, who so surprised her. She sat back as they passed out of sight.

Presently a whistle blew, and the train pulled out. Julia was so intrigued by the resemblance of the girl on the platform to Aglaia Armitage that as the Boat Express shook and rattled through the suburbs she walked along the corridor to find where the party was sitting. They were in the second coach ahead; she took a good look at all three. Yes, the girl really *had* dark brown eyes, and dark eyelashes too; and the older man's grey beard was slightly parted in the middle, she now saw. She went back to her carriage.

Soon a hand-bell, rung along the corridor by a white-coated steward, announced lunch. Julia had frugally brought sandwiches for herself and Watkins for this first meal; but she didn't suggest eating at once—she gave it ten minutes, and then again walked down the train, hoping to find that the party which interested her had gone to eat, so that she could examine the labels on their hand luggage. They had gone to eat, right enough—but there was no hand luggage!

When she sat down beside Watkins in her own compartment, Julia Probyn was conscious of an unwonted weight against the front of her thighs. This was caused by the "coffre-fort," that old ingenious American device by means of which ladies can carry currency about in almost perfect safety—a small canvas wallet, slung on webbing and straps from a belt round the waist, and worn under the skirt. Mrs. Hathaway, Julia knew, possessed several of these objects, and she had caused Watkins to produce the largest of them "for our money"; but in fact it contained a copy of the late Mr. Thalassides' will, and signed authorizations by Aglaia's lawyers and bankers in London to the Swiss bank "to give full information to Miss Julia Probyn" concerning the moneys in the numbered account. There was also a scrawl in Colin's rather crabbed writing, giving the name and address of the guardian-godfather who knew the number of the account—La Cure, Bellardon—and a cautiously worded note from the lawyers, suggesting that the Pastor of Bellardon also should give "all facilities" to Miss Probyn.

Colin had flown South from Glentoran on the plane after Julia's, the first on which he could get a seat; he had brought all these documents round to her club, and they went through them together—the other occupants of the half-empty room appeared mostly to be deaf or blind, or both. Julia read through the papers carefully. They were addressed to *Messieurs les Directeurs* of the Banque Républicaine in Geneva.

"Oh, so they do at least know the name of the bank," she said, folding them up and putting them in her handbag. "Only a photostat of the will, I see."

"Yes, but you also see that Judkins and Judkins have had it attested by a Commissioner for Oaths. Honestly, I think you've got everything you need now, bar the actual number, which old de Ritter, the guardian, will give you."

"Let's hope he will," Julia had said.

Experienced passengers on cross-channel steamers book a steward the moment they get on board to take their luggage ashore on the further side;

Julia, who usually flew to France, failed to do this. Her French porter as usual collected *eight* other people's luggage beside hers, and kept her and Watkins waiting for more than twenty minutes in the Customs shed before he appeared. This contretemps prevented Julia from checking on the movements of the girl with the extraordinary resemblance to Aglaia; through the dusty, dirty windows she thought she caught a glimpse of her boarding the Paris train, but she could not be sure.

The Swiss Customs examination on trains from Calais now takes place at Berne; sleepy, hungry, and feeling generally disheveled, Julia secured a porter, a tall fair middle-aged man, for their hand luggage, and deposited this, with Watkins, in the pleasant station restaurant—then she went off to the Customs. Another contretemps—their registered luggage had not arrived. Julia insisted coolly but persistently, in her rather moderate German, on being taken to see someone in authority, and was eventually led by the tall porter to a small office; here she made her complaint to two well-educated, civil-spoken men, who took down all details and asked where she was going?

"To Gersau—and the luggage must come on at once, *frei*," Julia said firmly.

Oh the delightful helpful Swiss, so unlike surly French officialdom, she thought, as her address in Gersau was noted, and she was promised that the missing luggage would be sent on as soon as it arrived in Berne. "This must have happened in France—in France *anything* can happen!" one of the officials said. "We regret the inconvenience to the Fräulein." Julia laughed, thanked him, and went back to the restaurant to tuck into coffee and rolls-and-butter with Watkins.

Emerging some two hours later from the high airy station at Lucerne, and crossing the open space outside it to the quay, the lovely heat hit them —blazing sun, brilliant sky, the cobbles and tarmac almost incandescent. "My word, Miss, I shall be glad to get into a cotton dress," Watkins observed. "But this is a clean, pretty place," the English maid added, casting an approving glance at the trim beds full of bright flowers. "This seems a clean country—I noticed the fields and gardens as we came along. That last train was clean, too. I do like things clean."

Watkins' desire for a cotton frock diminished on the lake steamer, whose swift passage made sitting on the deck too chilly. They went into the saloon, where Watkins continued her comments.

"My goodness me, Miss, do look at that! Is there any *reason* for a hill to stick up into the sky like a power-station chimney?" (This was Watkins' reaction to the Bürgenstock, seen end on.)

"Switzerland *is* like that, Watkins," Julia replied, laughing. "The whole place is up on end."

But though Julia was more familiar than Watkins with the power-station-chimney aspect of Switzerland, since she had twice spent three weeks skiing at Zermatt, she knew nothing whatever of the country beyond what could be seen from trains or ski-slopes, or learned from how its hotels are run; of the industrial and commercial, let alone the private life of its inhabitants she was completely ignorant, as most tourists are. Her enlightenment began at once, at Gersau.

This whole small place is compressed into a fold between two of the steep green ridges running down from the Rigi. Along the lake front is a fringe of hotels, restaurants, gardens and filling-stations—Gersau's public face; but up behind are large unsuspected houses in shady gardens, giving onto narrow quiet streets with occasional small shops, which supply the needs of the inhabitants rather than souvenirs for the tourist.

A tall stately old gentleman in a Panama hat was standing on the little quay, attended by a manservant in a red-and-black silk jacket; as Julia and Watkins stepped off the boat he raised his Panama and said, "Is it Miss Probyn? I am Rudolf Waechter," in perfect English, and then greeted Watkins—"Your mistress will be very pleased to see you." Julia was surprised to see no sign of a car or even a taxi, but none was necessary; their scanty luggage was placed on a handbarrow by the manservant and they walked, slightly uphill, barely two hundred yards before reaching a large plastered house with deep overhanging eaves, and passed through a heavy old door of carved walnut into a cool hall. Within, the staircase had walnut banisters, and there was old walnut paneling everywhere; Persian rugs and carpets covered the floors and even the stairs, and on the walls modern French paintings were skillfully juxtaposed with some lovely Primitives.

"You will want to see Mrs. Hathaway," he said, as he took her upstairs. "Luncheon will be at one-thirty, so you have time. Anna will show you your room, and then take you to her. It is very good of you to come yourself to bring her maid—and I am, of course, delighted to have you here."

On an upper landing Anna, a neat elderly maid, was waiting, and took Julia to her room, Watkins following. "Room" was an understatement; Julia had been given a suite consisting of a large bedroom, a sitting room, and a bathroom. Bedroom and sitting room both opened onto a deep balcony, set with luxuriously comfortable *chaises longues* and small tables, an extra room in itself. The whole thing was so exquisite that Julia almost gasped. She threw her hat on the bed, and then asked Anna where "Miss Watkins'" room was? Anna led them out onto the wide landing again—more superb rugs, Julia noticed—and opened the door of a pleasant bed-sitting room, also with an adjoining bathroom.

"Well, you will be quite comfy here, Watkins, won't you?" Julia said.

"Provided the water's *hot*," Watkins replied, turning on the tap in the basin. A cloud of steam answered her incredulity; a little abashed, she turned off the tap. "Yes Miss; it's a pretty room—and quite clean, too." Julia was satisfied; if Watkins passed the Waechter house as *clean*, she would give no trouble. She asked Anna to take them to Frau Hathaway.

Watkins had been put in a room next door to her mistress, who was housed in another lovely suite. Julia studied her old friend's appearance anxiously when Anna ushered them in, but it was clear that Mrs. Hathaway was, as she pronounced herself to be, very much better; her color was quite good, and her voice as firm as ever when she gave directions to her maid.

"I'm glad to see you, Watkins—I hope you had a good journey. Now go and unpack and get yourself straight, while I talk to Miss Julia. They will bring you some lunch in about half an hour; after that you must rest, and then learn your way about the house; and later you can make my tea, and do some washing for me." Watkins obediently made her exit.

"My dear child, this is so good of you," Mrs. Hathaway said. "I'm sure Edina was furious at having you reft away the moment you got to Glentoran, after so long. But Herr Waechter wouldn't hear of my going to a hospital, and he hasn't a large staff, admirable as they are; I really felt I couldn't impose the strain of having me waited on a moment longer than was necessary."

Julia said it was fun coming—"and what a marvelous house."

"Oh yes, it's bursting with treasures—partly inherited, of course—and then he has this passion for Rhenish Primitives and Persian rugs; he has spent a lifetime, and a fortune, collecting them. He only took a fancy to French painting much later—but just in time to get some good things. He has *three* Blue Picassos."

"Golly! But where did he get his money?" Julia asked, with her usual frankness.

"Oh, fine optical glass for precision instruments. Waechters are known all over the world for that."

"And does Herr Waechter still work at this glass performance?"

"Oh no—he only goes to Board meetings occasionally. A nephew runs it now."

"What are the inherited treasures?" Julia asked, surprised, in her English ignorance, that Swiss manufacturers should inherit any heirlooms.

"Oh, the furniture—a lot of it is beyond price; and some of the Primitives, and of course the house itself, which is over two hundred years old; that came from his grandmother, who was a Carmenzind."

"I saw that name on a shop as we walked up," Julia said. "I thought it so queer, and pretty."

"Yes, it's a great Gersau name." Mrs. Hathaway paused, and looked with shrewd amusement at her young friend. "I don't want to bore you, but did you ever realize that Gersau was an independent Republic, within the Swiss Confederation, till 1818, or thereabouts?"

"No—and it seems impossible! This tiny place a Republic? Like San Marino?"

"Yes, only perhaps even smaller. And its last president before it was absorbed was a Carmenzind; Rudolf Waechter's great-grandfather."

Anna at this point brought in a tray with Cinzano, ice, and slices of orange. Julia poured out for both, and sat down again.

"This is all quite fascinating," she said. "I had no idea that Switzerland was like this."

"Of course not, dear child. The English always think of the Swiss purely as a race of hotelkeepers, with a few hardy peasant guides thrown in— and, of course, as makers of cuckoo-clocks. Well they *are* hotelkeepers, though that is really our fault; it was the English who invented and patented Switzerland as the Playground of Europe. Even dear Rudolf Waechter, besides his glass business, has a controlling interest in three or four big hotels. But they have this private life as well, which has been going quietly on for centuries—and it is a very civilized life, as you will see in this house."

"I *am* seeing," Julia said.

"It can be combined with actual hotel-keeping, too," Mrs. Hathaway pursued. "Othmar Schoeck's parents—you know, the great composer, who died not so long ago—kept a delightful hotel in Brunnen, quite near here; I knew him well as a girl. I don't know who started the idea that hotel-keeping is a low, *deadening* trade."

Julia was just saying that so many English hotels were deadly as to suggest that the theory had its origin in England, when Anna again appeared, summoning her to luncheon, and bringing a tray for Mrs. Hathaway. "From now on, *Miss Watkins* will bring up all my trays," Mrs. Hathaway told the Swiss maid firmly in German. Anna smirked and nodded, and led Julia down to the first floor, on which were both the drawing room and the dining room.

The latter, where they ate a delicious lunch at an old walnut refectory table, was paneled throughout in the same wood; Julia, by way of making conversation, observed that it was odd to her to see such an ancient table made of anything but oak.

"Ah, but you see the walnut has always been our principal furniture tree, not the oak; and since we are not a maritime nation, we seldom imported mahogany." He drew her attention to the old carved dresser and other pieces in the room, including a near-Biedermeyer tallboy between the high windows. "You will notice that it is not *pure* Biedermeyer—and that is precisely what gives it its value. Here, from the eighteenth century, we copied foreign styles, but always with slight differences; if anyone shows you a piece of antique Swiss furniture which is *correct* Empire, or *correct* Biedermeyer, you may be sure that it is a fake."

Julia was delighted with her host. Over coffee in the drawing room, she asked him how he had come to know Mrs. Hathaway—explaining that she looked on her almost as a mother. She was touched by the way he told the story. Mrs. Hathaway, as a girl, had come with her parents to stay at one of the family hotels in Lugano—"I was the receptionist then; we must all learn our trade, from the bottom up! But there were dances on Sunday evenings, when I danced with her—and fell a little in love with her!" Julia loved the gentle reminiscent smile with which the old man said that. "We both married," he pursued, more briskly. "She had sons, I had no children. But our friendship we have kept."

Julia, delighted by this glimpse into the past, asked what Mrs. Hathaway had been like as a girl.

"*Plain,*" Herr Waechter said flatly; "and her mother did not dress her well. But she had a merry laugh, and great intelligence; also she was always what now I believe you call 'tough,' though the word was unknown then."

"And was it her toughness you fell in love with?" Julia asked.

The old man laughed.

"Miss Probyn, I never phrased it to myself in this way, but in fact I believe that was what I fell in love with."

Their heavy luggage arrived about four o'clock. There was nothing to pay, since the railway was at fault. Again Julia blessed the Swiss.

Mrs. Hathaway had to keep her bed for several days, but once Watkins had got the hang of the house, and could wait on her, Julia was fairly free, and her host insisted on taking her out with him in the car, which a chauffeur drove, when he had to go anywhere. The first of these occasions was a visit to his wine merchant in Brunnen; Julia in her ignorance was astonished at every meal by the excellence of the Swiss wines she drank, and was delighted at the idea. She was even more delighted by the reality. Accustomed to the urban precincts of London wine merchants, she was startled to drive into a cobbled yard flanked by a line of buildings backed up against a steep wooded hillside; when Herr Waechter, escorted by the foreman, walked all through the sheds, piled high with crates and barrels, to inspect the bottling of some wine in which he was particularly interested, she found it fascinating to see ferns and hazel boughs poking in at the barred windows.

They drove on to Schwyz, where Herr Waechter said he must see a nephew who made cement—"I have a small interest in the firm. And you should see Schwyz; it was the birthplace of the Confederation, and it is a charming town. I ought also to call on two of my sisters-in-law—widows, and not very interesting; but their houses are pretty." As they drove across the flat plain toward the twin peaks of the Grosse and Kleine Mythen, which stand up like two gigantic stone axe-heads above the small town, they could see the cement factory away to their left, its buildings all floury with grey dust. "It is rather a defacement," Herr Waechter said regretfully, "but it gives employment, and brings money. We seem compelled, today, to live in an increasingly ugly world."

But there was nothing ugly about the world into which he soon introduced her—that of the old Swiss families in the old town of Schwyz. They lived in large houses in big high-walled gardens; the houses themselves were as stuffed with walnut paneling and period furniture as his own. Julia got, that afternoon, an unusually intimate picture of the *original* European democracy—since the Greek and Italian republics have not survived. All these people kept hotels, or made watches, or machinery, or precision instruments; but their homes were in these ancient houses, and they could trace their ancestry back four or five hundred years.

A couple of days later they drove to Zürich. Herr Waechter had written a book on Swiss furniture, now in the press; he wished to discuss this with his publisher there. They lunched at the Baur au Lac (one of the best hotels in the world) in the glass-enclosed outside restaurant between the green-flowing river on one side, and the great garden, brilliant with flowers, on the other. The restaurant was full of people, all apparently German or Swiss—it was early in the season for Americans; Julia commented on the fact that there seemed to be no English. "I have so often heard people at home speak of the Baur au Lac."

"Oh, the English can't afford to come here any more," her host said, matter-of-factly. "Not with this quite ridiculous travel allowance, for which there is really no excuse at all! The pound stands well; this limit of £100 is purely a bureaucratic *idée fixe*." He paused, and sipped his wine. "In Switzerland," he went on, "we regret this folly very much. The Germans, whom you defeated, can come here and spend as they please; so can the

Belgians, who surrendered and left you *plaqués* outside Dunkirk; so can the French, who ran away! It is only the English, who stood alone for a year and a half defending European freedom, who may not travel in comfort on the continent they—and they *alone*—saved!" The old gentleman spoke the last words with great severity.

"Good for you, Herr Waechter!" Julia said with warmth. "I couldn't agree more."

The offices of Herr Waechter's publisher were as much of a surprise to her as his wine merchant's. She had once or twice been taken to cocktail parties given by London firms, and expected something of the same sort. Not at all. The car bore them up to a hillside suburb overlooking the city, where lilacs and laburnums bloomed along shady streets, and stopped outside a modern villa, with a plate on its gatepost bearing the words "Eden-Verlag." Herr Schmidt, the principal, a middle-aged man with a clever face, greeted her host with respectful warmth and bore him off upstairs, first installing Julia in a sunny room full of flowers and armchairs, and inviting her to amuse herself with the books which lined the walls. While Julia was examining these the door opened and a rather shaky little old man, with tufts of grey hair round his baldish skull, came in and introduced himself in bad French as Herr Schmidt's partner; he proceeded to point out various books, including several translations into German of novels by well-known English writers. Julia's inveterate curiosity suddenly moved her to ask him whether any of these people used numbered accounts. The question provoked an extraordinary outburst.

"Numbered accounts!" He almost spat out the words. "Oh yes, often we are asked to pay royalties into numbered accounts by people who do not wish to pay taxes at home! They come here and spend it on winter sport. But *these* can get their money when they want it—unlike the heirs of the wretched Jews and Poles and Hungarians, to whom it was refused by the banks." Again he almost spat the last word, his face twisted with a sort of despairing anger.

"Refused? But why on earth?" Julia asked.

"Because death certificates shall be produced before the bank will pay! And how many death certificates were given of those who perished in the gas chambers of Oswieczim"—he used the Polish name for Auschwitz—"or were beaten to death at Mauthausen, or died of starvation in Belsen and Buchenwald? So those who looked ahead and sought to make some provision for their children used their prudence in vain; the younger generation who escaped were denied their heritage."

"How ghastly," Julia said; though she was horrified, the little old man was so wrought up, and the story sounded so extraordinary, that she wasn't sure if she quite believed it. "It sounds impossible," she added.

"Oh, everything is possible! There was more than that," Herr Schmidt's partner went on. "The Lüblin Government, the Communist clique forced on us by the Russians, asked the Swiss Government to pay to them 300 million dollars of Polish money, deposited in Switzerland. The Swiss Government paid—I leave you to guess from where they got the money!"

"Good God! That really was too much," Julia exclaimed.

"Quite so." Her agreement seemed to soothe the little man; he went on rather more calmly. "This created a certain scandal; now the Government here is more discreet—other requests of the same nature have been refused. But all over Switzerland these banks are putting up wonderful new buildings—with the money of the dead, while their heirs starve!"

Julia was distinctly relieved that at this point Herr Waechter reappeared, and took her away. What she had heard disturbed and worried her; she wondered if it could be true, and longed to ask her host, but for some time she refrained, assuming that a man of eighty would be tired after such an expedition. But quite the contrary; the old gentleman seemed so brisk and spry, quite cheered up by his outing, that eventually Julia asked him what truth there was in the story of the death certificates.

He frowned.

"The old Petrus will have told you this, of course. It is true that payments are withheld unless a death certificate is produced; this is perfectly natural, and correct; otherwise the door would be open to every sort of fraud. And latterly matters have been arranged better, at least as far as Germans—Jews mostly, of course—are concerned; the German Government is very liberal about granting death certificates to those presumed dead, and also the United Nations circulates lists of names, partly from the very ill-kept records of the prison-camps, asking whether there is any evidence as to the life or death of those so listed—if there is no evidence that they are alive a death certificate is granted. But this was not the case in the first years after the war; the machinery had not been established, so the banks were helpless—they had to abide by their rules."

"Of course—I see that," Julia said. Then she asked about the payment to the Polish Government.

"Oh, everyone has heard this story!" Waechter exclaimed—"and here also the thing is complicated. No bank may pay out the money of a private individual to anyone but that individual or his legal heirs; that is why the private fortune of the late Czar of Russia is still lying in your banks of London, in spite of repeated requests from the Bolshevik Russian Government that it should be handed over to them. Government money is a different matter; one government may, quite reasonably, hand this over to the established successor of a previous government in a foreign country. What became of those lorryloads of gold bars which the Polish Government sent down through Rumania to Constanza when the German invasion threatened? *You* should know—your own Consul helped to carry them on board ship!"

Julia didn't know; she had never heard of this episode and enjoyed visualizing a sweating Consul humping gold bricks up a gangway in a hot Black Sea port.

"I've no idea," she said. "Do you know where it is now?"

"No. It has been suggested that it came here—we are such a repository! If it did, our government would have been perfectly within their rights in handing it over to the Polish Government. But though there has been endless talk about this payment, there is no evidence that it was really made; and never will be!" he added with finality.

Julia was fascinated by these glimpses of international finance, about which, like most people, she knew nothing. Herr Waechter obviously knew a good deal, and she decided to try to clear up the substance of another of the old publisher's complaints while the going was so exceptionally good —she asked if it was true that the splendid new bank buildings in Switzerland were really being paid for out of "the money of the dead," as old Dr. Petrus had said.

Herr Waechter fairly exploded.

"This is complete rubbish! and libelous rubbish too! I have already told you that machinery is now in operation to clear the accounts of those who died in the prison camps; but in any case our banks have no need of such moneys. When German shares and Mark obligations were far down, after the war, our banks bought them up—to the great relief of the holders! —and since Germany's wonderful recovery these have enormously increased in value; so much so that our banks hardly know what to do with their money! Very sensibly, they are using it to bring their premises up to date; this gives employment, and helps our young cement industry."

Suddenly the old man did look tired, Julia saw with compunction.

"I'm sorry I bothered you with all this," she said. "But I was upset by what that old man told me."

"Of course you were, and rightly. Justice and injustice, and human suffering are things about which *all* must be upset." He spoke with emphasis. "But may I ask you a question?" he went on. "How come you to know about numbered Kontos? From Dr. Petrus also? For the English public, I understand, has hardly heard of them, though many English, even in official positions, are now using them."

Julia concealed wariness by laughter.

"Are they really? Oh, what fun!" She thought quickly, and decided to use Paddy Lynch. "I have a banker friend who told me about them; that's why I asked Dr. Petrus whether any of his English authors used them."

"A banker in London?"

"No, no—in Casablanca."

"Oh, Casablanca!"

Julia laughed again, and broke off with an inquiry about a church they happened to be passing; Herr Waechter's historical enthusiasm deflected him, as she had hoped, from the matter of numbered Kontos. But all the way back to Gersau, through orchards that were pink drifts of blossom, she was worrying about one thing. Colin had said she had everything she needed to deal with Aglaia's numbered account; but she hadn't got the death certificate of Mr. Thalassides. And quite clearly, from what she had heard today, that was essential.

CHAPTER III

BELLARDON

ON THEIR RETURN Julia was met on the upper landing by Watkins, who followed her into her room.

"Mr. Colin was on the telephone for you at lunchtime, Miss. He seemed very much put about that you was out."

"Where from, Watkins?"

"London, Miss. He gave me a message, and said you was to have it the moment you came in."

"Well what *was* it, Watkins?" Julia asked impatiently. What could Colin want to ring her up for?

"He said—'Tell Miss Julia to get on with the job I gave her as fast as ever she can.' Really, Master Colin has a cheek, to be giving you jobs!—but that's what he said, and what's more he made me repeat it," Watkins said indignantly. (She had dandled Colin as an infant, and still could not take him very seriously.)

"Anything else?"

"Oh yes—he gave his orders as cool as anything! You was to stay here till you get a letter from him, but to be making arrangements meantime to

go and see the clergyman. He said you'd know who he meant. And he kept
on saying—'Tell her to hurry; it's urgent.' Three times, he said that."

"Thank you, Watkins. Tell Mrs. Hathaway I'll come along to her in a
minute or two."

As she washed and put on powder Julia considered. Mrs. Hathaway
really was much better. The doctor, who had been the evening before, had
said that in a week or ten days she would be fit to move; he recommended
that she should go to Beatenberg, above the Lake of Thun, for two or three
weeks—the air there was peculiarly beneficial. Watkins had by now come
to terms with Anna and the rest of the staff, so clearly dear Mrs. H. could
safely be left for the moment. And after supper she asked her host if she
might make a telephone call.

"Of course. To England?"

"No—to a place called Bellardon."

"Is that in the Canton de Vaud or the Canton de Fribourg? I know it is
in one or the other, but they are so intertwined that it is a little confusing."

"I haven't a clue," Julia said airily. "Does it matter which canton Bellardon is in?"

"Yes, certainly. You see here we have an automatic telephone system,
with a different call number for each canton—you dial that, and then the
number you want in the canton."

"Oh, not by towns? How odd! Well how am I to find out which canton
Bellardon is in?"

"The telephone book will tell us that." It did—Bellardon was in the
Canton de Fribourg. Julia looked through the Bellardon section, searching for the name de Ritter; it was not under R, nor under D.

"I can't find him!" she exclaimed.

"Whom do you seek?" Herr Waechter asked.

"A Monsieur de Ritter, at Bellardon."

"Oh, the Pastor—yes, such a brilliant man. Look under *Pasteur*, and you
will find him." And among the Ps, sure enough, Julia found the entry—
"*Pasteur de l'Eglise Nationale, J.-P. de Ritter, La Cure, Bellardon.*" She
dialed the two numbers, and was through in about fifteen seconds—the
Swiss automatic telephone system works like magic—and the Pastor himself
answered. Julia gave her name and said, a little deprecatingly and quite
untruly, that she was a friend of his goddaughter's, and wanted to come
and see him.

"Dear Mademoiselle, I have nearly 150 goddaughters!" the rich voice
answered gaily.

"All English?" Julia asked.

"Ah no! Only two English ones."

"Well Aglaia is the one, of those two, that I speak of." (In spite of the automatic telephone, Julia's instinct for caution made her reluctant to use the surname.) "But look, I want to come very soon, probably the day after tomorrow."

"Come from where?"

"Gersau."

"Then you must stay the night."

"Yes, but I don't want to be a bother. If you would just book me a room in the hotel I can come in and see you."

A loud, very engaging laugh came ringing down the line.

"Leave all that to me. Just come!—telephone your train, and we will meet you at the station. Au revoir." He rang off.

"He sounds frightfully nice," Julia said to her host.

"Jean-Pierre de Ritter? He is one of the world's charmers. So was his father, whom I knew very well indeed. They are an old Berne family."

Julia waited anxiously for Colin's letter next day. It didn't come by the first post, but she took occasion to tell Mrs. Hathaway that she would probably have to go away for a day or two, on a job for Colin—she knew that Watkins would have reported his telephone call to her mistress.

"More Secret-Service work?" Mrs. Hathaway asked. "You know, my dear child, I do think they ought soon to start *paying* you for what you do. It all comes out of the Estimates, after all—which means out of our pockets! —and I don't see why the government should have your services free."

"Oh, this is a private thing of Colin's," Julia assured her blithely. "Nothing to do with the Secret Service at all."

But Colin's letter, which arrived by the second post, promptly disillusioned her on that score.

"This business is turning out much more serious and more tiresome than I thought when I asked you to take it on," he wrote. "It seems that the old boy, along with his money, deposited some rather hideously important papers. I only heard this when I was having supper with H. last night. He's in rather a flap about it, as indeed everyone is, because we've heard that some *most* undesirable characters are onto this too, and may be taking rapid action of some sort about it. I didn't gather exactly what, but it is quite menacing. And when I mentioned that you were actually going to see you-know-who, H. begged me to lay you on and get you to function as quickly as possible. (He doesn't care to write to you himself, naturally.) But he laid it on me to tell you that it is really vital, repeat vital, that you should get these papers away from where they are and into your own keeping as fast as you possibly can.

So please get cracking, darling. Wire me when you are going, darling darling. Endless love, C."

Julia sat on her pretty shaded balcony looking out at the silver gleam of late spring snow on the mountains across the lake, and frowned over this missive. Hugh again!—how tedious to be mixed up in yet another of his jobs. But neither she nor Colin had ever used their call-note, "darling darling," to the other in vain in all their lives; they might jangle sometimes, and Julia, the older, get impatient with Colin's nerves and youthful official bossiness. But all in all she loved him as much as anyone in the world; if she couldn't help Colin without helping Hugh, so much the worse—but she would help Colin, come Hell and high water. She went and procured a couple of telegraph forms from old Herr Waechter—she guessed, rightly, that he was a person who still kept telegraph forms in his house—and presently took a telegram, printed in block capitals, down to the small post office. She was careful to use Colin's home address. The message read: "Yes I will darling but how tiresome Stop Starting tomorrow Stop Love." She signed it "Darling."

She refused a drive with Herr Waechter because she wanted to catch the afternoon post with a letter by air to Colin—sitting in her little salon she wrote hurriedly that she was going next day to see "the parson person"; it was all laid on, and she would do her best. In view of what both Petrus and Herr Waechter had said, she added: "What I haven't got, and *must have*, is a death certificate—they won't play without. You must take my word for this; I learned it quite by accident, but I *know*. If you can get it in twenty-four hours, post to the Parsonage; if it takes longer than that, probably better send here."

She paused at that point, and read Colin's letter through again. The passage about the "most undesirable characters" taking rapid action made her wonder if she ought to mention the curious episode of the girl at Victoria, but when she looked at her watch she decided that there wasn't time; she closed her letter and ran down with it to the post office. She looked out the trains to Bellardon, and put through a call to La Cure giving the time of her train, blessing the anonymity of the Swiss automatic exchanges.

She was off next morning on the first boat to Lucerne, and continued by train to Berne, where she had to change. There, looking from her new carriage window she caught sight of the detective! Julia watched him furtively; this time he appeared to be much more definitely on the lookout for someone than he had been at Victoria. She studied his face again, and found it more attractive than ever; it was intelligent, and the expression at once sardonic and *gay*. Curious, seeing him again like this; she wondered what he was up to. Could *he* be one of Colin's undesirable characters?

Julia had time in hand, and when the detective had entered the train she got out and went in search of a sandwich and a newspaper. Returning with both, hurrying through the subway, she ran slap into him. He stared —then gave his twisted grin, and half-lifted his hat. Clearly he remembered her. Slightly disconcerted, Julia regained her carriage.

The lowland agricultural cantons of Switzerland, like Vaud and Fribourg, are little visited by foreign tourists, and were as unexpected by Julia as Herr Waechter's house. Sitting in the train, munching her *Schinken-Brötchen*, she noted, with a country-woman's interest, the methods of the Swiss farmers: the fresh grass being mown by hand in narrow strips and carted off to feed the stalled cows; the early hay hung on triangles to be dried by air as well as sun; the intense neatness of the gardens round the houses, with rows of lettuce and shallots, and single sticks to support the French beans, at present only a green clump of leaves at the foot. The houses themselves surprised her; she had imagined all the Swiss to live in wooden chalets, but here, though deep-eaved, they seemed to be much more plaster than timber. On the horizon hung the blue shadow of the Jura.

She did not stay in the hotel at Bellardon, for the excellent reason that there is none! It is a tiny place, where tourists are unknown. At the station, where she was the only passenger to alight, Julia was met by a small dark-haired woman, rather beautiful, who said, "You will be Miss Probyn? I am Germaine de Ritter." The Station-master, the sole railway employee of Bellardon, piled Julia's luggage onto a small handcart with a long handle, like that used by Herr Waechter's manservant at Gersau; this she pulled after her out onto a small sunny street, saying easily—"My husband had to take the car, but it is only two instants to the house. We are so glad that you have come to us; we are devoted to Aglaia"—which made Julia feel fraudulent. They passed a grassy open space, closed at the farther end by the white-washed bulk of a church with a tall bell-tower. "We think our church beautiful," Germaine de Ritter said; in its solid simplicity, beautiful it was.

La Cure, the Pastor's dwelling, was a very large eighteenth-century house with painted paneling in all the rooms, and gleaming parquet floors —everything spotlessly clean. "Jean-Pierre will bring your luggage up when he returns for déjeuner—is this sufficient for now?" Mme. de Ritter said, lifting Julia's dressing-case off the cart. She carried it herself up the broad staircase with its wide shallow treads and polished beech planks, and showed her guest first her pretty bedroom—slightly defaced by a tall cylin-

drical black iron stove for heating—and then, across a wide landing, a
bathroom with basin and lavatory.

"It is a little inconvenient, only to have one bathroom, especially when
the children are at home," she observed; "but you see this house is Church
property, so it is not easy to have alterations made."

Julia asked about the children. There were eight, all grown-up except
Marcel, aged fifteen, who went daily to a *Lycée* in Lausanne; five were
married, and living near by; two others were in jobs in Geneva, but already *fiancés*. "I hope you will meet them all while you are here," Mme.
de Ritter said, and then excused herself. "I have to see to the déjeuner; it
will be at one-thirty, as my husband is late today. When you are ready, do
sit in the salon or the garden; make yourself at home." It was borne in on
Julia that her pretty hostess, so girlish-looking that seven adult children
seemed an impossibility, probably had to do the cooking—she learned later
that she did the entire work of the house.

Julia unpacked her dressing-case, installed herself, and then went down
to the garden. Here she found a curious mixture of beauty and utility.
Fine fruit trees bordered a well-kept lawn, there were seats and wicker
chairs on a flagged space under some pleached limes, and beyond these a
kitchen garden, well stocked with vegetables. But the flower borders were
rather neglected, and clothes-lines, from which hung an array of snowy
sheets, ran down two sides of the lawn. Julia went across and felt these;
they were perfectly dry. She went back to the house and found her way
to the kitchen, where Mme. de Ritter was busy with pots and pans on a
huge stove.

"The sheets are quite dry—shall I bring them in?" she asked.

"Oh, how kind you are! Yes, do. The linen basket is in there"—she
gestured with her head towards a door—"and the bag for the pegs." Julia
went into what had obviously once been a scullery, but now housed a vast
white-enameled washing machine and several old-fashioned wicker linen
baskets; she gathered up one of these and went out again to the garden,
where in the warm sunshine she took down the sheets from the lines,
folded them, and laid them in the basket. As she was carrying this load
back into the house she encountered her host.

"Ah, Miss Probyn! You are very welcome. Please let me take that—
Germaine has already set you to work, I see."

"No, I set myself," Julia replied, surrendering the basket, which the
Pastor carried through into the wash house.

"Ma chère, is luncheon ready?" he asked.

"In five minutes, Jean-Pierre. You said one-thirty, and at one-thirty you
will be served." His wife was perfectly tranquil, and equally firm. Laugh-

ing, the Pastor led Julia into the big cool salon, where the numerous chairs and settees were all stiff and rather upright—there was nothing to lounge in. On the walls were some rather attractive portraits in pretty old frames, covering, Julia guessed, at least the last three hundred years—several of them bore a striking resemblance to her host. Jean-Pierre de Ritter was a man of medium height, but he gave the impression of being small, partly because he was so excessively lightly built, with very fine narrow feet and hands; partly because of the squirrel-like rapidity of all his movements. He was handsome; clean-shaven, with merry brilliantly blue eyes under a massive forehead, the only big thing about him—this peculiar combination of figure and feature was repeated all round the room, on the paneled walls, looking out from dimly gilt frames in a variety of dress that spanned the centuries.

"We will not talk about my Goddaughter until this evening," he said at once. "I have to go out the moment after déjeuner."

Julia of course said the evening would do perfectly. Her host asked suddenly—"Do you speak French? Easily?"

"Yes, very easily."

"Then we shall speak French. It is simpler for me, and even more so for Germaine; she is French, a French Protestant from the Loire valley, where as you probably know there are a number of Protestant communities."

Julia didn't know—however, French they talked at lunch. It was all highly political and intellectual, and Julia was quite unable to answer many of her host's questions on what the English thought about the raid on the Rumanian Legation in Berne, the suicide of the Swiss Chief of Police, Dr. Adenauer's attitude to N.A.T.O., and the value of the activities of Moral Rearmament in Morocco. His own remarks on these subjects were shrewd and witty—Julia remembered that Herr Waechter had called him a brilliant man.

In the afternoon Henriette, one of the married daughters, arrived in a station wagon with the whole of her weekly wash, to be done in the vast *Pharos* in the ex-scullery. In theory she merely used her mother's washing machine; in fact Germaine did all the actual work while Henriette, in the garden, kept a maternal eye on her two pretty little girls and her toddler son of two, and did a little desultory sewing. She too talked, endlessly and very well, to Julia, who had undertaken to pick the spinach for supper; crouched over the hot crumbly earth between the rows of succulent green plants, Miss Probyn tried to make reasonably intelligent responses about the works of Kafka and Romain Rolland, and Gonzague de Reynolde's *"Qu'est-ce que l'Europe?"* This last she had read—and praised, throwing leaves into a basket as she spoke. Henriette, encouraged, asked if Miss Probyn admired Rilke?

Julia felt rather out of her depth in the rarified intellectual atmosphere of La Cure. She had always imagined Calvinists—surely the Swiss National Church was Calvinist?—to be terrific theologians, but completely *bornées* and inhibited otherwise; and here she was, utterly stumped on politics and literature by these same supposedly rigid people. Having piled her basket with spinach, she took it in to Germaine. In the wash-house were two more of the big linen baskets, full of clean wet sheets and towels. "Are these to go out?" she asked.

"Yes—but I will take them," her hostess replied.

"What rubbish!" Julia exclaimed. "Henriette!" she called through the window, "Come and help me out with your *linge!*" Turning, she surprised a rather startled and happy smile on her hostess's face. When Henriette came in they carried out the heavy baskets, and pegged the wet linen in the sun and breeze along the lines beside the lawn.

"Rilke my elbow!" Julia thought to herself. "Why not do one's own *work?*" She was becoming quite a partisan of her beautiful hostess. Henriette, as they stretched out sheets, continued to talk, now about her family, and from her lively chatter Julia learned yet other aspects of Swiss life. The Iron-Workers' Guild in Berne had given Henriette a small *dot* when she married, and were going to do the same presently for Marguérite, who was already *fiancée;* they were helping to pay for Marcel's education, as they had done for that of his two elder brothers. Julia was much more interested in this than in Rilke. Were there still Guilds in Switzerland, she wanted to know?

"Well at least there *were,* and there are funds still existing, to help those whose families have always belonged to the Guild. It is a hereditary thing —for of course Papa is not an iron-worker!" Henriette said, laughing. "But his family has belonged to this Guild for—oh, for centuries; so they help with the boys' education, and our dowries. It is very convenient, *en tout cas,* for we are so many, and Papa and Maman are not rich."

So that was why no maid and no drinks, and all the washing done at home, Julia supposed, as they went in and brought out a last basket of linen.

However there was Kirsch, locally made and excellent, with the coffee after supper. Then the Pastor bore Julia off to his study, where a business-like desk with a typewriter, and two shabby leather armchairs were looked down upon by shelves full of books going up to the ceiling: masses of theology, but also plenty of modern stuff in French and German, and in English too—Winston Churchill, Osbert Sitwell, Virginia Woolf, and of

course Galsworthy, for whom Continentals have such a surprising enthusiasm. Julia now pulled out of her bag the copy of Mr. Thalassides' will,
and the letters from Aglaia's lawyers and bankers. "As she is still technically an 'infant,' and as I was coming out to Switzerland anyhow, I was
asked to look into it," she said, realizing how lame the words sounded even
as she spoke them.

M. de Ritter drew up one of the old armchairs for her; then he spread
the papers out on his desk, and studied them.

"The authorizations are quite adequate," he said at length. "But I am a
little surprised that my Goddaughter's lawyers did not come to deal with
this matter themselves." He looked up at her, with a shrewd gaze.

"For one thing, I'm not sure that they even knew of the existence of this
numbered Konto till they were told," Julia said bluntly.

"Who told them, then?" he asked quickly.

"Aglaia, I imagine."

He tapped on the table, thinking; then he gave a sudden laugh.

"And if they do not know, how do you know? And why did they
authorize you?"

Julia laughed too—she liked him so much. But obviously she must come
out into the open—nothing could be done without him.

"Oh, why indeed?" she said cheerfully. "M. de Ritter, it's no good my
fencing with you. In fact there is more to this than Aglaia's fortune."

"The oil question, I suppose?" he said. "Oh dear yes, that was bound
to come up. But again"—he looked at her, in her cool summer frock of
lime-green silk, sitting so beautiful and relaxed in the shabby leather chair
—"Why *you*? Are you a very close friend of Aglaia's?"

"No. I told you a lie about that—I'm sorry. I've never even met her,"
Julia said candidly.

"*Tiens! De plus en plus drôle!* Well, there must be a reason—even for
your telling a lie! What is it?"

"Her fiancé is a cousin of mine, and as I was coming out here, he asked
me to undertake this errand."

The Pastor pounced on the fiancé aspect.

"Your cousin, you say, is her fiancé? What is he like? Is he well off?—
rich?"

"Yes, he's quite well off; he has a very large property in Scotland. He
doesn't need Aglaia's money in the least, M. de Ritter," Julia said crisply.

He smiled at her disarmingly.

"*Très bien!* You see I have to make these inquiries; there is now no one
but myself to guard the interests of this child; the aunt she lives with, her

poor father's sister, is a kind woman, but *peu capable*. And your cousin directs his *bien*, his property, himself, as my sons-in-law do?"

"No, not at the moment. His sister and her husband are running it for him."

"Oh? *Pourquoi?*"

"Because he has a job that keeps him abroad a good deal of the time," Julia said carefully.

The Pastor considered, again tapping the table; then he gave her a look so shrewd as to be almost sly.

"Abroad. And you say *he* assigned this task to you? Including the oil affair?" Julia nodded—but the Pastor's next remark came like a bombshell. "Is your cousin by any chance an agent of your government?"

Julia had to take a lightning decision. She had seen enough of Colin and Hugh Torrens to know that in their job Rule One is never to admit to Secret-Service activities, if it is at all possible to avoid this. But here speed was essential, and de Ritter was the key to the whole thing; she was really at the point of no return. To cover her hesitation she laughed.

"M. de Ritter, what a man you are!"

"Yes, but *is* he?" the Pastor insisted. "You see, when Aglaia was staying here last year she confided to my daughter Marguérite that she had recently met a young man who acted as a British Government agent, and that they were much drawn to one another. So naturally I am wondering, are this individual, and your cousin, the same person?"

"Yes, undoubtedly," Julia said, thinking how fearfully indiscreet it was of Aglaia to have spilt these particular beans to a foreign national. Strictly speaking Colin had also been wrong from the Service point of view to tell his semi-fiancée, with her disreputable mother and foreign stepfather, what his work was—but love was blind, of course. "To put your mind at rest," she pursued, "my cousin is much more worried about the official side of this affair than about your goddaughter's fortune." She added some warm praise of Colin—his simplicity, his charm, his conscientiousness, his enthusiasm for his work.

"Has he any head for *les affaires?*" her host asked, practically.

"For money? No, very little, I think. You and the bankers will have to occupy yourselves with all these billions!—money isn't his line at all; it doesn't interest him much. He could look after Glentoran—his place in Scotland—all right, when he retires. But M. le Pasteur, since you've guessed what Colin is, and what is at issue, will you let me explain the whole thing?"

He was so elegant about this.

"Do not let me press you—only tell me what I need to hear. But I should know this—are you, yourself, of the same profession as your cousin?"

"No. That is, not officially—I have accidentally helped him and his friends once or twice; that's all. I retain my amateur status!" she said smiling.

"Well now, tell me just as much as you please. You have satisfied me in regard to the personal aspect, which is the important one."

Julia liked him enormously for saying that—it fitted in so completely with the whole atmosphere of La Cure: the austerity, the elegance, the hard work cheerfully done; the affection, and the preoccupation with the things of the mind. Calvinists or no, these people lived in a wonderful world, and one seldom met with in the greedy materialistic twentieth century; the words "rat race," simply had no meaning at Bellardon! Much more at ease, she explained that initially Colin had only asked her to look into the matter of the inheritance—but then had come the telephone call, and the letter explaining that important documents had been deposited along with the money, which should be secured as quickly as possible. In fact, what she wanted was the number of Mr. Thalassides' account.

"You do not know me in the least," she ended, opening her bag—"but you have those letters from Aglaia's lawyers, and here is my passport."

He waved it aside. "A very poor likeness. Why must you hurry so much? We should enjoy a longer visit—my wife has lost her heart to you! The papers and the money are safe enough in the bank."

"M. de Ritter, that is just what my cousin's colleagues fear they may not be. They believe that other people are after them. That is why I have come here so suddenly—they say the matter is *de toute urgence.*"

"*Who* seeks them?"

"I have no idea—I wasn't told, except that it is the documents they are after."

He frowned. "It would be." He looked again at the papers on his desk. "But you have no death certificate for the old Greek! You can do nothing without that."

"I know. I wrote to my cousin yesterday to ask for it. I told him if he could get it at once to post it to me here."

"How can he get it at once? Thalassides died in Istanbul, in the Park Hotel! And in addition, to satisfy the bank the copy must be stamped and attested by the British Consulate. Latterly he held an English passport."

"Oh glory!" Julia exclaimed in English. "But all that will take *ages!*"

"At least it will take several days," de Ritter said. "So you see that you will have to prolong your visit!"

Julia didn't respond, because she was doing some of her usual practical thinking.

"I wonder if they know in London where he died," she said. "Oh, sorry. I love being here, only it's an awful imposition on your wife. But I think I must let Colin know about Istanbul."

"We will telegraph tomorrow, early," the Pastor said.

Germaine presently took Julia up to her room.

"At what hour would you like your *petit déjeuner?*" she asked.

"Oh, whenever you all have yours," Julia said, anxious to be accommodating.

"We breakfast at a quarter past six," her hostess said. "You see Marcel has to catch an early train to Lausanne for his school, and Jean-Pierre likes to be in the church at least by a quarter to seven, to have an hour to say his prayers in peace before the day's work begins. But this is early for you —I can bring you a tray in the *salle-à-manger* at any time. Just name the hour."

"Golly!" Julia muttered—and named the hour of eight-thirty. What people! she thought, just before falling asleep in the narrow but gloriously comfortable Swiss bed, with the smell of lilac coming in at the window.

CHAPTER IV

GENEVA

JULIA GAVE careful thought to the wording of her telegram the moment she awoke, and went down to breakfast with it written out on a sheet of paper.

"See my letter Stop Grandpa died in Constantinople and paper I asked for must be stamped and verified by our consulate there Stop Staying here pro tem Stop Hurry repeat hurry."

She signed it, "Darling."

The Pastor read this through carefully when she handed it to him.

"You have put 'stop' three times, when really the sense is quite clear without," he said, pulling out the pen clipped into his breast pocket. Julia snatched at his hand.

"No, leave it. It's the way they telegraph. Is it all right otherwise? I don't think it gives much away, do you?"

"No. Why"—he turned his blue eyes, usually so dancingly gay, onto her with a certain severity as he asked—"Why do you sign it 'Darling'?"

"Oh, that's a code word. It just means urgency, between Colin and me," Julia said airily. As he continued to regard her a little seriously—"Dear M. de Ritter, do take this from me," she said in English. "Would I be busting myself to secure Aglaia's fortune for her, if Colin were really a 'darling' to me? I do love him very dearly; we were more or less brought up together as children, and have never stopped being very close to one another. But that's all. And that's why I want to recover Aglaia's money for her—for them both!"

His expression relaxed.

"I accept what you say. But a telegram should be signed with a name, here."

"Well, 'Darling' is a name! There was Grace Darling, the girl in the lifeboat," Julia replied promptly.

He laughed loudly.

"All right! So now I take this to the Bureau de Poste, and meanwhile you stay with us. How nice!"

When a telegram like this of Julia's reaches a certain headquarters in London it sets all sorts of activities in motion. Tall men, with rather dead-pan faces, reach for their desk telephones and talk to one another, or walk along corridors to other rooms for conversations face to face; small men, usually in brown felt hats, scurry unobtrusively about Whitehall and the purlieus of the Strand. In this particular case, in a matter of hours men in rather loud check caps were hurrying through the steep narrow streets of Istanbul, and returning, frustrated by the innate Turkish passion for stalling, to their superiors. Ultimately there were even telephone calls between London and Ankara. And it all took quite a long time, as everything to do with Turkey does.

Meanwhile Julia, when she had breakfasted, asked to be allowed to ring up Gersau; she spoke to Herr Waechter, inquired after Mrs. Hathaway, and learning that she was going on well explained that she, Julia, would not be returning for a few days. "Please be sure to telephone if she gets worse, or wants me," the girl said earnestly. "But I feel sure that in your house, and with Watkins to harry, she will be perfectly all right unless she has a relapse. And I should really stay here—she will understand."

She heard his dry old man's laugh when she spoke of Mrs. Hathaway harrying Watkins, but he promised to do as she wished.

Julia spent the next five days very happily at La Cure, taking part in a form of life completely new to her. She got quite accustomed, when she went to the bathroom at 7 A.M., to seeing her hostess, in an enveloping check overall with a cotton kerchief framing her beautiful face, pushing one of those heavy lead-weighted polishing pads on a long handle to and fro across the broad beechen planks on the wide landing, or rubbing up the walnut table and the other pretty pieces of old furniture which ornamented it with *real* beeswax, mixed with turpentine in a small earthenware jar; the same of course went on downstairs in the hall, the *salon*, the *salle-à-manger* and the Pastor's study—and later in the bedrooms: theirs, hers, Marcel's. In the housework Julia was never allowed to take any part, except making her own bed, and this only under protest; but in other ways she did what she could to help Germaine. She took plates and cups out of the dishwasher and stowed them in cupboards; she picked peas and shelled them, sitting under the arbour of pleached limes in the garden; she gathered the first strawberries; weeded the borders, and propped up the superb white paeonies which filled them with twigs gathered from the rubbish-heap.

But these were morning occupations; in the afternoons the Pastor often took her out on his rounds to show her the countryside. This was green and gently rolling, with cherries ripening in the orchards and along the roadsides; here and there were small blue lakes. The villages were charming, and one or two of the old towns—like Murtag, with its broad street of lovely arcaded buildings—beautiful to a degree. Julia felt ignorant and foolish, in that she had never heard of Murtag; nor had she realized that half the Canton was Protestant, and half Catholic, as the Pastor now told her, pointing out the different churches—sometimes both in one village, more often a different form of worship in each settlement.

But most of all she was interested by her host's conversation. Where his work was concerned he was both intensely practical, and rather original in his views. His parish was vast and straggling—eighteen miles one way by twenty or more the other—and he scorched about it in a big Frégate— Julia was surprised to hear him say one day, when they were discussing the problems confronting the modern world, that he regarded *l'auto* as the enemy of the good life.

"I should have thought a car was essential for you, simply to cover the ground," she protested.

"It depends on how usefully I cover it," he said. "When I walked or bicycled thirty kilometers to reason with my parishioners about their misdeeds, or to pray with them, they listened to me, for they felt that I had taken some trouble on their account; when I drive up in a car they do not pay half as much attention, and will almost interrupt by exhortations to ask what she will do at full stretch! It has completely altered their attitude, and our relationship."

"Well, couldn't you still bicycle about?"

"Miss Probyn, I am sixty years old! and the work grows from year to year, as the State impinges more and more on individual lives. I spend half my day now at my desk, *tracassé* by filling in forms, or helping others to fill in their forms, when thirty years ago I could spend all my time on my proper task, that of a shepherd of souls."

But on the whole Jean-Pierre de Ritter was optimistic about the present, and the future, of religion.

"The eruption of evil in the world which the last twenty-five years have witnessed—first Hitler's Germany, then the Communists and their prison camps—has finally shut the mouths of those who formerly derided the idea of Original Sin, and equally of the deluded people who used to believe in human progress by purely human effort. Who now pays the smallest attention to Bernard Shaw or Bertrand Russell?—or the poor Webbs? Certainly none who have seen the photographs of what the Allied forces found in Belsen, or who have encountered Polish girls with big numbers tattooed in blue ink on their forearms in Auschwitz—or even who have read *Darkness at Noon.* No!" de Ritter exclaimed, standing on the accelerator in his eager emphasis—"The modern world has met Evil face to face, in Europe, at least, and whoever has truly seen Evil is ready, is eager, to look for salvation, redemption. And the only Savior, the one Redeemer, is Christ."

He shot past a line of farm carts, slewing dangerously over onto the wrong side of the road; and then proceeded at a more reasonable speed.

"It is to this that I attribute the quite remarkable resurgence of religion in Europe recently," he went on. "*We* have it here; in France it is mainly Catholic, and most remarkable—the Jacistes, the Jocistes, the Prêtres Ouvriers; and look at those amazing Whitsuntide pilgrimages from Paris to Chartres, 3,000 or more young people marching, praying, and hearing Mass, over the whole week-end of Pentecost. How is it in England?" he went on. "Have you the same thing?"

As so often while staying at La Cure, Julia found herself rather out of her depth. She had read *Darkness at Noon,* and she had heard of the French Worker-Priests, but she had no idea what *Jacistes* or *Jocistes* were, nor had she seen much sign of a religious revival in England, and rather gloomily she told her host so. "Of course there's been Billy Graham," she added.

"Oh, emotional Revivalism!" he said, in rather crushing tones. "But does that last?"

In the evenings she met the family: Gisèle and her husband came to dine one evening; Henriette and hers another; Antoine and his wife on a third occasion. Both the girls had some of their mother's delicate beauty, while Antoine was the spit and image of the Pastor. He worked at a rayon factory not far off; the two sons-in-law were "working farmers," living on land they owned—what the Scotch used to call "bonnet lairds." But Lucien and Armand, though they might have been forking dung or filling silage pits since 5 A.M., could talk about Galsworthy or Rilke with the best— could, and insisted on doing so, and on kindred topics. How was Auden regarded as a poet in England? Had the curious preoccupation of the not-so-young intellectuals with the Spanish Civil War died a natural death?

"Surely," Armand exploded—he was a blond giant of a man—"surely even Spender must realize by now that this all arose from an attempt to create a Communist enclave in the extreme West of Europe, out-flanking England and France?" And Julia, once again, had to confess that she had no idea what Spender now realized or didn't realize.

At last the death certificate arrived, direct by air-mail from the Consulate-General in Istanbul; the combination of the Turkish postage stamp and the Lion-and-Unicorn embossed on the flap of the envelope aroused the highest interest in the village *facteur* who brought the letters, rather to Julia's annoyance; it might, she thought, have been sent more anonymously. The Pastor was already out on his rounds in the parish, and till he returned for the déjeuner she had to pacify herself by cutting asparagus, and lettuce for the salad—in Fribourg they sow lettuces thick and cut them like hay, to save the bother of transplanting; Julia was amused by this curious trick. She was laying the table for luncheon when she heard her host's step in the hall; she hastened out to him.

"It's come!" she said. "So I must be off as soon as possible."

Jean-Pierre took this announcement, as he took everything, very easily. *"Quel dommage!* Germaine will be lost without her undergardener! However after supper we will arrange everything."

"Can't I go this afternoon? Colin said it was urgent," Julia protested.

"There is no train that will get you to Geneva before the banks close. No—we will deal with it tonight."

They dealt with it that evening in his study. Julia brought down the copy of the late Mr. Thalassides' death certificate, plastered with English and Turkish official stampings, the Turkish in ugly violet ink. The Pastor examined this, then pushed it aside, drew forward a sheet of paper, wrote rapidly, and put the sheet in an envelope.

"This is the authorization which I, as Aglaia Armitage's guardian, give you to collect the documents; it is incontestable. It gives the account *numéro.* I have told them that the *money* will not be taken away at this stage; her lawyers or her bankers can do that later—it is their affair. But I have instructed them to show you, if you wish, the certificates which give the extent of her fortune." He took a card out of his pocketbook, and scribbled on it. "Do not show the authorization I have given you until you are in conversation with one of these two gentlemen," he said, handing her the card. "They are two of the directors of the Banque Républicaine who know me well. If possible speak with Dutour; Chambertin is sometimes *un peu difficile*."

Julia read the card. It said—"*Je recommande chaleureusement Mademoiselle Julia Probyn, de Londres, qui voudra discuter des affaires bancaires.*" As she put the card away in her bag along with the other papers de Ritter chuckled.

"They will think *you* want to open a numbered account," he said. Then —"Where do you stay in Geneva?" he asked.

"I hadn't thought. What's a good hotel?"

"How are you arranged for currency?" he inquired.

"Oh, plenty."

"Well if you are not short of money you had better stay at the Bergues; it is delightful." He there and then booked her a room, and the following morning Germaine once again dragged her luggage down to the station on the handcart.

Julia, unlike many English people, was always ready to talk in trains. After changing for Geneva at Lausanne she found herself seated opposite a neat little man with a large brief-case, on which he was scribbling notes on narrow sheets of typed paper that looked like invoices. Julia's appearance of course produced its usual impact; he offered to put out his cheroot if she disliked the smell, inquired whether she wished the window up or down, and promised to show her Mont Blanc when it should come in sight. Soon they were in cheerful conversation—and it proved much more amusing to Julia than most casual conversations in trains. The neat little man presently explained that he held the Swiss agency for an English firm, which made surgical stays in a special air-light elastic weave—"Corsette-Air" was the trade name—and in Switzerland they had an immense sale; he named a figure for the firm's annual turnover which astonished Julia. She was even more astonished to learn that he had never been to England, and had never met any of the directors of the Yorkshire firm who manufactured "Corsette-Air"—all had been arranged by correspondence, through people who vouched for him. More peculiar still, he could not really speak English, but he could read it sufficiently well to understand the letters from Yorkshire.

"And do you reply in English?" Julia asked, fascinated by this odd setup.

Ah no, he always replied in German, "They get my letters translated, and reply to me in English."

To Julia it all sounded quite crazy; but if the sums he had named to her were accurate, obviously it worked. And the little man himself was so eager, so energetic and enthusiastic, that she could credit his making a go of anything. In his excitement over telling her about his work he quite forgot to show her Mont Blanc at the place whence it is visible—"*Ah, quel dommage!*" he exclaimed. "From Geneva one seldom sees it; in fact you may say never." Like so many Swiss he was bilingual; he told Julia in French how he wrote to his English employers in German, and how—he glowed with pride as he spoke—"Sometimes we even touch *la haute finance;* foreign business—not English, I mean; international. We are much used, because we are most discreet."

"How thrilling!" Julia said, with her customary easy warmth, which really meant nothing.

"Is it not? I see that Mademoiselle comprehends. Listen to this—only the other day I, Kaufmann, was called upon to act as intermediary between very important *agences* belonging to two different nations, and pass informations from one to the other!" The little man was quite carried away, between Julia and his own enthusiasms; the girl could not help smiling at his idea of discretion, but merely said, as warmly as before, that this was *formidable,* that he must lead a passionately interesting life—to which he agreed eagerly. Then, as the train began to slow down at the outskirts of Geneva, suddenly he became cautious.

"This is of course most confidential, what I have told Mademoiselle," he said rather nervously.

"But naturally. I am discretion itself!" Julia said soothingly. "And I am grateful to you for having made my journey so interesting." Whereupon the little man insisted on giving her one of his trade cards, and urged her to come and see him if she should be in his neighborhood. The card depicted on one side a rather fully formed lady wearing a "Corsette-Air," and on the other bore his name and address:

> Herr Viktor Kaufmann.
> Villa Victoria.
> Merligen-am-Thunersee.
> B.O.

Julia suppressed a giggle at the letters "B.O."—she already knew that in Switzerland they stand for "Berner Oberland"—not their usual English significance. She thanked the little man, put the card in a side pocket of her bag, and promptly forgot all about him.

The Hotel des Bergues at Geneva is indeed a delightful place; the Pastor had been quite right, Julia decided within the first five minutes. It is quiet, unobtrusively high-class, with excellent well-mannered service; it stands on the embankment beside the huge glass-green Rhône, close to where the river debouches from the lake, and exactly opposite the Île Rousseau, set with Claude-like trees. Upstream, on the lake shore, rises that exotic—and therefore so unSwiss—fantasy, the only fountain in Europe which springs a clear 300 feet into the air in a snowy jet which sways like a reed or a poplar in the breeze, glittering most beautifully in the sun against the distant blue shores. In theory the whiteness of the fountain's spray should be a *pendant* to that of the summit of Mont Blanc; in fact that tedious mountain seldom shows itself to Geneva.

She unpacked first, as was her habit, and then tried to telephone to the Banque Républicaine—it was already closed, the porter told her politely. So she went downstairs and strolled across the bridge spanning the Rhône to the Île Rousseau, where she observed with interest the wired enclosure reserved for the black swans, tufted ducks, and other varieties, and laughed at the typically Swiss notice about feeding the ordinary swans who hung expectantly in the strong current below the footbridge leading to the island: "Please give your bread to the keeper; he will arrange it suitably to feed the birds." She walked on to the farther side of the river, and strolled about a little; the whole place enchanted her, a city grey in tone, with an austere elegance combined with a certain simplicity. On returning to the Bergues she found that it had a tearoom close to the front hall; many people were having tea and cakes at small tables on the pavement outside, and Julia did the same, enjoying the warmth, the soft light, the shifting tops of the poplars on the island; and the grey profile of the other half of the city beyond the river, idly amused by the sight of the passers-by on the pavement beside her. One of these, a tall lanky man in a light suit of rather foreign cut suddenly checked, started, and came up to her, raising his hat—she recognized him as a man called Nethersole, whom she had occasionally met in London with her old admirer Geoffrey Consett.

Mr. Nethersole greeted her with the enthusiasm with which men usually greeted Julia, and sat down at her table. "What in the world are you doing here?" he asked.

"Oh, just sight-seeing. I'd never been to Geneva before. How beautiful it is."

"Yes, isn't it? I adore it. But have you seen the oddest sight of all?"

"No, I've only just arrived. What is the odd sight?"

"Oh my dear, the Palais des Nations! Well you'd better come and have lunch with me there tomorrow; I work there. Will you? One o'clock, in the restaurant. Oh, what a piece of luck this is!"

Julia accepted this invitation, mentally praising Mr. Nethersole's tact in not asking if she had seen anything of Geoffrey lately. (Anyhow it is always nice to be invited somewhere in a strange place.) Nethersole soon flitted off, and Julia decided to go up to her room and write a full account of La Cure to Mrs. Hathaway before dinner; between helping Germaine and talking with the Pastor, she had only sent her the scrappiest of notes. In the corridor beyond the main hall the lift doors were just closing; the lift-man politely opened them again for her, and she stepped in, saying *"Troisième."* Three other people were already in the lift; one of them was the detective.

This time he grinned very broadly indeed, and murmured—"How we do keep on meeting!" Julia put on her haughtiest expression, and made no response; she got out at the third floor, while he was borne upwards. This encounter disturbed her a little; if he really was one of Colin's *mauvais sujets,* it was rather tiresome that he should be staying in the same hotel. And half-way through her letter she went down again to the hall and procured from the *concierge* a small plan of the city; back in her room she looked out the Avenue de la République. It was only a short distance away, across the bridge by the island—fine, she would walk there tomorrow, and give no address to a taxi to be overheard by bellhops, hovering for a tip.

She woke next morning in good spirits; Julia had the priceless gift of sound sleep. Leaning from her window—she had no idea of her good fortune in being given a *front* room at the Bergues at twenty-four hours notice, nor that she owed this entirely to Jean-Pierre—she first looked entranced at the fountain, profiled golden-white in the sunshine against the blue lake. But what was that, looming mistily and incredibly high into the sky?—also golden-white, and immense? It could only be Mont Blanc; it was just where the chambermaid had told her to look for it the evening before. Utterly satisfied Julia rang for her breakfast, which she ate at her window; then, in high heart, she set out on foot for the bank.

The Avenue de la République is full of banks, all enormous, many of them new. The Banque Républicaine was one of the most grandiose of all: when she stepped onto a doormat 10 feet long, huge bronze and glass doors opened of themselves; within, marble pilasters flanked the doors opening off lobbies—there was no human being in sight. She pushed on through this mausoleum-like splendor into a vast central hall, rising to a height of three or four stories, and furnished with armchairs and sofas; there was no sign of banking whatever except for a few clerks behind glass walls round the sides. There was however a single desk at which sat a pimply youth, curiously inadequate to all this pomp and dignity; to him Julia handed M. de Ritter's card, and asked if she could see M. Dutour or M. Chambertin? The youth glanced at the card and went away, taking it with him—why not telephone, Julia thought, since there were two instruments on the desk. A long pause ensued—long enough to make her, at last, a little nervous. Eventually the youth reappeared accompanied by an older man, who led her to a lift and wafted her up to what he described as the *salle d'attente*.

The waiting room was as rich as all the rest—a big desk, heavy leather armchairs, a deep pile carpet, some quite tolerable modern paintings on the walls. But the sun struck full into the room, and it was hot and stuffy. Julia went over and threw open a glass door onto a balcony. This was surrounded by window boxes full of petunias and godetias—she was thinking how early it was for these to be in bloom when the door opened, and a man came in, holding de Ritter's card in his hand.

"I am M. Chambertin," he said. "What can I do for you?"

Julia took against Chambertin from the start. He was a short man; younger than she had expected, but somehow with an *elderly* expression, suspicious and slightly sour. As he seated himself behind the desk she decided that this was going to be a sticky interview; and sticky indeed it proved.

She began confidently enough, however.

"You are doubtless aware that M. le Pasteur de Ritter is the *parrain* and also the guardian of Mademoiselle Aglaia Armitage?"

"*Certainement,*" he said very coldly—indeed he seemed to stiffen a little at the girl's name.

"I come on her behalf—with M. de Ritter's authority, as you see."

"Mademoiselle, I do *not* see. This card refers only to '*des affaires bancaires,*' not to Mademoiselle Armitage at all."

Julia, apologizing, handed over the Pastor's letter. "I have other authorities also—pray have the goodness to regard them." She opened her large lizard bag and drew out the documents from England, which she laid before him on the desk: the copy of Thalassides' will, attested by his lawyers; the authorizations from Aglaia's bank and lawyers to hand over any or all of the property to Miss Julia Probyn, if so requested; finally the photostat of the death certificate, so liberally covered with official stamps. M. Chambertin, adjusting a pair of pince-nez, began to look at them, at first with a rather contemptuous air; but as he read through paper after paper his expression changed from contempt to one of bewildered consternation. "*Mais c'est impossible, cela!*" he muttered to himself; then he rounded quickly on Julia.

"Might I see your passport, Mademoiselle?" he asked. For the first time there was nothing disagreeable in his manner, only what she recognized as real concern. She handed over her passport—he studied it, looked at the photograph, looked at Julia, and then raised his hands in a helpless gesture of despair.

"This is all completely incomprehensible!" he said.

"Why?" Julia asked. "Surely these papers are incontestably in order? What is the difficulty?"

"Simply that Mademoiselle Armitage called here in person last week, and took reception of the money in the account."

"And took the—" Julia checked herself in time. "Took *everything* that you held in M. Thalassides' numbered Konto?"

"Yes—*all.*"

Julia stood up. She was tall; at that moment she was menacing.

"M. Chambertin, you have been duped! Miss Armitage sailed for the Argentine to visit her mother on the fourteenth of May, the day before I left for Switzerland myself."

"How do you know this?"

"It was in all the English papers. As M. Thalassides' heiress, whatever she does is news."

"*La presse* can make mistakes," Chambertin said, with the air of a man clutching at a straw.

"Hardly, in such a case. But in any event her fiancé would not; and he is my cousin." She paused, thinking with intensity of the girl Watkins had noticed at Victoria, and of her two companions. "Did Mademoiselle Armitage come alone?" she asked, sitting down again.

"But naturally not—she is not of age! Her guardian was with her, and gave the authorization."

Julia was a little shaken by this.

"Do you mean M. le Pasteur de Ritter?" she asked incredulously. "Did you *see* him? He says he knows you."

"No—I myself did not," Chambertin replied, a little unhappily.

"Then who did? I can't believe it was M. Dutour; he is a personal friend of the Pastor's too."

M. Chambertin looked more unhappy than ever.

"No. It was M. de Kessler, another of our directors, who conducted this interview."

"Does he know M. Jean-Pierre de Ritter personally?" Julia asked sharply.

"No, he does not." M. Chambertin's unhappiness was now marked.

"Ah. I expect these people carefully asked to see *him*, instead of you or M. Dutour," Julia said. "They are probably very well-informed." Her confidence mounted with her anger. "M. Chambertin, I think we had better see M. de Kessler."

"So do I," he agreed uncomfortably, and spoke into the desk telephone. He turned back to Julia. "I can assure you that Mademoiselle Armitage and her party produced correct documents. We are extremely particular in these matters."

"Oh, I am sure you are." But she pounced on the word "party." "There was a third?"

"I understood that the fiancé of Mademoiselle Armitage was also present."

"M. Chambertin, her fiancé is in London. I have been speaking to him there on the telephone. And you should perhaps know that I came to Geneva yesterday from La Cure at Bellardon, where I have been staying for the last week; therefore I know perfectly well; and M. de Ritter knows perfectly well that Mademoiselle Aglaia Armitage, for the past fortnight, has been on a steamer on her way to the Argentine. Certainly her guardian never came here last week. Would he have given me this letter of authorization if he had?"

Before Chambertin could answer the door opened and a white-haired man with a pleasant pink face walked in; he was really old, without any doubt.

"Ah, mon cher de Kessler, how good of you to come up," Chambertin said respectfully, rising as he spoke—it was evident that de Kessler was very senior among the directors. "May I present you to Mademoiselle Probyn?"

De Kessler beamed on Julia as he bowed to her, and then asked Chambertin, rather bluntly, what he wanted?

"A little more information about Mademoiselle Armitage's fortune. Mademoiselle Probyn has been spending the past week at La Cure at Bellardon, and brings me now a letter from M. le Pasteur de Ritter, in a handwriting which I recognize well, giving the number of the late M. Thalassides' Konto and requesting me to hand everything over to her, Miss Probyn. But I understand that you have already dealt with this matter yourself."

"Certainly—the account has been closed. Mademoiselle Armitage came in person—a charming young lady." He still only looked a little puzzled, and definitely repressive to his junior colleague.

"You saw her passport?" Chambertin asked.

"But naturally."

"And made a note of the number?"

"Certainly."

"She provided you with *les pièces justificatives* which satisfied you?"

"My good Chambertin, for what do you take me? I work in this bank for forty-five years! What is all this? Why these questions?"

"I too come on behalf of Mademoiselle Armitage," Julia put in, "and I fear very much that something may have gone wrong—some confusion have occurred. As you know, Mademoiselle Armitage is not of age, and cannot yet take control of her fortune."

"*Bien entendu*, Mademoiselle. But there was no confusion; she was accompanied by her guardian, who signed all the receipts." He looked more puzzled, now, and turned to Chambertin. "*You* know M. le Pasteur de Ritter? A man of a very old and respected Bernois family."

Again Julia spoke before Chambertin could reply.

"But you, yourself, are not personally acquainted with M. de Ritter?"

"Till last week, no—only by reputation."

Chambertin made to speak; Julia held up her hand like a school child who has his answer ready.

"M. de Kessler, this guardian who signed the receipts—was he tallish, rather stout, and with an iron-grey beard slightly parted in the middle?"

"*Exactement*, Mademoiselle," de Kessler said, looking relieved. Julia quickly put a term to his relief.

"M. Chambertin, would you be so good as to describe your old friend M. de Ritter to your colleague? He is more likely to believe you than me."

In pitiable embarrassment, but firmly, Chambertin said—"Mon cher, the Pasteur de Ritter, whom I have known for thirty years, is a short man, and noticeably slender."

"Clean-shaven, also, *n'est-ce-pas?*" Julia added.

"Yes—certainly." While de Kessler gaped Chambertin turned to Julia and asked—"How comes it that you know so well the appearance of—of the man who came and signed the receipts?"

"The impostor, you mean? Oh, I happened to see him, and the girl who was impersonating Miss Armitage, on my way here; they traveled to Calais on the same train."

De Kessler, now quite bewildered, said irritably, "Mademoiselle, what is all this talk of impostors and impersonators?"

Instead of answering him, Julia turned to his colleague.

"M. Chambertin, wouldn't it be as well to let M. de Kessler see the documents *I* have brought?"

"Certainly. *Les voici, mon cher.*"

De Kessler went round behind the desk, put on his glasses, and studied Julia's papers, muttering to himself as he did so—"The bankers, yes, and the lawyers; the executors, yes; and the British Consul-General in

Istanbul has *gestempelt* the death certificate." Last of all he read de Ritter's letter; then turned back and read the date aloud—*"C'est hier!"* Now thoroughly upset, he turned to Chambertin. "But this is impossible!"

"Oh no, M. de Kessler—unfortunately it's all too possible," Julia said. "You have been tricked by a gang of crooks."

The old man drew himself up (to Julia it was the most pitiable thing of all) and said—

"Mademoiselle, this does not happen with la Banque Républicaine!"

"Well, it has happened this time," Julia said crisply; she was sorry for the old man, but more important things than his feelings were at stake. She turned to Chambertin. "Do ring up M. de Ritter now, and ask him if he really came in last week and signed Miss Armitage's fortune away? That will settle it. I *know* he didn't; but it may satisfy M. de Kessler."

"Mademoiselle, I accept *no* statements made over the telephone," de Kessler said angrily.

"Oh very well—then we must drag the wretched man down here."

Chambertin was fluttering the telephone book. "Fribourg is 037," Julia told him, "and La Cure is 1101." When the call came through she firmly took the receiver. *"Allo? Ah, c'est toi, Germaine. Ici Julia. Est-ce-que Jean-Pierre est là? Ah, très bien—j'attends."* She noted the effect of all these Christian names on the two bankers while she waited, receiver in hand. When Jean-Pierre came to the telephone she spoke rapidly in English. "Listen, I am at the bank. There has been a complete disaster, which I would rather not discuss on the telephone. Is there the least possibility that you could come down this afternoon?"

"Only with great difficulty. Why?—what goes on?"

"We have been too slow. Those I spoke of have been ahead of us, and have gone off with everything. Someone else signed for them in your name."

"But this could not happen! Both the men whose names I gave you know me perfectly well."

"Of course they do. But unfortunately these persons must have known this too, and were sharp enough to ask for another director—a charming old gentleman who does not know you by sight, and so allowed himself to be duped." Julia found herself hoping that de Kessler did not understand English, but the hope was vain—she saw that cheerful pink face become crimson.

"Le vieux de Kessler?" came down the line.

"Exactement. And he now refuses to accept any statement on the telephone; that is why I must put you to this trouble. I do apologize; it is not my fault."

There was a pause. At last—"Yes, very well," the Pastor said. "Who received *you?*"

"M. Chambertin."

"Then please tell him I will be with him at half past four o'clock, *à peu près.*"

"I would rather you told him yourself—" and she handed the receiver over.

The Pastor had a very resonant voice, and Julia could just hear his words. "Mon cher Alcide, *what* are your co-directors up to? This is frightful, what has taken place. I shall be with you between four and half past four, and please arrange for your colleague to be present, and see that we are given admittance. Tell Mademoiselle that I will call for her at her hotel on the way."

Chambertin transmitted both these messages, adding afterwards to de Kessler—"*C'est bien Jean-Pierre*—I cannot mistake his voice."

Julia had been thinking as well as overhearing.

"M. Chambertin, surely these people ought to be traced, if possible. Did they give M. de Kessler any address?"

De Kessler said only La Cure at Bellardon, and for the demoiselle an address in London. "*Chez une certaine Madame Conway, à Kensington.*"

"That's Aglaia's aunt, of course—that's no help. They gave no indication of their movements?" she asked de Kessler.

"La demoiselle spoke of visiting Interlaken, to see the Jungfrau; nothing more. The fiancé spoke of making some ascensions."

"Ah yes, the fiancé. Was he tall, dark, with a markedly olive complexion, and the figure of an athlete?" Julia enquired.

"*C'est exacte*, Mademoiselle," the old man said.

Chambertin had a question to put.

"On which day did they come? Six days ago, you say? We must alert Interpol, and also the *Fremden-Polizei*, the Security Police. It is possible that they have not yet left the country."

"Wouldn't it be better to leave the police till M. de Ritter arrives," Julia counseled. She was thinking that she must try to ring up Colin from the Palais des Nations at lunch time.

"Mademoiselle, the reputation of the Banque Républicaine is at stake! There is not a moment to lose."

Julia refrained from pointing out that the bank had already lost six days.

"As M. de Kessler has their passport numbers, would there be any means of checking at the frontiers whether they have left or not?" she asked. "No, I expect not—those men in uniform just open your passport, take a good stare at you, snap it shut and hand it back. They couldn't possibly keep a record."

Chambertin smiled a little at this description.

"No, Mademoiselle, they do not. But they are quite observant, and this party of three, whom you seem to have observed very closely, might well be noticed. How was the aspect of the young girl, by the way?"

"Ask M. de Kessler," Julia said.

"She was blonde," de Kessler said, hesitantly.

"Yes, but her eyes—the color—and tall or short?" Chambertin asked impatiently.

"She was petite—and *très jolie,*" de Kessler said. Chambertin turned to Julia.

"Mademoiselle, can you help us?"

"Yes," Julia said. "This girl was certainly most carefully chosen as a double of Miss Armitage—needlessly, since the personnel of the bank failed to notice her appearance!" She could not resist that crack. "She is very short indeed, very slender, with tiny hands and feet, and though she is—or has been made to appear—ash-blonde, her eyes are dark brown."

Chambertin was scribbling.

"Perfect," he said. "And her clothes—did you observe these also?"

"Yes. A pale cream suit, a little blouse to match, a light brown overcoat— and a hat of cream Bangkok straw, trimmed with brown nylon lace to match the overcoat. Shoes and handbag of brown crocodile."

Chambertin went on scribbling. "Miss Probyn, you would be worth a fortune as a detective!" he exclaimed.

"I want to be worth Miss Armitage's fortune, M. Chambertin!" She looked at her watch—nearly twelve. "Could someone call me a taxi?" She wanted to tidy up at the hotel before going out to lunch.

She did not however let the taxi take her to the Bergues; she got out at the footbridge leading to the Île Rousseau, and then walked to the hotel. These types seemed to be madly smart; one couldn't be too careful. And there was that damned detective, too, actually staying in the hotel!

In her room she changed into a thinner frock—Geneva heats up in the middle of the day—and looked in the back of her engagement book to make sure that she had got Colin's office number. She had, and she would just have to risk telephoning there from the Palais des Nations after lunch; surely it ought to be one of the safest places. Anyhow Colin was usually pretty quick at picking up what she was driving at, either in their "darling darling" language or in Gaelic. But oh, why hadn't she written to him about the girl at Victoria? "Because one's afraid of looking a fool, one goes and *is* a fool," she muttered, as she put on scent and lipstick. She telephoned down for a taxi, which was waiting when she reached the hall; as she drove off along the *quai* beside the lovely green river, in spite of her frustration and worry she began to enjoy herself, and to look forward with pleasure to her luncheon with Nethersole. He was a curious learned creature; what his precise function with UNO, or whatever used the Palais des Nations, might be she didn't know, but he had many forms of strange knowledge, any one of which could make him valuable to international organizations.

CHAPTER V

GENEVA—THE PALAIS DES NATIONS

The Palais des Nations at Geneva is a very large, completely expressionless building. It isn't ugly, it isn't beautiful; it is just *big*, with a lot of flags fluttering in front of it from tall pale poles. It stands in spacious green grounds, with a parking space for cars all down the right-hand side of the broad entrance drive. Within, the bigness and the functional lack of expression are even more marked. An immense hall stretches to right and left inside the door, with racks full of folders, with polyglot girls in light overalls standing behind counters, casually and chipperly answering the questions of even more polyglot inquirers. The inquirers are not only polyglot but polychrome; every shade of color that the skin of the human race can take on, from splendid deep black to a pinkness like that of Monsieur de Kessler's, were exhibited to Julia's fascinated gaze standing in chattering knots on the wide marble floor as she made her way to one of the counters, and asked where the restaurant was.

"Lift to the twelfth floor; over there," a chipper girl said, without giving any indication of the direction.

"Over *where?*" Julia asked. "Could you take me, if you can't show me?"

"Oh sorry—on the right, round the corner," the girl said carelessly. "Lots of lifts."

Julia walked to the right-hand end of the huge lobby and went round the corner, where there were a great many very large lifts. The lift-men were much more polite than the girl—as indeed men usually are more polite than the teen-age girls who answer so many of the world's telephones. Julia was wafted to the twelfth floor in an outsize lift which opened into the restaurant itself; an elderly waiter came up to her politely, and asked her pleasure?

"M. Nethersole."

"*Par ici, Madame—*" and he led her out onto a broad balcony, where Nethersole and another man were sitting, having drinks. They both rose as she came up to the table; the second man was the detective.

"Ah, excellent!" Nethersole exclaimed. "How good to see you—and how good you look! I couldn't collect a party for you in the time, but here is John Antrobus, who says he doesn't know you, unhappy creature! John, let me complete your education by introducing you to Miss Julia Probyn."

Julia, already sufficiently disconcerted by her morning at the bank, felt that this was the last straw! For once she was grateful to Nethersole for his elaborations, which usually rather bored her; they gave her time to pull herself together, and she held out her hand to Antrobus saying coolly— "So now we really *do* meet."

"Why, have you met before un-really?" Nethersole inquired.

"Oh yes—Mr. Antrobus infests platforms! We bump into one another everywhere—and in lifts, too. He seems to cover the whole of Europe."

"This is most interesting. But first, what will you drink?"

"A Martini, like you. I'm dying for a drink." Nethersole ordered another double Martini, which was brought very quickly—but not more quickly than Julia was having to think. How could she best turn this meeting to account? Was it a coincidence? Was the detective in with the crooks, or on her and Colin's side? She wished passionately that she had bothered in London to learn more from Geoffrey Consett about what Nethersole really did; UNO—if UNO was what he was in—was of course liberally bespattered with fellow-travelers. But it was nice up there on the balcony; the air was sunny and warm, the gardens below were green, blue mountains rose in the distance. She relaxed.

His guest supplied with a drink, Nethersole returned to the subject of her earlier encounter with Antrobus.

"Oh, I was very forward at Victoria; I went up and spoke to him," Julia said airily.

"She asked me if I was a detective!" Antrobus interjected.

"Oh did you? Why? Do you think he looks like one?" Nethersole asked.

"Yes, I think so. Detective-Inspector Alleyne might look very like him, don't you think? And he was behaving like one, too."

Nethersole laughed.

"How do detectives behave?"

"Well, he was hanging about."

"Loitering with intent, did you think?" Antrobus asked.

"Well really it was the maid I was taking out who thought it."

"Goodness, Julia, do you still travel with a maid?" Nethersole asked.

"No, not still, nor ever!—I was taking her out to an old friend who has fallen ill out here. But Watkins is very shrewd, and she's been at endless weddings—always *plastered* with detectives to guard the presents. She was positive that Mr. Antrobus was one."

Both men laughed.

When they went indoors to lunch, in a long restaurant with big plate-glass windows giving onto the balcony, Julia deliberately abandoned that topic, and started another.

"Richard, what do you *do* in this peculiar place? Tell them about the Arabs, or the Walls of Jericho?"

"That sort of thing."

Antrobus supplemented this uninformative remark.

"Richard is a tremendous Arabic scholar, you know. Since Sir Denison Ross died, he has no peer."

"Oh, does UNO go in for *scholarship*? That's quite a new idea."

Again the two men laughed—and Antrobus said, "Specialized knowledge generally comes in usefully, even here."

Julia took him up on that instantly.

"Do you work here too, Mr. Antrobus?"

Did he hesitate? Barely.

"No, not really."

"At Victoria I remember you said that you were on business."

"How inquisitive you are! That was to put you off."

"And are you still putting me off? How does one work for UNO un-really—as you and I met?"

This time there was doubt about it; though Antrobus laughed, Nethersole at least was plainly embarrassed.

"Julia, I can't allow you to cross-examine anyone at lunch! Have some more smoked salmon."

So there it was! Some form of secrecy going on, and she didn't even know Nethersole well enough to be able to get the truth out of him later. "Oh yes please," she said; "I really like to make a *meal* off smoked salmon." As she helped herself she said cheerfully to Antrobus—"I'll apologize if you'd like me to; but like all women, since Fatima, inquisitiveness is my middle name."

"Oh don't apologize," the man said. "If we ever get onto Christian- or Mohammedan-name terms, I shall call you Fatima!"

Julia was unexpectedly pleased at the idea of being called Fatima by Antrobus. The luncheon passed very pleasantly indeed; both men were amusing and talked well—Antrobus in particular had a caustic vein which amused Julia, and a free and completely natural approach to any subject —she had never yet met a man so disengaged, or so totally devoid of self-importance. Long before the meal was over she had become far more interested in him as a person than in what he did, conscious though she was of her need, indeed her duty, to learn this—more than ever after Nethersole had so openly shut her up.

At one point, the talk turned on the great variety of Swiss trades; Julia, by nature so open, just stopped herself in time from telling how the Iron-workers Guild in Berne paid for the de Ritter boys' education, and quite casually substituted the little agent for "Corsette-Air." She made a funny story of it, with the letters in German going to Birmingham to be trans-lated; Nethersole laughed heartily; Antrobus laughed too, but after a half-second's pause—was there a flicker of surprise, of some extra interest, in the grey eyes under those sculptured triangular lids? Almost certainly Yes, for after a moment he asked "*Where* do you say you encountered this entertain-ing individual?"

"Oh, in the train—just a pickup," Julia replied airily. "*You* should know that I go in for picking people up!"

But in spite of her growing pleasure in Antrobus' company, when over coffee he offered to drive her back to the Bergues she refused firmly. "I'll make my own way back—I might like to walk. Besides, I hope Richard is going to show me the whole of this lunatic place. Isn't there a sort of Chamber of Babel, where they all shout at one another through micro-phones which translate as they go along?" Laughing, Antrobus was never-theless a little insistent—it was a long way, it was very hot, she would be exhausted, etc. Julia was pleased by his persistence, but couldn't help wondering whether possibly *he* wasn't as anxious to know about her busi-ness as she was to learn about his? In any case she was firm, and he left alone. When he had gone—"Would you really like to see the Salle des Nations?" Nethersole asked.

"Yes, if you can spare the time. But first I want to telephone."

"Where to?"

"London."

"What an idea! I never telephone. However I presume there is one up here."

This was a mistaken presumption. They were sent down to the main hall, where Nethersole made inquiries. Oh no—all extraterritorial calls had to be made from the third floor. On the third floor there was a whole array of telephone boxes.

"I suppose this is where the Press worthies queue up to send their ghastly nonsense," Nethersole said, regarding the glass cubicles with a cold eye.

"Oh, don't wait," Julia said. "Show me the Salle another day." She was suddenly nervous, afraid of being overheard, afraid of almost everything. Nethersole was very quick at the uptake, and said nicely—"I'll go and wait on the lawn; I'm in no hurry. But you ought to see the Salle, it's so portentous." Julia hoped fervently that he supposed her to be ringing up Geoffrey Consett.

The man at the desk was polite and intelligent; she made it a personal call, giving Colin's name and office number. Then she sank down onto a bench. In no time at all the man called out, "*Le numéro onze,* Mademoiselle." Julia bolted into box 11, and there on the line, as clear as if they were in the same room, was Colin's voice—"Hullo? Who is it?"

"Me—don't use names."

"Of course not, darling. What goes on?"

"Every sort of *desastre.*" She heard him laugh at the Spanish word. "No, it isn't funny. They've been ahead of us."

"What *do* you mean?"

"I'll tell you. Listen carefully; I'm going to talk Gaelic."

"Well speak very slowly, will you? Mine's got rather buried."

Julia had been thinking up phrases during the brief moments while she sat waiting on the bench. She now said slowly, using the archaic expressions of that archaic tongue—

"To the House of Gold, in this city, came a maiden who pretended to be one that she was not; *agus* [and] a youth who said that he was her betrothed—tall, dark-skinned, with the aspect of one who comes from the lands of the Sun's rising." She paused. "Got that?" she asked anxiously in English.

"I think so. D'you mean a Chink?"

"*No*—Middle-Eastern."

"O.K.—go on."

"With them came a *bodach* [old man] who pretended to be the guardian of the maiden."

"Hold on—the *what* of the maiden?" Colin asked in English.

"Guardian."

"Oh yes, I see."

"At the House of Gold these three spoke with another *bodach,* old and foolish, who believed their words, and gave them the parchments."

Colin's command of Gaelic was less than Julia's. "The *what?*" he asked in English.

"Documents."

"Oh God! Oh, damn! Why were you so slow? I told you to hurry."

"Yes, but you hadn't given me the one thing needful, you stupid—I had to wait for that," Julia said. She switched to Gaelic again. "Thus six days were lost; and six days since, these went and obtained possession of the parchments."

"As near as that?" Colin asked miserably in English.

"Yes."

There was a short pause. "Look, I'm finding this lingo rather a strain," Colin said. "Can't we play our old game?"

"Better not—this is much safer. I'll talk very slowly." She went on in Gaelic—"*Mo chridhe* [my heart], you should come to me at once."

"And if I cannot?"

"You must."

"To what place?"

"But to the city of the House of Gold! Take wings!"

She heard him chuckle at that—even in Gaelic there was a phrase for an airplane.

"But there, where do we meet, *m'eudail* [my jewel]?"

Julia herself paused, thinking how to say "Ring up," in Gaelic.

"You speak on a long thin thread with a small bell; you speak with him who is *really* the guardian of your betrothed one. He will tell you where we can meet. Got that?" she asked in English.

"Yes. Can you give me the number?"

"Better not." She switched back to Gaelic. "His name is not inscribed; seek the word 'shepherd.' Got that?" she asked again.

"I think so. All-same Niemöller, yes-no?"

"Yes. Good for you! The canton is Fribourg," she continued in English.

"Why that? I knew it."

"You'll see why. And on what day?" she added, again in Gaelic.

"Very soon."

"*No*, my heart. The day that follows. I beseech you!"

She heard Colin chuckle again.

"Goodness, what a memory you've got! Very well—when you say. I'm sure they'll let me go."

"Obviously they must. Till then." She closed this peculiar and mixed conversation in Gaelic, "Farewell, my heart"—to which Colin very modernly replied, "Bye, darling darling."

She paid the huge cost of a prolonged personal call from Geneva to London in the middle of the day, and then was borne down three floors to where Nethersole was patiently patrolling the rather poor turf which surrounds the Palais des Nations. Abstractedly, she allowed herself to be shown the portentous Chamber, with its pallid meretricious symbolic bas-

reliefs (so like the old Queen's Hall in London), its tables, desks, micro-
phones and press galleries—all the elaborate paraphernalia for international
propaganda, and the loud pretending that "there is peace, where there is no
peace."

"Rather dim, isn't it?" Nethersole said.

"Not dim—*lurid!*" said Julia with vigour.

She had little more than half an hour, when a taxi had carried her back
to the Bergues, to freshen up and be ready for the Pastor. She decided
to wait for him at one of the pavement tables outside the tearoom, so that
there would be no giving of names to the hall porter; certainly Antrobus—
she still thought of him as "the detective"—knew that she was staying
there, but since she had signally failed to learn what *he* was doing, there
was no point in giving away gratuitous information about de Ritter. She
ordered an iced *café-crème,* paid for it at once, and sat sipping it at a
table close to the hotel entrance; the moment the big Frégate drew up she
walked quickly to it, and was getting in at one door before Jean-Pierre
had time to get out at the other.

"*Tiens!* You are remarkably prompt! How are you?" he said, as he swung
left over the Pont des Bergues.

"Distracted, of course," Julia said. She looked calm and beautiful, which
is a very good thing to do if one is distracted—though few achieve it—
de Ritter glanced at her and smiled his shrewd smile.

"Distracted?"

"Yes. Aren't you? This silly old lunatic de Kessler has let these crooks
carry off all Aglaia's money, *and* the oil papers, whatever they are."

"It is serious," he agreed, as he pulled up outside the over-magnificent
portals of the Banque Républicaine.

The doormat didn't let them in at this hour, but a uniformed porter,
hovering behind the bronze and glass, did so at once, and took them, not
to the *salle d'attente* with the petunia window-boxes, but to a much more
severe apartment, where Chambertin and de Kessler awaited them.

Julia listened with interest to Jean-Pierre's dealings with the two bankers
—he tore them to shreds with such urbane skill. Chambertin presently said
that inquiries had been sent out by telephone, and that so far as could be
ascertained, no such party had crossed the frontier, outward-bound, in the
last six days.

"Then they must be waiting here—probably to meet someone; some
emissary. *Écoutez, mon cher* Alcide, surely you realize that for the present
any general alert, above all any publicity, is *most* undesirable? I imagine
you must inform Interpol, but do urge discretion on everyone. You understand, of course, that since the passports *ces types* used to perpetrate their

fraud on the bank were quite certainly forged, they may well use others for their departure. So the passport number may be of little relevance."

Chambertin agreed to this last point, but he was terribly worried. The Bank, he pointed out, was in a frightful position.

"What I would suggest, if I may," Jean-Pierre went on, "is that a description of these three persons should be circulated to the Swiss police, with instructions to make inquiries—it goes without saying with the utmost discretion—at all hotels in *le pays*. M. de Kessler can probably furnish a description?"

"Mademoiselle Probyn can furnish a much better one," Chambertin said acidly.

"But how?"

"Oh never mind how! I happened to see all these crooks when I was coming out," Julia said—"the *luckiest* chance." And presently she was dictating in French to an elderly male stenographer a description of the party she had seen at Victoria. "If *only* I'd kept the papers!" she exclaimed at the end. "They were full of pictures of Aglaia, and a photograph is worth *pages* of description."

"Why were they full of Mademoiselle Armitage's pictures?" Jean-Pierre inquired.

"Because 'Richest Girl in Europe' had just sailed for the Argentine. Of course she isn't that any more, unless those people are caught."

"You, yourself, have no photograph of her?" Chambertin inquired.

"No."

"In any case, must they not sign a *fiche* when they arrive at an hotel?" de Ritter asked.

"Yes, they must—but in what name will they sign?" Chambertin replied. "It all turns on whether they are using one set of passports or two. Naturally the *fiche* must match the passport. If only we had a photograph!"

De Ritter turned to Julia.

"*Et le cousin germain?* Might he . . ."

Julia interrupted him brusquely—"Let us leave that for later." She turned to Chambertin—"If I can produce a photograph, you shall have it."

Outside, in the car, Julia said—"If you can spare another half hour, let us go somewhere where we can talk."

"Then to your hotel."

"Oh no!—hotel walls have longer ears than any others!"

He laughed. "Then where?"

"Let's go and sit on the Île Rousseau—I love it."

There they went. Seated at a table under the trees by the river, looking up towards the lake, the snowy fountain, and the mountains beyond, Julia spoke in English.

"Colin is coming out tomorrow. I telephoned to him at lunch-time from the Palais des Nations."

"Telephoned to *Londres?*"

"Yes, certainly."

"But this must cost a fortune!" the Pastor said, looking quite shocked.

"A fortune is at stake!" Julia said—"and a good deal more, too. But the question is, where can he and I meet? I thought you might know of some modest pension here where he could stay. I don't want him to come to the Bergues."

"Why not?"

"Because there's a suspicious character staying there. I saw him on the platform in London when I saw those three, and now here he is again! So I'd rather Colin stayed somewhere else."

"At what hour does your cousin arrive tomorrow?"

"I haven't the faintest idea!—and he wouldn't have told me over the telephone, of course."

"Why not?"

"Oh my dear Monsieur de Ritter, people in his job don't *advertize* their movements, especially when something like this is going on."

"How very interesting! But how then can we establish contact?"

"I told him to ring you up at Bellardon when he arrives, and that you would tell him where to go. So do you know of a small, *obscure* place?" Julia pressed him urgently.

De Ritter considered for a moment—then he laughed his loud delightful laugh.

"Indeed I do. Bellardon is very small, and most obscure! Let him come and stay at La Cure; and you, chère Mademoiselle, shall return to us—we shall rejoice to have you—and there you can concert your plans in peace."

Julia considered in her turn—she hesitated so long that the Pastor was surprised, and asked—

"You do not wish to come back to us?"

"Oh, it's not that—I *adore* being at La Cure. Only it's rather an imposition on Germaine, and besides I'm just wondering whether we ought all to be under one hat."

"*Plaît-il?*"

"All three of us under one roof, if anyone tried something on. I don't want to be alarmist, but one never knows."

"I am not sure that I understand you."

For answer, Julia pushed aside her tawny-gold hair and showed the Pastor a long white scar running down one side of her forehead.

"I got that from a bomb in Marrakesh. The people who threw it were trying to blow up Colin, but they got me instead."

The Pastor looked at the scar in horrified amazement. *"C'est affreux!"* He reflected. "Such things are quite outside my experience. Nevertheless, I think Bellardon a good venue, and I must confess that I should greatly like to meet Aglaia's fiancé. What do you say?"

On the whole Julia said Yes.

"Then can I not drive you out tonight? How long do you need to *faire vos malles?*"

"Oh, I can pack in half an hour. But you mustn't pick me up at the hotel—I'll come in a taxi and meet you, somewhere where you can park inconspicuously. What about the station? People putting luggage in and out of cars all the time."

He laughed. "This is quite amusing. I feel as if I were living in a *Roman-Policier!* Very well—I will park in the courtyard, and will wait for you in that restaurant on the left of the station entrance, at one of the outside tables. This is extremely normal."

"That's right—normal is the ticket," Julia replied.

Julia walked across one side of the rectangled bridge to the hotel to pack, the Pastor returned across the other to get his car. In the hall of the hotel the concierge handed Julia a letter—it was from Mrs. Hathaway.

"As soon as you conveniently can, I should like it if you could come back here, and take me to Beatenberg. I am quite fit to travel now, if I have a courier!—and I think it would be well to give the staff here a rest. Herr Waechter has taken rooms for us at the Hotel Silberhorn."

She thrust the letter into her bag, packed quickly, and went down. In the hall stood Antrobus.

"Oh, are you leaving already?" he asked.

"Yes—I must get back to Gersau, where I have a friend who isn't well," Julia said, deliberately.

He looked at his watch.

"You will miss the last boat from Lucerne to Gersau tonight," he observed.

"No I shan't—I'm stopping the night with friends on the way."

"In Berne?"

"Well if it *is* any business of yours, *not* in Berne," Julia said tartly.

"Oh, excuse me. Berne is on the way, that's all. Anyhow *bon voyage*— I hope we meet again soon."

Julia hoped this very much too, but merely said—"On present form it seems almost inevitable, doesn't it?"

At that he laughed, and came out and handed her into her taxi. What a mercy they had settled to meet at the station, Julia thought, as she said, "À la gare!" to the porter. The Pastor had parked fairly near the restaurant; he rose from one of the little tables, her luggage was transferred to the Frégate, and soon they were speeding along the superb Swiss roads, the gentle countryside all golden in the evening light. It was late when they got in, but Germaine was waiting, pretty and fresh; the warmth of her welcoming kiss gave Julia a happy sense of home-coming. Over the excellent supper Jean-Pierre, to Julia's professional dismay, insisted on putting his wife into the picture thoroughly—Germaine was all interest and sympathy, and delight at the prospect of having another guest.

"Tomorrow? By then some more asparagus will be ready," she remarked. "You can cut it, Julia."

In fact it was just as well that Germaine had been told, for when Colin rang up next day the Pastor was out, and she answered the telephone. Recognizing an English voice—though it spoke excellent French—Germaine, who was much more security-minded than her husband, asked at once—"Would you care to speak with your cousin? She is here—Julie, I mean."

"Yes, if you please."

While Julia was telling Colin to come straight on to "the house of Niemöller's colleague," Germaine was consulting the time-table, and passed on directions about trains. When Julia had rung off she said—"Even if he spoke from the airport he will have time to catch that train." She brushed some fallen paeony petals off the table in the hall into her hand, adding— "Quite so much discretion is really hardly necessary here for internal calls; since everything is automatic there are no operators to overhear. But discretion never does any harm." She returned to her stove and Julia went out to cut the asparagus for supper.

"Cut some roses for your cousin's room," Germaine called through the kitchen window. "They are just beginning."

It was Julia who took the handcart down through the clean sunny little village to meet Colin; he gave his boyish giggle over this novel arrangement. "Don't kiss me at La Cure," Julia said, after his cousinly hug on the platform.

"Why ever not?"

"Jean-Pierre was a little suspicious because I signed that telegram 'Darling.' I told him it was just a code word, but don't go and wreck it all."

"Is he stuffy and portentous? How frightful."

"No. You'll see."

Colin saw, over a late tea in the arbour beside the lawn, now festooned with the washing of a daughter-in-law. The Pastor examined his ward's fiancé with the deepest interest, and when they repaired to the study to talk *les affaires,* Julia could see that he was favorably impressed by the young man's passionate concern over the loss of the documents, and complete indifference about the money—he never asked a single question about that.

De Ritter told Colin that the Swiss police, very discreetly, were on the lookout for the party, and asked if he could supply a photograph of his fiancée? Colin, jerking his thumb out, an obstinate look on his face, said that he couldn't. He however produced the information that in London it was thought improbable that the impostors had yet left Switzerland; it was considered more likely that they would wait in this ultra-neutral country to contact their principals and hand over their haul. The Pastor innocently asked who the principals were?—Julia laughed at him. "He couldn't tell you even if he knew."

It was settled that Colin should go on next day to Berne to see "our people" there, and take them Julia's description of the party of three; Julia then explained that she ought to return to Gersau, to take Mrs. Hathaway to Beatenberg.

"But how you come and go!" de Ritter exclaimed regretfully. "We like *long* visits."

"Some time, when the job's done, I'll come and pay you a proper one, and stay ages," Julia told him—and she rang up Herr Waechter to announce her return next day to take Mrs. Hathaway to Beatenberg.

Later the Pastor drew her aside. "I approve," he said. "A little immature still in some ways, but time will remedy that. *C'est un charmant garçon.*" Colin for his part, up in Julia's room, said—"He is most frightfully nice, isn't he? As an in-law I can't imagine anyone I should like more."

"He's only a godfather-in-law," Julia said. "But I agree."

Though Colin was going to Berne and Julia had to pass through it, they carefully arranged to travel not only by different trains but by different routes—he by Neuchatel, she via Lausanne—to the Pastor's incredulous amusement.

"But you are in *Switzerland!*" he said.

"So are some other people," Colin replied.

At Gersau next day in the *salon* Julia, idly turning over the pages of a fortnight-old *Paris-Match,* came on a page devoted to Aglaia and her story; there was a full-length studio photograph and, as often with *Paris-Match,* a snapshot (probably bought from a servant) of Colin and Aglaia together, looking very loverly, in the garden of some country-house. Julia was normally rather scrupulous about other people's newspapers, but in this instance she did not ask Herr Waechter's permission, but took the magazine up to her room and removed the whole page; she cut out the studio portrait, borrowed a large envelope, and posted it herself to M. Chambertin at the bank with a note clipped to it—"This is the likeness you require. J.P." The snapshot she put in her notecase.

CHAPTER VI

BEATENBERG AND THE NIEDERHORN

BEATENBERG IS a mountain village perched on a ledge facing South above the Lake of Thun; its chief claim to distinction, apart from its remarkably beneficent air, is the fact that it is over seven kilometers, or nearly five miles long. A bus careers at fairly frequent intervals up and down the straggling street, set with hotels, pensions, convalescent homes and shops from Wahnegg, at the head of the road up from Interlaken at one end, to the top of the funicular railway, going down to Beatenbucht to connect with the lake steamers at the other. There is no way up or down in between, only sheer cliff. The drive up from Interlaken in the Post-Auto is rather hair-raising: for much of the way the road is narrow, with blind hairpin bends, and the bus vast; it proclaims its advent by blaring out a pretty little tune on six notes, and cars squeeze into the rocky bush-grown banks to allow the great machine to edge past, its outer wheels horribly near the lip of the steep wooded slope. A notice in three languages at the front of the bus adjures passengers not to address the driver, but this is cheerfully ignored both by the local passengers and the driver himself—if a pretty young woman is on the front seat there is often practically a slap-and-tickle party the whole way.

By this route Mrs. Hathaway, Julia, and Watkins arrived at the Hotel Silberhorn. Since Herr Waechter, brought up in the hotel trade, had recommended the place they had expected something rather good, and were startled by the extreme smallness of the rooms: Mrs. Hathaway's, a double room with a cubbyhole of a private bathroom was quite small enough; as for Julia's and Watkins' singles, they were like prison cells, though each had a minute balcony with a chair—and all alike shared the view: the whole Blümlisalp range stood up, white, glittering and glorious, across the lake. The keynote of the hotel was extreme simplicity—coconut matting along the corridors, the minimum of furniture in the rooms—but the food was excellent. The plate-glass windows of the restaurant commanded the view, too; waitresses pattered to and fro across the parquet floor, their heels making a loud clacking noise; their activities were supervised by a grey-haired woman known as Fräulein Hanna, who appeared to be a sort of combination of housekeeper, head barmaid, and general organizer.

Like all English travelers in Switzerland today Mrs. Hathaway and her party liked to brew their own morning and afternoon tea in their bedrooms, partly because then it was *tea,* but also because these items were not included in the very high *prix fixe.* They all had small electric saucepans which would plug in in place of any electric light bulb; on seeing these objects Fräulein Hanna, far from showing any resentment, inquired earnestly what the voltage was?—it proved to match that of the hotel, to her manifest satisfaction. All three of course used Mrs. Hathaway's private bathroom; the hotel bathrooms were kept locked, and a charge of five francs, or nearly ten shillings, made for a bath. Watkins was outraged by this. "Well really! How do they expect people to keep clean? And with all that water running to waste downhill all the time!"

For the next two days Julia and Mrs. Hathaway explored their end of the village. They found a nice little shop close by, in a grove of pine trees, at which to buy their sugar and Nescafé; they walked gently up a fenced path between flowery meadows to the Parallel-Weg, a narrow road running parallel to, but a short distance above the village street; they peered in at the open door of the cow stable just opposite the hotel garden, and saw the huge Emmenthaler cows in their stalls, munching away at fresh-cut grass. Mrs. Hathaway delighted in the place—besides the exquisite view, here was peace, calm, and a native community leading its own pastoral life, untroubled by the tourists, who so early in the season were relatively few.

Colin rang up on the second evening to say that he was coming next day, and would Julia book him a room? He came up on the Post-Auto, which pulled up opposite a gasoline pump next to the cow stable; before dinner he and Julia strolled up the little path to the Parallel-Weg, and leaning back on one of the wooden seats, with not a soul in sight, he told her what he had learned in Berne. "They" had quite definitely not left Switzerland; they were waiting there to make contact with their principals, who would be coming in from abroad—meanwhile the Swiss police were conducting inquiries at all hotels.

Julia told him about finding the photograph of Aglaia in *Paris-Match,* and how she had sent it to Chambertin.

"Oh well, I think that was quite all right—really rather useful," Colin said.

"You'd got one all the time, hadn't you?" Julia asked.

"Yes, of course I had—but why should those bastards have it? If they'd had any wits they'd have looked at *Paris-Match* themselves." He sniffed the sweet air, and gazed across at the Blümlisalp range, now turning to a pale rose as the sun sank. "How nice it is here! Do let's relax for a few days till something happens. What's the food like at the pub?"

"Good," Julia told him.

In fact something happened the very next day. Mrs. Hathaway had quite got over the journey from Gersau, and was perfectly happy either sitting in the garden, or pottering up and down the village street with Watkins, so Julia and Colin decided to go up to the Niederhorn, the mountain immediately behind Beatenberg, in the Sessel-Bahn; see the view, and walk down.

The now universal practice of winter sports in Switzerland has conferred one great benefit on the travelers at all times of year. Every mountain with slopes suitable for skiing has been provided with a funicular railway, or at least some form of ski-lift, by which the lazy modern skier can be carried to the summit without effort, shoot down, be carried up again, and shoot down once more—these function in the summer too, so that any tourist can reach the tops of the lesser mountains. The Niederhorn Sessel-Bahn is one of the more elegant of these contraptions, with twin seats (slung from a strong steel cable) complete with footboard and a little sun-canopy overhead, into which an attendant clamps the passengers by a metal bar across their stomachs. Julia and Colin, so clamped, were wafted out of the small station and up through the tops of the pine trees. It was delicious sailing through the sunny air; people on other seats coming down on the opposite cable, a few feet away, waved to them out of sheer *joie de vivre*.

Halfway up they swung into a large shed, where the seats were hitched onto an overhead rail and hauled round by hand to be hooked onto another cable for the upper section of the journey; the sides of this shed were full of enormous white metal milk-churns.

"What *can* those be for?" Julia speculated. "The cows aren't up on the high pastures yet."

"How do you know?"

"Because they're still down in the village in their stalls—I'll show you. They're only taken up when the lower grass is finished, and it has grown properly up on the alps—a peasant was telling Mrs. H. about it. You can see that there's hardly a bite up here yet," Julia said, peering down; they were now above the tree-line and swinging over open pastures, still pallid and brownish after the recently departed snow. "Oh, look!" the girl exclaimed—"Those must be gentians. We must pick some for Mrs. H., she's mad on wild flowers." Colin saw brilliant blue stars shining in the drab grass. "Good idea," he said.

But on arrival at the small summit station it was at once evident that picking gentians would be a very bad idea indeed—large placards in four languages proclaimed that the whole *Niederhorn-Gebiet* was a Natur-Reserve, where the picking of flowers was most strictly forbidden. "Oh dear," Julia regretted as they strolled up to the top. Here they went over and looked down on the farther side, where the Niederhorn, while sloping up easily from the South, ends in a series of vertical cliffs, dropping some hundreds of feet to the Justis-thal, a long valley running in from the Lake of Thun. The valley is bounded on the farther side by similar cliffs; a thin white thread of road runs up through the flat green meadows along its floor.

"What's the little town down on the lake?" she asked.

"Merligen," Colin said, without consulting his map.

"Merligen? I have an acquaintance there," Julia said, remembering the little man from "Corsette-Aire." "Colin, wouldn't it be nice to take Mrs. H. to Merligen on the steamer and hire a car, and drive her up to the Justis-thal?—I call it a darling valley. Why Justice, by the way?"

"Two English missionaries, Justus and Beatus, originally converted this part of Switzerland to Christianity. 'Ence the word 'orse-'air," Colin said, using an old Glentoran nonsense. "Beatenberg, too. But one can't drive up the Justis-thal; it's a military area, where no cars are allowed."

Julia cautiously peered over into the green depths. "It doesn't *look* very military," she said. "I don't see any barracks, or anything."

"No, you don't; that's the point. The barracks are *in* the mountains. Those cliffs opposite, and these plumb under us here, are bung full of ammunition and guns and so forth—in some parts they even have military hospitals inside the mountains, so I heard in Berne. Terrific people, the Swiss."

Julia sat down on the yellowish turf and lit a cigarette.

"I'm beginning to think so."

Colin gestured back at the Lake of Thun, of which a segment was visible at the mouth of the valley.

"That's full of stores, too—years' and years' supply of butter and cheese and flour and corn, sunk in metal containers hundreds of feet down. These lakes are very deep."

Julia was entranced by this.

"But doesn't it get stale?—especially the cheese and butter?"

"Oh, they howk up the containers every so often, and empty them and put in fresh. A Swiss I met was telling me about it. The butter they always get out while it's still usable; and if the cheese is a bit dry they grate it and sell it in bottles."

They wandered on and came to a patch of still unmelted snow, dirty and pock-marked; round its edges small white crocuses were springing from the brown sodden turf, making a new snowiness to replace the old. "Oh, I wish I could take just *one* to Mrs. H.," Julia said.

"Better not—they mean what they say about picking flowers," Colin said. "I saw a type in uniform wandering about near the station. Come back to the pub and have a beer before we go down."

The pub was a long low building with a restaurant and a broad terrace outside, on which numerous people sat drinking beer or coffee at little tables; Colin and Julia sat there too and drank their beer in the sun. "It's a nice clean wash-place," Julia said, returning: "boiling hot water."

"I wonder how they get their water up here," Colin speculated. "There's no sign of a spring."

"Pumped, I suppose," Julia replied indifferently.

They had strolled and idled so long on the top that Julia said they had better not walk down, or they would be madly late. "Let's come up another day and walk right along and down to the village at the far end." Colin agreed to this, and presently they were swinging down through the air again, over the high meadows.

Now on the Sessel-Bahn you can see passengers traveling in the opposite direction a hundred yards away or more; and coming up towards them Julia now saw the girl she had seen at Victoria, perched in a seat beside the dark young man. "Colin, *look!*" she breathed.

Colin stared. "It can't be!" he exclaimed.

"No, it isn't. It's her double. But look well at the man—it's them all right."

Colin looked hard at the pair as they were borne past in the air, only a few feet away; then he and Julia discussed rapidly what to do. They decided that Julia should get out at the halfway halt and return to the summit, to see what she could of the pair; while in case she was not in time to meet them, Colin should go to the bottom and wait there—when they came down he would follow them, whether they took the bus to Interlaken, or the funicular to Beatenbucht and the lake. "They certainly can't get away at the top," Julia said, thinking of that dizzy range of lime-stone cliffs and buttresses.

"Unless they do what we were planning just now, and walk all the way across and down to Wahnegg."

"Oh, *she* couldn't. She was wearing the silliest little high-heeled shoes. Here we are"—and as they swung into the shed she called to one of the men who were maneuvering the seats round the circular rail leading to the lower section to unclamp her bar and let her out. "Der Herr *auch?*" the man asked.

"*Nein,* not the Herr." She sprang out. "Stick to them like *glue,*" she called to Colin, as he swung out of the shed and off into space.

Julia had to wait some time for a seat, and employed this interval, as was her habit, in ingratiating herself with the people on the spot, the men in blue dungarees who manipulated the seats at the halt; from them she enquired about the milk-churns. Oh, those were for water. There was no water at the summit; every drop had to be carried up in the evening after the Sessel-Bahn was closed to passengers, in the churns, and man-handled from the station some hundred yards to fill the cisterns of the restaurant. "Both guests and *Geschirr* [kitchen utensils] need water for washing," an elderly man said, grinning.

At last she secured an empty half of one of the twin seats, and was again borne upwards. She was tremendously excited, the more so after the delay at the halt; by keeping a sharp eye on the descending seats she had established that the pair she sought had not yet come down, nor did they pass her in the air. "Just keep your eyes open—that's all you can do," she adjured herself as she got out at the summit and began to walk up towards the restaurant.

This activity brought an immediate reward. A little below the path she saw on the grassy slope the sham Aglaia, a bunch of *Gentiana verna* in her hand, being violently scolded by one of the Natur-Reserve wardens. She ran down to them. The girl was in tears; obviously she could not make out what it was all about—there was no sign of the dark young man.

"The Fräulein does not understand," Julia told the official.

"The notice forbidding to pick flowers is also in English," he said indignantly.

"*Jawohl*—but the Fräulein must not have looked—I think it is her first journey abroad. Is there some fine to pay?" she asked, opening her bag.

"*Nein.* But let *das Mädchen* not do this again." He stumped off.

"Oh, thank you ever so! What did you say to him?" the girl asked Julia, as they began to walk up towards the restaurant. "He was being as nasty as anything, and I couldn't understand a single word!"

"He was scolding you for picking those flowers," Julia said.

"Why *ever?*"

"Because this is a Natur-Reserve, like our National Parks, and picking flowers is forbidden; there's a big notice in English to say so, just by the station. But I told the man that you hadn't looked at it, because it was your first trip abroad. Is it?" Julia asked, with a friendly smile.

"Well yes, ackcherly. I don't like it much, either—the food's so funny, and I can't talk to people, except the porter in the hotel, silly old thing! He *does* talk English, though."

The imitation Aglaia was obviously the commonest of little Londoners; too suburban for anything as genuine as a Cockney, and not very intelligent. Julia was thrilled by this piece of luck, but a little worried about the dark young man. She tried to play her hand carefully.

"Did you come up here alone?"

"Oh no. Mr. Wright—" she corrected herself hastily—"I mean Mr. Monro came up with me, but he likes climbing up things, and he's gone off. He said I was to stay on the terrace and look at the mountains—but I *hate* those old mountains, all snow and ice, and when I saw these little flowers in the grass I came down to pick some. I didn't know it was wrong. I 'spose I'd better throw them away, if there's all this trouble."

"No, give them to me," Julia said, and stowed *G. verna* in her bag. She was deeply interested to learn that the dark young man's name was really Wright, though he seemed to be calling himself Monro.

"Well, that's a good idea. Aoh!" The girl gave a little scream, and nearly fell—Julia put out a hand and caught her. One of those idiotic high heels had turned on a loose stone, wrenching her ankle; between pain and shock she could hardly walk. Julia, an arm round the tiny figure, dragged her up to the restaurant and sat her down on a stool in the washroom; she borrowed a pantry cloth from the cheerful Swiss maids and applied this as a cold compress, tying it in place with her own headscarf.

"Is that any easier?" she asked.

"Yes, a bit."

"Then let's go out and have some coffee on the terrace. Do you like coffee?"

"Not all that much—but the tea here is so lousy! You *are* being kind."

Julia ordered coffee for two. Perhaps she was being kind; certainly she was enjoying a most blessed stroke of luck, and set about profiting by it. "How long have you been in Switzerland?" she asked.

"Nearly three weeks. Mr. Borovali said it would be a nice holiday for me, but it isn't being, not so very—and now I've gone and hurt my foot." She showed signs of tears starting afresh. "I expect he'll be cross! They said at the Agency that he'd be so nice, and give me a lovely time, but he's very often cross."

Julia was rivetted by the word agency, and asked about it.

"Oh, the 'Modern Face Agency,' off Shaftesbury Avenue. I get my modeling jobs through them. Oh, not artists or the nude, or anything like that! —just modeling for the ads, you know. I tried for a mannequin, but I'm too small, even for Small Woman clothes. But I get a lot of quite good modeling jobs, shoes or jewellery, mostly—my feet are a treat for shoes. Oh, do you think this ankle will *swell?*" Tears again threatened. "My feet are my fortune, as you might say"—half giggling.

Julia realized that the little thing really had had quite a shock, and while she tried to console her about her ankle she ordered Kirsch for them both. "Put it in your coffee—it will do you good," she said. She was beginning to see a flood of light, and while the girl sipped, she thought about safe questions.

"Oh, that does taste funny! No, it's nice, really. Ta."

"Does Mr. Borovali pay as well as the Agency?" Julia inquired.

"Not quite—only £6 a week, but of course I get my keep for the month, and I'm to keep my outfit."

"Mr. Borovali has good taste, has he?"

"Oh, perfect. Some ex*quis*ite things I've got." The pretty little thing looked dreamily out at the glorious forms of the Bernese Alps, shining under the sun like the ramparts of Heaven. "Ex*quis*ite," she repeated rapturously—"Evening frocks and all. Mum wasn't so keen on my coming, just with two gentlemen, but really, the clothes alone have been worth it—and they've been quite all right," she added confidentially. She paused, and sipped again at her coffee and Kirsch.

"Mum isn't all that keen on the modeling, either," she pursued, "but a girl's got to live, hasn't she? I'm no good in shops, I simply can't get the bills right! And since Dad died I have to help Mum; I usually give her £3 a week."

This was said proudly, but very nicely—Julia was rather touched. She asked what "Dad" had done?

"Oh, in business." This too was said rather proudly. "Well ackcherly he was a traveler for a surgical equipment firm, really quite high-class. I sometimes wish he'd traveled in the garment trade; then Mum and I might have got things on the cheap." She looked wistfully at Julia. "That's a heavenly suit you've got on—d'you mind if I ask where you got it?"

Julia glanced down at her own soft, plainly-cut grey-green tweed. In the context she suddenly did mind telling this eager candid child its origin, but she couldn't think of a probable lie in time, and said, "Hartnell."

"Never! Well, it looks it." She fingered the stuff almost reverently.

"Where did Mr. Borovali get your things?" Julia inquired hastily. "That's such a pretty dress."

"D'you really like it? I *am* glad. He got them at a very good wholesale place, only they all had to be taken in, of course. But by the way, I oughtn't to call him Mr. Borovali—Mr. de Ritter he likes to be known as, on this trip—in case you should meet him."

"I'll remember—though I don't expect I shall meet him." She was thinking how to frame her next question.

"How shall you get back, with that foot?" she asked. "Have you far to go?"

"Only down to Interlarken. The bus goes from the bottom of this swinging-boat affair—goodness, isn't it ghastly? As bad as the Wall of Death, I think. And from the bus stop in Interlarken I 'spose Mr. Wright—sorry, I mean Mr. Monro—will just have to take a taxi to the hotel."

"I'm sure he will. Is it a nice hotel?"

"The Flooss? Oh, not too bad. It's right on the river, and you can see the steamers coming up to the quay, and watch the people going on and off. But Flooss is ever such a silly name, don't you think?—makes one think of floosies." She giggled.

From this description Julia surmised, rightly, that the party must be staying at the Hotel zŭm Flŭss in Interlaken, much praised by Baedeker, and was delighted to have this concrete piece of information for Colin. She felt it safe to ask this guileless child how long she was staying?

"Well I'm not sure. We should have been going home day after tomorrow, but some friends of Mr. Bor— I mean Mr. de Ritter's, that he wants to meet, haven't turned up, so we must stay on till they do."

"Oh well, if you're staying on we might meet again," Julia said brightly. "I'm up here at Beatenberg, at the Hotel Silberhorn, but if I come down I might look you up, Miss—?" Her voice hung on the query.

"Phillips—June Phillips," the girl said briskly. "I'd love to see you again—you're so kind." Then her face fell. "Sorry—I am *too* silly, with this foot hurting so! June Phillips is just my trade name; only I get so accustomed to using it. My real name is Aglaia Armitage."

"So if I came to the hotel I should ask for Miss Armitage?" Julia asked carefully. Presumably they were still using the forged passports, but she wanted to be sure.

"That's right." Then the pretty face clouded again. "D'you know, I'm not sure you'd better do that," June Phillips said worriedly. "Mr. B. doesn't seem to care for me to talk to people; there are some English people at the

Flooss, but if they start talking to me, he makes some excuse to get me away. Oh, I *am* so dull!"

How right Mr. B. was, Julia thought—in the circumstances he could hardly do otherwise, saddled with this utterly unpractical little creature. But she was sorry for poor June, wearing her pretty new clothes in vain. Before she had settled on some suitable response the girl pulled out an envelope with an English stamp on it.

"You write your name and address on that, do," she urged. "And your phone number. Then I could ring you up, if I was free any time."

After a moment's hesitation Julia did as she was asked—after all it didn't involve Colin in the least. As June Phillips pocketed the envelope Julia put a further question. "Surely Mr. Monro is a pleasant companion?"

"Well not all that much. He's all right, and of course he looks ever so distinguished; but if we come out like this he always wants to go off scrambling on rocks, or climbing up some mountain—which is no fun for *me*," June said energetically. "And the rest of the time he's generally binding away about a situation he lost in one of those Arab countries, and how unfair it was." She paused, and then leaned confidentially across the table. "I don't think he's really enjoying this job any more than I am, except the climbing—though he's paid much more than me."

"Oh really?"

"Yes!—and I do think that's unfair, too. After all, *he* isn't like anyone." She caught herself up, dismayed. "Sorry—I didn't mean that. I'm just *silly* today!"

Julia hastened to help her out. "Perhaps Mr. Monro is an expert about something," she said.

"Oh I don't think so, really, or why was he fired? But he has lived in these outlandish countries, and I think he knows these people that Mr. de Ritter is waiting for."

At this point the young man himself appeared on the path leading up to the restaurant; he was some hundred yards away. June Phillips gave a little gasp.

"Oh! There he is! D'you think you'd p'r'aps better go away? I mean, he mightn't like to see me talking to anyone. Only you've been so good."

"No, I shan't go away," Julia said firmly.

"Well you explain, will you?—how we met, I mean," the girl said nervously. "And by the way, on this trip he's supposed to be my fiancé," she added hurriedly. "Oh, it is all so difficult."

"Don't worry," Julia just had time to say before the young man rounded the corner of the restaurant and saw them. He paused, scowled, and strode over to their table. Julia spoke before he could.

"Mr. Monro?" He nodded, his relief evident at once.

"Miss Armitage has had an accident," Julia pursued blandly—"she has sprained her ankle rather badly. I happened to be close by, and did what I could for her, but I think she ought to get back to her hotel as soon as possible, and see a doctor."

"Oh, thank you, Miss—?"

"Probyn," Julia said, studying him. Probably a Greek or a Levantine or something like that, she thought, noting the weak mouth, the big melting eyes, the superb Greek-vase figure—a born gigolo. He thanked her again, rather curtly, and then rounded harshly on June Phillips.

"How did you come to have an accident? I told you to stay here on the terrace." There was no accent, except that it was not a well-bred voice; a Levantine educated at a second-rate English school, perhaps.

Julia's presence gave the girl courage to defend herself.

"Yes, but you were away such *ages*—and you never gave me money to buy a morning coffee, or anything! So I went down and picked some flowers, and a man came after me, and was nasty, and this lady came and sent him off. And then I hurt my foot, and she looked after me. More than *you* were doing!" June said, with a small display of spirit, like a kitten spitting.

"Oh well"—as he paused, rather nonplussed, Julia beckoned up a waitress and paid the bill—"Well, we'd better be getting back," he said to June. "Come on."

"Try your foot," Julia said to the girl. "Can you stand on it?"

June Phillips tried, and cried out with pain. "Aoh, it *does* hurt!"

"Damnation! What an idiotic thing to do!" the young man Wright exploded.

"Oh nonsense," Julia said. "If one neglects people, anything can happen. It's not in the least *her* fault." He stared at her. "Let's get her down to the Bahn—if we each take an arm she needn't put any weight on her foot."

"I'll carry her," the young man said; "she weighs nothing." And disdaining Julia's help he threw June over his shoulder like a sack and carried her, giggling, down to the Sessel-Bahn and in at the entrance on the far side. As the seats came up, were vacated, and pulled round the curve for the descent Julia nipped smartly ahead of the other two, secured a place, and was fastened into it by the attendant; June and Mr. Wright got into the next one. There is usually an interval of fifty to one hundred metres between the dangling seats, so as not to put too great a weight on the cable, and Julia reckoned that she would just have time to get hold of Colin and send him away before Wright could see him; since there was no longer any need to tail the party, it seemed to her rather important to do this. Her seat was launched, and she spun down through the sunny air, over the high pastures, among the fragrant pines—down, down, down, above the flowery meadows and the Parallel-Weg to the little bottom station. The moment the attendant unclamped the bar and released her she sprang out, waved to June, whose seat was just coming in, ran down the cement steps and walked rapidly along the zig-zag path leading down to the road and the big lay-by where cars and buses wait. From above she saw that Colin was there all right, half-perched on the retaining wall at the bottom of the path; but he was not alone—perched beside him, smoking a pipe and obviously engaged in most cheerful conversation was the detective.

Annoyance at this inopportune appearance quite overcame her pleasure at seeing Antrobus. *What* was he doing there just at this moment? Her original decision to get Colin away before Wright saw him persisted; but as she walked down the path towards the two men it occurred to her that it might be quite useful if *she*, at least, stayed to watch the impact of the impostor party on Antrobus—she might learn something, or she might not; anyhow worth trying. She slackened her pace—this had got to be planned *fast*—and glanced up behind her; June and Wright had not yet emerged from the station. In the last twenty-five yards she cast about for an excuse and hit on a poor one—all the same, she must try it on. She rounded the last corner and approached the pair.

"Oh hullo, Mr. Antrobus—how nice to see you again." She turned to Colin. "Colin darling, I'm out of gaspers. They have those beastly squashy local ones in that little shop just up the road; do go and get me a hundred, darling—fast, so that we can catch the bus."

"I've got quite a lot," Colin said, looking surprised at her knowing Antrobus.

"Oh don't be a *clot*, darling! *I* haven't, though I've got everything else." She hoped he would take this in. "Do *please* go, darling darling."

At this key phrase Colin obediently took himself off up the road—Julia was surprised to find that she minded a good deal being forced to use these exaggerated terms of endearment to Colin in front of Antrobus. However she turned to him calmly.

"Are you staying in Beatenberg, Mr. Antrobus?"

"No—I came up to have a look round. It seems a cheerful little place."

"Yes, I think it's delightful—so unspoiled. Where are you staying, then?"

"Interlaken—a most charming town."

Dead-pan double talk! Julia pushed ahead.

"So you know my cousin?"

"Who?—that beautiful young man? Your cousin, is he? No, we just fell into talk as we sat here—he said he was waiting for someone."

"And are *you* waiting for someone?" Julia asked recklessly, still rather unnerved by his appearance at this critical moment. Why was he *everywhere* when the impersonators were about? She glanced up the zigzags behind her—at last Wright had appeared, poor June again slung over his shoulder. Antrobus's glance followed hers; June's pretty face was hidden, of course, but Wright's handsome Near-Eastern visage was clearly visible. The man turned back to her.

"No," he said, looking her full in the face. "I was simply idling—Fatima!"

The name that in Geneva she had looked forward to hearing from him came, now, like a blow. Wounded, Julia blushed—her apricot blush that was so beautiful under her lion-colored hair. She was also at once angry and suspicious—was he lying, and trying to embarrass her *because* he was lying? She mastered her temper, and tried to think fast; well before Wright and his burden had reached the bottom of the zigzags she had taken a decision—not to conceal her acquaintance with that pair. Two buses, already half-full of passengers, were drawn up in the lay-by across the road, one for Interlaken, one for the Beatenbucht funicular—as Wright reached the level she went straight up to him and June.

"Let me help you, Mr. Monro. The left-hand bus is the one for Interlaken." Breathing rather heavily, the young man set June down; Julia took her arm. "Miss Armitage, how do you feel now? Come on, we'll get you a seat close to the door."

All this was well within earshot of Antrobus; in fact Julia spoke rather loudly, on purpose. She and Wright together supported the girl across the road to the lay-by, where Julia spoke in German to the flirtatious blond bus driver. "The Fräulein has had a *Fuss-Brechen* on the Niederhorn; she should have a seat by the door." The driver hopped out, heaved June in, and placed her on the front seat. The little thing leaned forward from the door to speak to Julia.

"Oh Miss Probyn, you *have* been so kind! I'll never forget it—never! If there's ever anything I can do for you, just let me know, and I'll do it!"

"I'll remember," Julia said. "Good-bye, dear. Take care of yourself." Impulsively, she mounted the step of the bus, leaned in, and gave the nice, silly little thing a kiss. Then she turned to Wright, who stood by with an open air of concentrated ill-temper not commonly seen outside Athens and the Middle East.

"Mr. Monro, do get a doctor to look at that ankle. I'm sure it ought to be seen to at once."

"O.K." Wright said sulkily. "Mind you, it's all her own fault."

"Oh don't be an *ass!*" Julia exclaimed angrily. "It's entirely *your* fault for going off to amuse yourself, and leaving her alone. And is that the way to talk about your fiancée, anyhow?"

Wright crumbled at once.

"Sorry," he said apologetically. "Yes, I did go farther than I meant, and —and it's all been a bit upsetting. Of course I'll get a doctor to her the moment we get down. Good-bye—thanks for looking after her." He got into the bus and sat beside June; the blond driver gave out tickets and collected cash in a leather wallet, and the huge vehicle pulled out into the road and rolled away.

Antrobus too had strolled across the road, and presumably overheard the whole interchange—his question as the bus rolled off suggested this.

"Friends of yours?" he asked expressionlessly.

"Which, the idiotic little girl or the revolting young man?" Julia asked rather sharply.

"Well really I meant both. They seemed rather a *unit* as they came down the path."

Julia could not help laughing.

"I ran into the girl up on the mountain today, and succored her when she sprained her ankle," she said; for once the truth was completely non-committal. "But I never met her before—*Bluebeard!*"

He laughed loudly.

"*Very* good! Only you see you kissed her just now, and then you addressed her rather dreadful escort as Mr. Monro. Your so infinitely more attractive cousin said *his* name was Monro, too."

Julia was worried by all this, but tried not to show it.

"Monro is a fairly common name in Scotland, isn't it?" she said. "Like Antrobus."

He laughed again.

"Quite true. But that young man doesn't look *enormously* Scotch, would you say?"

Julia also laughed.

"No. But don't Jews often take Scotch names? They seem to have a *penchant* for them."

"That young man isn't a Jew," Antrobus said positively. "A lot of other probables, but not that."

"What are your probables?" she asked.

"Levantine; or English father and Syrian mother, or English mother and Greek father—almost any Middle-East permutation and combination. But definitely not a Jew."

Odd that he should speculate like this to her, if he really was in with them, Julia thought—but perhaps it was just a blind. Anyhow two could ask questions.

"And have *you* never seen them before?" she said, remembering with almost passionate vividness the passage of three people down the platform at Victoria, under his very nose.

Before Antrobus could answer Colin came hurrying up to them, a flowered-paper parcel in his hand.

"There you are!" he said, thrusting it at Julia. "It wasn't *just* up the road, it was at least half a kilometer!" He saw that the Interlaken bus had gone, and looked at her inquiringly.

"Oh thank you, darling. Well look, we'd better hurry, or we shall miss our bus. Good-bye," she said coolly to Antrobus.

Colin also made his farewell to the detective.

"Good-bye," he said, much more warmly than Julia, holding out his hand. "You might do worse than come up here, if you want flowers and walks—I don't know about the birds yet. Let us know if you do—we're at the Silberhorn."

"Right—I certainly will, if I do come up. And don't forget to take your old friend who's so keen on flowers up to see the Alpine Garden at the Schynige Platte—she would love it. I'm probably going there tomorrow myself."

"Damn, there's our machine moving!" Julia exclaimed. "Come on!"— and she and Colin, running, leapt aboard their bus.

CHAPTER VII

THE SCHYNIGE PLATTE

"WHY DID YOU push me off?" Colin began at once. "*Did* you see them up on the top?"

"Yes—and learned a whole bagful. Tell you when we get in—no, it must wait till after lunch; we're fearfully late! But I pushed you off because I didn't want them to see you—him, rather; she's just a little cypher." She glanced round the bus. "What's all this about the Schynige Platte?" she asked—an English couple were sitting close behind them.

"Oh, it's some place above Interlaken where they've made a rock garden and naturalized the wild flowers and put labels on them, so that you can see what everything is; and there are little paths to walk about, and seats.

He's mad on wild flowers—and birds—and when I mentioned that Mrs. H. was keen on flowers too he said we ought to take her up. I think she could go; there's a railway right up to it, and a restaurant at the top."

"A good idea," Julia said. But at the hotel both she and Colin found it rather a trial to have to sit through lunch talking on indifferent matters, when she was bursting with her news, and he was impatient to hear it. The Schynige Platte seemed a useful topic with which to entertain Mrs. Hathaway; that lady was charmed with the idea, and when she went to rest declared that she should read it up in Baedeker while she was lying down. Colin and Julia repaired to a field below the hotel garden and sat in the shade of a mountain ash—the walls of the Silberhorn bedrooms, like those of many Swiss mountain hotels, were about as sound-proof as paper.

"Well now, *what?*" Colin asked.

Julia recounted her rescue of June Phillips, and the child's revelations. "Obviously Mr. Borovali, or whoever employs him, went round all these advertizing agencies and flipped through their photographs of girls with Pekes or outside banks, till they had the luck to find one who was passably like Aglaia. Then they engaged her for a month, and fitted her out, and brought her along as a sort of corroborative dummy."

"And why do you suppose they picked on this Wright person? Is he like me?"

"Not in the least, except that he's tall and has black hair. I imagine," Julia said, remembering June's words about Wright not being "like anyone," and her vexation at his larger salary, "that they routed round till they found someone with a knowledge of these oil countries; and as he's been fired from a job out there and has a chip on his shoulder, what could be better? I think June said something about his knowing these parties who are coming here to collect the blueprints—that alone would be ample recommendation, wouldn't it? And I feel he's the sort of creature who'd sell his mother's corpse before it was cold for her eyes, for that new operation."

Colin laughed.

"But anyhow, now we know where they are," Julia said. "So what next?"

Colin considered.

"Could he have had the papers on him today?"

"Definitely not, coming down. Pale corduroy slacks, silk shirt, and a silk wind-cheater—with no bulges! But where could he put them up there, and why?"

"Only that he went off alone like that."

"She says he always does—anyhow they've had a week to find a much better place to stow them in than the Niederhorn Ridge! How big would the papers be, by the way?"

"I've no idea. I should imagine a fair thickness, though."

"And foolscap size?"

"Julia, I don't know."

"Well do find out. Your department and their imaginings!—I never heard of anything so amateurish."

Colin grinned wryly. "How could we have seen them? They've been locked up in this damned bank."

"Oh well. Anyhow, hadn't you better ring up your firm in Berne, so that they can cause the appropriate department to pounce?"

"M'm. Yes. I had. They may know more now about how long the delay is likely to be."

"But why delay at all? Why not pounce tonight, or at least tomorrow?"

"It's not as simple as all that, in a foreign jurisdiction," Colin said soberly, rather impressing Julia. "However, I will get onto them."

"Well, when you do, do ask if they know anything about this Antrobus man. Have you ever met him before?"

"No—we just got talking."

"He doesn't belong to your outfit?"

"Not to my knowledge. Why should he?"

"Only because he keeps on turning up whenever your sham fiancée is about." She recounted the episode at Victoria; seeing Antrobus entrain at Berne for Geneva "on the very *day*, mark you, before these stooges went to the bank"; his presence at the Bergues, and also at Nethersole's luncheon. "And now he turns up here, *again* on the very day that June and the emetic Wright go up to the Niederhorn. You'd think he was watching them; if he isn't, he must be watching out *for* them."

"It is all a bit odd," Colin said thoughtfully. "But he struck me as a very decent sort of man. He's a member of the Alpine Club."

"Did he tell you that?"

"Well it emerged."

"You could have that checked."

"Yes, of course—I will." He brooded. "How well do you know this party who asked him to meet you in Geneva?"

"Not well at all—I met him a few times with Geoffrey. He's an archaeologist, when he isn't with the UNO. And I remember that Antrobus said he was a tremendous Arabic scholar," Julia said, trying to bring out all her few facts about Nethersole.

"Isn't he permanently with the UNO?"

"I don't think so—no. They lay him on when they want him, I gathered, and he goes if he isn't too busy digging up Jericho, or decyphering Qumran scrolls."

"The Qumran scrolls aren't in Arabic," Colin objected.

"Not? Oh well, anyhow he's in those parts a lot of the time."

"Middle East again," Colin said gloomily. "And of course a UNO part-timer could really be anything. Yes, I expect we ought to keep an eye on Antrobus."

"That shouldn't be difficult, as he seems to be keeping an eye on us," Julia said briskly. "But ask, Colin."

"I will. I'll ring up now, and give them this Interlaken address. They ought to be pretty pleased, J. dear." He strolled off up the steep field.

Julia remained under the mountain ash, relaxed and happy. "They" certainly ought to be pleased at this windfall. Of course it was not due to any skill of hers, merely to Wright's lack of conscientiousness—well what could you expect, with that face?—and poor little June's incredibly low I.Q. (She hoped that bloody youth really *had* got a doctor to look at the sprained ankle.) But it was a scoop, all right.

Colin, sooner than she expected, came slouching down across the meadow.

"*Were* they pleased?" Julia asked as he came up.

"No—no one was in. I shall go in myself; whatever you may say about the Swiss telephones, I don't care about that box here. The door won't shut, and there's always someone in the bureau next door."

Mrs. Hathaway took Colin's sudden departure as calmly as she took most things, when Julia told her of it before supper. She had a corner room, with Watkins' cell next door, so the question of being overheard hardly arose.

"How nice that his work should bring him here just now," Mrs. Hathaway said as she sipped Cinzano, gazing happily out of the window. "The only thing that surprises me is that there should be anything for the Secret Service to bother with, here; the Swiss are so *busy* over things like cleaning their cows."

Julia inquired about this.

"Oh yes. Have you noticed those iron rings in that high wall above the road, next to the glen with the waterfall in it?"

Julia nodded.

"Well those are where they *moor* their young beasts before they take them down to the market; they bring cloths and buckets to fetch water from the glen, and slosh the creatures down, there on the roadside. Isn't it charming?"

Julia agreed. But she had a notion of her own in her head.

"Did you read up about the Alpine Garden at the Schynige Platte? If it's fine tomorrow I thought we might go."

"Indeed I did!—and it is something I really do want to see. Yes, do let us go."

"You're sure you're up to it?" Julia felt a little guilty over her own motives for making this particular expedition.

"Well even if I do get a little tired, doing something I enjoy will do me good," Mrs. Hathaway said. "There are wise ways of spending one's strength, just as there are of spending one's money—and really the art of living is to recognize both."

The next day was superb, and they set out on the musical bus. The town of Interlaken, small as it is, possesses *two* railway stations: the West-Bahnhof, whence one entrains for Berne, and the Ost-Bahnhof, which serves Meiringen, Grindelwald, and the Lauterbrunnen valley. The Post-Autos all pull up outside the West-Bahnhof; trains flit from one station to the other, rattling across an open street and thundering, *twice*, over the Aar on iron bridges—Mrs. Hathaway however insisted on taking an open horsecab from one station to the other. A row of these ancient vehicles is always standing in the Platz, the equally ancient horses drooping their heads, the drivers smoking cheroots and gossiping. The party clop-clopped along the main street between small expensive shops and innumerable hotels, some also small, some large and rich-looking. But what startled and fascinated Julia about Interlaken was that the whole town was full of the scent of new-mown hay. The meadows are close round it, so that the sweet country smell is everywhere in what is indubitably a town. Towards the end of their drive they passed a building with the words "Hotel zŭm Flüss" across its façade; Julia gazed at it with deep interest. Beastly Wright, the enigmatic Mr. Borovali and poor little June were all housed behind that yellow front.

To reach the Schynige Platte one takes a train from the Ost-Bahnhof for Wilderswyl, a village at the farther side of the flat plain between the lakes of Thun and Brienz—part of this is occupied by a military airfield, whose hangars are turfed over to look like grassy mounds. Julia observed them with amusement; apparently the Swiss hadn't yet got round to stowing their operational aircraft in the bowels of mountains or at the bottom of lakes! But she was really keeping an eye open for Antrobus; there had been no sign of him at the Ost-Bahnhof. What a bore if he didn't come, after all! However at Wilderswyl, where they got out and stood waiting to be allowed to enter the funny little coaches with their red-and-white blinds which carry one up the mountain, there he was; and was introduced to Mrs. Hathaway. It was hot there in the sun, but when an official unlocked the doors of the small train he said—"Have you a wrap, Mrs. Hathaway? If so, put it on—it's often fearfully cold going up."

Watkins was carrying her mistress' wrap over her arm. She put it on. Then they climbed in and all sat together; Antrobus and Mrs. Hathaway got on like a house on fire, both staring out of the window on the watch for flowers, and pointing out to one another any treasure that they espied. "Oh, there's *Astrantia Major!*" Mrs. Hathaway exclaimed, "in the lower meadows do look!"

Julia was more pleased with Antrobus than ever because of his niceness and considerateness with Mrs. Hathaway. Presently it became really chilly in the windowless little carriage. But still there was more to see.

"Come over to the other side, now," he said. "In a stony valley we're just coming to, you *might* see a marmot." They all moved across, and there on the stone-flecked slopes they actually caught a glimpse of *two* marmots before the idiotic creatures fled whistling into their burrows, frightened by the familiar noise of the train.

"They look so like seals," Mrs. Hathaway said, delighted.

At the top they went straight to the Alpine Garden. It is a charming place, the wild plants grouped in situations approximating to the natural habitat of each, and every group with a metal label bearing its name; little paths wander to and fro, up and down; at intervals there are seats on which to rest and admire the splendid view. Mrs. Hathaway moved slowly along the paths, peering, examining, admiring. Presently they came on a girl in breeches and a blue gardener's apron who knelt beside a new bed, carefully setting in some tiny plants; she recognized Antrobus and got up, wiping the earth off her hands, to greet him in German with a rueful grin.

"Ah, you caught us completely over *Petasites paradoxus!* We learn from *you!*"

"That one *is* a paradox," the man replied, smiling.

As they strolled on Antrobus told Mrs. Hathaway about the girls, youthful botanists from Zürich University, who took care of the garden. "They share that house down by the entrance, and eat at the hotel. I often send them plants to identify, and they are so helpful and enthusiastic, bless them."

Mrs. Hathaway presently said that she would sit and rest for a little, and then make her way up to the restaurant. Antrobus suggested that he and Julia should take a short walk outside the garden and return for lunch. Mrs. Hathaway applauded this idea; so, in her heart, did Julia.

The Schynige Platte garden lies at just over six thousand feet facing South, on the top of a ridge running East and West above the Lake of Brienz; as with the Niederhorn, on the northern side this ridge falls away in vertical cliffs and buttresses; one or two tall rocky towers stand up from it. A path leads under the nearest of these, *Der Turm,* and Julia and Antrobus wandered along it across the open slopes. Here they were soon among the anemones, white and yellow—drifts of great sulphur and silvery-white stars nearly two inches across, flowering out of the rough pale grass— Julia fairly gasped at the sight. Then they climbed by narrow zigzags to the crest of the ridge. There were flowers up here too: the strange-looking Cerinthe and the tiny leafless Veronica, the minute blue heads on bare stalks among the white rocks—Antrobus named them all, as botanists do out of pure love.

On the crest itself they sat on a sun-warmed rock, looking out in front of them at that splendid group of Jungfrau, Mönch, and Eiger, all blazing and glittering under the sun. Up here there was nothing but "the peaks and the sky, and the light and the silence"—Julia herself was silent, suddenly moved; they sat so for a long moment. Then Antrobus turned to her.

"I get the impression that this says something to you?" he said.

Julia didn't answer at once. Then—"I never realized that anything like it was possible," she said, slowly.

He looked pleased. "But have you never been to Switzerland before?"

"Only in winter—Zermatt."

"Well when you've finished your cigarette we'll see more flowers."

Julia went off at a tangent.

"That's the Lake of Brienz down there behind us, isn't it?" she asked. "Is it true that it's full of stores, sunk on the bottom?"

"Yes, certainly. Who told you? Not that it isn't common knowledge; the very bus-drivers taking tourists over the Furka-Pass show them the entrances to the underground barracks and hospitals, and the embedded gun-emplacements."

"Couldn't the metal containers with all that butter and cheese be spotted from the air?" Julia asked. "Like those forts and circles that some-one used to photograph?"

"Not very well. It's much harder to photograph, or spot, objects under six hundred feet of water than under six feet, or a few inches, of soil. And strange planes cruising over these lakes would stir up a hornet's nest of Swiss fighters to buzz them. But who told you?" he persisted.

Julia regretted her question. She was in an idyl at the moment, and the need to mention Colin jerked her back to the world of reality, in which this delightful companion at her side might be an enemy—*the* enemy. The thought hurt her surprisingly.

"Oh, my cousin," she said airily, to conceal her discomfort.

"The second Mr. Monro?"

"Or would you say the first?" she answered brusquely, turning to look him straight in the face.

He smiled at her, and moved one hand in a gesture of brushing something away.

"Forget it!" he said gently. "I'm sorry I said that. Just for today can't we sink Fatima and Bluebeard to the bottom of the Lake of Brienz along with the butter and cheese, and simply enjoy ourselves?"

"I *was* enjoying myself," Julia said plaintively.

"Well go on! Do please. I'm so sorry; this is all my fault. And by the way I think Julia a much prettier name than Fatima."

She blushed at that—hard-boiled as she was in many ways, Julia could never control her blushes—and the man watched the apricots ripening in her cheeks.

"How did you know?" she asked rather defiantly. "Oh, Nethersole of course."

"Yes—don't you remember that he said you would complete my education?"

"At least you're continuing mine!—all these names of flowers."

"Ah, they're my besetting sin—flowers, and birds. Now I want to show you some more—come on."

They returned to the path below the Turm; there he stopped.

"Do you think you can manage this slope? It's quicker than going round by the garden. Better take my hand, though; this top bit is fairly steep." Without waiting for a reply he took her hand and led her down the grassy slope, tacking diagonally across it; he went rather fast and Julia, who had never acquired the mountaineers' trick of the loose-kneed descent—toes out, heels in, and practically sitting back on one's heels—found herself rather breathless when they reached the bottom. (Holding his hand was a faintly breathless affair, too.) Here in a grassy hollow stood three wooden sheds, long and low; these, Antrobus explained, were *Senn-Hütte*, the huts to which the peasants repaired when they brought their cows up to the high alpine pastures for the summer months for cheese-making. As they mounted up a muddy track on the farther slope—"Oh, here they are!" he exclaimed. "Coming up to get the place ready."

Down towards them came several men, steadying two enormous wooden sledges whose upcurved runners slithered in the greasy mud; the sledges were piled high with household and dairying effects—churns, cooking utensils, mattresses, blankets, tools, and topping all two wireless sets. These last made Julia laugh.

"Oh, that's the modern world," Antrobus said. "Today the radio is an essential, even for cheese-making." As the clumsy sledges passed he greeted the men in a language incomprehensible to Julia; they laughed as they replied.

"What on earth were you talking to them?" the girl asked.

"Berner-Deutsch—their patois. It's really more a very archaic form of German than anything else. I rather love it—Germans think it hideous, of course."

"How did you learn it?"

"I used to come here as a child, and played about with the peasant children. And I've gone on coming a good deal ever since."

"Oh yes—you climb, don't you?" By now they had reached the lip of the grassy hollow, and were on the broad track leading to the Faulhorn, and the great range opposite was again visible, glittering under the noonday sun. "Have you been up those?" she asked, gesturing at it.

"Most of them, yes. Do you see the Morgenhorn, that very silver one? It's the first to catch the sunlight in the morning as you look up from Interlaken; that's why they call it that."

"Pretty," Julia said.

"You've never climbed?" he asked.

"No—it never came my way."

"You should," Antrobus said, displaying the missionary spirit so strong in mountaineers. "I think you would—well, find the right things in it."

They wandered slowly on along the Faulhorn path; crossing a low ridge they came on another of those patches of old snow in a grassy saucer, surrounded by white crocuses as by a miniature snowstorm, held motionless three inches above the wintry turf.

"That's what I wanted you to see," the man said.

"It's exquisite," Julia responded.

They were so happy and *easy* together, there on the sunny mountainside, that at last she had the confidence to ask him, outright, what he was really up to.

But the attempt was a failure, lightly and gaily as she did it—"*Which* Mr. Monro are you really shadowing?" As he had done at Victoria he smiled, put a finger to his lip, and shook his head; then, serious all of a sudden, he took her hand and held it firmly. "My dear, I *can't* tell you," he said, very gently. "Let it alone, please. I asked you just now to sink Fatima and Bluebeard to the bottom of the lake. Whatever happens later, for this one day, this one lovely day, do let us just be Julia and John."

Her failure and his tenderness together quite overset Julia. She turned aside—she could not walk on, for he was still holding her hand in a firm clasp—both to conceal an unexpected stinging of tears in her eyes, and to think of an answer and then control her voice for it. He pressed her

hand, watching her averted head, and pursued, "Can't you just say—
'Yes, John,' and leave it at that—for today?"

She took a moment or two over it—oh, how difficult! Her watch was on
her free wrist, and she looked at it. Then she turned back to face him.

"'We maun totter down, John'—we shall be late else," she said.

The man, in his turn, was plainly a little shaken by the quotation.
"Oh!" That was all he said, but he raised her hand to his lips and kissed
it before he let it go. "But really we maun totter *up!*—quite a long way,"
he added, lightening the thing. "We mustn't keep your delightful friend
waiting."

As they walked back to the hotel Antrobus pursued the subject of Mrs.
Hathaway, who had evidently taken his fancy. "Is she inquisitive too?"
he presently asked.

"That's not fair," Julia said slowly. "If *I* mayn't ask questions, nor may
you!"

He laughed. "So sorry." But during lunch in the sunny glassed-in ve-
randa of the hotel Julia got the impression that Antrobus was rather warily
assessing Mrs. Hathaway. At one point she mentioned Gersau, and Herr
Waechter.

"Oh, you know him?" the man said. "Such a wonderful house—and
what a patriarch!"

"Well, if that is how you describe a childless widower!" Mrs. Hathaway
observed ironically.

Antrobus laughed, and they went on to discuss that so essentially Swiss
thing, the long bourgeois pedigrees, and the continuing industry and
wealth in the same families. "No 'Death of a Class' here," Antrobus said
at length.

"No. But don't you have to take neutrality into consideration?" Mrs.
Hathaway said. "The Swiss have escaped two wars, and the penal taxation
resulting from those wars. But if others had not fought, and died, and then
been taxed almost out of existence, would Switzerland still be free, and
able to enjoy her neutrality? I have often thought that neutrality, like
patriotism, is really not quite enough."

Julia, who knew that Mrs. Hathaway had lost two sons in their late
teens in World War I, watched with close interest to see how Antrobus
would deal with this.

"That is quite true," he said carefully. "I was over-simplifying. But I
still think that the social structure has something to do with it. The Swiss
really only have two classes: peasants—who as a class are always immortal
—and the bourgeoisie. In England we have at least four: the aristocracy;
the upper-middle and professional class; the artisans; and again the peas-

ants, whom we call 'country-people'; and of these the first two are of course by far the most vulnerable."

"And possibly the most valuable," Mrs. Hathaway said, a little sharply. "No—obviously true 'peasants' always preserve their precious country values, in spite of the wireless."

Julia put in her oar.

"But surely in Bolshevik Russia, where they aimed at a 'classless society,' they're now busy creating a new aristocracy all over again, of technicians?"

"A *technocracy*," Antrobus corrected her. "Specialized knowledge has its uses, but there is nothing particularly *good* about it. The word *aristos* means 'best,' don't forget." Mrs. Hathaway was pleased; she laughed.

Julia was keeping an eye on the time, and on Mrs. Hathaway for signs of fatigue; they finished their meal rather hurriedly, and caught an early train down. Antrobus went with them as far as Breitlauenen, where he got out to walk down, hunting for flowers in the forests on the way. "I'll bring you anything amusing that I find," he assured Mrs. Hathaway.

Julia had already procured, and carried round in her handbag, a time-table of the Beatenberg buses. This showed her that they would have nearly an hour's wait in Interlaken, and as the Hotel zům Flüss was quite close to the Ost-Bahnhof, curiosity prompted her to suggest that they should have coffee there, and then drive to the West-Bahnhof for their bus. Mrs. Hathaway of course agreed, and to the Flüss they went.

This charming hotel has two rather distinctive features. Opposite the entrance is a terrace, shaded by chestnut trees and set with tables, where light meals are served; also, for the convenience of passengers boarding or leaving the Lake of Brienz steamers, there is a side entrance giving access—as a discreet notice announces—to *Toiletten* for both ladies and gentlemen. Julia's party availed themselves of both. They ordered coffee on the pleasant terrace and drank it there, the air full of the scent of new-mown hay, and resounding with the song of blackbirds. A steamer drew in to the quay, and as they watched the passengers disembarking Julia thought of June, so lonely and "dull"—impulsively, she decided to inquire for her, and went in.

As an excuse she first asked the hall porter—who was bearded, fatherly, and chatty—the Swiss hotel version of the English family butler—if he could order them a horse-cab to catch the Beatenberg bus?

"Yes, certainly." Julia then asked if Miss Armitage was in.

The old man's expression changed instantly, and rather startlingly, to one of hostility and suspicion.

"No. They left this morning."

"Oh, I am sorry. I'd hoped to see her. How was her foot? Any better?"

The old porter thawed a little at that.

"Are you the lady who helped her up on the Niederhorn, and bandaged her foot? She said if you came I was to give you this—" he grubbed in his desk and brought out Julia's headscarf.

"Oh yes, that's mine. Thank you very much. But is her foot better?"

"*Ein wenig*, yes." The porter's suspicion did not appear to attach to June, and Julia pursued this promising line.

"I hope they did get a doctor to see her," she said, putting anxiety into her voice. "This young man seemed to me to take her injury rather lightly."

The porter scowled, and muttered something about a *frecher, ekeliger Kerl* [an insolent disgusting fellow] into his beard; aloud, and in English, he said—"Yes, Miss. The older gentleman told *me* to get a doctor, and I sent for Doktor Hertz; he is excellent; he has a fine Klinik in the town. I know everyone here. Thirty years I am *portier* in this hotel! So the Herr Doktor strapped up the foot, but he said she should use it as little as possible, and that he would look at it again tomorrow."

The porter was now obviously in the full vein of gossip; Julia, delighted, continued to probe.

"But now they have left? Oh, what a pity, since Dr. Hertz is so good! Did they leave an address? Though I have only met Fräulein Armitage once, I should like to know how she gets on."

"No, they left no address," the porter said, scowling again. "They left hurriedly—and with good reason! Oh, *das kleine Fräulein* is all right—she is simply an innocent! But the others!"—he shrugged, with an expression of ineffable contempt. "Curious customers, if you ask me."

Julia continued to pursue the June line.

"Really? I should be sorry to think that this young lady was not with nice people—she told me that she had never left England before, and she is so young. Her mother is a widow, too. Have you any idea *why* they left so hastily?"

The porter leaned over his desk towards her, and spoke in a lowered tone.

"The police came to inquire about them!"

"No!" Julia professed the expected surprise.

"*Aber ja!* Of course they spoke with *me*," the old man said importantly, "and I showed them the register with the names, and said that, as always, the passports had been sent to the *Polizei*—this is done in all hotels here. But then the police brought out a photograph and asked if I recognized it as that of the Fräulein Armitage? This is *most* unusual; in thirty years such a thing has never happened to me."

"And *was* it of her?" Julia asked, delighted at this evidence that her clipping from *Paris-Match* was being used.

"*Gewiss!* It was badly done, but certainly it was this poor young lady's picture—though why the *Polizei* should seek *her*, I cannot understand. And while I was looking at it—here at this desk, where we stand—up comes Herr de Ritter himself to ask some question of me, and sees the photograph, and may have heard the questions asked by the police, for all I know."

"Good Heavens! So then what happened?"

The porter was enjoying his dramatic recital.

"Oh, I know my duties! It is not my business to give away our clients to the police, whatever I myself may think of them. 'Mom*ent*,' I say— and of Herr de Ritter I ask, 'Yes, Sir, what can I do for you?' He inquired of me then about the times of the steamer to Iseltwald; I gave them, and he wrote them down—ah, that is a cool one!—while all the time the photograph of Miss Armitage lies on my desk, under his eyes! He looked well at it, and at the two police—though these were in *Zivil*." (Julia knew that he meant plain clothes.) "And he thanked me, and went away."

One up to Mr. B., Julia thought; crook or no, he had good nerves. "And after that?" she asked.

"Oh, the police went off—to make a report, I suppose," the porter said, with some contempt—"being now satisfied that the Fräulein Armitage is here. But less than an hour later she is no longer here! Within thirty-five minutes the valet comes down with the luggage; they pack, pay their bill, and off! Would not anyone think this odd?"

"Very odd indeed," Julia agreed. "And the police made no attempt to hold them?"

"*Ach nein!*—the police had gone. And now the birds are flown!"

"*Did* they go to Iseltwald?" Julia asked.

"No. They simply went across to the Ost-Bahnhof. I told Johann, who took their luggage, to note where they booked to; but they had a *carnet* of *Ost-West* tickets, as all who are wise do in Interlaken, and they used those. So one knows nothing. From the West-Bahnhof one can travel to anywhere in Europe."

"All most peculiar," Julia said slowly. "And did you tell the police they'd left?"

"Fräulein, guests are guests!" the porter said pompously. "As I said before, it is no part of my duties to lay informations to the police. If they ask questions I answer them, as in the matter of the photograph—but that suffices."

"How very right. If I ever marry a crook I shall come and stay at the Flüss!" Julia said, and went out to rejoin Mrs. Hathaway, leaving the porter bowing and laughing. "Don't forget our cab," she called over her shoulder.

"Dear child, how long you've been! *Can* they get us a cab?" that lady asked.

"Oh yes; all laid on. I'm sorry I was so slow; the porter was rather a gossipy old thing," Julia said carelessly, and Mrs. Hathaway asked no further questions—she was tired as well as tactful. But all the way back to Beatenberg in the bus Julia was *distrait* and rather silent. The reference of the porter at the Flüss to June as "an innocent" exactly matched her own impression of the pretty, silly, good-hearted little thing who proudly gave a lot of her wages to support "Mum," now that "Dad" was dead; and she was filled with a slow, cold anger that international crookery should get hold of such a helpless creature and use her simply as a commodity to serve their beastly purposes. "Expendable!" she muttered angrily, thinking of June's boredom, and how she had now been reft away from the excellent Dr. Hertz, who would have seen to her ankle, her source of livelihood.

"What did you say, my dear?" Mrs. Hathaway asked.

"Oh sorry, Mrs. H.—I was talking to myself. I must be going round the bend!"

"Nonsense, dear. I think soliloquies aloud are a sign of intelligent emotion—after all, where would Shakespeare have been without them? But do look out on the right—oh, no, now it's on the left—these awful hairpins!" —as the bus negotiated another, playing its little six-note tune. "There! Do you see that Enchanter's Nightshade? Unmistakable!—but it's practically *blue.*"

Julia tried to pick out the small dull plant which so excited Mrs. Hathaway from among the heaths, whortleberry bushes, ferns and other greenery which clothed the bank above the terrifying road. "Oh yes, so it is," she said. "How odd!" Then she returned to her private preoccupations. She was no longer so pleased at the use to which her clipping from *Paris-Match* had presumably been put. It was almost certainly her fault that June's ankle was now going to be neglected. But when she sent the photograph to Chambertin she hadn't met June.

COLIN RANG UP after tea. "Where on earth have you been all day? I tried to get you three times."

"At the Schynige Platte."

"Oh. Well something very boring has happened. I gave my friends here that address, but I think the locals must have been a bit slow off the mark—anyhow, your new acquaintances have gone."

"I know."

"*How* do you know?"

"I just happened to find out. And it was the locals who scared them off, bumble-footing round with a certain photograph, quite openly."

"Any idea where they've gone?"

"None—I couldn't learn that."

"Well can't you learn it? Do try. It's too maddening their vanishing into thin air like this, just when we thought everything was taped. And now we've heard that their principals, who were delayed, are probably arriving by air within the next forty-eight hours."

"Arriving where?"

"Wherever my would-be bride and her escorts have stowed themselves."

"Her beastly escorts!" Julia exclaimed. "Much they care about her!"

Colin ignored this.

"Well darling you see it's pretty urgent. Do you think you can find out some more, as you're on the spot?"

"No, I don't see how I can, since they now know that the *polus*"—she carefully used the Highland word for the police—"are after them."

"They do definitely know that?"

"Yes—I told you. That's why they left at half-an-hour's notice."

"*How* boring. So we've absolutely *no* clue?"

"No. Oh by the way, what about the detective?"

"The who?"

"The man you met yesterday. *Is* anything known of him by your friends?"

"Damn! I forgot to ask."

"Oh really, you *are* tiresome! I begged you to get a line on him."

"Sorry, darling. But does it really matter?"

"It could matter a lot." Julia felt that it probably mattered most to her, but did not say so. "Find out—don't forget again," she adjured Colin. "Are you coming back?"

"Don't know yet. We may have to be spread pretty thin at these airports. But do try to think something up, darling; because if they keep the girl under cover, as I imagine they will now, we really have no clue at all."

"No clue at all." Those last words of Colin's stuck in Julia's head all the evening, while she saw to Mrs. Hathaway's supper in bed; they were with her as she stepped out onto her balcony last thing, sniffing the scent of the opening rowan blossom from the tree in the meadow below, and looked across the darkling lake at the Blümlisalp white under the moon. Another phrase of Colin's nagged at her while she undressed—"if they keep the girl under cover." She visualized June locked in her bedroom, starved, anything; people like Wright and Borovali could easily be remorseless, now that the child had both served their turn, and given them away. She got into bed, but was too troubled to sleep. Suddenly there flashed into her mind the recollection of the Mass that Father Antal, the old Hungarian priest, had said in the private chapel at Gralheira, in Portugal, on behalf of Hetta Páloczy, another girl in ruthless hands—and how by a miraculous coincidence Mrs. Hathaway had found and rescued her. Here there was no priest or chapel; the little Catholic church in the village only opened on Sundays. But prayer was always prayer; Julia hopped out of bed, and kneeling on the scanty mat which covered the pine flooring beside it she prayed urgently for safety for June. Then she hopped in again, and slept soundly.

She woke in the morning with a bounce, as the young and healthy do, and went out in her nightgown onto the little balcony. An early steamer was crossing the lake from Spiez toward Merligen, hidden behind a ridge running down from the Niederhorn; as Julia watched it, idly, an idea stole into her mind of itself, as ideas sometimes do. The little man from "Corsette-Air" lived at Merligen—and hadn't he said that he had been asked recently to act as intermediary between *agences* of different nations, and pass information from one to the other? Had he said *agences* or *agents*? She couldn't be sure; she hadn't been paying much attention. But if there were people like him who did this sort of thing, might it not be just worth while to see him again, and try to find out a little more about the nature of the "informations" he transmitted?—learn more of how these things were done? It didn't amount to a clue—but the idea of going to look him up, having come into her head, persisted. Merligen was so near—she would lose nothing by going. It was only the vaguest of hunches, it might be all a fantasy; but her hunches and fantasies had sometimes served well in the past. Had she still got that card? She routed in her bag—yes, there it was—

> Herr Kaufmann.
> Villa Victoria.
> Merligen-am-Thunersee.
> B.O.

Her *bouilloir* boiled, and she made her tea and drank a quick cup; had a bath in Mrs. Hathaway's cubicle of a bathroom, and dressed hastily. It was probably all a nonsense, but Colin, poor sweet, had been so urgent, and she had nothing to do—Mrs. H. ought to keep quiet today, after yesterday. On her way down to breakfast she looked in on that lady, and found her none the worse for her exertions; she had slept well. "But I don't feel like being very energetic today."

"Much better not—keep quiet and rest. I'm flipping off on a tiny expedition the moment after breakfast; with any luck I shall be back for lunch, but don't wait."

Ninety-nine elderly ladies out of a hundred, in the circumstances, would have asked where her young friend was going? Mrs. Hathaway did not, which was one reason why everyone loved her.

"Very well, dear child, I won't. It's a lovely day for an *Ausflug.*"

Julia, as Colin had done two days before, went down in the funicular at the end of the village to Beatenbucht, and thence took a trolley-bus along the lake shore to Merligen, at the mouth of the forbidden Justis-Thal. This proved to be a sweet little place, dreamy and tranquil in the spring sunshine, looking across the lake to the shapely blue pyramid of the Niesen behind Spiez; there was a single large hotel on the shore, many old châlets, and an endless crop of small new villas, mostly on streets inland from the lake—but what startled and pleased Julia was that the whole little town was white and sweet as a bride's bouquet with bushes of syringa and *Spiraea canescens,* flowering in every garden. After inquiries she made her way to the Villa Victoria, in one of the new streets; a neat paved path between the usual bridal bushes led up to the front door. Julia, wondering a good deal how she was to work this interview, rang the bell.

The door was opened by a rather sour-looking middle-aged woman in a spotted black-and-white apron, with her hair in a net. Julia asked if she could speak with Herr Kaufmann.

"I am Frau Kaufmann," the woman said, not at all agreeably.

"Ah, good day. Is your husband at home? I come to inquire about surgical stays."

Reluctantly, casting on Julia the suspicious glance that ugly women so often bestow on beautiful ones, the woman admitted her, and led her from the cramped little hall into a rather modest-sized room, obviously a sitting room-cum-office: a huge safe stood against one wall, a very large desk heaped with files and papers under the window; a nouveau-art sofa and armchairs, covered with a pattern which suggested an electrical discharge, were grouped round a nouveau-art fireplace. Julia was enthralled by this fresh version of a Swiss interior—one in which, moreover, thousands of pounds worth of business was conducted annually.

"My husband is away," the woman said then; "he had to leave suddenly, for Lugano. I expect you know that his business is really wholesale? What firm do you represent?"

At this point piercing screams in a child's voice were heard from somewhere upstairs. *"Warte ein Augenblick, Franzi,"* the woman called. But Franzi would not wait; he renewed his screaming. With a snort of exasperation and a hasty, *"Entschuldigen Sie, bitte,"* the woman left the room and could be heard stumping up the small narrow staircase, and speaking to a child in the room above.

Julia, without the smallest scruple, instantly went over to the outsize desk and began to examine the papers left strewn on it, clear evidence of the owner's hasty departure. There were some invoices, clipped together, several letters with the *"Corsette-Air"* letterhead from the firm in Yorkshire, all in English—nothing to help her there. But tucked in under the blotting-pad, only one corner peeping out, she came, with her inveterate curiosity, on an open envelope; she drew out the letter and read it. It was in German, from a chemist in Berne, and read: "Our client, Herr B., left his recent address today. He may shortly be calling on you in person to deposit a valuable consignment of goods." Julia looked quickly at the date—*yesterday!* H'm—her "Herr B." had undoubtedly changed his address yesterday! Could the Borovali outfit be one of the *agences*, or *agents*, for whom Herr Kaufmann had recently been asked to act as an intermediary, to receive and pass on "informations"? "Goods" might perfectly well mean blueprints—this letter could possibly mean something. Hastily she scribbled down the chemist's name and address in her diary; she just had time to put the envelope back under the blotter and sit down on one of the hideous chairs before Frau Kaufmann reappeared, with apologies. The little boy was ill, she said; he had measles, and the fever made him fretful. But now, about the Fräulein's firm?

Julia expressed sympathy about the child—"But I had better speak with Herr Kaufmann himself. When does he return?"

"I await him tomorrow, or even tonight. *Übermorgen* would be better for the Fräulein to come."

"Then I will call again. It does not press," Julia said.

The woman asked her name.

"That is unimportant—I will give it when I return." Then she asked if she could take any message to the doctor, or the chemist, in the town?

"Thank you, no; I telephone," the woman said, disagreeable to the last.

Walking down the sunny little side street between the snowy gardens, Julia wondered whether Franzi's screams were another wonderful stroke of luck or whether the letter meant nothing? Anyhow, she thought, Colin ought to have that chemist's name and address, just in case. She decided to telephone from the big hotel by the lake; Berne is a longish call, and she knew from the Silberhorn that Swiss hotels have a little machine in the Bureau which clocks up both time and price—but of course she had to risk giving Colin's number in Berne to the Bureau-Fräulein.

Mr. Monro was out. When would he be in? "No idea." A cheerful English voice spoke.

"Well please ask him to ring up his cousin"—she gave the Silberhorn number—"as soon as he can; but only after three-thirty."

"O.K.—good," the cheerful English voice replied. "Have you got some news for us?"

Julia laughed. This might be half-clever, or too amateurish for words. But she did not want to lose time.

"Nothing hard," she said down the telephone—"but there is an address that I think it *might* pay you to keep an eye on—round the clock."

"Fine! I've got a pencil. Go ahead."

Julia gave the chemist's address, and had it repeated. "And the phone number?" the voice asked.

"Oh please look that up yourself!" Julia exclaimed—she wasn't going to say over the telephone that she hadn't had time to write it down.

"O.K." the cheerful voice said again. "That shall have attention. Thanks very much."

After paying for her call Julia ordered an iced Cinzano, and sat on the terrace beside the lake—a drink was always cover of a sort. And while she drank she reflected. Yes, on balance she had probably done right to give the Berne chemist's address to an unknown voice—but still she was worried. Oughtn't the Villa Victoria to be watched too? If there was anything in her wild guess about the chemist's letter, Mr. Borovali might call at any moment to drop the papers, and that old sourpuss Frau Kaufmann would pop them in that huge combination safe, and then how could they be retrieved? She lit a cigarette and pondered, gazing at the Niesen—and finally came to another decision. Yes, she would chance her arm with the local police.

At the police station she handed over her card and asked for the *Herr Chef*—she had no idea what the German for "Superintendent" was. Rather to her surprise she was shown into an inner office, where a tall middle-aged man, with fair hair turning grey, courteously asked her her business?

Julia, in her very moderate German, inquired if he spoke English?—"I can express myself better in my own language."

He smiled at her.

"Fortunately, Fräulein, it so happens that I do; I spent some time in England before joining the *Polizei*."

"Oh, I am very glad." Julia did not smile; she spoke slowly and seriously. "All I ask of you is to listen to something I have to tell you. You do not know who I am, though here is my passport"—she gave it to him—"and I do not expect any response to what I tell you; that will be a matter for you and your superiors. Can you spare me five or six minutes?"

This rather portentous opening caused the official to assume the cautious noncommittal mask of police all over Europe. "Please speak," he said.

"I believe the police in Switzerland have been circulated everywhere with the photograph of a young English girl," Julia said; "a girl accompanied by two men, one old and one young." She opened her note-case and took out the small snapshot of Colin and the real Aglaia which she had cut out of *Paris-Match* at Gersau, and handed it across the table. "This is, I think, the same young lady."

The official took up the photograph and examined it; then went to a cupboard, unlocked it, and took out and laid on the table a coarse photostat of the portrait of Aglaia which Julia had sent to Chambertin. He compared the two—then, completely po-faced, he turned to Julia.

"And so, Fräulein?"

"In this town there lives a certain Herr Kaufmann—at the Villa Victoria; an agent for 'Corsette-Air,' a foreign firm selling elastic stays. Probably you know his name."

"*Natürlich*," the man, still po-faced, said.

Julia, feeling that she might be making fool of herself, nevertheless kept steadily on.

"I have reason to think it possible that the two men accompanying the young lady whose picture you have there—a Mr. Borovali, though his passport is made out in the name of de Ritter, and the young one, whose passport is in the name of Colin Monro—may possibly call at the Villa Victoria. If they do so, it would almost certainly be to dispose of some documents of the highest importance, which they obtained recently by fraud from the Banque Républicaine in Geneva. The photograph you

have there"—she put a pink-tipped finger on the photostat—"has been circulated, I think, mainly with a view to the recovery of those documents."

Still superbly po-faced—"And so, Fräulein?" the official asked again.

"Nothing, really," Julia said, "except that it might assist your superiors,
who took the trouble to send you that photograph, if a watch were kept
on the Villa Victoria. I think you were also furnished with a description
of the two men: the one elderly, grey-haired, with a grey forked beard,
the younger very tall, slender, black hair and an olive complexion. If two
such people came to the Villa they would very probably have the stolen
documents with them, and it might be useful to the bank, at least, if these
documents could be apprehended." She rose. "That is all." She made to
leave, as expressionless as he—only no blankness of expression could really
make Julia look po-faced.

The official remained seated.

"Just one moment, Fräulein; please to sit down again."

Julia sat down, and the man studied her with a long gaze in which
surprise, curiosity, and suspicion were blended.

"The Fräulein shows herself remarkably conversant with the personages
in an affair which is apparently a crime; and, as you say, you are unknown
to me. Have you any documents with you which would throw light on
your status? The Fräulein will recognize that the circumstances are a
little peculiar."

"I have nothing but my visiting card and my passport, both of which
you have seen," Julia said, rather stiffly. "But if you wish you can telephone
to the Pasteur of the Église Nationale at Bellardon: he is the *real* Herr
de Ritter, and knows me well—I have stayed twice at La Cure within the
last three weeks. And he is fully conversant with the whole affair."

The police official made a note, and then asked—"The Fräulein is staying
in Merligen?"

"No, at Beatenberg; the Hotel Silberhorn."

"And do you know the present whereabouts of this young lady?" he
asked, touching the police photograph.

"But naturally not! If I did, I should have gone also to the police there,"
Julia said.

The official reflected.

"Please excuse me for a moment," he said, and left the room. Julia
began to wonder if she was going to be put in the cells, or whether he had
merely gone to ring up Bellardon—and, again if what she was doing was
quite idiotic. She pushed her wooden chair over to the window, opened
it—Julia was always opening windows—and sat looking out. Below her
were more gardens, white and fragrant with spiraea and syringa; beyond

them, across the lake, rose the Niesen, with snowy gleams beyond. There is a certain reassurance, for some people, in the mere presence of mountains; Antrobus had not been wrong in his guess that Julia belonged to this fortunate group. She waited quietly in the bare official little room; she did look at her watch and saw that it was just after twelve; but she had warned Mrs. Hathaway that she might not be back for lunch. She was feeling perfectly tranquil when after a few minutes the greying-blond police officer returned. But the question he instantly put to her was rather upsetting.

"Fräulein Probyn, can you explain to me *why* you connect Herr Kaufmann with the persons of whom you have been speaking?"

Julia hesitated, and thought. The little "Corsette-Air" man's remarks about touching *la haute finance,* and acting as an intermediary for agencies of foreign powers seemed to her far too complicated and tenuous for this blunt intelligent man, with his official limitations. Much better stick to the letter she had read less than two hours ago. She opened her bag and took out what she had scribbled down in the Villa Victoria.

"A certain chemist in Berne," she said carefully, "wrote yesterday to Herr Kaufmann, to say that 'Herr B.' might call on him shortly to deposit, 'A valuable consignment of goods'; he also mentioned that 'Herr B.' had left his recent address 'today'—that is to say yesterday. And yesterday morning Mr. Borovali left the Hotel zŭm Flüss in Interlaken at less than an hour's notice, with that young lady and the young man." As she spoke she reached out and took the snapshot of Colin and Aglaia, and put it in her bag.

"You require this?" the official asked.

"Yes—it is mine. In any case it is not the likeness of the young man who is Borovali's collaborator."

"Then of whom?"

"Of quite a different person, well-known in English society, whom I happen to know. This photograph will not help you, and you already have an adequate likeness"—she chose her words carefully—"of the young lady in the party." She paused. "I am sure you have already been informed that she is impersonating someone else."

The man turned po-faced again. As Julia took up her passport from the table and put it in her bag—

"And the name of this chemist in Berne?" he asked.

"Oh yes"—she opened her bag, read it out, and as he wrote it down, once more closed her bag.

"You return now to Beatenberg?" the man asked.

"Yes, immediately; I'm late already—I shall miss the *Mittagsessen*." Once more she rose; the official said—"Adieu," and opened the door.

"Good-bye," Julia said, and went out into the sunny little street to find the trolley-bus.

It was nearly a quarter to two when she got back, but Fräulein Hanna had saved her an *assiette anglaise* (a dish of mixed cold meats, in which veal and tongue predominated) and a bowl of salad—the kind woman told her that *die alte Dame* had made a good meal, and was gone to rest. Julia made a good meal too, and then went up to her room and brewed some Nescafé, which she drank on her balcony, idly watching more hay-cutting in the field below, and wondering whether she had really achieved anything by her morning's excursion. Was it all a mare's-nest, and would the Merligen policeman *do* anything?

Presently she was summoned to the telephone—it was the Pastor.

"My dear Miss Probyn, what have you been up to? Stealing edelweiss in a *Natur-Reserve*? The police have been here to inquire about you."

"Oh, splendid!" Julia said heartily; he laughed loudly.

"Oh, the English! You really love *all* police, don't you? But you are all right? You are not being troubled?"

"Not yet."

"Any news of these individuals?" he asked, with a change of tone.

"Yes, I met two of them, but they've flitted."

"Please?"

"Gone away—we don't know where to."

"And you actually *saw* them?—how extraordinary! But what has happened today, to cause this interest?"

"Oh, I had a wild idea, so I went and reported it," Julia said airily. "I'm glad they paid some attention—I wasn't sure they would."

"Our *Polizisten* do not pay attention to wild ideas as a rule," the pastor said, again merry.

"Well I hope you gave me a good character," Julia said. Like Colin she found that the door of the telephone box wouldn't latch, and there were two or three people in the small lounge outside, which gave onto the garden—she wanted to cut the conversation short. "How is Germaine? —and the family?"

"All very well. Your cousin is with you?"

"Not at the moment. Give Germaine my love. Good-bye."

Julia went upstairs feeling on the whole rather pleased. At least the Merligen police hadn't completely ignored her visit; and if they had been activated to the point of ringing up Bellardon, they might possibly do something about the Villa Victoria. She washed out some handkerchiefs, humming a little tune, happily, as she did so; she was just plastering the hankies on the windowpanes to iron them—that invaluable trick of the experienced traveler—when there came a tap on the door.

"*Herein,*" Julia called—and in came Fräulein Hanna, with a distressed face.

"Fräulein Probyn, I am most heartily sorry, but the *Polizei* are here, and ask to speak with you! I tell them that it must be a mistake, but they give your name, and insist they must see you."

"Oh never mind, Fräulein Hanna, it's quite all right." She paused, and thought. "But I don't want Herr Schaffhausen upset. Where are they now?"

"They wait *im Bureau.*"

"Then shall I come down to them, or were it better that they come up and see me here? There are people in the *Kleine Saal,* aren't there?" [The *Kleine Saal* was the small hall containing the telephone box; the Bureau opened off it.]

"*Jawohl.*"

"Well then bring them up to me here, in the lift—that will be less noticeable. Don't worry," she said, seeing the big kind woman's troubled expression. "You will see, there will be no unpleasantness."

"It is *höchst unangenehm* that they come to trouble the Fräulein at all," Hanna said indignantly. "All this nonsense about passports! But it is perhaps better so—though *das Fräulein* should not have to receive strange men in her bedroom." She went out, and returned in a couple of minutes with two large, pink-faced countrified policemen, whom she ushered into that exceedingly small room, with its single wicker armchair and the wooden bed with its white honeycomb quilt. "Shall I remain?" she asked earnestly of the English girl.

"No, dear Fräulein Hanna; I thank you, but do not give yourself this trouble," Julia said easily. "Very probably I can help *diese Herren* better by myself." This was said in German, and the two pink faces manifested simple relief. Hanna, casting a baleful glance at them, went out.

"*Also, meine Herren,* how can I be of service to you?" Julia asked—as she spoke she sat down in the solitary chair. "I wish I could ask you to be seated, but as you see there is only the bed."

The Beatenberg police did not fancy sitting on the bed; they stood. It was only a formality, the slightly senior one explained—could they see the Fräulein's passport? Julia produced this, and the man wrote down her name and the passport number, in a black notebook.

"And the Fräulein entered Switzerland, when?"

"The date is *gestempelt,*" Julia said patiently. "Allow me to show you."

She took the passport and showed him the entry stamps, nearly four weeks previously.

"And since then the Fräulein has been where?"

At dictation speed Julia gave him all her movements: Gersau, with her host's name and address; La Cure at Bellardon; the Hotel Bergues at Geneva; Bellardon again; Gersau again; and finally here at Beatenberg. All policemen write incredibly slowly; so did the Beatenberg worthy, poising his notebook on the small bedtable—however at last he closed it with an elastic band.

"And *das Fräulein* expects to remain here?"

"For the present, yes. But *mein Herr,* I would like to make one request of you."

"And that is, Fräulein?" He looked suspicious at once.

"That you do not cause the *Polizei* in Gersau to disturb Herr Waechter with their inquiries. He is an old man, and it might upset him to have the police calling at the house and asking about his guests. This cannot really be necessary—you know that I am here, and since when, and the police at Bellardon have already verified my presence at La Cure, on the dates I have given you."

A slow look of surprise gradually disturbed the bland pinkness of the older policeman's face.

"And may I ask how the Fräulein knows this?"

"But because the Herr Pastor himself telephoned, only now, to tell me so!" Julia said merrily. "He asked if I had been stealing Edelweiss on the Niederhorn—he has laughed very much."

The two policemen grinned a little, though evidently shocked by such levity. "*Die Edelweiss* are not yet in bloom," the younger one added seriously.

"*Nicht?* But please hear me," Julia pursued earnestly. "With the old Herr Waechter it will be otherwise; *he* will not laugh, he will be distressed. If it is really essential that you verify my presence in Gersau on these dates, can it not be arranged that the *Polizei* there speak only with his servant Anton—Anton Hofer? He is in the house for twenty years. I beg this favor of you."

Julia's earnestness gained her point. "It shall be done as the Fräulein desires," the older one said. "Have no anxiety. *Schönsten Dank,* Fräulein, for your cooperation." They bowed themselves out, rather awkwardly, past the end of the bed.

Julia was just wondering whether she ought to ring up Herr Waechter herself, and warn him, when Anni, one of the waitresses, came in to say that *die alte Dame* was about to take tea in the garden, and desired to know if the Fräulein would join her? Julia ran down, and found Mrs. Hathaway and Watkins sitting at a table on the gravel, under clipped chestnuts, which constituted the garden of the Silberhorn.

"I thought we would have tea out here, as it's so fine," Mrs. Hathaway said, "but these cakes are not very nice."

"Hadn't we better have some sandwiches or bread and butter instead?" Julia asked, and ran in to Fräulein Hanna and asked for tongue sandwiches and bread-and-butter to be sent out at once.

"How went it with the *Polizei?*" the Swiss woman asked.

"Oh, they couldn't have been nicer; just a technicality," Julia said, reassuringly.

"They should not have come," Hanna said. "The older one is my cousin —I shall speak with him at Mass on Sunday. Troubling good, polite, *excellent* Herrschaften." Julia, laughing, returned to the garden; there she found Antrobus sitting at the table, and the tea tray littered with botanical specimens. As he rose to greet her she experienced an almost frightening pang of pleasure.

"Oh, how do you do? Bringing your finds to be identified?" she asked teasingly, to conceal her delight.

"Do *look,* dear child—Mr. Antrobus has brought me the red Cephalanthera," Mrs. Hathaway said exultingly. "*And* Sweet Woodruff—you know it grows in the Cotswolds, smell how fragrant it is." She held up a small flower rather like the common bedstraw, only larger, with frills of leaves in sixes all up its stalk.

"Delicious," Julia said.

"They make a drink of it here with white wine," Antrobus said; "they call it *Mai-Kop.* And the peasants call the plant itself *Waldmeister.*"

"Master of the Forest is a much more imposing name than Sweet Woodruff," Julia observed.

"I've sometimes wondered if it mightn't really be the same idea," Antrobus said—"Woodruff merely a corruption of 'Wood-Reive,' the Warden of the Wood."

"How charming; that had never occurred to me," said Mrs. Hathaway. "They make a drink of it in Austria too," she added, "only there they call it *Mai-Bowle.*"

Julia again smelled the potent scent of the small flower—she liked to think of two different nations using the delicate, precisely-shaped little plant to make a spring drink, and calling it by two such pretty names as May-cup and May-bowl. "I wonder if it grows here," she said—"if I could collect enough I'm sure Fräulein Hanna would make us a *Mai-Kop.*"

"It's rather early for it as high as this," Antrobus replied—surprising

Julia, who had not yet grasped that the seasons in Switzerland depend partly on altitude, and that a difference of 3,000 feet may also mean a delay of two or three weeks in the flowering of plants. "But the woods round Interlaken are full of it," he went on; "if I can I'll bring up a good bunch tomorrow."

"Then you must bring it up in time to have the brew made, and stay and dine," Mrs. Hathaway said happily; she was greatly taken with Antrobus.

"I should be delighted to do that, if—if I'm not called away," the man replied, for once showing a trace of embarrassment.

"Oh, are you leaving?" Mrs. Hathaway asked, a note of chill coming into her voice. She belonged to a generation which was accustomed to having its invitations accepted or refused, but not left hanging in the air.

Antrobus did his best.

"Dear Mrs. Hathaway, I hope very much both to be able to bring you the Sweet Woodruff tomorrow, and to dine with you and drink the product. But I am not altogether my own master."

"Oh." A pause. "Then who *is* your master?" Mrs. Hathaway asked, implacably. Julia listened enchanted to Mrs. H. turning the heat onto the detective—what *would* he say? She might learn something.

What he said struck the girl at once as being a cover-story.

"My master is one of these modern Juggernauts, the Press Barons," he said. "They are very arbitrary, and quite unpredictable." He put this out with a rather graceful aplomb, but Mrs. Hathaway, unmollified, regarded him with a steady look which had all the quelling effect of an Edwardian dowager raising her lorgnette to her face. The very fact that she so liked and approved of this man made her all the more severe, now that his behavior fell short of her standards.

"Oh, you are a journalist?" she said at length. "I should never have suspected it."

Nor should I, and I don't believe it for a moment, Julia thought to herself—if that was all he was, why had Nethersole made such a fuss when she asked what he did, at lunch at the Palais des Nations? But she saw Antrobus, at the old lady's tone, actually blush—the ready unconcealable blush of a fair-skinned man. She intervened.

"Mrs. H., dear, what's wrong with being a journalist? Aren't I one?"

"Not very seriously, my dear—and only with a very nice Press Baroness!" She turned to Antrobus. "Well, if Lord X, or Lord Y, or Lord Z, whichever your so needlessly ennobled 'master' is"—she put a sardonic stress on the word master—"leaves you free tomorrow evening, it will be delightful to see you at dinner. Seven-thirty. Won't you have another cup of tea?"

Not unnaturally in the circumstances, Mr. Antrobus declined a second cup of tea; he took his leave rather hastily, striding out of the garden on his long legs, got into a large car which he had parked near the cow-stable across the street, and drove off.

"I never saw a car like that before," Julia said, as she watched him go. "I wonder what on earth it is."

Mrs. Hathaway was often unexpected—she was now.

"It's a Porsche," she said. "I've seen them in Vienna. Porsche was the man who designed the Volkswagen, and later he made this car too, bigger and faster. Rather expensive for a journalist, I should have thought— they're practically racing cars."

"Mrs. H., what a lot you know! But I think you were rather hard on that wretched man," Julia said.

"Mr. Antrobus? Why is he wretched?"

"He wasn't, till you made him so. I expect he has quite a sunny nature really," Julia said, trying to sound casual.

Mrs. Hathaway studied her young friend with a speculative eye. Why this concern for Mr. Antrobus? She spoke carefully.

"My dear, I am sorry if I have distressed you on his account. I was taken by surprise—his neither accepting nor refusing an invitation was so unexpected, in *him*."

"I daresay he really couldn't help it," Julia said. In fact she had learned nothing from Mrs. Hathaway's pressure except that Antrobus could lie, but not very well. And would he come to dinner tomorrow, after this?

They sat on for a short time while the air cooled, and the white peaks across the lake turned to a richer gold; the pine forests on the slopes in front of them assumed a quite extraordinary color—a sort of rosy bronze with the deep softness of velvet. Presently Fräulein Hanna came stumping out across the grey gravel on her thick grey-stockinged legs.

"One demands Fräulein Probyn *am Telefon*."

Julia went in to that insecure telephone box in the *Kleine Saal*. The voice was Colin's; he sounded cross.

"Darling, what *are* you up to? You seem to have stirred up an absolute hornet's nest among the local *polus*, just when we wanted to do everything as quietly as possible. What goes on?"

"I don't know for sure if anything goes on at all," Julia said, not in the least disturbed. "I just had a hunch, and acted on it. The bobbies have been here too," she added, gurgling.

"Hell! Whatever for?"

"Just to check on *me*. They were quite sweet."

"Why did you send them to see the parson?"

"Oh, as a Swiss 'reference as to character'—really the only one I've got except Mrs. H.'s old boy-friend, and I made them promise not to worry him."

"I think you're *quite* mad," Colin said.

"Could be. Time will show. But I hope someone is keeping an eye on that chemist's, darling darling—I really think that might pay off. Your colleague with the nice voice seemed to be willing to."

"Oh yes—that's being taken care of. I wish to God I knew what all this is about."

"Well when are you coming back to hear? I don't think I'd better telephone the whole story, automatic or no."

"I don't know—as soon as I can. But do try to keep *quiet*, will you? This may be rather a crucial forty-eight hours." He sounded tired, anxious, and overwrought to Julia, who knew his voice so well.

"Bless you, I'll try to. Oh by the way"—she paused for an instant—"what about the detective?"

A click indicated that Colin had already rung off.

CHAPTER IX

INTERLAKEN—THE CLINIC AND THE GOLDEN BEAR

A LITTLE before nine on the following morning Julia was finishing her breakfast in the restaurant, vulgarly scraping up the black cherry jam off her plate with the delicious Beatenberg bread when once again she was called to the telephone. An obviously Swiss voice asked, in uncertain English—"It is Miss Probeen who speaks?"

"Yes."

"Miss Probeen herself?"

"Aber ja, unbedingt," Julia said reassuringly. "Who wishes to speak with me?"

"One moment please, Fräulein." There was a pause, a faint confused noise of voices "off," and then Julia heard June's unmistakable sub-Cockney tones—"Is that Miss Probyn?"

"Yes, Julia Probyn speaking. Is that June?"

"Yes. Oh, I am glad I've got you. You couldn't come down and see me, could you? I *am* so unhappy!—and my ankle's so swollen, it's terrible. The two gentlemen have gone off, so I thought you might come and see me."

"Of course I will. Where are you?"

"Oh, in ever such a funny little hotel—not a bit like the Flooss! And it's got such a silly name, the Golden Bear. Whoever heard of a golden bear?" June demanded, with a fretful giggle.

"But where is it? What town, I mean?"

"Oh, poor old Interlarken! I don't know why we had to come here; it's ever so small, and one can't see the steamers—well reelly one can't see anything! And we rushed away from the Flooss in such a hurry, I couldn't pack properly; and here there's no room to hang anything. My dresses will be ruined, staying in the cases, and not folded right."

"I'll fold them for you."

"Oh you are sweet!—I *would* be glad. But can you come *soon?* You see I don't know when they'll get back, but not before dinner-time, I don't think."

Julia guessed that by "dinner" June meant what she called luncheon.

"I'll come down at once. Not to worry," she said, employing an idiotic phrase which she hoped would appeal to June; she was rewarded by a happy giggle, and—"Oh, lovely! 'Bye 'Bye."

Outside the telephone-box Julia hastily consulted the bus timetable which is such an essential feature of life in Beatenberg. The next bus for Interlaken left in five minutes; she raced upstairs, collected a jacket, looked in on Mrs. Hathaway with—"Flying off—can't stop—back sometime"—and ran down again, and along the graveled garden to where the downward bus pulled up, between the cow-stable and a petrol-pump. She just made it, and got the front seat of all, next to the driver.

This happened to be the blond man whose goings-on had exasperated Watkins on the day they arrived. So early in the morning the passengers were mostly local Swiss; they all referred to the driver as "der Chrigl," the Swiss-German dimunitive for the name Christian—and from him, on the way down, Julia inquired how to find the Golden Bear. In the Cantonal-Platz, he told her. "It is a very small hotel; few foreigners go there," der Chrigl observed, eyeing her a little curiously—and most dangerously—as he swung his vast machine round one of the hairpin bends. "But the Fräulein cannot miss the big golden bear over the door—it glitters."

The Cantonal-Platz is in the old indigenous Interlaken, which few tourists ever see. Deep-eaved plastered houses line narrow streets, many of which end at the river. Local trades are carried on here—timberyards, warehouses for coke and briquettes or for wine, shops for second-hand clothing; Julia paused before a very small window indeed, in which a splendid pair of climbing-boots was displayed for twelve francs, or roughly one pound. She was tempted to go in and try them on, remembering Antrobus' suggestion that she ought to climb; but June was more important, and she walked on. Presently she found the Cantonal-Platz, a very small square, most of one side of which was occupied by the Hotel zum Goldenen Bären and its garden, as usual shaded by clipped horse-chestnuts; exactly opposite stood a rival hostelry, the Gemsbock, also with a garden. But there was no mistaking the one she sought, for in the strong sunshine a large gilt bear glittered—der Chrigl had been quite right—over the entrance. The small door stood open and Julia tapped on it—a middle-aged woman in black, wearing a grey-and-white flowered apron, emerged from the dark interior of the little hallway.

"*Grüss Gott,*" Julia said. "Could I speak with Miss Armitage?"

The woman, who had a pleasant kindly face, had smiled at the Swiss salutation "God greet you," but at the name "Armitage" her expression became troubled and hesitant. "I am not sure that the Fräulein is *zu Hause,*" she said doubtfully.

"*Aber ja,* I know she is! She has spoken with me only a short time ago *am Telefon,* and I wish to see about her foot," Julia replied firmly.

"*Ach so!*—you are the friend! *Ja, die Arme,* it does not go so well with her foot. Please to enter."

This interchange confirmed Julia's suspicions about how Borovali and Wright probably dealt with June. She followed the woman along the narrow hall and up two flights of steep stairs; at the top, at the far end of a tiny corridor, the woman in the *grisaille* apron threw open a door, saying —"Fräulein Armitage, you have a visitor!"

In a little, low-ceilinged room June was sitting in a small cheap armchair by a small window looking out over the Platz, her injured foot propped on a stool; several pieces of luggage, half-opened, with clothes coming out of them, stood about the floor. Besides the bed and the inevitable commode there was a washstand with a ewer and basin, a slop-pail under it; a small chest of drawers on which stood a cheap blurred mirror in a wooden frame, and a row of pegs for clothes along the wall in one corner. That was all—the Golden Bear was clearly a very simple hotel indeed. June greeted her in a way which Julia found quite upsetting.

"Oh, you *have* come! Well in a way I knew you would, if you promised —but reelly sitting here, I began to think I'd have to live and die in this room! Oh, I do wish I could go home!" As Julia went over to her the little thing stretched up her arms and gave her an almost passionate hug.

"How is your foot?" Julia asked. "Has the doctor seen it again?"

"No, and it hurts ever so. I am so worried—if it loses its shape I shall be finished for modeling! But I'm not allowed to go out, and Mr. B. says he doesn't want the doctor coming here just now."

Julia could well understand Mr. B.'s attitude, wicked as she thought it.

She pulled down June's stocking; above and below the strapping the flesh was purplish and unwholesome-looking.

"Dr. Hertz must see this," she said. "Just wait—I'll go and arrange it."

"Mr. B. will be mad," June said, half-alarmed.

"Let him be!" She heard June giggle as she left the room and ran downstairs. From a tiny office off the dark hall she telephoned; Hertz was in, but could not leave his clinic.

"Then I bring you one of your patients—Fräulein Armitage, this young English girl from the Flüss."

"Very good—it is time I see this foot again."

"Well please see her *sogleich*, when we come," Julia said firmly. "I think it is urgent, and we shall not have any time to spare."

"Agreed. Give her name when you arrive."

Julia asked the woman in black to send for a taxi. "I take the Fräulein to the doctor; her foot is very bad."

"But she should not leave the hotel!—those are the wishes of *der Herr*."

"If you do not let her go, I shall be forced to fetch the *Polizei*," Julia said. "It is essential that she sees the doctor."

The woman gave in. "Heinrich!" she called—from the kitchen regions a rather dirty youth appeared, and was dispatched to fetch a taxi. Julia went upstairs again, pulled a foolish velvet slipper onto June's bad foot, unhooked the pale tweed coat which she had seen at Victoria from one of the pegs, and helped the girl into it. Then an idea struck her.

"Where are your hats?"

"All in the hatbox, over there."

"Have you one with an eye veil?"

"Oh yes, a lovely one! I've only worn it once, when we went to a bank in Geneva. I'd love you to see it."

Julia was already pulling hats out of a vulgar tartan-covered hatbox, doubtless Mr. Borovali's choice, and laying them on the bed. "This one?" she asked, reluctantly admiring Mr. B.'s astuteness.

"Yes, that's it." June hobbled over to the dim little mirror on the chest of drawers, powdered her face, added—quite needlessly—to her lipstick, and skillfully arranged her pale hair with smart strokes from a semicircular nylon brush—as she watched this process Julia noticed that a much darker shade was beginning to show at the roots of the pretty *cendré* hair. Hm!

"Have you always been as fair as this?" she asked casually, while the girl was adjusting the hat to a becoming angle.

"Oh *no*," June replied, without the slightest hesitation; "lovely brown hair, mine is; sort of chestnut, with goldy lights in it. But for this job Mr.

Borovali wanted me a real ash-blonde so in the end I agreed. Mum simply loathed it!—but he paid me twenty quid, in cash, just for the color of my hair; and I thought that was worth it."

"It's frightfully becoming," Julia said. "Now stop titivating and come on down; the taxi will be waiting. Pull your veil down." Slowly, they crept down the dark narrow stairs.

Dr. Hertz's clinic was at the far end of the town, beyond the Bahnhof-Platz; it was clean and functional, with trim nurses in attendance, one of whom ushered them into a waiting-room deplorably full of patients—Julia followed her out into the corridor.

"Please inform the Herr Doktor that Fräulein Armitage is here. He knows that she cannot wait, and will see her quickly; we have spoken on the telephone."

The nurse put on the face of obstruction common to nurses the world over. "The Herr Doktor sees his patients strictly in rotation," she said smugly.

"*This* patient the Herr Doktor will see next," Julia said. She took out a card and wrote June's false name on it. "Have the goodness to take this to the Herr Doktor immediately."

"He is with a patient," the nurse said sulkily, barely glancing at the card.

"Naturally—I do not imagine that he sits alone in his surgery!" Julia said laughingly. "But you can enter and give the card." She could hear voices from behind a door a little way off, and moved toward it. "If you do not, *I* do," she said.

The nurse gave way, and took in the card; in a moment a short man in a white coat, with grey hair and a pale clever face appeared, her card in his hand.

"You bring Miss Armitage? Good—in five minutes I see her." He said this in English, and disappeared again.

In the surgery Dr. Hertz frowned as he removed the strapping from June's foot.

"This has been on too long. I arranged it for less than twenty-four hours, and it is now two days"—glancing at a card on his desk. "I went to the hotel on Tuesday, as arranged, and you had left, giving no address." He felt the ankle skillfully while he scolded, his hands more sympathetic than his voice. "Where have you been?"

"We went to another hotel," June said feebly.

"Then why not leave an address?" He pressed a bell on his desk, and a young man, also in white, appeared. "An X-ray, at once; and I want the films promptly." Another nurse came in with a wheeled chair, and June was propelled out.

Julia turned to the doctor.

"Is it serious?"

"I think not, but it is better to know. But what is this nonsense of changing hotels and leaving no address?" He spoke in the arbitrary manner of a clever busy professional.

"Just a nonsense, as you say," Julia replied, looking him straight in the eye.

"So?" He was surprised at her tone. "And this man de Ritter, her guardian—why is he so careless of her health?"

"Well, he just is. Therefore I should like you to inform me, exactly, about her condition, and what treatment she ought to have."

"You are a relation?" the Doctor asked, with a certain incredulity, studying Julia's beautiful calm face, and the indefinable distinction of her clothes and her whole appearance.

"No—just a friend. But quite as much in loco parentis as Mr. de Ritter," Julia allowed herself to say, thinking of "Mum," and again angry at how June was being treated as utterly expendable.

The doctor continued to eye her steadily and curiously.

"Then may I have your address?" Julia gave it.

"And hers? She is with you?"

"No." Julia thought quickly. "Dr. Hertz, I am going to take you into my confidence; and I beg you for the moment to trust me, and not to ask any more questions, for this child's sake. I would prefer not to give you her present address, for if you were to call there it might put her, I believe, in actual danger."

He stared at her. "This sounds like a detective story!"

"It is a detective story," Julia said coolly. "But if you will tell me, when you have seen the X-ray, what needs to be done, I will see that it gets done, somehow or other."

He studied her again. "You ask a great deal; but for some reason I trust you," Hertz said. "I will come to you when I have seen the X-ray; meanwhile I must attend to my other patients. Will you wait?"

"You are very kind," Julia said as she went out.

She sat in the waiting-room; quite soon the girl was wheeled in, giggling and saying that X-rays were ever so funny, and after very little delay they were summoned back to the surgery to hear the verdict. No, no bones broken, only a severe sprain. The foot should be kept up, but the patient should use it a little every day, to prevent stiffness. Hertz eyed June carefully—in spite of all her make-up she looked pale, and somehow slack.

"Get her out of doors," he said to Julia. "Let her sit in the sun and amuse herself. She is altogether below par."

"Very well. Thank you." Julia inquired about the fee, which seemed very small, and paid it.

Out in the street—

"Well now, as he says you're to use it a little, see if you can hobble along till we find a carriage," Julia said. "Then we'll go and eat cakes somewhere, and look at the shops." With Julia's arm to support her, June got along quite well—"It doesn't hurt nearly so much now," she announced. "You *are* good, to take me there. Was there much to pay?"

"No, hardly anything."

"Well I'll pay you back when Mr. B. pays me."

"Aren't you paid by the week?"

"No—he said he'd give it me in a lump at the end," June said. "I wish I *had* a little cash on me sometimes, I must say. I can't even buy a paper."

Just then one of the open cabs came by—Julia hailed it. "Where to?" the driver asked.

"To wherever they have the best cakes," Julia told him—the man whipped up his horse. "In Interlaken, if one will eat cakes one goes to Schuhs," he said. In fact, though Julia did not know it, the cakes at Schuhs in Interlaken have an international reputation. They went into the comfortable old-fashioned place (alas now pulled down) and sat at a table beside windows giving onto the Hohe Matte, the great grassy open space bordered and intersected by avenues of limes and horse-chestnuts which the municipal authorities, wisely regardless of building values, have preserved right in the center of the town—across it one looks straight up the Lauterbrunnen Valley to the Jungfrau, framed between interfolding pine-clad slopes.

June was a wholesome little creature with a healthy appreciation of physical pleasures, including food; but of this her experience was rather limited. Cups of foamy creamy chocolate, and Schuhs' melting deliciousnesses in the way of cakes—chestnut, caramel, coffee, or cream—were something she had never dreamed of; she devoured one kind after another, saying at intervals—"But this is ex*quisite*!" Presently, sated, she looked out of the window at the Jungfrau in her green frame.

"Now I call that a pretty mountain," she said.

"That's the Jungfrau."

"No! I saw it once on a poster, and I've always wanted to see it—I told Mr. B. so—and he said we'd see it in Interlaken. But you don't see it like this from the Flooss—and from that old Bear you don't see anything!"

Presently they went out and walked along the main street. June Phillips was just the sort of person at whom the window displays of the Interlaken shops are aimed: the bracelets of edelweiss in imitation ivory, the carved wooden bears, the handkerchiefs luridly embroidered in blue gentians or pink Alpenrosen—she was ravished by them all; the word "exquisite" was never off her lips.

"Oh, I *should* like to get that! I do wish I had some money," she said at length, stopping in front of an outsize edelweiss brooch in a glass case.

"Isn't it rather big for you?"

"Oh, I could never wear it; it's not my type at all. I want it for Mum."

Julia melted to her. She groped in her purse and found that she had 150 Swiss francs in notes, as well as some silver. She handed June the notes. "Here you are."

"Sure you can spare it?"

"Yes, quite sure," Julia said, liking this nice child more than ever, and more than ever hating beastly Mr. Borovali, who wasn't paying her by the week. In deed and in truth she couldn't spare it very well; she had left England so hurriedly that she hadn't bothered to lay on her journalist's allowance. But the Bergues had been very expensive, the Silberhorn was not cheap, and even things like her run to Merligen and this down to Interlaken mounted up. But at a pinch Colin could pay for the Merligen trip!

They went in and bought the brooch. June was rather tempted by a carved wooden holder for toilet-paper, which played a tune as one pulled on the roll; she shrieked with laughter when the shop girl demonstrated it, but decided against it. "It's ever so comical, but a tiny bit vulgar, don't you think? I don't believe Mum would care about it." For herself she bought nothing but a handkerchief embroidered in gentians of a deplorably violent blue; she got another of these and gave it to Julia.

"There!—now we both have a souvenir of how we met! I'm quite thankful I picked those silly flowers—if I hadn't I'd never have got to know you."

Julia was more moved by this than she expected. Out in the street June suddenly began to wilt. "Oh, my foot does hurt! Is it far to that old Bear?" Julia again hailed one of the open carriages trotting by, and they drove off. Glancing at her companion she noticed that she had pushed her eye-veil up to examine the brooch and handkerchiefs.

"Pull your veil down, June," she said.

The child obeyed at once, but asked "Why on earth?"

"Oh, it's so much prettier, and Mr. Borovali didn't want you to be seen much outside, did he?"

"No. Oh mercy, I do hope they aren't back yet. What's the time?"

"Only just twelve. Anyhow I'll deal with them if they are there."

"I *hate* this job!" June burst out nervously, as the cab turned into a side street. "I don't know what really goes on; I mean, it's all so peculiar. I believe there's more in it than meets the eye. I do wish I were out of it!"

Julia instantly tried to profit by this frame of mind.

"It must be very worrying for you," she said. "But June, can you tell me one thing? When you were at the bank in Geneva, did Mr. Borovali take anything away with him?—papers and so on?"

"Oh, I'd tell you anything! Where should I be without you? Lose my foot, as like as not! Yes, masses of papers was what he took—they were carried in on a sort of tin tray. There was two lots—one whitish papers, some with red stars on them; and then there was a great big envelope with *blue* papers in it. Ever so funny, they were, Mr. B. had them all out to look at them, and they had white lines, well sort of drawings, on them— he looked ever so pleased when he got those."

"What did he take them away in? Not the tin tray, surely?"

June giggled.

"No—a black sort of leather bag, like businessmen carry. Thin as misery it was when we went in, and stuffed out fat when we came out, like this" —she held up her small beautifully-shaped hands some six inches apart.

"Did *you* have to sign anything?"

"Aoh no—Mr. B. did all the signing. I just told the old gentleman that Mr. B. was my guardian—of course I called him Mr. de Ritter. That was what they told me to say beforehand, and it seemed all right then; I mean, I know it was telling lies, but that seemed so little to do for a month's keep, and all my outfit—and the pay as well. But now . . ." she paused.

"Yes?" Julia prompted.

"Well now I'm beginning to think there's something really screwy about the whole thing," June said worriedly. "It's partly Mr. B. turning so nasty lately, and keeping me shut up; if there was no harm in it, why doesn't he go on being nice, like he was at first? If people get nasty, it generally means there's something wrong behind it, in my opinion. What do *you* think?"

Julia had been doing a positive blitz-think ever since June first burst out about hating the job; wondering, given the child's extreme innocence and bird-wittedness, whether it would help her to give a guarded warning about the character of her two companions, or whether it would be safer to leave ill alone. She hedged.

"It does all seem rather odd," she said. "Did Mr. Borovali ever tell you *why* he wanted to be called Mr. de Ritter, and Mr. Wright to be called Mr. Monro?"

"No, not *why*. He just said that was the job. But if you ask me the real reason, I haven't a clue," June replied—so airily that Julia had an impression that the girl might be hedging in her turn. In any case she, Julia, who had such an ample clue, decided not to enlighten her as yet.

"Oh well, I shouldn't worry too much," she was saying when the cab pulled up before the Golden Bear. In the hallway she asked the woman in the *grisaille* apron if *die Herren* had returned? They hadn't, and she ordered June's lunch to be served in her room—"The Fräulein is tired, and Dr. Hertz says she must rest." In fact she put her to bed and then, as she had promised on the telephone, she unpacked all the suitcases, shook out the clothes, and repacked them, folding them neatly on the bed across June's knees and feet.

"Goodness, you are a lovely packer! Where did you learn?" June asked.

"Oh, I travel a lot," Julia said carelessly, going on with her work; June watched her in silence for some time, and then surprised her with a question.

"How did *you* know we went to that bank in Geneva?"

Julia straightened up from a suitcase, startled; to gain time she lit a cigarette. "Sorry—what did you say?"

"I asked how you knew we'd been to that bank in Geneva?"

"But June, you told me yourself that you'd worn that hat with the eye-veil when you went to the bank, and what you'd been told to say."

"Oh yes, so I did. But why did you ask me about the papers Mr. B. picked up? And what he took them away in?" The girl had suddenly turned suspicious, with the ready suspicion of the under-educated and under-privileged. Julia decided that up to a certain point it was no use hedging any more. She went over to the bed.

"Listen, June. You know as well as I do that your *real* name is June Phillips, and that Mr. Borovali paid you twenty pounds to dye your hair to impersonate a girl called Aglaia Armitage, who really has got ash-blonde hair."

"So what?" June asked defiantly.

"So nothing. I went to the bank on behalf of the *real* Miss Armitage, to see about her money, and found that some other people had been there before me and taken it away. That's all—quite enough too, I think, to make me want to know what's become of it."

"So you're a spy? That's why you've been nice to me? Oh!—oh, my God, what *am* I to do? Now there's no one." She burst into tears.

Julia waited and let the poor little thing sob herself out, her face buried in the pillow; she was distressed for her, but sooner or later this had to come out. Presently June stopped crying, and raised a sad and swollen face.

"Oh, I'm sorry I said that. I don't know whether I'm coming or going!—

and now my foot and all. I do *wish* I could get home." She began to cry again. Then, with a sudden flash—"But I must have my clothes and my pay!"

At this point a maid brought up June's lunch on a tray; it was ample, and smelt good. Julia arranged it all: poured out the soup, set a chair by the bed and put the other dishes on it, gave her a hanky to dry her eyes, and started the girl on her meal—to her astonishment, in spite of all those cakes at Schuhs June tucked into it with a will, while Julia finished the packing. Then she looked at her watch, and went over and sat on the bed.

"June, will you listen to me?" she said—"I shall have to go in a minute." Her mouth full, the girl nodded.

"When I saw you up on the Niederhorn," Julia went on, "I recognized you as the person who was pretending to be Miss Armitage; and when I went down to help you with the man who wanted to take you up for picking those gentians, I *did* want to get in touch with you, and find out anything I could. But then you hurt your foot, and we talked, and you told me about yourself; and we've talked again today. And now I want to help *you*. I hope you believe that. I think you're a good girl, really; and though you must have known that it was wrong to tell lies for money, I think perhaps you didn't fully understand what you were being used for."

June clutched at this.

"Well yes, I did know it was wrong, in a way; but the little they told me, I thought of it as a bit of a fiddle—rather a lark, really, just to show up at that bank and say Mr. B. was my guardian and Wright my fiancé. As if I'd marry *him!* And then to have my lovely outfit. But I am sorry now —I wish I'd never done it. You don't think"—again there was a return of that curious anxiety—"that it's doing any *real* harm, do you?"

Julia wondered what this odd little being meant by "real" harm, when another girl's fortune had been stolen.

"I hope it won't," she said soberly. "But we must get Miss Armitage's money back, you know."

"Oh yes, I see that. And you'll forgive me?—please do. I'd no idea it was a friend of *yours* that the money belonged to."

Julia could have laughed at this further example of modern morality.

"Yes, of course I forgive you. Now do look after that foot, and if you move anywhere else be sure to let me know—I expect to be at the Silberhorn for another ten days at least." She looked again at her watch— twenty to one; she didn't want "Mr. B." to catch her in June's room.

"Oh, I will," June said earnestly. "You've been so sweet. I'm ever so sorry I was nasty just now—all along you've helped me, whatever your reasons."

"That's all right. Good-bye, dear."

June held out her arms—awkwardly, over the tray—and gave her a long kiss. "You will forget what I said?" she muttered.

"Yes. And you'll trust me?"

"Oh, I will. Who else have I to trust to, out here?"

"Trust in God," said Julia, and went out.

CHAPTER X

INTERLAKEN—THE GOLDEN BEAR AND THE GEMSBOCK

WHEN JULIA left June's room she found herself in that little dark narrow corridor, now feebly lit by a single electric bulb, presumably left on by the maid who had brought up the tray; in its faint glow two glassy eyes shone out at her—startled, she went over to look. A stuffed marmot, rather moth-eaten, occupied the blind end of the passage, standing on a plaster rock; Julia laughed softly to herself—how Swiss! Turning from the animal, she examined the corridor. It only had four doors: June's and three others. Were Wright's and Borovali's rooms up here too, she wondered? Softly, carefully, she tried the second door on June's side; it was locked. Feeling that she might be taking a foolish risk, but unable to resist the temptation, she went silently back toward the marmot, with its silly seal's face, and tried the last door on the left, opposite June's. To her surprise it opened, and she stepped into a small room exactly like the one she had just left, even to the pegs on the wall in one corner; on these, carefully suspended from a coat-and-trouser hanger, hung a wind-breaker and a pair of pale corduroy slacks. Julia recognized them at once; she was in Wright's room.

Her heart began to beat rather fast. She moved cautiously over to the window, which gave onto a timberyard shaded by an immense walnut tree; beyond, over a vista of shingled roofs rose the steep wooded ridge of the Harder-Kulm, its pine-toothed crest cutting the sky like a green saw. She looked round the sparsely furnished apartment and now noticed that there was a communicating door with the next room, which stood ajar; she tiptoed over and looked in. In the ewer on the washstand just opposite was a huge bunch of Waldmeister; she pushed the door a little further open—standing at the chest of drawers under the window and methodically going through its contents stood Antrobus.

For a moment Julia paused, undecided whether to advance or retreat;

then, the fact that he was rummaging through what were almost certainly Mr. Borovali's clothes suddenly gave her, she thought, the answer to the question that had been tormenting her for days, and the relief was so great that she gave a little gasping laugh. The man looked round.

"Well, well, if it isn't Fatima!" This time the name didn't come like a blow at all; his voice was almost caressing as he turned to her. Still utterly taken aback, Julia came in and sank down on what was presumably Mr. Borovali's bed; the only chair was covered with underclothes from the chest of drawers.

"How on earth did you know they were here?" she asked.

"I didn't, till you showed me. I saw you and that pretty little creature, Miss Armitage's stand-in, driving along in a *Fiaker*, and followed you. At Cambridge I used to be a tolerable half-miler, but one doesn't need a great turn of speed to keep up with an Interlaken horse-cab," he said grinning, as he came and perched beside her on the bed.

"I think we'd better clear off," Julia said, suddenly nervous—partly from his proximity.

"No, we've got lots of time. They took packed lunches with them—I asked the old Frau downstairs." He was perfectly at ease. As for Julia, a dozen questions were battling for priority in her head—a rather foolish one came out.

"Why on earth do you suppose they leave their doors unlocked?"

"They didn't. But I happen to be rather good at opening doors." He pulled a bunch of curious-looking metal instruments from his pocket. "A burglar, you see, rather than a detective," he said gaily.

Julia was rather irritated by his nonchalance.

"Don't you think it's about time you came clean?" she asked crisply. "What you said just now about that poor little creature being a "stand-in" *sounds* as if we were on the same side; but I have to be sure. Can you give me any proof that you are? Colin doesn't know you."

"My dear girl, do relax," Antrobus said gently, putting his hand on hers. "No, your delightful cousin doesn't know me, and I didn't know him when we met up at Beatenberg. But he and I are on the same job."

"Then why didn't you know him?" Julia asked suspiciously.

"Oh, the two branches—the same initials, but different numbers, you know. We tackle things on rather separate lines."

"None of that is proof," she objected.

"You are perfectly right—it isn't; and you are also quite right to make sure. I see that you are every bit as good as Torrens says."

Hugh Torrens' name upset Julia afresh; that was still a sore subject.

"How does Major Torrens come into this?" she asked, trying to sound indifferent. "Do you know him?"

"Of course. He's rather big brass, whereas your cousin is very junior. Look, do stop worrying, Julia, and let me explain. Will you?" He asked this in a very beguiling voice.

"I wish to goodness you *would*—I think we've been fencing about quite long enough," she said.

"Very well. Let's begin with the birth of the Dragon, like the man who wrote the Life of St. George." Julia laughed a little. "I did rather wonder," Antrobus pursued, "what you were up to when we kept on meeting in all the relevant places—Victoria, and Geneva, and so forth. And when you seemed in such close touch with that girl up at Beatenberg, kissing her in the bus, I became definitely suspicious. So naturally I rang up London to make inquiries, and was put on to Torrens; and he told me all about the really splendid job you'd done in getting Dr. Horvath out of Portugal. It was you who arranged the hide-out for him with that duke who breeds sheep up in the North, wasn't it? At Gralleira, or some such name."

This really *was* proof, and Julia did at last relax, with infinite relief. But her next question surprised him.

"Do they know your name in Berne?"

"Who? The outfit your cousin works with? Of course. Why?"

"I do wish Colin wasn't such a *clot!*" Julia said. "I've kept on asking him to check on you there, and he never has. If only he had, I should have known where I was."

"Well do you know where you are now?" he asked, very kindly.

"Oh vis-à-vis *you*, yes at last, thank goodness!" But the form of the question revived her anxiety on June's account—anything might happen if Borovali caught them in his room. "Look, have you finished your detection in that chest of drawers?" she asked—"because if so I do think we ought to go. Merligen is no distance away—they might come back quite soon."

"Why should you think they have gone to Merligen?" the man asked, staring at her.

"Oh, just a little private detection on my part."

"Goodness, was it you who triggered off the Merligen thing?" He shouted with laughter. "Do tell me all."

"I simply won't, here." She got up off Mr. Borovali's bed, and watched with interest the meticulous care with which he rearranged all that worthy's effects in the drawers he had been examining, polishing the knobs and edges with a silk handkerchief as he closed them. Finally he gathered up the dripping bunch of Sweet Woodruff from the ewer on the washstand, and mopped the stalks on the bathtowel. "That will tell him nothing

—he'll just think it's his own feet!" he said, grinning. "All right—where are you going now?"

"I rather thought I'd like to wait and see Mr. B. and Mr. W. come back," Julia said. "But how do you relock this door? And don't talk in the passage, or the child will hear. Wait till we get down."

Again with deep interest she watched him polish the door handles, and relock the door of Wright's room with one of his skeleton keys. Halfway down the stairs—"Where do you propose to conduct *this* piece of detection?" he asked over her shoulder.

"There's another little pub just across the Platz, and I thought of having a beer or something in the garden there. It has a nice spindly hedge one could see through—I noticed it."

"All right—I want a beer, anyhow."

The other hotel, the Gemsbock, had a small garden enclosed in the hedge already observed by Julia; over its door a wooden chamois confronted the gilt bear. Julia sat down at a table on the extreme left of the entrance, exactly opposite the door of the Bear.

"Perfect," she said in a satisfied tone. "We can see everything, but from outside you can't see a thing—I looked as we came across."

"How thorough you are!" Antrobus said, as he sat down opposite her. "Now, please tell me why you want to watch these individuals' return?"

"To see if they've been able to drop the papers in Merligen, of course."

He gave her a long amused stare.

"You evidently know more about Merligen than I have yet been told. But how do you expect to know, simply from looking at them, whether these unpleasing creatures have left the papers there or not?"

At this point a pretty waitress in a cotton frock and a lace-trimmed apron came up and asked what they wished?

"*Bier,*" Julia said.

"*Hell oder dunkel?*"

"*Hell,*" Julia replied. In German "Hell" merely means light beer; Antrobus also ordered "Hell," and the pretty maid tripped away.

"Well go on," Antrobus said.

"They carried off the papers from the Banque Républicaine in Geneva in a black brief-case, stuffed out fat. If they come back with a thin brief-case, or none, I shall deduce that they unloaded the goods at Merligen; if they bring it back as fat as ever I shall hope that they've been stymied there, and still have what we're after with them."

"How do you know about the brief-case? Oh, the little girl. You kissed her in the bus to some purpose!"

"Don't!" Julia said sharply. Her relations with June were beginning to trouble her, they were so equivocal.

"So sorry. But what put you on to Merligen in the first place?"

"Well really, I don't know what the British Government pays you for!" Julia said. "I presume you draw a tolerable salary, since you run a Porsche on it, and yet you never seem to put two and two together. Don't you know that 'Corsette-Air' has their Swiss agency in Merligen? I told you and Nethersole how I met the little man who runs it in the train, just to make a story—and somehow I got the impression that you *did* know something about them."

"Can you tell me why you got that impression?" he asked, rather seriously.

"Oh, you looked so dead-pan!" the girl said. "People like you and Hugh never seem to realize that that blank expression can be quite as much of a give-away as registering emotion of some sort. Nethersole laughed; you didn't, till later, and that made me begin to wonder. I hadn't given two thoughts to the little man before that."

Antrobus regarded her across the table. "You are slightly alarming," he said—"especially because your appearance gives so little indication of these gifts! Well go on—my blank expression focused your suspicions on 'Corsette-Air.' So?"

"When B. and Co. left the Flüss Colin asked me to try to find out where they'd gone, so I went to Merligen to call on Herr Kaufmann at his villa."

"And what did you find?"

Julia told him what she had found, and how she had reported to the local police. "But can you tell me one thing?—*are* they watching that chemist in Berne? Because I do think . . ." she broke off with a sudden exclamation. "Hullo! Here they are!"

Peering through the hedge she and Antrobus saw two figures crossing the little Platz toward the Golden Bear—one with a greying beard, the other the young, sinisterly handsome, creature whom Antrobus had seen up at Beatenberg; he carried a black brief-case positively distended by its contents. Both men looked hot and out of temper.

"Hooray!" Julia said under her breath. "They've not been able to unload them."

"No, it looks as though you'd stopped that earth. But I'd better find out." He made to rise, as the two men entered the other hotel.

"Oh wait a moment, for goodness sake! There's something we must settle."

"What?" he asked rather impatiently.

"We must arrange something about June."

"June? Oh, is that the little creature? Why do we have to settle anything about her? She's an accessory to a major fraud, and as such liable to quite a long sentence."

"Oh, accessory my elbow! She's a nice, harmless child whom these horrible crooks have roped in—well bribed in—for their own ends, and they'd be absolutely merciless to her if she got in their way, or was a hindrance. They've been pretty merciless already"—she recounted their visit to the clinic and the state of June's foot.

"Oh, that's where you took her?"

"Yes. But look—when you pounce, as I suppose you will in a few hours, can't you do something about her? That ankle of hers needs attention—it's her livelihood."

"What a nice person you are," he said. "But my dear, I'm not the one to do the actual pouncing—that's up to your cousin and his show."

"Oh." Julia was taken aback. "Why?"

"I told you. I deal with the local people; Colin's lot work with Interpol and the Special Police, who handle international crime. We work in, of course; and that's why I really must go and telephone now."

"Who to?"

"Well first to Merligen, to find out if B. and W."—Julia grinned at the familiar phrase—"succeeded in getting into the Villa Victoria or not. Then I shall report to Berne; telling them the new address, of course."

"And then will Colin and Co. pounce?"

"I expect so." He got up, and then sat down again. "Really, I think I'd better explain the whole setup, as you seem to be playing these uncontrollable lone hands—and I'm sure no one can stop you! They'd be foolish to try, really, because 'the Fatima touch' does seem to produce results."

"What is the setup, then?"

"Twofold. Rather complicated. Large sums have been extracted by an elaborate fraud from a Swiss bank, and naturally the Swiss authorities wish to recover that, lay the thieves by the heels, and save the bank's good name. But we"—to her surprise he paused, and looked at her consideringly.

"Well, 'we' what?" Julia asked impatiently.

"You do know what your cousin is after?" he asked. "I don't want to be the one to tell you."

"Oh really!" Julia exploded. "No, I know nothing! Except that Colin wrote that some vital papers were in the bank along with the cash; and the Pastor spoke of 'the oil question'; and June has described seeing 'blue papers with white drawings on them' put into that brief-case we saw just now. So I deduce blueprints for a hidden pipeline, or an atomic-powered submarine oil-tanker, or something. But does it matter?"

"Yes, it does matter," Antrobus said. "However, you're so near the mark that it makes no difference! Well, our people aren't worrying very much about the late Mr. Thalassides' fortune, or whether the real Miss Armitage recovers it or not; but they *do* want those blueprints—and they don't want even the good neutral Swiss to see them. That's why your cousin's outfit must do the pouncing; the Swiss police can have the cash, but Colin and Co. must get what they want *first*."

"I see."

"Good." Again he got up.

"No—sit down." Grinning a little, he obediently sat down once more. "We still haven't settled about *June*," the girl said. "You rode off onto all this stuff about your separate branches. But when Colin's lot does pounce, what will happen to June?"

"My dear, how can I answer that one? I probably shan't be there. Can't you get your cousin to deal with that?"

"No!" Julia said. "That's absurd. As you said yourself, Colin is very junior, and presumably cuts no ice at all. *We've* got to do something about June."

He looked at his watch.

"I am so sorry," he said rather formally, "but I positively must go and telephone now, or I shall be falling down on my job. Where can I find you? Where shall you lunch?"

"Nowhere!—here; I haven't thought."

"Well lunch here, or anyhow stay here for the next half-hour. We might lunch together, and try to plan something for your little stand-in." Julia agreed, and Antrobus went off.

She ordered a Cinzano—beer made one so sleepy—and sat on behind the hedge, thinking where June could be parked. The Silberhorn was not much use—it was too close. Then where? Gersau? No—Herr Waechter was too old to have that sort of thing put on him. After a moment it came to her—La Cure would be the ideal place, if Jean-Pierre and Germaine would take the job on; and she believed they might. She went along to the little hotel, which was even humbler than the Bear; the telephone was in the open hall, but she had the good fortune to get Jean-Pierre himself, so the conversation could be in English. Julia explained, with calculated vagueness and no names, what her idea was.

"I see," the Pastor said at the end. "You wish us to house for an indefinite time a very uneducated English girl, who is connected with criminals. Yes, of course we will gladly."

"You're an angel!"

"Not in the least. I am supposed to preach Christianity; and what is

Christianity *about*, but things like this? When do you want her to come?"

"I don't know yet. It may be at rather short notice, I'm afraid."

"Ah well, Germaine always has rooms ready." He paused, and then said —"Do not answer if I am being indiscreet, but could this be *la jeune personne* who has recently purported to be my goddaughter?"

"Yes—who else?"

"Then *raison de plus* for my entertaining her!" the Pastor said, with his infectious laugh. "A godchild is probably still a godchild, even at one remove! *Alors très bien;* I shall await your *coup de téléphone.*"

Julia went out into the garden again. This was marvelous. But as she sat looking up at June's window on the extreme right of the Bear's front door, she wondered how on earth she was to extract the girl from that innocent-looking little hotel. Perhaps Antrobus could help, though he wasn't very sympathetic about June.

Before she expected him he reappeared and stood beside her.

"Goodness, I never saw you come."

"No. Back entrance—no need to be seen too often. Now let's go and eat something."

"Did they leave the papers at Merligen?" Julia asked, as he led her out through a back gate into a small alley.

"No—you fixed them there. The local police were lurking in the next-door garden, and they saw them and cleared off. That was rather inspired of you."

"Where do we eat?" Julia asked, turning the compliment off.

"Oh, a nice little place, in the main street."

They did not however walk to it along the main street. Antrobus shepherded her down to that delightful hidden feature of Interlaken, the narrow path leading almost from one end of the town to the other along the river bank, flanked on one side by backyards, gardens, walls and orchards, and on the other by the broad viridian-green current of the Aar, twisted into swirling patterns by its own speed. Close above the surface of the great river, swifts skimmed to and fro, the bronze of their slender bodies and back-curved wings vivid in the sun, in exquisite contrast with the color of the water. A little farther on, where trees overhung a backwater, a loud alarmed chittering of birds brought her to a halt.

"Oh do look! There's a whole family of young redstarts. Let's hurry; Papa and Mamma are in such a fuss, poor sweets."

"Birds, too?" the man asked.

"Only the commonest."

At that moment a train crashed along the farther bank, to recross the Aar farther down to the West Station.

"So like the Swiss to have the intelligence to keep the railway outside the town," Antrobus said.

"I was thinking that in Schuhs this morning," Julia replied. "God knows what they must sacrifice in ground-rents to keep that open space right in the heart of the town."

"The Hohe Matte? Yes. Of course you may say it's an enlightened self-interest, because of the *turismo*—but how *un*enlightened our own self-interest is! Can you imagine the humblest Swiss municipality allowing Adelphi Terrace to be destroyed, simply to get inflated rents for office buildings? But London allowed it."

In the main street, Antrobus led Julia into the garden of a small restaurant, as usual with tables set in the shade of trees. A waitress brought the menu. "Have you eaten Brienzerli?" he asked.

"No—what's that?"

"A strange little fish from the Lake of Brienz—rather like smelts. Care to try them? All right, we'll have those—and Wiener Schnitzel, do you think? They do them quite well here; the chef is a Czech refugee. What for an *apéritif?*"

Julia asked for White Cinzano.

"How comes it that you know that? It suits this climate so much better than anything else." While they smoked and sipped the fragrant aromatic stuff—"Now," Antrobus said, "let us make plans for your little protégée."

"In fact I've made mine."

"Already? What is your scheme?"

"Well you'll have to help with the preliminaries. She's to go to La Cure at Bellardon."

"Good Heavens! Will they have her?"

"Yes."

"Do they know she's the fraud?"

"But naturally. The Pastor said a godchild was a godchild, even at one remove," Julia said, with her slow laugh.

"He must be a remarkable person," Antrobus said slowly.

"Oh he is. Such a charmer, and absolutely boiling with Kafka and Rilke and all that."

"Kafka and Rilke don't by themselves necessarily produce actions like this," he said.

"Not? I've never read them," Julia confessed. "But when I thanked him he said—'This is what Christianity is about.'"

"Extraordinary," Antrobus muttered, broodingly.

"Oh, is it? I don't see why. Don't you know any Christians? I know several, and this sort of thing is really common form with them," Julia pronounced, thinking of the Duke of Ericeira and other people in Portugal. "Anyhow, have you never read the New Testament?"

While he was laughing the Brienzerli appeared; crisp little fish fried a golden brown, though with much bigger heads than smelts—Julia tucked into them eagerly. "Goodness, I *am* hungry. And these are delicious." Antrobus was hungry too, and they ate practically in silence; having finished Julia asked—"Did you get Berne?"

"Yes."

"When do they pounce?"

"Not today."

"Why not?"

"Because they rather hope that if they wait till 'the principals' come from the organization that is after the papers it *might* be possible to snaffle them too."

"Any idea who these principals are? Sheiks or emirs, one supposes; but wouldn't they be rather noticeable if they turned up in long robes and a silver-plated airplane or a solid-gold Cadillac?"

He laughed.

"They won't do that. The principals almost certainly represent a particular financial and political interest which supplies the gold Cadillacs to the sheiks and emirs."

"I see." She paused, frowning. "Yes, I see. Look, John, we ought to get that child away before all this starts." She stopped as the little waitress put the veal and salad before them.

"Have you a plan for her actual removal?" he asked.

"Not yet. It was no good trying to arrange anything till I had somewhere to put her; which I hadn't, this morning—and anyhow I should be rather frightened of letting her know of a plan in advance."

"Why? Is she unreliable?" His voice was cold; Julia realized that for Antrobus June was still simply one of a gang of criminals, a willing accessory to a fraud.

"Yes, completely unreliable," she replied readily. "Not from vice; it's simply that she's so frightfully *silly*."

"Then what do you propose to do? Just walk in and sweep her off?"

"Not unless those two murky characters are out of the way—I'm sure they'd shoot us both for tuppence! No, this is where *you* come in. You're in touch with the local police, who I presume will now be hovering nonstop in the Gemsbock garden. Can't you arrange for them to give me a ring when B. and W. go out, so that I can hustle down and collect June?"

"No, that wouldn't work. You see for one thing *you* are now on their list of suspects." He grinned at her.

"*Oh* how unfair! They ought to be grateful to me; and so ought you, and Colin's lot."

"I am," he said, suddenly serious. "And so will your cousin's superiors be when they have digested the facts—which I shall give them. But I don't propose to furnish those facts to the Swiss at this stage."

Julia munched her veal.

"I don't suppose Chambertin told them, either," she said, forking salad into her mouth.

"Chambertin of the Banque Républicaine? What might he not have told them?"

"Only that I sent him the photograph of the real Aglaia Armitage which was circulated. That's why Borovali and Co. fled to the Bear."

"How *do* you know that?"

"Oh, the porter at the Flüss told me—Mr. B. came down at the very moment when the photograph was lying on his desk in front of the police."

He shouted with laughter.

"Oh Fatima, Fatima! You don't need to open doors; everyone tells you everything! Not that I'm surprised, mind you—if I were a Swiss policeman or a hotel porter I should tell you everything myself!"

"Well I do think it's hard that *one* detective can't let me know when Messrs. B. and W. go on their next little trip," Julia persisted. "But if they can't I do think *you* might."

"My dear, if I possibly can, I *will*. Of course I ought not to, and I can't altogether share your affection for the little impersonator. Probably I shall be compounding a felony! But I agree that anyone would be better away from B. and W."

"Well give me all the notice you can," Julia said. "Bellardon is a long way away."

A clock struck from one of the towers of the two churches, the Catholic and the Protestant, which stand side by side at the eastern end of the Hohe Matte, the chime ringing out through the sunny hay-scented air.

"A quarter to three! I must race, or I shall miss my bus," Julia exclaimed.

"You've had no coffee."

"Can't be helped," she said, rising. "Thank you for the *lovely* lunch—and do let me know when Mr. B. goes to have his beard trimmed at the coiffeurs."

Antrobus had risen too.

"Would it be a great nuisance to take this with you to Mrs. Hathaway?" he asked, holding out the now rather drooping bunch of Waldmeister, which had lain in the shade on the gravel under his chair.

A chill of dismay struck Julia.

"No, of course. Does that mean you aren't coming to dine?"

"Yes, please God I am. But the longer this little herb is steeped in the wine, the better our *Mai-Kop* will be." As he spoke a horse carriage came clopping along—Antrobus hailed it, paid the driver, and handed Julia in.

"There—now you won't have to race," he said. She leaned out towards him.

"Why on earth did you tell that frightfully silly story about being a journalist to Mrs. H.?" she asked, rather anxiously.

"To tell you the truth, I lost my head. I do occasionally—in fact quite often!" he said, grinning at her—if a grin can express a *double-entendre*, that one did.

"Well keep it tonight—and think up some corroborative detail," Julia said urgently. "You can't fool Mrs. Hathaway at all easily."

"I'm sure not! I'll do my best." As she drove off—"Sorry about the coffee," he called after her.

Julia enjoyed the short drive. Her overmastering feeling was of relief at the knowledge that Antrobus was on their side. It would have been impossible—well, to let oneself go at all with a person who was in league with crooks; but as it was. . . . She didn't finish that sentence; anyhow, he was coming to dinner tonight.

On the Bahnhof-Platz the Interlaken Post-Autos always draw up next to a long set of roofed open-sided platforms into which trains clank across the street on their way back from the far side of the river. These huge buses carry both mail and passengers—hence their name. The Beatenberg bus was still nearly empty when she drove up; she got in and took the front seat.

"You found the Golden Bear?" the driver asked, as he gave her a ticket.

"Yes. It seems a nice little place."

"It is very small," der Chrigl said disparagingly.

"The personnel are agreeable," Julia said, irritated by his contempt.

"Oh, the old Frau Göttinger is all right, and she gets good girls to serve her—that is quite true. She is my aunt! I expect you saw her—old, and wearing black."

"With grey flowers on her apron?" Julia asked, instantly intrigued by the possibility of a link with the Golden Bear through der Chrigl.

The fair man laughed.

"Oh, those old black aprons with the grey flowers! She will never wear anything else. They aren't made any more, but I believe she has two dozen of them! You have friends staying there?" he asked rather curiously.

"One friend, yes."

At this point a gaggle of passengers arrived to board the bus; a train from Berne had just come in. The driver busied himself with their tickets, while Julia looked on idly, wondering how, if at all, she could use him and his aunt for information about Borovali's movements. Suddenly, among the group waiting to get in she caught sight of Colin, most oddly accoutered: shorts, a beret and a hideous tartan wind-cheater, with an outsize rucksack on his back and heavily-nailed climbing boots—the very picture of the native tourist on holiday. She grinned, and at that moment he saw her too; he gestured towards the rear of the bus. Julia turned and deliberately looked the other way. Drawn up on one of the further platforms was an empty *Wagons-Lits* coach with black-and-white placards at both ends; these, to her great surprise, read, "Dortmund–Interlaken."

"Goodness, fancy through sleepers coming here from Germany," Julia muttered to herself; she regarded Interlaken, though a bewitching place, as definitely what Americans would call "small town." The Berne train, clanking along towards the river and the Ost-Bahnhof, gave some treble hoots before it crossed the street; insular Julia laughed; she still thought trains running about loose in towns funny. She was relieved by Colin's prudence, especially in view of the driver's connection with the Golden Bear, though she was glad that he had come back. But as the bus roared along the flat road through the Interlaken suburbs, and ground its way up through the woods hooting its little tune, it occurred to Julia that with Colin at the Silberhorn tonight the stroll with Antrobus, on which she had been counting when Mrs. Hathaway had gone early to bed, might not come off as easily and inevitably as she had hoped.

This idea upset her to a degree that was rather frightening. Was she losing her head? She found herself running over in her mind phrases Antrobus had used: "What a nice person you are!" "Birds, too"—and what he had said about telling her everything if he were a Swiss policeman or hotel porter. But when you added them up, they really amounted to nothing more than that he enjoyed her, which men practically always did in her experience. She shook herself mentally; she was behaving like a schoolgirl!

The bus gradually emptied itself along Beatenberg's interminable village street. When it pulled up at the foot of the Sessel-Bahn Colin got off, and went striding up the path towards the station—Julia wondered what on earth he was up to. However after she had arrived, handed the now very withered bunch of Waldmeister to Fräulein Hanna, looked in on Mrs. Hathaway and reported this, and that Antrobus was definitely coming to dine, and was quietly brewing tea in her room, there came a tap on the door, and in walked Colin.

"Hullo! Are you staying here after all?"

"Certainly. Only I didn't want to advertize it, so I walked along the Parallel-Weg and popped down. Do I see tea preparing? Good—I'm frightfully thirsty."

"You'll have to have it in the glass; I've only got one cup."

"No matter."

"Are some of the others watching the airports?" Julia asked in a lowered voice, as they sat rather crampedly on the balcony in two wicker chairs, and she poured out tea.

"No. We hear they're probably coming by train now," he replied in the same tone.

"Oh." She was suddenly struck by the recollection of that Dortmund–Interlaken sleeping-car which she had noticed down at the West-Bahnhof. "From Germany?" she asked.

"Yes, almost certainly. But why on earth should you think so?"

Julia explained what she had seen.

"That could be quite useful," Colin said. "I didn't know about those through sleepers."

"Who will watch the trains?" she asked. "Antrobus, I suppose, as he's down in Interlaken."

"Why Antrobus?" Colin asked, in his most carefully neutral voice.

"Oh, he came clean this morning," Julia said, with her warm laugh. "In spite of your *total* clottery, you silly creature, I do now know that he's in with your lot—but how *idiotic* that neither he nor you knew about one another."

"He had no business to tell you," the young man said. "After all, he knows nothing about you."

"Dear child, he knows *everything* about me—Morocco, Portugal, and all."

"How?" he asked sharply.

"Quite simple—rang up London to ask, and was put onto Hugh." She reddened a little at that name. "Anyhow he was more or less compromised into telling me, because I caught him red-handed in the Golden Bear, going through Borovali's effects!"

"That's where they've shifted to, is it? In Interlaken?" She nodded. "How did you find that out?"

Still in a low voice Julia recounted the events of the morning, beginning with June's telephone call; Colin listened attentively.

"How I wish all international crooks employed such *morons!*" he muttered fervently at the end. "This June girl is a piece of cake! Of course they had to use her for her face, but she is God's gift to us."

Julia proceeded to tell him that God's gift must be got away promptly—

"before you start clamping down on those unsavory characters, B. and W."

"Where can she go?"

"Oh, they'll take her in at La Cure, any time."

"Good Lord! Does that delightful Pastor know what she's been up to?"

"Of course. When he and I went to the bank together he heard the whole story. He doesn't mind a bit."

"Good Lord!" Colin said again.

"More tea?" As she refilled the glass—"Why the fancy dress?" Julia inquired.

"Ah—well—perhaps slightly less obviously English. You see we think that Borovali and Wright almost certainly *won't* hand over the papers to their principals in Interlaken itself; much more likely on a sight-seeing tour of some sort. So when I tag along I want to look as Swiss as possible."

"Oh, very crafty! But how did you get hold of this idea of the excursion meeting?"

To her surprise Colin's dead-white face suddenly reddened like a girl's.

"Well—in fact—look here, J., I apologize for ticking you off last night about your goings-on at Merligen. My superiors took a different view, and they were quite right; we got some 'bugging' arranged for that chemist's telephone in Berne, and that produced this information about the meeting."

"*And* their coming by train?"

"Yes." Colin's face got redder still.

"Oh ho!" Julia said cheerfully. "So the chemist, all innocent, rang Mr. Kaufmann at the Villa Victoria, and he—or sour-puss Mrs. K.—rang Mr. B. at the Bear, I suppose. Did you get any date for this *Ausflug?*"

"Not hard, no. But most likely tomorrow or the day after."

"Ah—that's why Antrobus felt safe to come to supper tonight." She felt that Antrobus might have told her some of this himself.

"*Is* he coming to supper?" Colin asked, looking pleased.

"Yes—Mrs. H. invited him. She rather fell for him, and then fell away again!" Julia said laughing. "But look, Colin"—she paused.

"Yes?"

"Well, he and I might have something to discuss, rather privately, after Mrs. H. has gone to bed." Julia as she spoke reddened as deeply as Colin had done a few moments before. "So if you could contrive not to be too much in evidence, darling—"

He studied her face, more beautiful than ever scorched by the blush, with affectionate curiosity.

"Very well. Is this *it*, Julia my sweet?"

"Oh, how do I know? Clear out now, there's a lamb. I *must* have a bath."

DINNER THAT NIGHT was rather a success. Julia, who bought clothes so skillfully and so expensively that they lasted almost forever, put on the green brocade dress which she had worn at a royal wedding in Lisbon nearly two years before; Antrobus startled everyone, and delighted Mrs. Hathaway, by appearing in a dinner-jacket. He bowed over her hand, and expressed his great pleasure at being able to come—Mrs. Hathaway was completely mollified. Fräulein Hanna had done wonders with the Waldmeister, and the May-cup was delicious; so were the soup, the tiny local trout, and the steaks. Small the Silberhorn rooms might be, but the food was admirable, and so was the view—beyond the window the snows of the Blümlisalp turned a tea-rose pink, faded to pale gold, and then to a cold lavender-grey. Within the brightly-lit room the curiosity of the English party was aroused by a table close by, evidently prepared for some celebration: broad mauve-and-white ribbons were stretched across it from corner to corner, mauve-and-white bows were pinned here and there, and posies of mauve flowers lay at each place.

"What can it be?" Antrobus speculated. "What does one celebrate by half-mourning?" Julia inquired of Fräulein Hanna, and learned that it was a Swiss silver-wedding party.

"Oh well, I suppose half-mourning is quite appropriate for that," Antrobus said. "The onset of middle-age, and so on. After all, what color could they have? White is bridal; red—well presumably all passion is *nearly* spent; green—oh, perish the thought! And blue is too dismal—so far as I know no one has composed 'Silver-Wedding Blues.' No, I think mauve is very well chosen."

Mrs. Hathaway, laughing, agreed. She was pleased with Antrobus for taking the trouble to make this sort of civilized conversation; all her former approval of him returned. Colin sat rather silent; Julia put in a slightly *cassant* drawled observation from time to time—so as not, as she said later to Antrobus, to leave everything to him and Mrs. H.

For she got her stroll. After coffee in the *Kleine Saal*—Mrs. Hathaway was still too cautious about evening chills to risk having it on the balcony —Colin offered to escort the older lady to her room; when he came down he asked Antrobus to excuse him, as he had some letters to write.

"You two don't want a little chat about unfinished business?" Julia asked helpfully. Colin said No.

"We can have that tomorrow morning, can't we?" Antrobus said to the young man. "What about 10 A.M. in the Englische Garten?—you know, by the river, with the superb silver poplars and the monument to the man who built the railway up to the Jungfrau-Joch? I shall be sitting on a bench, reading the *Times* and listening to the blackbirds."

"I *don't* know, but I will find it, and be there," Colin said. "Good night. 'Night, Julia." He took himself off.

"Is anything upsetting him?" Antrobus asked.

"I'm wondering." She glanced round the small room, where two other parties were sitting. "It's stifling in here—let's go into the garden," she said.

The garden was empty; the graveled paths and the now clothless tables were clearly illuminated by the big arc-light across the street. Julia went over and leaned on the parapet above the hayfield.

"Colin worries," she said to Antrobus, as he came and leaned beside her. "Especially about his job—always. He's so keen. And I expect you've heard about the line-tapping, and that the principals are expected to come by train now, from Germany."

"Yes, I heard that this afternoon."

"Personally I fancy those through sleepers from Dortmund to Inter-laken," she said. "*Wagons-Lits* passengers give their tickets and passports to the attendant in order not to be woken up at the frontier; so even if the passport officials were alerted, they'd have a frightful job rousing up all the women with their hair in nets in the upper berths."

He laughed out loud.

"What a splendid scene! No, I don't think the Swiss would go as far as that—too bad for tourism! But *all* passengers, even in sleepers, have to tumble out and pass their luggage through the Customs at Berne; and there someone, I hope, will be keeping an eye open tomorrow—improbable— and the day after, and the day after that."

"And then give you a ring about people booked through to Interlaken?"

"That, roughly, is the idea."

"And you loiter with intent at one of the Bahnhofs, and tip off Colin, in his incredible hiker's outfit, who to follow?"

"Some arrangement of the sort, if we are lucky."

"Well can't you tip *me* off, so that I can go and snatch June while B. and W. are going up to Mürren or the Jungfrau-Joch to hand over the doings?"

He laughed rather grimly.

"Julia, I've told you already that I will if I *can*. You are so persistent!

—one would think nothing mattered but your little criminal and her ankle!"

"I'm not sure that anything else *does* matter, quite so much. Certainly not beastly Sheiks and Emirs and their revolting oil for revolting airplanes!"

"You're incorrigible!" he said, with an unwilling laugh. "Anyhow, I think I have a better idea. How would it be if I could arrange to have B. and W. summoned to the police station on some excuse about passports tomorrow? And meanwhile you nip in and carry off your meretricious little protégée?"

"How long could they be kept at the police station?" Julia asked, thinking of all June's clothes and make-up, and how slow the limping child was. "Anyhow she isn't meretricious; that's the last adjective to apply to her."

He ignored this.

"Say half an hour."

"Could you make it three-quarters? If you can do that I could work it."

"Probably yes."

"Is this a *hard* offer? Because if so I ought to ring up the Pastor and lay him on. He's frightfully busy always, and it's quite a drive from Bellardon to Interlaken."

"Oh do for goodness sake leave that till later!" the man said impatiently. "You can't talk from that hopeless box now, with those people sitting just outside. All this is so boring, really, and it's such a divine night. Come for a stroll. Do you want a scarf or something?"

His impatient urgency delighted Julia. It was indeed a divine night; too warm for her to want any sort of wrap, she said. They crossed the street and took the narrow little path up towards the Parallel-Weg, passing the cow-stable where the enormous Emmenthalers, chewing the cud gently but audibly in the darkness, exhaled the sane and sweet smell of cows' breath, delightful to the country-bred—Antrobus paused and looked in through the open half-door which a shaft of moonlight penetrated, touching some of the huge peaceful hindquarters. "Sweet beasts" he murmured. The moon was near the full, and its light strong; out to their right it illuminated the white-and-yellow hotel cat, sitting watchfully on the verge of the high uncut grass waiting for field mice. "I love that cat," Julia said, pointing it out.

When they reached the Parallel-Weg they turned along it in the direction of the Sessel-Bahn; the forest was some distance above them, but isolated trees studded the fields here and there, the moonlight throwing their shadows sharply onto the silvery sheen of the meadow grass.

"What is this tremendously strong scent?" Antrobus asked suddenly, stopping short.

"Rowan."

"What?"

"Mountain-ash I suppose to you. It's just coming into flower—the whole place smells of it."

"Delicious," he said, walking on. "Clever of you to know what it is."

"I think it so odd that you *don't* know it," Julia said. "After all, aren't you supposed to be Scotch? It's such an amusing tree—the great antidote to fairies."

"What *do* you mean?"

"Oh yes—in the West Highlands in old days practically every garden had a pair of rowan-trees planted at the gate, with their boughs twisted together to form an arch; the fairies can't go through that, you see."

"Can't they fly over the hedge, or wall, or whatever?"

"Apparently not—the entrance is the entrance, and if you protect that, you protect all."

"How charming. Yes, of course it's the same idea as the Chinese putting those short isolated walls at the entrance to their courtyards—the devil-dodgers. Demons can't fly or climb either, it seems; or even make right-angle turns."

"What fun! You've been in China, then?"

"For a short time—before all this Communist beastliness really got going, thank goodness. I'd sooner have positive swarms of demons than Mao T'se-t'ung!" He stopped again beside one of the wooden seats which the Swiss so thoughtfully place along their paths. "Let's sit," he said, and taking her elbow drew her down beside him.

Julia's heart began to throb a little. She felt shy and nervous, though this was exactly what she had hoped for all day—to walk and sit in the moonlight with John Antrobus. He had chosen the seat well. The meadows sloped away below them, broken to the left by the bends of a small stream which tinkled musically between flowery banks; from other cow-stables down by the village came an occasional note, deeper and even more musical —Swiss cows wear their bells all night, and any movement of the great beasts gives off this soothing sound. Away across the darkling lake the Blümlisalp stood up, white in the moonlight, above the dark silvery-velvet shimmer of the forest slopes in front of it. The air was full of smells: a resinous whiff from the pines up the hillside, the sweet breath of summer in the meadow and, sharper and more intense, the almost savagely pene-trating scent of rowan-blossom. Antrobus looked round; a mountain-ash stood a little way behind the seat.

"There's another of your anti-fairy trees," he said. "I shall always know that smell from now on."

"It seems to smell stronger out here than at home," Julia said.

"Practically all flowers smell stronger, and are more intense in color in mountains," he observed. "Odd, with their very short blooming season. Or perhaps that is the reason—*carpe diem*, if you know what that means."

"Gather ye roses while ye may," Julia replied readily.

"Quite so." He paused—when he spoke again it was hesitantly. "I have an idea that there are roses you and I might gather—together. But I don't know how you feel about it."

"I'm very fond of roses; they're one of my favourite flowers," Julia said lightly—but a slight breathlessness in her voice belied the flippancy of her words. He turned, and put an arm round her.

"I really do like you *very* much," he said. "Do you like me at all?"

"Yes."

"Enough for a kiss?"

"Well for a little one, anyhow."

He put his free hand on her farther shoulder and drew her round towards him, saying—"A little kiss? A butterfly kiss?" He brushed her cheek with his eyelashes, as children do. "A shower of kisses, I think, if they are to be so very little."

He gave the shower of little kisses in a rather absurd way, all over her face—cheeks, temples, eyelids, even the tip of her nose; but it was done so lightly and gently that Julia was somehow reassured, to the point that presently she twisted her head round and gave him a kiss in return.

"Oh sweetheart, that *is* nice of you. Are you all right? Happy?"

Julia was very much all right, and very happy indeed, but she was irresistibly reminded by his words of a sentence in Harriette Wilson's *Memoirs,* and gave her slow laugh. " 'Amy, Amy, does it feel nice?' " she quoted.

Antrobus gave her a little shake.

"What a monster you are! Am I so like poor Lord Berwick?"

"Well not to the point of being a peer, unless Antrobus is just an alias!"

He laughed gently, then settled himself more comfortably on the seat, and drew her head down to his shoulder. "Really, how very pleasant it is to be able to be together like this, at ease and safe, instead of on guard and suspicious the whole time. Don't you agree?"

"Completely. And all totally unnecessary, if the Secret Service weren't so *inept.* How idiotic of them to send Colin out here without either letting you know about him, or telling him about you."

"Oh don't *bind,* darling! I told you we're in different branches. Anyhow it's all right now—for goodness sake forget it, and look at the Blümlisalp."

They did this very satisfactorily for some time, talking a little, happily, with an occasional kiss as punctuation—Julia found his lightness of touch and his percipience extraordinarily delightful. But presently through the still air the little six-note tune of the Post-Auto came up to them.

"Goodness, that must be the last bus going down!" she exclaimed. "John dear, we must race back."

"Why?"

"To ring up the Pastor about fetching June tomorrow. They go to bed early at La Cure."

"Why?" he asked again.

"Because Jean-Pierre starts saying his prayers in the church so early; breakfast is at six-thirty, to let Marcel catch his train to school at Lausanne. And it will be nearly ten by the time we get down."

"I wish you weren't so conscientious!" Antrobus said. "No, I don't really; I see that, however surprisingly, conscientiousness is part of you. Well, one last one, darling."

But their last one wasn't a little kiss at all, and it left Julia rather shaken. When he let her go she hurried ahead of him, with her light graceful step, along the Parallel-Weg, and practically ran down the narrow stony path between its silvery wooden railings that led past the cow-stable.

"That cat's still there," he called to her.

"Oh, so it is. It's a sweet wussker." In the hotel garden she paused. "We'd better say Good-night now—when I've finished with the Pastor I must tuck Mrs. H. up, and I can't leave her too late."

"Good-bye, stern daughter of the Voice of God," Antrobus said, taking her hand and kissing it. "Though why a woman with a face like yours should trouble to be *good* as well, I can't think!"

Julia brushed that aside—she knew all about her face.

"What time shall I tell him to come?" she asked. "We never settled that. When can you have B. and W. dragged round to the police station?"

"What time would suit you?"

"Oh, *late* morning. It's a long run from Bellardon, as I told you."

"Have them there at 11:45, and not released till 12:30?"

"*Perfect.* Good-bye. Thank you for the Waldmeister—I must say it makes a lovely drink." She ran up the steps into the hotel.

The *Kleine Saal* was now empty, and she rang up the Pastor at once. "Jean-Pierre? Ici Julie. English please. It's for tomorrow."

He made no fuss, merely asked—"At what time?"

"Twenty past twelve—very exactly. Can you manage that? I made it as late as I could."

"Yes, certainly. Where?"

Julia hadn't thought where. After an instant's hesitation she gave the address of Dr. Hertz's clinic; it was in a quiet part of the town, and the presence of a limping young lady would arouse no comment. "Wait outside, would you? I shall be bringing her and her gear in a taxi."

"*Plait-il,* 'gear'? *Qu'est-ce que c'est?*"

"Luggage."

"Has she much 'gear'?"

"Mountains!"

His rich laugh came ringing over the line.

"*Ma chère,* your criminal friends are very unpractical! I thought burglars always traveled light."

"Not this one," Julia said, laughing too. "Bless you for this."

"You will not come with her? We should like that so much."

"No, I can't come now. I will later on; I'd love to."

She gave this answer quite instinctively; after they had rung off she wondered why. Because she didn't want to leave the neighborhood of Interlaken while Antrobus was there?—or simply because she wanted to see his and Colin's job through? With all the honesty she could muster—and Julia was rather honest—she realized that it had simply never occurred to her to leave before the papers were recovered. She went and tucked Mrs. Hathaway up, and then tapped on Colin's door.

"Nice walk?" he asked, with a puckish grin.

"Very nice," Julia said, grinning back—then she told him of the plan to evacuate June next day.

"Why you fuss so about that really rather unworthy little creature I can't imagine," Colin said—"nor why Antrobus gives in to you about it. Well yes, I *can* imagine that! But honestly, Julia, in this job it's much better to leave emotion out of it altogether."

"Oh really? Like Mata Hari, I suppose?" she responded blithely, at which the young man gave an unwilling laugh.

"That was passion—a very authentic and useful tool. But I can't believe that you have any passion for this June girl—whatever you may feel about Antrobus."

"Blast you!" Julia said, without heat. "Anyhow, though both you men seem to forget it, there is such a thing as charity—which is quite independent of emotion *or* passion. Good night." She gave him a cool affectionate kiss, and went out.

Colin left on an early bus to make his contact with Antrobus in the English Garden. Soon afterwards June again rang up Julia.

"I've got something to tell you, something I overheard. I think you'd like to know it, and I'd like to do something for you."

"Splendid. But don't tell me over the telephone. I'm coming down to see you this morning."

"Oh, how lovely! Oh—" a drop in the voice. "You'd better not come when *they're* here. They're out just now."

"They won't be there when I come," Julia said. She wondered if she should give a hint about getting packed, but decided against it. "Is the foot better?" she asked.

"Oh yes, a lot. Thank you ever so."

"I'm so glad. Be seeing you." She rang off before June could reply.

Well before eleven-thirty Julia walked into the garden of the Hotel Gemsbock, carrying a parasol tilted over her shoulder in the direction of the Golden Bear, concealing her face from any observers on that side of the square; she ordered coffee, and sat behind that convenient hedge, watching the small sunny Platz. As usual it was almost empty: a workman wheeled a handcart full of briquettes across it from the coal-merchant's establishment opposite the timberyard, and presently a neatly-dressed man, obviously Swiss, came walking in from the direction of the Bahnhof-Platz. This individual came into the Gemsbock garden and sat down at the table next to hers; he ordered a beer, and then opened a newspaper, but from time to time he too seemed to be looking through the hedge. At precisely 11:35 two figures emerged from the Golden Bear, those of Mr. Borovali and Mr. Wright—they both looked exceedingly out of temper. As they passed the Gemsbock the neatly-dressed man downed the last of his beer, put a couple of coins on the table, and rose and walked out into the sunshine—Julia, peering through the privets, saw that he was casually strolling along behind the pair.

"A detective!" she muttered gleefully. And she too paid, walked across to the other hotel and up, past the marmot, into June's room.

"However did you know they'd be out just now? They've only just gone," the little thing said, after giving Julia a warm kiss. "They've had to go to see the police about our papers—furious, Mr. B. was. But how did *you* know?" The old ugly suspicion showed signs of reappearing. "Are you in with the police?"

"The Swiss police? No," Julia said firmly. "Does it matter how I knew? Do you want to get out of this show or don't you? You said you did, and so I've come to do it."

"Go home?"

"Yes—quite soon. Not to England today. Yes or no?"

"Oh, *yes!*"

"Then there's no time to waste. We must pack your things and get you away before they come back." As she spoke Julia brought the tartan hatbox to June's chair by the window, and began to collect the hats which were perched here and there round the room—"There, now you be packing those while I do the rest."

This calm assumption of authority quelled June; obediently, though unskillfully, she began to pack her hats. "What a mercy you packed all my frocks yesterday! Did you know then?" she asked.

"No, yesterday I hadn't a clue!—I just packed them because you wanted them packed. Which case do your night-things go in?" The work went on; after some minutes June asked—"Where am I going? To be with you?" This with eager hopefulness.

"Not just now—my hotel is too near. You're going to stay in the country with some friends of mine, darling people; they'll look after you, and get a doctor to keep an eye on your foot." As she spoke Julia made a mental note to mention June's ankle to Jean-Pierre.

"English friends?" June inquired, pausing with a hat in one hand.

"No, Swiss; but they both talk English. You'll love being there, and I shall come over as soon as I can." She noticed the hat June was holding; it was the one with the eye-veil. "Don't pack that—you'd better wear it." She removed the hat and perched it on the ewer. June giggled—but she had another question.

"Will I be able to get a set there? My hair's frightful, with Mr. B. never letting me go out this last week or more."

Julia suppressed a laugh. Her brief impression of Bellardon had not led her to suppose that it could supply a set of any sort, let alone a rinse, which June would certainly want; the dark line along the roots of her bogus ash-blond hair was becoming rather marked.

"Oh, Germaine will see to all that," she said easily.

"Who's Germaine?"

The question brought Julia up with a round turn. Should she say "Mme. de Ritter"—and reveal that June was actually going to stay in the house of the man whom Borovali had been impersonating? She had never thought of that aspect when she arranged this hide-out for the girl.

"Oh, she's his wife—the wife of the gentleman who's coming to drive you over," she said, falling back on June's ghastly idiom. "Look, which coat? And what case do the shoes go in?" While she coped with these various problems of June's she was packing at high speed. When June was arranging her face and hat she went downstairs and spoke with Frau Göttinger.

"The little Fräulein is leaving now. Could the valet bring down her luggage? And a taxi be called?"

Frau Göttinger was startled, put about.

"*Die Herren* leave too?"

"So far as I know, not; only *das Fräulein. Her* bill I can pay," Julia said; she had borrowed a supply of Swiss francs from Colin before he left for this express purpose, rather to his annoyance.

The old woman drew herself up, a most dignified figure in her shabby black and her curious apron.

"The Herr de Ritter booked the rooms, therefore *he* shall pay the bill," she pronounced firmly.

"*Sehr gut*—as you wish," Julia said, smiling her slow smile. "But can one fetch a taxi while the *Gepäck* is being brought down? We are a little in haste."

Frau Göttinger bent on Julia then a glance suddenly full of meaning—comprehension? complicity?—the girl could not be sure. But Heinrich was summoned by an imperative shout to bring down June's luggage, and a girl in an apron stained by cooking was bidden to go and fetch a taxi. "*Aber die Schürze zuerst abnehmen!*" Frau Göttinger said, brusquely pulling off the soiled apron. "*Schnell, Luise.*" And five minutes later Julia, June, and all June's luggage drove away from the Golden Bear, that very *ungilded* cage; to Julia's surprise the old woman gave the girl a kiss, saying, "*Gott geh mit Dir, mein Kind.*"

"What did that mean, what she said?" June inquired, as they turned out of the square.

"God go with you, my child."

"Oh. Oh how funny." A pause. "Rather nice, wasn't it?" June said thoughtfully.

"Very nice indeed. Now June, we haven't much time; will you tell me what it was you overheard, that you thought I should like to know?"

"Oh, I heard the two of them, Mr. B. and Wright, talking about those papers we got from the bank, that I was telling you about. It seems they want to give them to some people coming from outside, from *Germany*, I think; and they were discussing where to do it—on the quiet, not here in Interlaken."

"And did they settle where they would do it?" Julia asked casually, though she was burning with interest.

"Yes. On a bus tour!" June brought out, with her usual giggle. "Mr. B. said there was a bus that 'does all three passes'—whatever passes are! Not passes at a girl, I don't suppose; not in a bus! Anyhow that's what they said—'the three passes tour.' And when these Jerries come—tomorrow, so I understood—Mr. B. and Wright will go on the same bus, and give them the papers somewhere on the way."

"Thank you very much, June."

"Does that help you? I want to help you."

"Yes, it helps me a lot." The taxi, Julia observed, was now approaching the street in which Dr. Hertz's clinic stood—hastily, she rode at her next fence.

"Listen, June. You know that Mr. Borovali isn't really Mr. de Ritter, don't you?"

"Yes, of course."

"Well to get you away from him—Borovali—I had to arrange for you to stay somewhere, and the only nice place I knew of out here was the house of the *real* Mr. de Ritter, who's Aglaia Armitage's guardian. So I've fixed that up, and we're meeting him now, in a minute, and he will drive you home, and he and his wife will look after you till I can come and take you back to England."

June was absolutely horrified—her reaction startled Julia by its violence. "Oh Miss Probyn, I *can't!* Not go and stay with that man. Oh, this is awful! Let's stop!" She started to hammer on the glass of the taxi; Julia pulled the small hands away and held them.

"June, don't be foolish. He knows all about it."

"Knows about *me?* Pretending to be that heiress, and all?"

"Yes, everything."

"And just the same he'll have me in his house? But that other girl that I'm so like, whose money Mr. B. has taken, is his godchild!"

"Of course. But when I told him the trouble you were in, and asked if they could put you up, do you know what he said? He called you his 'goddaughter at one remove.' Don't worry, June—it will be all right."

"Well! He must be someone!" June exclaimed. "I never heard anything like it; really I never did. But are you sure . . ."

At this point the taxi stopped outside Dr. Hertz's clinic; across the street Julia saw with satisfaction the Frégate drawn in to the curb, and Jean-Pierre himself standing smoking a cigarette in the sun. She jumped out and went over to him.

"There you are! This is so *very* good of you. But look, the little creature is in a panic; I had to tell her your name, and that you were the reality which her horrible Middle-Eastern slave-driver has been impersonating, and it has upset her terribly. So can you be tremendously reassuring?"

The Pastor wrung her hand, laughing heartily.

"How nice to see you! I only wish you were coming with us. I will do my best—it is really a main part of my profession to administer reassurance! Is that her, in the taxi?" He started to cross the empty street, but checked midway. "Good heavens, what an extraordinary resemblance! For a moment I thought it was Aglaia herself."

"That's what those beastly people engaged the poor little wretch *for*," Julia said moving on. Jean-Pierre caught her arm and halted her.

"But how could they find her? This is so strange."

"Oh, she's a model. She sits to be photographed for advertizements—mostly her feet and ankles—to display shoes. All they had to do was to ruffle through the files in the advertizing agencies till they came on someone reasonably like Aglaia. In fact this girl, June Phillips, really has *brown* hair; they had it bleached for this job."

"This is horrible," Jean-Pierre said, slowly walking forward again.

"Of course. The modern world *is* horrible, beyond belief; personally, I regard the atom bomb as one of its more respectable features."

Jean-Pierre's loud laughter at this observation was still filling the small quiet street as he approached the taxi, and this produced a slightly reassuring effect on June when he went up and opened the door.

"Good morning, Miss Phillips," he said, shaking her hand. "I am so glad that you are coming to pay us a visit, and so is my wife. All our daughters are married, and we miss them; we shall enjoy having a young girl about the house again." He told the taxi-driver to cross over and pull up behind the Frégate to simplify moving the luggage from one car to the other; the man did so. June had made no reply to the Pastor's welcoming words; when Julia went to help her out she saw that tears were pouring down the pretty foolish little face.

"June dear, what *is* the matter? Do stop crying, and come into the other car. You've got to drive quite a long way, you know."

"He's too good and too kind!" June sobbed out. "I can't understand it. I don't deserve it."

"Which of us deserves all the kindness we get? I know I don't," Julia said. "The only thing we can do is to give as little trouble as possible to the people who are being kind to us. Come on—hop out."

During this interchange the Pastor and the taxi-driver had been switching June's luggage from the cab to the car; when the girl got out and hobbled along to the Frégate Jean-Pierre looked at her with concern.

"But she is lame!" he said to Julia, when June had been bestowed in the front seat.

"Yes, she sprained her ankle the other day, up on the Niederhorn. I wanted to tell you about that—Dr. Hertz has been treating her here, but a *good* doctor ought to see it from time to time. Her feet and ankles are her bread-and-butter. She may use it a little, and she can get up and down stairs all right; but I'm afraid she won't be mobile enough to be much help to Germaine. I *am* sorry—I ought to have told you about this before, but I was concentrating on getting her away."

"That aspect is quite unimportant," he said, brushing aside any possible inconvenience from having a female criminal, who was also *lame,* foisted on his household. "As to her foot, it can easily be seen to; I often have to go to Lausanne, where the doctors are *hors concours.*" He paused.

"I'll get all that paid, of course," Julia said, thinking that in view of June's information about the bus tour the Secret Service, in the shape of Colin or Antrobus, might well pay for the child's medical expenses.

"Another aspect of no importance," Jean-Pierre said, quickly though smilingly. "Many of our doctors do half their work for love, as I believe yours do also."

"I dare say they did before the Welfare State came in," Julia replied rather acidly. "But most of that has been spoiled now."

"So? That is very sad. But I am thinking—should not Hertz perhaps see her before she leaves? Here we are precisely at his clinic."

Julia looked at her watch; it was exactly half-past twelve.

"There's not time enough to be safe. Anyhow he saw her yesterday. No, I'd rather you cleared off at once. Good-bye. I can't thank you enough for doing this. My love to Germaine." She went and leaned in at the door of the Frégate.

"Good-bye, June dear. I shall be coming to pick you up very soon, and meantime the Pastor will get a doctor to keep an eye on your ankle."

"The what?" June asked—the word "Pastor" had caught her ear. "Is the gentleman a Minister? Dad was Presbyterian."

"Really? Yes, I think it's all more or less the same," Julia said, trying vainly to remember how much Calvin and John Knox had had in common. "You can ask him. Good-bye. Thank you very much for what you told me just now; that may be quite a help."

Once again the little Londoner startled Julia.

"*You* won't go after them on this bus trip, will you? Oh don't, *please!* They both carry revolvers!—and Mr. B., he'd stick at nothing."

"No, I'm sure I shan't. Don't worry, June dear—bless you." She gave the girl a quick kiss, and turned and bade Jean-Pierre good-bye. With the utmost satisfaction she watched him maneuvre his car round at the end of the street and drive back past her, waving as he went. Anyhow June was sorted. One job cleared up, and a main one.

The taxi-driver was patiently waiting. "*Das Fräulein* desires to return to the Bear?" he asked.

"No, not to the Bear." Where should she go to try to put a call through to Antrobus?—she had his number. "To Schuhs" she said, getting in. Surely a big place like Schuhs would have a telephone box?—and please God with a door that *shut!* Like all English visitors to Switzerland she glanced anxiously at the meter as they drove off; to her surprise it registered only the minimum price. Julia spoke through the front window.

"You have been paid to the clinic?"

"*Ja. Der Herr* paid me, while *das Fräulein* was consoling *das Mädchen.*"

Julia laughed rather wryly to herself. Switzerland might be the oldest democracy in the world, but even among its taxi-drivers social *nuances* were recognized: she was "The Small Lady," poor June only "The Girl." As the taxi passed along towards Schuhs she caught sight of two men, one tall and graceful, the other rather stocky and bearded, turning down the little side street that led towards the Cantonal-Platz—Wright and Borovali, both looking as sour as vinegar. What would they say when they found their wretched captive gone? Poor Frau Göttinger! But she was well able to defend herself. At the sight of the two discomfited crooks Julia laughed again, this time with full-hearted pleasure.

CHAPTER XII

THE PASSES

THERE WAS a telephone box at Schuhs, and Julia got Antrobus at once. "I have a little news-item," she told him.

"Where are you speaking from?"

"Schuhs."

"Have you had lunch?"

"Goodness no!—I've only just finished off-loading the little party."

"Then why not come and eat something with me? Where we lunched yesterday? Was that all right?"

"Yes, lovely. I shall have Brienzerli again! When?"

"Now. It's not two minutes from where you are."

"All right."

She wandered along the walk beside the Hohe Matte, lingering to smell the newly-mown hay and to gaze up the valley at the Jungfrau; when she turned into the garden she saw, with a small throb of delight, Antrobus already seated at a table, two misty glasses of iced Cinzano before him. He got up.

"Darling, you've taken rather a time. What have you been doing?"

"Looking at the Jungfrau," Julia said, sitting down.

"Quite a good excuse, as they go. Now take your drink—half-way through it I hope you will feel strong enough to pass on your news."

Julia did this after a couple of sips—she was boiling over with her information.

"On the Drei Pässe Tour!" Antrobus exclaimed. "How ingenious!"

"Why?"

"Because on that trip the bus makes *five* halts: on the top of the Grimsel; on the top of the Furka; a long stop at Andermatt for lunch; a pause again on the top of the Süsten-Pass; and finally all the more energetic passengers get out at the upper end of the Aares-Schlucht, to walk through it and be picked up again at the bottom—after having coffee and buying picture post cards. So there's a vast choice of places for a brief-case to change hands in."

"What's the Aares-Schlucht?"

"Oh, it's 'a sight.' In fact it is rather spectacular. The Aar runs through a very narrow gorge between vertical limestone cliffs, three hundred feet high or more, and the water races along between them frighteningly fast— in fact everything about it is rather frightening, especially those unclimbable walls."

"How does one walk, then? Is there a beach?" Julia asked.

"No, there's no beach. To exploit the place the ingenious Swiss have built a little sort of gallery-path all through it, fastened to the rock on steel brackets, thirty feet or so above the water; it's barely a yard wide—no place for people who easily get giddy."

"It sounds horrible. Let's hope the other side have bad heads for heights! Not that that will worry Colin."

The waitress came to take their order; when she had gone Antrobus said—"I must get hold of Colin and pass this on. Your little creature has done us quite a good turn this time."

"Did he find you all right this morning?"

"Oh yes. But he was fairly sour."

"Why?"

"That's what I was going to ask you. Is he in love with you?"

Julia laughed out so loudly that heads turned in their direction.

"Don't make so much noise!" Antrobus said, with a hint of irritation. "What is the joke?"

"Only that he's engaged to Aglaia Armitage! I'm sorry, John—but he really can't be jealous about you and me."

"Was he never in love with you? That seems unlikely."

"Yes, I suppose a bit, when he was finishing with Eton and I was a pre-deb. But it was much more that we were tremendous muckers, and *did* everything together, as we had ever since we were small children. Anyhow all that is as dead as mutton." She paused. "Listen; June said another thing—that B. and W. always carry revolvers. Has Colin got one?"

"I shouldn't think so—no. They're such a nuisance at the Customs; draw attention, and all that."

"Well when he goes along on this tour I think he *ought* to have one. Can you supply?"

"Not myself—I don't carry one either. But I can get him one from Berne, I expect."

"In time? Do you know when this bus starts?"

"Yes. 7:30 A.M., and it wanders round the hotels, picking up passengers. I shouldn't think it would bother with anything as small as the Bear; I expect B. and W. will board it at one of the big places like the Victoria."

"Then he ought to have it tonight," Julia said anxiously. "He'll have to come down to sleep here anyhow, to be in time. Can you fix that?"

"Yes. If you will excuse me for a moment I'll go and telephone at once— then it should be here by tea-time."

While he was doing this the Brienzerli arrived, and Julia began on them —no sense in letting them get cold. When Antrobus returned he said— "You do fuss about Colin, don't you? Are you still in love with *him?*"

"Oh don't be such a clot, John. That was practically in our infancy! And would anyone of my age stay in love with someone who wasn't in love with them?" She said this with complete sincerity, but even as she spoke a little pang of anxiety struck at her heart. If Antrobus *wasn't* in love with her—and she couldn't be sure—would she be able to stop falling more and more in love with him?

His answer was not altogether reassuring.

"It's been known to happen," he said, with his rather twisted smile. "Anyhow I don't know what your age is."

"Do you want to guess? No, I hate rubbish about one's age. I'm twenty-eight."

"You're so *posée* that I should have given you thirty. But clearly you'll be quite as beautiful at forty-five as you are now; you have bones and eyes, which don't change, as well as your fantastic coloring."

This was in a way more open than anything he had said yet, and Julia's coloring promptly showed one of those modifications which so exasperated her. She changed the subject abruptly.

"Couldn't we go too?"

"Where? On the bus tour?"

"Well not in the bus. In your car, I thought—just follow on and be there at all these halts. I'd adore to go over those passes."

"Yes—I want very much to take you over them sometime. But I'm not sure that tomorrow is quite the moment—we couldn't concentrate on views and flowers if we are keeping lynx eyes on B. and W. all the time."

"Oh." Her dove's eyes mourned at him. "Oh John, couldn't we do some of it?"

"You beguiler! Yes, I think we might do a short run, but I shall have to check with Berne and make sure that they don't want me here."

"Oh do that!" Another idea struck her. "How do you think B. and W. will react to June's having flitted? I saw them coming back from the police station, and they looked frightfully soured—but of course they didn't know about June then. Do you suppose it will make them alter their plans?"

"They can hardly do that at this stage. In their place, I should be only too thankful to be relieved of such a liability as that little nitwit!—she's served their turn, and ever since she can only have been an embarrassment, even before she started turning King's Evidence to you! But I dare say it will bother Mr. Borovali quite a bit."

"Here is something else, while I think of it," Julia said.

"More information?"

"No." She paused, considering how to present what she had to say. "Did you tell Berne just now about the bus tour?" she asked.

"Yes." He looked a little surprised.

"Were they pleased?"

"Delighted. I was congratulated warmly on my 'local sources'!" he said, smiling at her.

"Fine. However, as you very well know, your local source is not me, but June Phillips," Julia said.

"My dear, so what? What's biting you?" he said, leaning across the table, upset by her change of manner.

"Money," Julia said firmly. "I know your people pay their local sources for 'hard' information, and often for information that isn't 'hard' at all— soft as putty, half the time! What is this rather crucial information about the bus tour worth to Berne? What would they have paid a genuine local source for it?"

He stared at her in surprise, his expression slowly stiffening.

"I have no idea," he said, rather coldly.

"Oh nonsense! Of course it's your business to have a very good idea," Julia replied brusquely. "You are *such* a bad liar, John! Anyhow I want three hundred francs for it. Probably miles below the real tariff, but I think that should be enough for my need."

"May I know what your need is?" he asked, a little less coldly. "If you are really short of cash of course we can help you out; you have done a great deal for us. Merligen, and the Bear, and now this."

"*And* the photograph the police used," Julia reminded him. "Personally I think three thousand francs would be much nearer the mark!"

"I don't disagree. In fact it is hardly possible to put a cash value on what you have done in the last three or four weeks. Only I didn't realize that you wished it to be on this basis." His tone was very cold indeed.

"I shall slap you on both sides of your face if you make any more remarks like that," Julia told him, in her slowest tones. "I hadn't realized that being offensive was in your repertoire at all."

He blushed.

"I do apologize. Pray forgive me. If I was offensive—and I see that I must have sounded so—it was because I am so taken by surprise at your raising the question of money."

"That's simply because you never use your imagination. Look—June Phillips, to whom the British Secret Service owes most of the information on which they have been, and tomorrow will be acting, has injured her ankle, which is her livelihood. She has got to see doctors, and they will have to be paid. I paid Hertz's bill here—myself. But now she's gone to people who are as poor as the traditional Church mice, and I want three hundred francs—damn it, it's only twenty-five pounds!—to cover her medical expenses while she's with them. Isn't what she's given you worth that?"

"Fully. Only you see she may be involved later in criminal proceedings."

"Well if you must be hateful, *be* hateful," Julia said calmly. "Goodness, what a creature you are! Anyhow I'm not asking you to give it to her, only to me—the so useful intermediary."

His grin appeared, again oddly accompanied by his fair man's blush. "How savage you can be! We both seem to be getting revelations about one another today." He took his wallet from his pocket, counted out five hundred-franc notes, and handed them to her across the table. "Will that cover your little criminal's medical expenses, do you think?"

"Should do. Thank you very much." She stowed the notes away in her bag, without the smallest embarrassment. "Well-earned," she said.

"Oh Julia, you are fantastic! You appear so sophisticated, and then suddenly you go and behave as naturally as a charwoman!"

"I like nature better than sophistication," Julia said, tackling her veal; she was glad to have got the money for June's foot.

Presently Antrobus returned to the subject of Mr. Borovali.

"We have an informant at the Bear," he said. "I expect he will let me know what the reaction there is to your little friend's departure."

"If you mean Heinrich, the valet, he's practically a mental deficient! However I dare say he'll get his facts from the chambermaid, who's quite bright, and I'm sure like all chambermaids peeps and listens through key-holes."

Antrobus laughed, but went on considering things from his own angle.

"On the whole I don't think you had better go up to Beatenberg on the bus," he said presently. "If this driver happens to have called on his aunt at the Bear for a free beer while he was down in the town, and hears that *you* carried that girl off, it might conceivably lead to complications, given the suspicions the Swiss police already entertain of you! And one never knows who is in whose pay."

"Thank God June is now in yours!" Julia said cheerfully, patting her handbag.

"Oh really! Anyhow, why not take a taxi?"

"To *Beatenberg?* It would cost the earth! And please don't expect me to start embezzling Miss Phillips's salary, because I won't."

He laughed again.

"You really are *quite* monstrous! I can't think why I should like it, but I do! Well, if you can wait a few minutes while I do some telephoning, I'll take you myself. If your cousin has gone up again—I'll ring him—I could see him about coming down tonight at the same time, and kill two birds with one stone."

"Poor birds—me and Colin! Very well."

"He is a ring ouzel, a mountain bird," Antrobus said unexpectedly. "You are a thrush."

"I don't sing."

"No, but you are rather thrush-colored, and your speaking voice is extremely musical."

While Antrobus telephoned Julia sat under the chestnut avenue along the edge of the Hohe Matte; the Porsche was parked by the restaurant, but he told her not to sit in it. Presently he came back and they drove off, spinning through the old wood-built town on the Beatenberg side of the Aar, where pear-trees, white with blossom, were trained up against the dark timbers of the houses; then across flat meadows into the forest, where the road began to climb. The Porsche made nothing of the ascent, and took the hairpin bends at a speed that startled Julia. "Nice car," she said.

"I like it, yes. It's competent—like you!"

"I'm not fast!"

"Well, you're not slow!" They laughed, once more at ease together; as the car swung up the mountainside they heard from far below the bus's theme tune, softened by distance.

In Beatenberg Antrobus drew up by the little *épicerie* where Julia and Watkins habitually bought sugar and Nescafé.

"Would you very much mind walking from here to the hotel, and telling your cousin to come down and talk to me? I told him I was coming."

"Not in the least—but why the precautions? We all dined together last night, quite openly."

"Well everything is rather hotting up now—one can't take too many precautions. Good-bye, my dear. I'll leave word with Colin where you and I are to meet tomorrow."

"Oh, *are* we going? Lovely!"

"Yes but I must concert everything with him first. Up to a point this is his show."

"Colin won't want me anywhere about," Julia said. "I don't think he's ever quite forgiven me for stalling him in Morocco."

"Well, in the last resort he must do what *I* say, here."

"Right—I'll send him along. Thank you for my good lunch."

Later that afternoon Colin—sure enough with a rather ill grace—told Julia that she was to go down on the bus which reached Interlaken soon after half-past nine—"Then you just potter along the main street towards the Ost-Bahnhof, on the right-hand side, till he picks you up. Kerb-crawling, I call it!"

"But you'll have started ages before that!"

"Yes, thank God! Julia, for Heaven's sake don't *please* go and do anything silly tomorrow. This is important."

"Yes—and who found out where this important meeting was to be? Don't be so *pomposo*, Colin!"

"Sorry, J. dear. You've been doing wonders for us. But you see this is my first really big job, and I don't want to bog it."

"I'm sure you won't, darling." She planted a forgiving kiss on his dead-white cheek. "The Lord love you! Oh—" she paused. "He *is* getting you a revolver, isn't he?"

"Yes. Was that your idea?"

"No, June's. She says B. and W. always carry them, and I don't want you to be at a disadvantage."

"It isn't usually done," Colin said, disapprovingly.

"Well I'm glad it's going to be done this time."

On reflection that evening Julia found herself disturbed about the scene at lunch. She was not pleased with the way Antrobus had behaved—was it necessary to put things so offensively? But she was not too pleased with her own behavior, either. Julia knew from long experience that when people lose their hearts it makes them liable to lose their tempers, too; had she reached that stage? the whole thing was on quite a small scale, but still it was disquieting. *Why* had he used that harsh voice, those unpleasant words, to her? And all right on top of their rose-gathering together on the Parallel-Weg the evening before. Somehow it didn't fit; there was a sense of something wrong somewhere. As she went to bed she hoped fervently that tomorrow's excursion might show her more where *he* stood; alas for her, she feared she knew her own position only too well! The words "or crossed in hopeless love" rang in her head as she went to sleep, though she could not recall either the poet or the poem.

Well before ten o'clock on the following morning Julia, idling along the right-hand pavement of Interlaken's pretty, innocent main street, was overtaken by the Porsche. In Switzerland traffic drives on the right, hence cars have a left-hand drive; as Antrobus pulled up she got in beside him almost before the car had stopped, and they shot off again, swinging left presently over the road bridge across the Aar at the end of the Englische Garten, to take the main road to the east along the northern shore of the Lake of Brienz. Julia had never been out of Interlaken on this side before, and looked about her with interest. Between gently sloping fields studded with great walnut trees and patches of pines they came to Brienz, a hot little town tucked into an airless cauldron between the hills; on to Meiringen, up the wide trough-like valley which separates the Bernese Oberland proper, with the great peaks of the Finsteraarhorn, Schreckhorn, Wetterhorn and Jungfrau groups, from the complex of lesser mountains to the north of it. On and on, till by several huge and quite ferocious hairpin bends they approached the summit of the Grimsel Pass. Water-filled valleys stretched away on their right, as steep-sided as Norwegian fiords; somehow they had a rather unnatural look, and Julia inquired about them.

"Oh yes, they're artificially drowned," Antrobus told her. "It's all part of the hydro-electric system. The Swiss have everything!—everything to make life *clean,* that is to say: limitless water-power to electrify their railways and factories; wood for building and for burning—no stinking smoke or grimy coal-dust anywhere. Limitless limestone for cement, limitless meat and butter and milk and cheese. If they could strike oil they would be almost completely independent of the outside world, except for coffee and chocolate!"

"Are they likely to strike oil?" Julia asked, as the car entered a cutting between high banks of snow.

"Geologically it's perfectly possible, down by the Jura. But they're quite lucky enough as it is."

The summit of the Grimsel Pass is a rather bare and forbidding place, especially when snow lies, as it did that day, in patches between the grey outcrops of rock rising from the dark and largely barren soil; to Julia it was rendered even more forbidding by the large numbers of parked cars and the swarms of tourists in bright locally-purchased woollen caps and pull-overs. Several huge motor buses were also drawn up in a lay-by.

"Can one of those be *them?*" she asked, ungrammatically.

"Oh no—they'll be over the Furka by now, heading down to Andermatt. Look, there's the road up to the Furka"—he pointed out to her the white loops twining up across a slope above the valley which lay immediately below them, a valley down which another road ran. "That's the great through route from eastern Switzerland," he said. "Now, shall we have a cup of coffee here? I've brought lunch for later on."

They had coffee in the small restaurant, with its racks of picture post-cards and steamy windows. Julia was impressed in the "Ladies" to find a spotless towel and scalding water practically on a mountaintop; when she returned to the single room where one ate or drank Antrobus was in jocular conversation with the landlord over glasses of Kirsch—another awaited her at their table. She sat sipping it, while the incomprehensible syllables of Berner-Deutsch went on at the far side of the room by the rather primitive bar; presently Antrobus came over to her, followed by the coffee.

"They didn't hand over the stuff here, anyhow," he said, looking cheer-ful. "Borovali and Wright certainly came in and had coffee—they're rather recognizable—and B. was carrying the brief-case, still very fat indeed! The patron *thinks* he saw them just speak in passing to a woman at another table, but he won't swear to that—he's always so rushed when a bus comes in."

"A woman!—what sort of woman?" Julia asked in surprise.

"Fat; middle-aged; ill-dressed; German, he thought. She had a little man with her."

"But would they use a woman for this sort of job?"

"Oh yes—and a middle-aged couple of German tourists is an excellent disguise, especially if the woman is the senior partner. So un-German!"

"Had she a *big* handbag? I mean, she'll have to have something to put the papers in."

"Oh blast!—I never asked about that."

"Can't you ask him now?"

"The patron? No, one mustn't go back over questions. I had to pretend that B. and W. were friends of mine, who might have joined some other people on the trip."

After their coffee they walked across the bare slopes, beyond the range of most of the tourists, looking for flowers. Little was out at this altitude so early in the season, but Julia exclaimed in delight over some tiny things only three or four inches high, with small veined white chalices, golden hearts, and narrow upright channeled leaves of a bluish silver, three to each stalk—she knelt down on the damp black earth to examine them more closely.

"How *lovely!* I never saw anything so exquisite. What on earth are they? Some sort of baby lily?"

"No, it's *Ranunculus pyraenaeus.* They are beautiful, aren't they? I'm glad you've seen those—they're not very common."

Julia, still on her knees, looked up at him with incredulity.

"John, don't be absurd! One of the few things I *do* know is that a *Ranunculus* is a buttercup; and they are yellow, and have *round green* leaves."

He laughed at her delightedly, as she knelt there on the cold sodden ground, her tawny-gold head profiled against the blue ranges beyond the valley.

"All the same it *is* a *Ranunculus,* darling." He stooped and picked one, and as he did so the delicate veined petals fell off, exposing the tiny conical seed head, still covered with golden stamens. "There—isn't that exactly like the heart of one of your yellow buttercups?"

"Could I pull one up?" Julia asked. "Mrs. H. would so love it. But if the flowers fall it's no good."

"One won't matter—let's find a plant in bud." He took her hand and pulled her to her feet. Presently they came on some plants with closed buds, and with a pocket-knife Antrobus carefully extracted one from the soil. He took out a small polythene bag and stowed the small object in it, closing the top with an elastic band. "Polyethylene bags are the answer to carrying flowers about," he observed. From another pocket he took a cardboard box, and put bag, flower and all into it.

Julia would have liked to go farther and see more—to say nothing of keeping close to Colin—but Antrobus said No. "We've sent a man up to Andermatt, where there's the long halt to eat, in case your cousin needs reinforcements there; you and I, I thought, would have lunch up on the Süsten Pass, and then go down and loiter in the Aares-Schlucht, in case they should come that way."

"Would they be likely to do the hand-over in a place like that?"

"You never know. Anyhow there's a bird there that I should like to see if I could."

"Oh—combine business with pleasure!" Julia said blithely, as the big car hummed gently down the hairpin bends.

It was a brilliant day in early June; the sun was so hot that in the valley Julia threw off her nylon windbreaker and sat in the open car in her thin pull-over—up near the Süsten Pass, however, she put it on again. The top of the pass was crowded with cars. Antrobus with some trouble found a space, turned, and parked facing downhill before they went off to eat their lunch, sitting on an outcrop of rock a considerable distance above the road. Up where they sat there was space and peace, but the slopes down by the road were thronged with people: hikers eating lunches out of paper bags, car travelers feasting from elaborate picnic-baskets; several parties had even set up canvas chairs and tables, and were eating at those—meanwhile charabancs came up, paused for five minutes, and passed on, ceaselessly. Julia surveyed this scene with astonished distaste.

"It might be the Portsmouth Road on a Sunday," she said.

"Well today is Saturday; this is the weekend traffic. At mid-week it's much quieter."

"You're *sure* they aren't in any of those buses?" she asked, as two more huge vehicles coming up from the St. Gotthard and Andermatt side maneuvred into a parking-space and disgorged a swarm of tourists.

"Quite sure." He looked at his watch. "We're at least an hour and a half ahead of them. Have another roll."

Julia realized that she had been foolish to hope for any manifestation which might make Antrobus' attitude to her more defined on this expedition—the teeming crowds made anything of the sort out of the question. She accepted her disappointment philosophically, and concentrated on two things she could always enjoy, scenery and food. Antrobus had rather surpassed himself over their lunch. Instead of the usual fairly tough-crusted *Brötchen* with slices of ham in them, hard-boiled eggs, and an apple and orange, normally provided by Swiss hotels, he had brought delicious squashy Bridge rolls lined with smoked salmon, *pâté de foie gras,* and Emmenthaler cheese; there was a polythene bag of fresh lettuce, and a box of Carlsbad plums.

"You do yourself well," Julia said, taking another *pâté* roll.

"Why not? In nice places, eat nice things. This is rather beyond my usual style, I may say—laid on for *you,* Julia."

"Thank you, John. I do like food."

"So I observe—and applaud."

After they had eaten they drove down again to the main valley, and on to the lower entrance of the Aar Gorge. Here a small restaurant was flanked by a large car-park, where Antrobus left the Porsche; the restaurant had a sort of open-air extension, roofed over and full of little tables, now thronged with holiday-makers—Antrobus walked past them towards the ticket gate.

"There," he said, pointing to a framed drawing on the wall—"that's what I should so very much like to see."

The picture was of a small bird poised, apparently in perfect comfort, against a vertical surface of rock, on which it appeared to maintain its hold by long curved claws; its beak was slender, and also curved. Otherwise, apart from rather defined light and dark markings round the head and on the wings, it was thoroughly insignificant.

"It looks rather like a Tree-creeper," Julia said.

"Naturally. It's his first cousin, the Wall-creeper—only this fellow has red splashes here, and here." He touched the drawing with his finger. "But this particular bird is rather rare; the Aares-Schlucht is one of the few accessible places in Europe where one may hope to see it, because the gorge is so enclosed. And this is unusually low for it; its normal bottom level is 7,000 feet, and here we are not much over 2,000. Come on in—there's a pause between the buses just now, so we might have a chance. He's rather shy."

While Antrobus got out a handful of coins to buy their tickets, Julia idly looked round at the crowded tables behind them. At one, fairly close to the ticket *guichet*, sat M. Chambertin. She touched Antrobus' arm—"Half a moment."

"What is it?" He was all impatience for his bird.

"There's Chambertin," she murmured.

For a moment the name failed to register.

"Who?"

"Chambertin, from the Banque Républicaine—sitting there, reading a newspaper. Do you suppose *he's* waiting for them too?"

Antrobus frowned, and walked back towards the car-park. "That wretched von Allmen must have told him," he muttered, vexedly. "He promised to leave this part to us. Has he seen you?"

"He's reading his paper so hard that I think he must have," Julia said. "Shall I thwart him?"

Antrobus thought for a moment. "Yes, do," he said then, grinning. "It may cramp his style. I've never met him." As they turned back towards the restaurant Julia saw, sitting several tables away from the banker, the man who had come into the Gemsbock garden the previous day and shadowed Wright and Borovali when they went to the police station.

"He's got his detective in tow, too," she said.

"Where?"

"Three tables to the right of the door—the very ordinary-looking little man."

"By Jove, so he has! Well really that is rather much, to bring Müller along! All right—go and accost him, Julia."

"Shall you come too?"

"Yes, I think I will. Damn, now we shall miss that bird! There are more buses due soon."

Antrobus watched with amused satisfaction Julia's manner of accosting the banker.

"Oh, how do you do, M. Chambertin? What a surprise to see you here! But how nice to meet again." Chambertin rose, quite as embarrassed as the Secret Service man had hoped, and greeted Julia fussily.

"I am on holiday," he explained, needlessly. "I have a little villa near Spiez."

"Oh how nice. Are you going to look at the Aares-Schlucht?" Julia pursued. "So are we. This is my friend Mr. Antrobus"—Chambertin bowed, with noticeable coldness. "There is a rare bird here which he desires to see. Are you interested in birds?"

"Not birds—no. They are not a subject of mine. I am here simply *en touriste*, sight-seeing."

Antrobus, still resentful that the Interlaken Chief of Police had obviously betrayed his information about the bus-tour, which he had given him the evening before, to the bank, now decided to add to the other man's discomfiture.

"Not even interested in birds of prey, M. Chambertin?" he asked, with a sort of deadly relish.

"In *no* birds, Monsieur." Chambertin raised his hat—of which the tourist effect was increased by a tuft of chamois-tail stuck in the back—to Julia, bowed, and abruptly stumped off into the restaurant with a cold *"Au revoir, Mademoiselle."*

"*Not* pleased to see us," Julia murmured.

"No—nor I to see him, and his flatty. This may complicate things." He looked at his watch. "Their bus is due at the top end in about half an hour. For goodness sake let's go in and see if we can spot *Tichodroma muraria* meantime."

"Heavens, what a name!" Julia observed.

They went in and walked along that strange little wooden pathway propped out precariously over the grey-green rushing water. The Aares-Schlucht is both deep and narrow; its cold, grey limestone walls limit the sky above to a thin pale line; a deadly chill comes up with the loud sound of the water racing by so close below—on Julia the whole place produced a highly disagreeable, almost an uncanny impression. "Why any bird should *choose* to live here!" she remarked.

"Walk very slowly, and don't make any abrupt movement," Antrobus said, taking a pair of Zeiss glasses out of the big poachers' pocket of his tweed jacket; he returned the leather case to the pocket, slung the glasses by their narrow strap round his neck, and then focussed them carefully on the opposite wall of the gorge. For the moment no tourists seemed to be

coming through it, and they walked slowly forward, Julia constantly looking at her watch, her companion incessantly scanning the opposite cliff.

"There it is!" he exclaimed suddenly. "Oh what luck!"

Julia, standing behind him and following the direction in which his
field-glasses pointed saw—a little ahead of them and rather high up—a
tiny bird, grey like the rock, but darker and splashed with crimson, with
white spots on its tail, fluttering about on the farther rock wall.

"It's not a bit like a tree-creeper," she said rather resentfully. "It flits like
a butterfly, it doesn't creep." Her resentment was partly an echo of her
disappointment with this whole expedition, as far as her relations with
Antrobus were concerned, and partly of the irrational dislike which she
felt for the Aares-Schlucht as a place. Once before, in Morocco, she had
felt a similar irrational dislike for a house and garden in Marrakesh—but in
Marrakesh, within an hour or two, she had been blown up by a terrorist's
bomb.

Antrobus ignored her remark. The bird was slowly moving forward, upstream; he followed it, and Julia followed him. "I wish it would come down
a bit," he said. "Oh damn, what's this?"

"This" was that the path now dived into a tunnel hollowed out of the
rock; Antrobus hurried through it, Julia still following—when they
emerged he eagerly scanned the opposite cliff. The bird, though now
abreast of them, had gone higher up than ever.

"Little brute!" Antrobus said, watching the small creature intently pecking at a thread-like crevice in the rock, clasped to the vertical surface by
its claws. He looked about him to see if there was any means of reaching
a level nearer to that of the bird. The cliff on their side was obviously impossible, but oddly enough behind them, close to the exit from the tunnel,
a slender iron ladder, reddish from the remains of oxide paint, rose thirty
feet or more against the rock wall, though for what purpose it was impossible to guess.

"Corn in Egypt!" Antrobus exclaimed. He moved stealthily back towards
the ladder and began to climb up it with slow, wary movements.

"It may not be properly fixed—do be careful," Julia said, alarmed
at this maneuvre, for the ladder was fastened against a bulge in the cliff
which projected out over the racing water below.

"No, it's quite firm," he called back—the noise of the river was so loud
that the sound of their voices could hardly disturb any bird. Julia watched
him anxiously as he climbed steadily upwards, pausing now and then to
raise his binoculars and peer at the wall-creeper which, having apparently
struck a rich vein of grubs or insects in the crevice, clung there absorbed,
exactly as in the picture, prodding diligently with its slender beak. The

ladder did appear to be quite firm, and one way and another Julia felt that the bird was becoming rather a bore—reassured, she stopped watching Antrobus, and looked about her.

Some hundred yards away, coming downstream towards her along the narrow plank-walk, where two people could barely walk abreast, she saw Mr. Borovali, moving partly behind a stout woman in a hideous tartan coat, with an enormous tartan shoulder-bag slung over her arm; a short distance behind them came Wright and a small man with a broad Teutonic face, who, like Chambertin, wore a green felt hat with a chamois-tail stuck in the back. Wright was carrying the black brief-case, still distended.

"Yes, do the switch-over in the tunnel!—I see!" she muttered to herself as she returned to the foot of the ladder; there she called up urgently to Antrobus, who had now reached the top and was staring entranced through his Zeisses at *Tichodroma muraria*.

"John, here they are!"

No response. In her fresh and different anxiety she actually shook the ladder. "John, they're *here!* Do come down."

At this moment an immensely loud tune suddenly blared out from somewhere close by, filling the chasm and echoing from wall to wall. This, though Julia could not know it, was produced by a young man round a bend in the gorge blowing the *Alpen-Horn,* a musical instrument nearly ten feet long whose principal if not its only merit is the enormous volume of sound which it can produce. As these trumpet-notes suddenly echoed and re-echoed between the high walls of the narrow cleft, three things happened more or less at the same moment. The stout lady came to a halt, looked behind her, and started to walk back in the direction whence the sound came, followed by Borovali, who laid a restraining hand on her arm, clearly trying to stop her. Antrobus started, and nearly lost his balance on the ladder; the wall-creeper flew away.

CHAPTER XIII

THE AARES-SCHLUCHT

JULIA, CONVULSED with unseasonable laughter, once more called up from the foot of the ladder, shaking it—

"John, do please come down! They're *here!*"

"Why on earth must the municipality cause anyone to make that filthy row? Now it's gone," he said indignantly, starting to climb down. Naturally he had to do this backwards, and therefore could not see, as Julia did, what was taking place on the plank-walk some distance upstream. The stout lady, apparently determined to go back and see the *Alpen-Horn* in action, steadily returned on her tracks, ignoring Borovali's imploring gestures, but within twenty yards she came face to face with Wright and his short Germanic-looking companion. The wooden path was so narrow that it was impossible for people to pass one another without good will on both sides, including a certain flattening of the person against either the rock wall or the rail overhanging the water—and Wright displayed no such good will. On the contrary, he stood scowling, effectively blocking the stout woman's path. There was an altercation, diagramatically visible to Julia, though of course inaudible because of the roaring noise of the river; arms were raised in angry gestures, the woman tried to push past, Wright continued to obstruct her, Borovali wrung his hands. While this was going on Julia saw Colin coming round the bend in the gorge and approaching the other group.

"Now, what were you shouting about?" Antrobus asked Julia, wiping traces of red paint off his hands with a tuft of grass snatched from the rock-face. "I couldn't hear a thing."

"Look," Julia said, pointing.

The four people now formed a sort of angry knot, completely blocking the cat-walk.

"Which of them has the stuff, Wright or the woman?" Antrobus asked hastily.

"How should *I* know? He's still got the brief-case, but she has a bag big enough to hold the Treaty of Versailles," Julia replied.

Antrobus started forward towards the group as Colin bore down on them from behind, but they were all so engrossed in their altercation that they never noticed the two Englishmen till they were almost upon them. Colin, saying *"Verzeihung"* and *"Pardon"* very politely, pushed right in among them, and with a swift movement wrenched the black brief-case out of Wright's hand; the next second he was racing away in the direction whence he had come. Wright whipped out a revolver from the pocket of those pale corduroy slacks which Julia had so recently seen hanging up in a bedroom in the Golden Bear; but Antrobus leapt onto the slender rail like a cat, took one step along it past the three solid bodies of Borovali, the German man and the German woman, and even as he sprang down behind them onto the plank-walk knocked up Wright's wrist—a little pale puff of limestone dust showed where the bullet had hit harmlessly on the cliff overhead.

Wright, furious, instantly tried to turn the revolver onto him; Antrobus struggled to wrest it out of the other's hand—they grappled confusedly on the narrow path. The stout woman now took a hand; raising her enormous tartan bag she bashed at Antrobus' head with it—Antrobus ducked. The bag was one of those open-topped ones, and out of it now fell, not the Treaty of Versailles or any other documents, but a positive shower of packets of chocolate, bags of biscuits—which burst—oranges, bananas, and some knitting; finally a tiny pistol dropped onto the planking among the edibles. This, with a quick movement of one foot, Antrobus kicked off the boards into the river, while he went on wrestling with Wright for the possession of his revolver.

Meanwhile Julia, who had come forward from the foot of the ladder to watch what was going on, saw that Colin's get-away with the black brief-case was hopelessly blocked by some twenty tourists, who now came round the bend in the gorge, whence the *Alpen-Horn* continued to blare out its cheerful notes, in a solid block. He checked, looked behind him, saw her, and came running back, right up to the others.

"Over to you, darling," he shouted above the roar of the river, and pitched the black brief-case clean over all their heads; it fell with a plonk on the boards at Julia's feet.

But there were more than two revolvers in that party—June had been quite right. Mr. Borovali now extracted one, not without trouble, from somewhere about his stout person, and called out—"Please put up your hands, all of you. I am armed."

Antrobus paid no attention whatever to this; he was entirely concentrated on his struggle with Wright, who was as muscular and elastic as an eel. "Look out, John!" Julia called to him, snatching up the brief-case as she spoke. But just then a second revolver shot rang out. For a moment Julia thought that Borovali had fired, but she was wrong; Wright had managed to put a shot through Antrobus' leg. Antrobus lost his temper, and exerting the unnatural strength of fury and self-preservation heaved the younger and lighter man up and pitched him bodily, revolver and all, over the railing into the swirling Aar below—the onlookers saw the dark head sink, rise, sink again, rise again, as he was whirled along between the rocks; he was attempting feebly to swim when the green waters bore him out of sight round the bulge in the cliff against which the ladder stood.

Again several things happened more or less at once. Julia, ignoring Wright in the river, from behind twitched Borovali's revolver from his outstretched hand while he stood staring dazedly at his colleague in the water, and slipped it into the pocket of her windbreaker; Colin hurried up to Antrobus; the group of tourists, hearing revolver shots and seeing a man thrown into the river, recoiled, pressing one another backwards—all but one burly individual, who thrust his way to the front demanding, in the unmistakable tones of an English policeman—"What goes on 'ere?"

No one paid much attention to him. Antrobus had sunk down on one knee; from the trouser on his other leg, stuck out awkwardly in front of him, blood was streaming over the plank walk, soaking into the biscuits and packets of chocolate from the German woman's bag. Julia, in an agony, called out "Oh Colin, do see how bad it is."

Antrobus heard her.

"Clear off, Julia—the key's in the car. Take that thing away—Colin will see to me."

This told Julia that Antrobus, in spite of his struggles with Wright, realized that Colin had passed her the black brief-case. For a moment she hesitated—there was John, pouring with blood before her eyes; could she leave him? It was in fact Borovali who decided her to do what Antrobus asked—he wheeled round on her, saying—"It is you who took my weapon?"

"Goodness no! What weapon?" But Julia was full of a blind instinctive rage—at the injury to Antrobus, and at all these crooks who had brought it about; above all she was furious with the German woman. Even as she spoke she nipped past Borovali and snatched the vast tartan bag off the fat creature's arm, and then turned and ran like a deer down the plank-walk into the tunnel, leaving the others staring after her.

She ran all the way through the tunnel too—only when she was approaching the exit did she slow down. Oh gracious, would the man want her ticket? John had got them. But the official at the gate was busy with a swarm of tourists eager to enter, and when she said, "Just now I came in with the *Englische Herr*," he let her pass.

In the open restaurant the first person she saw was Chambertin, no longer sitting at a table but standing talking with two other men, one of whom she recognized as Müller, the detective who had sat in the Gemsbock garden, and shadowed Wright and Borovali to the police station. She hurried over to them.

"M. Chambertin, can you get hold of a doctor? Mr. Antrobus has been shot."

"Shot? Where?"

"In the leg," Julia said idiotically, thinking only of Antrobus.

"But in what circumstances?" Chambertin asked, looking concerned.

"Oh, by those ruffians in there—in the gorge. And one of them is in the river," she added needlessly, with a rather hysterical laugh.

The man who was not Müller rounded sharply on her.

"How came he in the river, Fräulein?"

"Oh, go in and ask! There are dozens of people in there who saw it all." She turned to Chambertin. "But do get a doctor quickly, can't you? He may bleed to death," she said urgently, and started away towards the car-park.

Chambertin followed her, and while she was fiddling with the controls on the dashboard of Antrobus' big Porsche, all completely unfamiliar to her, he poked his head in at the window.

"And you, Mademoiselle? Where do you go now?"

"But to my hotel. I have a friend there, an English lady, who is unwell. I must get back to her."

"Your hotel is in Interlaken?"

Julia noticed that the man who had asked her how Wright came to be in the river had also come up to the car, and stood beside Chambertin, listening intently. Was this the Swiss police chief, von Allmen or whatever his name was, who had given away the business of the bus tour to Chambertin? Anyhow she could only speak the truth.

"No, up at Beatenberg—the Silberhorn. Good-bye, Monsieur Chambertin—do *please* get a doctor at once." She let in the clutch and shot away out of the car-park.

Spinning down the road towards Meiringen, through it, and on towards Brienz, Julia, in spite of her anxiety about Antrobus, began to do some hard thinking. Since she had got both the brief-case and the German lady's tartan bag presumably she had got the papers, there on the seat beside her in the car—including the documents which John didn't want the Swiss police to see. And John had entrusted her with the job of taking them away, and "clearing off." Well, she *had* cleared off; but she would like to find out as soon as possible if she really had got "the doings," as she privately phrased it; and then she must think of somewhere to put them. If the third man with Chambertin was the Interlaken Chief of Police, or any form of police, he now knew her address, and nothing could stop him from searching the hotel. Oh dear!

Brienz has a rather narrow street, which on fine weekends is apt to be packed with cars. Julia was more than once brought to a halt where single-line traffic was coming towards her—and she noticed in her driving-mirror that a small grey Volkswagen, with two men in it, was immediately behind her. Through Brienz, in the open country beyond, she slowed down with the idea of looking at the contents of the two cases, and waved the grey Volkswagen on. But it did not pass her—it slowed down too. "Oh, bloody police car, I suppose," she muttered irritably, and shot on again.

The Porsche, if pressed, had the legs of the Volkswagen; Julia pressed it, and soon left the smaller car behind and out of sight. Then she again thought hard. Where could she go, short of the Hotel Silberhorn, to examine the contents of the two bags without interruption?

The inside of a ladies' lavatory is one of the few places where a woman can be certain of being alone and undisturbed, and as Julia drove along the shore of the Lake of Brienz she remembered the large, exquisitely clean "Ladies" in the Hotel zŭm Flüss at Interlaken, which she had visited when she brought Mrs. Hathaway down from the Schynige Platte. The very thing!—moreover it was not on the direct route to Beatenberg, but lay in the opposite direction, involving a double-back on her tracks, which might throw those snoopers in the grey car off the scent. Grinning with satisfaction, she swung over the road bridge across the Aar at Interlaken, turned left, and passing the Englische Garten with its dull statue and its beautiful silver poplars pulled into the open car-park where the Brienz steamers have their landing-stage. The *"DAMEN"* at the Flüss had, she remembered, a separate entrance giving on to this; no need to go through the lounge past the chatty old porter. Grasping both bags, Julia hastened in at the side door, through the outer washroom, and into one of the actual lavatories; there she bolted the door and began to examine her booty.

She had worried rather on her way as to whether the black brief-case might be locked, but it wasn't; the two clips sprang up at the touch of her fingers. Eagerly she raised the flap and looked in—to see large quantities of old newspapers! Then it occurred to her that the documents might have been wrapped in these, and she hastily unfolded and shook out every single copy of the *Journal de Genève*, the *Gazette de Lausanne*, and the *Continental Daily Mail*, thinking as she did so that these must represent Borovali's and Wright's tastes in newspapers respectively. No—only newspapers. Could everything have gone wrong, and John been wounded for nothing? However there remained the German lady's tartan bag—she had already noticed as she carried it in from the car that in spite of the loss of all those comestibles which had been poured out in the Aares-Schlucht it did not feel like an *empty* bag; in fact it was quite heavy. (At the Aares-Schlucht she had been too hurried and upset to notice anything.) Stuffing the useless newspapers behind the lavatory seat, Julia, her fingers actually trembling, tackled the tartan bag.

In it, just below the broad imitation-leather band which bound the open top there was a second compartment with a zip fastener, running the whole length of one side of the bag. The zip was secured with a silly little imitation-gilt padlock, but it was a cheaply-made affair; Julia fished a tiny nail-file out of her handbag, slipped it through the ring of the padlock, and wrapping her handkerchief round her fingers wrenched the thing off, and pulled back the zip.

Inside she found a very large, stiff, shiny envelope, heavily sealed with black wax; as well, bundles and bundles of papers, folded narrow and long, some tied with white tape, others not fastened at all. She examined these first, looking them over rapidly. Julia had been left a considerable fortune by her grandmother, and she was perfectly familiar with the appearance of certificates for debentures, stocks, and shares; the only thing which startled her about these was the colossal size of the figures, typed or written in—here was Aglaia's fortune, and it must be *vast*. But that was not what John cared about. She turned to the big envelope, and hastily pulled out her Biro pen from her bag—the slender oval end of a Biro is perfect for opening envelopes without tearing them—rolled it along under the flap, cracking the black wax of the seals, and drew out the contents.

"Blueprints," a word so casually used in the press for any project for the future, when they are scientific and technical really *are* blue—blue, with the design for the machine or plan showing up on them in white lines. Such sheets, just as June had described them, Julia, sitting on the lavatory seat in the Hotel zǔm Flüss, now unfolded—and then most carefully folded up again along their original creases. With things like these she was quite unfamiliar; she had no idea whether she was looking at the plans for a nuclear-powered submarine tanker or for the pumps on an underground pipe line from Kirkuk to Iskenderun, emerging into the Mediterranean on Turkish soil. The drawings of one or two large bulbous-looking objects reminded her, vaguely, of Colin's account of the huge under-water containers in which food for man and beast was even now stored in the green depths of the Lakes of Thun and Brienz—but this could hardly interest the Swiss. She was faintly intrigued, too, by another set of papers, drawn in ink on bluish paper with a linen pattern; but these seemed merely to be duplicates of the blueprints. What she did realize was that she had got, here, under her hand, the documents that both John and Colin were so desperately anxious to secure; and she must, absolutely *must*, somehow contrive to hand them over to one or the other without letting the Swiss police, or anyone else, see them first.

It struck her at once that this might not be so easy. Whether or not the grey Volkswagen was a police car it had been on her tail, and its passengers knew the number of the Porsche; if it was *not* a police car, but belonged to some nefarious associates of Borovali or the two Germans, so much the worse. But in any case Chambertin and the man with him knew that she was staying at the Silberhorn, and nothing could stop the Swiss police from —perfectly properly—searching her room for missing property.

Julia considered. The blueprints were much too big to be stuffed down her bosom, in the good romantic manner, and her own handbag was too small to accommodate them. Some people say they think best in their bath; Julia thought to quite good effect, perched on the seat in a ladies' lavatory. What Chambertin—and hence the Swiss police—really wanted was Mr. Thalassides' fortune, entrusted to the Banque Républicaine and, by fraud, stolen. Good—they should have it; sooner or later they would have to hand it over to Aglaia Armitage anyhow. She picked up the certificates representing that fortune from the tessellated floor, where she had left them while she looked at the blueprints, put them in the black brief-case, and snapped it to; then she replaced the stiff envelope containing the blueprints in the inner compartment of the tartan bag.

"One for John, one for the Swiss," she murmured, gurgling—for an idea had come to her about the disposal of the tartan bag which made her laugh. She looked at her watch—twenty to six. There *ought* to be time, if Colin got back fairly soon. Carrying her three bags, she went out to the Porsche.

Julia had guessed—rightly, as it happened—that if the grey Volkswagen *was* a police car it would go straight on up to Beatenberg, and look for her at the Hotel Silberhorn; its occupants could have no means of knowing that she had doubled back to the Flüss. There was no sign of it on the parking-place by the quay when she left the hotel, nor on the Bahnhof-Platz by the West Station—she looked carefully there as she passed, and then drove on, as fast as the low-hung Porsche could take the hairpin bends, up through the scented woods to Beatenberg.

But she didn't go to the hotel. Instead she drove into the big lay-by at the foot of the Sessel-Bahn where cars and buses park, left the car, and went up the zigzag path to the little station. She took a ticket to the Niederhorn itself, and was soon swinging up between the treetops, through evening air sweet with scents drawn out from grass and flower and tree during the long warm day—and as she sat swaying she took out the local bus timetable, which had on the back the hours during which the Sessel-Bahn was open. Yes, passenger traffic went on up to 2030 hours, or till 8:30 P.M.—how tiresome the continental habit was of having no A.M. and P.M.; one always had to do these complicated sums! It was now nearly a quarter to seven—that was cutting it pretty fine; please God Colin *did* somehow come to the hotel at once. If he didn't, she would just have to come up again.

At the midway station, where the twin seats are pulled round by hand from the lower steel cable to the upper one, Julia got out, clutching her three bags.

"The Fräulein does not go on to the *Gipfel?*" the man in dungarees, who was conducting this maneuvre, asked in surprise.

"No, not tonight." While he was slinging two more seats round the curved rails she walked over to the group of milk churns which stood in a far corner ready, as she already knew, to carry water up to the hotel on the summit when the passenger traffic was over for the day. Lifting the lid of the remotest churn of all she slightly bent the tartan bag and stuffed it into this odd receptacle; then she replaced the lid, and walked back to the man in dungarees.

"Do you use *all* the churns now, to carry up the water at night?" she asked casually, when a pause occurred in the traffic.

"Ah, Fräulein, no; not now—this is not the high season. In July and August, yes; sometimes we are loading these vessels till after midnight! But at present it is not so bad."

"So how many containers do you use now? All?"

"Oh, it varies—but certainly not *all*. We fill these nearest ones, and load them up; the hotel sends down word how many they need."

This satisfied Julia. It was highly unlikely that the blueprints would be soused, even if she and Colin were a little late. She got onto the next seat that came down empty, and was carried away through the bright air, down to the road and the car; then she drove on to the Silberhorn.

There were three cars drawn up on the graveled space outside the hotel, where normally there were none except at lunch time—one was a grey Volkswagen. Grinning a little, Julia avoided the main entrance and went in by a little door which led directly into the bar; there she encountered Fräulein Hanna, who left off polishing glasses, took her arm, and led her with a certain urgency out into the long broad corridor which served as a hall.

"Fräulein Probyn, the *Polizei* are here again!" she said agitatedly. "And another gentleman also."

"Are they? What are they doing?" Julia asked; as she spoke she hung the black brief-case up on one of the many coat hooks which adorned the hall on both sides, and slung her windbreaker over it.

"They speak with Frau Hathaway; but they have asked first for you."

"Where are they?"

"In the garden."

"Is the Herr Monro here?"

"No."

Julia walked quickly through the *Kleine Saal* into the garden. It was nearly half past seven; Mrs. Hathaway ought not to be out too late—and she ought not to be worried.

Mrs. Hathaway however did not appear to be in the least worried when Julia reached the garden; she seemed to be having a party. Chambertin, and the man Julia had seen with him at the Aares-Schlucht restaurant were sitting by the old lady, drinking Cinzano and laughing; Müller, the detective, and two other men sat at another table, trying to make conversation with Watkins, who was refilling their glasses.

"Oh my dear child, there you are at last! These gentlemen have been wondering what had become of you; they want to see you about something, it seems. I gather you already know M. Chambertin—and this is Herr von Allmen, the Chief of Police in Interlaken." Nothing could have been easier than her voice and manner.

"So I had guessed," Julia said rather coldly, as she returned von Allmen's bow. "But look, Mrs. H. darling, you don't want to get chilly, after your illness—now that I'm here, hadn't you better go in and get some dinner? It's quite late."

"Oh no—we're having such fun. Aren't we?" she asked of her two guests. "And I'm sure they won't mind my hearing whatever it is they want to ask you about."

It was obvious to Julia that both men did mind considerably being forced to interview her in the old lady's presence, and she knew Mrs. Hathaway well enough to be sure that she realized this too, and was doing it on purpose. She rejoiced at Chambertin and von Allmen's evident embarrassment.

"Before anything else," she said to Chambertin, "please tell me about M. Antrobus. Where is he? Has a doctor seen him?"

"Yes, Mademoiselle. It so happened that there was an English *infirmière* in a party of tourists who were passing through the gorge when" —he coughed—"when the accident happened; she attended to M. Antrobus at once, and put on a tourniquet. Meanwhile we had telephoned to Meiringen for a doctor and an ambulance, and he was brought out with the least possible delay; he was carried very carefully—our *brancardiers* are excellent."

Julia was enormously relieved at this news, though the idea of an English hospital nurse coping with John on the plank-walk struck her as distinctly funny. But the mention of a tourniquet worried her—that sounded as though the bullet had punctured an artery.

"Where is he now?" she asked again.

"In Dr. Hertz's clinic down in the town, here. He expressed a very strong desire to be in Interlaken rather than at Meiringen."

"Oh, I'm so glad. He'll be perfectly all right with Hertz," Julia said happily.

"You know the Herr Doktor Hertz?" von Allmen asked, looking surprised.

"Yes. But now, M. Chambertin, what is it that you and the Chief of Police wish to ask me about? I don't want to keep Madame Hathaway out of doors too long. And oh darling Mrs. H., could I have a Cinzano too? It's been such a day."

"Watkins, you haven't given Miss Julia anything to drink," Mrs. Hathaway said mildly.

"Oh, I'm sorry, Madam. I've got some spare glasses here. There, Miss," the maid said, bustling over from the other table.

"Thank you, Watkins." Julia took a good gulp of the Cinzano, gratefully, and then turned again to the two Swiss, with an expectant face. She saw them glance at one another doubtfully—it was Chambertin who spoke.

"Mademoiselle Probyn, when this—this episode—took place in the Aares-Schlucht this afternoon, I understand—from *several* witnesses—that you picked up a black leather case full of papers, and carried it away."

"Certainly I did. Didn't you see it lying on the seat of the car, when you and Herr von Allmen came and asked me where I was going?" Julia asked coolly.

"Yes, I did see it," Chambertin said, irritated by her tone; "and if you had not driven off in such haste I should have spoken of it at once. But the papers in that case, Mademoiselle, are the property of the Banque Républicaine, which I represent, and I wish them to be returned to me."

"They're really the property of Miss Armitage's trustees, aren't they, which your poor old M. de Kessler let a lot of impostors steal from him?" Julia replied—eliciting a glance of startled delight from Mrs. Hathaway. "What have you done with the impostors, by the way? Have you laid the old one, Borovali, by the heels?—and did you fish the young one out of the Aar? I told you he'd been thrown in."

Von Allmen's face, at this point, would have repaid observation.

"For the moment Herr Borovali is in our hands," he replied cautiously. "But it would interest me to know, Fräulein Probyn, how it comes that you are so familiar with the name of this individual?"

Julia took her time over replying to this. If she mentioned June it might lead to more questions, and then trouble at La Cure, and possibly poor little June arrested too.

"Really, I think you'd better ask M. Chambertin about that," she said. "He will tell you that it was I who supplied him with the photograph that was circulated all over Switzerland, and enabled you to trace Borovali to the Flüss. And when you lost him there, I found him again at the Golden Bear."

"Dear Julia, did you really? *How* entertaining," Mrs. Hathaway interposed. Julia turned to Chambertin.

"What have you done with the two Boches?" She realized that the local chief of police was still rather at sea where she was concerned, and that she was likely to get more out of the banker.

"Unfortunately, Mademoiselle, technically we have nothing against them; they claim that they were simply tourists, quite unwillingly involved in this affair."

"Oh I see," Julia said, thinking of the tiny revolver that had dropped out of the tartan bag, and what its inner pocket still contained, in a churn halfway up the Niederhorn. "So back to Dortmund on tonight's sleepers, I suppose."

Once again von Allmen's face would have repaid observation—and got it, from Mrs. Hathaway. But he was a senior police official, and as such kept to his point.

"In any case, Fräulein Probyn, you admit to having obtained possession of these papers. Where are they now?"

"Hanging up in the hall here, with my jacket. I'll show you in a second, but first, do tell me where Mr. Monro is?"

"In the hospital at Meiringen. He has a concussion."

"Colin? Good heavens! How on earth did that happen?"

"Fräulein, when a person is thrown into the Aares-Schlucht, bones are liable to be broken," the police chief said repressively. Chambertin looked embarrassed; Julia laughed rather hysterically. Why did von Allmen know Borovali's real name, and not Wright's? Or had he forgotten? Or had someone thrown Colin into the river too? Before she could work out, or ask, the answers to these questions the Interlaken bus rolled past, and drew up beyond the cow-stable across the road—a moment later Colin himself walked in from the farther end of the garden. The girl got up, and flew to him.

"Have you seen John?"

"Antrobus, do you mean? Yes—I've just come from there. He's perfectly O.K. in that clinic; he says the nurses are charmers. The doctor's operating this evening."

"Operating? What for?" Julia was horrified.

"To take out the bullet. It won't be much, that man Hertz says, but they can't leave it in. I say, have you got those papers all right?"

The urgency in his voice caused Julia to look at her cousin more attentively than she had done so far, concentrated as she was on Antrobus; Colin looked battered, almost bruised, by the day's events, and his anxiety about the job.

"Yes rather—both lots. They weren't in the black brief-case, though."

"Then where?"

"In that tartan bag I snatched from the German Frau."

"But she emptied that out; all fruit and stuff!"

"Ah yes, but there was an inner pocket, and all the doings were zipped into that. There was nothing in the brief-case but old newspapers. I expect the eats were just camouflage."

"Where on *earth* can they have done the switch?" Colin speculated. "I never let them out of my sight for a moment."

"Even in the loos? That's where I'd expect. In lots of these Swiss pubs the *Herren* and *Damen Toiletten* are side by side."

"So they were, in Andermatt!" he exclaimed. "And they all went there in a bunch together. The man from Berne went into the Gents, and I was hovering outside, but I didn't see anything—there was a huge crowd, as there always is when a bus tour makes a halt."

"Well, I bet the greedy Frau took the brief-case from Wright in the corridor, did the switch inside, and handed it back to him as she came out. They must have had the old newspapers on them somewhere—no, I expect they were in the black case all the time; the real papers aren't all that bulky."

"You've actually looked at them?" the young man inquired anxiously. "Is what *we* want there?"

"Well a great big envelope of those drawing things."

"Where are they now?" Colin asked, almost trembling with excitement.

"In two places. What you and John want is where no one would ever think of looking; we must fetch them as soon as we can. What the Swiss police and old Chambertin want—Aglaia's good money—is hanging up here in the hotel." She looked at her watch. "Goodness, we haven't a minute to lose! Come and get a drink from Watkins, while I satisfy these types and push them off." She moved across the garden.

"Good God! Are *they* here?" Colin said nervously—he now saw who was sitting with Mrs. Hathaway.

"Oh yes—I was tailed all the way from the Schlucht," Julia said cheerfully. "And I did my *triage* in a 'Ladies' too. What goings-on the Swiss lavatories have seen today!" She spoke to the maid as she passed. "Watkins, I know Mrs. Hathaway has some whisky—could you get some for Mr. Colin?"

"Of course, Miss. I'll fetch it." She bustled away.

Von Allmen was looking distinctly restive as Julia returned to Mrs. Hathaway's table after this colloquy, Colin beside her.

"Monsieur Chambertin, I don't think you've properly met my cousin

Colin, have you?" She turned to von Allmen. "And Herr von Allmen, this is *really* Mr. Monro; the young man in the hospital at Meiringen is a Mr. Wright, though he has a forged passport in the name of Monro."

The police chief had risen for the introduction and bowed politely to Colin; but he looked thoroughly disconcerted at Julia's last remark, and threw an angry glance in Chambertin's direction. Julia flowed on. "And now, shall we go and get those papers you want, Monsieur Chambertin?"

They went through the *Kleine Saal* to the lobby, where Julia reached down the black brief-case from under her nylon wind-jacket and handed it to Chambertin.

"You'd better look at the papers, and see that everything is there, hadn't you?" she said.

"Most certainly. But where can we do this?"

The lobby at the Silberhorn leads into a sort of coffee-room adjoining the bar, with french windows opening onto a broad terrace or balcony which commands the view; since dinner was already going on in the restaurant both these places were empty. But a few people were still in the bar; Chambertin went through onto the terrace, followed by von Allmen, and sat down at one of the small tables, on which he placed the brief-case. "Where is the key?" he asked.

"It isn't locked—I never saw a key."

"*Incroyable!*" the Swiss exclaimed. He opened the case, drew out the papers, and from his pocketbook took a sheet of paper covered with spider-fine handwriting and figures; this he spread out on the colored tablecloth and then, taking the papers one by one he began to go through them, ticking off items on the sheet of paper as he did so.

"Oh good, you've got a list," Julia said. "Well while you're checking it, will you excuse me? I must take Mrs. Hathaway to get some dinner; she's stayed out far too late as it is."

"Fräulein, I shall require to get *your* account of what took place in the Aares-Schlucht, and of other matters," von Allmen said as she made to leave.

"Yes, of course. But can't that wait till the morning? I shan't run away, and my friend is still a convalescent; I must take care of her."

"Very good. Will half past nine tomorrow morning be too early?"

"No, perfect. See you then." She hastened back to the garden, where Colin was drinking whisky—"Wait here," she told him, and led Mrs. Hathaway through the whole length of the hotel to the restaurant, where the heels of the waitresses were clacking on the parquet as they served the rather sparse guests.

"Dear Julia, what are those men doing? Have they gone?" Mrs. Hathaway asked.

"Not yet—they're checking!" Julia said laughing. "And the policeman is coming back to interview me tomorrow morning!"

"Well now do sit down and have something to eat, dear child, and Colin too," Mrs. Hathaway said comfortably, unfolding her napkin and buttering a roll while she waited for the soup.

"No, I can't eat yet; Colin and I have got to go out again," Julia said, casting a horrified glance at the restaurant clock, which said five minutes to eight. "Ask Fräulein Hanna to keep something hot for us. I'll come up to see you last thing."

On her way through the coffee room she encountered Colin. "Where do we go?" he asked eagerly.

"Half a moment." Through the huge windows Julia could see Chambertin and von Allmen talking; neither the list nor the envelope were visible on the table. She went out to them.

"Are the papers in order, M. Chambertin?"

"*Grace à Dieu,* Mademoiselle, yes," the Swiss said, deep relief in his voice. "On the part of the Banque Républicaine, I wish to thank you for what you have done to recover them."

"*De rien!*—it was a pleasure," Julia said. "Au revoir. Till tomorrow morning, Herr von Allmen." She almost ran out to the car, followed by Colin, and shot down the pretty winding road to the foot of the Sessel-Bahn, where she again swung the Porsche into the lay-by.

"Can't help it if they see the car—we must get up there at once," she said, and darted up the zigzag path to the little station.

CHAPTER XIV

BEATENBERG

"WE ARE ABOUT to close, Fräulein," said the man at the entrance who sold tickets, making no move to produce any.

"We only want to go as far as the midway halt," Julia said pleadingly, making doves' eyes at him. "And you must send some of the chairs up there to take the water on to the hotel, musn't you? They've been busy today, *am Weekend.*"

"The Fräulein seems to know a great deal!" the man said with a smile, as he gave her the tickets. "Is she *einheimisch* [native-born]?"

"No, foreign. But so much I know!" Julia said, smiling too. "*Schönsten Dank.*" The man drew round one of the twin seats, clamped the metal bars across their stomachs, pulled a lever, and launched them on their airborne career up the mountainside.

"What on earth *is* all this?" Colin asked, as they swung through the pine trees, whose branches were still set with small upright tufts of a brilliant carmine; these are the cones, which later bend over on the branch to droop downwards, turning brown in the process. "Are the papers up here? If so, why on earth?"

"Simply to have them somewhere where that infernal von Allmen would never think of looking," Julia said. "I don't know if Chambertin knows that they were in the same pigeonhole as all Aglaia's stocks and shares—if he doesn't, he ought to, and I didn't trust him not to put von Allmen onto the fact. John was furious that he'd told him about the bus tour."

"But why up here?" Colin persisted.

"You'll see in a moment, if we aren't too late! Oh goodness, I hope I can find the right one again! Anyhow it's no good fussing—we are in time or we aren't, I can or I can't. Tell me, is it true that there was a hospital nurse as *well* as a bobby in that lot of tourists? Chambertin said there was, and that she put a tourniquet on John's leg."

"Yes—she was a splendid person. She took off Antrobus' trousers to get at the place; he was furious! But she simply ignored him. It really was a damn peculiar scene," Colin said, grinning at the recollection; "I wish you'd been there. That nurse kneeling on the planks, completely professional in her rather dim civvy clothes, doing the necessary and ordering me about; the policeman—who came from Wolverhampton, just to add to it—booming on about 'culpable homicide in the presence of witnesses'; and the German woman bellowing that her bag had been stolen. Why *did* you take her bag, by the way?"

"I don't really know; I just felt angry with her. Anyhow it's lucky I did, since that's where everything was. Go on."

"Oh well, just when I'd gone and cut a bough off a bush to twist the tourniquet with, and another female tourist had contributed her scarf to fasten it, that old bank manager comes processing through the tunnel, complete with the Swiss police—who took depositions from everybody on the spot."

"How? I mean in what language?"

"English. That von Something man speaks it perfectly, and the busload of tourists have had the day of their lives—especially the constable from

Wolverhampton!" He paused. "Then the ambulance men arrived with a stretcher and lugged Antrobus out, and the rest of them all came back to Interlaken on the bus, I suppose."

"And you?" Julia asked.

"I waited to see the ambulance go off, and then got a lift in a car, and somehow persuaded the people in it to tail the ambulance—they were quite amused when I said there'd been an attempt at murder!" Colin said, giggling.

"Ought you to have said that?"

"Oh don't be silly! The whole place was buzzing with it. Do you suppose anything or anyone on earth could keep those tourists' mouths shut? Anyhow they took me to that clinic place, and I went in and saw Antrobus, and then came on up here."

At that point they reached the midway halt. The man in dungarees stared in surprise at seeing passengers arriving so late, but grinned amicably at Julia when she called to him to let them out—he was busy shifting churns, but did as she asked. So many churns had been moved to be filled with water—and were even now being loaded by another man onto the seats, by day occupied by tourists, for their trip up to the summit hotel— that Julia rather lost her bearings; she went from one of the tall white-metal vessels to another, lifting off the lids and peering in, while Colin looked on, an expression of delighted comprehension beginning to dawn in his face.

"Ali Baba and the Forty Thieves," he muttered—just as Julia, with an exclamation of satisfaction, bent down and from at least the twelfth churn pulled out the tartan bag.

"Oh, you clever darling! No—they'd never have thought of looking here," he said, and dealt her a shattering blow on the back.

"The Fräulein is removing something?" said the man in dungarees, coming over.

"Only something I put in when I was up here earlier this evening," Julia said, making more doves' eyes at him. "Now, can we go down?"

"Ah, Fräulein, it is after the hour. I ought not to allow this."

"Oh, but *do* allow it! I'm so tired, and we shall lose our way in the forest in the dusk, if we have to walk," Julia beguiled.

The man lifted a wall telephone, spoke, and then beckoned them into a seat. "For the Fräulein," he said, clamping them in—Julia said *"Schönsten Dank"* again as they swung out of the shed.

In the air—safest of places—Julia showed Colin the shiny envelope and its contents; he examined them carefully, and replaced the blue sheets.

"That's IT!" he said triumphantly. "Do you know, I think I'd better take this on to Berne at once."

"How?" Julia asked. "There are no more steamers to Spiez tonight I don't think, even if the funicular is still running. I should leave it till tomorrow."

"I could drive there in Antrobus' car."

"Have you got a map?"

"Not a roadmap—no."

"I think you'd better come and have something to eat, and take these things on in the morning," Julia said. "If Chambertin *has* put von Allmen on to suspecting something, there'll probably be road blocks all the way to Berne!"

Colin laughed, but he was overruled—and when they drove up to the hotel the sight of one of the local policemen, lurking near the front door, reinforced Julia's arguments. "Let's have supper, and then take them up to Mrs. H.—she'll look after them. Trust *her!*" she said.

Late as it was, Fräulein Hanna had kept them some soup and cold chicken and salad; in the bright lights of the restaurant Colin's youthful face, always white, showed the marks of fatigue and strain. The restaurant was of course now empty, and Fräulein Hanna did her watchful hovering from the servery door at the far end; they could talk freely, and did. Colin spoke of his panic when he found his retreat blocked by the tourists in the gorge, and of the worrying day-long watch on Wright and Borovali. "I spotted the German couple fairly soon, because they were practically the only other non-English people in the bus; but those Post-Autos are so huge, and so crowded, it was hard to be sure that nothing passed from one hand to another. Goodness, I am thankful we got them in the end! Where's that bag now?" he asked, with a sudden recurrence of nerves.

"Here, under my chair," Julia said tranquilly.

After supper they went up in the small cramped lift and tapped on Mrs. Hathaway's door. The old lady was already in bed, wearing a very becoming lacy Shetland bed-jacket; she greeted them gaily.

"So there you are at last! But have you had anything to eat?"

"Yes, a lovely supper, just now. Hanna is an angel. But look, Mrs. H. darling, we want you to do a tiny bit of secretion for us."

"Dear child, don't one's glands do that? I'll do anything I can, but I can't answer for my glands!—I believe they get a little sluggish at my age."

Julia, laughing, opened the zipped pocket of the tartan bag and drew out the big envelope.

"All we want you and your glands to do is to keep this safe for Colin till tomorrow morning," she said. "There's a policeman hanging about downstairs, and we don't want him, or anyone else, to get it."

Mrs. Hathaway sat upright in her bed. "Pull out the top three pillows," she said to Colin—he did so. "Now put that thing on the bottom one, and put the others back." The young man did as he was told, and Mrs. Hathaway leaned back again, comfortably, against her four pillows.

"That should do," she said. "And now, may I know what I am hiding?"

"Just some papers that were stolen," Colin said. "Julia got them back, and I'm taking them to Berne tomorrow."

"Oh, I see. To your organization, I suppose. Well I hope no one steals them from you on the way. But Julia, I thought you were handing over some papers to M. Chambertin and that nice police chief?"

"Ah, I was—but these are different ones; they are for Colin's 'organization,' as you call it, in Berne. The Swiss aren't to see these—they might be nosey about them," Julia said.

"I see," Mrs. Hathaway said again. "All right—leave them with me." She glanced at Colin. "My dear boy, you look quite exhausted. Do go to bed."

Colin stooped down and gave her a kiss. "Bless you, Mrs. H.—I think I will. Have you got such a thing as a Soneryl, by any chance?"

"No—Seconal is my bedfellow. Julia, in that little drawer in the night-table." Julia got out the bottle. "These are the small ones; you'll need two," Mrs. Hathaway said, shaking them into her hand—"or even three. And don't make *too* early a start. I assure you that I will look after your papers." Colin blew her another kiss and went out.

"What *has* he been doing, to make him so worn out?" Mrs. Hathaway asked. "And is Mr. Antrobus really hurt? If it isn't too secret, I should rather like to know what has been going on, Julia."

"You look quite tired enough yourself," Julia said; she had already noticed that her old friend was rather white. "You stayed out too long. Do you think you got chilled?"

"Oh no, it was quite warm. Only it was a little bit of a strain when those men came and asked for you—you see I was completely in the dark, except for guessing, and I tried just to keep them going."

"Well now you shall hear it *all*," Julia said firmly—"only I think you'd better have some brandy. Where is it?"

"In the hat cupboard—the key's in my bag. You had better have some too; I think there are glasses."

There were, charming miniature cut-glass goblets; when these were filled, and being sipped, Julia told Mrs. Hathaway the whole story of the theft from the Banque Républicaine, of her encounter with June on the

Niederhorn, and finally of the events of the day itself. "Poor Colin, you see, has been tailing these crooks since seven-thirty this morning, and in an agony of anxiety all the time, because this is his first big job, and he was terrified of falling down on it."

"Yes, I do see. Poor boy! And quite an agitating dénouement; the shooting, and those tourists in the way, and then Mr. Antrobus throwing that man into the river! So unexpected from such a civilized person."

"Oh, do you think so?" Julia inquired with interest.

"Superficially, yes. Though mind you, I think he is probably *capable de tout,* in every respect."

Julia laughed, a little uneasily, at that last remark.

"And you have bestowed the poor little girl, June or whatever her name is, in a safe place?"

"Yes. With Aglaia's godfather, M. de Ritter—the people I went to stay with. He fetched her yesterday."

"Ah, that is what you were doing! Well now, my dear child, I should like to know a little more about these papers that are in my care. Colin spoke of taking them to Berne tomorrow. To the Secret Service? Have we got people there?"

"Yes. I believe we have them more or less everywhere."

For the third or fourth time that evening Mrs. Hathaway said, "I see"—thoughtfully. Then Julia rinsed out the brandy glasses in the basin, kissed her old friend good night, and went downstairs and rang up the clinic.

A nurse answered. *"Justus-Klinik. Hier spricht Schwester Berta"*—and of the Sister Julia made her inquiries. Yes, the operation had gone well, and the patient was sleeping; the *Herr Doktor* was very satisfied. No cause whatever for *Angst.* Could one see Herr Antrobus tomorrow? Julia asked. Very probably—but better to ring up the *Herr Doktor* about ten o'clock to make sure that visitors were allowed. Relieved, Julia went to bed.

She too was tired, and slept late; it was not far off nine when she hurried into the restaurant, where sun was pouring in through the huge plate-glass windows. Colin was already seated at their table, tucking into bread and black cherry jam—he looked a different being from the exhausted creature of the night before.

"Sleep well?" Julia inquired.

"Far *too* well—that's most wonderful stuff of Mrs. H.'s; no backlash, either. But I must get off as soon as I can."

"That policeman is still on the door, or a relief—I looked on the way down."

"I know—so did I. But if I put the envelope in my rucksack he'd hardly search that, would you say? And I've decided not to take the car; I shall go down by the funicular, take the boat to Spiez, and on by train."

"That's a much better idea," Julia said, buttering bread and pouring out her coffee. "Unobtrusiveness is the ticket, every time. You'd better get off before von Allmen comes to interview me, though."

Colin ate such a vast breakfast that Julia finished nearly as soon as he did; nevertheless he hustled her over her last half-slice, in his impatience to be off. He raced upstairs ahead of her to collect his rucksack; they met outside Mrs. Hathaway's door, and went in together—like Colin, Mrs. Hathaway looked much better for a night's rest, and greeted them gaily.

"Good morning, dear children. Colin, I see you have had a good night; I'm very glad."

"Wonderful, Mrs. H. And now I'll just relieve you of that envelope, and push off to Berne."

"It's gone," Mrs. Hathaway said.

"Gone? Gone where?" Colin asked, in an agitated voice. "Did they get in after all? I thought . . ."

"Colin, you *must* learn not to get into such a fuss about nothing," Mrs. Hathaway said, interrupting him peremptorily but calmly. "*I* sent it off, by post—that is to say, Watkins has taken it to the post office."

"But where have you sent it?" Colin tried to control the anxiety in his voice.

"To the Embassy in Berne. No one ever dares to interfere with Embassy mail and with all these police about, and you known by sight, I thought it much the safest way."

Julia began to gurgle. "Oh, splendid, Mrs. H." Colin was not pacified. "But this has nothing to do with the Embassy," he said worriedly.

"Of course not. So I marked the inner envelope, "NOT TO BE OPENED. TO BE CALLED FOR." And now you can either telephone to your superiors and let them know where to collect it, or go and tell them in person. But in the post, I think it can't be held up, whereas anything might have happened if you had taken it yourself."

There was a tap on the door, and Watkins came in.

"There you are, Madam—the receipt for the registered letter," she said, tendering a minute and rather grubby piece of paper to her mistress. "Good morning, Mr. Colin. Miss Julia, the police are downstairs; they want to see you again, that Hanna says."

Julia rose resignedly from her seat on the foot of the bed. "Oh very well," she said. "I'll come up when I'm through, Mrs. H."

"Do. And Colin, in your place I should wait up here till Julia comes

back. You can sit on the balcony. Watkins, find yesterday's *Times* for Mr.
Colin."

During her talk with Herr von Allmen, Julia was mainly preoccupied
with getting the thing over in time to ring up Dr. Hertz at ten. They sat
out on the long balcony, at that hour in the morning practically unoc-
cupied. The police chief opened his inquiries by asking why she, Julia,
came to be in the Aares-Schlucht with Herr Antrobus the previous afternoon.

"We were looking for a bird," Julia said.

"*Um Himmel's Willen!* A bird?"

"It's called *Tichodroma muraria*," Julia said briskly. "It lives there. It's
very rare. We saw it, too—such luck! It's very pretty." She began to describe
the wall-creeper.

Von Allmen, exasperated—as Julia had wickedly hoped—interrupted her
description.

"A German lady who was present said that her bag was stolen—by
someone resembling you, from her description."

"Does that trouble you?" Julia asked. "Surely you know that she was the
receiving end of the fraud on the bank?"

Von Allmen would not let himself be out-faced. "Do you admit to taking
her bag?" he asked.

"Of course—I'll get it." She walked into the lobby, and returned with
the tartan bag. "She had it full of things to eat, chocolate and so on," she
remarked, laying it on the table between them.

"Why did you take it?" he pursued, suspiciously.

"Because she hit Herr Antrobus with it—that's when all the food came
tumbling out," Julia replied readily. "And because she was a nasty, fat,
greedy woman, and I wanted to annoy her! So I just snatched it."

Von Allmen gave a short unwilling laugh at this.

"Give it back to her, if she hasn't gone off to Dortmund, and you mind
about her so much," Julia added, encouraged by the laugh. "It's hideous."

But von Allmen was too astute to be deflected from the purpose of his
inquiries.

"In any case I retain the bag," he said. "And now, Fräulein, I return to
a question that I asked you yesterday evening, to which you evaded giving
a direct answer. How comes it that you know the real names of these two
fraudulent gentlemen, M. Borovali and M. Wright, so well?"

Julia was disconcerted, but she determined not to show any hesitation.

"Last night I referred you to M. Chambertin for the answer to that," she
said. "I do so again now."

"Why are you unwilling to tell me?"

"Because really I don't see what this has got to do with you at all," the girl said rather haughtily. "You are questioning me as if I were a suspected criminal, when in fact—again as I mentioned last night—it was I who supplied the photograph which enabled you to trace the real criminals in the first place, and when you lost them, I found them again for you. What have *I* done wrong?"

"Except for a little bag-snatching, nothing that I know of," the police chief said, with a small placatory smile. (Good police at some point always try to placate the subjects of their interrogations.) "Where did you get the photograph?" he asked smartly, with a quick change of subject.

"Out of *Paris-Match*." She paused to watch the effect of this, which was satisfactory; von Allmen looked rather nonplused for a moment. Only for a moment, however; then he ploughed doggedly on.

"This photograph was of the young lady in Mr. Borovali's party, who impersonated the heiress?"

"Look, Herr von Allmen, don't treat me as a fool!" Julia said. "Would *Paris-Match* bother with the photograph of an impersonator? Of course it was of the real heiress, Miss Armitage, who left for South America not long ago."

"Then how did you know that the resemblance would help us?"

"Because I saw *all* the impersonators on the platform at Victoria, when I was coming out here," Julia replied fearlessly. "I was struck by the girl's likeness to Miss Armitage, and looked at them all carefully. That is why I was able to describe them at the bank, and establish the fact of the fraud. You heard M. Chambertin thank me for this—are the Swiss police not also grateful?"

"Undoubtedly, Fräulein." Von Allmen sketched a bow. But he was still not to be deflected from his inquiries.

"This young lady, who played the part of the heiress at the bank, has disappeared. Do you know where she has gone?"

Julia was frightened—this was *it*. Playing for time—"Why do you ask me that?" she said. But she guessed the answer before it came; that bloody Müller had probably seen her drive June off in the taxi from the Golden Bear. Had he tailed them to the clinic? Or questioned the taxi driver? She decided to stall completely.

Von Allmen duly gave the answer she expected. "You were seen to drive her away, with her luggage, from the hotel."

"Why not? Is there a law in Switzerland against rescuing young girls from the hands of international crooks? I know you don't allow women the vote," Julia said unkindly, "but is what I did a crime?"

The police chief looked annoyed when she spoke of the vote, but he kept his temper admirably.

"My question is, *where* did you take her? And a second one—where is she now?"

They stared at one another, both stubborn and remorseless, across the table with its red-and-white checked cloth, for a long moment. Then—

"I am not going to answer either of your questions," Julia said, very slowly and deliberately. "I am alone with you, without a lawyer; I know nothing of Swiss law, so I don't even know whether you are entitled to cross-question a foreign national like this. I can ring up our Embassy and find out, of course." Again she stared at the police chief across the table; her doves' eyes could become as hard as onyx when Julia was determined. Suddenly, at something she half-saw in the man's face, her expression altered completely.

"Herr von Allmen, need we oppose each other?" she asked, in quite a gentle voice. "I know you must do your duty, but are we not really on the same side?" Surprised, the man's face also relaxed; he half-nodded. "I have seen quite a lot of this wretched girl," Julia went on. "She is an ignorant child, hardly out of her teens, who works for an advertizement agency to support her mother, a widow."

"Ah, this is how they found her?" von Allmen interjected.

"Precisely. And she took on the job because those brutes bribed her with a lot of pretty clothes! She's vain, and silly, and as stupid as a rabbit," Julia said candidly—"but she's fundamentally a good, honest girl, who had really no idea of the use to which she was to be put. And because I was a little kind to her—quite by accident—she determined to help *me*, rather than her beastly employers, and rang me up to tell me that the papers were to be handed over on the Drei-Pässe tour."

"*Unmöglich!*" von Allmen exclaimed, thoroughly startled.

"But certainly. So she, not I, is the person you and the Banque Républicaine ought to be thanking for their recovery."

"But Herr Antrobus knew this," the police chief said, still incredulous.

"Only because I told him, after she had told me. She warned me that they were armed, too. Now, do you *still* want to harry and pursue her? Or arrest her, and frighten her out of her wits?" She paused—the man was silent. Julia leaned across the table, her eyes again doves' eyes.

"Look, Herr von Allmen, I have sent her away to good kind people, who will look after her until I can take her back to England. Can't you just *lose* her, like you lost the others last week? You've got back the money, you've caught the real criminals—can't you forget about her, and allow her to disappear?"

He laughed a little at this outrageously barefaced request.

"Fräulein, she cannot cross the frontier. All posts have been told to look out for her passport."

"Yes of course. But that was a bogus passport anyway—your frontier officials won't be looking out for one in the name of Phillips."

"This is her real name?" He drew out a notebook.

"No, don't write it down!" Julia said, stretching a long, faintly tanned hand across the table, and laying it on the notebook and von Allmen's hand together. "*Please!* This is off the record—aren't we working together, now?"

The police chief, rather slowly, withdrew his hand from under Julia's, and put the notebook back in his pocket. Instead of answering directly—

"It was she who told you their names?" he asked.

"Not *told*—she's so frightfully stupid that she kept on letting them slip out," Julia said, half-laughing at the recollection. "But I can easily get her a fresh passport, in her real name."

"Is this so easy?" the Swiss official asked, looking rather shocked.

"Goodness yes! I'm always letting my passport run out, or losing it, and having to get a new one. Any consulate can do it."

He looked more shocked than ever.

"Actually I expect horrible Mr. Borovali has got hers," Julia pursued blithely. "If she has it, I shall burn it—and if he has it, *you* can burn it!"

Von Allmen laughed out loud.

"And we are told that the English are so law-abiding!" he said.

"So we are—only we realize that laws, like the Sabbath, are made for man, and not man for the law. Also"—her voice changed—"we are a merciful people. I believe you are, too; who invented the Red Cross? Be merciful, Herr von Allmen—and you shall obtain mercy."

There was a long pause. Julia forced herself not to look at her watch, though surely it must be ten o'clock by now? But June was the first thing. At last von Allmen spoke.

"Fräulein, I have had a long experience in administering the law, which you treat so lightly; but I have never yet encountered a person who appeared to be at the same time completely unscrupulous, and also good! This is very curious."

"Oh, I'm not good—only merciful on occasion!" Julia said lightly. She did not press her appeal—this rather oblique response was probably as much as she could expect; at least he had not refused outright. Better finish now —and at last she did look at her watch; it was five past ten. "Herr von Allmen, have we finished? Because if so I ought just to go up and see my old friend before I go down to the town—she got rather overtired last night."

"I am sorry for this. Please convey my compliments to Frau Hathaway
—that is a most gracious lady," von Allmen said.

"Yes, isn't she? She liked you so much too," Julia said. She held out her
hand. "Good-bye—thank you for being kind."

"Have I been kind?"

"Well I rather think you're going to be! *Auf-wiederluoge!*" she said,
laughing, and ran away to the telephone box.

She was too late for Dr. Hertz, who was on his rounds, but the *Schwester* with whom she spoke said that certainly it would be possible to visit
Herr Antrobus; he had slept well, taken a good breakfast, and had little
pain. Relieved, Julia went up to Mrs. Hathaway's room, ascertaining on
the way from Fräulein Hanna that the *Polizei-Chef* had driven off.

"All serene," she said as she entered—at the sound of the door opening
Colin came in off the balcony. "I'm not in prison, and von Allmen has
gone. He sent you his respects, Mrs. H.—you've made a hit."

"What did he want to know?" Colin asked.

"Why I was in the gorge yesterday, and what I'd done with June. I told
him that Herr Antrobus and I were looking for a bird in the gorge, and
gave him its name—he hated that," Julia said, laughing. "And I refused flat
out to tell him where June was. But it all went very well—we parted
friends."

"How extraordinary!" Colin said, beginning to jerk his double-jointed
thumb in and out. "He didn't ask about the papers?"

"Not a word. He said the Hun Frau had accused me of snatching her
bag, and I said of course I did, because she was using it as a weapon on
John! He's taken it off. I shouldn't worry, Colin—either Chambertin didn't
know about the prints, or if he did, he didn't tell von Allmen."

"That all sounds very satisfactory," Mrs. Hathaway said. "The police in
most countries are quite reasonable as a rule, if one treats them sensibly."

"Now, Colin, are you going to Berne?" Julia asked. "If so you'd better
drive down with me and get a train—much less hanging about than with
the steamer."

"Yes, I must go and report," Colin said. "There are bound to be repercus-
sions from the Swiss end, and I hope to Heaven there won't be a fuss with
the Embassy."

"Colin, I am quite sure there won't," Mrs. Hathaway said. "Anyhow if
you go with Julia you will be in Berne as soon as the package. Dear boy,
do keep that thumb of yours quiet; it makes such a disagreeable sound."

"Yes, go and pack your ghastly great rucksack, quickly," his cousin adjured him. "I want to be off in ten minutes."

Colin got up—at the door he paused. "I ought to see Antrobus, and let him know what's happened."

"*I'll* tell him; I shall be seeing him," Julia said impatiently.

When Colin had gone—"Have you heard how Mr. Antrobus is?" Mrs. Hathaway asked.

"Yes, I rang up just now. The operation went all right, and he slept well, and ate a huge breakfast."

"The operation?"

"Oh, didn't I tell you that part? That revolting Wright shot him through the leg in the Schlucht, and they had to take the bullet out, and stitch up the artery. That was why he threw Master Wright into the Aar—he felt a little cross with him."

"No wonder," said Mrs. Hathaway.

CHAPTER XV

INTERLAKEN—THE CLINIC

"Ah, there you are at last. I expected one of you before this," Antrobus said, when a nurse ushered Julia into his small austere room at the clinic next morning.

"Couldn't get away before—I was stuck with von Allmen. He came to cross-examine me about the goings-on in the Schlucht," Julia said, seating herself in the single wicker chair, with its bright cretonne cushions. The sight of Antrobus lying rather flat in bed, in pyjamas, a cradle over his right leg, brought about in her a set of emotions so strong that she spoke even more slowly and casually than usual.

"Why didn't Colin come?"

"He's gone to Berne to report."

"I think he might have reported to me first," Antrobus said.

"There wasn't time. Anyhow I can tell you all he can, and a good bit more," Julia replied, rather chilled by his tone.

"I don't see why the rush to get to Berne. However, as you're reporting you'd better report. Is everything all right? Did you get the papers?"

"Yes, I got them. They weren't in the black brief-case, though."

"Good gracious! Then where were they, and how did you get them?"

"They were in the Hun woman's tartan bag—I snatched it as an after-thought."

"And where are they now?"

"Well all old Thalassides' stocks and shares I gave to Chambertin; the drawings . . ."

"Yes, what about them?" he interrupted sharply.

"They're in the post to the Embassy in Berne. That's why Colin's raced off—he wants to be in time for his people to ring up the Embassy to say they'll call for them."

"Why on earth did you do anything so idiotic as to post them to the Embassy?" he asked, quite irritably.

"I didn't. Mrs. Hathaway did. Look," the girl said, becoming irritated in her turn by his carping manner—"if you want to hear my report, I'll report, but I don't see why I should be scolded by anyone. If I hadn't snatched that bag, by now your papers would be safely on their way to East Germany or wherever, and you'd have got nothing but a brief-case full of old newspapers." She was upset that this meeting was turning out so disagreeably.

"Not really? So they did manage to switch after all. I wonder where —your cousin swore he'd never taken his eyes off the black case."

"He had to take them off Frau Dortmund when she went into the lav at Andermatt, which is almost certainly where it happened," Julia said, and rehearsed what Colin had told her.

"And when did you find out that this had been done? I still don't understand about the need for posting to the Embassy," Antrobus said.

"Of course not, till you're told," Julia said, trying not to upset him further. "Do let me tell you what happened; but I don't want to be bullied until you know the facts."

"How tough we are!" he said. "All right, my dear—tell me your story in your own way."

"I'm afraid your leg must be hurting you," Julia said. "I believe pain does make people bloody-minded." The patronizing tone of his last remark had hurt her very much.

He held out a placatory hand.

"I can't reach you—come nearer." She kept her seat. "Oh very well—I'm sorry. Will that do? Now tell me."

Julia told—of her encounter with Chambertin and von Allmen at the Schlucht restaurant, of finding herself tailed by the grey Volkswagen, and of how she had examined the contents of the two bags in the ladies' lavatory at the Flüss; Antrobus laughed at that.

"Very neat. So then what did you do?"

"Divided them. I put the lolly into the black case for Chambertin, and the blueprints in the other bag for you. John, such an odd thing . . ." his praise had restored her equanimity.

"What?"

"Some of the drawings looked rather like Colin's description of those under-water food containers that are sunk in the lakes here; I mean there was a line that looked like water-level at the top, and measuring in meters up to it. Only there were pipes and things going out of the containers as well, as far as I could see—of course I was in a hurry."

"Have you mentioned that resemblance to anyone else?—Mrs. Hathaway, for instance?" he asked sharply.

"No. Why?"

"Well don't—don't speak of it to anyone."

"All right. Am I ever to know what they are?"

"Sometime, perhaps, Fatima!—as a reward for saving them. Now go on telling me about your complications."

"Well sure enough when I got back to the pub, there was von Allmen with Chambertin, and the grey Volkswagen, and spare police, and all." Antrobus laughed.

"What were Chambertin and von Allmen doing when you got to the Silberhorn?"

"Being beguiled by Mrs. Hathaway!" She continued to recount her and Colin's doings, including handing over the blueprints to repose under Mrs. Hathaway's pillows. "I thought that a rather safe place," she concluded.

"So do I," Antrobus said, laughing again. "But why post to Berne?"

"That was her idea. When Colin and I went up this morning, she told us she'd sent Watkins to post it to the Embassy. Things are pretty safe in the post," Julia said. "Personally I think it was a sound notion. If Colin had taken it in by hand anyone could have slugged him on the way—as it is he'll be there by the time it's delivered, and his people can ring up, or go round in false beards and collect it, or whatever you all do."

"The Ambassador won't like it," Antrobus said, looking dissatisfied.

"Well he won't have to lump it for more than an hour, if that," Julia replied cheerfully. "That is, if no one *does* slug Colin. If they do I don't know what happens—I go in with a chit from you, I suppose, to the anonymous office." She was laughing.

Antrobus didn't laugh. He reached out and pressed a bell. When the nurse appeared—"*Telefon, Schwester, bitte,*" he said; the nurse nodded, and disappeared.

"Goodness, can you telephone from your bed?" Julia asked.

"Yes—there are plug-ins in two or three of the rooms here, like in American military hospitals; there's one in this. But they're rather slow. Meantime, tell me what von Allmen asked you."

"How I knew Borovali's real name, mostly. And if I'd stolen Frau Dortmund's bag, and why?"

"I should rather like to know that too. What moved you to snatch the bag? It seems almost like direct inspiration, since you'd got the brief-case. Why did you?"

"Well really because she'd tried to cosh you with it, I think," the girl said rather slowly, the ripe-apricot stain beginning to appear in her cheeks. "And she was so *fat!*" she added, rather hurriedly.

He studied her face, with its betraying blush, with remorseless steadiness. Julia had expected him to laugh, or at least grin, at her last words, but he did neither. "I *see*," he said slowly, still looking at her; Julia became uncomfortable under that steady noncommittal scrutiny. She lit a cigarette, got up, and went over to the window, which looked out on a trim plot with the usual Swiss town-garden mixture of espalier fruit trees, vegetables in soldierly rows, and narrow edgings of bright flowers.

"And how did you answer the one about Borovali?" Antrobus' voice from the bed recalled her. "That involved your little friend, of course. Did you tell von Allmen where you had stowed her? I'm sure he wanted to know."

"Yes, he did—and I didn't tell him," she said, turning round.

"Oh! How did he take that?"

"Poorly, till I told him that it was she who had provided the information that the papers would be handed over on the bus tour. That shook him quite a lot—and I suggested that in view of the service she had rendered the Swiss police, he should leave her alone."

"Did he agree?"

"Not in so many words. It must be awful to be police or lawyers, and never be able to say anything straight out," Julia said. "But I don't think he will make any trouble—or let anyone else make any. I told him I should take her home myself, when Mrs. H. is fit again."

Now Antrobus was laughing.

"In fact you got away with it? What a getter-away with things you are, aren't you?"

Again Julia was hurt by the detached amusement in his voice—it was so unlike his former frequent praise of her skill, his warmth towards her.

"It's just as well, for other people, that I do sometimes get away with things," she said, turning back to the window.

Before Antrobus could answer there was a tap on the door, and the nurse trotted in with a telephone which she set down on the bed-table; she plugged it in at floor level, saying—"Now the Herr can get his connection. I return"—and trotted out again.

Antrobus reached out and set the instrument down in front of him on the honey-combed coverlet; the movement hurt his leg, and he gave a grunt of pain—"Ouch!" This upset Julia still more. "Shall I go out?" she asked, while he twiddled the dial.

"No, it doesn't matter." He lifted the receiver to his ear—his intent expression showed her that she was completely out of the picture for the moment.

"Hullo? Oh, Philip—John here. . . . Yes, everything's fine. . . . No, not according to plan in the least, but perfectly successful. . . . No, I shan't be coming for a few days yet. . . . Because I'm in hospital. . . . No, nothing much. . . . Yes, there was a bit of a fracas. . . . Exactly— young Colin is on his way in to you now; he'll tell you everything. . . . No, but as good as . . . He'll *tell* you, I say. Don't *fuss*, Philip—it's cast-iron. . . . News for me, did you say? . . . Yes, I got the letter you forwarded, this morning; the hotel sent it round by hand, but it didn't say where to . . . Having *Tommy* as a colleague! Oh, how perfect!—I've always longed to get out there. . . . Well really, Philip, I can't say exactly how soon; I've had a bullet through an artery, and the doctor won't commit himself about dates just yet—he only stitched it up last night. . . . Yes, of course—tell them I shall report the moment I can move. I can't wait to get out there!—I've wanted to see those mosaics all my life. . . . Of course I shall look in on you on the way—there will be one or two points to tidy up. . . . What? Oh yes, the two main ones, who are what matter. I expect you'll get the Interpol report tomorrow, or later today possibly. Not the ones from outside. . . . No, technically impossible. . . . No, lay off the third; that's of no importance. . . . Listen, Philip, did you hear me tell you to *lay off*? Well do what I say. . . . No, I won't explain anything now. You can give me a ring after you've actually laid hands on the things; my number is"—he gave it. "And don't get impatient when you ring up—the machine has to be lugged upstairs to my room. Good-bye."

Listening to one end of a telephone conversation is always a tantalizing business, but a shrewd listener can usually pick up a certain amount of the drift. Julia gathered quite clearly two essential points: that Antrobus had told his colleague in Berne not to pursue June, and that he was being transferred to another assignment. A place with mosaics—where would that be? She thought at once of Ravenna, but that was too near—he had said "out there." Then probably Istanbul—she remembered hearing about an old American restoring famous mosaics in Santa Sofia. But what struck her with painful force as she listened was that he was longing to go; there was no hint of regret or reluctance in his words or, more important, in his voice—he was all happy eagerness. In fact—she swallowed a little as she faced and digested the wretched knowledge—he didn't mind leaving her in the least. He had just been enjoying himself, but he didn't care—he didn't care at all.

The last few minutes of the conversation gave her a chance to pull herself together, nor did she stop paying attention even after she heard her new-found happiness being knocked from under her feet by a few words —she registered that Antrobus was safeguarding June. That was something vital. But while she went on listening, her mind was at work. So he'd had the letter announcing his transfer this very morning, before she came; that would account for his being so different—if anything could decently account for the alteration between his attitude today and his behavior up on the seat under the rowan tree. Write it off—a lost option, Julia said to herself. She took out her compact and began to powder her nose as Antrobus replaced the receiver.

"Well, I expect you heard that I've done my best to prevent your little friend from being chased," he said.

"Yes, I did. I heard everything. Thank you."

"I think that what with you mopping up von Allmen, and the fact that she did really turn King's Evidence, it ought to be all right," he said. "But she'll have to have a fresh passport, you know."

"Of course. But if your Philip has the Passport Control Officer in Berne on a string, you might pass a word to smooth our path."

He laughed. "Very well—I'll do that. You both deserve it."

"Yes, don't we? Where would the poor old Secret Service be without us?" Julia said. Talking about concrete things like getting June home had done her good, taking her mind off her private misery—she cracked back at Antrobus almost without effort. But it was not without effort that she now said—"And you're being transferred, I gather?"

"Yes. I was only laid on here for this bank affair, because I know the people."

"But did they know in London *beforehand* that Wright and Borovali were going to rob Mr. Thalassides' numbered till?" Julia asked, startled.

"Not *who*, or *how*—no. But there was a hint that an attempt would be made to get hold of the blueprints; that's why I came out; and why you were able to accost me at Victoria!" he said, smiling.

Julia didn't smile—she could no longer bear to recall that lighthearted moment. But her curiosity mastered her pain.

"How on earth did Borovali come to know the account number? That seems so extraordinary."

"We don't know. He comes from the Middle East, as Thalassides did, and practically everyone there is as crooked as a dog's hind leg! There was certainly a leak somewhere—more likely east of the Piraeus than in London. But he *did* know the account number, and the lawyers' names, and got hold of a faked death-certificate, as well as writing-paper with their letterhead; and then forged the signatures."

"Must have been a minor leak in London too, mustn't there? Some trumpery underpaid clerk with a pregnant wife or a girl-friend with extravagant ideas, I expect," Julia said. "Poor toad! He was exploited just like June, no doubt. How I do hate and *loathe* the way international crookery plays on these silly ignorant creatures."

He looked at her rather earnestly. "You really are always on the side of the angels, aren't you? I like that," he said, with more warmth than she had yet heard in his voice that morning. But what good was it for him to like this or that about her, if he didn't like her enough to mind going two thousand, or whatever it was, miles away?

"Oh, I hope I am," she said, in her most casual voice. "No point in being on the side of the devils, that I can see, unless one's a Commie." And as he laughed—"Where *are* all these mosaics? Istanbul?"

"Yes. I've always longed to be there," he said, with the same eagerness that she had heard while he was telephoning.

"I thought Ankara was the capital nowadays," Julia said, still using this protective disguise to her feelings. "Why won't you be up there?"

"Oh, so many things really go on in Istanbul still," he said, "in spite of the Cabinet and the Embassies being stuck up on the plateau. Of course one will be going to and fro—I believe the wild flowers round Ankara are amazing: they say one of our Ambassadors, between the wars, found a new species, unknown to science, within a hundred yards of his newly-built Embassy!"

"How nice," Julia said, rather tepidly.

"Don't publicize this," he added.

"Oh don't be absurd, John! *Really!*"

"I apologize," he said at once. "That was stupid of me. What can I do by way of reparations?"

"Well, as I don't suppose I shall be seeing you again, you might tell me what those blueprints are of," the girl said. "And *don't* call me Fatima!" she added hastily.

"Do you dislike that? I didn't realize. I suppose it was rather a silly joke."

She couldn't tell him that in fact she had greatly enjoyed his calling her Fatima, and that was just why, now, the name had become unendurable.

"Rather a moderate one," was all she said.

"But why shan't you be seeing me again? I shall be in this bed for at least a fortnight, that man Hertz says. I hoped you would be coming to bring me flowers, and cheer my loneliness."

"Hopes are nearly always dupes, whether fears are liars or not," Julia said. (Really, this was a little much.) "My pan is overfull of fishes as it is, and now that Colin's job is done, I must start frying away."

"What fish?"

"Mrs. Hathaway, who overdid herself last night coping with bankers and policemen!—I must look after her till she's fit for the journey to England. And then shepherding June home. Goodness, I suppose we shall all have to travel in a bunch!—Watkins will *hate* June." As Antrobus laughed she said—"Don't ride off on side-issues, John. Pay me my reparations!"

"I wonder why you want to know so much," he said, looking at her speculatively.

"Never mind. I just do. Come on—tell. What *are* those container things?"

"You do really realize that I've no business to tell you this at all, and that you must keep it a deadly secret?" he said.

"Oh yes—and I do really realize that but for me they'd be in enemy hands by now, and therefore that much deadlier. You seem to have forgotten that."

"I shall never forget that," Antrobus said. "Neither your inspiration or whatever it was in snatching that bag, nor your resource in securing the papers afterward." He paused. "Couldn't you bring that chair a little nearer?"

"No—it has lead in its legs," Julia said, making no attempt to move the light wicker construction. "No one can overhear you—don't stall. Tell."

"Well, old Thalassides was a bit of a genius in his way; at least he had the gift of looking further ahead than most people. And with the Middle East the way it's going, he thought that nuclear-powered submarine tankers would be a much better way of moving oil about than overland pipelines, with grasping little oil-less States demanding exorbitant transit dues, or blowing up the pumping stations if they happened to lose their tempers."

"Sound enough," Julia commented.

"So he conceived the idea of having submarine pumping stations on the sea bed, offshore from these coastal oil-producing places like Bahrein or Kuwait, with underwater pipelines leading into them from the land, and nozzles and so on to make the connection with the intake tubes from the tankers. I'm not an expert in these things, but roughly, that's the idea. Just a junction, you see."

"Oh yes—and then frogmen with aqualungs go down and operate it when the nuclear tanker has anchored itself alongside. How ingenious."

"Exactly. I believe they're to be made of Perspex, to let in as much natural light as possible—though I fancy there will be electric lighting too. But of course the whole thing is immensely complicated—the door and valves for ingress and egress, and so on."

"Oh, like the *Schnorkel* thing in submarines?"

"*No*, dear; that's the mistake everyone makes. Like the Davis Escape Hatch is what you mean. Anyhow old Thalassides and his experts got the whole thing worked out, and *drawn* out. And if Russia gets too much of an ascendancy in the Middle East, as she shows every sign of doing, it might save the life—or at least the mobility—of the free world if these things were in operation. That's why you really must keep all this completely dark."

"And that's why Frau Dortmund, and all our other enemies, wanted the blueprints so much. Well, I think I ought to have the D.B.E.," Julia said briskly. "Which of all these old Dames, Civil Servants or professional do-gooders or what have you, have done anything more useful than June and I have?"

"None of them; nothing so important. You've rendered a *major* service. But you won't get it, and I shan't recommend you for it."

"Why not? 'For Services Rendered Abroad' sounds very like the Honors List, to me."

"No. It's all much too serious. Anyhow, what on earth do you want to be a Dame for? Dame Julia Probyn—at your age, you'd look a fool!"

"Yes, I suppose I should," Julia agreed candidly. "Still, I think I might have *something*. What about the Order of Merit? 'Julia Probyn, O.M.'— I don't think that sounds at all bad. Surely I measure up to some of the people who get it?" She rose as she spoke. "I ought to be getting back to Mrs. H. Do you need soap or gaspers—or some paperbacks? And do you want anything fetched from your hotel?"

"As a matter of fact I do—I made a list, hoping that someone would be a ministering angel!" He reached for his wallet on the bed-table, grunting again with the pain of the movement, and took out a sheet of paper. "There—it's rather a lot, I'm afraid."

Julia scanned the list.

"Oh, I can do that quite fast—I'll have the things from the shops sent in. But are you going to keep on your room at the hotel, or do you want everything packed and brought round? I can't do all that today."

"No, I'm keeping the room—if you could just throw what I've listed into one of the suitcases and get it round here it would be a great help. I *should* like to be able to shave!"

"Right, I can manage that. But telephone to the hotel to authorize them to let me take away your property."

"I'll do that, of course."

"And what shall I do with the car? Leave it outside the door here, or what?"

"I think you'd better keep it while I'm laid up," he said, after a moment's consideration.

"Oh, that's absurd," Julia said, thoroughly taken aback.

"Why? I should have thought you might like to take Mrs. Hathaway for some nice drives."

Julia was silent, considering in her turn. It would of course be absolutely lovely to be able to drive Mrs. H. about in the Porsche, but as things were, she couldn't be under any obligation to John.

"You might even slip down occasionally to cheer me up," Antrobus added, before she had spoken.

"I don't expect to have time for that. I think, No—though thanking you for the kind thought," Julia said, as lightly as she could. "Tell me where to leave it, and when I've brought your things round here I'll go back on the bus."

"I think you are making the wrong decision," he said, after studying her face. "I think you've earned a free car. I wish you'd take it."

Again she was silent. How quick he was to guess her reason for refusing. She stood irresolute, torn between the delightful prospect of driving Mrs. Hathaway about and her reluctance, now, to accept anything from John. On the other hand she didn't mind what she accepted from the Government—certainly she had earned something from the Welfare State, which lived (or rather moved) on oil, if she had helped to secure its future supplies. And was it much good trying to safeguard her personal position with someone as astute as John? Was it ever, really, all that important to safeguard one's personal position, even if it were possible?

She moved over again to the window, and stood looking out on the military array of vegetables. *Men* didn't worry about their personal position: Geoffrey Consett hadn't, Steve hadn't, Hugh Torrens hadn't; they had all simply thrown their personal positions away, thrown them *at* her, openly imploring. She suddenly remembered, with a curious twisted pang, how Colin up at Glentoran—was it really only six weeks ago?—had remonstrated with her for leading men on and then rubbing them off—especially Torrens, to whom he was devoted. And now she had been led on and rubbed off herself! Oh, but for women it was different, at least by convention; very few Englishwomen, at any rate, were Claire Clairmonts, shamelessly pursuing their Byrons to the point of running from one villa beside Lac Leman to the other in their nightgowns, across the dew-grey meadows. She giggled a little at the picture; she had always thought Claire a funny phoney. And accepting the use of a Government car for a fortnight was hardly the same as running about in one's nightgown to pursue a lover.

"What are you laughing at?" Antrobus asked from the bed.

"I thought of something funny."

"May I know what?"

"No." Suddenly she found that she had taken her decision. "And it's No to the car, too," she said, quite gently. "Can I leave it at the garage of your hotel here, and let them cope?"

He looked at her rather fixedly.

"My dear, why not use it?"

"You must answer my question before I answer yours. Can your hotel cope?"

"Yes, of course. But I still don't see why not."

Julia went over towards the bed.

"You'll have to learn to understand a lot of things before you're through," she said lightly. "Good-bye. Don't forget about June's passport." And ignoring his outstretched hand she walked out of the room.

CHAPTER XVI

INTERLAKEN—BELLARDON

GOING INTO Antrobus' room at his hotel, and collecting and packing his more intimate accessories, like sponges and pyjamas and shaving things was strangely painful to Julia. All this might have become part of a common life with him; now it wasn't going to. She went through the job methodically, then made the purchases on his list, and took everything round to the clinic. The nurse who answered the bell said *"Der Englische Herr"* wished to see the Fräulein when she brought his luggage. He asked this most urgently."

"Tell Herr Antrobus that I regret it much, but it is too late," Julia said, looking at her watch. It *was* late; she would barely have time to get the

Porsche back to the hotel and catch her bus—but everything between her and John was too late now. She drove away very fast.

The drive up to Beatenberg was long, hot, and wearisome; even the little tune on the horn was a burden, like King Solomon's grasshopper. She had hardly sat down to lunch with Mrs. Hathaway, when the good Hanna came to summon her to the telephone. Dreading Antrobus' voice, she walked along to the *Kleine Saal;* but it was Colin who spoke.

"I thought I'd just let you know that everything is perfectly all right. I got in so soon that we were on the doorsteps of H.M.'s Personal Representative as the postman walked up!—so no fuss at all. Everyone here is delighted, naturally."

"Good—I'm very glad." At once she thought of June. "Look, could you talk to Philip, whoever he is, and arrange about a passport for my little friend? I'll ring Jean-Pierre and get her home address, date of birth, and so on. Can *she* sign the form? She's only eighteen."

"I must look that up—hold on."

Julia held on. Quite soon Colin was on the line again.

"Here you are—'between the ages of sixteen and twenty-one, children must have individual passports, but the application must be signed by a parent or guardian.'"

"Oh, that's all right," Julia said easily. "I'm sure Jean-Pierre will sign as her guardian like a shot."

"The Pastor isn't a British subject," Colin reminded her.

"Oh, so won't that do? Well then send me the form, and ring John and tell *him* to sign as her guardian!—he promised he'd see that it was arranged."

Over their delayed meal she told Mrs. Hathaway that the vital papers had reached the Embassy safely; she replied cheerfully to the good lady's inquiries about Antrobus. But it was with infinite relief that she slipped away to her cell-like room; there she had a good cry, and then lay down on her narrow bed and slept for an hour or more.

Later on she had plenty of time for thinking, and did a lot of it, reviewing her acquaintance with Antrobus from beginning to end. It was an unhappy process. Julia was as remorseless with herself as she frequently was with other people, and, alas she had to face it—in the common but all too accurate phrase, John Antrobus had simply been "amusing himself" with her; she had lost her heart and her head, and been had for a mug.

But she was too fully occupied to mope. She wrote to the Pastor asking him to send her the essential facts for June's fresh passport in her proper name; she told Mrs. Hathaway the girl's whole story, and explained that June would have to travel home with them. "I've got to take her, and I should so much like to go with you and act as courier—I could save you all trouble. But I'm afraid Watkins will be terribly despisey about her; servants are such frightful snobs! And precious June is in the lowest range of the lower middle class! She'll amuse you, I think; but I'm worried about Watkins."

"I will deal with Watkins," Mrs. Hathaway said, in a most convincing voice. "Yes, do let us all travel together, dear child; you will be the greatest help."

The application form arrived from Berne, and the facts as to June's birth and parentage from Bellardon, by the same post. Colin's covering letter was not helpful; he had changed his tune since that enthusiastic telephone call.

"Here you are—but please don't try on any funny-business about forged signatures of guardians! We don't want to run into trouble."

Julia, anyhow overwrought, was infuriated by this. Here was Colin, like almost all junior officials, just making difficulties for their own sake. She filled in the form with everything except the signature of the parent or guardian, and then rang up her cousin's number.

"Oh, is that you? I want to speak to Philip."

"Philip Jamieson? Do you know him?" He sounded astonished.

"I want to speak to him," Julia repeated. At least she had now got the man's surname—but was he a Major or a Colonel, like so many of them?

"But look here," Colin was protesting, "you can't bother him unless it's urgent. If it's just about that infernal girl's papers, tell *me* what you want."

"What I want is to speak to Philip Jamieson. Do please get him."

"Well hold on—I'll see if he's free."

Of course he was free; in a few moments Julia recognized the cheerful voice she had heard when she rang up from Merligen, saying—"Is that Miss Probyn? What can we do for you? We're prepared to do almost anything after what you've done for us! May I congratulate you on at least three separate excellent performances?"

"Oh good. Yes, there is something you can do. I want the P.C.O. to give a passport to a British subject to whom you really owe much more than you do to me! Colin is being rather tatty about it. It's this tedious parent or guardian business, as she's technically 'an infant.' Her only parent is her mother in London, an old widowed prole."

A jolly laugh came down the line.

"Don't worry. Have you got the date and place of birth, the parents' names, and so on?"

"Yes, I've got all that."

"How is she going to get home?"

"I'm taking her myself."

"Where's the document she came out with?"

"I should think in the Super's safe in Interlaken," Julia said. "I imagine horrible Mr. B. had it."

"Highly probable! But check, will you? Meanwhile shove in the form, and I'll see that she gets a travel document to take her home."

"Oh thank you so much."

"Shall you be coming to Berne yourself?—if so, we might meet."

"Possibly," Julia said.

"Well let your cousin tell me if you do make any sort of stopover. Good-bye."

In fact a stopover in Berne was inevitable. While Julia went to La Cure to fetch June, Mrs. Hathaway and Watkins would stay there to break the journey. Arranging all this in Cook's hot office in Interlaken, Julia found it hard to resist the temptation to go round to the clinic and see how John was, but she did resist. At Mrs. Hathaway's suggestion, she wrote an article on the economic self-dependence of Switzerland for *Ebb and Flow*; this didn't help much since, all through, it recalled John's remarks on the subject, and the places in which he had made them. Then Mrs. Hathaway said they must write to June's mother and tell her about her child's return. Julia did this too.

It was gradually borne in on the girl that these various suggestions of Mrs. Hathaway's were made with a purpose—to afford her, Julia, distraction. On the first two days after that disastrous interview in the clinic her old friend had asked her how Mr. Antrobus was—Julia said that she hadn't heard. After that Mrs. Hathaway rang up the clinic herself and made her own inquiries, the results of which she passed on casually to Julia. Mrs. H. had evidently guessed that something had gone wrong, but she was the one person whose perspicacity Julia did not dread. Sometime, she would tell her all about it—had not Mrs. H. said that Antrobus was *capable de tout*? She speculated occasionally as to whether John himself would attempt any further approach, even if only a note of thanks to her for packing and bringing round his things; but she guessed that he would not, and he didn't. This rather raised him in her estimation; he had recognized the double import of the message she sent by the Sister when she dropped his luggage—"Tell him it is too late." It *was* too late for anything more—even for the casual kindnesses of taking flowers or cigarettes. It was over.

Colonel Jamieson—Philip proved to be a Colonel—in due course sent a travel document for June. "Here are your protégée's tickets," he wrote.

"I know how tiresome the travel-allowance is." An inner envelope contained a first-class ticket from Berne to London, and vouchers for a sleeper and meals.

Armed with all these, Julia was ready to go to Bellardon. It was raining when der Chrigl drove them down, sounding his musical horn; the upper forests were shrouded in mist, and they splashed through puddles crossing the Bahnhof-Platz, where the cab horses stood with dismally drooping heads, their coats streaked and dark with moisture. Apart from Mrs. Hathaway getting her feet wet, Julia was quite glad that the skies should weep as she left darling Interlaken, the sweet, beautiful little town where she had been so exquisitely happy and so miserably unhappy.

In Berne she insisted on going with Mrs. Hathaway to her hotel, and seeing her safely installed; then she drove back to the Haupt-Bahnhof and took the train for Lausanne. Just before it pulled out another passenger got into her carriage—with something like horror Julia recognized Herr Kaufmann, of "Corsette-Air."

He recognized her too—nothing could have been more genial than his manner.

"Ah, Mademoiselle, *quelle chance!* Mademoiselle goes again to Geneva?"

"This time only to Lausanne," Julia said. It was positively uncanny, sitting opposite this cheerful little man, with his natty summer suit and his brief-case, to think that she had penetrated into his house, spoken with his wife, heard his child screaming, and burgled his desk for vital information—while he now greeted her so warmly. Had the sour-faced Frau Kaufmann suppressed all mention of her morning visitor—or had he failed to put two and two together? She inquired politely how his business was going?

"Oh, very well indeed. Of course from time to time there arrive *des embêtements,*" he pursued, confidentially. "One expects to bring off a *coup,* and behold, something goes wrong at the last moment." (Like Hell it does! Julia thought to herself. But obviously the Frau had at least not described her.) She spoke sympathetically, and ventured the hope that he had experienced no serious contretemps—she was burning with curiosity to hear what else he would say. Herr Kaufmann shrugged philosophically. These things were all in the day's work!—only one did not like to disappoint clients.

Julia, who had so successfully caused two of his clients to be disappointed, made appropriate sounds—again, it seemed uncanny that he should be telling her this. The little man then said, politely, "Now this time, Mademoiselle really *must* see Mont Blanc! It is a perfect day—all the peaks are clear."

In fact it was a perfect day. The weather had lifted, and the Lake of Geneva shone a brilliant blue in the sun; at the right spot, this time, the little "Corsette-Air" man pointed out to Julia Europe's highest mountain standing up like a vast pearl in the blue sky above the blue water.

At Lausanne she got a porter and was making her way to the platform for Bellardon when suddenly Jean-Pierre appeared, waving his black felt hat above his so un-clerical grey flannel suit.

"Ah, there you are! I came on the chance; I had to be in Lausanne this morning."

As they sped through the green fruitful countryside she asked after all the family; Jean-Pierre in his turn informed her that the Banque République-licaine had formally announced to him the recovery of the whole of Aglaia Armitage's fortune.

"The letter was not very informative, so I rang up Maurice Chambertin; like all bankers he was extremely cautious, but he allowed me to gain the impression that you had played a major role in this affair."

"Well really June played a much majorer role than me," Julia said, not very literately. "However, this is how it was"—and she gave him the whole story.

"Made the exchange in the *toilette!* That was very *rusé!*" the Pastor exclaimed on hearing about Andermatt; he bellowed with laughter when Julia recounted her *triage* of the papers in the ladies' lavatory at the Flüss.

Julia asked if the police had been after June in any way. "Of course she is involved, up to a point; she did impersonate Aglaia."

No, there had been no difficulties. "La Cure is not registered as a hotel—though often it very much resembles one!—so I do not have to show the passports of my guests to the police. But I must say I feared trouble of some sort, since she was known to have been associated with that gang. How did you manage to avert it?"

"Oh well, one way and another," Julia said, with studied vagueness. "Your police are really very nice, I think." She wanted to keep the Berne office out of it.

"I expect they also think you very nice," he said slyly.

They stopped in the nearest town to Bellardon for Jean-Pierre to make some household purchases for Germaine; Julia got out too, and stood in the little street in the hot sunshine. When the Pastor returned he threw his parcels into the back of the car; as he held open the door for her to get in he saw her face in the strong light.

"You look exhausted!" he exclaimed—"no, overstrained. This whole affair must have worn on your nerves, I think?"

Julia agreed that it had been rather anxious work. She had not realized that her unhappiness actually showed in her face, and was upset.

"Well, with us you shall rest, and restore yourself. At La Cure there is, thank God, always peace. Oh—have you the new passport for *la petite?*" he added, as they drove off.

"Its equivalent, anyhow. She can get home."

When they arrived Germaine and June met them on the doorstep; Julia noticed the surprise in her host's face when the young girl threw her arms around her neck and kissed her, saying—"Oh, it's simply *lovely* to see you again! And thank you for sending me here; I am so happy," she added. Germaine too commented on how tired Julia looked, and after lunch dispatched her to her room to rest.

"*No*, June; you are not to go up now—you can talk with Miss Probyn later."

"I thought I might unpack for her," June said. She was hobbling about quite actively with the aid of a stick shod with rubber; she spoke perfectly unresentfully.

"You shall help me with that presently, June," Julia said. She went up to her old room, and before lying down looked out of the window. Washing still hung along the lines beside the lawn, little apples were beginning to swell in the orchard trees; the lilacs and paeonies were over, but the familiar benign sense of peace and kindness reigned. She threw open a suitcase and took out a wrapper. As she lay down to rest she murmured—"Blessed place!"

She got an even stronger sense of the blessedness of La Cure from seeing June there. The little English suburbanite, so many of her values completely shoddy, was the oddest possible inmate of that Swiss household; yet there she was, perfectly at home and as happy as a bird, with no sense of strain on any side—and moreover making herself quite useful. Germaine exercised on her the quiet discipline normal in those fortunate families where tradition is still strong; and June, obviously with great contentment, did as she was told.

The child duly came up after tea to help unpack; Julia was again struck by her ease of movement. "Your ankle seems much better," she said.

"Oh, it's wonderful! That surgeon or whatever he is, in Lawsanne, pulled it about—oh it did hurt!—and then he said I was to have massarge for it."

"But can you get massage here?" Julia asked.

"No, but there's a very good massoose in that little town where Mrs.

de Ritter does her shopping, so they've been taking me in—I haven't missed a single day. They *are* kind! And the swelling's nearly all gone—look."

Julia looked, as the girl held out her foot—the injured ankle had almost returned to the delicate perfection of the other one.

"How excellent—I am so glad," she said.

"Yes, but how's it all to be paid for?" June asked, with her usual directness. "That surgeon!—and an English girl who came and stayed a night here told me that Swiss massooses charge the earth, in our money. And these people are *poor*, reelly," June said, staring at Julia with wide eyes. "Look at Mrs. de Ritter!—up before six, and doing all the housework, as well as the cooking. I asked her why she didn't have a girl in to help, and she said she couldn't afford it! I don't want them to spend money on me."

"I've been given the cash to pay for all your medical expenses," Julia said.

"Who by?" June, true to her type, was incredulous.

"The bank," Julia lied swiftly. "*You* gave me that tip about the bus tour, and the bank people were so pleased that when I said your ankle needed treatment, they gave me the money."

"Oh, I am glad. And that girl, the proper Miss Armitage, will get her money back all right?"

"Yes."

"I can't think now how I ever came to do a thing like that," June said thoughtfully, smoothing and folding sheets of tissue paper on the polished top of the heavy old walnut chest of drawers. "Mum said I was silly to go in for it; but it was worse than silly, it was downright wicked, helping to steal another girl's money. Oh,"—with one of her birdlike hops to a different subject—"what's happened to Mr. B., and that nasty Wright?"

"Mr. Borovali is in prison," Julia replied, deliberately.

"What, for stealing the papers and the money?" June had turned pale. "What about Wright? Is he in prison too?"

"Not yet—he's in hospital with a concussion," Julia said—still, in spite of everything, relishing the recollected picture of Antrobus hurling that disagreeable young man into the Aar. "But he'll go to prison too, as soon as he's well enough."

"Out here?"

"Yes. The crime was committed here."

"Oh." June, still very pale, again stared at Julia, her brown eyes wide. "And what about me?" she asked. "Shall I have to go to prison too?"

"I hope not—I've tried to prevent it. You see you did something that's called 'turning King's Evidence,' and when a person does that . . ."

"Oh, I *never!*" June interrupted indignantly. "That's when a wide boy gives away his pals! I never did anything like that."

"No, I don't suppose you would call Wright and Borovali your pals, exactly," Julia said calmly. "But in fact you did, didn't you, at one point decide to help me instead of them—and told me about the bus tour? That's what is letting you out."

June began to cry.

"Oh, I never thought I'd be called King's Evidence! That's a nasty thing!"

Julia was startled afresh by June's highly peculiar moral code—for clearly she had one, of a sort.

"Which do you think is worse—to let down two crooks like Wright and Borovali, or to steal another girl's money?" she asked. "You did let them down, granted; but what you were helping them to do before you you changed your mind was plain theft. Which is worse? *Think,* June—you don't think enough."

June sniffed and dabbed at her eyes with, Julia noticed, the gentian-embroidered handkerchief bought in Interlaken.

"Oh yes. 'Thou shalt not steal!'—Dad was always saying that. Yes, the stealing was the worst, and I'm glad I helped to stop it. But 'King's Evidence' is a nasty word to have tacked onto one!"

"Do try to make up your own mind, June," Julia said rather impatiently; "don't be fooled by words." June's attitude to the phrase "King's Evidence" was, she thought, an astonishing example of the frightening power of certain words among the ill-educated—purely emotive, bearing no relation to morals or conduct. It was like the Trades Unions' idiotic use of the word "black," which is really only short for "blackmail"—of the public at large.

The girl's reply, when it came after more sniffing and eye-dabbing, surprised Julia.

"These people here, the de Ritters I mean, don't care a thing about money. I never knew anything like it! And they're good, and *enjoy* being good. Can you beat that? She's so beautiful, and she dresses quite well, but she does her hair in that fearfully old-fashioned way, and never uses lipstick—she says the Pastor's congregation wouldn't like it! I will say, they make you think!"

"Well have they made you think whether you did right or wrong to help me to recover Miss Armitage's fortune, which you set out to steal?" Julia asked remorselessly.

"Oh yes, I'm sure now that that was right. Only 'King's Evidence' *is* a nasty word."

"Well it's the word that will keep you out of prison, please God—nothing else will," Julia said.

June said nothing more, but continued to unpack; in the bright light from the high window Julia noticed that the dark line at the roots of the girl's hair was now very marked.

"You didn't do anything about a rinse?" she asked. "Wasn't it possible?"

"Yes, I found I could have had one in Lawsanne, but I didn't like to ask for it," June replied. "I was worrying about them paying, of course; but even if I'd had the money, I should have felt funny, suggesting a rinse to them! But one of the daughters, Hahnriette they call her—she brings her wash for her mum to do; as if *she* hadn't enough work!—said she'd set my hair if I washed it, so I did. Washed my hair in Lux, imagine!—but it came out lovely, as a matter of fact. And Hahnriette set it a treat, don't you think?" She turned her small head this way and that, to display Henriette's set.

"Hahnriette and Gisèle have the sweetest kiddies," June pursued. "They run round after me, though I can't speak a word of French; I teach them English words, and they love it." She paused, seeking to express a meaning new and unfamiliar to her. "This is the queerest setup ever! They're all poor, and they're all good, and yet they're *happier* than any people I've ever known."

After supper that evening June went out to the kitchen to help Germaine put the plates in the washing machine, polish the spoons and forks, and generally tidy up; Julia sat with Jean-Pierre in his study. She thanked him for having June, and then brought out the five hundred francs which Antrobus had given her. "Will this cover her doctor's fees, and all this massage, which is having such a wonderful effect? And then there is the petrol for taking her to and fro."

He sat looking at the notes on his desk, but made no move to touch them.

"Where does this money come from?" he asked.

"From my cousin's colleagues. I asked for money on her behalf, and was given it." She blushed a little, remembering that uncomfortable scene at lunch. "But I told June a lie about it," she added. "I said the bank had given me the money."

"Why?"

"Oh, do you ask that? How could I let her know about the Secret Service? She's so fearfully silly."

"You do not like her? We have received the impression that she is devoted to you; and you have been very good to her."

"Not all that good—I've made use of her for my own purposes, or rather for Colin's. I've worried about that—I was really trading on her affection. But at least I did her no harm—in fact getting her here (thanks to you) has been a major benefit."

"Why do you say that?" he asked.

Julia told him about her conversation with June, and the revolution beginning to be effected in the child's muddled values by her stay at La Cure; Jean-Pierre laughed a great deal at the girl's dismay over the words "King's Evidence."

"Yes, this is how they think now," he said. "Crime is reputable, but to report a criminal to authority is shameful!"

"Well is this enough for her massage, and the surgeon, and the petrol?" Julia asked, touching the notes.

Now Jean-Pierre looked at the money.

"This will be exact," he said. "The extra petrol I would gladly have given. You have begun a good work on this child, and if we have contributed to it, that is our privilege. Will you be able to keep in touch with her?" he pursued.

Julia was taken aback by this question. The idea of visiting June in England had never occurred to her, and was distinctly dismaying. She was kind by nature, but it was a spontaneous kindness, lightly given and soon forgotten.

"Do you think I ought to?" she asked.

"But obviously. Any redemptive work needs to be followed up, followed through. What future do you envisage for her?"

Julia was positively horrified. It had never occurred to her for a single second that she was doing a "redemptive work" for June, and the future she had envisaged for the girl was the same as her past—going on having her feet photographed in pretty shoes for advertizements. She had taken quite a lot of trouble to insure that this employment could continue, but she had never looked any further, and she told de Ritter so, frankly.

"I could see her from time to time, of course," she said at the end. "But this job seems to suit her very well."

"You really think so? A job that simply involves advertizing her body, or parts of it? If she is as foolish as you seem to think, I should have thought it rather dangerous."

"I haven't thought about it at all," Julia said flatly. "I'm not a do-gooder! She makes her living from her feet, and I've tried to help her to go on doing that—and to keep her out of prison!" She resented these problems suddenly being thrust upon her. "Have you got other ideas?" she asked.

"Yes. But you are tired tonight—we can discuss them later. Germaine will take you to bed. Here you shall rest."

THOSE DAYS at Bellardon did Julia a lot of good. As the Pastor had said, there was peace at La Cure; almost more useful to her state at the time was the being immersed in the life and concerns of a quite different set of people, who knew nothing of her private trouble. But the presence of Germaine's grandchildren introduced a new idea in connection with June.

"This young girl really has a great gift for children!" Germaine exclaimed one day, looking from the kitchen window into the garden, where Gisèle sat sewing in the arbour while her infants swarmed round June, who was folding paper caps for them out of an old copy of the *Gazette de Lausanne*. With Julia, Gisèle had just hung out a line of newly-washed sheets along the lawn, and one of the children went and fingered them, leaving muddy marks.

"No, 'Toinette! Naughty!" June said, and slapped the fat little hand. 'Toinette pouted and cried a little, but two minutes later she was cuddling up to the English girl as confidingly as ever—'Meess June, *fates-moi un papper-cap.*'" Julia had already noticed that June, herself half a child, not only enjoyed playing with the children but in fact kept them in order with the flat, matter-of-fact competence of working-class people, untroubled by psychological theories; if a child did wrong it was slapped, least troubling of punishments.

"It is really a pity that she could not take a position as *bonne d'enfants* out here," Germaine pursued. "There is such a demand for English nurses and governesses, and they are well paid. Would not this be a more wholesome employment than being photographed for advertizements?"

Julia hesitated. On her arrival she had resented the Pastor's attempt to saddle her with the responsibility for June's moral welfare—partly from sheer fatigue; but earlier she had also resented, fiercely, the use to which June had been put by international crooks. The Modern Face Agency had let her in for Mr. Borovali—what would they let her in for next time? Being a *bonne* in some respectable Swiss family was obviously a much more wholesome form of employment. But Julia was always practical.

"She'd teach any little Swiss she was with an appalling accent," she said.

"So? All the same they would learn *some* English, and she is a person who can rule children easily, which is the essential." Germaine turned away to her cooking.

Julia left Bellardon with a strong sense of privilege that Fate and Colin between them should have sent her there; it would have been a real loss not to have met Jean-Pierre and Germaine, and seen the calm beauty of their lives. As for June, at the hot little station she burst into tears, and threw herself into Germaine's arms.

"Oh, you have been so good! I'll never forget it. And I've been so happy. Give my love to the kiddies when they come over—I shall miss them like anything."

Jean-Pierre wrung Julia's hand.

"Come back! *Ne manquez pas!*"

The long train from the frontier drew in; Julia kissed Germaine, June pulled herself up the high steps; they both leaned from the window as the train pulled out. The Pastor waved his black hat in farewell. "Remember that he who has put his hand to the plough must not look back," he called, his resonant preacher's voice carrying above the noise of the train.

"What on earth did he mean by that?" June asked, when a curve in the line hid Bellardon, and they sat down.

"I can't imagine," Julia said; she could in fact imagine only too well, and was still a little reluctant.

June had some ideas of her own about her future, and promptly put one to Julia.

"Miss Probyn, you said Mr. Borovali was in prison. How long will he be there?"

"Oh, seven or eight years, I should think, at the very least. It was a big robbery, with forgery and all sorts of other things as well."

"Can he pay me my screw from prison?"

"No, certainly not. And for your own sake you'd better forget about that," Julia said. "You don't want seven years in prison yourself, do you?"

June's face puckered with dismay.

"Oh no!—that would kill Mum! But who *will* pay my salary? Six pounds a week I was to get, and it's six weeks now. I can't afford to lose my pay."

"No one will pay you anything, and you mustn't ask for it." Julia foresaw the foolish child possibly tackling the Agency on this head. "Don't you realize that you will be tremendously lucky if you escape going to prison yourself? Don't be a fool, June."

"But I ought to have my pay!"

"No you oughtn't—not for helping to commit a crime! Anyhow the bank gave me over £40 for you, because you turned King's Evidence"—

Julia deliberately used the distasteful phrase. "That is more than six weeks pay. Let it go."

"Well if you say so, I will," the young girl said. "Only I meant to repay you the money you lent me in Interlaken out of what Mr. B. was to give me. Never mind—I'll save up and pay you back." She glanced up at the broad racks above their heads, loaded with luggage. "At least I've got my outfit," she said, in a satisfied tone. She paused. "Anyhow I don't feel now that one ought to worry so much about money—I mean not after staying with the de Ritters. Rich or poor, they couldn't care less! But one can't get out of the habit all at once, and everyone else I know does."

On arriving in Berne Julia put their luggage in the *consigne;* then they walked through the warm bright evening to the hotel where they were to dine with Mrs. Hathaway.

"There wouldn't be time to see the bears, I 'spose?" June asked. "This is Berne, isn't it? Mr. B. said there were real bears here, and that they'll eat buns if you give them to them on a stick. He said he'd bring me to see them when it was all over. I *would* like to see a real bear!"

"No, there isn't time now," Julia said, thinking how well the hatefully astute Borovali had taken June's measure, and offered the appropriate lure and bribe to every facet of her character: her vanity, her cupidity, even her childishness. "But sometime when I'm in London I might take you to the Zoo," she said recklessly. "There are bears there. I expect you've been, though?"

"No, never. It's such a long way from Malden. Oh, I should love that."

At dinner, June soon got onto quite comfortable terms with Watkins, with whom Mrs. Hathaway had clearly dealt to some purpose; but she was a good deal overawed by Mrs. Hathaway—with her height, her grey hair, her assured manner and incisive way of speaking. In fact the older lady went out of her way to be nice to the young girl, inquiring about her foot, her advertizing work, and her mother; but June was too abashed to give more than brief answers—there was none of the giddy outpouring to which Julia was accustomed, though a direct question as to whether her mother was not lonely while she was away at work elicited the fact that "Mum" belonged to a whist-club, which occupied all her spare time.

"She's like a real dowager on the films, isn't she?" June observed to Julia as they were washing and tidying-up before going to the train. "One can just see her wearing a tiara at some grand ball!" Julia, who took the dimmest view of the utterly phoney dowagers usually displayed on films said that the thing about Mrs. Hathaway was that she was *kind.*

"Oh I'm sure she is—only I mean she doesn't look it," June said. "Dowagers don't, do they?"

June was thrilled with their sleepers. "I told her I'd sleep on top, Miss, because of her foot," Watkins said to Julia; "but she says she has a fancy for the steps."

"There was none of this when we came out," June observed, climbing down from the top berth. "Sat up all night, we did. I call these beds lovely—and this"—she patted the little ladder. "And the washbasin is ever so clever, folding up like that."

"Now, shall you be all right, Watkins?" Julia asked.

"Oh yes, Miss."

"Good night, then"—Julia returned to Mrs. Hathaway.

"Yes, they're fine," she said in answer to a question. "I wish this train would leave, so that we could go to sleep. Are you very tired, Mrs. H.?"

"No, not in the least. But I think I will unpack, and get ready."

"I'll curl up on top while you do," Julia said, and climbed a little ladder like that which so pleased June.

"Do smoke," Mrs. Hathaway said, quickly taking what she required from her dressing-case. "Here's something for you," she said after a moment, and handed up a small pewter saucer with rather florid ornamentation. "The worst feature of top bunks in sleepers is no ash-tray. I thought you could carry this in your bag for journeys. Don't lose it—it's an old one."

Julia was examining the small object delightedly.

"It's quite beautiful," she said. "Darling Mrs. H., how very good of you. It's the perfect thing. Where did you find it?"

"In an antique shop here. Rudolf Waechter came over a couple of days ago to say Good-bye, so I asked him to help me—all the *antiquaires* here know him too well ever to try to swindle him. He thinks that it's not Swiss, or it would be plainer; possibly South German. But it is quite a good piece—probably seventeenth-century."

Julia climbed down the ladder and gave her old friend a hug. "Mrs. H., it's too darling of you! Why should you give me an antique ash-tray?"

"Why not?" Mrs. Hathaway replied, kissing her in return. "But do go up aloft, or I shan't have room to move." When Julia had obediently re-climbed the ladder Mrs. Hathaway spoke again, measuredly.

"Apart from the fact that I wanted to give you a pretty ash-tray to travel with—instead of that horrible tin lid that I so often see you carrying about! —I felt that you ought to have some tangible reward or memento, however small, of what you have done. Our officials can't do it, so I thought *I* would give you something."

Julia was almost ready to cry, touched by the charming present and by Mrs. Hathaway's feeling that she deserved a reward, but tormented by the fact that she so *didn't* want any reminder of this Swiss trip. The up-and-down conversation went on.

"Rudolf Waechter sent you his best wishes—he said he was too old to send you his love," Mrs. Hathaway remarked from below. Then, with a smart switch of subject—"What are you going to do about this child June?"

Julia, touched a moment before, felt a little impatient even with her beloved Mrs. H.

"Why should I do anything about her?" she asked, knocking ash from her cigarette into the little pewter dish, perched on the green blanket of the upper berth.

"Oh, surely you can't get out of it?" Mrs. Hathaway said, opening the washbasin and preparing to brush her teeth. "Is there any real difference between the slopes of the Niederhorn and the road from Jerusalem to Jericho? And if ever anyone fell among thieves, she did."

Julia was silent, at last rather ashamed of her reluctance to "take on" June. She told Mrs. Hathaway of Germaine's suggestion that the girl might take a post as a *bonne d'enfants* in Switzerland.

"I think that an excellent idea," Mrs. Hathaway said. "If it was arranged through the de Ritters one could be sure of her being sent to a suitable family. But what is she to do till her hair grows brown again?" she asked, as she washed her face. "That nice Colonel Jamieson, whom I met at the Embassy at luncheon, said something about its being inadvisable for her to return to Switzerland till her hair is brown again, and she has a proper passport saying so."

"Oh, go on with modeling her feet—she doesn't need her hair for that," Julia said. She paused. "Someone ought to call on the Model Face and hint to the Manager not to give her any more outside jobs, don't you think? You'd do that much more impressively than me, Mrs. H.—could that be your share in this Good Samaritan effort?"

Mrs. Hathaway laughed. "Very well." As she spoke the stuffy train at last pulled out; the blessed air came in at the window as the express began to roar across a darkened Europe, in fact Julia had to climb down and raise the shutter so that Mrs. Hathaway should not get chilled as she undressed. "Are you coming to bed?" that lady asked, when she herself was comfortably installed.

"Not just yet, if you don't mind; I thought I'd stay up till the frontier, in case there's any bother over June's travel-paper—that attendant man pulled rather a face when I gave it to him. But are you dying to have the lights out and go to sleep? If so I'll undress now; I don't a bit mind confronting officials in my nightgown."

Mrs. Hathaway laughed again.

"No, I'm not at all sleepy; I'd like to talk for a little."

"Good." Julia perched on the little snap-up pull-down seat attached to the wall, and lit another cigarette.

"I had a letter from Edina in Berne," Mrs. Hathaway said. "She asks us both to Glentoran—she and Philip were dreadfully disappointed that I dragged you away the moment you arrived. So you will come up with me, my dear child; I think you need a rest," the older woman said firmly.

Julia began to feel nervous.

"I've just been having a holiday," she protested.

"*No*, dear child; not a holiday at all. First you were nursing me, and then having some very wearing experiences. One can really rest at Glentoran. It is peaceful there."

Julia nodded. There was always peace at Glentoran, as there was at La Cure; a different *ambience*, but the same peace. Only what did Mrs. H. mean by "wearing experiences"? She looked at her old friend's wise, kind face, framed between the white pillows and the mahogany panels, and saw there what made any attempt at concealment useless. Suddenly she burst into tears. Mrs. Hathaway leaned out and stroked her hand.

"You had every excuse, but I am sorry that it should have happened," she said. "A most charming man, but a *coureur*."

"Was that why you said he was *capable de tout*?" Julia asked, wiping her eyes.

"Yes. I said it because I thought it; I wasn't warning you—one doesn't warn people of your age. But I did recognize both his quality—which is great—and his charm, and I became rather alarmed on your account."

This speech was immensely comforting to Julia; it made her feel less of a fool.

"There really *is* good in him, don't you think?" she asked. "As well as all his things, like birds and flowers and climbing?"

"Yes, I think so. Only at his age he should be less self-indulgent and more scrupulous," Mrs. Hathaway pronounced. "His serious weakness is that he hasn't realized this. But you may have taught him something."

"I felt such a beast, not going to see him," Julia said, immensely relieved to get all this secret trouble at last presented before the incorruptible tribunal of Mrs. Hathaway's standards.

"Oh no, you were quite right. When I telephoned from Beatenberg he was always begging to see you, but I said that you were too busy. I think he took it in, in the end," the old lady said.

The train slowed to a halt; from the darkness outside came the demand,

"*Les passeports, s'il vous plait.*" Julia got up, her little seat flipping up behind her.

"I think I'll just go and lurk," she said.

"Leave it to the man, unless there is trouble," Mrs. Hathaway said.

In the corridor Julia found Watkins lurking too, but for a different reason.

"I said I'd just let her get undressed and into bed," the maid said, with a nod towards her and June's compartment. "Is Madam in bed? She ought to be."

"Yes, all tucked up some time ago," Julia replied.

"That's right. Has she got her Fishy water?" Watkins asked, with a jealous interest in her mistress's welfare.

"Yes—and a cork in the bottle, so it won't spill. Would you like some Vichy, Watkins?" Julia asked.

"Oh no thank you, Miss. I only tried it once, and fishy it tasted to me! Why are we stopping? Is this a town?"

"Not really—it's the frontier, where they inspect the passports."

"Ah. Will *she* be all right?" Watkins asked, with another nod in the direction of the sleeper door. "She seemed a bit worried about her passport —something wrong with it, I gathered."

"She's got a new one," Julia said. Oh, dear foolish gabbling June!—How much else had she told Watkins? She soon learned some of it.

"You know, Miss, she's really a very decent little girl, if she is a bit flighty and silly," the maid pursued. "She gives a lot of her pay to her mother, to help her out—a widow's pension isn't much! But I don't fancy the idea of her going on doing all this modeling. It's my belief that these Agencies lead young girls astray, as often as not—I mean I think they're often agencies for other things than adverts! And she's silly enough, in a way, to be taken in by anyone. Couldn't you get her into some decent job, where she'd be safe? She'll take anything *you* say, that I'm positive of; she thinks the world of you."

Julia, glancing down the corridor, saw the frontier officials in a huddle outside the *Wagons-Lits* man's little cubbyhole, going through the passports of the sleeper passengers—she watched them, and was immensely relieved when they went out to by-pass the sleeping-car on their way to the next coach.

"Good!" she muttered. "Yes, Watkins, I think there is a chance that I might find quite a nice job for Miss Phillips, and I mean to try, presently. Good night."

"Good night, Miss," the maid said, and after a tap on the door re-entered her compartment.

Julia stood a moment longer in the corridor. First the Pastor; then Mrs. H.; now *Watkins!* Undoubtedly June was her neighbour; there was no escaping that fact. But June's pretty, silly face was not the memory that she must carry home from this journey whether she would or no; it was the memory of a gothic face, with triangular eyelids and a twisted smile. Tears smarted again behind her eyes; she brushed them away angrily—goodness, what a fool she was! Anyhow there would be peace at darling Glentoran, and in time she would forget. Like Watkins she tapped on a polished wooden door, and went in and rejoined Mrs. Hathaway.

ABOUT THE AUTHOR

Ann Bridge is the wife of a British diplomat with whom she has traveled around the world. Over the years, she has shared her unique international background with the many devoted readers of her novels, and many of her own personal experiences have provided settings for her charming amateur-detective heroine, Julia Probyn. In *Julia Involved*, three exciting Julia Probyn stories—*The Lighthearted Quest, The Portuguese Escape,* and *The Numbered Account*—have been brought together so that the wide circle of Julia Probyn admirers can follow again her adventures in international intrigue, courage, and love.